*C*lio wrenched her eyes from the gardenia, sinister and glowing, and found that she was crying. . . .

She flew down the stairs, panting, her heart pounding. . . . With shaking hands she unlatched the front door of the house and rushed out, into the street, into the warm night air, into the comforting, anonymous darkness.

Into the arms of the man who had been waiting for her all night. . . .

LADY KILLER

Michele Jaffe

BALLANTINE BOOKS • NEW YORK

A Ballantine Book
Published by The Ballantine Publishing Group
Copyright © 2002 by Michele Jaffe

ISBN 0-7394-2546-3

For this volume there can be no better godmother than Susie Phillips, with whom I first learned to appreciate all the secrets a text can contain—and conceal. I can only hope that among its pages she will find some small measure of the pleasure that I have long been blessed with in her friendship.

The Vampire, also known as a Bloode-Sucker or fiend, comes originally from the Northern Countries. Contrary-wise to what others have said, he is often faire of complexion, and mayhap shows none of the fiend without. A man once had a vampire for a Friende a good many years before he discovered the truth of the matter, and then only when it was too late and he saw his wife dying of two pricks in her neck, and his friend with blood upon his lips.

Concerning the Vampire, t'are those who say he is e'en such a one as rises from the dead, but this is wrong, for the Vampire is a living being, and takes to his blood sucking so that he may prosper, and grow stronger, from others. For him, the blood is as food for us, and he must have it, lest he weaken and die. This is the cause that he shall be known to strike in a regular way, just as we must eat our victuals and drink ale at our regular times or we will perish. So that he will suck blood every day or every week, as he list, but regular like always or else he will bee sick unto death.

This noorishment he taketh only by night, being a creature who loves the darkness, and thrives upon it. So that as the Moon, no longer young, waneth in her course and grow slimmer, even so the Vampire grows fatter, which is to say, more powerful. And on every such night as there is no Moon, when between her monthly courses she doth hide her face, on that night will the Vampire be at his most powerful. Woe awaits he who thinks he can strike the Vampire down on such a night, for he has the power of the Devil in him most strongly then, and will be invincible.

And I say 'he' but really there is also the other kind, the female or 'she-vampire' who is the same in every respect, save this one: that she is far more dangerous.

—From *A Compendium of Vampires and Other Fiends*, London: 1545

Prologue

I was getting hungry by the time she came in, but waiting is nothing new for me. I have spent the better part of my life waiting on women. Still, I held my breath when she opened the door. I didn't want her to know I was there, not yet anyway. She liked surprises, I knew, because I had seen her two days earlier with that silver piece in her hand. She had stood in the stable yard and twirled around and hummed to herself in happiness at the surprise. I hoped she would hum for me, too. In fact, I was counting on it.

I waited until she had slipped out of her cloak and settled herself on that squalid mattress she called her bed before I entered. At first she pretended to be asleep, but when she finally looked up, I could see that she recognized me. I was delighted. It is always a pleasure to be recognized, to be seen as you long to be seen, especially when so much time has passed. I smiled broadly to show her how happy she had made me.

Silly, idiotic girl. She started screaming then, turning her head from side to side to appeal to the others, as if they would help her, as if they could feel pity. I almost fancied one of them had whispered to another that they thought my choice was unworthy, but when I turned around they were all still silently looking on as I had found them.

I owed them something, too. They brought her to me, they put her in my path, and I repaid them by letting them watch. An audience is a powerful stimulus. But I would not let them comment. You see, it was only for me to determine worthiness. Only I could make the selection, only I knew why. No one else could understand.

I explained that to her, explained what she was destined for. I wish you could have seen the expression on her face. It was better than I could have imagined, more beautiful than any word-sharping poet could ever describe. I was overtaken with emotion and I lifted her to my breast and held her tight.

I admit that I cried. Don't look so surprised. What would you have done in my place? It was a beautiful, magical moment. I showered my tears over her, cleansing her, and then I followed them with my lips. I dried them with my mouth, kissing her cheek, her jaw bone, her chin. With each kiss I could feel her excitement growing, feel her pulse quickening. I felt as though I could see the blood throbbing just beneath the skin, just out of sight. I heard her voice then, calling to me, singing out to me, begging me for succor, for mercy, for release. I looked up once to memorize the dear expression on her face.

And then I sank my teeth into her neck.

God it was good to be back.

Chapter 1

It was no use. Clio Thornton had tried squinting, closing one eye, and glaring at the book lying open on the desk in front of her, but nothing made it look any better. The two rows of columns refused to add up to the same thing, or even anything, besides nothing. She was broke.

The squealing of door hinges interrupted her thoughts and she just had time to shove the ledger under her desk before a woman in a silver gown rushed into the room.

"Today is the day," the woman trilled. Her steps were being dogged by a monkey in a dark blue velvet doublet with two gold medals pinned to it. "Don't you dare say that word to me, Clio Thornton, that word you are always saying: impossible. I am completely sure. I, Princess Erika, have seen the portents in the bottom of the water jug."

Princess Erika set the jug down firmly in the middle of Clio's desk.

"Look for yourself," she offered, and Clio leaned forward. The monkey, having taken up a post on Clio's shoulder, looked also.

"It's cracked," Clio said. The monkey nodded.

Princess Erika, whose nation of sovereignty no one—including the princess—seemed to know, drew herself up to her full height and demanded, "Clio, what am I going to do with you? You call that cracked? That is a sign. A great sign. A very, very great sign. Today, this very morning, fortune comes knocking."

Despite the state of her finances, Clio received this news with great calm. During the two years that they had been neighbors, Princess Erika's prophesies had become legendary throughout London, because whatever she predicted could be counted on with certainty never to occur. In her career as a seer, Princess Erika had only once made a correct prediction, and that only by accident. Her reliability was held in great esteem by many—travelers had begun to frequent her rooms to receive her solemn assurance that they would die on their next voyage, and merchants sought her recommendations on which ventures she guaranteed to fail. But Princess Erika longed, more than anything, to be a true prophet, and she continued singing out her predictions, dauntless in the belief that if she just found the correct vessel for her portents, all would come out right.

This morning she had returned to the water jug, which explained her enthusiasm. Once, two years earlier, Princess Erika had looked in her water jug and correctly predicted that the heavens would shower diamonds over London. But since then—barring a wild prophesy about Clio's future, which was more poetic than predictive—the jug had remained silent. Despite its past success, Clio was not optimistic about its results.

Which was why, when at that moment there was a

knock on the main door of the house, she was so surprised that she nearly fell out of her chair, sending the
ledger thumping to the ground and disturbing the monkey who had settled in for a nap.

For an instant, all time seemed to stand still and the
two women just stared at one another in euphoric disbelief. Then Snug, a former, highly unsuccessful, liberator of
others' possessions, and now the head steward-gardener-
cook-tinkerer-majordomo-housekeeper-fix-anything-man
of Clio's household, showed their guest into the study.

Many people had come to Clio for help during the
years she had lived in London, but none of them appeared
less like a harbinger of good fortune than the dark-haired
boy who now entered. He looked as though he were not
merely unfortunate but almost anti-fortunate, as if he
had not smiled in years and had no plans to do so anytime soon.

Above all, he looked hungry. Without waiting for him
to speak, Clio rose and began to move quickly in the direction of the kitchen. But she had not taken three steps
when she felt the boy at her side, tugging insistently on
her arm. Clio remembered reading about boys that if you
showed weakness once, they would never respect you.
Although this boy was as tall as she was, he was only half
her age, which Clio felt gave her the clear upper hand,
and she determined not to go anywhere with him until he
yielded to her superior authority and ate something. But
to everything she suggested—a piece of bread, a bowl of
jam, even a little meat pie (which Toast, the blue-velvet-
clad monkey, indicated he would be willing to consume by snapping his fingers and pirouetting)—the boy
simply shook his head and pulled harder at the fabric of
her gown.

It did not take Clio's years of experience with people in trouble to realize that the boy was either unable or unwilling to speak. And that unless she went wherever he wanted to drag her, he was not going to leave off tormenting her sleeve until every thread on it gave way, which would not be long given that the gown was almost as old as the boy. With a sigh she persuaded him to come into the kitchen just long enough for her to stuff two meat pies into a cloth bag, thrust it into the boy's hand, and set out at a run behind him, trailed by Toast.

The crowds grew thicker as they progressed down Knightrider Street, changing from dark-coated men of business to rowdier soldiers and sailors as they crossed Water Lane. Several people stopped to stare at the strange procession of boy-woman-monkey, but Clio did not notice, her mind completely taken up with wondering what this mad dash might mean. As they approached Alsatia—the quarter of London referred to by the respectable as Devil's Keep, and by its denizens as Little Eden in honor of the number of houses of pleasure located there—she had the sudden, sickening thought that perhaps the boy was one of Captain Black's minions, sent to waylay her. Just then the boy turned down an alley and stopped in a bare courtyard that fronted a tiny building, so small it looked like a child's play house. He stood next to the door, trembling, as if afraid to enter.

"You keep our visitor company out here," Clio instructed Toast, whose eyes never left the bag of meat pies in the boy's hand. Assured that her young charge was going to be closely watched, Clio pushed the door open and stepped inside.

Her stomach rose into her throat and she had to steady

herself against the cupboard next to the door as the sight and the stench hit her like an invisible punch. A hundred hands stretched out toward her, a hundred eyes stared unblinkingly at her above red-gash mouths. A severed ear lay on the table in front of her, next to a nose, a golden braid, and what looked like it could have been a face. There were only empty sockets where the eyes should have been, and a large swath of beige matter showed where the ribbon hair had yet to be sewn on.

The dolls hung in rows along three walls of the room, the hooks in the backs of their gowns making them lean forward, leering, grasping, casting crazy shadows across the planked floor, but it was not these that made her knees sway and the knot in her stomach tighten. Beneath a window against the far wall there was a mattress. And on the mattress, dangerously still, lay a girl.

Clio felt a spasm of sadness and horror when she registered that the girl was dead, and then stopped feeling anything at all as her mind took over. This was not the first mysterious death she had been involved in—her solution to the mystery of Ellis Wittington's drowning two years earlier and her role in catching the notorious Butcher of Buckinghamshire that past April had earned her the two medals from the queen, which Toast now wore on his doublet—and she knew what to expect, but she never got over how clear her thoughts became in the face of tragedy. *Unnatural girl, thrives on the misery of others,* she heard her grandmother's disapproving voice say in her head. She pushed it aside and turned back to the task at hand.

Clio looked around the room, memorizing it. She noted the dolls, arranged by dress color, then the small statue of a saint at the foot of the bed, the worn-through boots, the bug-infested straw mattress covered with a patterned piece of fabric—no doubt to brighten the room—and the bouquet of flowers on the window sill, undoubtedly put there with the same end. She noted the two sets of muddy footprints on the floor, one made by the sort of small feet Clio had always longed to have and appearing to correspond with the boots next to the mattress, the other set larger but following the same path from the door to the bed.

Finally, when she had taken everything in and her nose had adjusted to the smell of death enough to keep from gagging, Clio crossed the floor and stood next to the body. Deep green bracelets of bruises circled the girl's wrists, but no other wounds were immediately apparent. Bending, Clio brushed aside the plait of dark hair that covered the girl's face.

She recoiled. Huge, glittering eyes stared out at Clio with an expression of acute terror and the dead girl's mouth gaped open in a silent scream. *No.* Clio could almost see the words forming the syllables. *No, don't please no, NO.*

Clio tried to close her own eyes but she could not. She could not free her gaze from the lifeless one of the corpse, and as she looked, she felt a prickling fear crawl over her. It started at her feet and swam slowly up, until her entire body was tingling. She heard a scream in her ears, in her head, and felt a line of clammy perspiration form down her back. Her heart pounded as she struggled to swallow, but she could hear it over the screams.

There was a noise behind her. The cupboard! She had not looked inside the cupboard, and he had been hiding there. The girl's face, her scream, had been a warning. There was something coming for Clio. She heard a board creak. The hairs on her arms stood up. She could smell his sweat as he moved up behind her. Another board creaked.

She wrenched her eyes from the girl's and swung around. A sound rose in her throat, then stopped. From every wall the dolls leered at her, grinning ghoulishly. But there was no one else in the room. She was alone. The door to the cupboard was closed. Her heart thudded. She had imagined the whole thing, there had not been anyone there. She was alone. Her heart slowed. Alone. She swallowed hard and turned back to the bed.

That was when she really knew terror. The hideous death mask of moments before had vanished. The girl was lying on her back peacefully. Her eyes were closed. Her lips were pressed together, and almost curved into a smile. She was still dead, and there were still bruises on her wrists, but there was no sign of the horror Clio had seen in her face.

Clio forced herself to breathe to keep from screaming. Breathe, think, breathe. It was a trick of the light. An illusion. It was nothing, a fake—it had looked so real— there was a logical explanation for it. There was, damn it—but the fear, the fear had been real. It had been the girl's fear, locked somehow in the air of the airless room. She knew it, the fear of someone about to die.

It had looked so bloody real.

Clio shook her head, shaking away the feeling that she was lying to herself. She had never had a premonition in her life, she did not even believe in them, but she knew with unwavering certainty that something horrible had happened in this place. She concentrated on focusing her thoughts, on pressing the chilling vision down into the darkest corner of her mind. *It had been so real.* She would consider it later, rationally, logically, objectively. Right now she had work to do. She still had no idea of how the girl had died, she reminded herself, let alone who she was. Work to do. Seizing on this, Clio moved her eyes from the serene face. Behind the girl's head, wedged in the corner between the mattress and the wall, was what appeared to be a dark blue silk kerchief, similar to one Clio had at home, its fine fabric looking startlingly out of place in the humble room. Clio reached across the dead girl's body to finger it—

And froze.

What stunned her was not so much what she saw, but how unsurprised she felt seeing it. It was as if she had known—had known even as she mistook shadows on the girl's face for a scream—what she would find. She blinked twice, just to be sure, but this time there could be no trick of light. Just at the point where the woman's neck met her collarbone, on the smoothest, purest part of her neck, were two dark brown dots, slightly larger than pin pricks, but much, much more deadly.

Although Clio had never seen anything like them, she knew instantly what they meant. The Vampire of London was back.

"Impossible," Clio whispered to herself. She had been in Nottingham looking for the missing daughter of a baronet when the vampire first made his appearance three years earlier, but she remembered the stories and had the news sheets about his crimes in her files. Twenty-four London women died that summer at the vampire's hands, and scores of others perished indirectly by being forced to sleep with their shutters closed in airless rooms during the long, hot months. Families bankrupted themselves buying mirrors when the belief that a vampire could not bear to see his reflection gained popularity, and herbologists got rich selling "secret essences" guaranteed to be anathema to demons when applied to the neck. The behavior of vampires past was closely analyzed by the leading lights of Oxford and Cambridge for clues as to his method of selecting his victims, but the London fiend's preferences remained a mystery. He seemed to strike indiscriminately, preying on women of all complexions and social classes. Their only common denominator was that they were all young and smallish in stature. The inanimate figure lying on the bed in front of Clio was both young and diminutive, so it was not any lack in the victim that had made Clio whisper *impossible*. Nor was it because she had never really credited that the vampire existed. It was quite simply because the Vampire of London was dead.

Or supposed to be. He had been killed three years earlier, shot down in broad daylight as he tried to escape pursuit by stealing a boat and making off down the Thames. Two hundred Upstanding Citizens saw the first shot go into his thigh, saw him waver, and then watched as the second shot went directly into his heart. Two hundred Upstanding Citizens saw him look toward his assassin with surprise, saw him stretch his throat to yell, "You'll be sorry Dearbourn," and saw him fall backward into the swirling rapids of the Thames at the base of London Bridge. Two hundred Upstanding Citizens saw the body pelted against the strong supports of the bridge once, twice, three times, until it was sucked into the powerful vortex of the river and disappeared entirely. No one had ever survived a fall that close to the bridge's supports—even the most seasoned boatmen avoided the rapids at all cost—but the river was dredged religiously anyway, for three months, without a sign of the vampire's body. Two hundred Upstanding Citizens swore that the vampire was dead and the entire city of London rejoiced.

But Clio knew something that the Upstanding Citizens did not know, a detail that had been kept secret by the special commission the queen dispatched to look into the public menace. She knew that next to each corpse had been found a pure, white gardenia. And now, looking at the windowsill next to the mattress on which the dead girl lay, Clio saw what she had failed to see before. There was not a bouquet of flowers there. There was *a* flower. A white gardenia.

Two hundred Upstanding Citizens, Clio thought grimly, were wrong.

Clio, rational and unafraid and not at all having trouble keeping her breathing steady, rose from the bed and crossed the floor. She looked more closely at the larger set of footprints now. The previous night's short rain had been the first London had seen in over two weeks, which meant that both the girl's muddy footprints and those Clio tentatively assigned to the vampire had been made last night, between an hour before midnight when the rain started, and three hours afterward, by which time the ground would have been dry. Clio filed these observations away clinically, as if she had never seen a dead woman scream, and was about to leave when her eye fell again on the cupboard.

The door was not quite closed. It had been closed—hadn't it?—when she looked before, but now it hung open, just a crack, just enough for someone to be watching her, just enoug—

Clio crossed to it and threw open the door. It was empty. EMPTY she told herself. But she stood looking at it, into it, for a moment, to steady herself. Nothing like this had ever happened to her before. Not in the course of an investigation. Cool. Levelheaded. Unafraid. Those were the words people applied to Clio. She did not believe in supernatural killers—there were enough bad people in London alone to logically explain all the murders in the world, she had said numerous times. No need to go into the realm of true demons. She had not even believed in the Vampire of London when she first heard about him. She knew that if she had been in the city at the time, she would have found a logical explanation for his behavior. She was convinced that he was no more than a man cloaking himself in a legend.

But suddenly, for the first time, she had to wonder. No *man* had ever survived the rapids that sped under the supports of the Thames. No *man* had ever resurfaced from that particular swim in the river. But the Vampire of London had. Shot through the heart, he had survived. Which meant . . .

Reason came to her aid. No man *had* survived, but it did not mean that no man *could*. Things were not necessarily what they seemed. It was just this room, this place that was playing with her mind, the heat, the smell, the dolls, and the fact that she had not really eaten anything in two days.

The vampire was just a man, she told herself firmly. A

girl had been murdered by someone and she simply had to find out who. This was no different than any other investigation she had undertaken, she was just hotter, and hungrier, her mind was playing tricks, but it would stop, now. She gave the cupboard a scornful look, cast a final glance at the corpse, and stepped out into the courtyard.

Toast had climbed atop a stump of wood and was delivering one of the lengthy performances for which he was named—consisting largely of lifting an invisible glass and drinking it down with intermissions of loud and somber sounding twittering—while the boy sat on the ground before him. From the way he rolled his eyes at her, Clio could tell that Toast was finding the boy an unsatisfactory audience, probably because he had not yet yielded up the packet of meat pies, and the monkey was only too happy when she sat down next to the child.

The boy turned hollow eyes to her, then gestured with his head toward the room and pointed two fingers at his neck.

"Yes," Clio said, searching his face, "I saw them. The pricks. Did you find her like that?"

The boy looked down at his lap, his face hidden by his dark hair, and nodded.

"When? Today?"

The boy nodded again.

"Is she your sister?" Clio asked. The question was almost unnecessary. Their features were very similar and the girl looked to be only three or four years older than the boy, but Clio wanted to be sure.

The boy answered in the affirmative, this time raising his face to hers. Anger flashed across his hollow eyes, and then expectation.

Despite his lack of speech, Clio understood the boy's request instantly. "Of course. As soon as I have settled you at home, I will dedicate myself to learning who hurt your sister," she replied. For most people in London, such an assurance from her would have been all they needed to sleep more soundly in their beds, because Clio's reputation for wresting the truth out of mysteries was well known. There were a few skeptics who suggested that a person who would willingly take into their home any being—man, woman, child, animal—who merely *seemed* hungry or lonely or even just sad could not be nearly as intelligent as Clio was said to be, but her supporters far outnumbered her naysayers. People had begun to come from all over England not only to seek her aid—which was how she supported her menagerie—but merely to cast eyes upon her, causing the ancient ruin of a house she and her companions occupied on the corner of Milk and Honey Streets to become something of a tourist attraction, rivaling even the gallows at Tyburn in popularity. Indeed, so often did visitors stop her neighbors on the street with the question "Which house is Clio Thornton's?" that they had forgotten the true name of the rambling old building with the rose bushes growing over the facade and now called it simply Which House.

But Clio's assurances seemed not to placate the boy at all. He frowned and poked a finger in his chest, then pointed at her. When she appeared not to understand, he did it again.

"*Oh,*" Clio said finally. She tried to smile a boy-soothing smile. "That is a very kind offer, but I am afraid that I only work alone. The best way for you to help me would be to go and eat—"

The boy shook his head fiercely and again went through the pointing regimen.

Clio began to worry that she had not been firm enough with the boy at the beginning and she felt a twinge of panic. When she said she only worked alone, she had been telling the truth. Those who kept track of such things could tell you that Clio Thornton had solved exactly 203 mysteries in the past three years, and she had wrestled with all of them solo. She might turn to others for information, but she always worked by herself. It was a rule she had made years earlier, and it was a rule that no one, especially not anyone under the age of thirteen, was going to get her to break.

She frowned at the boy, trying to look simultaneously maternal and intimidating and authoritative, and he frowned back at her in blatant defiance. She puffed out her cheeks and he puffed out his, she squinted at him and he squinted back, she bit her lip and he bit his, too, with even more vehemence. Clio had received enough lectures on the evils of stubbornness during her growing up to be able to teach an Oxford course on the topic, but she felt she had never really understood its drawbacks until now, and finally, when he out-sneered her, she had to concede that she had met her match.

She gave in with a sigh. "Very well. You can help me. However, if we are going to do this together, it must be very clear that I am in charge." The boy looked past Clio, as if he could not hear her. "That means that you will do whatever I say," she repeated. "Otherwise, I shall find this fiend alone. Do you agree?"

The boy frowned slightly and then gave a slow nod in agreement.

Clio, who had not realized she was holding her breath, exhaled loudly. "Good. Excellent." Now that he had agreed to be led by her, he no longer looked quite so formidable and Clio felt herself relax slightly. As she did, she remembered the piece of blue silk she had taken from next to the mattress. She held it toward him and asked, "Have you ever seen this before?"

The boy fingered the fabric, then shook his head, and shook it again when she asked if it had belonged to his sister. Having confirmed that the kerchief had been imported into the house, and recently, made finding its owner a top priority. Perhaps whoever left it there saw someone around the property before the girl died. Or, perhaps it belonged to whomever—*whatever*—killed her.

It had been so real.

Clio did not know if it was the memory of the girl's face or the feel of a hairy arm brushing against hers that made her shudder. She looked down and was just in time to see Toast bring the blue handkerchief to his face and sniff it suspiciously. Then, before she could stop him, he turned into the alley and dashed out into the press of people on the main street.

Now it was Clio's turn to do the dragging. Without pausing to think, she grabbed the boy by the arm and set out after the monkey. During the several-year term of their acquaintance, Toast had demonstrated two outstanding qualities: a tendency to purloin small objects, and an incredible sense of smell. Generally he exerted these only in pursuit of meat pies, but on occasion, and Clio hoped this was one, he had been invaluable in helping her track down suspects by following their scent. If Toast could find the owner of the kerchief, Clio would certainly be closer to finding the killer. Possibly much, much closer.

Her mind keeping pace with her feet, Clio forced herself to consider that Toast might be leading her directly to the Vampire. Even if one discounted that he was a demon, he was indisputably a most cunning, dangerous criminal. It had taken a madman to capture him, and even then, as Clio now suspected, the capture had been only temporary. What in the queen's name did she plan to do against someone like that?

She had never faced a murderer alone before, and never a fiend. Suddenly the knife she always carried in her bodice for protection when she went out on investigations felt very small and ineffectual. But even as she considered the wisdom of turning around and waiting until a constable could be found, she saw Toast turn abruptly and go into a tavern door and she knew she had no choice but to follow him. As she reached the tavern and saw the sign with a picture of a heavily made-up woman hanging over it, Clio felt a flicker of surprise and relief. Despite its name, the Painted Lady Tavern was one of the most respectable houses in the area, more often hosting poets and playwrights than the ruffians and rakes who crowded the benches at other establishments.

What was more, she knew the proprietor well. Indeed, Clio had recovered Lovely Jake's prize pig for him that spring, and so was relieved to see him standing behind the bar as she entered. Whispering to her young companion to stay by the door and not move, a request to which she got only a barely visible sullen nod, Clio scanned the length of the dimly lit room looking for Toast. It was empty except for a solitary figure hunched over the table near the stairs and snoring loudly, around whom Toast was dancing ecstatically.

The thought that a vampire would sleep all day in order to be fresh for his kills flashed through Clio's mind, but was quickly dispersed by a hearty welcome from Lovely Jake.

"Miss Thornton, it is an en-orm-ous pleasure to see you," he boomed. Lovely Jake had earned his nickname playing the Maiden in numerous plays to packed playhouse crowds in his youth three decades earlier. Although it was hard to imagine the now enormous man as a captivating damsel, his voice, particularly when he chose to exercise it, could still command the attention of even the farthest boxes. He was exercising it now. "How is the Triumvirate these days?" he bellowed, as if in proof. "They have been *off scene*, if you will pardon me a theatrical expression, this long month. Have they a new project afoot?"

"It's a pleasure to see you, too," Clio said quietly, her eyes not leaving Toast. Then, moving close to Jake, she stood on her toes, pointed in the direction of the sleeping figure, and whispered, "Who is that man?"

Jake looked remorseful. "It would bring honor to us both if I could speak his name," he replied, in his idea of a confidential whisper, audible in Southern Kent. "But I cannot—nay, I must not. I do hate to wear the mask of secrecy, but you see, I took a stack of gold as long as my shoe and promised to, as we thespians say, *stand mute upon my mark*." Clio eyed Jake's enormous shoe and felt her heart sink. There was no way she could match that offer. "I can tell you this, though, my dear Miss Thornton," Jake went on. "That is neither a happy man, nor a content man. His role upon the stage of life hangs heavy upon him. I begrudge no man my company, but one would think he would have had enough of it by now. He has been here, much as you see him at this moment, since yesterday midday, or as we say in the theater, *intermezzo*, and I must confide that I do not see any sign of *exit, End Act I*, on the near horizon."

If the man at the table had been in the tavern since the previous noon, there was no chance that he had made the muddy footprints Clio had seen at the doll house, which meant there was little chance he was the vampire. Clio's relief that she was probably not facing a fiend just now was undermined by what that meant: the murderer was still out there, possibly getting ready to kill another victim. Her only consolation was the bizarre dance that Toast was performing around the sleeping man. The monkey's sense of smell was as unerring as a dog's, so there had to be something linking this man to the dead girl. Impatient to question the sleeping man at once, she just nodded her thanks to Lovely Jake and headed straight for the table.

The man was snoring contentedly, his head down over his arms, his body covered with a red silk cape. Clio stood over him, watching him sleep for a moment, then suddenly remembered the expression of horror she thought she had seen—*it had looked so real*—on the girl's face.

She was not afraid. She was not afraid. She was *not* afraid.

She cleared her throat and said, "Excuse me."

The man resettled himself in the crook of his arm, but did not stop sleeping—or snoring.

"Excuse me," Clio said again, this time louder.

Still nothing. Rationalizing that Jake would not allow her to be killed *center stage* in his tavern, Clio ventured closer. She tapped the man on the crown of the head while bending near his ear and whispering "excuse me" directly over it.

Miles Loredan, Viscount Dearbourn, was feeling belligerent. He would not kill whomever had replaced his head with a pumpkin, that was all right, but the scurvy villains who were trying to carve it out were going to find themselves facing the sharp point of a sword. Wasn't it enough that they had pulled him from wonderful oblivion? Did they need to compound their sins by beating his head with cudgels? What had he—

A vague thought seeped into his ale-soaked head, a memory of his cousins towering over him several days earlier, as they left the Turkish bathhouse, and promising that if he was not home by four bells to prepare for his betrothal ball, they would send an escort who was sure to rouse him. Aha, Miles realized triumphantly, the devils playing squash-the-squash with his head were his cousins' minions of evil. Perhaps if he showed a sign of alertness the minions might go away. And if that didn't work, he would fight them to the last man.

With great effort, he snarled and opened one eye.

Then very quickly opened the other one. What he saw in front of him, a dancing monkey and an elf, was surely an apparition. He had not reckoned on real demons and was beginning to worry that they might be harder to kill than normal men, when he raised his head completely and saw that he had made a mistake. There was a dancing monkey. But the elf was a woman. A woman with a smear of dirt on one cheek and a tattered gown and long brown hair and enormous, challenging brown eyes. An absolutely stupendous looking woman.

There was only one thing to do with a woman like that. Reaching out, Miles pulled her toward him and pressed his lips hard against hers.

She tasted like a memory, like summer, and youth, and his favorite kind of ink all rolled together, and he could have gone on kissing her all day if she had not pulled away, leveled a knife-sharp look at him, and said, "You moldy mongrel."

It was not the kindest thing anyone had ever said to him, but coming from her it sounded lovely. As did the "You contemptible, cantankerous cur," and the "You repellant rat terrier," that followed, along with the probing question, "How dare you sit there and stare at me with such insolence?"

Miles would have liked to reply it was because he could not help himself, that he had never before been pegged down by the *Dog Breeders Almanac*, but he was completely speechless, another first for him. Instead he smiled.

"You would grimace at me, bug-eating beagle?" Clio demanded, her glare intensifying as she rubbed the place on her chin where his overgrown whiskers had abraded her.

His cousins had really outdone themselves, Miles thought. Listening to her was almost better than kissing, he decided, brushing a lock of dark hair from his forehead so he could watch her more easily, but only almost. Taking advantage of a lull in her tirade, he reached out, this time pulling the woman all the way onto his lap. She smelled delicious. He licked the comparison between himself and a spineless spaniel from her lips and kissed her deeply.

That was when all the demons of hell attacked him. Someone punched him from behind and the girl pushed away from him from below, and nearby someone else was twittering. When he could finally collect his thoughts, he saw that the monkey seemed to be making a toast to a young boy standing behind him, who had the defiant posture of a pugilist. Next to the boy, speaking soothingly, was the woman, but her expression was anything but soothing when she turned it on Miles.

Clio was having to work hard to convince herself not to run the man through with the small knife she always carried, when she was spared the argument by the arrival of three rough looking armed men. They pushed past her and surrounded her potential victim on all sides.

Not actually trusting her restraint even in their presence, she grabbed the boy's hand, made a sign to Toast, and almost ran out into the open air. Clio was heedless of the racket that followed her from the Painted Lady, heedless of the gruff voice of one of the armed guards saying, "Come along, Lord Dearbourn, your cousins sent us to escort you home," heedless of the fact that the boy was growing winded trying to keep up with her, heedless that she was muttering to herself. She stalked down the street, completely absorbed in thought, or rather thoughts, for there were two that cycled around in maddening relay between *how dare he?* and *who was he?*

If anyone had told her that answering those questions was going to cost her everything she had, everything she believed, everything she held most dear, she would have laughed and said "impossible."

She would have been wrong.

She was heedless of the dark-caped figure who slid from shadow to shadow, following her home.

Chapter 2

"Just dump him in there," the tall man instructed, and the three guards who had carried Miles from the Painted Lady tipped him headfirst into the tub of iced water sitting at the center of the sparsely furnished chamber.

The guards left then, and for a moment the room was completely still. There was only one chair in the vast space, so Crispin, Tristan, and Sebastian stood around the tub, watching impatiently, while Ian turned to his wife, Bianca, who was standing off to the side, and asked, "Are you sure this won't kill him?"

She looked up from the conversation she was having with her sister-in-law, Sophie, and shook her head. "I never said that. I said it would not kill a woman. My medical expertise only applies to women. I make no guarantees about your part of the speci—"

Before she could finish, there was an enormous splash and Miles leapt from the tub. "What in Hades did you think you were doing?" he demanded, glaring at each of his cousins in turn. "Are you trying to kill me?"

"You did say death would be preferable to going through with your betrothal," Tristan reminded him.

"I believe the exact words were 'even a long painful

death would be preferable,' " Sebastian corrected. "Be glad we did not take you at your word."

"Besides, Bianca assured us that the cold water probably wouldn't kill you," Ian pointed out. He paused before adding, "It did seem the fastest way to make sure you were sober."

Ian's words hung in the air. He had said what none of them wanted to, and now they all braced for the inevitable maelstrom that followed any mention of Miles's drinking.

Miles stood in the middle of the room, his clothes dripping wet, clenching and unclenching his hands. He was looking down at the water puddling on the bare floor, but the tension in his body was palpable, and every one of his cousins was holding his breath anxiously.

It was a scene that very few people could have imagined, or even believed. Because Crispin, Ian, Tristan, and Sebastian were four of the six richest, most powerful, and most dauntless men in Europe—four of the six men who, as the Arboretti, were hailed, worshiped, envied and courted by princes, merchants, and beautiful women everywhere. The word 'Arboretti,' describing as it did not only the six cousins but also their enormous shipping enterprise, could conjure blushes behind both the gilded doors of the most exclusive boudoirs and the solid oaken ones of the most respected counting houses, although generally not for the same reasons. Between their wealth, connections, charm, and courage, the Arboretti could have anything they wanted. Which made Crispin, Ian, Tristan and Sebastian, four of the six men least likely to worry about antagonizing anyone, particularly anyone dripping wet and much the worse for drink.

But Miles was not just anyone. He was the second

youngest of the Arboretti, and in many respects more like a younger brother than a cousin to all of them. In a way they had raised him themselves, since he had spent most of his youth avoiding his father's insults by hiding out at their houses, and each of them felt a concern for him that went beyond mere affection. Especially right then.

During the previous three and a half years, Miles had willfully become something of a stranger to them, to everyone really, first because of Beatrice and then, after her death, by purposely holing up at his country estate and refusing all visits. The other Arboretti knew that he had overseen the training of the queen's forces in hand-to-hand and sword combat before the battle against the Spanish Armada, but after that he had slipped out of sight. From the scant information available to them—that he descended into his wine cellar every morning sometimes for days on end, and that when he arrived in London six months earlier it had been found to be completely empty, with not even a single cask left filled—his cousins surmised that he had been spending his days and nights brooding in the lonely company of a decanter. But it was just a surmise. He would not volunteer any information about that period, and they had all experienced his wrath enough times when they dared ask to have stopped inquiring.

Despite his listlessness and the fact that he never opened his eyes more than halfway, he still looked like Miles, the man who could fall in love with five different women in the time it took most fellows to unknot their boots; the man whose poems had once spawned a national craze and whose three year silence the publishers of London continued to bemoan on a daily basis; the man who still had the best collection of timepieces in England, but no longer cared to keep them working; the man whose habit of pushing his unruly locks from his forehead had become a hallmark for gentlemen of fashion, even now that he never bothered with it anymore and just let his hair hang limply in his eyes; the man who had been without question England's best swordsman, but now used his skill only in drunken brawls; the man that women nicknamed the Viscount of Dreams and took to their bosoms with a willingness despite his long-standing betrothal that made the other Arboretti—let alone the rest of the men of Europe—mope with envy; he still looked more or less like that man, but he was not the same.

The smile for which he had once been famous had been replaced by a sneer, his love poetry had turned into such sharp parody that no London printer who valued his neck would dare to touch it, his brilliant wit had become biting sarcasm, and he now considered friends only those who would drink with him without challenging his behavior. His apartments, once among the most comfortable and sumptuous in London, were now empty of all but broken clocks, the brand-new furniture stacked in towers against the walls, still swathed in the wrappers it had been delivered in three years earlier. Not that it mattered, since he was rarely to be found there, preferring to pass his days and nights in unsavory taverns. On his worst days he provoked fights, during which more than one man had been injured mortally. But even on his best days there was a brittleness about him, an uneasiness, and a deep unhappiness.

His cousins felt for him enormously, both for his loss of Beatrice—they had never before seen him devote himself so entirely to a woman—and for the approach of his arranged marriage. As they had grown from boys into young men, they had all aided him in avoiding any meeting with his prospective bride, agreeing wholeheartedly that half a lifetime was long enough to spend with someone you hated and he need not start any earlier than necessary. Together they had all toiled over the "love letters" Miles's parents forced him to write, packing them with such extraordinary poetic confections based on the portraits of her he received yearly, that Mariana had been moved to publish them, an event which Miles claimed set back the reputation of English composition by sixty years. If the thought of marrying someone not of his own selection had not been bad enough, the decision to publish those missives and the poor taste it showed would have caused Miles to break the contract, even though it meant the loss of his immense fortune, were it not for his strong sense of duty and honor. His cousins respected him for that, even as they suffered at his hands.

All of which—his unhappiness, their suffering—had only intensified in the weeks leading directly up to his nuptials, that is, up to this night, the night he would at last meet his betrothed (whom he had for years called the Monster). Tonight was the first in a series of ten days of celebration that would end in the most sumptuous and anticipated wedding of the year. Anticipated by everyone except the Arboretti, who dreaded it more than they would have dreaded the gallows. It was their responsibility to see to it that Miles was presentable, if not entirely present, at all the festivities. And given the way he looked at that moment, unshaved, in the same clothes he had been wearing for three days, now dripping wet, that was going to be quite a chore.

Especially if he went into one of the rages generally

occasioned by any mention of his drinking. As the seconds spread into a minute, the tension with which the Arboretti awaited Miles's retaliation became so thick it was almost edible.

"Actually," Miles said finally, and with a surprisingly small amount of surliness, "It was not the water I was talking about. It was that pack of ruffians you sent to bring me home."

The collective exhaling of breath in the room could have launched the heated air flotation device Ian had been working on for years.

Crispin recovered his wits first. "They were not ruffians," he pointed out. "They were more like well paid thugs. One of them said he had worked for the queen."

"I believe he said the Queen of Bawds," Sophie corrected her husband in a semiwhisper.

Miles grunted. "It is not as though I won't have enough bullying after my marriage. Given what awaits me, you might have considered sending a slightly kinder escort. Say a young woman. With long brown hair. And brown eyes. And a smudge of dirt on her cheek." Miles nodded to himself then and gazed out into the distance. "Oh," he added suddenly. "And no monkey."

All four of Miles's cousins raised an eyebrow, a family trait, but only Tristan spoke. "Right," he said, working to keep the surprise out of his voice. "We'll note that the absence of monkeys would be welcome next time."

"Good." Miles pushed the lock of hair off his forehead, and glanced at the large clock that stood opposite him. None of them knew why he kept it there, it had never shown the correct time even when it was well looked after—just now it said it was three o'clock when it was easily half past four—but today it seemed to have a strange effect on Miles. When he spoke again the hint of Old Miles was entirely gone, replaced by surly irritation. "Don't you have anything better to do than wait around my apartments gaping at me? I have to go make myself presentable for this evening, and if it pleases you, I would rather not have an audience."

Ian stepped forward to stop him. "Before you go, you should read this note from L. N." L. N., Lucien North Howard, earl of Danforth, was the youngest of the Arboretti, and the most mysterious. None of the cousins had ever met him, though not for lack of trying. It was not simple curiosity that drove them, but also the fact that, according to the terms of their grandfather's will, L. N. was the official head of the Arboretti. Still, the words "His Lordship is abroad," spoken by his solemn steward, were the only real evidence they had for his existence. That and the train of beautiful women who spoke of him in terms reserved by the ancients for their deities, and pined for him openly throughout the courts of Europe. They had hoped that their mysterious cousin would at least put in an appearance at Miles's ball, but his expression on reading the note suggested their curiosity would not yet be satisfied.

"He regrets to say he will be unable to attend this evening," Miles announced. He crumpled the note into a ball and let it fall to the ground, adding audibly, "Lucky bastard."

He did not see the expressions on his cousins' faces as he stalked out of the room, but Miles hoped they showed resignation and disappointment. It was ironic, he thought, that the one day he really had been doing exactly what he seemed to be, the one day when he actually had spent the last twenty-four hours in the company of a decanter, was the day when he had almost let his carefully wrought disguise slip.

It was not that Miles did not spend a good deal of time in taverns. He visited them almost daily, seeking sanctuary. They were the only places he felt at ease, the only places he could easily sleep. Nor was it that he did not drink. He did, every day. But only at home. Only at night. And only alone. "Insurance for pleasant dreams," he used to say glibly as his manservant Corin brought in the carafe of wine he would go through between midnight and dawn before he could fall asleep. But that was before. Now it was more like five carafes. And now he did not bother to make excuses.

Miles closed the door of his inner chamber with a desultory shove and silently locked it. Then, moving with an animation and purpose his cousins would not have believed, he crossed to the large clock that stood against the wall, opened its false-front panel, inserted a strange looking key, rotated it three times and ducked inside.

The troubled looking sailor who slid out of Dearbourn Hall half an hour later went unnoticed by the crowds that had massed to gawk at the illustrious guests arriving in their hackney carriages and litters for the party. Garlands of lemons with their glossy leaves decked the facade of the house, and four-dozen footmen in the immaculate yellow and gold livery of the Dearbourns stood before the door to lead away horses and escort guests in. This was a party unlike any other in English memory, bringing together not only the elite of the London social whirl, but also celebrities from the worlds of art and theater. The arrival of Sir Francis Drake and entourage garnered a loud cheer from the crowd, as did the appearance of Sir William and Lady Elizabeth Porteous, the famous travel writers, and that of Christopher Marlowe, an up-and-coming playwright. But by far the biggest sensation of the evening came when Lawrence Pickering, the best-loved hero of the battle of the Spanish Armada, descended from an elaborate coach with the wry smile that was setting every heart in London aflutter that season on his face, and a stunningly beautiful but unknown woman on his arm.

The stir caused by Lawrence's arrival outside Dearbourn Hall was audible even over the din of conversation in the Great Hall within. Lady Mariana Nonesuch, Miles's betrothed, stood at one of the windows overlooking the main door, observing the commotion below with a dreamy smile on her lips.

"Don't the coachmen with their lamps look like a sea of diamond angels, Doctor?" Mariana asked the bearded and brooding man at her right. Without waiting for him to answer, she rushed on, addressing the rest of the small group that surrounded her. "Oh! It is all so darling. That is ten war heroes including the admiral," she enumerated. "Eight poets, six members of the Star Chamber, two of Her Majesty's former lovers, three playwrights, and five artists, in addition to all the regular guests. Poor dear Cecilie, she will be so jealous. She had only three war heroes—none of them admirals—and no poets at her ball. I shall have to do my best to let her know that her place in my heart is unchanged."

Lady Alecia Nonesuch, the betrothed's grandmother, inclined her head, setting aquiver the two "copied from life" purple doves that sat atop her enormous silver hairpiece. "It is like you to think of others' distress even as you prosper, my dear."

"Oh! I feel acutely the pain of others. When one is blessed as I am, one must always be magnifamous."

"Magnanimous," the bearded doctor corrected.

"Doctor, you are too literal," Saunders Cotton, the young man standing on Mariana's left, interjected then. "My lady's soul cannot be defined within the language spoken by such as you and I."

Mariana gave him a soulful look. "Darling Saunders, you must not mock me. You know that I am only a mcek little thing, a baby dew drop, and easily overwhelmed by your superior mind."

Two patches of color appeared on Saunders's cheeks. "Lady Mariana, I would never insult you. Never. I would rather stab myself through the heart with this knife," he took something that looked like a child's toy from his waistband, "than let it be said that I offended you. Please, my lady, free me of the stain of your displeasure or let me die."

"Calm down, Saunders," Mariana said, not at all displeased by this show of loyalty from her grandmother's secretary. "I forgive you. And I do hope you are right about the bodice of this dress."

"There is no question." Saunders replaced his toy dagger at his waist. "As soon as he sees you in that gown, the viscount's first thought will be that you must have jewels for your beautiful neck. Only a monster could react otherwise."

"Oh! The darling viscount does particularly like to talk of my neck in his letters," Mariana mused. "He has compared it many times to the threads woven by the

fates, so thin and delicate that it is a wonder they can utterly destroy a man's life." She smiled to herself for another instant, then, exhibiting one of the rapid changes
in mood to which she was prone and which young men
found so fascinating, she frowned. "I do wish he would
get here. This party is tedious."

As if on her command, the crowds passing in front
of Mariana to pay their respects drifted to the sides,
and Miles appeared before her. Corin had been promised twenty pounds by the Arboretti if he produced his
master in good condition, and he had earned his money
in hard labor. Miles was resplendent, radiating wealth,
power, elegance, and good odor in equal measure.

But there was nothing Corin could do about his mood.
Miles's face had grown blacker and blacker as the hour
of the ball approached. The vitality had drained from his
movements, his eyes had slipped back down into slits,
and his face was once again a mask of bitterness. There
had been a time, Corin was aware, when all of that was
merely affect, but as the day of his marriage approached,
it had begun to sit naturally. Even the drinking, which
had been a cover to allow him to gather information in
taverns, had assumed a more real aspect, as Corin knew
from the ever larger pile of empty decanters he collected
from his master's bedside each morning.

But as much as he would have liked to be, Miles was
not drunk as he entered the ball. Unable to bring himself
to really examine the woman he would be spending the
rest of his life with, he instead focused on her companions, bowing to each as the introductions were made.
One of them looked familiar to him, but it took Miles a
moment to recognize the young man called Saunders, the
son of a country squire he had met years ago, beneath the

patina of a tall, gangly gentleman that he now wore and the cloud of absurd cologne that circled him. Next to him, his arm through Mariana's, was some sort of bearded foreign professor of indeterminate origin with an accent that hurt Miles's head. On the other side of the bride stood Lady Alecia, her grandmother, whose quivering coiffure made Miles a bit nauseous, and behind them, whistling to himself in a corner, stood Mariana's father, Sir Edwin Nonesuch. Of all of them, Miles decided he liked Sir Edwin best, mostly because nothing about him made Miles queasy.

But he did feel queasy, right through Lady Alecia asking him how he did and him saying fine, right through Sir Edwin giving him a menacing scowl before fading back into the wainscoting, and especially through Mariana curtseying to him with an "Oh!" and a sigh and asking if he could not hear the baby rabbits raising their little voices to sing in doleful—"dulcet" the foreign professor put in helpfully—tones at their union. It took Miles a moment to recover from the shock of this question. He was still mouthing the words "baby rabbits" to himself, soundlessly, when Mariana went on.

"This, darling Viscount, is Saunders Cotton, my grandmother's secretary," Mariana explained, gesturing to the man Miles had recognized, who promptly blushed. "And this—" she pushed forward the bearded fellow, "—is Doctor LaForge, the famous scholar and my tutor. Of course you have heard of him."

"It is a pleasure to make the acquaintance of a being of such greatness as you possess, monsieur le viscount," La Forge said, bowing low and averting his gaze from Miles's like one who dare not look upon a great idol.

Miles gave the man a smile with an amazing resemblance to a sneer and muttered something under his breath that sounded to his cousins like "simpering puppies."

Mariana heard it too and clapped with delight. "Oh! I knew as soon as you set eyes on me our spirits would frolic together like baby clouds at the start of a new day. I have always wanted a puppy! Oh! Do have your man bring one to me, darling Viscount. One with large, soft eyes that speak of his sweet baby soul. Like mine."

Much to the horror of the Arboretti, Miles smiled. It was not a real smile but one of the ghostly new expressions he used when he was about to flay someone alive verbally. But before he could begin, a bell was rung at the other end of the hall and the crowd grew silent.

A middle-aged man, with his hair slicked to the side and very red lips, cleared his throat, and all eyes turned to him. He looked down at a piece of parchment he was holding, then up at the crowd. "It was the wish of his late Lordship, the current viscount's father, that this letter be read on the opening day of the celebration of his son's marriage," the man began without introduction. "He left it in the care of my father, his business agent, but my father being infirm, he asked me to read it in his place."

The man licked his lips and began to read.

" 'On this, the first day of July in the year fifteen hundred and sixty-five, in gratitude for Sir Edwin's saving my life, I do hereby betroth my son to the first-born daughter of my dear friend Sir Edwin Nonesuch. Twenty-five years from today, her hand shall be joined with his in marriage, and her fortunes likewise. From the day of her twenty-fifth birthday forward, Sir Edwin's daughter will be sole heir to my son's estate. Only if the Deity sees fit to take one of them to himself*

before that day, will this betrothal be voided. Other-
wise, it is my firmest wish that it proceed. To that
end, I pledge my son's complete obedience. If my
son should prove to be craven or unworthy of his
blood and my title, if he should behave with dishonor
and break this contract, then I disown him, and order
that he shall forfeit his entire fortune to Sir Edwin
Nonesuch.' "

Craven or unworthy. The words that bound Miles to
the damn contract. They were like an incantation, guar-
anteeing his obedience. If his father had not included
them, had not yoked his son's honor and character to the
betrothal, Miles would have extricated himself long ago,
willingly giving up his fortune in exchange for his
freedom. Miles had always thought that those last words
were designed to goad him, to be a challenge to him, a
thorn in his side. He could still hear his father's predictions about him—that any son who was more interested
in what made a gun work than how to fire it, any son
who would not back his father in a fight when someone
called him a thick-headed beast, but would happily jump
into a fray to stop some leprous tramp from being
robbed, that any son who kept his father from disciplining his mother with the cat-o-nine-tails when the
bitch deserved it, was unworthy and cowardly and a
failure and would bring dishonor to the Dearbourn title.
Miles would be damned before he fulfilled those predictions by backing out of the betrothal.

"Unfortunately for Sir Edwin, it does not look as
though anyone is thinking of breaking this contract," the
man who had been reading joked with an artificial smile.

The assembled company laughed politely at the remark,

and raised their glasses in a toast to the bride and bridegroom. Beaming at the adoration she felt communicated
to her in waves from every corner, Mariana gave a low
curtsey, exposing an expanse of alabaster bosom that
at least one man in the room would have killed to call
his own.

That man was not Miles. His attention no longer held
by the reader, he turned it to the glass of sparkling wine
someone had given him, and, having gulped that, to
Tristan's glass, which he pried from his cousin's fingers.
Slowly, he began to feel better. He was just about to
reach for Sebastian's when he saw Mariana shudder.

He wiped his mouth on the back of his sleeve. "Now
that my fortune is yours, you might spend it on getting a
proper dress made," he told her with an unflattering
glance at her bodice. "There is no reason for you to go
about half-exposed and freezing like that."

"Oh! Listen to his divine similitude for me," Mariana
trilled to her companions, ignoring the doctor's whispered correction "solicitude" as she leaned toward Miles
to confide, "A heart such as mine, darling Viscount,
needs no covering, but must remain unexhibited so it
may rise to the heavens."

"Uninhibited," the doctor whispered.

Miles stared at her dumbfounded.

"I knew you would understand, darling," she went
on, awash in smiles. "I knew you would see that only
jewels might come near it without fear of damage. I have
already reserved an emerald pendant on a pearl choker
at Beaumond's, Viscount," she explained, naming one of
London's most expensive and most garish jewelers.
"You need only send your man to buy them. Darling

Beaumond said he would await your bill of credit until the baby birds cease to fly and all upon the earth perish."

S'teeth I hope that happens soon, Miles thought to himself, utterly undone at the prospect of having to spend the rest of the evening, not to mention his life, with this woman. He felt like a seasick sailor in the middle of a storm whose arms were broken and whose boat had sprung a bad leak. Then, suddenly, he saw a life raft. "Of course you shall have the jewels. In fact, I shall see to them, and the puppy, right this moment if you can spare me your company."

The word "jewels" had a marvelous effect and Mariana could not dismiss him fast enough. Just the instant before, he had been prepared to rid himself of the viscount title forever so that he would never need to hear it on her lips again, particularly coupled with the words "darling" or "baby," but he was now glad to have it, if only because the rents from the lands associated with it might bring in enough income to purchase him a lifetime of jewel-induced liberation. "This first meeting has surpassed my fondest imaginings. You are an even more incredible woman than I ever dared dream," Miles said as he bowed in departure, and meant it acutely.

While Mariana rejoiced at her conquest of the darling viscount, so like a lonely baby horse until she came— "Oh! He is utterly smitten, isn't he Saunders?"—Miles barreled past his guests in search of wine. Or liquor. Or poison. Anything to dispatch him from his misery for at least a moment. He finally located a long table covered with savory delicacies, and spotted a carafe of sparkling golden wine at its far end. His fingers had almost closed around its neck in a fair approximation of what he wished someone might do to Mariana, when he felt a hand on his arm and a smooth voice whispered in his ear, "You are looking marvelous, my lord. Even better than I remember."

Lady Starrat Peters gave Miles a wide smile as he turned to face her. "Of course," she said, appraising him, "it might only be the clothes. I would have to see you out of them to know for certain if you have changed. Are you busy right now?"

Miles had known the beautiful Lady Starrat for many years and had been fond of her, both because of her wit and because she had been one of Beatrice's only friends from childhood. There had been a time when a proposition like the one she had just made would have amused and intrigued him. But now the idea of such intimacy with another person left him more than cold. The only company he was interested in at that moment was the company of the wine decanter in his hand.

"Don't look so shocked, Miles," Lady Starrat laughed. "I was only going to ask you to dance."

Miles gave what was supposed to be a smile. "It would be a pleasure, Lady Starrat, but not tonight. I have some important business to attend to." She did not need to know that it consisted of downing as much wine as he could absorb.

Gripping a full decanter—his "business partner"—tightly in one hand, Miles had just begun threading his way to the door of the Great Hall when there was a chorus of screeches behind him followed by a thud, a clatter, and the feel of an object sailing into his back.

The Arboretti, who had been following close on Miles's heels to ensure that he did not leave the party, stopped dead in their tracks.

"Isn't that—" Sophie whispered.

"Do you sce—" Bianca asked.

"What the devil—" Tristan and Sebastian said simultaneously.

"A monkey," Crispin pronounced with enormous surprise.

"And a woman," Ian added

"With dark brown hair—" Crispin went on.

"—Brown eyes—" Ian put in.

"—And a smudge of dirt on her cheek," they whispered in unison.

Miles, who had swung around ready to give his cousins hell for their overblown attempts to keep him from his own damn wine, found himself speechless for the second time that day.

Clio was not much better, but she had a better excuse. Miles at least knew where he was. Only minutes before she had been alone in her library, reading at her desk by the flame of a single candle, and now she found herself standing in a great hall blazing with light and filled with the cream of English society.

She had spent the early part of the afternoon having the girl's body removed to a cool-house. Afterward, she had gone to ask questions of the dead girl's employer, Mr. Wattles the doll maker, but instead had spent an hour listening as his wife explained that he only did the dolls to make ends meet because really, you see, he was an artist and had several important patrons, very important, who valued his skill at being able to take off a face from a drawing and make it come to life in the round, just as sure as if it were looking at you. The only useful piece of information she had been able to extract from the Wattles was that the boy's name was Inigo.

He had followed her everywhere, and it was only once

she had convinced him she was taking the investigation seriously that she had been able to persuade him to eat something. Although he was dropping from exhaustion, he had refused to stay in the bed Clio had made up for him in the big room with the angel heads carved in the ceiling unless she stayed with him, so she had sat next to him, humming him the song her ancient nurse used to hum for her and holding his hand, until he had fallen into a fitful sleep. She had then retired to the library, putting Toast on the gold cord that doubled as his leash and looping it around her chair to keep him from waking Inigo. When she had procrastinated as much as she possibly could, she gave up and opened her household ledger.

It was the most depressing book ever written, Clio had thought to herself as she again tried squinting. For a moment she could almost pretend that what she was looking at was a sea scene, with a wave caressing the prow of a sailboat over which the sun shone, but as soon as she stopped squinting the traitorous wave once again became a six, the boat showed itself to be a four, and the sun was revealed as a zero.

640. Six hundred and forty. Not an offensive number in itself, Clio knew, but very, very bad when written on the debit side of a ledger as it was on hers. Six hundred and forty was the number of pounds she needed to keep her household—and her creditors, who were not even really *her* creditors but were now her responsibility—content for the next six months. And six hundred and forty was about five hundred and forty pounds more than she currently had.

She knew the money Baroness Von Sturman still owed her for having recovered her prized black tigers would take care of ten pounds, and the job she had done clearing the famous pugilist Thomas "Lay-Ye-Down-To-Rest" Barlow of the charge of killing his mistress would bring in another thirty, but even with the addition of her quarterly allowance there would still be over three hundred pounds unaccounted for. As if to underscore the deficiency, a booming voice wafted down the stairs from the floor above announcing the end of the Roman Empire. Such an announcement could only mean that the Triumvirate—Masters Pearl, Williams, and Hakesly—had almost finished their newest theatrical masterwork, about the end of the Roman Empire, which meant that the time for disappointing her friends by telling them that she could not fund its debut would soon be upon her.

Clio had just begun to think that the six looked more like a noose with which the four—which looked like her—was about to be hung, when her attention was drawn to Toast's growing agitation. Assuming that it was designed to show sympathy for her and the growling her stomach was doing—she had begun to limit herself to one meal a day, and today she had sacrificed that to be sure the hungry boy had enough—she patted him on the head, put the ledger aside, and reached for her copy of *A Compendium of Vampires and Other Fiends*. But she had not gotten past the half title when Toast gave an enormous jerk, pulled the leg off her chair, and sent her somersaulting onto the ground.

She had recovered quickly enough to grab the end of the gold cord, but not fast enough to keep him from leaping out the open window into the street outside. Her protests only made him pull harder, and he led her on a strange chase through the narrow backways of the city. She had a vague notion that they were headed toward the queen's palace, but the warren of alleys and byways that ran between the larger houses of London was unfamiliar to her, and it had been all she could do to keep up with the dashing monkey. They were rushing down what appeared to be a dead-end passage when Toast stopped abruptly, turned his head, cocked it to one side, and then jumped through an open ground-floor window. Clio tried to pull him back, but the expression on his face when he turned it to her—urgent, without a hint of mischief—was one she had never seen, and she had resolved to follow, guessing this had something to do with finding the vampire. With Toast leading the way they wound through a maze of dark and empty corridors and up an unadorned flight of service stairs that ended at a closed door. Toast did not pause but threw himself with all his might against the door until it burst open, and then dragged her into the middle of the glittering room in which she now stood, depositing her squarely in front of a man.

He looked like a version of the man she had met that afternoon, the man in the tavern, but not the same version, because instead of a stubbly slovenly wreck, this man was a picture of aristocratic elegance. A picture she recognized. She was so astonished that she dropped Toast's leash, allowing him to make directly for the refreshment table, while she gaped at the familiar man, who was now making a low bow. She only had time to think, *No, not him,* when he began to speak.

"I am delighted to see you," he said, his voice a deliciously rich rumble, his teeth even lovelier than she remembered. "I had been hoping for an opportunity to apologize for my conduct this afternoon, but I had no idea you were on the guest list."

There was a rustle in the crowd and then a piercing voice announced, "She most assuredly was not," from the other side of the room. "You just could not stay away, could you?" the voice asked, addressing Clio.

Clio did not need to turn around to identify the speaker, but she forced herself to do it anyway, tearing her eyes from the man in front of her. Giving a low curtsey, rendered somewhat more difficult by the fact that she discovered she was still clutching *A Compendium of Vampires* in her hand, she looked Lady Alecia Nonesuch in the eye and said, "Good evening, grandmother."

Clio was accustomed to being unwelcome by her family, but the twin looks of disgust bordering on hatred that shown on the faces of her grandmother and her cousin, Mariana, were unique in her experience. Not that she could really blame them. After all, she had been receiving her quarterly allowance for the last five years on the single condition that she never bothered any of them, a condition that had been redoubled upon the last payment with the stipulation that if Clio did anything to disrupt Mariana's upcoming nuptials to Viscount Dearbourn, if she so much as showed a lock of her unbeautiful hair during any of the proceedings prior to the wedding, her allowance would be cut off for all time, and other bad, nameless things, would happen to her.

And here she was, bursting into the exact center of her cousin's betrothal ball, practically accosting the man Mariana was to marry, wearing a tattered gown that was barely acceptable inside her house and certainly not fare for a gala like this. Hoping that making a rapid departure would at least allow her to keep some part of the allowance that she had never needed as desperately as at that moment, she turned to look for Toast.

She saw only Miles. "It appears that introductions are unnecessary between all of you," he observed with a surprised gesture in the direction of his betrothed, "but allow me to introduce myself. I am Miles Loredan. The Viscount Dearbourn. Who are you?"

Clio did not have time to wonder at the strange tone in which he pronounced his title. "I am Lady Clio Thornton and it is an honor to meet you my lord, and if you will accept my apologies I shall be going good night I am sorry to have intruded," Clio said in a single breath.

"Surely you could spare me one dance before you go, Lady Thornton," Miles asked, all memory of his business meeting gone.

Clio's heart was racing. "No," she said, stepping backward, away from him. "I cannot."

He lowered his voice. "I promise there will be no repeat of my earlier behavior."

"It is not that, it is only—" Clio began to protest but was cut off by her grandmother.

"Yes, by all means, Clio. Dance with the viscount. One would so enjoy the entertainment of watching you stumble around the room."

Miles shot Lady Alecia an unfriendly look for these words, but he was smiling when his eyes returned to Clio. "It would do me great honor. Unless of course you need to get back to your reading." He leaned down slightly to see the book in Clio's hand, then stood abruptly. "What are you doing with that?"

All at once, Clio saw the beginning of a solution to her financial problem. Part of her mind knew that there were a thousand reasons it was a bad idea, a very bad idea, but it might also be her best option. Giving Miles a timid half smile—the first he had seen from her—she set the book down on the refreshment table and said, "I shall explain it as we dance."

The room buzzed as Miles led Clio into the middle of the floor and signaled to the musicians to begin a lively volta. Other couples rushed to join them, jostling to be nearest to the mystery woman for better observation, and even Mariana could not resist, dragging an embarrassed yet enraptured looking Saunders out onto the floor with her when Doctor La Forge refused. Theories about Clio's identity circled the room faster than the dancers' feet, ranging from the pedestrian—that she was the illegitimate child of the queen—to the more obscure—that she was one of a band of fairies sent by the Spanish to bewitch England—and everything in between. The Arboretti were somewhat inclined to this latter theory, if only because they could think of no other explanation for the rapid metamorphosis the woman called Clio had worked on Miles. Everything about him that has been wrong suddenly seemed right, and the smile he was giving her was the most Miles-like smile they had seen in years.

Lawrence Pickering, who with his companion had been detained by well wishers on their way up the stairs and had missed the stunning arrival of the girl with the monkey, now stood with Crispin. "Miles and his betrothed certainly make a charming couple," he said, gesturing at the dancers.

"They do," Crispin agreed. "But that is not his betrothed."

"Oh. Oh, no."

"Exactly," Crispin nodded. They watched as Miles

and his companion spun around the room, stunned by the unfamiliar sound of Miles's good-natured laughter.

Clio, whose experience with dancing had been limited to the miserable forms she was forced to run through at Mariana's birthday celebrations, had always thought it was an idiotic pastime designed only to humiliate, but Miles was a sublime dancer and she found that she was having a not entirely horrible time. Indeed, for the first few rounds, she lost herself in the pleasure of dancing with him—of feeling his golden eyes on her, of laughing with him—to such an extent that she momentarily forgot about her plan.

And then he reached out and touched her cheek— unable to stop himself, he had to wipe that smudge of dirt off, he had been thinking about it all afternoon— and the feel of his thumb gently caressing her made Clio miss a step. Or was it Miles who missed a step, Miles who was so undone by the softness of her skin—my God, if her cheek were that soft, what would the rest of her be like—Miles who held her against him for the briefest second—roses, that is what she smelled like, delicate wild roses—Miles who felt her heart beating hard against her dress.

It was then that Clio caught sight of her grandmother nodding knowingly *(You see, you cannot dance. You are a bad, wicked girl)* from her place at the edge of the room. Then that she saw her grandmother frown in her direction even as she discussed something with an over-dressed gentleman at her side. Immediately she recol-lected the reason she had agreed to be led onto the dance floor in the first place.

"You asked about the book, my lord," she began

when Miles had released her. She found she was slightly out of breath.

"I did?" Miles asked, then smiled, recalling. "I did." He led her in a weaving step among the other dancers. He found he did not want to talk about it much. "None of my business, certainly."

"It is, actually," Clio said. "I am reading it because I believe that the Vampire of London is back."

Miles did not miss a step. "Impossible. He is dead."

Clio nodded. If anyone should know, it would be her companion, since he was the one who had succeeded in hunting him down and shooting him after the fiend killed his beloved mistress Beatrice. Clio had read all about it in the news sheets, and it was upon this that she had based her plan. "I know that he is *supposed* to be," she agreed as they came together in a turn, "but this morning I saw the body of a dead girl. With two pricks on her neck. And a gardenia."

Miles pulled her toward him so they were dancing closer together. "How do you know about the gardenia?" he asked, his face serious.

Clio waved the question away with a shake of her head. "That doesn't matter. What matters is that a girl is dead and others may die and I want to see to it that does not happen."

Miles spun her out, then back, and asked, "Just how do you propose to do that?"

"I am going to find the vampire," she said, turning away.

Miles turned her back. "I have already found him. And killed him."

"I think you are wrong," Clio said, her eyes challenging

over her shoulder as they glided among the other dancers. "And I can prove it."

"Indeed?" Miles slipped her arm through his. "How?"

"By bringing him to you," Clio explained. Their conversation stopped while they entered a long arch made by the arms of the other dancers.

"I see," Miles resumed on the other side. "And exactly what would motivate you to do that?" He swung her in a wide arc.

"Money," Clio answered simply, not sorry that the turn had taken her out of his immediate gaze. "I propose that you pay me to find him."

Miles's feet kept time, but his mind left the dance. Even as he pulled Clio toward him, he was remembering the night he caught the vampire. The long scar across his stomach where the vampire had tried to drive his knife into Miles's heart was the only physical evidence he had of the horrible battle, but the memory, the memory of that man standing next to the girl, of his lips . . . He could not let the woman now in his arms see what he had seen.

"Not only will I not pay you to find him," he announced in the voice of one accustomed to requiring—and receiving—obedience, "it would be foolish for someone like you even to look."

"Foolish? Of someone like *me*?" Clio spat out the words. She pulled away from him and there was anger burning in her eyes. "Why? What is wrong with me? Do you think I am incapable of it just because *you* failed to capture him?"

Miles heard only two words. *You failed* resounded in his head, and everything instantly went white. Then his mind became completely, acutely, clear.

The events of the evening snapped through his memory one after another—*I have already reserved an emerald pendant on a pearl choker. The vampire of London is back. Pay me*—and a clear picture of what had happened took shape. He stood still in the middle of the floor, his hands on Clio's shoulders, his eyes looking at hers but not seeing them, a terrible smile on his face. "Will you and Mariana stop at nothing for money?" he sneered. "This was a rather elaborate ruse, making up that story about a dead girl. Elaborate and tasteless." He pulled her forcefully toward him and his eyes bored into hers. "Next time, don't tax yourself. Just have Mariana ask for my purse directly."

"What in the queen's name are you talking about?" Clio asked, numbed by the expression on his face.

"You said it yourself. You want money from me. But you made an error. I rarely pay women for services they perform with their clothes off, and never for those with their clothes on."

Clio wanted to slap him hard until his cheeks burned but willed herself to keep her fists clenched by her sides. Her hands were trembling, but not for the reason Miles thought. Pushing past him, she grabbed Toast who had by that time successfully decimated the meat-pie table and was proposing the health of the entire assembled company with real wine, and stalked from the room. She tried to keep her pace slow and dignified, but she knew what was about to happen and wanted to get away before it started.

The first hiccup came as they stepped out of Dearbourn Hall, and they multiplied as she and Toast made their way quickly through the quiet streets. Clio hated the hiccups, not because they were uncomfortable, but because of what they said about her. They were a sign of the war that raged inside her, a war between the violent urges that seized her and her efforts to keep them at bay. She only got the hiccups—and always got them—when she had forced herself to subdue the powerful impulses that smoldered within her. Her hands had trembled with the back-and-forth pull of violence and restraint, and she was appalled, as she always was, by the realization that she had wanted to do another person harm. She had never acted on one of these impulses, had never hurt anyone, but that did not mean that she never would, and the prospect horrified her. *You carry a devil inside you,* she could hear her grandmother's voice saying, *just like your father,* and despite how hard Clio fought against believing the words, the hiccups were always an undeniable reminder.

Don't think about them, she admonished herself. Don't think about the hiccups or your grandmother or Mariana or Viscount Dearbourn, or dancing—

She stopped walking and stooped down to look Toast in the eye.

"Why did you take me there tonight?" she demanded. "Was it only for the food?" At the word food her stomach rumbled.

Toast shook his head but reached into his doublet and produced a slightly mangled meat pie, holding it out to her. When she refused it, he pushed it at her more insistently.

"No bribes," she hiccuped. "Tell the truth."

Toast held the meat pie out to her with one hand and put his other on his hip, with an expression—one worthy of Inigo—that said she would absolutely get no more information from him until she took the savory pastry. Many people would have felt ridiculous taking orders from a monkey, but none of them knew Toast, or were as hungry as Clio was. She acquiesced, devouring the meat pie in three blissful bites between hiccups. Then she picked Toast up and brought him level with her eyes.

"Did our going there have something to do with the vampire?" she asked seriously. "With the kerchief you smelled today?"

Toast nodded and began looking agitated.

"Was he there? The man you smelled?"

Toast nodded again, squirming in her grasp to turn and look over his shoulder at the street behind him. Even by the dim light of the waning moon, it was easy to see that it was deserted.

"Was he the man I danced with?"

Toast relaxed slightly, shaking his head in negation.

"But he was there." Clio spoke the words as much to herself as to the monkey, setting him back on the ground. He ran ahead of her and she followed, letting the implication of her words seep in. The vampire had been at the ball. Given that her conversation with Miles had not been exactly private, he probably knew she was looking for him. And only Toast seemed to know his true identity. Her fastest route to finding the murderer, she concluded, was to keep him on a very short leash.

For a moment she wondered at what was really driving her forward. It was not simply that she wanted to catch the girl's killer. That would have been enough, but she knew there was more. There was something deeper she was looking for, something personal.

She quickened her steps to catch up with Toast—her best chance at a solution—who was skipping down the street in front of her. Thinking it was a game, he increased his pace, too, and she had just opened her mouth to tell him to stop when a hook shot out of an alley, grabbed him, and dragged him, shrieking, away.

By the time Clio reached the alley the shrieking had stopped and there was no sign of her monkey in sight.

Chapter 3

Clio's hiccups were gone. She ran headlong down the alley, struggling to listen over the sound of her panting, her eyes straining in the darkness. She slowed her pace, concentrating, and even still she almost missed it.

"I've got you," a voice said behind a door just beyond her on the right. Clio crept back and put her ear next to it, listening.

"How would you like to feel these, eh? They're sharp, they are. Sharp enough to teach you a lesson you'll not soon forget."

Clio pushed the door open and walked in. Toast, gagged, was hanging upside down by his legs from the large hand of a red-faced man. She had never been in this room before but she had been in the shop just beyond it, and she recognized the man with the hand as its proprietor, Arthur Copperwith, apothecary, slightly less than sober.

"Aye, Miss Clio," he greeted her. "Saw this little devil running down the street and thought I'd show him what I think of his behavior."

Clio kept her voice level. "What exactly has Toast done, Mr. Copperwith?"

"What's he done? Why, what he always does. Robbed me blind, that's what he done. Just the other day when you were in the store purchasing my serum. Snuck in here and helped himself to almost my whole stock of ourali."

The behavior the apothecary was describing was not beyond Toast, Clio knew—he had a way of making anything edible disappear into the folds of his doublet and had in fact produced a handful of lavender lozenges after their last visit—but Clio had read about the herb Copperwith claimed Toast had taken and knew it was poisonous, smelled bad, and was decidedly inedible. Plus, Clio had made it a practice to keep a close eye on Toast in public for that reason, and did not recall him leaving the front of the store during their last visit. "Are you sure?" she asked, frowning.

"Sure as this little devil is a monkey," Copperwith nodded. "You came in to get my famous serum, and after you left I walked back here for a little nip and what do I see but half my supplies gone."

Clio looked at Toast. "Did you steal anything from this room?" The monkey shook his head furiously and Clio turned her gaze to the apothecary. "He says he did not do it. Couldn't someone else have taken it?" Clio suggested.

The man was unmoved. "Says he did not do it, does he?" He gave Toast a violent look. "Didn't have any other customers that morning. Had to be your friend. But that is the last time." He brandished the pair of shears he had been holding in his free hand and brought them to Toast's ear. The monkey wriggled in the man's grasp, looking at Clio desperately. "Going to make sure he listens to me good next time I warn him."

"Wait," Clio commanded. "Put him down." When Copperwith gave her only a suspicious frown in reply, she rushed on. "I will pay you for whatever he took. But don't hurt him."

The shears receded slightly from Toast's head. "Pay me? When?"

"Tomorrow," Clio answered positively, as if she had crates of gold inconveniently filling her foyer. "But you must put him down."

Copperwith reluctantly, and not gently, lowered Toast to the floor. He scampered over to Clio and leapt into her outstretched arms.

"Thank you," she said. She examined the monkey to be sure he was intact, then asked, "How much do I owe you?"

Copperwith looked around the storeroom for a moment, adding. "Ourali is mighty rare. Comes over from the New World, got to steal it from savages you know. And I'm about the only person around who's got it. Should be eleven pounds twenty. But since you are a good customer, I'll let you have it for ten pounds."

Ten pounds was enough to feed Which House for a month, albeit not extravagantly, but one did not haggle over one's best friend's ears. "You may send someone for it tomorrow," Clio agreed, wondering where the money would come from.

Copperwith glared at Toast for a moment, then nodded. "You be careful Miss Clio. Just a bit of that stuff and you'd be dead faster than you could say a prayer, and he stole enough to kill off half London. I wouldn't want the little devil near me with that poison on him."

"Thank you, Mr. Copperwith," Clio said as she untied the gag from Toast's mouth. "I'll be cautious."

"I was you, I'd lock that monkey in the house and never let him out again," the apothecary said as he opened the door to let them out. "He's going to get you killed, Miss Clio, mark my words."

"I would trust Toast with my life," Clio replied, little guessing how soon she would have to.

The Great Hall at Dearborn House had long since ceased to vibrate with the sounds of men laughing, women's heels clicking, gossips whispering, gallants complimenting, and fine silks swishing when Lord Edwin Nonesuch entered his mother's chamber to ask if she heard the internal whistling outside her window that was keeping him awake.

Thirty-six women with distinct and highly varnished expressions looked at him from under thirty-six distinct hair-arrangements as he crossed the threshold. Or rather, thirty-seven, for Lady Alecia herself sat among the busts that held a portion of her famous collection of hairpieces, scrutinizing them.

No one knew exactly how many wigs she had, but she could go for more than two months without appearing in public in the same one twice, each more elaborate than the last, and all made of real human hair. Her most valued pieces were those taken entire from the heads of the dead or dying, and it was these that stood arrayed around the room. Every time she acquired a new treasure of this stature she had a stand for it made in the exact image of the person whose hair would sit atop it. Indeed, she had earned a bit of a reputation in France for delaying the execution of a golden-haired shepherdess, supposed to be a witch, long enough to allow an artist to make a sketch of her face that could later be applied to a bust. By far the most esteemed piece in her collection was the Anne Boleyn, which had reportedly been scalped from that unfortunate at the very moment of her execution. She had just had that bust redone, having deemed the older version too morbid, and it was toward the now smiling face of that doomed queen that Lady Alecia gestured.

"Do you think Annie would be better tonight?" she asked her son before he could speak. She was on familiar terms with all of her heads. "The Mary Hatfield kept getting in my eyes last time and distracting me, but I worry about sending the wrong message," she explained. "It is really a question of whether one prefers to play the seductress or the murderess."

Edwin frowned. "Why should it matter? Who will see you in bed? Did you hear someone—"

"Bed?" Lady Alecia laughed hollowly, interrupting him. "Whatever gave you that idea, Edwin? We shall not be abed for many hours."

For a moment Edwin looked at her in horrified silence, then he mouthed the word, "No." Finally finding his voice, he said it aloud. "No. We cannot. You promised we would not do it again."

Lady Alecia's face hardened. She reached for the Mary Hatfield—the famous murderess who had served a pie made of her husband and children to the neighbors who had come to support her in her time of loss; she would have gotten away with it, too, if the bullet her husband had lodged in his kneecap had not gotten caught in one of the guest's throats—and lifted its long brown tresses carefully to her head. "I promised no such thing."

"But you will ruin us," Edwin said, almost stuttering. "You will destroy us all. As soon as anyone finds out, we are done for. Do not do this, mother," he implored.

Her expression was anything but maternal. "You are a fool, Edwin. You have always been a fool. No one knows anything about it. They do not even begin to suspect."

"But how long do you think you can cover it up?" Edwin whined.

Lady Alecia clucked with disapproval. "Idiot. Don't you see? Everything is perfect. Something happened at the ball tonight that I could only have dreamed of. No scandal will ever touch us."

"I don't understand."

"You wouldn't and I don't care to explain it. But trust me." Her voice softened as she finished pinning the wig on and turned to look at her son. "Haven't I always been right before?"

Edwin hesitated. "Yes."

"And I shall not fail now. This is it. The moment and the means of our triumph are here. We need only grasp them."

"But someone is going to have to pay," Edwin half pled, half moaned.

"Someone will," she assured him, picturing the face in her mind, and the long, brown hair—similar to the wig she was now wearing and yet much more precious to her—that she had coveted for so long. "Someone will."

I wonder if the hairpiece could be done in time for Mariana's wedding, she thought as she left the room, dragging her son behind her. *It would look so lovely with my dress.*

* * *

Miles stood at the open window of his room, drinking. From his position he could have heard the hum of crickets and occasionally have seen the faint glimmer of a firefly, but what he was hearing and seeing was not outside. It was in his head, a dreamlike vision he had seen many times before, a vision he tried to keep at bay.

Three years earlier he had begun purging himself. First of love. Then of hate. He had intentionally organized his life so that slowly, all emotion faded from him, like the ink of an old manuscript, growing fainter and fainter until its traces were impossible to make out. He felt nothing now; his insides were blank. He had his work and his wine and everything in between was empty. He was like an elaborate binding that endured even when the pages it contained had yellowed and crackled away.

Only three things remained. Anger. Pain. And the vision.

She lay on her side, her hair splayed like a golden curtain out over the crisp white linen of the pillow, one arm thrown over her eyes. Her wrists were blue and green and purple with bruises. There were dark marks on her smooth shoulders where someone had held her struggling body down. And on her neck were the two brown pricks.

"Liar," Beatrice's voice said in his head with the rich Devonshire accent it acquired when she was angry. "You said you would always protect me. You failed, Miles. This is your fault."

You failed you failed you failed.

He drained his glass and reached for the carafe again.

*   *   *

The Royal Astrologer, up early to cast the queen's chart for the next day, looked up at the sky and made the following notation in his book: *4 hours past midnight. Moon—one degree beyond half-full. Waning.*

Chapter 4

Clio awoke suddenly, hitting her knee against the edge of the old chest in her study. In the space it took her eyes to focus, she realized that she had been sleepwalking again, and that this time she had gone all the way downstairs. Outside it was a bright day and the foot traffic in the street was already heavy, but Clio felt as though she were still engulfed in night. She tried for a moment to catch the tail end of a vision—a memory?—she had seen right before she awoke, but it was gone. In its place she was left with only the vague notion that it had been important.

"Drat," she cursed under her breath, rubbing her bruised knee. Arthur Copperwith, Apothecary's, Anti-Perambulation Serum had worked for three nights—for three blissful nights she had both laid down and awakened in her bed—but apparently its efficacy had worn off. He had warned her that might happen, that she might have to increase the dosage, but she still felt discouraged. And somehow she did not think the problem was with the dosage.

Limping slightly, she followed the sound of voices back toward the kitchen. It was a large room made of rough-hewn stones with an enormous fireplace in one wall and a wide table in the middle. She had always loved kitchens—she spent most of her time growing up sitting by the fire and reading and trying to be invisible— and she especially loved this one because it was large and filled with light, and because it was hers. Or would be, she thought with a grimace, until she ran out of money.

"The dawn arisith," a male voice boomed at her as she entered, and she traced a mock curtsey in her nightgown.

"Good morning, Mr. Hakesly," she said.

"Good morning, dear patroness," he replied with a slight bow.

Clio looked around the kitchen. "Where is Mr. Williams?"

"Quiet you two," the other man sitting at the table shushed. "I've got to get this down." It was Mr. Pearl, the scribe of the group. "Mr. Hakesly, on your cue."

Mr. Hakesly pointed to Inigo who was seated at the other side of the kitchen near the fire, holding two flat pans. At Mr. Hakesly's signal, Toast dove for cover and Inigo brought the pans together with a resounding crash. A voice from above them began shouting "Bosun! Bosun!" and Mr. Williams burst into the room through the window, arms waving, hair frothing. "Mariners, fall too't, yarley! Blow til thou bust thy wind! We'll blast—no, no, no." He stopped abruptly and shook his head. "Too blustery. Scare an audience senseless like that."

"I said before, and I maintain that it's coming through the window that's wrong," Mr. Hakesly said. "Come in from stage left and you've got a winning scene."

Mr. Williams muttered something about no one ap-preciating innovation and disappeared out the kitchen door—stage left—while Mr. Pearl diligently crossed out part of what he had written and dipped his quill in ink. Over his shoulder, Clio could read the words "Bosun, bosun" in his tiny, precise script at the top of the page.

Mr. Hakesly, Mr. Williams, and Mr. Pearl, known in the theater world as the Triumvirate, had been writing plays together for more than forty years, with an unprecedented absence of success. Not one of their plays had ever made it beyond the third act before being booed off the stage, shut by the censors, or pulled for lack of audience. Not that this bothered them. They went on writing because they loved it, and because they were certain that their masterpiece was just around the corner. And because, with Clio supporting them, they did not have to worry about eating.

"I'm sorry I interrupted, I didn't know you were rehearsing," Clio apologized, but Mr. Hakesly waved it away.

"Always a pleasure to see our muse. And I want you to know, we've been studying our charge." He nodded toward Inigo, sitting poised with the pot lids. "We think the boy has a future as an artist. Look at this." He held up a very good drawing of Toast.

Clio was impressed, but before she could say anything, Mr. Williams called from the corridor, "Are we rehearsing or are we going to chat all day?"

Chastened, Mr. Hakesly gave Inigo his cue. Toast hid, the pots clanged, and the scene began again, again ending abruptly, this time in a collision between Mr. Williams and the vegetable basket. He was in the process of extricated himself from a cabbage when he looked down at his hands and saw that he was holding a paper.

He turned it over twice as if he did not recognize it, then said, "Oh, Clio, there was a messenger at the door. He left this for you."

Clio took the note, ran her fingers over the familiar seal, and slit it open. As she read it, she began to scowl. Asking the Triumvirate to keep an eye on Inigo, she carried the note upstairs with her, where she changed from her tattered nightgown into one of her tattered day gowns. On the way back down, she reread the message and her scowl deepened. She was just crumpling it into a tight ball when she reentered her study.

It was a long room that ran the length of the house, with small-paned windows facing both onto the street and into the back garden. The walls housed shelves full of books, between and along the top of which were diamond-shaped inlays of gold and cherry-colored wood. A cherry mantle carved with medallion portraits of the seven muses picked out in ivory surrounded the deep fireplace, now unlit, and a worn but still richly colored rug in greens, blues, and creams covered the wood floor. The beams of the ceiling were whitewashed and painted with green vines and pink flowers, echoing the pink roses that clung to the facade of the house and pressed against the windows as if eager for entrance. There were a dozen chairs of different shapes and sizes arranged around a large trunk at the end of the room nearest the street, each with different colored cushions in varying stages of disintegration. At the other end of the room, closer to the garden, was a massive, scarred, and vaguely lopsided wooden desk. It, and most of the books, had belonged to Clio's father and were her only inheritance from him— besides, of course, her wickedness.

There was a man standing in front of the desk when she came in. He turned as she entered and her scowl became a smile at the sight of him. "Elwood! I cannot thank you enough for coming," she said, taking his hand in both of hers.

"You know I would do anything for you," Elwood replied earnestly. He had practiced declaring his feelings to Clio so many times in front of his mirror that for a while he had been perpetually hoarse. Now he cleared his throat, clearing away the words that her presence always inspired, and said instead, "I would have been here sooner but the streets are a mess today. Not only was there a huge explosion last night, but apparently every dressmaker in London has been called in to fray the hems and sleeves of their finest gowns, and footmen from every house have been sent out and told not to return unless they bring a small monkey with them. A bidding war broke out in Southwark over what was supposed to be a fine specimen, but turned out to be a bear cub." He looked at the threadbare dress Clio was wearing, and then at Toast as the monkey crept into the study and leaped onto her shoulder. "Is there any chance you had something to do with these new fashions?"

Clio groaned. "You heard about the Dearbourn ball."

"I hear about everything."

It was true. Until the war with Spain two years earlier, Elwood had worked for Lawrence Pickering, the king of the London underworld. His job had been to collect and store all information about people whose last names began with the letters "A" through "F," and he had continued in that occupation in the employ of the Special Commission for the Security of London after his boss had retired, rising to the rank of deputy commissioner. He and Clio had met during one of her first investigations, and since then she had found him an invaluable resource. And a very good friend.

"But I do not suppose you called me over just to learn about the latest styles, or to have me tell you that there is a very good engraved portrait of you in today's *News from Court* report on the ball," Elwood continued, then eyed her closely. "You look like you haven't eaten in days, Clio. Your urgent message would not happen to have anything to do with the state of your finances, would it? Your ledger was lying open on the desk and I happened to glance at it."

Clio shook her head. "No. There is nothing you can do about that."

"I have some money saved and—"

Clio put up a hand to stop him. "Absolutely not. That debt is my fault and a result of my stupidity and mine alone to see to."

"You are not stupid, Clio," Elwood said softly. Then, taking a cue from her vehemence he asked, "Does the debt have something to do with Justin?"

She looked at him, then looked away, and nodded. "Don't say it. I know you warned me against him. It was just that—"

That what? Clio asked herself. That she was a fool. She had known without a doubt that she was not in love with Justin Greeley. She knew what it felt like to be in love, because for ten years she had been in love with someone else, quietly, secretly, and completely. But that man could never love her back. She did not need Princess Erika's water-jug prediction that she would "not

experience true love until the fireflies came out at noon"—
that is, never—to tell her that.

And so when Justin had said he was in love with her,
she had decided that was enough. He understood her
heart was not his yet, Justin had said, but he would wait,
because it was worth it. She was worth it. And he
loved her.

It was the first time anyone had said anything like that
to her. Anyone. After a childhood of being told she was no
good and unwanted, it felt so wonderful to hear those
words that she had entirely lost her head. So what if
kissing his thin lips was not entirely pleasurable—perhaps
somewhat less pleasurable even than the kisses she had experienced the day before. So what if he insisted on taking
over her investigations, and mocking her for reading so
many big books, and laughing off her suggestions as the
ideas of "his silly, foolish little girl." He had loved her.

Said he loved her.

Elwood had tried to caution her, but he had been able
to give her no concrete information—Greeley starting
with a "G" and therefore being outside his provenance—
and so she had believed every word Justin had spoken.
When he told her that he wanted to be with her forever
but first needed a small loan, she had given it willingly,
even happily. It was only once he had disappeared that
she learned he had taken her bill of credit and used it to
secure an even larger loan, in her name, with Captain
Black, London's most dangerous and notorious thug and
a man she had sworn to destroy if she ever had the
chance. It was only after Justin was already living with
another woman in Paris that she had learned she now
owed an enormous debt to the person she considered her

mortal enemy, who refused to delay its repayment from ten days hence except under terms of exchange—Toast—which were unacceptable to her. It was only then, when relief mixed with her anger, that she knew he had been right, that she was a silly and foolish girl. It was only then that she knew how stupid she had been.

But that was her problem and her fault and she would not get anyone else involved. For the moment, anyway, she had a far more pressing matter to distract her. According to her previous night's rereading of the news sheets about the Vampire of London's last appearance, he never went more than a day without killing. Apparently no body had been found that morning and since the Vampire seemed to go to pains to ensure that his kills would easily be located, that meant there had been none the previous night. Which meant, in turn, that there was a very good chance that tonight, unless she found him first, a girl would die.

"Read that," she said to Elwood, holding out one of the three-year-old news sheets she had been studying the night before and letting Toast curl his tail around her finger.

"Comtesse Helèn DuPont held services for her beloved dog Wilimena last Monday. As in life, the corpse of Wilimena was dressed in a delicate pink tulle skirt—"

"No. Above that."

Elwood's eyes moved up the page. "Serena Mayhew became the Vampire of London's most recent victim," he read aloud, then met Clio's eyes with a questioning look. "That one?"

"Yes."

"But that happened three years ago. Why are you interested in it now?"

"Because, as you no doubt have heard, the Vampire of London is back." She slid into the chair behind her desk, into the familiar relief of work. "I want you to tell me everything you know about him."

Elwood frowned. "You are not proposing to find him, are you?"

"That is exactly what I am proposing. I already have a client. Why?" Clio looked at him challengingly, and her look was mirrored by Toast. "Don't you think me capable of it?"

Elwood sank into a seat opposite her. "I think you capable of anything, Clio. It is just that the Special Commissioner will not like your involvement."

"As a matter of fact, I have had a message from him this morning on that very topic."

"Then he knows? And he does not mind?"

"Not terribly," Clio said. Her eyes slipped away from Elwood's and she went sort of sideways in her chair. Toast, deciding things were getting dicey, leapt from her shoulder to the bust of King Henry the Eighth that stood behind her, and sat on his head. "He said something about my 'getting any help from his office' I might desire, and him wishing me the best of luck if I should choose to undertake the inquiry."

Elwood eyed her. "I assume the word that proceeded the phrase 'getting any help from his office' was 'never' and that his wishing you the best of luck was intended as more of a threat than an encouragement."

Clio shrugged and tried to look innocent. "Who can say. Words are so tricky and I am just a stupid woman."

Elwood sat forward, genuinely concerned. "Look, Clio, I know how you feel about the commissioner, but this is not the sort of investigation to undertake as a personal vendetta. I know he said some dreadful things to you—"

"He said that I was not fit to find anything besides puppies and even those might prove too taxing for me," she quoted. "He said that women should stay at home and look lovely, and since I did not have a proper home and could not look lovely if I tried, then I should throw myself into the Thames."

Elwood winced. "Yes. Well, you have to admit you provoked him."

"By solving six of his last eight cases before he even had any idea where to look?" Clio demanded.

"I was more thinking of the part when you described him as a corrupt and contemptible cur—"

"I only did that because of what he said about the dogs," Clio interrupted, sitting up straight.

"—whose powers of observation were worse than those of a tit mouse, and whose mind made caterpillars look intelligent," Elwood finished the quote.

"I do not see how he could be annoyed with me for that. If he had an ounce of sense he would admit it was all true. Anyway, in the interests of not overtaxing what little mind he has, I thought I would direct my questions to you rather than him. He must be very busy." She smiled convincingly at Elwood. Behind her Toast, who shared his mistress's estimation of both the Special Commissioner and dogs, clapped approvingly.

Elwood cleared his throat and tried to seem stern in the face of her smile and the monkey's encouragement. "What did the commissioner's message say, Clio?"

Her shoulders sagged. "Everything I already told you,

plus what you guessed about him never helping me, and, for added measure, that they had a 'very good man, a very special man' working on finding the vampire, who would work better and find the fiend faster without any 'infernal assistance from foolish and meddling females.' He closed by suggesting that there were probably puppies lost in London that needed my help finding their way home."

Elwood pressed his lips together for a moment, deep in thought. Then he sighed, looked into her lovely face, and said, "What do you want to know?"

Miles had awakened with a pounding headache and a gnawing feeling of unease, neither of which he could recall acquiring. Nor was he quite sure how he found himself in bed. Or, for that matter, who was breathing deeply next to him.

He threw open the bed curtains and was blinded by a wave of brilliant sunlight. Squinting, he looked over at the adjacent pillow. Golden hair curled over a small face, from which one brown eye peeked at him. His companion seemed to smile, then started to pant.

"Corin," Miles shouted into his room. "Corin, who put this bloody hound in my bed?"

"It's not a hound, sir, it is a retriever," Corin corrected in the tone of an authority. "And a very fine specimen if I might commend my own self in selecting him." He moved to the bedside, holding out a bowl filled with steaming brown liquid, which Miles grabbed and gulped down. "He crawled in by himself when I went out this morning. Although it doesn't speak too well for his intelligence, I think he likes you."

As if to prove the truth of this statement, the puppy climbed up on Miles's bare chest and began licking his nose. Setting down the now empty bowl, Miles lifted him off gently and put him back on the bed, where the dog set to work on his fingers. "Would it bother you terribly to explain what the hell he is doing here," he asked finally, but not as gruffly as he would have liked.

"He is to be a gift from you to Lady Mariana. Unless you want to keep him. I can find another. It seems that puppies are not much in demand today."

"I do not want to keep him," Miles said with only partial finality as the ball of fur nibbled playfully on his pointer finger. "I would bore him to death. And I think one will be enough in the household."

"You might reconsider. It's so rare to find someone who will put up with you." Corin answered the look of death Miles sent his way with an innocent smile. Then the smile faded and he added in a more serious voice, "Besides, another one of your guard dogs was killed last night and we still can't figure out how."

Miles's jaw clenched—that was the fourth one in two weeks—and his eye flitted to the wall behind Corin. To his left was the large clock that led to his attic offices and which showed the correct time. And to his right, on the mantelpiece of the fireplace, stood another clock, the duplicate of the one in the other room. This one's hands pointed at three.

Corin noted the direction of his master's gaze. "That is why I woke you. Something has come up."

Miles was out of bed and half-dressed by the time Corin had the clock open. He finished dressing as they ascended, and was tying the last of the laces on his leggings when they reached the landing just below the roof. Without pausing, he followed Corin through an inconspicuous door into a large room, that, despite the absence of windows, was filled with light flooding in from the opaque glass panes that made up its ceiling. Those who had heard of the extraordinary knot-garden Viscount Dearbourn had installed on his roof to please his new mistress three years ago little guessed that the birds its plants attracted were carrier pigeons winging messages across England, or that many of the shrubs were elaborate fakes, below which lay a nerve center far more delicate and far reaching than any set of roots.

Eight desks were occupied by young men, all of them in the yellow and gold livery of the Dearbourns. They were dressed as footmen, but the papers over which they were poring were not instructions for the running of the household. They were instructions for the preservation of a kingdom. England.

This was the realm of one of the most trusted of Queen Elizabeth's advisors. His official title was Lord High Commissioner for Security of the Kingdom but he was referred to by the few who knew of his existence only as "Three"—and then only in whispers.

The naval victory over the Spanish armada was widely credited to Sir Francis Drake, vice admiral of the navy, and Lawrence Pickering, the hero, but both of them, and everyone at the highest levels of government, knew the real credit belonged to Three. It was Lawrence Pickering who sailed the *H.M.S. Phoenix*, but it was Three who mapped its course, Three who organized the deployment of the English forces, Three who—by spreading the word that England was five times stronger than she really was and vulnerable in two places that she really wasn't—managed to lead the English to triumph despite being massively outmanned and outgunned by their enemy.

But while many English cheered their victory, those at the top knew that the war was far from over. Realizing that they could not outmaneuver the English at sea, the Spaniards had very cleverly begun undermining the country from within. Shortages of vital supplies from food to coal were natural during a war, and with such shortages came dissatisfaction. The Spanish took advantage of this, liberally distributing the gold they brought back from their American territories to anyone who would work for them within the borders of England, using it to sow discontent and encourage smuggling, particularly of high-quality English gunpowder. They thus created a second front to the war, and a much more difficult one. Unlike armor clad soldiers or ships of war, these enemies were difficult to spot, and, once spotted, even more difficult to subdue. For the past half year, Three's attentions had been focused on this invisible war, a delicate game of chess whose board was the island of Britain and whose stakes were the life of a real queen and her subjects.

Three was not a spy—although he did occasionally venture out to collect his own information—but rather the man who decided what to do with the information Elizabeth's spies procured. Three knew from personal experience that people believed what they saw and he designed the defensive strategy for England based on this knowledge, fortifying her against her enemies by working to create illusions of strength and weakness, preparedness and vulnerability. His men monitored sales of gunpowder and poison, carefully watching for any signs of instability within the kingdom of England. He was a problem solver, a strategist. And Queen Elizabeth's most potent secret weapon.

Speculation about his true identity abounded among both those friends and enemies who were privy to his existence—he had discovered the week before that his enemies called him "The Wasp" in honor of the pain and destruction his work caused them—but only the queen and the men in this light-filled garret knew who he really was.

Miles Fraser Loredan, Viscount Dearbourn, the third person behind the queen in charge of England's security, saluted each of his men as he passed by their desks on the way to an open door at the rear of the room. In the country the operation occupied the entirety of his wine cellar, but when he was forced to relocate to London because of his wedding, his headquarters were jammed into a much smaller space. Despite the somewhat cramped atmosphere, Miles felt an enormous sense of freedom as he entered, as if, only here of all the spaces in his vast town house—in these hot, crowded attics, stuck above even the most humble of his servant's quarters—was he actually at home. He took a deep, satisfied breath, and looked toward the broad man with gray hair sticking out of his head like a bottle brush standing in the open door of his private office.

The man's tan and the wrinkles around his eyes were his badges of honor from having served Her Majesty's Navy for three quarters of his fifty years of life. They were the only such badges he had, being one of the most irascible seamen in that organization, whose most notable career achievement was having spent more time in the Brig than any other sailor alive.

Most men, even those unaware of his reputation, steered clear of Tom Furious on sight, but then most men did not know that Tom's visits to the Brig were precisely timed, or that he was actually the brother of the current minister of war and closely related to seven other royal advisors, or that for thirty years he had been the Navy's most confidential and successful courier of information.

When any of the "broken" clocks in Miles's house pointed at three, it meant that his attention was needed urgently. And the presence of Tom Furious only confirmed the importance of the situation.

"Tom. It is not every week I get to see you twice," Miles said as Corin directed him to a seat and began pulling shaving implements out of a dumbwaiter hidden behind a painting. "Has there been some new word about the smugglers?"

Tom shook his head. "No. Nothing there. Pickering is still working on it, even if he is a bit distracted just at present. Seems he ran into a bit of trouble last night and lost some of his men. But that's not why I'm here."

Miles took in Tom's serious expression. "What is it, then? Did someone find Castillo?"

Tarquino Castillo was Miles's most recent recruit, a high-level secretary to the Spanish ambassador who had lost faith in the honor of his sovereign after King Philip refused to discipline one of his favorite nephews for seducing and then abandoning Castillo's sister. Their first meeting had been in an old Turkish bathhouse in Madrid, a locale Miles selected because, with the steam obscuring their faces but not their words, it allowed information to be passed anonymously. Since then they had continued to rendezvous at such places, and Miles had used his pre-betrothal ball visit to a bathhouse with his cousins the day before to schedule a meeting. But Castillo had not arrived. Which meant that there was a very good chance that somewhere in London, Castillo's broken and tortured body was being circled by flies.

The thought of what had probably befallen his agent was a potent reminder for Miles of why he worked so hard to keep his cousins away from him, why he continued to isolate himself, why he had made himself into Three, a figure with no family and no friends, why the only companion he allowed to get close to him was a full decanter of wine. At least a decanter of wine could not get itself killed because of you. Even his damn guard dogs—

"I'm afraid there's still no word from Castillo," Tom said, interrupting Miles's thoughts. "It is something else." He handed a single page of paper crudely printed with thick black gothic letters and woodcut images in two columns to Miles. "I got this from the printer on the way over. The ink's still wet."

Miles cast a cursory glance at the paper, then, pushing Corin's hand with the razor away, leaned over to study it. His eyes had a hard, faraway look in them when he was finished. "They are sure?"

"Aye. Special Commissioner certified it. That girl was killed by the Vampire of London."

"Gardenia?"

"Yes, there was a gardenia. He is back, Three. No question about it. At first we thought it might be a stunt by the Spanish, but it looks like the real thing. And Queen E wants you to make finding him your top priority. She is worried that if people get nervous, there could be riots. Which is just the sort of instability Spain could take advantage of. Three, she is worried that if he is not stopped quickly, this could be the end."

Miles nodded, but his eyes were still unfocused. "Of course. It is a matter of domestic security. Of protection."

"Aye. She has told the Special Commissioner to give you all the information he has, everything, and his full assistance."

Corin smirked and said, "I bet he was whistling with joy at that news."

Tom nodded. "I'd say he was not exactly delighted, but he knows he's in over his head." He fastened his eyes intently on Miles. "Queen E asked if you might refrain from describing to him again the ten ways he reminds you of a caterpillar, Three, at least until you find the vampire."

"That is going to be tough," Miles admitted. "The resemblances are striking."

"When you feel the urge to abuse someone, Queen E wants you to turn your attention on your own men. They are also there for support, but for the sake of secrecy we think it best if you undertake this as a private party. Shouldn't be hard to account for since the last word on his lips before he went down before was your name."

You'll pay for this Dearbourn.

The smile that Miles's contemplation of the Special Commissioner had started, vanished. He looked grim. "I remember."

"What Queen E is most concerned about," Tom went

on, "is this notion that the vampire gets stronger as the moon grows dimmer. Seems we are at half-moon now, and according to the astrologers, no moon in nine days. And when there is no moon it is supposed to be impossible to kill him. That means you only have—"

"I know what it means," Miles interrupted.

"Right," Tom confirmed. He was watching his boss closely. During the early days of their collaboration, Tom had thought that Miles's cold, generic code name, Three, was perfect. Like a number, the boy had no heart, no personality, no humanity. He seemed to have extended his job of building defensive structures to his personal life, fortifying himself with an impenetrable psychological wall. But over the years of their working together, Tom had realized he was wrong, and had come to suspect that perhaps Miles was only too human underneath. The austere personal credo that he had caused to be carved into the molding above his office door—"Trust no one, believe nothing, the only certainty is death"—began to read less like the ideas of a cold investigator, and more like the words of a man who has been deeply and personally hurt. Tom had grown not only to respect, but to care deeply about the man called Three. He was also one of the few people who could see through his emotional armor, and right now he did not like what he was seeing. "Are you feeling all right, Miles?" he asked, his use of the name showing the depth of his concern.

"Yes. Fine." Miles settled back into his chair and let Corin return to work on his face. "I want to meet with the Special Commissioner this morning," he said to Tom. "In the meantime, give me all the information you have."

Tom complied and Miles nodded thoughtfully as if he were listening, but all he really heard for the two hours of the briefing was *This is your fault. You failed.*

Chapter 5

"This is your fault. Do not think to shift the blame to anyone else. You did this yourself," Lady Alecia reiterated needlessly, setting her ringlets aquiver. "You are wicked and evil. That is how your father was. And how you are."

"I know," Clio said, her head bowed. "I broke my promise. I take full responsibility."

"Broke it?" Lady Alecia snorted. "You decimated it. You made a scene. A scandal."

"A debutante," Mariana put in prettily.

"Debacle," Doctor LaForge corrected.

Lady Alecia kept her eyes on Clio. "You mortified us. And you will pay for it. You will refrain from such behavior in the future, Clio," she informed her granddaughter. "You will not set foot in Dearbourn Hall unless specifically requested to do so."

Clio was only too happy to agree. Indeed, she had no desire to set foot in the place ever again, and would gladly have been anywhere else at that very moment. She had known the summons from her grandmother would come, it was inevitable after her appearance the night before, and she had known she would dread it and the withdrawal of her allowance it was sure to result in, but what had surprised her on the way from Which House was that even more than seeing her grandmother, she dreaded running into the Viscount Deerhound, as she had taken to calling him in her mind. She had been immensely relieved when she arrived and found that he would not be present at the interview.

Not that she could blame him. She had herself felt woozy walking into Mariana's apartments. She had no doubt that her cousin and grandmother were responsible for the decor themselves, it had the unmistakable stamp of their taste. Three of the walls were covered in bright blue silk overstitched with green, gold, purple, and indigo threads to look like peacock feathers, all surrounded by gold moldings. The remaining wall was mainly taken up with a huge fireplace, whose beautiful medieval mantle had been gilded, and over which hung what had to be the largest mirror in London, held up by two baby angels. They were made of gold, as were all the sconces from which three dozen candles shined. Every piece of furniture was upholstered in the same fabric as the walls, and the floor was covered by the thickest, most silky looking, and most hideously overpatterned Turkish carpet Clio had ever seen. All in all, the effect was eye-popping.

Her grandmother—wearing the wig Clio had named "the Medusa"—and her cousin were seated on an oversized settee, at right angles to one occupied by the man she remembered having been introduced to once as her grandmother's secretary. On a table between them lay a plate filled with hazelnut cakes, the one thing that Clio and Mariana had in common, the one thing they both loved. Despite his protests, Clio had decided to leave Toast at home in the interest of reminding her grandmother of as little as possible of the scene she had caused the previous night, but she was half wishing he had come, if only to smuggle a few of the hazelnut cakes out in his doublet. From where she was standing, Clio imagined she could smell them, and she began to fantasize about what they would taste like, the crisp outer crust giving way to a soft—

She forced herself to look away. Against the wall, the faded form of her uncle, Sir Edwin Nonesuch, was hunched over a chess table opposite the morose looking Doctor LaForge. The vacant expression on Sir Edwin's face could have given anyone fierce competition in the "Daftest Man in England" contest if there had been one. Sir Edwin was the one member of her family for whom Clio felt any real affection, the one member of her family who had ever deigned to smile at her and wish her a good day, and for the first time she was glad that his mind wandered, because at least that meant it was not imprisoned in this hideous room which, despite being large and high-ceilinged, felt small and claustrophobic. Indeed, the sooner she could leave there, the happier she would be.

This was confirmed when her grandmother started waving about that morning's edition of *News from Court*. "You even had to intrude yourself upon the public eye, didn't you?" Lady Alecia asked, accusingly. "You could not allow us—"

"Did you hear someone whistling?" Sir Edwin asked abruptly, starting forward in his seat. He looked across the chess table. "Infernal noise. Kept me out of my bed all night. Did you catch it, too, Doctor?"

Doctor LaForge looked embarrassed. "*Non,* monsieur," he said with a tight smile, then redirected his attention to Lady Alecia. "You were saying, madam?"

Mariana, a dreamy smile on her face, spoke instead. "Do not worry, Papa, I am sure it was just the mother dew drops singing to their babies in the moonlight."

Sir Edwin scowled at her and sat back, muttering under his breath. Clio was thinking that she liked him better than ever, when she realized Mariana was speaking to her.

Mariana's smile was still there, but beneath it Clio could see the hard determination in her cousin's eyes. "You must not be so hard on poor, dear, Clio, grandmama. She cannot help herself. She has always been so eager for the merest thread of attention. The opportunity to have so many people talk about her must have been too strong to overcome. Poor thing, no one has paid any attention to her since that awful low woman with the horrible teeth and that dreadful Dover accent she had as a nurse died." Clio tried to interject that the nurse had been from Devon, but Mariana was unstoppable. "No one has noticed her at all since then." Mariana leaned forward and addressed Clio directly. "I ache for how much *you* must ache to know that all your efforts last night have gone to waste."

Seeing Clio on the verge of speaking, Mariana put up a hand. "I know," she said feelingly. "You don't have to say anything. I can see your pain in your eyes. The eyes of a baby butterfly who has lost his way."

"There is no such thing as a baby butterfly," Clio pointed out.

Mariana ignored her. "Poor, dear, misguided Clio. Remember how you used to pretend to get presents on my birthday? *My* birthday. Just so people would pay attention to you. I never begrudged you that. I was always content to share with you, even though I knew you made it all up. How sad I felt for you that there was no one who would bother to send you gifts. That no one ever wished you a happy birthday."

Her words, or rather their truth, stung Clio, but she hid her reaction under a blanket of sarcasm. "Your kindness to me was really astonishing."

"I know." Mariana prided herself on her graceful acceptance of compliments. "Even now, I feel sorry for you and the ruin of your plans."

"What plans were those?"

"To wreck my wedding, like you always try to wreck everything of mine. That is why you came to the ball last night. I understand you cannot help it. That, like the baby duck, it is in your nature to follow me everywhere and nip at my heels. But it shall not work. Everyone is too busy discussing the Vampire of London." Mariana leaned forward. "Do you know when he first appeared?"

"Three years ago," Clio answered, without enthusiasm. This quiz did not seem poised to expedite her leaving, or her devouring the hazelnut cakes.

"No!" Mariana said triumphantly. "He first appeared the year I was born. When I was a baby duck myself. In *my* village. Isn't that exciting?"

Clio refrained from pointing out that she had herself been born that same year, just a week earlier in fact, and in the same village. "Are you sure?"

"Of course. And I know why." As if to build suspense, Mariana leaned over to study the plate of hazelnut cakes, picked one of them up, broke it in half, sniffed each half suspiciously, tried a taste, made a noise that indicated it was delicious, ate both halves, and then returned her gaze to Clio. "I fear what I am going to say will upset you, dear Clio, but you are not the only one who feels a fascination for me. There are others. I think the vampire is one of them. I think he has come back for my wedding."

A guttural noise, almost like a sob, came from Lord Edwin's corner. Everyone turned to where he was sitting, his eyes glassy, his face blanched, his mouth working. "Mother," he said finally in a voice that sounded like it had traveled miles. "Mother."

"Speak of this no more," Lady Alecia commanded with a frown at Mariana.

"Why?" Mariana tossed her head adventurously. "I have no fear of his acollation."

Doctor LaForge sighed. "Adulation."

"It is upsetting your father." Lady Alecia leaned toward her granddaughter and explained in a furious whisper. "You know very well that his sister, Clio's mother, was killed that same year by that horrible, horrible man—"

"My father," Clio volunteered, in case Mariana did not understand.

Lady Alecia glared fulsomely at her before resuming, "—and that he has never recovered from the blow of her loss. One shall not speak of anything that happened in those dark days."

"But—" Mariana began to protest and was cut off.

"Was the vampire caught?" Clio asked, despite this warning.

"One shall not spea—"

"Like the fly, like the fly, like the fly," Lord Edwin chanted from against the wall, as if it were a nursery rhyme.

"That is enough, Edwin," Lady Alecia told him, then turned to Clio. As she did, her face changed into what

Clio thought of as her "wicked abbess" expression, a mask of beneficence barely concealing a core of cruelty. "Now Clio, we summoned you to inform you that as a result of your behavior yesterday your allowance has been revoked. However, in honor of Mariana's wedding, we deem it appropriate that you share in our good fortune. In commemoration of the happy day we shall set aside a small sum for you." She paused, waiting for Clio's professions of gratitude. When they did not come, she went on. "You may collect the purse here, that morning, before Mariana's wedding."

"It shall be a birthday present!" Mariana said, clapping her dainty hands. "Just like when we were girls. Only this time you really will be getting something. Oh! I am so happy for you dear Clio. For once you will know what it is like to be cared about." Her eyes got large and misty with the enormity of her heart. "I want you to know that I understand why you behave wickedly, like you did last night. I understand how hard it must be to know that you are unlovable, that no one wants you."

Clio took her leave quickly, and not only because it was evident that Mariana was about to embark on a series of "Poor dear Clio" statements that was going to make her head ache, or because the numbers in her ledger loomed larger than ever. For reasons she could not understand, Mariana's words, her family's dislike of her, still hurt, even after all these years. She did not know why, or how, she could care about them, why she craved their approval, their affection, but some part of her did, and some part of her was wrenched by their treatment. Was she really as awful—as unlovable—as they thought?

Her cheeks were burning and her eyes filled with

tears as she rushed through the corridors of Dearbourn Hall. She wished she could be angry with them, angry and resentful, but her rage was turned against herself, for her weakness, for caring what they said, caring that no one had ever wished her a happy birthday, that no one ever would. And not just caring, but crying.

Silly, foolish, stupid girl. She heard Elwood's kind words—*you are not stupid, Clio*—through her tears, but she was certain that if he really knew her, he would realize he was wrong. Crying! Letting her cousin make her cry! What was happening to her? She felt like she was peeling apart. First death's head visions, now breaking down in unfamiliar corridors. Breaking down anywhere. She did not—*would not*—care that her birthday always went unmarked, *would not* care about Mariana and Lady Alecia. She stopped to wipe her eyes and as she did a golden puff of fur scurried around her ankles and set to work licking the tears off her boots.

She bent down and picked him up, and he reached out his tongue to lick the tears off her face as well. It tickled so nicely that despite the fact she refused to have anything to do with dogs, she laughed to herself, which is why she did not hear his footsteps.

Miles felt a pang of jealousy such as he had not known in years, watching Clio's expression go from delight to disgust as her eyes moved from the puppy's face to his. After Mariana's reaction to the puppy—or rather, baby dog—that morning, which included shrieking, attempting to kick it, and declaring that she hated it and never wanted it to come into her presence again—Miles had half wished to change places with it, but not nearly as much as he did now.

"Oh," Clio said when she saw him. "Here." She extended the puppy toward him. When he made no move to take it, she set the dog down and began walking quickly away.

"I owe you an apology," Miles said, following her closely.

Clio waved his words away.

"I treated you badly last night. I am sorry."

Clio kept walking.

"Also, I should tell you that this corridor only goes to my bed chamber. Unless that is where you wish to go?"

Clio stopped and glared at him. "I think that was a record. Three seconds before you insulted me. Bravo. You are making progress." She turned and began marching back the way she had come.

"That is not fair," Miles said from behind her. "Last night I went at least five minutes before offending you."

"I was taking an average," Clio replied. The sound of Miles's laughter stopped her and she whirled around. Her face was stark, her voice almost desperate as she said, "Please. Please just leave me alone."

Miles closed the space between them. "What is wrong, Lady Thornton?"

Clio swallowed hard. They stood facing each other, in silence, as the clock at the end of the corridor ticked off the seconds. Up close, he did not look detestable. Nor did his ears, chin, lips, eyes, hair, teeth, neck, chest—what she could see of it, at eye level—nor did his hands, hands which were moving up to cup her face, soft warm hands, hands caressing her cheek, hands tilting her head back, lips . . .

She pushed past him at a run. It was not the way her knees got tingly that made her rush from him. It was not the fact that his personality suddenly seemed entirely un-detestable that made her career down the stairs, almost tripping, and fly through the front door of his house. It was the fact that she felt them coming on.

The hiccups.

And she did not know why. She searched her head as she ran, searched for any sign of violence, any desire to harm anyone, but could find none. Certainly she would never be averse to strangling Mariana, but that was a different impulse than the deep, scary violence that prompted the hiccups. Once outside the gates of Dearbourn Hall she slowed, but the hiccups came quickly, fast like they did when she had to work hard to suppress her rage. Her primary emotion was not rage, however, it was fear, fear that she no longer even felt the violence inside of her. Fear of what she might be capable of. Fear of herself.

She was walking blindly, clenching her fists into tight balls, moving with the crowds that filled the streets but not hearing them, not seeing them. The hiccups meant one thing. She wanted to hurt someone. And she did not even know it.

Just as she did not know the identity of the person who pushed her into the street in front of an onrushing coach. Her surprise paralyzed her and she stood, unable to move, looking at the horses rearing above her. For an instant she was aware of every detail of her surroundings as if they had all been frozen in amber—the perspiration of the horses flying like raindrops from their necks, a shabby looking boy running down the street in the opposite direction, the shouts of the people around her, stopped, hanging in the air in individual syllables, the gold puppy leaping high into the air, a figure in one of the second floor windows of Dearbourn Hall observing, a familiar looking man with a mustache dressed in a fancy red doublet staring at her with a smile and then winking (winking!), a butterfly alighting from a flower eight feet away, a rivulet of water between the smooth gray stones of the street, an orange skidding past her feet, mud on her boots, mud on her boots, mud on her boots—and then, slam, everything started moving again and she was moving also, flying, and the horses had brushed past her and no one was shouting and the man across the way had vanished and the gold puppy was jumping up and trying to get into her arms but he couldn't because someone was holding them at the shoulders and she looked up and it was the viscount and his lips were moving and what he was saying was, "Are you all right?"

Clio blinked, realized that her hiccups were gone, then nodded. "Did you see a man in red?" she asked.

Miles frowned. Of the questions he would have expected someone to ask after he had saved their life—are *you* all right, what happened, where am I, what can I ever do to repay you—"Did you see a man in red?" was very low on the list.

"Are you sure you are all right?" he asked again.

Clio nodded impatiently and pulled away from him. "I am fine. But I have to find that man."

"I did not see anyone in red," Miles said, but then, he had not exactly been paying perfect attention.

He had been glad if slightly surprised to see Clio Thornton in the hallway of his house, principally because he was on his way to call on her and her appearance would save him the trip. He was going to her house to find out everything she knew about the Vampire of

London, and to order her not to attempt to unmask him herself, to leave it to him. He was damned if he was going to have Lady Clio Thornton's death on his conscience as well.

Then there she was, miraculously on the threshold of his room, and instead of inviting her in and asking her questions he was about to kiss her.

It was ridiculous. He had not kissed anyone—besides, of course, Clio at the Painted Lady the day before—in over two years.

He had not wanted to. After Beatrice's death he found that physical intimacy only left him feeling lonely. The mere thought of kissing any of the women who sought his attention had almost repulsed him. Unlike the thought of kissing Clio.

The man known and feared as Three did not kiss women, he lectured himself. It was a distraction and a nuisance—who had time, with someone killing his guard dogs, a smuggling investigation in process, the Vampire of London on the loose, and his impending marriage to Mariana? He would not kiss Clio Thornton. And definitely not in the middle of the street.

Her mouth, when Miles brought his lips to cover it, was more succulent and delicious than anything he had ever tasted in his life.

Clio stood on her tiptoes, and he bent down over her, gently, softly brushing his lips against hers. Butterflies, satin, blades of grass, honey, rose petals, marble, none of them were right for the feeling of his lips on hers. They were barely touching, and yet Clio was astonishingly aware that this was different than what she had felt with Justin Greeley. This was achingly, impossibly wonderful.

Miles felt transported back in time, back to a moment before the pain, the enforced emptiness, before the vision. Before Beatrice.

The kiss lasted less than two seconds.

It was Clio who ended it, pulling away sharply. She reached her fingers up to her lips, touching them where his mouth had been, kicking herself mentally. This man was betrothed to her cousin. He could never be hers, he would always be one more thing that she lost, one more person who was fascinated by Mariana and repulsed by her. *How hard it must be to know you are unlovable,* she heard Mariana say again. She was not jealous, it was different than that. She just needed never to see him again.

"Good day Lord Dearbourn," she said, then spun and walked away.

Miles did not follow her. It had been Clio who ended the kiss, but Miles who was charred by it. He had won his peace by ridding himself of all those emotions, emptying himself (and his wine cellar) and he would not go back.

But where would his peace be if he let Clio Thornton be killed by the Vampire of London? Where was his peace anyway?

"Wait," he shouted, moving quickly after her. He wanted to let her go, wanted to force her to go away from him, forever, but he could not. He had to make sure she would do nothing that got her killed. "I need to talk to you," he said when he caught up with her.

Clio did not stop moving. "About what just happened?" she asked in a stilted voice, not looking at him. "Don't worry, it—"

"No. About the vampire."

Clio walked on in silence, still avoiding his gaze.

"I want your promise that you will not pursue him," Miles continued when it was clear she would not speak.

Now Clio looked up at him. "I will make no such promise. Why should I?"

"I will pay you."

Clio gave a harsh laugh. "My lord, although it may be hard for you to believe in light of what just happened, and although I would very much like your money, I have my pride. I am no more inclined to take money from men for no reason, than you are to pay women who work with their clothes on."

"Very well. Then I will pay you to look into something for me." Miles could not understand how he had failed to see this option earlier. He had been briefed on her investigations and impressed by her success—as well as by the way the Special Commissioner's face looked near exploding whenever her name was mentioned.

She stopped walking. "Into the vampire?"

"No. Into a household matter. Someone has been killing my guard dogs and—"

Clio put up a hand, interrupting him. "Have you been speaking to the Special Commissioner?"

"No," Miles lied. "Why?"

"I was trying to decide if you said that innocently or maliciously."

"And what did you conclude?" Miles smiled his most innocent smile.

"It does not matter." Clio shook her head and began walking again, this time faster. "I do not do investigations involving dogs."

"That is a very strange rule. Why not?" Miles asked, genuinely curious.

Clio waved his question away. "I have a great many strange rules. You would not enjoy working with me."

Miles had to stifle a laugh. "Perhaps you should allow me to determine what I would and would not enjoy, Lady Thornton. If you are refusing because you think the investigation is somehow beneath you, I can assure you, the situation with my dogs is very grave. They were not poisoned or strangled and—"

"I am sorry. Even if I were willing to undertake a case chasing puppies around, I would have to decline. I already have a client."

"Who?" Miles demanded, suddenly serious again.

"I do not divulge the names of my clients to men who chase me down the street. Another of my strange rules."

Miles decided not to contest her description. "Does this client want you to find the vampire?"

Clio shrugged.

"It would be a mistake for you to attempt to unmask the Vampire of London on your own, Lady Thornton."

"It would be impossible for me to do it any other way. I only work alone."

"Not this time," Miles told her. "Not against this fiend."

"I am not sure I believe he is a fiend. I am not convinced this is anything more than a clever, and somewhat theatrical, murderer."

Miles's voice was low, serious. "You are wrong, Clio. I did not believe it was a vampire either, but I do now. And I can prove it to you."

Clio did not reply for a moment, letting his words, or rather, one of them, sink in. Then she asked simply, "How?"

"I can tell you what I saw the night we captured him. But only if you agree to work for me."

"I have already told you, I do not investigate dogs."

"I understand. I will pay you to help me find the vampire." The best way to ensure that she did nothing to put herself in danger was to oversee her actions himself, Miles realized. "But it must be on my terms. We work together. You do what I say. We share information. I know more than anyone else about the vampire, but I will only tell you if you are in my employ."

The audacity of the Deerhound knew no boundaries, Clio thought to herself. He would be perfect with Mariana. Who did he think he was, the Lord High Commissioner for the Security of the Kingdom? Did he really think she would allow him to command her? She would find the money and the information some other way. Even dealing with the Special Commissioner would be preferable. With enormous relief, she saw her front door in the near distance. She was just formulating an appropriate response to his kind offer when she noticed the figure pacing back and forth in front of her house like a sinister sentinel. The apothecary's apprentice.

She had entirely forgotten about the ten pounds she owed Arthur Copperwith. She reached for her purse, but then remembered that she had not bothered to bring it with her because it was completely empty. Her mind racing, she looked from the sentinel to the Deerhound, and had an idea.

"Let me understand," she began, casually. "In order to learn what you know, I have to let you pay me?"

"You have to agree to work for me, yes," Miles nodded.

"Very well. My consultation fee is ten pounds."

Miles held out two large round coins to her, but she shook her head and gestured for him to follow. "Give them to him," she announced, pointing to the shabby looking man standing menacingly in front of her door. "He is a sort of guard," she explained, as Miles handed over the money.

Closing the door on the "guard's" toothless grin, Miles followed her into the cool, dark-paneled vestibule of her house. The noise of the street disappeared, replaced by the muffled sound of someone proclaiming the end of the Roman Empire in another room, accompanied by a twittering that Miles recognized as the monkey's. The scent of the light pink roses that covered the facade floated on the air, and grew stronger as Clio led him into her study, where a bunch of them were haphazardly arranged in a water jug. The room seemed filled with Clio's presence, with her scent. It would be a good room for sleeping in, Miles thought.

A tall, gangly looking man wearing an alarming wig, whom Clio addressed as Snug, followed them in.

"You saw the gentleman outside," Snug asked delicately.

Clio signed. "Yes. He has been satisfied. But remind me that I need to have a talk with Toast. A long talk." The tone in her voice made Miles glad that his name was not Toast.

"Very good. May I bring anything for you and your, ah, visitors?" Snug looked at the little gold puppy, now covered in dust, who was chasing his tail around Miles's legs.

"Take him," Clio pointed at the dog, "to the kitchen and give him some refreshment. Nothing for the viscount. He would not want to trouble you."

Miles could have sworn that Snug sneered at him. He followed Clio toward the back of the room, and took the chair she motioned him into as she moved behind a mammoth desk. She settled back in her seat, leveled her eyes at him, and said, "Prove to me there is a vampire. Tell me what you saw."

Much of what happened in the course of his seventy-two hour pursuit of the Vampire of London three years earlier had grown cloudy in Miles's memory during his recovery from the knife wound to his abdomen, but there was one image that did not dim. He could use a drink, he thought, and considered asking for a glass—or better, a carafe—of wine, but one look at Clio's intent expression changed his mind.

He took a deep breath, pushed his hair off his forehead, and began speaking. "We had been pursuing the Vampire for two days when we finally found him, and even then it was more luck than skill. Every member of the queen's guard was sent out into the streets and told to watch for a man who fit the vague descriptions we had collected from witnesses. Even this was guesswork, since half the people claimed he was tall, the other half that he was short, some said he had blond hair, others red. Nor was it helped by all of the theories that were circulating. We had several false calls—one poor man caught in bed begged us to arrest him just to keep his wife away from him when she learned he had a mistress—but finally we found the right man."

Miles's voice changed, became almost colorless, as if he were giving a report to a committee, and he looked out the window. "One of the guards had seen a short, young girl go into a building, followed—a half hour later, when her light had gone out—by a figure in a cape wearing a cap with light hair showing beneath it. I stationed my men around the building to stop his escape and I went in alone. The door to the girl's room was ajar, and I was able to enter without making a noise. There were no candles, but the moon was half-full and it was possible to see everything in the room." He paused, swallowing again. He wished he had asked for that drink. "There was a bed against the far wall. A man leaned over the bed, a man in dark clothes. He was small—" Miles remembered his surprise, surprise that someone that slight could be so dangerous— "and fair, that much I could see from behind. I inched close to him, until I was within lunging distance, and I touched his back with my sword."

"He turned around slowly and faced me. His cap was pulled low, casting a shadow over his face, and his hair hung over his forehead but I could see his eyes, huge and glassy, and his mouth and teeth, dripping blood. Blood from the woman behind him. Blood from where he had punctured her neck. The wound was so fresh it was still bleeding. There was blood everywhere, on his clothes, on her pillow." Miles brought his eyes to Clio's. They looked haunted. "I saw him sucking her blood, Lady Thornton. There can be no other explanation—he is a vampire."

Clio had to agree, or at least, almost. There was something about Miles's narrative that bothered her, but she could not put her finger on it. As he had been speaking, Toast had come in and settled himself on her shoulder, placing a soothing hand around her neck. Despite his comforting touch, she felt numb, as if she had been in the darkened room, as if she had seen the glassy eyes, the bloody mouth. For a moment, neither she nor Miles spoke, locked in their own thoughts.

Clio broke the silence. "If it is true, if he is a vampire as you maintain, then what has he been living on these past three years? There have been no notices of vampire attacks anywhere in England. Have you read *A Compendium of Vampires*?"

"Yes, I have a copy of it in my library. And I know it says that the vampire needs regular infusions of blood to survive. My guess is that he went over to the continent. I have already written to my business agents in Venice, Milan, Rome, Paris, and Prague to see if anyone has reported any unusual deaths."

Clio pondered this, and as she did, she felt herself wavering, both about the possible existence of a vampire, and about the advisability of going through with her plan as she had devised it earlier. Maybe this once she should lift her prohibition on working alone. Maybe she should consider collaborating with the Deerhound and his agents in Venice, Milan, Rome, Paris, and Prague. Not to mention with his purse. But then she remembered how she had felt when he said her name, how she had felt when he kissed her, how it had been like waking up into a dream, how she had sworn off all partnerships of any kind for any reason and particularly partnerships with men who made her feel that way when they kissed her and said her name, not to mention those who were betrothed to and most likely in love with Mariana, and she knew she was better by herself. Safer.

"Snug," she called out, breaking the silence. When the man appeared in the doorway she said, "Please bring the viscount his dog. He is leaving."

Miles stared at her. "I beg your pardon? We have only begun our work."

Clio shook her head. "You said you would only tell me what you knew if you could pay me—"

"—Hire you," Miles corrected.

Clio shrugged. "It amounts to the same thing, doesn't it? Well, you paid me ten pounds, and I got ten pounds of information. I doubt you have anything else of interest to impart, so I'll not make you pay me any more. It would not be ethical. Of course, you would know the value of your information better than I would."

Miles's face hardened into the mask of a man accustomed to being obeyed. "This is not a jest. I hired you. And I expect you to do what I say. Right now, I expect you to answer my questions. After that, we shall see."

"You can pay me to listen to you, Lord Dearbourn, but your entire fortune would not be adequate to secure my obedience. Good day, Viscount."

Miles realized then that there was only one way to handle a woman as stubborn as Clio Thornton, and that was to give her exactly what she wanted. "As you like, Lady Thornton," he said, his voice cool and formal and one hundred percent viscount as he rose from his seat. "Do what you wish. I apologize for my unwanted intrusion and I will not bother you any further. I wish you the best of luck with your investigation." He bent over to pick up the puppy and was about to leave the room when a man with incredible white hair stopped him in the doorway and cried, "Perfect, perfect, perfect!"

The man was looking not at Miles but at the puppy squirming in his arms. "Just what we need," the man proclaimed. "A dog will liven up that banquet scene like nobody's business. No one else has done a scene with a puppy before. That'll smite them!" And without another word, he scooped the puppy from Miles's grasp and disappeared.

"Mr. Williams," Clio called after him with alarm. "Mr. Williams you must bring back the viscount's dog. Mr. Williams!"

"Let him keep it," Miles said. Maybe it would bite her. Then he traced a formal bow, turned on his heel and strode from the room.

Clio made a face at his receding back, which was echoed by Toast. She was reviewing and revamping a list of his hateful qualities and had just determined that the less time she spent with him the happier she would be, when Snug entered the room.

"This was delivered while you were out. Apparently you forgot it last night at Dearbourn Hall." He held out a bound volume that she recognized as her—or rather, her father's—copy of *A Compendium of Vampires*. She took it and opened to the point where a marker had been placed, then stopped.

It was a single piece of paper, unfolded. Written on it in careful black letters was the phrase: *You do not know what you are.*

Clio had no idea what the words meant, but she suddenly felt chilled through.

Mrs. Wattles, wife of Mr. Wattles the doll maker-cum-artist, bustled into the front of her husband's workshop, out of breath. Between having to run her own errands now that their maid-of-all-work had been taken by the Vampire of London, and having to stop at every one of her London acquaintances to share that news as she did so, she had traversed the city more than once that day and, not being a small woman, her feet hurt awfully.

She cast a longing glance at the large carved chair that stood next to the table, but did not let herself stop. Just one more errand and she would be through. Huffing slightly, she made her way to the back of the workshop, where her husband (famed for his ability to reproduce a lifelike face from a sketch) was bent over his work.

"Mr. Wattles," she announced as she came in. "Mr. Wattles, I have brought the newest picture from Lady Alecia. She says she needs the bust right away and you are to stop all your other work."

Mr. Wattles raised his head from the face he was molding. He wore a large magnifying lens over one eye that made him looked like a lopsided fish. "That lady thinks she owns me, she does," he complained, reaching out for the folded paper his wife was holding. "I didn't even hear there'd been a hanging. Whose head is it this time?" His wife shrugged and walked gingerly away, the large chair beckoning to her from across the room.

He brought the picture, which was clipped from a news sheet, close to his face, and his surprise was so great that his unmagnified eye grew almost as large as his magnified one.

"Mrs. Wattles," he called to his wife's retreating form. "Mrs. Wattles, come see."

Something in her husband's tone made her return quickly. She took the paper from him, studied it for a moment, then met her husband's eyes. "Isn't that—?"

"Yes," he nodded. "That is what I thought, too."

"Do you suppose we ought to tell someone?" Mrs. Wattles asked, slowly.

Mr. Wattles thought for a moment, then shook his

head. What he said was: "Isn't any of our business, is it?"

But what both of them were thinking was: Lady Alecia is a *very* good customer.

"Poor Inigo," Mrs. Wattles murmured under her breath at regular intervals during the remainder of the day. "Poor, poor boy."

Chapter 6

No one had ever seen a barge as large or as luxurious as the one anchored in the Thames in front of Dearbourn Hall, nor had anyone ever imagined a banquet so clever. There were a dozen lemon-ice swans floating between the candied violets that covered the surface of the crystallized sugar pool—the viscount himself had developed the machine that made the swans really glide across the surface—and long tables filled with food. No one had dreamed of a juggler as charming as the one who produced gilded gillyflowers specially grown to smell like oranges for all the ladies as he wandered about, no one had ever counted so many monkeys so delightfully dressed to match their owners in one place before, no one had thought there could be musicians so handsome, or heard birds so sweet-voiced, or conceived of lanterns so cunningly decorated with the Dearbourn crest—in short, never had there ever been a party as marvelous as the one Mariana had orchestrated for herself, at "the dear Viscount's" expense. And it was not even halfway done when one member of her entourage made a low bow to his mistress and a lower one to her grandmother, and slipped away from the festivities, complaining of a headache.

He had one, too, and who wouldn't who had to listen to the insidious preenings and whinings of those two bitches Mariana and Lady Alecia, all day and all night. While they had been traveling in France and Italy for Mariana's "edufication" it had been fine, there had been enough of a distraction. But now they and the waiting were beginning to wear him down, and he was only too happy that the end of his project was nearly in sight.

He breathed more easily as he slipped out a side door of Dearborn House and made his way into Alsatia. His appearance was innocuous enough that he was almost invisible. Neither the women lingering on the street in search of a last catch for the evening, nor the thugs waiting to accost drunken noblemen out on a spree, bothered with him, and he arrived at the Painted Lady Tavern entirely unmolested.

"Who comes strutting upon the stage?" Lovely Jake demanded from behind his hand of cards, then looked up, saw the new arrival, and nodded. "Ah, it is only my good boarder, back from his revels. Would you care to join us in a hand of Primero?"

"No, thank you, I am very tired," the man refused vaguely, and the other players were just as happy.

"Odd fellow," he heard one of them lean over and whisper to Lovely Jake. "Doesn't look quite right in the head."

He was up the far stairs and had the door of his room closed so he did not hear Lovely Jake's assurances that "he but wore a mask" as the thespians said, and was actually a very interesting fellow. Afterward, when they were shown the evidence of his disguise, one of them remarked that the mask line had been closer to the truth than Jake reckoned. Of course, Jake was dead by then and in no position to say whether or not he had known that the light-haired, disturbed looking fellow dressed in dark blue who left the tavern less than a half hour later had really been the same man as his strange boarder.

Nor did the women on the street or the thugs recognize him from earlier, but there was something about this new appearance that kept them away even more efficiently. When questioned afterward, one of them even remembered commenting that the fellow, "made the blood run cold in the veins, he did. Could I identify him if I saw him? No. But I would know that feeling again anywhere. I wouldn't have wanted to be alone with him, not for the queen's pearls, and the other girls felt the same."

But the man did not care what they, or anyone, thought of him. He had one thing to do, one thing only, and there was only one person who could help him. Three years he had waited to return to England to put the demons to rest. Three years of planning, and scheming. Three long years. It had been worth it.

Or at least, it soon would be.

He paused for a moment to massage his thigh—the bullet that bastard Dearbourn had shot at him was still lodged inside and it pained him when he tried to walk too quickly—then made the final turn and stopped outside a house. Two of the windows were still lit, but he knew they would grow dark soon. He could wait. Waiting was what he did best.

As he assumed his position outside the house, he glanced up to study the moon, noting with a trained eye that it was a sliver smaller than it had been the previous evening. "Good night," the man known as Vampire of London then whispered into the darkness. "Sweet dreams."

"Looked like he was up to no good," the char-woman who had passed the man on her way to work reported during the hearings of the Special Commissioner later. "Looked like he was putting a curse on someone."

In his tower at Westminster Castle, the Royal Astrologer licked his pen and wrote: *4 hours after midnight: moon—exactly half full. Waning.*

Chapter 7

She was not alone.

That was Clio's first thought when she woke with a start. It was more a perception than a certainty. The room was completely dark, she could see nothing, but she could sense the presence of another person. Close to her. Behind her? To her right? God she was thirsty.

She sat entirely still, listening. And waiting. Like the man who had been waiting outside her house.

At first she heard nothing. Then she saw a shadow move and heard a moan and a sharp crack to her left. She swung her head toward it. A surge of relief coursed through her.

The shutter on her window swayed back and forth in the breeze, wailing softly and rapping against the side of the house each time. That was the crack she had heard. There was no one in the room with her, it was just the shutter flapping. How foolish of her to leave it un-latched, she thought. Inigo was sleeping in the room just below and the banging would surely wake him, as it had no doubt woken her.

That, and her thirst. Her throat was so dry it hurt, and her lips were cracked. She licked them and tasted a drop of blood. What time was it? The half-moon outside trailed light in through the open shutter, shadows moving as the wind rustled among the leaves of the old apple tree. In the dim light she could make out the familiar contours of the battered old armoire that held her enormous wardrobe of two dresses, the mirror with the faded green enamel leaves around it that had belonged to her mother and was now so warped that it made everyone's face look like a parody of melancholy, the outline of her bed. Why was she sitting on the chair instead of lying on the mattress, she wondered, but her thirst distracted her attention to the table next to her bed that held the water jug.

The room was obviously empty, but the feeling of being not alone persisted. It must have been something she had been dreaming. Something from a dream. She rose, her eyes locked on the water jug—God she was thirsty—and then gasped.

The pain seared through her, up from her ankle, as soon as she put her weight on it. Sitting back down quickly, she examined her left leg, and saw that there was an enormous, crudely wrapped bandage around it. She had absolutely no recollection of having hurt herself, no recollection of having come to her room at all, actually. Had she fallen and hit her head? But her head felt fine, except for her thirst.

How did she get here? She remembered watching Toast scurry around the house vainly attempting to avoid the puppy, who had developed a violent crush on him. And she recalled dinner, one of the best they had eaten in recent weeks, because of the cartload of food Elwood had sent. It contained no note, but she knew it was from him because no one else would have bothered, and no one else would have remembered her passion for hazelnut cakes and sent a dozen. She must have eaten three of them before getting tired and going to doze off in her study. An image of the numbers on her ledger floated into her mind, seeing them from the side, as if she was lying next to them, and then nothing. Three whole hazelnut cakes—not the little ones like Mariana's but proper full sized ones with sugared syrup drizzled over them—could have that effect on anyone, she reasoned. No wonder she was thirsty.

She looked at the water jug again. If she were very careful, she could reach it without having to step on her injured leg at all. She stood and hopped toward it. On her last hop she tumbled forward onto her bed, hitting her sore left ankle against the table leg. She winced in pain, but then forgot her pain altogether.

Lying diagonally across her bed was a girl she had never seen before. On her neck were two round pricks. In her hand was a gardenia. Clio opened her mouth to scream and tasted blood.

In that horrible instant Clio understood. She understood why she had been so unsurprised to see the pricks on Inigo's sister's neck, understood how she had so clearly seen the girl's fear. She understood why it had all made so much sense to her. It was because she had seen it all through her own eyes and forgotten it. Because she had been there. Because it was her. She was the vampire.

Clio swallowed back her scream. *You do not know what you are,* the note had said that morning, but she did now.

What? You think you know?

Demon. Fiend. She had always known there was violence living inside her. *Just like your father,* her grandmother had said, and she understood now, better than ever, what she had meant. "The vampire as a child is impossible to love," she remembered reading in the compendium. It all fit together. Her father's interest in the occult and the supernatural, the vampire's appearance at the time of her birth, her mother's death whose cause no one talked about directly. All the years she had wanted to know more about her father, all the questions she had asked that had been evaded or ignored, she now understood why. She had indeed inherited her father's wickedness, just as she had inherited his blood.

His *taste* for blood.

These thoughts streamed through her head as she stood paralyzed, looking down past the girl, her eyes fixed on the gardenia. It seemed to glow, pulsing white in the moonlight, a perverse symbol of purity, a sign of her wickedness. All at once, the half-seen images she was always trying to recall when she awoke flooded over her, coming to life in her room, fantasy and reality meshing together.

Clio looked up and saw hovering in front of her a portrait of a woman, wild-eyed. In the space between reality and imagination Clio watched the woman in the picture lift a kerchief to wipe her lips, a blue kerchief, like the one she had found near the first girl, like the ones she had received as a mysterious present the year before on Mariana's birthday. That was when Clio saw it wasn't a portrait at all. It was a mirror, her mother's mirror with the green leaves, the mirror in her room, and the woman was a reflection. A real reflection. Of her. Clio looked down and saw that she really was clutching a blue kerchief in her hand, and that it was stained with blood.

She had known it all along. It was as if, all along, something inside had been waiting to get out, waiting to tell her. Waiting for her to understand that she was the vampire.

Wicked girl!

Clio wrenched her eyes from the gardenia, sinister and glowing, and found that she was crying. Why was this happening now? What was making her do these things? Words and images swam together before her eyes—a screaming corpse, those laughing dolls, dirty footprints, mud on her boots, a man winking at her, cracked lips, her thirst, her godawful thirst—and she knew she had to get away, away from the body, away from her house. She had to leave before she hurt someone else. Heedless of the pain in her leg, she ran. She would turn herself in, she would kill herself, she would get away. She would not hurt anyone again.

She flew down the stairs, panting, her heart pounding. Her thoughts were a jumble—please don't let them wake up, please don't let me hurt anyone, what are you what are you *what are you*? With shaking hands she unlatched the front door of the house and rushed out, into the street, into the warm night air, into the comforting, anonymous, darkness.

Into the arms of the man who had been waiting for her all night.

Chapter 8

"I had expected you earlier. You can't imagine how long I have been standing here."

At first Clio did not know him, in his dark suit with the cap pulled low over his forehead. But then recognition dawned and she fought even harder.

"Get away. Let me go. You must let me go." Her voice was desperate, almost pleading.

He had not planned to reveal himself, had planned merely to follow her, see where she went, before letting her know he was there. It was the plan he had devised that afternoon, after he had followed her back to her house, but the way she had looked when she ran out the door, the dangerous expression on her face, changed his mind. Now he held her at an arm's length and examined her.

"Clio," Miles asked with genuine concern. "What is wrong? Has someone hurt you?"

Clio shook her head tensely. "I am fine. Just let me go. Please. Leave me alone. I must be alone."

Her eyes were wild, and refused to meet Miles's gaze.

"Clio, you are not fine. You must—"

"I would be if you would just leave me the hell

alone," she spat at him. "Get away from me. Don't you understand? Don't you see that I am dangerous? That I am wicked? That I will hurt you." Her voice changed. "Oh, God, Lord Dearbourn, for your own good, you must go away."

"What do you mean you are dangerous?"

Tears were running down Clio's cheeks. "I am the vampire, my lord. I am the killer."

Miles looked at her in silence for a moment. "That is not possible." Then, his eyes narrowed. "Is this some sort of jest?"

Clio's face changed again, this time into a malevolent smile. "You think so, my lord? Not possible? Come and see." She began to lead the way across the street, then stopped. "But you must promise me, after you do, that you will do nothing to stop me from turning myself in. That you will see to it I am not left alone until I am in custody. Do you promise?"

Miles nodded.

"No," Clio insisted. "You must say the words."

"I promise. I promise I will not leave your side until you are turned in," Miles assured her, and she took his arm and led him into her house. Instead of turning left into her office as he had done that day, they went directly up two flights of stairs. They turned, then passed through a crooked doorway.

Two strides took Miles to the side of the bed. His eyes, already adjusted to the dark, spotted the dark pricks on the girl's neck immediately.

He swung around to face Clio. "When did you do this?"

Her eyes looked strange, dangerous, again. "I don't

know. I woke there," she pointed to the chair, "and found her as you see her now. But there can be no question it was me. This is my room."

"What do you mean you 'found her'? Didn't you put her there?"

Clio shrugged. "I have no recollection. I can't remember anything that happened tonight. But I suppose that makes sense. I suppose my mind blotted it out. That is the logical explanation. It would also explain why I did not remember killing the other girl, two days ago."

"That, or the fact that you did not kill either of them," Miles pointed out. He turned back to the bed and leaned over the corpse. At first he thought the girl had a bruise on her cheek, but he saw it was just a flower-shaped birth mark. She did have rings of bruises on her wrists, however, and scrapes on her knees and shins below the hem of her gown. The gardenia was clutched in one of her hands, but the other was closed, in a fist. He took it and pried it open.

"Light a candle," he instructed without turning around.

Clio did not know why, but she obeyed him, then moved with the taper to his side. In his hand he held a small lead token, of the type sold as collectable souvenirs at major fairs. Each fair minted its own tokens and impressed its own logo on them. This one showed a crude portrait of the queen, marking it as a token of the once-a-year fair that had opened that day in Smithfield, just outside the walls of London.

"Have you been to the Jubilee Fair?" Miles asked Clio.

"Not in my right mind. There is no telling what I might have been doing out of it," she answered bitterly.

He turned to face her. "I do not believe that you killed this woman."

"Why?"

"For one thing, because I have been standing outside your door all night." When she opened her mouth to protest, he rushed on. "There is no way you could have entered, or left, by that means. So you would have had to come through there—" he gestured toward the window whose shutter continued to moan weakly in the wind, "—dragging the girl behind you. Which seems unlikely given that she is heavier *and* nearly a head taller than you are."

"Why couldn't I simply have induced her to walk up with me? Why would I have had to drag her?"

"Look at these marks." Miles pointed to the scrapes that ran up the girl's shins and over her knees. "Unless I am mistaken, we shall find that they match in width the supports of the ladder that is leaning against the house outside your window." Clio looked out the window and noticed for the first time the ladder Mr. Williams had been using that morning in rehearsal. But how had Miles noticed? Before she could ask, he went on. "For another, the last time I saw a vampire, his mouth was dripping with blood. There is not a spot of blood on you except a touch on your lips and that is because they are so dry they have begun to crack. Besides, if you did kill her, why would you bring her to your house? Your room?"

"Perhaps I was trying to show myself. So I would know. I read about a madwoman doing something like that once. She did all these horrible things and never remembered any of it, it was as if she were possessed

by a demon. And each time the demon got more powerful until finally he was going to take her over and
the way he did that was by showing her all the evil she
had done. Perhaps the vampire part of me is getting
stronger."

"I think it is more likely that the vampire wants to
make it look like you are responsible for the deaths of
those girls than that you are possessed."

"Why would the vampire do that?"

"Shift the blame. It would be a good way to get you,
and anyone to whom you reported the news that you
were the vampire—say the Special Commissioner—to
stop investigating."

"But if I were arrested or turned myself in and another
girl was killed, then it would be clear it was not me,"
Clio pointed out. "This would only work for a short
time."

Miles glanced outside and saw the waning moon low
on the horizon. "Perhaps that is enough." He crossed to
Clio's armoire and opened it. "Are these the only gowns
you own? This old one and the tattered one you are
wearing?"

It took Clio a moment to realize what he was doing. "I
am sorry if my wardrobe does not meet with your approval, my lord," she answered acerbically. "If I had
known you would be pawing my clothes, I would have
improved the selection, I assure you."

Miles almost smiled with relief. She had begun to
sound, and even look, like Clio again. "It rained tonight.
If you had been out of the house, your clothes would
have been wet. The girl's dress is wet. But it seems that
your entire wardrobe is dry."

He was right. Her clothes were all dry and the girl's were wet and that meant that she had not dragged the girl there, had not been out of her house.

But she could have had another set of clothes. A vampire outfit. An ensemble she left stashed somewhere. And—

"There is something else, my lord."

Miles, who had again been looking at the girl's body, faced Clio. "What?"

"My ankle. When I woke up, it was sore, and in a bandage. But I don't remember having done anything to it."

"What do you remember of yesterday?"

"Not very much," Clio said, avoiding his eyes. Not anything about his lips. Or about what it was like to kiss him. "I spent the afternoon in my study and dined and then fell asleep. But downstairs. Not here. I do not remember coming to bed."

"Perhaps you tripped on your way up the stairs."

It was not impossible. Indeed, it was distinctly possible. But it also seemed like the sort of thing she would remember.

"Did you drink anything?" Miles asked.

"Are you suggesting I drank too much? That I was drun—"

Miles interrupted. "No, you hardly seem like the type to gulp down a decanter of sack." *And you should know.* "I was wondering if your drowsiness might have been induced. It is easier to put a sleeping powder in wine than in food."

"You think someone drugged me?"

"It is a possibility. Can you think of anyone in your household who would do that? Your cook, or baker, or footman?"

The degree to which he had misestimated the size of her staff almost made Clio laugh. "Why not the yeoman of the buttery?" she asked earnestly.

A crease appeared between Miles's brow. "It could be him, certainly. I did not see a butter shed outside so—"

"You are right. We have no buttery. I guess that rules him out. And also the idea that I was drugged. At least by anyone in my household. Besides, the cake I ate was not made here. It was delivered by special messenger in a basket of food."

"Who was it from?" Miles demanded.

"A very good friend. Someone who would have no interest in drugging me."

"Are you sure?"

"I don't know about your friends, my lord, and I can already see the appeal of drugging you myself, but I am fairly sure that none of my friends would be up to it."

"That is too bad."

"Why, would you prefer that I were drugged? Is that how you like your women?"

"Oh yes," Miles replied with such apparent sincerity that for a moment it looked like Clio might explode. "Actually, I had something else in mind. As I see it, there is only one good explanation of what happened: Someone— most likely the vampire—waited until they could be sure you were asleep, then dragged a body up through your window. Very few people would undertake that kind of operation unless they could be assured that you would not wake up. A convenient way to ensure that would be to send you drugged food. A readily available herb like mandragora would do the trick perfectly."

He was right, but that was not what made Clio's eyes

grow huge. "The vampire was here," she said, almost whispering. "If I am not the vampire, he was here, in this room, tonight. With me." Clio shuddered, then looked right at Miles. "But if he was," Clio went on, "why didn't he kill me?"

Miles opened his mouth, and then closed it. He did not know. Nor did he know why he was so damn hell-bent on convincing Clio Thornton that she was not a vampire. Perhaps she was. He could use a drink. Maybe there was more than one of them, maybe he had killed the Vampire of London last time and Clio was merely a replacement. But somehow he did not believe it. Clio was a connection to the vampire, but not the vampire herself.

Or at least he hoped not.

Where had that come from? He did not care what happened to Clio Thornton. *Liar!* No matter how brave she was, no matter how smart, and how— No matter what, she was not his responsibility. He had given that up, the kind of caring that engendered responsibility, with Beatrice's death. He looked around for a carafe of wine. The only duty he owed now was to his queen, to find the vampire. That was the only reason he was staying so close to Clio. That and the fact that he did not want her death on his conscience. The only reason he had hovered around her house all night was to be sure that nothing happened to her.

But something had happened. He saw her watching him, the strain showing on her lovely face.

No. She was not his responsibility. She had refused his help that afternoon, flat out. She was damn lucky that he had decided to spend the night in the shadows next to her house at all. If he hadn't been there, who knew what she would have done, he asked himself. But his conscience would not relent. *This is your fault.* He remembered the tears running down her face when she first ran out of her house. *You failed.*

"Do you have a manservant you can summon?" he asked abruptly. His manner was cool, condescending even, and the question sounded more like a command.

Clio blinked at the change in him. "Why?"

"I want to send him to get my carriage. You can't walk all the way to Dearbourn Hall with your ankle like that, and I doubt you would let me carry you."

"You are absolutely right, I wouldn't," Clio said, outraged. "Nor can I imagine what makes you think I would go home with you. Why would I go anywhere with you?"

"You have no choice. I cannot protect you well enough if—"

"Is that what you call what you were doing in front of my house tonight? Protecting me?" Her tone was sarcastic.

"No. I was spying on you. Since you wouldn't allow me to work with you, I thought I would watch you work. See where you went. What you did."

"You admit it?"

"I can deny it. If you prefer I can say that I thought ten pounds was a rather steep price to pay for a few minutes of your time and I wanted to be sure I got my money's worth."

"That's strange," Clio hissed. "I felt the ten pounds was only marginally adequate compensation for having to spend that long with you." Then she reached behind her back and began untying the laces of her gown.

"What the devil are you doing?"

"I know how you feel about paying women who are dressed," Clio explained. "I thought perhaps you would get your money's worth more quickly if I took my gown off." She had never done anything like this before in her life and she flushed red with anger.

Her pinafore and overskirt fell to the floor, leaving her standing in only a knee-length chemise. It had been fine once, but years of wear had made it almost transparent.

It was a good thing Miles no longer felt desire *(liar)* because if he did he would probably have been feeling it. Damn he wished he had a drink. The room suddenly drew itself in and became smaller, cramped, as if the air were heavier, as if it were somehow compelling them to stand closer together.

There was something about seeing her standing like that, so small and fragile and unutterably beautiful, that sliced through Miles's anger. "That won't be necessary," he managed to choke out before she pulled her chemise over her head. "I think we are all settled up."

"Good," Clio said with a sharp nod, releasing the hem of the gown. "Good. Then there is nothing to keep you here. You may go."

Yes. He should go. She did not need him. And he definitely did not need her. Mucking around with his investigation. Interfering with his life, making his breeches feel like they had shrunk ten inches in the past two minutes. What was it, six in the morning, and he had not yet been to bed? It was not as though he did not have more important things to be doing. What was he thinking, wasting his time pacing up and down in front of her house?

But there was definitely some connection between her and the vampire, and he had to find out what it was.

"I cannot just go." Miles did not sound apologetic. "You see, I promised to stay with you until you were in custody."

Clio waved that away. "That is not important anymore."

"I am sorry, Lady Thornton, but a man of honor always keeps his promises."

"A man of honor does not torment innocent women by throwing promises they extracted during moments of strain back in their faces," Clio pointed out hotly

"It is an interesting point," Miles acknowledged. "But you are wrong. I am bound. You are stuck with me." Clio opened her mouth to say something, no doubt comparing him unfavorably with a foxhound, but he cut her off. He was rather enjoying himself now. "Even without my promise, you have to concede that it would be irresponsible of me to leave an admitted fiend alone to do more harm."

"I am not a fiend. You said so yourself."

"And you said yourself 'I am the vampire.' "

"But that was before. Everything has changed."

Miles raised an eyebrow. "Has it? Are you really convinced?"

Clio bit her lip and turned to look out the window into the waning night, hugging her arms around her. The stars still glimmered faintly and the sky was the vibrant blue that marked the moment just before dawn. Until recently, this was a time of day that always made Clio a little sad because it marked the end of the night. She loved the night, loved the stillness of the city air and the velvety darkness, loved the glow of the moon and the twinkle of fireflies. At night, anything seemed possible. It was only during the day that reality took hold, that reason and logic reasserted themselves, that all her hopes and dreams seemed impossible once again. But now this had happened and the peace she had felt at night vanished. Would she ever get it back?

If I am not the vampire, why didn't he kill me?

You are not what you think you are.

What did it all mean?

The simplest explanation is the best, Clio had learned in her investigations. And the simplest explanation certainly was not that her friend Elwood had drugged her, dragged a dead woman up a ladder into her room, and left the lifeless body lying across her mattress with a white gardenia in its hand. No, the simplest explanation was that she herself was the vampire.

"I can prove you are not," Miles said then, as if he had heard her thoughts. "I can show you that you are not the vampire, but you will have to obey me."

Clio turned to face him. "How?"

Miles did not know why he had not thought of it sooner. It was the perfect means of keeping an eye on her. Keeping her safe. "You suggested the method yourself: If you were locked up and another body surfaced, it would be clear you were not the vampire. Correct?"

Clio thought for a moment, then nodded.

"Therefore you have two options: Either I can take you to the constables, or rather," he said, remembering a certain tone in her voice, "to the Special Commissioner, and have you locked up until another girl dies. Or, you can have me as your constant companion until then, but be able to continue your investigation. The choice is yours—the Special Commissioner, or me." Miles added, "I would, of course, pay you for having to put up with my company."

Clio narrowed her eyes at him. "I don't want your money."

"You will," Miles assured her. "I know you will find it hard to believe at first, but I can be very bothersome. Tedious, even."

"I can't tell you how you surprise me."

Miles ignored her. "I had to pay you ten pounds to compensate for inflicting myself on you for half an hour today," Miles calculated, "so at that rate, two days would cost about a thousand pounds. Would five hundred up front, as a retainer, and five hundred when the job is done suit you? It should not take more than two days for another body to arrive. If it is longer, we can renegotiate."

Clio stared at him, stunned. Five hundred pounds would pay off her debt to Captain Black. A thousand would keep Which House fed for years. It was an absurd sum to offer for a job of detection.

She was immediately wary. "Why are you doing this? Why do you care what I do? Where I am?"

"I don't," Miles answered bluntly. "I care about finding the vampire. As far as I can tell, whether you are the vampire or just the person he is trying to frame, you are the closest link I have to the truth."

She remembered all the news sheets she had read from three years earlier. "Are you doing this because of Beatrice? Because you still love her and want to avenge her death?"

Something tensed in Miles's cheek, but his voice stayed level. "You are very good at asking questions. That will be useful at the fair."

Clio, who had opened her mouth to protest his change of subject, said instead, "The fair?"

"Yes. I propose that we start with a visit to the Jubilee Fairgrounds. Perhaps someone there can tell us who she—" he gestured at the dead girl on the bed, "—is, and who she left with last night. Perhaps someone there saw the real vampire."

Clio might not have been to the fair, but she had read about it, and knew that by law it was supposed to close at midnight. "But it's nearly dawn. Who will be there?"

"Everyone. It is only once the booths licensed by the crown have closed that the fair begins to get interesting."

"I am only going along with this for the money," she announced to him.

"Really? I thought it was my charm that convinced you," Miles replied dryly.

Clio felt as though the reigns of the investigation had slipped away from her. For one final moment she considered telling him to take her to the Special Commissioner instead, but then the thought of his thousand pounds and what it could mean convinced her.

That and the fact that he might be the only thing standing between the innocent women of London and death at her hands.

Even in the kind, rosy light of dawn, the Jubilee Fair looked disreputable. The air was filled with shouts—people hawking everything from leather belts and knives to love, good breath, and long life—and scented with a mixture of lemons, roasted chickens, spilled ale, women's perfume, and soot. The place was entirely singular, entirely unforgettable.

And entirely unfamiliar to Clio. She felt her spirits lift enormously. To her, even the hastily constructed shanties of Jubilee Fairgrounds looked beautiful because she was sure she had never been there before.

"This is the first time I have seen any of this," she said to Miles as they walked between the stalls, Toast perched on her shoulder to avoid being trampled. The opening lines of an old ballad came unbidden to her mind. *The first time I did see you dear, my heart in me did pound, I knew that day as I know—*

"What are you humming?" Miles demanded sharply.

"Humming?" It took Clio a moment to realize that in her excitement, she had been. "It is something my nurse used to sing me to make me go to sleep," she said. "I don't even think it has a name."

Miles nodded, but his eyes had a faraway look. "It is called 'The First Time I Did See You Dear.' A very good friend of mine used to sing it often." It had been Beatrice's favorite, one of the vestiges of her early life in the country. He used to love it when she sang it to him because he knew it meant she was happy, loved seeing the sweetness that still hovered unextinguished beneath her ever more polished exterior. Or at least, had until—

A woman in a red satin gown festooned with fake gems and ribbons barreled into him with a coy smile. "Good evening lovie," she began with an exaggerated wink in Miles's direction. "Look like you're a man who could show a lass a good time. A real good time, if you know what I mean." Before she could elaborate, her eyes fell upon Clio, and her smile vanished. An expression almost of terror took its place. "Oh. You. Never mind," she said, hastily backing away before turning around and running into the crowd.

"I am sorry, my lord," Clio said with a frown. Had the woman been afraid of her? "I seem to have scared her off. If you'd like, I can wait in the carriage."

Miles looked down at her to be sure she was joking, and found she was not. "That won't be necessary."

"But she was beautiful," Clio said, with real awe.

"I suppose some might think her beautiful."

Clio frowned at him. "If you are trying to spare my feelings by understating your admiration, you need not, my lord."

"Thank you. I shall remember that in the future."

His eyes seemed to be laughing at her and Clio was suddenly strikingly aware that the man whose hand was on her elbow *(The first time I did see you dear)*, the man who was looking at her with genuine interest in his intense golden eyes *(My heart in me did pound)*, the man whose lips were close enough for her to touch *(I knew that day as I know now)*, the man whose proximity was filling her head with old songs *(That my true love I'd found)*—that this man was her cousin's fiancé, that he could never be hers, and that he was probably in love with Mariana just like everyone else.

Clio moved away abruptly. *Bad girl* she heard her grandmother screeching, and had to agree. Coming here, going anywhere, with the Viscount Dearbourn was a mistake. She would have been better off with the Special Commissioner. At least she would not have imagined kissing him, or kept wishing that she were beautiful, or had a lovely gown like the woman in red, a gown that made men swoon. What would it be like to be that sure of yourself, Clio wondered, remembering the woman's smile at Miles. What would it be like to know you were beautiful, that people desired you, that they loved you?

"Like a slice of heaven" a voice answered her thoughts. Clio looked up and realized it was a question, not a statement, put forward by a man selling sweetmeats from a tray. "Rose water and almond paste and sugar, that's what that is. Or perhaps a lemon-and-sugar sweet for the lady? She loves a good lemon sweet, I can tell you."

How did he know that? Clio wondered.

Miles gave the man a coin, and selected three of the large lemons with hollow sugar straws in them, giving one to Clio and one to Toast.

"You'd better take the whole lot of 'em, if this is the smallest coin you got," the sweet-seller told Miles.

Miles shrugged. "You keep the difference."

The sweet-seller's eyes grew wide. "You are a gentleman, sir, a true gentleman, and I thank you, sir." He leaned over to Clio, who had been watching the exchange with perplexity, and said, "You done well this time, sweetheart."

"Tell me," Miles said, drawing the man's attention. "Have you seen a girl with a birthmark in the shape of a flower on her cheek, here at the fair?"

The sweet-seller seemed to think for a moment, then shook his head. "Can't say that I have, but then I don't notice all of them. Now if she had a birthmark here," he made a gesture toward a region below his neck and above his stomach, "that I mighta remembered."

Clio and Miles got similar responses from a dozen other people they asked, including a man whose body was entirely wrapped in snakes, three girls who offered to paint birthmarks on their "cheeks" for Miles's personal and private inspection, and a woman who proposed to sing a song that the girl with the birthmark would not be able to resist and would cause her to appear before them in a matter of minutes from anywhere in the world.

But despite these handsome offers, Clio felt increasingly uneasy as they pushed deeper into the fairgrounds. There was something in the way people eyed her that began slowly to erode her sense of relief.

"Try yer luck, win a brooch," a stooped figure croaked from a booth next to her, and Clio jumped.

"Are you all right?" Miles asked. He had been watching her closely, and had seen her expression go from enjoyment to concern. "You look pale. Perhaps we should come back later."

Clio shook her head. "No. Now. I want to find out now. Whatever there is to find out."

"Three tries for a penny, sir," the stooped figure went on. It appeared to be a woman, and if her looks were anything to go on, she was old enough to be one of the original Fates. "Try your luck and win a brooch. Guaranteed to bring long life to the winner. Try it for the lady, sir," she cooed at Miles, blowing stale breath in his face and pressing three wooden balls into his hand. "Hazard is but a penny, sir, and all you have to do to win is get one of those balls into this basket."

Miles shook his head.

"Almost the lady's birthday, my lord. Brooch would

make a fine present, it would," the woman continued her sales pitch, and Miles was about to relent, merely so he would be allowed to leave, when he saw the color drain from Clio's face.

He dropped a penny on the woman's table, then put an arm around Clio and led her to one side of the crowd where a felled log provided a place for them to sit. "What is wrong?" he asked.

"She knew it was almost my birthday," Clio stammered. "No one knows my birthday is tomorrow. *I* nearly forgot. How did *she* know that? How *could* she have known that? Unless I was here earlier and told her."

Miles exhaled with relief and had to repress a smile. "Is that what is worrying you? What she said about your birthday?"

Clio's eyes unclouded slightly in her surprise at his tone.

"I can assure you she says that to all her customers," he went on. "Most of the couples you see strolling around here probably never met before tonight," Miles explained, aiming for delicacy. "It is merely a ruse to get more people to spend more money. I suspect if you asked three quarters of those women they would say it was 'almost' their birthday, if it meant they could pry their companions' purses open a bit wider."

"You mean they are prostitutes? And she thought I was a prostitute also?" Clio asked.

"That is not what I meant to imply," Miles said quickly. He braced himself for her anger.

"How marvelous!" Clio declared, smiling. "No one has ever thought anything like that about me before. I read in a book once that prostitution was the only honest life for a woman," she rushed on. "Because there are no lies between a prostitute and her client, not like between a husband and wife or a man and his mistress."

"I think Aretino meant that as a satire, not a suggestion," Miles said quietly, astonished at her reading.

Clio ignored him, musing aloud. "Perhaps other people here think I am a prostitute as well. Perhaps it is only because I am with you that no one has approached me."

"If you would like I can wait in the carriage," Miles offered.

"Yes, perhaps that would be better," she agreed quickly. "If you wouldn't mind."

"Lady Thornton, I will have to insist—"

Clio burst into laughter. "I was only fooling, my lord. You need not look so ghastly." Clio leaned in and scrutinized him. "I don't know how you do that. You seem to grow both taller and older simultaneously."

Her face was too close to his. Her eyes, her nose, her lips. The curve of her eyelashes over her cheek when she blinked. The angle of her chin. Her playful smile, her even teeth, the dry crack on her bottom lip, the wisp of her hair that had escaped from its pins and hung between their faces, the slight flush on her cheeks, the smell of roses, the line of her smooth neck, the question in her eyes—Miles was aware of all of them, aware with every inch of skin on his body. He reached out with a finger, caught the truant tendril of hair, and pushed it back behind her ear.

Then he stood up, pulling her up with him. "We should go."

Clio's mind buzzed confusingly for a moment. "But we have not learned who the girl is," she reminded him. "Or who she was seen with."

"We'll have to do that another way. I think I am too tired—"

A man careened out of one of the establishments along the back wall of the fair, known as Sinner's Alley, stumbled against Clio and then fell, unconscious, at her feet. Before she could bend over to make sure he was still breathing, another man, face red with anger, followed him out of the establishment, wielding a twig broom.

"Don't come back until you can pay," the broom-brandishing man yelled at the man on the ground, whacking him a few times for good measure. "I ain't running a church here, Ginny, so we don't give out no charity." He raised the broom to give Ginny another whack, and found it stuck.

"I think he's gotten the message," Miles told the man from behind.

"This ain't none of your business, sir," the broom-brandisher told him, swinging around and giving Ginny a chance to crawl to safety. "Ain't nothing to do with—" He broke off, spotting Clio. A smile spread over his face. "Well I say. I knew you'd be back. I told Flora so, I did. We'll see her again, I said. And there you are."

Clio looked behind her to see who the man could be speaking to, then raised a hand to her chest. "Me?"

"You think I mean some other pretty young thing with a monkey? Hell, lass, I haven't seen anyone get taken with the flavor like you since my own Mary, rest her soul."

"You must be mistaken," Clio said. "I have never been here before."

The man looked skeptically from her to Miles. Then he winked. "You got nothing to worry about. He won't care if you was here earlier. The gentry all love my place. They all got a bit of the hunger for it, too. Don't you agree, sir?"

Miles, who seemed to be paying only marginal attention, said, "Oh yes. Of course. You are very correct."

"Told you." The broom brandisher shot another wink in Clio's direction. "No need to hide it from him. We'll not tell him how much you won though, that can be our secret. But you best come inside so you're not standing on that ankle of yours."

"What did you say?" Clio demanded.

"It must be hurting something fierce after that fall you took trying to get closer to the pit," the man elaborated. "You'd do well to sit down."

"You know about my ankle?" Clio asked. Her voice was strangely hoarse.

"Course I do. Didn't I have my Flora bandage it up herself. Didn't I have her—"

"Flora," Clio repeated the name. Her face was ashen. "You call her that because she has a birthmark in the shape of a flower on her cheek."

The man nodded. "It was my sister's idea. She's buried now, near the old house in Devonshire, but she left me Flora. Thought the flower on the girl's cheek meant good luck. And the girl has been good luck, at least for me. Never was another who could sing so sweetly. Makes a man's heart glad to hear her."

"Where is your niece now?" Miles asked abruptly.

"Last I saw her I think she was going to bed," the man told him. "That's where all good girls ought to be now. Excepting those who have the taste like your friend here. Once you got the taste, you don't want to sleep or eat or do anything. The taste gets into you and you always got to have more."

"What taste?" Clio half whispered. "The taste for what?"

"What taste?" The red faced man laughed at the ridiculous question. "Why, the taste for blood."

Chapter 9

Taste for blood, taste for blood, taste for blood.

The horrible feeling of being trapped in a nightmare was back, wrapping itself around Clio more and more tightly until it was almost suffocating. *You are not what you think you are.*

What you think you are, you are.

You are exactly what you think you are.

She had been at the fair the night before. She had hurt her ankle. She had met Flora. And she had killed her.

Clio took a deep breath. "My lord, may I speak to you apart?" she asked Miles. The moment of her confusion had passed. She felt calm, in control. Relieved. She knew what she had to do.

Miles had been worried that the broom-man's words would upset her. Her tranquility was a relief.

"My lord, I would do this myself, but I am afraid I might bungle it. Would you please tell that gentleman that I killed his niece and that you are taking me to the Special Commissioner? There is no need to bother him with the details of my being a vampire, he seems to know. After that, I propose we go directly to Newgate or the Tower, or wherever they put criminals of my type."

"What are you talking about?"

"We have incontrovertible proof that I am the vampire. There is no reason for me to remain in your custody any longer."

If she had not looked so serious Miles would have been tempted to laugh at her idea of incontrovertible proof. But there was nothing funny about her expression, or her intent. "Very well," he said finally. "You stay here and I will go and speak to the gentleman, as you generously called him. Then we will discuss the question of where to take you."

Clio nodded and stood ramrod still while Miles approached the man. A few words were exchanged, which Clio could not hear, but she saw the man's eyes grow huge as he looked at her. Then he spun around and doubled over, holding on to Miles for support, and Clio felt as though her heart would burst. The man was sobbing, absolutely uncontrollable, and it was her fault. When he turned back he had tears streaming down his face and Clio saw that he was avoiding looking at her.

"Get that filthy bitch away from me," he said and began to sob again, so hysterically it sounded like laughter. Clio shuddered and looked away.

Her entire body felt heavy, leaden, solid with grief and self-loathing. She barely saw or heard anything as they left the fair, did not even notice the man who said, "Good to see you again, sweetheart." She was only slightly aware of Miles's hands helping her into his coach and of his following her in after giving orders to his horsemen.

They were reentering the city gates when she spoke. "Thank you for telling the gentleman about Flora. He seemed very distraught. He must have loved her very much."

"Yes. Certainly." Miles debated informing her that what he had told the man had nothing to do with Flora but rather was an off-color joke about a man who confused his wife and his dog, and that Flora's uncle had been laughing rather than crying, then decided against it.

"Did he remember Flora leaving with me last night?"

"I didn't ask him."

"I guess it does not matter," Clio conceded. "Still, I would like to know how I spent my last hours. I wonder if there is something that triggers me to act like a vampire, or if it just comes upon me all at once." She paused. "Poor Flora. Will her uncle come to Which House and get her body? I suppose it would be more courteous for me to have it delivered. Do you think I should offer to pay for the funeral?" Before Miles could even dream of how to answer her questions, she went on. "I *would* have to go and kill someone beloved."

Miles shook off his astonishment. "Clio, you did not kill that woman, you did not suck her blood, and you are not a vampire."

"Of course I am." She leaned forward. "If I am not, why are you taking me to Newgate?"

"I'm not," Miles replied. "I am taking you to Dearbourn Hall, although I am beginning to think I should take you to Bethlehem Hospital."

Clio looked surprised. "But at the fair, you told me—"

"I did not tell you anything. I led you to believe I was going to do what you said because it was the only way to get you into my coach. When we arrive at my house, we will have a very long conversation in which I explain to you, for the final time, that you are not the Vampire of London."

"Impossible. Flora's uncle recognized me. He knew about my ankle. He knew about my taste for blood. He even—"

"He recognized a woman with a monkey. And I am more inclined to see his information about your ankle as proof that you were not there than as proof that you were. The idea of you tripping over yourself to get a better view of a cockfight is one I cannot believe."

"A cockfight?" For the first time there was a crack in Clio's practical armor. "You mean where two birds fight one another to the death in a pit and people bet on it?"

"Yes. I'm sure you've read a book about it. That is the entertainment that Flora's uncle's establishment provides. That is what he meant by 'a taste for blood.'"

"Are you sure? A taste for cockfighting?" For a moment, Clio felt relief again, but it vanished as quickly as it had come. "If you don't believe I was at the fair, if you don't believe Flora's uncle saw me, then is everything that happened just a coincidence?"

"No." Miles shook his head. "It might have been, if it weren't for your ankle. The fact that your ankle was hurt makes this far more sinister."

"Yes. It means that it was me."

Miles worked to control his growing frustration. "No. It means that someone was impersonating you here, and whoever it was hurt their ankle—by accident or on purpose—so *your* ankle had to be hurt, too. Whoever is masterminding this is not leaving anything to chance." But there was more to it than that, Miles knew. This business with the ankle suggested that the goal was not merely to frame Clio, but something else, and if it was as Miles surmised, it was something extremely disturbing.

"Why would the vampire impersonate me? That makes no sense at all."

"It wasn't the vampire, but someone working with him. Wittingly or unwittingly."

"How do you know it wasn't the vampire?"

"Whoever impersonated you had to be a woman, and I cannot believe the vampire is a woman. A woman with a hurt ankle would not have been able to haul Flora up that ladder and into your room."

Clio thought for a moment, then looked at Miles, almost with pity. "Impossible. I am sorry, my lord, but that makes no sense at all. There is no need to go about making up demons and demon accomplices who traipse around London with the idea of doing me harm for unknown reasons when everything fits into place if you simply assume I am the vampire."

Miles leaned forward. "You—are—not—the—vampire," he said slowly. "Are you enjoying this? It is almost as if you *want* to think you are a fiend."

"It makes more sense." Clio's voice was soft as she spoke, and it took Miles a moment to realize what she had said.

"Why? Why is it so easy for you to believe you are wicked?"

"Because I am," Clio answered plainly. "Because I have always been. I have bad thoughts, thoughts about hurting people. Once, when we were girls, I hurt Mariana. I—" Clio stopped then, and her eyes got huge. "I bit her," she whispered finally. "I bit her. I had forgotten, but now I remember. I bit her and she screamed and looked terrified and grandmother locked me in my room for a week." *You are evil, just like your father.* That was when the comparisons had started, Clio remembered.

"Just once?" Miles interrupted her thoughts. "You only tried to hurt Mariana once? My cousins and I tried to kill each other at least a dozen times between the ages of four and fourteen, with, I suspect, less provocation."

"It was not the same," Clio told him. "It was not a joke. And then, since then, there have been the hiccups."

"Hiccups?" Miles was clearly skeptical.

"Sometimes I feel violent and angry, like I am filled with a strong desire to harm someone, and when I don't, when I hold myself back, I get the hiccups. But I have had them more and more often, recently. Sometimes even when I don't know I am angry or upset. It is as if violence has been building inside of me, trying to get out. I am evil, my lord. You have to understand that. I should be sent to Newgate before I can harm anyone else. I should be chained up and flogged and beaten for what I have done."

"No one should be beaten," Miles said sharply.

Clio looked at him, but whatever she had seen in his face out of the corner of her eye was gone. "It would be better for everyone if I were locked away."

Miles could not have agreed more. It was the only way to ensure that she would be safe. And that he would know where she was. "Lady Thornton, you are not evil, and I will not send you to Newgate," he said, trying to strike a tone between imperious and polite. He was almost ready to tell her that even if she were sent to Newgate she would end up in his custody, but decided against it. "You are coming back with me to Dearbourn Hall where you will remain until another body is found. At that point, once you have been convinced of your innocence, you can decide to stay or return to your own house."

"Absolutely not. I cannot go to Dearbourn Hall. I mean, I will not go."

"Why?"

Clio hesitated. There were a thousand reasons she could give, none of them revealing the fact that her family reviled her. She countered with a question of her own. "My lord, do you possess anything so precious to you that you would rather suffer than lose it?"

The query caught Miles by surprise. "Yes," he answered finally. "My cousins."

"So do I. My home. The only thing I have. And if my grandmother finds me at Dearbourn Hall, I shall lose it forever. Compared with that loss, the loss of my freedom is nothing. Please take me to Newgate."

Miles regarded her with an indecipherable expression for a moment, then said, "Your grandmother is not in the habit of coming to my apartments. You can stay there. There's nowhere else for you anyway, the rest of the house is full." Watching her mouth open he added, "And there is no use protesting—you have no choice."

"You mean I am your prisoner?"

"No. You are simply going to be forced to enjoy my hospitality."

"Can you explain the difference?"

"It would take some time. It is very subtle."

"Yes. I have noticed your subtlety. Along with your wit. And charm."

"You are very kind, but you don't need to flatter me."

Clio blinked at him, and was torn between the desire to laugh and the desire to hit him over the head with a blunt object. "Why are you doing this? Is it because of Beatrice?"

"I suggest you refrain from mentioning that name in my presence again."

Clio frowned. "Then why?"

"Because it seems to me that whoever has gone to all this trouble to frame you would be overjoyed if you turned yourself in—it would save them a lot of work—and I would hate to give them that pleasure. In addition, I do not care to spend another uncomfortable night pacing the street in front of your house."

"Neither of those is a real answer."

"No," Miles conceded thinly. "But they are the only ones you are going to get."

Clio suddenly felt very tired. Although it was only nine o'clock in the morning it felt as if it had been a very long day. She was tired of fighting, tired of worrying, tired of trying to reason with the irrational Deerhound, tired of trying to keep her thoughts straight, tired of trying to remember why she was evil, or why she wasn't, tired of trying to recall where she wanted to go, and where she did not, tired of trying to keep her eyes open, and hold her head up and ignore the regular rhythm of the coach wheels as they bounced up-down-up-down-up-dowwn-up-dowwnn-up-dowwwnn-up-dowwwnnnn . . .

Miles carried Toast and Clio up the back stairs of Dearbourn Hall to his apartment without waking either of them. He would deposit Toast on a chair and her on his bed and then find Corin, he decided. But as he pulled the downy linen coverlet up over Clio's sleeping form, her fingers curled gently around his. Unable to disentangle himself despite his best efforts *(liar)*, he kicked off his boots and lay down next to her. In less than a minute, he had fallen asleep.

The wine decanter stood on the table next to the bed, untouched for the first time in months.

The working clock in Miles's bedchamber quietly marked the passage of an hour, and Miles and Clio slept.

Four men arrived unexpectedly at Which House to deliver a handsome new armoire to Clio's bedroom and remove her old one, now strangely heavy. Snug was sure he had seen one of them before, and Princess Erika felt certain—whether it was a premonition or the sight of a sliver of yellow sleeve peeking out from beneath the cuff of one of their shabby work robes—that there was a mystery afoot concerning the viscount Dearbourn. This affiliation was confirmed when one of them reappeared shortly with a note saying that Clio was engaged on a very secret investigation on behalf of the viscount and would not be back for several days, accompanied by a purse containing five hundred pounds "as a retainer for her services." In the kitchen, the Triumverate began work on a new play about enchanted servants.

The clock counted off another hour.

Three new silk gowns were delivered at a side entrance of Dearbourn Hall by a young apprentice from the studio of Octavia Apia, London's most sought after dressmaker. A generous tip kept her from probing too hard for the name of the gowns' recipient.

Two hours went by.

The man known as the Vampire of London sat at the writing table in his room at Dearbourn Hall, carefully studying a document. He had to force himself to concentrate, not to mention stay seated. Every time he heard a chambermaid pass in the corridor, he jammed the document into a hiding space he had created between the top of the table and its base, and moved next to the door, hoping for a snatch of gossip. At last he heard what he had been listening for, the news that another body had been found. But when he discovered that no one knew where, or by whom, his face went white.

"Looked like he might faint he did," one of the chambermaids told the Special Commission later.

"Or like he was real angry," the other suggested.

The hands on Miles's clock traced a complete circle.

A shriek echoed through the west wing of Dearbourn Hall as Lady Alecia discovered that one of her favorite hairpieces—indeed, the one she had been planning to wear to the wedding—was missing. Corin held off rousing his master but promised that a full search of the house would be made, and pretended to consider Mariana's order that the malefactor be severely flogged.

Another hour passed.

Doctor LaForge entered the library, then passed into the reading alcove at its rear. He slid a volume with dark blue binding off the shelf, inserted a piece of paper between the eleventh and twelfth pages, and returned it to its place.

Ten minutes later, Mariana's maidservant Jocelyn entered the alcove, looked over her shoulder to make sure she was not observed, removed the same book from the shelf, and left.

Three quarters of an hour ticked by.

Responding to a summons from Mariana, Corin was relieved to hear that he was not expected to give a report on how the footmen were progressing in their search for the thief of Lady Alecia's hairpiece. Rather, he was told that because one member of Mariana's entourage was feeling low, the program for the night was being changed from a ball to the latest craze in entertainments, "a tablooviant."

"Tableaux vivant," Doctor LaForge corrected her.

"Darling Saunders suggested it," Mariana went on to Corin, ignoring her tutor. "It is the rage in Europe and I shall have the first one of the season here. Everyone must dress up like characters from famous works of art. I shall go as the goddess Diana. She is the one with all the baby animals around her, isn't she?"

"I believe that is Saint Francis," Doctor LaForge put in, but was again unheeded.

Half dreading and half dreaming of Miles's reaction to this change, Corin dispatched three-quarters of the footmen on the staff to spread word of the substitution, and the other quarter in the search of "darling baby birds" to adorn Mariana's costume.

Throughout Dearbourn Hall, clocks chimed five.

An apologetic and somewhat breathless Corin wakened Miles then, who frowned when he heard about the tableaux vivant, frowned harder when he saw what he was supposed to wear, and frowned harder still when he learned of the missing wig. He used his special key and disappeared up the hidden staircase inside his clock. If Corin had been surprised to find his master in bed with a woman, he did not show it.

The clock ticked on undisturbed by his passage, and undisturbed Clio slept. After a few hours, she began to dream.

She was small, a little girl, and she was walking around a fair, holding a man's hand. He bought her a sugared citron. It was the first time she had tried one.

"Do you like it?" the man asked, and she nodded, even though she wasn't sure. She wanted the man to be glad.

"I knew you would," he said, happily drinking the juice out of his own. "You are just like your daddy, and daddy has a taste for them."

Clio felt a surge of happiness then, for being with her father, being like her father. She held his hand tighter, willing him never to let her go, and he pushed her hair off her forehead affectionately. She raised her face to smile at him and tell him she loved him, too, but he was gone. Instead she saw a sign floating above the heads of the fair crowd with something written on it in large black letters, and she knew instinctively that it contained a crucial clue. She ran toward it and for an instant she could almost see the letters, almost make them out—

She awoke abruptly. In the split second between unconsciousness and consciousness, Clio caught one last glimpse of the spinning sign and the letters froze in her mind. N-E-V-E-R-D-E-S-I-R-E. Never Desire. Could that be what it said? Could that be the clue? It felt right, almost. Never desire. It made sense, sort of.

"Is there something you need, Lady Thornton?" said a voice behind her, and Clio's eyes shot open.

She must have walked in her sleep again. She was standing in the middle of what should have been a beautiful room. Even in the pale darkness she could make out the expensive sheen of the smoky gray velvet that covered the walls, but instead of furniture there were only crates stacked in the corners. To her right was a set of windows, under which stood four trunks with clothes spilling out of them. To her left was the lofty bed from which she had presumably sleepwalked, its striped hangings supported by lightly silvered pillars in the shape of ancient columns. And at her feet lay an overturned wooden box from which had been spilled a glass figurine in the shape of a headless bear, the bear's head, a handful of checkers, a sling shot, and what had once been a small gold table clock, which was now a not-so-small pile of gold coils and gears. Clio bent to pick it up, but the voice behind her—Corin's voice—stopped her.

"Don't worry about the clock," he said amiably. "It was one of the first His Lordship made and hasn't functioned right in years. Besides, we've more than enough around—" he made a wide gesture with his arm, and Clio saw that while there were no chairs in the room, there were indeed three other clocks "—and it will be good for His Lordship to have something to work on." Noting the uncomprehending look on her face, and the fact that—despite the warnings Miles had given him about the tantrum she would throw when she awoke and the demands she would make to be taken to prison—she was not speaking, he rushed on. "I can have a bath ready in ten minutes if you like, and these gowns are for you." Corin opened a hidden door in the wall behind which lay a built-in cupboard containing three dresses, each one ten-thousand-times lovelier than the one the woman at the fair had been wearing. "They are only temporary, of course, until Octavia can get your measurements." When she still had not said anything, he asked, "Are you all right, Lady Thornton?"

Clio gazed at him. "I am still dreaming, aren't I?"

But any doubts about whether she was awake or asleep were put to rest when she moved to take a step forward. The pain that shot up through her ankle brought back the events of the previous night with astonishing clarity, as did the appearance of Toast, who came dashing into the room with a clatter. If she were still dreaming, she would definitely have dreamed a better-behaved monkey.

He jumped up and down in front of her for a moment, then reached for her hand and tried to drag her through a partially open door. Clio looked at Corin. "Is there food through that door?"

"Yes. It just arrived. I did not know what he liked to eat, so I had the kitchen send up a bit of everything."

"That is exactly what he likes to eat," Clio told him, "as often as possible." She addressed the monkey. "You go on, Toast. I am not hungry."

Toast threw his chin up at her, a gesture of intense disdain, and crossed his arms.

"Really. I—" Anything further Clio would have wanted to say was drowned out by Toast chattering at her intensely. Deeming argument futile, she rolled her eyes and allowed herself to be led out of the bedroom.

Clio had been wrong. She was famished, and Toast lost no time in pointing this out to her. Corin had taken the liberty of dismantling one of the furniture towers to find a round, leather covered table and two chairs, and it was here, next to a window, that Clio and Toast dined. From this point Clio could see the rooftops of London in the growing twilight and below them, the small clusters of coachmen and grooms who had deposited their parties at Dearbourn Hall an hour earlier, and would wait outside all night until their services were needed. Over roasted capon stuffed with brown bread and parsley, Corin answered her questions about how she had arrived there (carried up by His Lordship), if the residents of Which House knew where she was (yes), whether any constables had gone there looking for her (no), what she had done all day (slept), if she had, um, been alone (Corin was afraid he did not know), and where His Lordship was at that moment (posing as a hunter in a recreation of a Titian painting in the Great Hall before a crowd of four hundred assembled guests).

"You must be joking," Clio said. She felt remarkably better.

"No." Corin confined himself to that one syllable because otherwise he might have been tempted to share with her the choice expressions Miles had used before departing, and he did not feel that was his place. "He asked me to extend to you his compliments and make myself available should you need anything. Is there anything you desire?"

Clio started to shake her head, then stopped. His words triggered her memory of the end of her dream, of the words Never Desire. Again she felt that they were almost, but not quite, right.

"I think I could use a library," she answered finally. She always found being surrounded by books conducive to thinking, and perhaps looking over *A Compendium of Vampires* would help her sort her mind out and reveal to her the meaning hidden behind the spinning sign. It would certainly force her to stop thinking about the dresses she had glimpsed shimmering in the cupboard, especially the purple one. Because Clio Thornton of Which House did not think about clothes—about the pitifulness of her two dresses, about the fact that she had never had a new gown, about the sound that new silk would make as she walked, providing she did not trip, about what it would feel like next to her skin—ever, and definitely not during investigations in which she was the main suspect.

"A library," Corin repeated. "It might take me some time to transfer the entire library here. Is there something in particular you were looking for?"

"Yes. Or rather, no. Sort of. If you would just show me to the library, I could find it myself."

Corin mustered a tight smile. "No, no. Please. You must let me get it for you."

Clio was about to protest his politeness when something about his words stopped her. "What do you mean, I *must* let you get it for me?"

Corin's smile became fixed. "The viscount said you did not wish to be seen, and since the house is filled with people, it was his suggestion that you stay here."

"Suggestion?"

Corin sighed and the smile disappeared. "Order. He said I was not to let you leave his apartment." He watched her and was glad to see how calm she seemed. Miles had warned him that she might be upset to learn that she was, for a time anyway, a prisoner, and had especially told him to be on the look out for hiccups, but she showed no sign of them. Indeed, she did not seem to be bothered at all.

"I see," Clio said, idly toying with one of the serving spoons as she mentally explored ways she could sneak out of the apartment. She was so preoccupied that she let the spoon slip from her fingers and onto the floor.

Clio was startled out of her thoughts by a loud thud, followed by a groan, both of which emanated from somewhere around her knees. She looked down and saw that Corin had bashed his head on the underside of the table when he went to pick up the serving spoon and was now lying unconscious at her feet.

She hesitated for almost two seconds. Then she checked to ensure he was breathing, rose from her chair, calmly moved past his inert body, and made her way to the door.

She was unhappy about having to leave Corin alone with his injury, but it was not really her fault. If Miles had not ordered her confined to his apartments, she probably would have had the manservant bring her the *Compendium* and would not have been so distracted by her own plans for escape that she failed to warn him before he hit his head. But she was certainly not going to sit quietly and be held prisoner.

It was Miles's fault, therefore, that she left Corin slumped unconscious on the floor. His fault that she was forced to sneak out of the apartment and, clinging to the shadows, go in pursuit of the *Compendium*. His fault that in the interests of drawing minimal attention to herself she left Toast dozing on his chair next to the window and went alone. His fault that an hour later she was gulping for air in the small reading alcove off the side of the library, her heart racing, her lips pleading, in desperate fear for her life.

Chapter 10

Occasional bursts of applause from the Great Hall below filtered into the library as Clio combed its shelves. She had never seen so many volumes in one place. Even the finest libraries in England comprised only a hundred or so titles, but this one had to have at least four times that. She ran her fingers over the leather spines of the books with appreciative awe and a good measure of envy. As a child, books had been Clio's refuge from her family. Every problem, every question, every irrational occurrence could be explained by a book—it was simply a question of finding the right one. What would it be like to have such a collection, she wondered to herself. To know you could read any book you wanted, at any time. To have all of human knowledge, everything you might ever want to know, stored away on shelves in a room in your own house—

Never desire, her mind flashed, and she remembered what she was doing there. What she needed was merely *A Compendium of Vampires,* not all human knowledge. The Deerhound had said he owned a copy, and she had not seen it in his apartment, which meant it was most likely here. Somewhere among the hundreds of books.

She started on the shorter and more manageable walls

of shelves in the reading alcove but found that every title was related to fighting or waging war. She had no idea that there were so many books on defense and keeping enemies at bay, but somehow it did not surprise her that Miles's library would be filled with them. She counted fifteen books on the fortification of castles and the construction of unassailable walls, four on how to wield a sword, sixteen on the construction and use of cannons, one about fire and its many uses as a weapon, and another on water power. Every conceivable substance that could be used in combat had at least one volume dedicated to it. She found a copy of a book on gentlemanly comportment, which seemed slightly out of place, but nowhere did she spy a copy of the *Compendium*. She had just stepped into the main library to continue her search when she heard the sound of muffled laughter in the corridor outside. It grew louder and stopped in front of the double doors.

"We can be alone in here," Clio heard a voice say and had barely enough time to duck back into the reading alcove and pull its door mostly closed before the couple entered the room. She blew out her candle, leaving her in total darkness, and peered through the crack between the door and the wall. If someone was coming her way, she wanted to know so she could be ready with an excuse, or at least try to pretend she was just casually taking a nap under the table. But it was immediately apparent that the two people standing at the far end of the library were not interested in her.

The tall, broad man was wearing a floppy peasant's cap and not much else. The short toga of an ancient hunter did very little to conceal the rock hard planes of his thighs, and the boots that laced over his calves seemed only to highlight rather than disguise their solid power. His arms looked like they had been sculpted from tanned marble as they reached forward and lifted his companion, a woman in a slightly tattered gown that seemed to float around her, to his lips.

There was no question that the man was handsome, even almost as handsome as Miles. But although many women had been guilty of mistaking the two, Clio knew instinctively that it was not the viscount. Which allowed her to watch with shocked interest rather than envy as the woman slid to her knees and slipped the hunter's toga up over the man's stomach.

"You can see better from over here," a voice whispered in Clio's ear, and she felt a hand close on her arm.

As she turned around, she was immediately aware of two things: that there was a lamp burning in the alcove that had not been there before; and that she had been wrong in thinking the man in the other room was almost as handsome as Miles. Because the real Miles, who happened to be standing in front of her, was a hundred times more handsome, a hundred times more . . . more everything.

And her reaction to his presence was a hundred times more intense. His eyes smoldered in the lamplight, glowing with yellow flecks like hot, molten gold, and for a moment she entirely forgot about hating him for locking her up. And about breathing, swallowing, or blinking.

"Look," he whispered, and gestured toward an opening in the wall just above her eye level. Still too stunned to say anything, Clio stood on her toes to glance through it. She could see the entire library now, in more detail, as if it, and the couple at the end of it, had moved closer.

"It is the other side of the mantle clock," Miles explained without waiting for her to ask. "You are looking out between the sun and the moon. There is a circle of glass over the face of the clock that magnifies everything."

But that was not what was magnifying the strange sensations inside of Clio. Swallowing hard, she turned around. "What are you doing here?" she whispered.

"I came to haul you back to my apartment, where you will stay until I say otherwise," Miles explained succinctly. "I had not counted on finding Sebastian and Lady Starrat," he gestured through the clock, "as well. That means we are trapped here."

Sebastian Dolfin, Clio thought to herself. One of Miles's cousins. No wonder the two men looked something alike. "What do you mean trapped?"

"They are setting up for the next painting downstairs and in the intermission the corridors are swarming with people. The only way to get back to my apartment unseen is through the service door behind the table that Sebastian is, ah, using." Miles's gaze flitted from the clock to Clio. "Perhaps we can pass the time with your explaining why you had to knock my manservant out and go roaming through my house without my leave."

"I did not knock him out. He hit his head," Clio replied defensively. Her eyes narrowed. "Perhaps you can explain what right you have to hold me hostage without my leave. I thought I was not your prisoner."

"I thought you did not want to be seen."

"I wasn't seen. No one has seen me."

"Not yet, but there are four hundred people out that door who might. Besides, as a host it is irresponsible of me to let a potential demon wander about free."

"I am not a—" Clio began, then stopped herself. She could not say it.

Miles shook his head, disappointed. "For a moment I thought we were making progress. At any rate, you will do what I tell you from now on."

Clio tilted her head up to study him. "Everyone always obeys you, don't they?"

"If they are wise."

Good God, he was pompous. There was a slight pause, and then Clio asked, "Is it very painful?"

Miles frowned. "What?"

"To be that way."

"What way?"

"So insufferable. And conceited. I read in a book once that tyrants often die young because of the great effort it costs them to act so imperious. You look drained."

It was not true. At that moment Miles looked more possessed than drained, but Clio decided not to quibble. Instead she rushed on. "Does it bother you awfully when people do not do what you say?"

"Not at all," Miles told her through somewhat clenched teeth.

"Good. Because I intend to go out of my way to disobey you whenever the opportunity arises."

"I fear you will have to find another hobby. Your opportunities will be few and far between when you are manacled to my bedpost."

"You would not dare."

"The temptation is strong. Very strong."

"Why? Why do you insist on hovering over me as if I were a baby lion cub and you were my mother?"

Miles's face suddenly really did look drained. "Please refrain from mentioning baby animals to me."

Caught off guard by this telling flash of vulnerability, Clio blurted, "Don't you love Mariana?" When he did not reply, she prompted him. "Don't you? She is very beautiful."

Miles chose not to answer.

"Oh," Clio reached a hand up to cover her mouth. "I am sorry. Then you must still be in love with Beatrice."

Somewhere inside Clio knew she had made a mistake. It was not just the way Miles's eyes changed, or the way his jaw became set, or the way his hands clenched. Or rather it was. Because the strikingly handsome man that Miles was when he was calm became, when angered, a sublimely sensual animal whose proximity made Clio's heart pound, and pound harder when Miles, all six and a half sublimely sensual feet of him, moved toward her. "I believe I asked you not to introduce that name into conversation, Lady Thornton." He leaned down, bringing their faces closer. "The state of my affections is none of your concern. But the increasing state of my displeasure is. You still have not explained why you deemed it necessary to knock Corin unconscious with a blunt object."

"I did not knock him out," Clio corrected but without force. Her mouth had gone completely dry, making it hard to speak, or remember what she meant to say. "And I should think—" she broke off abruptly. Her eyes became huge. "Never mind. I am sorry. It will not happen again. You—You should go."

Miles frowned. "What are you talking about?"

"Just go," Clio ordered him in an urgent whisper. "Now."

But it was too late. The first hiccup sounded like a thunderclap in the small alcove.

Something that might have been amusement flashed in Miles's eyes, and the tension in the room changed entirely. "So these are the famous violent hiccups," he commented.

Clio was too terrified by what she might be preparing to do to him to muster a glare. "Go—" she hiccuped, "—away."

"You really should try to be quieter," Miles advised, stepping even closer. "We don't want to disturb them." He tilted his head in the direction of the other room.

Clio backed away from him until she ran into the wall, her mind racing. "I would have no trouble being quieter," she whispered through clenched teeth, trying to swallow back her hiccups, "if you left me alone." She hiccuped twice.

"Does it bother you awfully when people do not do what you say?" Miles asked with a faint smile.

She seemed to especially want to hurt him when he smiled. "This is no joke," she told him, almost pleading through a pair of hiccups. "Please." She hiccuped. "You had better leave—" she hiccuped, "—before I attack you—" she suppressed a hiccup, "—viciously."

Instead of moving away, Miles closed the space between them. "Do you really want to hurt me?"

Clio could feel the battle to suppress her violent urges intensifying inside her, the hiccups coming more rapidly as he got closer, straining her restraints, pushing them to their limits. Her entire body felt warm, like she was seething—or rather, melting—with rage. "Yes," she announced in a hoarse whisper, hiccuping three times. "I do. I must."

"Go ahead," Miles challenged, gazing directly into her eyes. "Show me that you are violent. Show me—"

Clio never got the chance to give him the disembowel-
ment he so richly deserved. She did not hear the squeak
of the alcove's doorhandle, but Miles did, and he realized
instinctively that there was only one way to keep whoever entered from seeing her.

His mouth came down over hers at the exact moment
the door opened. It was an old and hackneyed trick, but
it worked. The newcomer took two steps into the room,
said, "Oh, my. Pardon me," in a low voice, hesitated for
a moment, and quickly backed out, reclosing the door
behind him. The encroachment took exactly five and a
half seconds.

The kiss went on considerably longer.

Long enough for Clio to realize that reading ten books
about such matters, even one in Italian with illustrations,
was not enough to teach her what it would be like. Long
enough for her to understand that the kiss they had
shared the day before had encompassed only a sliver of
kissing possibilities. Long enough for her to feel her
entire world shift under her, for her to feel her body
pulse with a sensation that was simultaneously hot and
chilling, thrilling and terrifying, for her to feel like she
was being spun around and around by a mad whirlwind.
Long enough for her to realize that what she had been
feeling was different from violence.

Long enough for Miles to know it was a very bad idea,
that he might as well take out a dagger and start giving
himself deep, painful gashes. At least those would heal in
time, he told himself. What feeling her lips against his
was doing was irreversible damage. Three would not do
what he was doing. He had just wanted to show her that
the hiccups were not a sign that she was a fiend, to get
her to stop thinking she was the vampire. So she would

go home and leave him alone. He had just wanted to demonstrate a logical point—

Without taking his mouth from hers, he lifted her up, turned her around, and seated her on the edge of the library table, pulling her closer. They kissed in gulps, as if they had been starving, famished for the other's touch. Her chest pressed against his, and he could sense the pounding of her heart beneath the thin fabric of her dress. He reached his hand up to feel it and her hand followed, resting atop it, their fingers entwined. Clio raised her other hand to the back of his head and urged his mouth over hers, opening her lips to his tongue, meeting it with her own. She did not know what she was doing, only that she wanted it to go on forever, until the explosion that was kindling inside her took place. And it might have, if the clock in the wall behind them had not abruptly struck midnight.

The chime startled both of them, shattered the space they had created, and they separated. Their eyes did not meet as the clock rang out twelve times. They were both lost in their own thoughts, their own self-recriminations, their own narratives of why that had been such a bad idea and should never happen again. When the last chime died down, Clio swallowed hard and addressed herself steadfastly to Miles's thumb.

"Thank you, my lord. That was remarkably efficacious."

Miles let his eyes settle on her chin. "Efficacious?"

"Usually I have to wait for the hiccups to go away. It can take hours. Although I have never had a bout of them as acute as that one, your treatment was swift and effective. I wonder that I have never read about it." She spoke in a tone a curious alchemist might use about a promising experiment.

"I am glad I could help."

"Yes," she said, distractedly. It turned out that speaking to Miles's thumb was not as neutral as she had hoped, because he kept moving it, rubbing its tip lightly along the edge of his index finger in an oval, which by some power she did not understand, made her body feel like it was being rubbed by the tip of his thumb in an oval, or if not exactly feel that way, then wish that it were feeling that way, which made it utterly impossible for her to move, or breathe, or think about what he was saying or what she was saying or really anything other than how to get him to touch her.

"—safe to return to my apartment," Miles was explaining.

Clio nodded. Then she gasped, looked directly at him and whispered, "I think I hear someone else coming."

"What—?" The rest of Miles's words were lost as she pulled his lips toward her. They kissed for a moment, then he moved away slightly and asked, "You did not hear anyone, did you?"

Clio hesitated for a moment before shaking her head.

"Did you learn that in a book?"

She shook her head again. "No. From you. I was trying to be subtle."

Miles contemplated her from the vantage point of the tip of her lovely nose. There was no question that she was going to make him ache. He was already aching. In all the salient parts of his body, and some parts he had forgotten he possessed. A smart man would say thank you very much and leave.

He cleared his throat and said, "I would advise against it."

Clio looked away from him. "I am sorry. I just—"

"Against your trying to be subtle," he went on. He was not a smart man. "You are very bad at it. However, I do not think you are unredeemable." Miles turned her face back to his. His eyes melted into hers and his voice was molten. "Perhaps I can give you some lessons." His lips brushed the place where her neck met her shoulder blade. "In fact," he said, his mouth skimming along her delicious collarbone and making Clio tingle all over, "I think you should put yourself entirely in my hands. But you must obey me implicitly. Do you agree?"

Clio moaned slightly.

"I shall take that as a yes."

Even if she had been able to speak, any possibility of protest drained from Clio as all ten of his fingertips caressed her shoulders. She closed her eyes, leaned back, and exposed the expanse of her neck to him. Miles kissed it softly with his lips, and felt her tremble.

A sensation, half awe and half anxiety, suffused him. What the devil was he doing? He had not felt desire, real desire, in a long long time, but he felt it now. Or something like it. It did not feel like he remembered. It was stronger, less focused on a single part of his body and more all encompassing. Alarm bells clanged in his head, and an image flashed into his mind, the image of a sign that hung on the door of a condemned building near his house in Venice, a board painted with a crude skull and crossbones and the words *DANGER, DO NOT ENTER!* in red. *DANGER! DO NOT ENTER!* his mind screamed at him. Turn back.

She was a virgin. He could not marry her, so he could

not make love to her. And there was no question that was exactly what he wanted to do. What he was about to do.

Nonsense. He only wanted her pleasure, only wanted her to understand that she was not the vampire, that her hiccups were not violent. His desire for her was ephemeral, illusory, like the illusions of strength he created to mislead his enemies. That was why it felt so different. It would go away and leave him unscathed. He was in control. He was not fooled. He just wanted to make her feel good, to make her see she was not evil. He would not let things go too far.

He saw an uncut quill on the desk beside her, a tight, pointed goose feather. It would be perfect. As long as he only touched her with that, and his lips, as long as he did not let his fingers feel her skin, he would be fine. And she would learn her lesson.

DANGER! He lightly traced the letters along the line of Clio's bodice with the feathery side of the quill, just to prove to himself they held no menace, and followed them with his lips. He placed a kiss at the start of the shadowy valley between her breasts—how perfect they looked—and felt rather than heard her wavering sigh.

DANGER!

Feeling his lips nestled between her breasts, feeling his hair brush against her chin, Clio had thought she was in ecstasy, but when he let the feather he was holding dip into her bodice and brush against her nipple, she knew she had been wrong. The sensation was so powerful that it left her gasping, and she gasped harder as he pulled her bodice down slightly and lightly caressed her breast with his lips.

Her nipples were small and dark and perfectly smooth and the most beautiful things Miles had ever seen. He suckled her gently, reveling in the slight noises she was making, thrilled when she brought her hands behind his head and, twining her fingers in his hair, pressed his face against her harder. Her joy at his touch sparked something old and forgotten inside of him. The ache in his body grew almost overwhelming, but he ignored it. It was not real, just an illusion.

He kept his lips on her breast but moved the hand with the feather lower, until it was resting on the inside of her right ankle. Then, kissing her, he dragged the plume up, moving it in a long slow S along the curve of her calf, dipping it to caress behind her knee, winding it up and then inching it, with excruciating slowness, along the tender inside of her thigh. He used his other hand to push the skirt and petticoats of her gown up, and his fingers accidentally brushed the supple skin of her leg.

He felt a spark pass through his body and his self control deserted him. Bringing his mouth to hers he kissed her hard, and moved the hand not holding the feather to the buckle on the wide leather belt of his costume. This was not desire, it was need, blistering and relentless in its heat. He had to feel her around him, had to bury himself in her, had to feel her touch on his body. Clio's hands were there, too, trying to help, fumbling with the buckle. Her palm strayed over the bulge in the fabric of his short breeches and it was his turn to gasp.

"I want to touch you, my lord," she whispered. "I want you to feel what I am feeling."

Her fingers hesitated over the lacings of his leggings and for a moment he could imagine just how it would feel, how it would feel to have her touch him, to have her in his arms, to make love to her on the desk, on the floor, in every room of his house, how it would feel to make love to her over and over again for weeks, for years, to learn every part of her, touching her and tasting her, being entirely with her, no restraint, no control, to give himself to her entirely.

But he was not his to give. A surge of anger flared through him, white hot and repellant, and he pulled away from her, but not before her lips could brush against his cheek.

That touch, her unsure, nervous kiss, quenched his rage. Gently, he lifted her hand away from his body, and held it in his own as if he were weighing it. "Not now," he said, huskily. He was doing this so she would know she was not evil. "Now is only for you."

He kissed her differently then, tenderly, sweetly, and moved his lips along her neck, along her collarbone, to the smooth globes of her breasts. With his lips kissing the edge of her right nipple he tightened his hold on the feather and used it to trace the outline of the triangle of curls where her legs met.

Clio gasped and stopped his hand. "My lord, I think something is wrong. There is nothing subtle about what I am feeling."

Miles kissed his way up from her delicious breasts and caught her eyes with his own. She was blushing gorgeously. "You are perfect," he said, his gaze unwavering, his voice a low purr, his lips close to hers. "Don't be afraid," he whispered, his eyes locked hypnotically into hers, and Clio was lost. Releasing his hand she let him slide the feather between her thighs and trace a tight circle over the aching place there.

Clio shed her reserves, laying her whole self at his disposal, withholding nothing. Using the tip of the plume, Miles darted over her sensitive nub, petting it with the lightest and most subtle of touches, making Clio shiver in blissful agony. When her eyes darkened and began to look almost purple and her moans grew sharper, he turned the feather sideways and let the edge run up and down her entire length, up and down between the swollen petals of her body, dragging it slowly back and forth in a long figure eight. She bit her lip then, biting back the cries inside of her, and the pressure between her legs built with every smooth, gliding stroke.

Clio felt as if she were ascending, flying higher and higher with each flick of the feather across her body, rising to dizzying peaks, swooping up and up and up. Miles pressed the plume into her, so the hard rib at its center was massaging her, then spun it, wet with her moisture, from side to side along her entire length. "Oh, my lord," she whispered, closing her eyes. "Oh, Miles, please do not ever stop."

It was the first time she had spoken his name. His self control deserted him. He moved his face close, placed his lips over hers, and began to stroke her with his thumb. He could not help himself. He had to touch her.

The haze Clio had been in evaporated and her body felt like it was ablaze. Miles teased her lips with his tongue and ran his thumb in a wide circle over her once, then again, pressing against her with the roughened tip of his finger harder and harder. He caressed her like that, in wide lazy circles, until she was panting and gasping and begging him for release, for death, for whatever he was planning. When she was too lost to even beg Clio felt his other fingers join his thumb, all of them at once, all five of them surrounding her and pulling gently at her and then sweeping against her in a long oval that sent waves rippling out across her body. She felt his fingers spread her wide, felt his thumb again, harder now, petting the slick tip of the most sensitive part of her, pressing it up and around and up and around. One of his fingers slid into her tight passage, just slightly, but the place he touched made the feeling become so much more intense that Clio was certain she was levitating. With his finger inside her, his thumb rubbed over her hot, wet pearl in one last circle, and she exploded. She felt a little burst inside of her, and then a larger one that echoed in every part of her and made her feel like she was careening through the air, spiraling down and down and down, in a thrilling descent that left her gasping and ordering him to stop and begging him not to. She closed her eyes and threw her head back and moaned in pleasure, and wonder, and joy.

When the echoes of her pleasure against his finger had slowed, when her eyes had lightened and the purple flecks had gone back into hiding, when her gasps and moans had become only sighs, Miles whispered, "You are spectacular, Clio Thornton."

Clio felt like she might cry. She was happy in a way she had never been before, exquisitely happy, exquisitely satisfied. She closed her eyes and reveled in the feeling of having Miles next to her, the warmth of his hand resting possessively on the small rise of curls between her legs, the little trills of pleasure her body was still sending. Every night for ten years she had fallen asleep thinking about what it would be like to be with him, the man she had fallen in love with as a girl, the man who had captivated her heart from afar, and now she knew. It was better than anything she could have imagined.

For one moment, her life was perfect. And then her

eyes opened wide and she spoke the three words that had been in her mind all night, and the moment was gone forever.

Chapter 11

"I love you," were not the words.

What she said was, "Never desire. Devonshire."

"Thanks" or "Lovely" or "Oh" or "Gazooks" or even "I am hungry" were all things Miles would have been unsurprised to hear. But not that.

"Devonshire. Never desire," she repeated.

"Are you all right?" Miles inquired with real concern.

Clio gave him a glowing smile. "I was momentarily thrown off by the 'h', but now I understand," she explained without explaining anything. "Devonshire. That is what the spinning sign said. The letters just got a bit mixed up."

"What sign?"

"The sign in my dream. That doesn't matter. What matters is that Devonshire has something to do with the vamp—" Clio stopped and her eyes got a faraway look in them. "Flora was from Devonshire."

Miles slid his hand from her thigh and turned away from her. After a pause, he said, "So was Beatrice."

Clio spoke to his back. "Maybe that is how the vampire chooses his victims."

"Yes. Or maybe it is a coincidence."

But Clio knew her dreams were usually more accurate than that, bringing together things she had read or seen without realizing it. "I wager that if we go through the accounts from three years ago we will find that all the women were from Devonshire." Miles turned around and his expression was skeptical. "Do you have a better idea?"

"I have the news sheets from three years ago in my apartment," Miles said, not replying directly. "We can go there to study them."

Clio waited for a moment before sliding off the table. Her knees were not functioning properly and she wobbled slightly. Miles reached out to steady her and found himself instead pulling her against his chest. She came to him desperately, fiercely, and he wrapped his arms around her tight. They stood like that, holding each other, not talking, not breathing, for a long time.

"We had better go," Miles said finally, stepping away from her and breaking the embrace. His voice sounded unnaturally loud in his ears.

Clio nodded. They left the alcove and entered the now empty library without speaking. As they approached the door leading to the service corridor, Clio bit her lip and seemed to hesitate. She raised her eyes to his. "Thank you, my lord," she said quietly.

Miles scowled. "For what?"

Clio gestured behind her. "For that. In there. On the table."

Something flickered behind Miles's eyes. "You are welcome."

"That was—no one—I mean—well—nothing like that has ever happened to me before," she said, fumbling. She was blushing beautifully and her eyes were slightly misty. "I felt—It felt—You made me feel extraordinary."

DANGER DANGER DANGER!

"I see," Miles said in a tight voice.

Hearing the strain in his tone, Clio rushed to reassure him. "Do not worry. It won't happen again."

For a moment he stopped walking and looked down at her, and she had the feeling that he was looking through her, inside her, looking for something.

"No," he said finally. "It won't."

Something she could not give him.

They walked the rest of the way to his apartment wrapped in silence.

The figure flitted out the servant's entrance of the west wing of Dearbourn Hall, and, looking furtively over a shoulder, made its way into the bushes. She paused to get her bearings, then rushed toward the agreed-upon meeting place, a shrubbery copse which would be almost impossible to see from the house.

He was already waiting for her when she arrived, and she threw herself into his arms. "I have been dreaming of this all night," she whispered. "I could not wait for all those tedious people to be gone so we could be alone together."

Her companion murmured something back, some endearment or other, enough to make her feel that he was paying attention, then asked, "Did you bring it?"

She reached into her sleeve and pulled out a key. "This was the only one I could find." She held it out to him, playfully. "Come and get it."

It had been easier at first, these meetings, but now he had to grit his teeth when he took her in his arms, and tonight he had a bad headache. The charade of waiting on her was getting boring, exhausting, but it would not have to go on much longer. She was just a pawn, just a playing piece to be maneuvered and sacrificed as part of master strategy for revenge. Just a little longer, he told himself. Buy yourself just a little more time. You are so close. So damn close.

So close he could taste it. He pulled her toward him roughly, wrenching the key from her hand as he kissed her hard. Her lip started to bleed and the taste of her blood excited him even more and he pulled open the bodice of her gown.

"Oh, my darling, you mustn't," she protested, but he knew she liked it, liked the pain, liked the fear. He pushed her down into the bushes and took her, took her not for the first time, but for the first time really enjoying it. He was so close. It was not her face he saw as he pumped himself into her, it was another face entirely, a face that grew sharper and sharper as he got closer and closer to his release, a face with brown hair and those odd-colored eyes, eyes that would bulge when they saw what he had done. He would have his revenge; he would have his triumph. All of them would pay and pay and pay, he thought, and each time he pounded into her harder and harder and harder.

Beneath him, the woman moaned as he pushed, moaned and panted as he shoved roughly into her, clawed at him as he thrust himself into her one final time, pouring his seed into her, ripping her open.

Afterward, they lay together in the bushes. "Darling. Darling, I love you," she whispered intensely. She was clinging to him, her hands clammy with sweat.

The man known as the Vampire of London left her

lying in the bushes, a trickle of blood streaking down her legs, and made his way back to his apartment. They could not dare to be seen together like this, that was how he explained his abandonment each time. The truth was, the bitch revolted him.

Minutes later the woman reentered the house. On her way to her bed she paused in the room with the peacock walls to study her face in the huge mirror over the mantelpiece. There was a becoming flush on her cheeks, but other than that, no signs of her meeting with her lover. She was certain that no one would ever know.

The room was a mess. Every drawer of the beautiful carved desk had been crudely pried open, every glass and ceramic and inlayed box smashed. The window treatments, which had been woven in Florence especially for the chamber, had been ripped down and lay in tattered puddles of silk on the floor. Upholstered chairs had been sliced open, their straw understuffing ripped out and strewn over the carpet, which was stained with yellow and reddish-brown spots. The armoire gaped open, its contents—forty dresses—splayed on the floor, loose threads showing where diamonds and rubies and pearls and emeralds had once been sewn on to them. A painting of the Virgin Mary with baby Jesus that had been done by Raphael, a present Miles had given Beatrice two months earlier, had been pulled off the wall, to reveal the safe behind it. Its contents, a queen's ransom in jewels and gold, were gone. A single emerald glinted in the back, having weeks earlier slipped out of a necklace and not yet been replaced.

Only the bed had been left untouched by the attack. Sort of. In the middle of a tangle of sheets, Beatrice was stretched, bruised, over a sea of pillows. She lay on her side, two pricks on her neck, dead. But in the vision she spoke to him.

"Do you see this, Miles" she asked, gesturing around at the destruction of what had been the most sumptuous apartment in London. "You said you would make me happy. You said you would protect me. You promised to care for me. But you abandoned me. Like I knew you would."

Her voice echoed through Miles's thoughts, ricocheting from past to present, from the woman in his bed beside him now to that other woman, from Clio to Beatrice, from this empty chamber to that one and back again. He wanted a drink.

"You talk of love, but it is all lies. Liar liar liar," her voice grew more hysterical. "Protect me. Fine job you did protecting me. Caring for me. Look at this. Look at this!" she shouted, and the voice mingled with other voices in his head, his father's, his own. "You did this, Miles. This is your fault. All your fault."

(No. NO. I did love you. I tried. I TRIED!!!)

"You failed, Miles."

That was the last time a woman had shared Miles's apartment. Sitting up in bed now he shook his head, shaking the images and voices back into obscurity. He squinted into the dark of the chamber, looking for the telltale glint of a carafe. There wasn't one. Damn Corin. Why had the manservant believed him when he said he wouldn't be needing any wine? The fool should have known better.

Miles raked a hand through his hair. The look in Corin's eyes when he had given the order—easy words, "I won't be needing a decanter tonight"—came back to him, an expression of wonder and relief. He was sure his cousins would have shared it. It pissed him off. Damn them all. He had the queen and the admiralty breathing down his neck on the one hand, and some breathtaking fool of a woman claiming to be a vampire and keeping him from his investigation on the other. He deserved a drink. Why couldn't they just leave him alone, leave him to drink himself into oblivion or peace or whatever he was drinking himself into. Why did any of them care if he had a couple of glasses of wine before bed? What the hell difference would it make to anyone?

Out of the corner of his eye, he saw Clio stir. She was probably getting ready to chastise him about his drinking, too. Having her here was a mistake. He should never have consented to share a bed with her, even if there was no other place to sleep in his chamber, even if they were both dressed, even if the mattress was huge. Although the desire he had felt for her in the library had fizzled out as they poured over the old news sheets together, her presence still made him feel . . . like he wanted a drink. Tomorrow he would order Corin to unpack all the furniture so he could sleep somewhere else. Anywhere else. Away from her.

Who did she think she was, barging in, disobeying him, knocking out his household staff, challenging his orders? Some woman who did not know the first thing about manners. Or how to flirt. Take her eyes, for example. Those eyes that flared purple when she had climaxed. Had other men seen them do that? God he wanted a drink. She just looked out of them, challenging, direct, instead of using them to convey a hint of mystery, a spark of desire. Instead of making a man feel like he was the most interesting creature she had ever stood near, she made him feel like she suspected him of some nefarious deed that she would soon be finding out and sending him a bill for. She had no notion of how to be seductive. Or coy. She was totally uncouth. Totally uncultivated. Totally uninteresting.

Damn his throat was dry. The key thing was to get her the hell out of his bed and his house and never see her again. Which meant finding the vampire and proving to her that she was not one. Why was she so damn determined to believe she was a fiend anyway?

It had happened again that night. He had hoped that the kiss had worked to show her that her hiccups were simply a sign of strong desire, not necessarily the desire to do violence, but she had gone right on willfully crediting she was a fiend. Acting on her suggestion, they had looked through the old news sheets and confirmed that all but two of the girls killed by the vampire three years earlier were from Devonshire. Not only that, it appeared likely that the remaining two were as well.

"But what does it mean?" Clio had asked, dropping the papers with frustration. "I wish we knew what it meant."

Miles had been about to agree with her when something tugged at his memory. "Perhaps we do." He picked up the small blue volume and started flipping through it.

"What is that?" Clio asked.

"It's that perennial favorite, the *Compendium of Vampires*," he told her absently as he skimmed the pages. "I remember reading something about this. Something that explained how vampires chose their victims."

She frowned. "Where did you get that book?"

"I took it from the reading alcove when we were leaving. It was sitting on the table."

"Impossible."

Miles looked up. "Why?"

"I looked all over the alcove for it and it was not there, much less on the table."

"Then it must have appeared by divine intervention."

"Or by the office of whomever it was that entered the room while we were there."

"It would make sense that someone in my household was looking at it," he said, brushing it off. He had not wanted to think more about those moments in the reading alcove than necessary. "Here, look at this."

Studiously avoiding touching her, he had extended the book across the table to Clio, his finger indicating a passage:

"They say that the Vampire must have the blood of whatever creature had the Nursing of him as a child, so that if he was put out to nurse with a Goat, it will be a Goat he requires, or a Cow, or a Sheep, or a Woman, of whatsoever type she be. Only this blood will he have a taste for, and only this blood will be sweet to him. For whatsoever creature whose blood he takes, the Vampire has afterward a soft place, as for his mother who gave him life, or one with whom he had dined often and eat well. So therefore will he take away a token from them, as a memento, or in the French, soovineer, for to re-member them by.

And in one family there might be only one Vampire of four siblings, and ye can know him by his bad behavior, because even from a youth he will not be like the other children, and he will try to harm them, so he may lick their blood as if by chance and not give himself entire away. For this reason, and for his wickedness, the Vampire as a child is impossible to love."

Miles had been surprised by the shocked expression on her face when she raised her eyes and looked at him. He did not know that the words "impossible to love" seemed to vibrate on the page in front of her, or that in her head she heard Mariana's voice repeating *You are unlovable, you are unlovable*, taunting her, in an eerie echo of the book. *You are unlovable. Impossible to love.*

It won't happen again. No, it won't. IT WON'T IT WON'T IT WON'T IT—

"Why did you show me this?" she had demanded in a voice that shook with emotion. "What you said before made your position quite clear."

He had not tried to conceal his confusion from her. "What the devil are you talking about?"

"About your wanting nothing to do with me."

"I beg your pardon?"

"There is no need to hide behind excuses. Just say that you have changed your mind and you want to send me away from your house. Send me to Newgate." When Miles appeared too bewildered to speak, Clio went on. " '*As a youth he will not be like the other children and try to harm them, so he may lick their blood as if by chance,*' " she read aloud. "I told you, I did that. When I bit Mariana."

"Please. Please do not say you are going to start claiming to be the vampire again."

"How else—"

"I was talking about the paragraph above that," he had interrupted her forcefully. "Where it says that the vampire drinks the blood of *'whatever creature had the nursing of him.'* Since our vampire kills only women from Devonshire, we can assume he comes from Devonshire. You see? And since you are not from Devonshire, it cannot be you."

She had looked up at him with excitement then, but it faded quickly. "My nurse. My mother died when I was just a few months old and a nurse brought me up. She was from Devonshire."

Of course, Miles had thought grimly then. He had been a fool to think it would be that easy to persuade her. He realized that what struck him most, besides the depth of her belief in her wickedness, was that her concern was not for herself, but for the people she might hurt.

Miles's concerns were precisely the opposite. Whoever was setting out to frame Clio had done it with a perfection bordering on the obsessive, right down to the risk they had run in hurting her ankle. The fact that no constables had been alerted by an anonymous tip to check her house for bodies told Miles that the vampire's plans for Clio Thornton were not as simple as having her arrested for his crimes. He seemed determined not merely to get her into prison, but to convince her that she was a vampire so she would turn *herself* in.

"He is like a hunter setting a trap, but a trap you must spring yourself," Miles had mused aloud before they went to bed—damn he could use some wine—and his words came back to him now. Even as he spoke them he had known that was only half an explanation, and it left a crucial question hanging: Why? Why was it important to the vampire that Clio think herself guilty?

Answering that was the key to understanding—and catching—his enemy, Miles knew. And there was only one way to find out. Sitting up in bed, his mind roved over different plans until he found the one he liked. It was simple, and, with Clio locked in his apartment, would be both easy and safe to implement. Plus it should get quick results. Which would mean that soon she could be home and he could get on with his life.

He told himself that this was a pleasing thought.

With Clio locked in his apartment. Yes. That was the key. Lock her up so she could not bother him anymore, could not distract him, or worry him or . . . S'teeth he wanted a drink. With her out of the way, he could finally undertake a real investigation. From now on, this would be between him and the vampire. *You failed,* he heard Beatrice whisper in his head. *You failed.*

But not this time. This time the vampire would die.

Clio's leg brushed his then and her bare foot came to rest on his calf, taking him by surprise. Undoubtedly it was not the quiet pressure of her foot against his leg, the feel of her arch curving around his muscle, the warm touch of her body on his, that made him relax. Undoubtedly it was not the nearness of her, the softness, the canny comfort of her proximity, not the knowledge that she would be there in the morning, next to him, just as fiery and stubborn and antagonizing and beautiful as she had been that night, that made his tension, his anger, his pain, drain from him in a rush, as if it had never been there. It was the fact that he had a plan he liked, the fact that he was about to catch the vampire, that affected all that. Undoubtedly.

For a moment, he stayed very still, unable to move. Then, carefully so he would not disturb her, Miles lay back down on the bed.

In ten minutes he was asleep. He had forgotten all about wine.

4 hours after midnight: Moon—one degree less than half-full. Waning.

Chapter 12

"Try to explain again what you mean by the words, 'she just slipped away'?" Miles demanded that evening as the clock struck seven.

"Just that, sir," the footman said, his voice quivering. "She was here one moment and then the next, no one."

A muscle stood out on the side of Miles's jaw and inadvertently the footman flinched. "Do you think you could explain how one woman could get by all six of you?" he asked, directing his scorching gaze at the group of men assembled before him. "Three of you were trained by the queen's guards. If this is the best England has to offer, we would do well to surrender to our enemies right now. Answer me!"

A gangly youth with bright red hair stepped forward. He was the newest, and therefore the most foolhardy. "I believe she must have sneaked out behind one of them crates when we was watching the monkey, Your Lordship," he offered.

"Really?" Miles's voice could have flayed the skin off a rhinoceros. "I thought perhaps she had jumped from the window."

"No," the youth said, perking up. "I was watching the windows. No one got out that way."

"This room is on the third floor," Miles pointed out to him, his voice cool as iron. "Anyone 'getting out that way' would be lying splattered on the ground." He turned from them and faced Corin. "Where did we get these bloody idiots?"

"Now, sir, I think you are being over harsh. T'was your order that sent them unpacking the boxes. 'Might as well be useful if they're going to sit around guarding her all day,' were, I believe, your exact words." No member of Miles's family, let alone his household, would have dared to do what Corin had just done, but then none of them knew the man Corin had adopted as his master three years earlier quite as well as he did. "If I might make a suggestion, sir," he went on, "her monkey is still here. I am sure she will come back soon if we just wait."

"I am afraid that is not an option."

"Why?"

"Because in less than an hour every news sheet seller in London will be spreading the word that she was arrested this afternoon as the Vampire of London," Miles explained in a lowered voice through clenched teeth. "Which would make it very inconvenient for her to be seen in the street."

"Maybe we could use the monkey to find her then," Corin volunteered. "He might be able to lead us to her."

The vein in Miles's jaw continued to throb, but not as acutely. "You propose I go searching the city with a monkey on a leash? Who knows where the hell she is? I wouldn't put it past her to be having tea with the queen."

"She was not dressed for a royal visit, sir," the red-haired youth who had been contorting his neck to hear put in helpfully. If he had been smarter he would have known that the appraising look Miles gave him indicated that his life expectancy had just been cut in half.

"Get rid of him," Miles muttered under his breath.

"Can't," Corin told him. "Nephew of the chancellor of the Exchequer. The CE especially requested an important posting for him."

"Then post him somewhere important. Maybe somewhere in Spain. Give him to the Spanish Army. Let him do his damage on their side rather than ours."

Corin took the boy aside and dispatched him to the kitchens to await further "vital and confidential" instructions. Then he rejoined the group.

"I want you to take the monkey and these three men and head into the city," Miles said to his manservant, pointing to three of the footmen. "You," he said to one of the remaining two, "go to Which House and see if she stopped there or left word. And you," to the final footman, "alert the guards we already have stationed. As soon as you find her, sequester her and send for me. I will bring her back myself."

"If I had known that I would have waited and let you carry me home in your coach," Clio said as she slipped in between the shoulders of the gawking footmen. "It would have spared me a great deal of pain in my ankle."

Miles swung to face her. "When did you get here?" He hoped to hell she had not heard what he told to Corin about the news sheets.

"Just now."

He relaxed slightly inside, but his expression remained grim. "Where the devil were you?"

Clio regarded him for a moment, trying to decide how much she felt like goading him. If things had not gone so smoothly that afternoon, she might have been tempted to ask him by what authority he was holding her prisoner and if clenching his jaw that much was as painful as it looked, but as it was she was in an excellent mood and let him off easily. "I was visiting a sick friend," she told him.

And it was almost true. Norton Nitely had greeted her from his plumped up bed with the words "It is infinitely kind of you to pay your last respects this way, dear Clio. I fear it is the end for me this time."

"New houseboy," Astor had whispered to her as he passed out of the sumptuous chamber with a tray. "He's jealous as an old maid."

"I heard that," Norton called after him, the sternness in his voice belied by the fond expression on his face as he watched Astor's receding back. He briskly motioned Clio over to the bed. "I just do this dying man routine to make him feel important," he confided to her. "After twenty-three years together, you know, I don't want him to worry about the state of my affections." Then he sighed. "He has been spending an awful lot of time with that new footman, though. You would not consider hiding out in the kitchens for a few days and—" He stopped speaking when the violence of Clio's head shaking became apparent.

"No, under no circumstances and never," Clio said firmly. "Besides, it would be a waste of your money. You know he is devoted to you."

"Yes, I suppose you are right. But if he found out I'd hired someone to keep an eye on him we could have a huge row, and then afterwards—"

"—Afterwards your heart pains would act up," Astor said, coming into the room again. "And you would be even less entertaining to deal with than you are now." He tenderly brushed the hair off the other man's forehead, seated himself on the bed, and looked at Clio. "What can we do for you, love? I assume you did not drop in simply for the pleasure of watching an old couple bicker."

Something inside of Clio tightened as she looked at the two old comrades. They were so happy together, so content in one another's friendship. She had met them four years earlier when they hired her to take care of a small matter involving the theft of a prized French chair in which King Francis the First was said to have made love to his mistress three times. Over the course of their acquaintance, she had learned that Norton Nitely and his business partner Astor Buff-Carter were not at all what they seemed. Their partnership was much more than financial; and their business in European furniture was merely a cover for the fact that they were very highly skilled con men.

Working selectively—only on aristocratic families that could afford it and those who mistreated their horses—Norton and Astor would insinuate themselves into a household and siphon off good pieces of furniture, but so gracefully and with such aplomb that they would actually be thanked for it in the end. Their success was based on the fact that they knew more about the nobility than anyone else in England, more about many aristocratic families than the scions themselves, and could therefore pass themselves off as long-lost relatives of almost anyone they chose at any time.

It was this knowledge that Clio had come to tap. If

she accepted Miles's arguments that she was not the vampire—which she could afford to do by day since the vampire seemed only to kill by night—then she knew that it was probably a man. A man who, according to Toast, had been at Mariana and Miles's first betrothal ball. A man from Devonshire. Which meant that all she needed was to ascertain which males on the ball guest list had been from Devonshire. Once she had done that, she would turn the tables on him.

It was Miles who had given her the idea. "He is like a hunter setting a trap," he had said the night before about the vampire. *A hunter* she had repeated over and over in her mind that night as she lay in bed next to him, trying to block out the memory of his kiss, of his words, of his touch, trying to ignore the desire that was pulsing through her. *(Do not worry, it will never happen again. No, it won't.)* Trying above all not to cry.

He is a hunter. And I, she had realized suddenly, am the prey.

But not for long.

She supposed she could have gone to Elwood with this. He was, in fact, originally from Devonshire. But she knew he would demand to know why she wanted the information and she did not want him involved. Plus, she could not get around the fact that accepting that she was not the vampire meant accepting that someone—possibly even Elwood himself—had drugged her. So she called upon Norton and Astor instead.

"Who on this list is from Devonshire?" she asked, holding out the three sheets of paper on which she had transcribed the names of those invited to the ball.

"Conceivably we could all be, if we went back far

enough," Norton told her, dropping the guise of the invalid entirely. "There are those who think Devonshire is almost Eden. But I assume you mean in the last two generations."

Thus narrowed, Norton and Astor found six names on the list for Clio. Two of them were very elderly and slightly infirm, making it unlikely that they had hauled a girl up a ladder, and one of them was the woman, Lady Starrat, who had been entertaining Miles's cousin Sebastian in the library the night before. This left only three real candidates. Clio proffered her sincere thanks to Norton and Astor and was just about to take her leave, when she thought of something.

"What about the Mayhew family? Serena Mayhew?" she asked as she rose from her chair. Serena Mayhew was one of the two victims of the vampire that Clio and Miles had been unable to definitively link to Devonshire the night before.

"Mayhew," Astor repeated, tapping a finger on his cheek. "Married?"

"I do not know. Why?"

"There was a Serena Arlington from Devonshire, who married Lord Winston Mayhew," Astor hazarded.

"But he was from Kent," Norton put in. "One of our 'friends.' Man was a real tyrant. Do you remember how we found his horses?"

"He said it was his son that beat them," Astor reminded him.

"Hogwash," Norton declared. "That man was a—"

"What about Theolinda Rightson?" Clio introduced the other victim's name in a desperate effort to change the subject. She knew from experience where their tirades over the treatment of horses could end up if not checked immediately.

"Rightson?" Norton repeated, frowning. Then his face brightened. "Oh yes, of course. Rightsons of Devonshire. Old family. Not much money. Kind to their livestock, though. Sent their boy Samuel to London to make something of himself. Wonder what became of him."

Under other circumstances Clio might have stayed to discuss that interesting question, but since there were no Rightsons on the guest list she had in her hand and since she had quite a lot to do before it grew dark, she kissed both men on the cheek and left.

From Norton and Astor's she went to see that word was spread warning women from Devonshire to be on their guard, and took out a small advertisement in the news sheets that anyone with information about the vampire should communicate with her, just in case either the fiend or the Special Commissioner thought his attempts to scare her away had worked. Then she headed to Which House, where a brief consultation with her client had been enough to secure the fact that he and his sister were also from Devonshire and a brief check of *A Compendium of Vampires* had confirmed one of the premises on which her plan was based. With her copy of the *Compendium* stashed on her person, she had gone to complete her final errand, depositing the five-hundred pounds she owed Captain Black in the hands of one of his thugs. The nearly quarter moon was lightly visible in the sky and the sun was just setting as she slid into the servants' entrance of Dearbourn Hall and made her way back to Miles's apartments.

She had felt a brief pang at Which House when she had looked at a calendar and realized it was her twenty-fifth birthday and that it, like the twenty-four that preceded it, was going to pass unnoticed, but she reminded herself that she did not care. Besides, paying off her debt had left her feeling light, almost giddy, especially toward the Deerhound, whose purse had enabled it. That, coupled with the fact that by the next day she would have caught the vampire, assuming she was not the vampire herself, had worked to erase her disappointment and put her in a very good mood.

Miles was having none of it. "What sick friend? Why did you visit a sick friend?"

His deep glower only made his eyes look more golden and did nothing to dull Clio's happiness. "I went hoping I would catch whatever he has and pass it on to you," she explained. "I read in a book once that certain ailments can be almost instantly fatal."

"He? You went to visit a man?"

"Two of them, actually. Handsome ones. Does that make you jealous, my lord?"

Miles knew she was only teasing, but the hell of it was, it did. He was flat-out jealous. Worse, he found himself checking over her clothes to see if they looked tousled in any way. Not that he could tell with the tattered state they were in. Damn this woman. "Why haven't you put on any of the gowns I had sent in for you?" he demanded.

"I—I couldn't," Clio replied, the challenge draining from her voice. "They are too lovely. I couldn't wear them."

"You can and you will," Miles said, dead serious.

"Right now. And you won't go out again. Anywhere. Do you understand?"

"No."

"What do you mean, 'no'?" Miles snarled.

"Why would I put on a beautiful dress if I cannot go anywhere in it? That makes no sense. Surely even you must see that, my lord."

Miles could have sworn he heard a snicker coming from Corin's direction, but he ignored it. He moved closer to her. "You will put it on because I asked you to." His eyes were burning into hers. "And then you will wait in my chamber, here, until I come for you."

"What if I choose not to?"

"I do not recall saying that you had a choice. But I will tell you that if by some miracle you manage to break through the cordon of guards and leave this apartment again without my permission, I will personally find you, bring you back, and see to it that you are tied up in such a way that it will be impossible for you to get out again. I hesitate to take such steps now, but I will if I must. Do you understand?"

"Oh yes," Clio said. "I am very good with short words."

Miles ignored her. "I must make an appearance at this ball, but in two hours I will be back and we will dine together and discuss your behavior today."

"I have nothing to discuss, my lord," Clio said, tilting her head back to look at him defiantly.

He reached out and rested his fingers lightly under her chin. "That is good, because I plan on doing all the talking." Then, as if to make his point early and often, he turned on his heel before she could respond and strode out the door.

Clio stood in the middle of the room staring at the place he had just vacated.

"Do not let him upset you, Lady Thornton," Corin advised, coming to stand next to her. "He is a bit rigid in his expectations for obedience."

"Why is he like that?" Clio asked.

"I wish I knew. Been this way as long as I've known him."

She looked at the manservant. "And yet you stay."

"Gives a man a challenge, doesn't it? There's no effort required to serve a good-tempered master. But a fellow like our viscount takes a bit of work."

Clio found herself smiling at Corin. "I am sorry I got you in trouble last night by sneaking away. How does your head feel?"

He waved her words away. "No apology necessary. My head doesn't hurt much. And the pain was worth it just to see the expression on our lord and master's face when he saw you were gone." He looked at her closely. "Don't misjudge him, Lady Thornton. He's a good man."

"I know," Clio said quietly.

Corin nodded. "I thought you might."

They stood in silence for a moment, until Clio added, "I am afraid I don't bring out the best in him."

"Now I disagree, and I know his cousins, the Arboretti, do, too," Corin told her. "They were saying it to me just today. Our Miles hasn't been this exciting to be around in years."

"Exciting," Clio repeated doubtfully.

"Aye. Used to be you could count on him being either surly or churlish. But since you've been around, he's become unpredictable. It makes things more interesting."

Before the clock struck midnight, things would become much more interesting than any of them had bargained for.

The man known as the Vampire of London stood at the window of the peacock chamber and looked at the moon. He knew the words on the news sheet were a lie, because he knew where Clio Thornton was. Indeed, he had watched her slip out the servants' entrance of Dearbourn Hall earlier that day, and back in that evening.

He did not like that she was there. He did not like her at all. He would deal with her, he decided, teach her to meddle where she did not belong, make her pay for her stupid and insulting bluff. He would take care of her. No one and nothing was going to get in his way. Not when he was this close. Not when—

He was startled by the sound behind him. He swung around to glare as a footman entered through a hidden service door in the wall. "Excuse me, sir," the servant said. "I was sent to find Sir Saunders Cotton. Have you seen him?"

He stared at the footman for a moment, then moved his stare to the door he had come through. "No." He smiled. "No I haven't."

The footman had backed out of the room and run so quickly down the corridor that he collided with two maidservants bringing platters of food for the party, and was fired on the spot. "I didn't mind a bit, though, I tell you," he testified before the Special Commission later. "Would have quit myself that very night. No way I ever wanted to see that smile again. Poor Lady Thornton. Must have suffered at his hands something awful."

* * *

"Must you go so early, darling Viscount?" Mariana said with a pout. "The fireworks will not begin for hours."

The words "for hours" had never sounded so much like "forever" as they did when she spoke them. "I am afraid I am not feeling well," Miles said lamely. "I was visiting a sick friend today and I fear I have caught whatever he had."

Mariana's hand shot up over her mouth. "Oh! You are ill." She backed up hastily, nearly tripping over one of the three dozen monkeys that seemed to have accompanied every female guest. "In that case, by all means, go. With my delicate constipation—"

"—constitution—" Doctor LaForge corrected.

"—I am very susceptible. Like a baby bird. I should not want to get ill before our wedding."

"No, that would be a tragedy," Miles said, trying to repress his joy at this new discovery. If he could somehow manage to be ill for the entire duration of his marriage, then he could keep Mariana and her delicate constipation at a good distance. "Good night, Lady Mariana," he said with a loud cough and a bow.

"Good night, Viscount darling," she shouted to him, almost sprinting in her efforts to get away. Then she turned and spoke to the man at her right. "Do you think I am in any danger, Saunders? Oh! I feel my heart palpitating already."

"Please do not fear, Lady Mariana. I am sure you are fine. If I may say so, I have never seen you look so well. The blush on your bosom only makes the jewels upon it shine more brightly."

Mariana smiled at him and slipped her arm through his. "Dear Saunders. You are so malodorously kind to me."

Doctor LaForge, walking behind the couple, opened his mouth to make a correction, then shut it. Miles could not have agreed with him more.

For the first time, an interaction with Mariana had put him in a good mood, and Miles almost smiled at his cousins when he brushed past them on his way up the stairs. Without realizing it, he had begun to whistle as he walked down the empty corridor of his wing of the house, and he whistled louder as he crossed into his apartment.

The transformation was astonishing. In the course of one day the rooms had gone from impersonal, cavernous spaces to comfortable chambers that looked like someone might live in them. Might even *want* to live in them. But even as he contemplated this change, the hint of a smile that had been on his lips disappeared. Because, despite the candles burning in the sconces and the handsome furniture, it was clear that the rooms were empty.

Or almost. Slumped unconscious against the wall opposite him was the body of a footman. Next to him lay a large block of quartz, just the right size to knock a man out, and the equally unconscious body of Toast. As he approached the man and the monkey Miles saw that the door to one of the service corridors leading out of his chamber was slightly ajar. He paused just long enough to be sure that both the footman and the beast had a pulse, then plowed down the corridor.

Four men. Three of his special footmen plus Corin. He had left four men guarding her, and she was gone.

There was no way Clio could have orchestrated that herself. Sneaking past Corin the night before was one thing, distracting his guards earlier another, but he had chosen these men for their skill and after what had happened that afternoon they would have been more careful. And her monkey had been hurt as well. She would never have left Toast if he were injured. No, this was different. This had to be the work of someone else.

Miles swallowed hard, forcing himself to concentrate. The corridor came to an end abruptly, junctioning with another that ran across the middle of the house. To the left lay the library and Mariana's wing. To the right were the kitchen and the stables. Think, damn it, Miles commanded himself. If you were trying to make off with a woman, which way would you go.

To the right. Miles did not have far to travel before his hunch was confirmed. Guard number two lay sprawled across the top of a staircase that led directly to the kitchen. Miles did not even bother to check this one's pulse but leaped over him and took the stairs four at a time. A grown man hit on the head remained unconscious for anywhere from one to ten minutes, Miles knew, but not usually more. That meant that he was not that far behind them.

Hopefully. And even then . . . Ten minutes could be a lifetime in the hands of a fiend. What if it was the vampire who had her? What if he was hurting her right now? What if he was digging his teeth into her neck right now, into that beautiful neck, the neck that had trembled when he kissed it, the neck that had tasted like—

Guard number three lay at the bottom of the stairs in a heap.

This is your fault. He never should have gone to the ball that night. He never should have trusted her with only four guards. He should have stayed to protect her. *This is your fault, Miles. You failed.* He should have been there, with her, the whole time, he should have stayed with her no matter what, if he loved her he never should have abandoned Beatrice that way, and then she would never have gone to that place, would never have left the house, would never—

Tripping over Corin's leg outside the stables, shook miles back into the present. A horse was missing, a gelding, and without pausing, Miles leaped on the nearest animal, which happened to be saddled. He left the stable yard at a gallop and skidded into the street, looking left and right for hoofprints.

A low whistle from a tall hedge next to him drew his eye. He urged his horse over to it, and peered inside. His mouth fell open.

"You said two hours. You are late," Clio said.

Miles stared at her, dumbfounded.

"I know you are going to be angry, but before you begin hollering and hurling insults, let me explain."

"I never holler," Miles said in a voice that was as filled with menace as a poison dipped sword.

Clio shuddered. She wished she had taken the footman up on his offer of a weapon. "I need to do an errand. Three of them actually. And I need you to come with me. To make sure I do not hurt anyone. I knew if I behaved like a civil person and asked for your assistance, you would say no. So I was forced—by you—to behave uncivilly. Since we are outside already, though, and since I went to all this trouble, won't you help me?"

Miles had to clench his large hands into fists to keep from ringing her neck. "Are you a lunatic, Lady Thornton?"

Clio seemed to consider the question. "Possibly. I might be the vampire, remember. That is why I need your help."

"Absolutely not." Miles's refusal was firm but his voice almost shook with fury. "You are coming back into the house with me right now."

Clio nodded and coaxed her horse just out of range of his grasp. "I thought that might be your response. I wanted to give you a chance since you insisted that we work together, but I knew it was futile. This partnership will never work. Good-bye, Lord Dearbourn." She dug her heels into the gelding's flanks, and began to gallop down the street.

The tempest of conflicting emotions raging within Miles did not affect his reflexes, and he was chasing after her before she had gone even three yards. The relief he felt at seeing her safe was entirely eclipsed now by fury and outrage, and if Clio thought that by disappearing into the night she could escape their brunt, she was very wrong. As soon as they got wherever they were going, he would wring her neck, then throttle her, then holler and hurl insults at her, then wring her neck again, then lock her up, using chains this time, lock her in a corner of his apartment, an uncomfortable one, and leave her there, perhaps for months. And he would damn well force her to wear one of those new dresses. And to ride her horse like a proper lady, not astride like a man.

He saw her look over her shoulder but was so absorbed in glaring ferociously at her and making plans for her torment that he did not bother to turn around, which was why he did not see Corin and Toast and the three guards waving her off triumphantly. But Clio saw them, and saw Miles on her heels, and something inside her fluttered. He looked magnificent when he was angry.

She glanced at the fronts of the houses they were passing, squinting to identify the crests. At the fifth one she reigned in her horse and deftly steered it into the alley that ran along the house.

"What the dev—" Miles began, but Clio silenced him with her finger to her lips.

"Shhh. We do not want to rouse the staff."

"Whose staff," Miles asked, whispering despite himself.

"Lord Mosley's. That is his house right there." She pointed to the building on their left with two windows in the wall. The open shutters on one of them moved lazily back and forth in the evening breeze. "His personal apartments are on the second level. If you will hold my horse, I will go in first."

Miles blinked at her for a moment. "Are you suggesting that you plan to enter Lord Mosley's personal apartments by climbing through that window?" he asked finally.

"Exactly. I knew you would be a good accomplice. Here," she handed him the reins, and, steadying herself with a hand against the side of the building, stood with her feet in both stirrups. The reason for her choice of a male saddle was now clear, but Miles had other more important things to think about.

"You mean, you expected me to follow you?" he asked, grabbing her by the wrist.

Clio avoided his gaze. "I do not think this is the best time or place for this discussion. We do not know when Lord Mosley might come home."

Miles sought her eyes. "Answer my question."

"Yes. Given your dislike of being disobeyed, I thought it likely that you would follow me."

Miles did not like being tricked. Or lied to. Or understood quite so well. "And you figured that once I did I would just sit here outside while you broke into a gentleman's house?"

"Of course not." Clio was aghast. "As soon as I am inside I will let the rope down for you to climb up. I would not leave you out here idly."

"I cannot tell you how that relieves me," Miles said in a tone so controlled it was almost inhuman. "What exactly does Lord Mosley's house contain that requires you to rob it?"

"Oh," Clio said, as if everything were now clear. "I am not robbing anyone. We are just going to do a search." She decided he did not need to know about the notice she had put in the news sheets that day to stir the vampire into action. He was already overreacting.

"A search?"

"Yes. A search for evidence that he is the vampire."

Miles goggled at her. "You think Lord Mosley is the vampire?"

"No. I think nothing of the kind. That would prejudice my search. I am leaving my mind a blank until I have evidence one way or the other." Clio examined him closely. "Are you all right, my lord. You look as though you have stopped breathing."

She was not far off. Miles cleared his throat. "Would

you mind explaining what sort of evidence we are looking for? And why the hell you think Lord Mosley might possess it?"

"Not at all, but perhaps we could do this back in your apartments? When we have finished? As I mentioned before, we do not have unlimited time and I should like to be thorough."

"My apologies if my questions inconvenience you, Lady Thornton—"

"That is quite all right. I promise I will answer all of them later."

"—But I refuse to be a party to this illegal entry unless you give me some explanations."

Clio sighed. "It is quite simple," she explained, but paused as Miles made a strangled noise. "Really, it is. You need not sound like a—a baby bear cub dying."

"I told you not to mention baby animals to me."

"Then do not interrupt with needless whining. I thought you would be pleased. This entire investigation is based on two principles you suggested. First, the assumption that I am not the vampire. And second, the idea that the true vampire is like a hunter, hunting for me. I decided I would make him the prey."

"Marvelous," Miles commented at the information that he had been the instrument of his own torment. Leave it to Clio Thornton to concoct that.

"Fewer interruptions would make this go faster," she suggested helpfully. "Anyway, we know the vampire is from Devonshire. And, if we accept your assumption that I am not the vampire, we know it is probably a man. I also happen to know that he was in attendance at your betrothal ball two nights ago."

Miles sat forward. "How the devil could you know that?"

"The reasons are mine. You would not find them compelling."

"Try me."

Clio sighed again. If she had known he was going to be this difficult, she would definitely have borrowed the footman's sword. "It was my monkey, Toast. He smelled something at the house of the first victim. And then he smelled it again at your ball. He told me it was the same smell—the same man."

"He told you?" Miles raised an eyebrow. "Can you communicate with all animals, or only monkeys?"

"I cannot say. I don't seem to be having much success communicating with you," Clio shot back. "I trust Toast's sense of smell. He—" she paused. "Do you remember, two days ago, at the Painted Lady, when I woke you?"

Something that might have been a smile passed over Miles's lips. "Yes."

"Whose cloak were you sleeping under? I have not seen you wear it since then."

"I haven't the vaguest idea. It was on me when I awoke. I must have left it there. Why?"

"Because Toast led me there as well. But he says you are not the man he smelled. At any rate, whomever it was attended your ball. So I merely looked over the guest list, found the names of the three men who were from Devonshire, and decided to search their houses."

"Amazing. And just what are we looking for?"

"The *Compendium* says that the vampire has a 'soft

place' for those he has killed and therefore always takes away a memento or souvenir. I thought first we could look for those souvenirs."

"You think the vampire just leaves these lying around?"

"Perhaps. But even if we did not find anything, I was planning to take some small object, like a handkerchief, to have Toast smell it."

"Why didn't you just bring him with you and let him roam around the place? Really make yourself at home?"

"I considered it," Clio replied seriously, "but his behavior can be a bit unpredictable. Particularly in houses with well-stocked kitchens."

"Of course," Miles said in a dangerously tight voice. Then he cleared his throat. "Let me see if I understand. You propose to break into three gentlemen's houses looking for souvenirs and kerchiefs?"

Clio looked indignant at the suggestion. "No. Only two. One of them is not a gentleman. One of them is a vampire."

"Oh," Miles said hollowly. "That makes it different."

"Exactly. Now let go of my arm so I can climb up."

Miles stared at her. "Absolutely not. This is the most absurd plan I have ever heard. It will not work."

"How do you know?"

"Because I am a sentient creature. My God, Lady Thornton, think about it."

"I have thought about it, Lord Dearbourn, and I think it has a strong chance of success."

"You are wrong."

"Oh really?" Clio retorted. "Prove it."

"How do you propose I do that?"

"By going through with it. If my plan does not work, if we do not find evidence in any of the houses of the three men from Devonshire, then I will be forced to concede that you are right. We are here, now. There is no reason not to at least try it. Unless, of course, your objection comes from some other source."

"Such as?"

"That you are afraid to be outdone by a woman."

Miles clenched and unclenched his jaw five times. "There is nothing I can say that would dissuade you from doing this, is there?"

There was one thing, Clio realized with shock, but the chances of him saying it were so small as to be nonexistent. "No."

He rolled his eyes, then moved them from her to the wall to think. When he looked at her, he found himself thinking that it was not such a bad idea, and grudgingly admiring her ingenuity in getting him out of his house. No one besides Corin had dared to flout his authority so directly in years, and he should have been angry with her. But he wasn't, not really, and he found that distracting. The wall offered no such distractions.

Spreading the word that Clio Thornton had been arrested as the vampire was only part of the trap he had prepared, and he was fairly certain he would have his man by the next day. All he needed to do, he realized, was to stall her until then. After that, she could go back to Which House and he could go back to his—

His whatever he did before he met her. Drinking. Ordering her to stop her investigation was not going to work. He needed to divert her but without letting her know what he was doing. It was an interesting challenge.

"Very well," he agreed, sounding deliberately displeased. "If we search your suspects' rooms and find nothing linking them to the vampire, then you must promise to admit that I am right. And to remain in my apartments without trying to escape."

"I will. I do."

"Then I will go along with your scheme. But only if we search all the houses tonight."

Clio paused and studied him. That was how she had originally planned to do it, but his insistence made her suspicious. "Why?"

Miles raised one eyebrow. "Why not? We had better get started if we are to finish before they all come home."

It hit Clio then. He was hoping that they would rush and miss something. "No. We will not have time to do an adequate search if we do them all tonight. We will do one a night for three nights." She looked at him challengingly.

Miles rubbed his chin, ostensibly in thought, but his hand worked to cover his smile. "Fine," he said with stoical resignation. "One a night for the—Wait." He interrupted himself, his expression changing. "I think I hear someone coming."

Clio's eyes got large, until she understood what he was doing. "That is a cheap trick, my lord," she scolded, trying to twist out of his grasp. "It might have worked last—"

Miles put a hand over her mouth to quiet her. In the silence that descended on the alley then, she made out the faint sound of hoofs at the far end. "Get your horse behind me," he whispered to her, and was relieved when she complied. The moonlight was very faint in the narrow passage, but there was enough of it to flash off the drawn sword of the man who was riding toward them.

"You're surrounded," the man shouted. "Hand over the girl at once or prepare to die. The choice is yours."

Chapter 13

"I am afraid I will have to disoblige you," Miles replied, not apologetically. "I don't really like either of those options."

"Do as I say and no one will be hurt," the man warned again.

"What will you give me for her?" Miles asked.

"Your life, you fool. Now hand her over."

"My life," Miles mused. "Not much of a bargain. I think I'll fight instead."

"You are making a mistake," the unknown man cautioned. "There are four of us."

"Actually it is you who have made a mistake," Clio told the man from behind Miles. "His Lordship is an excellent fighter, probably the best in England. Now that he is aware there are four of you, he knows he shall have to throw the two knives he keeps in his boots toward the outer walls of the alley to get the two men stationed there, and then unsheathe his sword to run the third through the middle. As to you, I am sure he would give you his choice of a pistol to the heart or beheading."

Before Miles could suppress his surprised laughter enough to silence her, or the man could respond, a sound like the sound made by three horses rapidly backing out of an alley was heard. "Cowards," the unknown man shouted after his fleeing accomplices. Then he turned his horse and moved slightly forward. "Do not worry, Clio, I am not afraid. I know he made you say that. I will save you from this beast without them."

"Friend of yours?" Miles asked Clio over his shoulder.

Clio had thought the voice was familiar, but it was not until the man stepped into a patch of moonlight that she was sure. Even still, it took her a moment to recognize him, because his hair was different and he had grown a mustache. "Justin," she said with an undertone that Miles would not have wanted to hear connected to his name. "What are you doing here?"

"Saving your life, and I'm just in time by the looks of it," Justin Greeley replied. "I always said you'd get yourself in trouble without me around to look after you, my silly foolish girl."

Miles did not at all like the man's condescending tone and was going to say so, but Clio got in first.

"I thought you were in France," she said. "With Plucky."

"Plootie," Justin corrected. "And you know that was just a passing affair. I had to have some solace after you broke my heart."

"I?" Clio was aghast. "*I* broke your heart?"

Miles could not figure out why Clio sounded so surprised. It made perfect sense to him.

"Of course. You said you could never love me, that you loved someone else and always would. You could have given me no greater blow. I went off with Plootie to try to block out the memory of you, erase everything that we were together from my mind. But try as I might, I haven't been able to stop loving you. I know I can make you happy. Just as soon as I kill this man who is abducting you. Unhand her, sir."

"How did you find me?" Clio demanded.

Miles had been wondering the same thing, between bouts of wondering who the man was that Clio was in love with, and what kind of a fool Justin was to think that anyone—especially someone named Plootie—could erase Clio from his mind.

Justin turned over a palm to show how easy it was. "I followed you from your house this afternoon."

"Why didn't you just call on me there?"

"Don't forget, Clio, I know you better than you know yourself." There was that condescending tone again. "You would have had some silly little fit of pique because I hurt your feelings. You never would have agreed to see me."

"Of course I would have. Why shouldn't I?" Miles was about to open his mouth to suggest a number of reasons, including the fact that this Justin person was, to use a phrase of hers, a moldy mongrel, when Clio went on. "Just because you abandoned me, ran off with another woman, and left me enormously in debt to that scoundrel Captain Black? What makes you think you would have been unwelcome?"

If Miles had been harboring any doubts about the sordidness of Justin's soul, they were put to rest now. Abandon Clio for another woman? The man was not only evil, he was an idiot.

"Ah, Clio, you always were wretched at concealing your feelings," Justin opined. "You see, you are mad at me. But I will make it all up to you. As soon as I rescue you."

"For your information, I do not need you to rescue me. Lord Dearbourn was not abducting me, he was assisting me. He is my partner in an investigation. And we will be far more productive if you leave and let us attend to it."

Justin shook his head sadly. "Clio, angel, I know I hurt your feelings, but you have to understand. Come with me. Let me talk to you. It can be how it was before. We can be close," he licked his lips and winked at her, "like we used to be. Remember how you enjoyed that?"

"I have no interest in being any closer to you than I am right now," she told him. "As a matter of fact, a bit more distance would suit me quite well."

This was the stuff to give him, Miles thought, and a grim smile crossed his lips. He was thinking that maybe three thousand miles would be a good distance.

"Come on, Clio," Justin urged in a voice that sounded greasy to Miles. "You know you have missed me and our—" he winked again, "—long conversations."

Ten thousand miles, Miles revised. Or the moon. The moon might be a good distance. A good place for that man Clio was in love with, too.

Clio was glad it was too dark for him to see her blushing furiously, but Miles felt the heat of her embarrassment. "The only thing I am missing from our relationship, Justin, is five hundred pounds. Now go, before *you* are missing something. Something vital."

Justin opened his mouth to speak, but Miles judged that the time had come for him to intercede. The removal of vital organs from the man was just his kind of job. "You heard the lady. Leave."

Justin jabbed his heels into his horse and sprinted forward toward them, his drawn sword aimed right at Miles's heart.

"You are mine, Dearbourn," Justin shouted and his sword made contact with Miles's sleeve. Then, to Justin's utter amazement, it clanged against the wall and fell from his hand. As far as he could tell, Miles had barely even flicked his wrist.

Miles slid out of his saddle, picked up the sword, and held it out to his stunned opponent. "If you are really interested in fighting, dismount. There is no need to endanger our horses."

Justin stared at him. "You will regret this, Dearbourn. I am an expert swordsman."

Miles smiled and his beautiful teeth shone in the moonlight. "Excellent. It has been a long time since I had a worthy opponent."

Justin snatched his sword from Miles's hand, but did not dismount. "It's going to have to be a bit longer. I do not engage in unofficial duels like a ruffian," he said disdainfully. Then he looked over Miles's shoulder and nodded. "Now boys. Get her."

Miles turned around just in time to see a man grab Clio, drag her from her horse, and sling her over his shoulder. He sensed rather than saw another man to his left, and a third, to his right, both on foot. They must have sneaked up the alley from the back while Clio and Justin were talking. Miles cursed himself for having been so distracted. He could not remember another time anything like this had happened to him. Without taking his eyes off the form of Clio and her assailant as they receded down the alley, Miles's hands dipped toward his boots. Something glinted and made a whistling noise, and suddenly the two men on foot each let out a howl. Justin, whose horse had been pounding up the alley toward Miles, abruptly reigned in when he saw the two knife points glinting out of the thighs of his accomplices.

"Hurry, Reynolds, he is gaining on you," Justin shouted after the man who was making off with Clio.

"Yes, Reynolds," Miles whispered, practically in the man's ear, "hurry." Before the man could take this very good advice, Miles brought the side of his hand down against the back of Reynolds's head at a precise angle he had learned from his cousin Sebastian, sending him careening unconscious to the ground. Miles caught Clio's body before she fell with him, and cradled her in his arms.

"Clio, are you all right," he asked, but her head simply lulled from side to side. There was a slight bump on her forehead and it looked as though Reynolds had struck her to keep her from fighting. "Clio," he said, more urgently, shaking her slightly. Out of the corner of his eye he saw Justin, still mounted on horseback, approaching. There was nowhere to put Clio down and no time. Holding her close to his body, Miles spun around and gave a flying kick, sending Justin's sword hurtling toward the wall. It hit with such force that the hilt broke off and the blade bent.

"You are next," Miles told Justin through clenched teeth, Clio's unconscious form cradled against his chest. "If you are lucky, you will just be able to hear the sound your head makes as it hits the wall before your brains explode. It is a very satisfying noise."

Before Miles had even finished speaking, Justin had

turned on his horse and fled. It would have been a pleasure to go after him and make good on his threat, but he
had more important things to think about. He looked
down at Clio and gently brushed his lips across her forehead. "Clio," he whispered. "Clio can you hear me?"

This time she stirred slightly. Her eyes came open, and
focused on his face. She smiled up at him, the most brilliant smile he had ever seen, and said, "I read once that
you kept knives in your boots, but I did not know it was
true." Then her lids fluttered closed and she went limp in
his arms.

"May I come in?" Clio asked from the doorway of
Miles's workroom. Two hours had passed since their return to Dearbourn Hall. Two hours during which Miles
had plenty of time to think. And fume at her. And berate
himself.

How had he let her get hurt? He had been distracted
listening to her, applauding her in his mind, and he had
made a grave error. It would not happen again. And
what had she meant when she said that she had read he
kept knives in his boots anyway? Had she been following
his exploits? Did she read what the news sheets wrote
about him? Did that mean—

From now on he would keep himself aloof from her.
He would not allow her to be a distraction. Nor would
he allow her to bend him to her will, to go dragging him
around the city, to disobey him blatantly, willfully and
with the assistance, he now suspected, of his staff. No
one disobeyed him. What had happened was at least as
much her fault as his. If she had not disobeyed him, she
never would have been in danger. What if he had not

gone after her? What if Justin's attempts to take her away had succeeded? The two men writhing in the alley had been kind enough to admit that Justin had paid them each a hefty sum for their assistance in getting the girl. What had he wanted with her?

He did not care. His only interest in Clio Thornton was in keeping her alive and out of trouble while he found the vampire. Tonight he was going to ask her questions and she was damn well going to answer them. Tomorrow he would damn well catch the damned vampire. And then Clio Thornton would be safely out of his damn life forever.

Forever.

By the time they got home, Clio had been semiconscious. Despite her protests, Miles had ordered her into his damn bedroom to take a bath and change her damn clothes. She was filthy and her gown had literally fallen to pieces when she was dragged off her horse. He was not surprised that she obeyed him. Obedience never surprised him.

But he was surprised now when he looked up and saw her standing on the threshold of his room.

DANGER!!!

The air in the chamber behind her was still steamy from her bath, and seemed to cling to her in a glowing aura. Her long straight hair hung loose over her shoulders, and two thin braids framed her face. She was wearing one of the gowns he had ordered for her, the dark purple one. It was cut significantly lower than her old dresses, and was significantly more fitted. Where her previous attire left almost everything to the imagination simply by nature of its shapelessness, this seemed designed to outdo the imagination with its devilishly engineered lines.

If she had been beautiful before, now she was staggering.

Miles barely noticed.

Not the way the gown brought out the deep purple flecks in her brown eyes. Not the subtle curve of her breasts, framed by the V of the bodice into a shadowy, fragrant valley. Not the grace of her neck, which would really look better with the Loredan amethysts around it. None of it. Let whomever she was in love with drape her with his family jewels. Miles was too damn angry at her, and if she thought that appearing in a new dress and looking like some kind of goddess was going to make him rise from his seat and take her in his arms and beg to be allowed to make love to her and forget all about his wrath, she was wrong. He scowled at her darkly and tightened his grip on the restraining arms of his chair.

Clio swallowed hard and fortified herself with a deep breath, telling herself she was *not* disappointed. She had never worn a gown like the one she was wearing now, of fine silk, beautifully cut by a master designer. By the standards of current fashion, its single color and the gem-less hem of the skirt were very plain, but Clio thought it the most glorious garment she had ever beheld. Slipping it on had been an almost erotic experience. The silk was incredibly thick and smooth and cool against her skin, like a caress. It rustled every time she moved and seemed to float around her. For the first time in her life, as she surveyed herself in the mirror that had been placed against one wall of Miles's bedchamber that day, she felt elegant. And graceful. And almost lovable.

For a moment, as she had gazed at her reflection, she began to hope it could be like her dream, the dream she had begun having ten years earlier. It began with her gliding into a room. Over the years it had changed—initially, with her limited experience, the room had been a kitchen, the only place she had ever been comfortable. Next, fueled by the stories she read in news sheets, it had been a crowded ball room with a secret alcove off the side filled with padded chaise lounges. Now it was the outer chamber of Miles's apartment, the room where he was diligently working at the round, leather-topped table. But no matter the room, the dream was always the same. He would look up, and his heart would stop beating and she could see in his eyes that he thought her beautiful. "Clio," he would whisper, saying her name with reverence. "Clio Thornton, you are spectacular." Then he would cross to her and take her in his arms and say, "I want to make love to you right here, right now."

But given the look he was leveling at her, that hardly seemed possible. There was no spark of recognition, no moment when he looked up and his heart stopped beating. His eyes made it clear that what he was seeing was a drab woman foolishly garbed in a dress designed for a princess. She looked idiotic, and out of place, and clumsy. And as if to confirm all of that, she tripped for no reason as she moved into the room.

"We'll have to have that gown shortened," he said coolly, and it was the only evidence she had that he had even noticed what she was wearing. Then he looked back down at the papers that were spread over the table. "In half an hour we will dine together and discuss your behavior tonight, and in the future. Until then, I am busy. You may amuse yourself as you wish so long as you do not leave this apartment."

You are clumsy and foolish and silly, Clio reminded herself as she moved numbly toward the chair on the other side of the table and sank into it. Just like Justin had always said.

Justin. What had he been doing tonight? She found it hard to believe that he was trying to save her, despite his words. But if he was not saving her, then he was kidnapping her, and that was even harder to imagine. That Justin had never loved her was clear; why he would bother to risk his life trying to get her was not. He seemed so much smaller and less worldly when she had seen him tonight than she remembered. Perhaps that was why she had not recognized him before. Because now she was almost positive that it was he who had been the man in the red doublet, the one she suspected of pushing her into the street in front of Dearbourn Hall two days earlier. The day she had come to see her grandmother. The day she had kissed Miles on the street.

If only she were not wearing the ridiculous dress, then maybe she could sit comfortably and figure all this out. She wished that Toast had not been sent to sleep in Corin's chambers, wished that somehow she was not entirely alone with Miles. Wished that her best friend was not a monkey. She felt her lower lip begin to tremble and commanded it to cease. She would not break down in front of Miles. Her eye fell on his copy of *A Compendium of Vampires* then, and she opened it to the page that was marked with a tightly braided yellow ribbon. She would work. It would be a perfect distraction. There had been something tugging at her mind all day, a persistent annoyance, the subconscious knowledge that a fact or an idea was out of place, and maybe, just maybe if she concentrated on the book it would come to her. Not cry, work. The words on the page were familiar to her, she had read the passage a dozen times, but she forced herself to study them anyway.

"Concerning the Vampire, t'are those who say he is e'en such a one as rises from the dead, but this is wrong, for the Vampire is a living being, and takes to his blood sucking so that he may prosper, and grow stronger, from others. For him, the blood is as food for us, and he must have it, lest he weaken and die. This is the cause that he shall be known to strike in a regular way, just as we must eat our victuals and drink ale at our regular times or we will perish. So that he will suck blood every day or every week, as he list, but regular like always, else he will be sick unto death."

Clio paused here to assess if she felt "sick until death" from lack of blood sucking. She did feel sick, there was no question about that, but she thought it had more to do with Miles than with any absence of human blood in her diet. Not really relieved, she read on.

"This noorishment he taketh only by night, being a creeture who loves the darkness, and thrives upon it. So that as the Moon, no longer young, waneth in her course and grow slimmer, even so the Vampire grows fatter, which is to say, more powerful."

She glanced at Miles, considering telling him she thought it barbaric to treat books as if they were scrap paper and underline things in the text, as he so clearly had in this passage—and why only every few words? Very distracting—but he was not looking at her.

"*And on _every_ such night as there is no _Moon_, when between her monthly courses she doth _hide_ her face, on that night will the Vampire be at his most powerful. Woe awaits he who thinks he _can_ strike the Vampire down on such a night, for he has the power of the Devil in him most strongly _then_, and will be invincible.*"

What would it be like to be invincible, she wondered. There were a few things she might try if she were invincible like—

She forced her eyes back to the page.

"*_And_ I say 'he' but there is also the other kind, the female or 'she-vampire' who is the same every respect, save this one: that she is far more dangerous. For though she look like a _comely_ woman she hath the strength of ten men when the bloode is in her, and may do bold acts, and daring.*"

Bold acts and daring. If she were looking for evidence that she was not the vampire, she had just found it. The female vampire was prone to bold and daring acts and she felt prone to neither of those things. If she were bold and daring, she would march over to Miles, tell him that it was wrong to write in his books and also casually mention that she wanted him to make love to her, and see what happened. But she knew what would happen. He would laugh at her. He, who had made love to the most beautiful women in England, would want nothing to do with her. She had been a fool to think he might. What was she? A dull, poor, plain, unwanted, unlovely woman who no one had ever bothered to wish a happy birthday and whose only real friends were a bunch of equally unwanted and possibly insane people, and a monkey. What would the Viscount of Dreams want with her?

But the night before, for just a moment in the alcove— Clio's indignation flared. It really was not fair of him to act the way he had toward her one night, to touch her and kiss her and say—say whatever he had said, if he was just going to glare at her the next day. How dare he treat her that way? Very well, he was angry at her, but as far as she could see he had no right to be. He was just as much to blame about her faked escape from his apartment as she was, maybe even more. After all, if he had not locked her up as a prisoner she would not have had to escape. If he had not made it so steadfastly clear that he intended to ignore her wishes and demean her ideas, then she might have consulted him. They were supposed to be partners, not jailer and prisoner.

And even if he was not attracted to her, he did not have to treat her like a baby sheep who needed constant shepherding, incapable of knowing its own mind or protecting itself from dangerous wolves. She wanted only one kind of protection from him: protection of others from herself. Despite the fact that she felt neither bold nor daring, she could not yet discount the fact that she might be the vampire. But that was all she wanted. And that should not interfere with her investigation in the least.

She was just marshalling her arguments when his voice broke into her thoughts.

"It is time for us to talk," he said, rising and walking around the table so that he was standing in front of her.

She raised her chin and looked at him defiantly. "I completely agree. And I already know what you are going to say."

Miles raised an eyebrow. "Really?"

There was something about having him look at her that made her stomach flutter. "Yes. And I do not feel I owe you an apology for dragging you out of here today. You left me no choice. You treated me unfairly. I thought we were supposed to be partners but instead I was your prisoner."

He seemed to consider, not so much her words as her, and she could tell he found her lacking. "It is an interesting point. But you must admit you got me out of the house under false pretenses. It would seem to me that partners should not keep secrets from one another."

She cleared her throat. What had she been meaning to say? "In the interests of having no secrets, I shall tell you that I am very mad at you."

His face was a cold mask. "Really? Why?"

His expression made Clio shudder and for a moment she could not remember. "Because you have not let me pursue my investigation. Because you have treated me like a baby sheep."

"I see. A baby sheep." He bent toward her so their faces were almost touching and his eyes were hooded. "Exactly what would you have me treat you like, Lady Thornton?"

Clio could feel his breath on her cheek, could smell

him, his unmistakable smell, an impossible mixture of hazelnuts and virility. Her heart was racing and her breathing was shallow. "Like a person. Like a woman," she said.

"Ah," Miles replied, a long exhaled syllable.

"Ah? Is that all you can say?" Clio was outraged. "My lord, your behavior to me is absolutely unacceptable."

Miles scrutinized her and she could see a vein in his jaw throbbing. "And just how should I behave, Lady Thornton?"

"With respect," she said forcefully. "You should share your information with me. And consult me about the investigation. Not pace around me as if I were an exhibit at the fair."

"Share information," Miles repeated as if the words were scalding his tongue. "Very well, Lady Thornton, I will share some information with you. I will share with you the fact that you were wrong about what I was going to say before."

"I was?"

"Yes." He paused. "I was not going to ask for an apology."

"You weren't?"

"No." Miles straightened himself to his full imperious height. "I have no use for your apology, and only a fool asks for what he knows he will not get. No, I was going to ask—" He gazed down at her face, her lips slightly parted, her eyes expectant, wondering. And purple.

Miles's mind took flight. There were a thousand strong reasons why he should not do what he was about to do, and not one of them was powerful enough to stop him. Lowering himself onto one knee so their faces were level, he brushed the lock of hair from his forehead and said, "I was going to ask if I could make love to you."

Chapter 14

"Impossible," Clio breathed and she realized she had been swallowing back hiccups for the previous five minutes.

Miles recoiled. His expression grew instantly distant, walled. "Of course. In that case, we should get back to our investig—"

Clio brought her lips to his with a hunger born of ten years of dreaming and Miles responded by sweeping her into his arms and holding her tight. He had told himself that it was not her that he desired but something else, something no one could give him. But he had suspected, with instincts honed through years of studying defenses, that he was lying to himself. And now, feeling her against him, he knew.

He pulled away to look at her. For one moment the wall that was always there vanished and in his eyes Clio saw a swirling mixture of desire and awe and pain and something else. Then his lips crushed hers again, and she saw nothing at all.

Miles covered her with lavish kisses, hundreds of them, her cheeks, the hollow below her throat, sampling her, memorizing her. Her flavor overwhelmed him, her suppleness, her willingness. His tongue licked her lips, urging them apart. Never had anything, anyone, felt so right to him. Clio Thornton was not a woman, she was *the* woman. The woman he wanted, the woman he needed.

Time was suspended as he held her against him, but when her lips opened to his it began again, hurrying, insistent, implacable. They had no time to lose. As if she felt the urgency, too, Clio grabbed for the laces of his breeches, fumbling with inexpert fingers, giving him half caresses that made him gasp. Miles reached down to help her, his fingers wrapping around hers, their hands getting in the way of one another, until clumsily, laughing together, shyly and boldly at once, they had unloosed and untied and unhooked everything that kept them apart. The clothes between them fell away, stripping away all reserve, and they stood together, wondering at one another, first apart, then skin on skin, warm tight planes pressed against each other as closely as possible.

Miles was more beautiful and awe inspiring than any of Clio's dreams had prepared her for. She ran her hands up his back, along his shoulders, tracing the lines of the muscles of his stomach, their perfection only enhanced by the deep scar that cut across them. His body was astonishing, powerful and firm and warm and soft and trembling and precious. She felt his heart beating in his chest, against hers, pounding in time with hers. She wanted to know everything about him, explore every part of him, right away, instantly. She dropped one of her hands down and timidly touched the hard shaft standing between them. It sprang toward her and she felt Miles's heartbeat stop. Then it started again, racing faster than before as she lowered her eyes and wrapped her fingers around his warm smoothness. "I never knew anything could feel like this," she breathed.

"Neither did I," Miles gulped back. Her hand, her eyes, on his member felt extraordinary. Each time she moved her fingers he felt pulses of intense sensation from the base of his feet to the tips of his ears. It was as if she were not touching him in one place, but everywhere at once, at his very core, arousing him, igniting him, spreading sparks through her fingertips. She was otherworldly, an enchantress. She was his. At least for tonight.

Her eyes rose to meet his and he kissed her with the full force of his desire, thrilled when she answered, kissing him hard, passionately, everywhere, responding unlike any woman had ever responded to him before. As they kissed she stroked her hand along his length, then rubbed her palm against his tip. Instinctively she found the sensitive place where it met in two round petals and ran her thumb over it.

Miles staggered at the sensation. "If you do not stop, I shall explode," he whispered to her.

"I thought that was the intention," she whispered back with a coy smile.

Something about her tone brought Miles's reason flooding back. What the hell was he doing? Summoning all the self control he possessed, he stilled her hand with his own and looked at her. "Clio, you know I cannot marry you."

"Do you want to stop, Miles?"

Miles shook his head grimly. "No. But it is, it would be—"

"—Dishonorable of you to take my virginity," Clio finished the sentence for him. She knew what he was saying, what he was trying to ask. "I understand. But you do not need to worry, my lord. Nothing you could do will dishonor me." Then she smiled up at him, a smile more potent than any touch, and said, "Make love to me, Miles. Here. Now."

He could deny her nothing. Tenderly, he lifted her onto the round table he had been working at, positioning himself between her thighs. Her hand was resting on his member but he willed himself to ignore it, concentrating instead on her. Using his nose he tilted her face up to his and kissed her softly once, deeply once, then began to move his lips lower.

Working with the dedication of a new-world conqueror, he planted kisses down her arms, along her hips, across her thighs, leaving trails of singing sensation behind. Clio felt his mouth leave a feathery kiss on the inside of her wrist, and a slower, deeper one on the palm of her hand, felt his lips close around each of her fingers, pulling them into his mouth, slowly, one at a time, wrapping his warm tongue around them, letting his teeth glance over them, meeting her eyes with a mischievous smile. He was touching only her hand, a hand she had been in possession of her entire life, and yet she felt like she was going to ignite. His mouth strayed down her legs then, to her feet, and when he ran his tongue over her arch and between her toes while his fingers slid slowly up her thighs, Clio thought she was going to lose her mind. She watched, unable to move, as Miles parted the soft brown hair between her legs with one finger and placed a gentle kiss on the bundle of nerve endings gathered in a tight knot there.

Clio could wait no longer. She pulled his head up so it was level with hers and, kissing her taste on his lips, begged, "Now. Please, please be inside me now."

Miles gave in. He rubbed his stiff shaft along her body, making himself slick and wet with her moisture. Then he braced himself against her opening and stroked her with his fingers and when she bucked against him, demanding him, he pushed the top half of his length into her.

He felt something give, felt her body opening for him, welcoming him home, and he plunged himself entirely into her. She was impossibly tight, impossibly narrow, impossibly wonderful.

"*Miles!*" she cried out in a tone equally divided between pleasure, surprise, and pain, and he stopped moving and began to pull out of her. She wrapped her arms around him. "No, don't. Not now. Please no."

Miles was rigid. "But I hurt you." Understanding came all at once. "Oh god, Clio, this is your first time. But I thought—You said—"

She looked at him intently. "I said nothing you could do would dishonor me, Miles, and I meant it. I knew that you would never make love to me if you knew I was a virgin. And I wanted you to. I want you to. Please, please do not stop."

"Clio, *amore*, you should have told me. I could have made it better for you. There were precautions, other ways. Other things we could do."

"It could not be better, Miles," Clio said, and she smiled exquisitely. "Nothing in the world could be better than being here, with you, now."

Passion, desire, tenderness, and a fierce sense of possession surged through Miles like fire, his heart aching and pounding. He had never felt so good in his life. She was his. She had given herself to him, to him only. He was the luckiest man alive. He would make sure she did not regret it, would never regret it. He pulled her close and kissed her on the lips. "Just wait," he said, raising one eyebrow and giving her a sly smile, the one she loved. "This is only the beginning."

His voice resonated inside her and she felt herself open more widely for him. Carefully he slipped part of his length back into her, then pulled out, slowly, letting only the beginning of him stay inside. He did that again, this time reaching out with his palms to stroke her nipples, and she arched her back, taking him in deeper, and wrapped her legs around his waist.

Pain disappeared into a hundred other sensations—fullness, warmth, sleekness, contentment, desire, curiosity—as Miles moved slowly in to and out of her. There was so much to learn, so much to experience. Each touch of Miles's hands was extraordinary and different. His palms teased over her nipples until they grew hard, and then he lowered his mouth to one of them, sucking it in at the exact moment as he slid into her.

With his mouth still on her nipple, he slipped two of his fingers between their bodies and she felt him touching her, pressing the little pink bud of her pleasure against his organ as it glided into her. "More," she moaned and he smoothed his fingers over her harder and quickened his thrusts into her, overwhelmed by her response to him. Lifting his mouth and his free hand from her nipple, he lowered her back until she was lying on the table in front of him and he was standing above her. With one hand he cradled her from below so that her hips were level with his, and he kept the other on her sensitive kernel, teasing it, plying it, touching it with devilish precision. She was a masterpiece, perfection, the most sensual woman he had ever known. Nothing he had ever done before had come close to feeling how this felt.

Clio wrapped her legs tighter around him, pressing her body against him wildly. The sensation of having one of his hands on her bottom, stroking her from behind, and his other hand above while his body slid into her was more than she could bear. As she sensed him growing thicker inside her, pressing more forcefully against the walls of her tight passage, as his fingers glided over and under her, following the channels of her own wetness, she knew her control was giving way. She gasped and felt the first hint of her release, felt herself tighten around him, and begged him to stop.

"Wait," he told her through clenched teeth and she did and suddenly she felt something a thousand times more powerful again, sparking over her, glittering through her body, along his body, growing brighter and brighter until she could wait no longer. She reached up and pulled him so he was laying on top of her and whispered, "Now, my love. Now."

Hands and legs and lips and arms and bodies entwined and moved together as a single entity. Being inside of her was unlike anything Miles knew, unlike anything he had ever dreamed of. They hovered suspended on the gleaming edge of their release and then Miles thrust into her one more time and the room seemed to fill with sparks and light and noise and they soared together, exploding into and around each other, laughing and shuddering and hollering and clinging to each other desperately, fiercely, possessively.

They lay panting and gasping and sweaty on the table, eyes closed, not speaking, until they were both breathing again. Even then the silence continued, each of them lost in their own thoughts. Miles was telling himself that she had not called him "my love" before but rather simply said "Miles," which could sound like "my love," when said quickly. Clio was telling herself that when he said "amore" he had not meant "my love" but had rather been using it as a general term of endearment, such as one might use to a friend or close acquaintance.

And then Clio whispered, "gardenias."

Miles, still inside her, propped himself on one elbow. "What?"

"Gardenias. Something had been bothering me all day, and that is what it was. *The Compendium* says that the vampire will take souvenirs, but does not say anything about him leaving them. But our vampire leaves gardenias. We should go to the flower market and learn who has been buying them." Clio smiled at him. "Making love with you has a splendid effect on my memory."

Miles kissed her lips and wondered if he could ever get used to the way her mind worked. He knew he could never grow bored of it. "Tomorrow I will send someone to the flower market to inquire," he told her. Then, reluctantly, he pulled himself out of her and rolled onto his side. He winced as he noticed the smudge of blood between her legs. "*Amore*, I am so sorry I hurt you."

Clio reached up and brushed the hair off his forehead. "I am not. It hardly hurt at all. And besides, it was worth it."

"Because you figured out what had been bothering you all day," Miles said in a blank voice.

"That. And because it was wonderful."

Miles's heart beat hard. "I am glad you think so." He kissed her fingertips, then kissed her mouth sweetly and gathered her to him. He felt none of the loneliness that had followed his other flings, and he knew he would not. Clio was not like any other woman he had ever known.

And nothing he had felt with her just now was anything like any other experience he had ever had.

Clio rested her cheek against his shoulder. "I read in a book once that at the height of pleasure a woman might feel like she was in heaven, but I would swear, my lord, that you made me see stars."

Miles had to laugh. "I wish I could take credit for what Louise Labé was describing in her poems, but I think those are the fireworks over the river."

Clio sat up slightly, her eyes alight with excitement. "You have read Labé? You read French, too? Have you—" Then she cut herself off, realizing what he had said. "Fireworks? Real fireworks? Here?"

Miles looked at her with awe. She was without question the most intelligent woman he had ever met. And the most beautiful. And she was his. At least for tonight. "Would you like to see them?"

"Yes." She hesitated. "But only if we can watch them together. Only if I can be with you."

Miles found he could not reply. Instead, he lifted her from the table and held her close against his chest. He carried her into his bedroom, from which the fireworks below were visible through a window, but they did not stop there. Pausing to pick up a strange looking key, he turned and inserted it into the housing of his clock. Clio watched with astonishment as the front of the clock sprang open, revealing a staircase. They went up, past a small landing, and emerged on a large patio that covered the top of Miles's wing.

It had once been a formal knot garden, Clio could tell, but now all the hedges looked wild and overgrown, and its precise design was barely discernable. The entire place had a neglected feeling, like an uncivilized oasis in the middle of an ocean of civility. It was the highest point for miles in each direction, and the view, across London on one side, across the river on the other, was extraordinary. Clio spun around, taking in the entire panorama, her eyes aglow with pleasure.

"What a spectacular place," she said breathlessly, moving to stand next to Miles. Her toes crunched over piles of rose petals that had blown over the terrace, filling the air with their scent, her scent. Miles wrapped his arms around her from behind and they stood, naked in the middle of the city, alone together, looking out at the river where towers of fireworks were flaming on four barges.

"Magical," Clio whispered, awed by the gold and red and green streams of sparks billowing into the sky.

"Magical," Miles repeated, his cheek rubbing against the crown of her head.

She turned and looked up at him and saw that his eyes were closed. "You are not even watching."

"I can see fireworks anytime," he told her. "But you will only be mine for a few days."

I will always be yours Clio wanted to tell him, wanted to scream at him then, but she knew it would not be good for either of them. It would be her secret. And she would not think about it until they were apart.

Seven days. She had seven days with him. "I read in a book once that if a woman kisses a man the right way, she can restore his virility in a matter of minutes," she told him in an offhanded tone.

Miles smiled, wondering how his friend Tullia d'Aragona would feel to know her *Dialogue about the Infinity of Love* had been quoted in such a context. "Are you trying to tell me that you want to make love again?"

"Yes," Clio admitted.

"Do you remember what I said about being subtle?" Miles inquired. Now he was looking at her and his eyes, reflecting the fireworks, were the color of melting gold.

"No," Clio shook her head from side to side slowly. "You had better refresh my memory."

"I said that you were bad at it."

"No you didn't," Clio corrected. "You said that you would give me lessons." She stepped away from him and spun around, her hair flying out behind her, her head tipped back. "Here I am. Teach me."

As he watched her spin and spin, Miles could have sworn for the second time that night that she was glowing. Then she stopped and threw herself into his arms, and all he could think about was how on earth he was going to keep her there.

They made love again, more slowly this time, with showers of colored sparks cascading around them and then, when the sparks were gone, by the light of the fireflies that gathered on the bushes. Afterward, they lay knitted together in a sea of rose petals, with Miles's head on her chest. Clio was just about to fall asleep when she felt Miles look up.

"Clio," he whispered. "Clio, I forgot something."

Clio ran her fingers through his hair. "Umhmm?"

"Clio, this is serious."

"What is it?" she asked lazily.

"I forgot to tell you something important."

"Important? What?"

"I forgot to say happy birthday." He leaned over her and kissed her. "Happy birthday, *amore*." Then he smiled into her eyes, lay his head back onto her chest, and fell asleep.

Clio turned and watched the fireflies, gracefully shifting among the leaves, and heard Princess Erika's voice in her head. "You will never find true love until the fireflies come out at noon," she had predicted. Perhaps not. But for a few days, Clio thought to herself, she would come very, very close.

She closed her eyes and wrapped her arms more tightly around Miles. She was in paradise.

Twenty-four hours later, she was in hell.

4 hours after midnight: Moon—two degrees less than half-full. Waning.

Chapter 15

"I think I hear someone coming," Miles whispered to Clio. "Wake up, *amore*. You have to hide."

Clio smiled at him without opening her eyes. "You do not need to be subtle with me," she informed him in the voice of someone who is still asleep and does not know what they are saying and would likely shoot themselves if they did, particularly if what they then said was, "I will do anything you want so long as you call me *amore*. You may kiss me if you wish."

Miles would have liked to, very much, but it was not just the fact that she was totally unaware of what she was saying that stopped him. It was the ever louder sound of voices on the other side of the threshold that did it. He and Clio had moved from the privacy of the roof to his apparently public bedroom several hours earlier, and he was already regretting it. He was about to leap from the mattress and cut the voices off at the pass when the door opened, beating him.

"Tough night?" Tristan asked as he crossed the threshold, followed by the rest of the Arboretti. "You look a bit feverish."

Miles felt feverish. He had quickly pulled himself up and bent his knees, making a sort of tent beneath the covers into which Clio's body fit snugly, but the presence of her between his legs was not exactly calming. "I was up late," he said with a frown. "Perhaps you can explain why you have decided to barge in on me like this."

"We were just passing by and thought we would visit," Sebastian told him sweetly.

Under the covers, a Clio who was somewhere between waking and sleeping, reached out and lightly touched Miles's member.

Above the covers, Miles made a noise that was a cross between a wail and a snort.

"Very well. You are right. Sebastian is lying," Crispin admitted. "We came because you disappeared early last night and we heard from your betrothed that you were ill. We wanted to make sure you were feeling all right. Apparently Doctor LaForge is sick this morning, too."

"Actually, Crispin is lying as well," Ian, the elder statesman, told Miles. "We came to make sure you had not run away. And that you would be attending the baby animal ball tonight."

"I am not sure that is a good idea," Miles said in a curiously taut voice. He appeared to be addressing his sheets.

Ian frowned. "I beg your pardon?"

"Oh God," Miles gasped, gripping the covers in his hand. "Oh God."

"None of us are thrilled about going either," Ian said, "but I don't think you should be quite this alarmed."

Miles would have liked to differ with him, would have liked to say that he was feeling something so sublime, so different from anything he had ever felt before, that he knew it was cause for serious concern, but any ability he had to speak left him when, timidly, Clio circled the tip of his shaft with her tongue and then covered it with her mouth.

"Ahhllgooohh!" Miles groaned.

"What?" Crispin asked.

"I—" Miles gulped as Clio planted teasing little kisses along his length—"think"—she curled her fingers around him—"the ball"—her palm slid up his shaft—"tonight"—her thumb rubbed back and forth against his tip—"will be"—she sucked him entirely into her mouth—"remarkable."

The last word came out more as a sigh than a word, but Sebastian, who was standing closest to Miles, caught it. "Remarkable. Are you planning something we do not know about?"

"Yes," Miles said. "Oh yes." Clio's mouth roved up and down him now, the fingers of one hand following, the fingers of the other gently caressing him from beneath. He gasped.

"Are you all right, Miles?" Crispin asked, leaning closer.

Miles panted slightly as her thumb ran up the entire length of him. "No. I am in a bit of agony. I think you should all leave."

"You really are ill. Do you want me to send for a doctor? Or for Bianca?" Ian asked.

"No," Miles replied quickly, gasping again despite himself. "I will be fine. In a moment. It will pass soon. I will come to see you then."

"You are sure?" Tristan asked, hovering near the threshold.

"Yes!" Miles shouted, but not at them. As soon as the door was closed, Miles threw back the covers.

That was a mistake. Because as marvelous as what he

had been feeling had felt, seeing Clio's small form curled between his legs, her hand on his shaft, her lips wrapped around him, utterly undid him. Looking at her, feeling her, he hovered on the edge of his release for less than half a second and then plunged over it, exploding into her mouth in wave after wave after wave of sparkling passion.

"*Clio!*" he shouted with exaltation, panting and moaning her name. It was the sweetest sound she had ever heard.

When he could move again, he pulled her up his body and held her against his chest and kissed her on the lips. Those lips.

"Clio Thornton, what have you done to me?" Miles asked. His body was tingling, his mind was reeling, his ears were ringing, and he was lying in bed with the most beautiful woman in the world.

"I'm not sure," she answered candidly. She opened and closed her mouth a few times, experimenting with the slight ache in her cheeks. "I read about that once in a book, but I do not know what to call it." She blushed slightly. "Did I do it right? Was it pleasant?"

Miles shook his head. "It was most definitely not pleasant."

Clio looked alarmed. "I did it wrong. I am sorr—"

"Definitely not pleasant," Miles interrupted. "More like extraordinary. Sublime. Spectacular."

"Really?"

"Yes. And a bit excruciating. As a matter of fact, I think it is time for me to retaliate."

"What do you mean?"

Miles did not answer, but used his body to tip her onto her side. He stretched himself out behind her, his chin resting on the top of her head, his chest pressed close to her back. Sliding one arm underneath her, he let the other trail along the curve of her waist, to her hip, then let it rest there. "Look in front of you," he whispered in her ear.

Clio's eyes had been closed as she reveled in the sensation of his body pressed against her back, and when she opened them she inhaled sharply. In the mirror that had been propped against the wall, she could see herself, naked, extended to her full length, amidst the tangle of white linen sheets. Behind her rose the planes of Miles's body, his cheek leaning now against her cheek, his arm possessively draped over her stomach. As she watched, he let his tongue slip out and trace the curve of her ear, then turned his eyes back to the mirror and held her gaze. She felt the heat of his hand moving down her stomach, the soft caresses of his fingers as they combed through the brown curls between her legs.

"You are so beautiful, Clio," he whispered to her, kissing her forehead, her cheekbones. "Look at how lovely you are."

Clio could not answer, could barely even moan, as, her eyes locked on his, she felt his fingers enter her. She sighed with awe as his thumb and pointer finger pulled her taut, while his middle finger snaked over the glistening surface of her rose-colored bud. Each move he made echoed wildly in the cavern of her body, and she felt as though inside of her a spring were being coiled tighter and tighter.

"Put your hand over mine," Miles commanded her, and she did, her fingers lying over his, over the fingers that were touching her. In the mirror she saw only his eyes, but she felt his hand on her, her hand on his. The rhythm of them both caressing and stroking her body, the feel of his fingers under hers, of her fingers touching herself, too, was driving her wild. Her fingers slipped off of his, so that she was touching herself while he held her open, but her glance never left his. She stroked herself tentatively at first, then more forcefully, stunned by the exciting feel of her fingers on her slick wetness. She grew hotter and bigger under her own touch and she felt her nipples turn to hard points. All the while his eyes did not leave hers in the mirror but watched from behind, incinerating her with their heated gaze. She could feel his body growing hard behind her, could tell that looking at her aroused him as much as having him look aroused her. This awareness of him observing her as, for the first time, she brought herself to a climax, wound the spring of her self-control to its limit. Looking only at him, only into his gaze, she felt herself let go, felt pleasure twist and curl in wild eddies through her body, springing along every sinew, filling her with warmth and joy and finally almost painful pleasure. Her release came not once but three times, first by her hand, then with the additional pressure of one of Miles's fingers on her very tip, then with his whole hand pressed over hers, with their fingers twined together, together pressing and stroking and buffing at her until she hollered his name and shuddered against him.

Miles held her tightly against him, waiting for whatever strange burst of insight she was going to share with him in the aftermath of her climax. He heard nothing but felt her lips move against his chest and strained to make out the words.

"I love you," he thought he saw her say. But of course, that was just his imagination.

What she had really said, what she said again a few moments later, was "Food."

"Food?" Miles repeated. "What does that have to do with the vampire?"

Clio tilted her head so she was looking at him upside down. "Nothing. I am hungry." Her expression altered and she flipped onto her stomach so she was facing him. "But I am wrong. It does have something to do with the vampire. Because, you see, I feel fine. And if I were the vampire, and if I had not killed anyone since we found Flora, I would not feel fine at all. I would be ill."

"Does this mean that you will believe me now? Or rather, believe that you are not the vampire?"

"Probably," Clio answered cautiously. "It would be good to know if a body was found last night."

Miles slipped out of the bed. Without bothering to pull on a robe he crossed to the door, opened it, and summoned Corin. Clio meant to listen to their conversation, but she could not drag her eyes from his body, from the curve of his bottom, the muscles that rippled in his back as he leaned against the door frame, the way his thighs and calves looked like the models for an antique sculpture. He was spectacularly beautiful, and even more so when he turned around and sauntered back to the bed.

"No new bodies have been found," he reported, then, feeling her eyes on him, asked with amusement, "What are you looking at?"

Clio swallowed hard. "I felt it last night, but I did not realize how big and thick it was."

"You really should not say things like that, Clio, not if you want me to stay sane," Miles whispered, acutely aware of the fact that he was growing hard.

"What do you—oooh," Clio said as the direction of her gaze changed. "I was talking about your scar."

"My scar," Miles repeated as if the words had no meaning. "Oh. My scar. On my stomach."

"You got that three years ago. In pursuit of the vampire," Clio said. "When you caught him sucking that woman's blood. You almost died."

"Yes," Miles nodded.

"I am glad you didn't."

She had sounded so sincere when she said it, as if it really made an important difference to her whether he lived or died, and Miles had been thrilled. But that had been seven hours ago. Now, seven hours and five carafes of wine later, Miles knew better. Now, thanks to Justin Greeley's kind visit to him, he saw it all with piercing clarity.

Late that morning, when he had come back from reassuring his cousins that he was fine, he had found her pacing his room, brimming with excitement. She had shown him the news sheet that reported her arrest, assuming the vampire had planted the story and seeing it as evidence that the fiend was getting desperate to get rid of her.

He should have gone along with it. He never should have told her the truth. But he had been convinced that she would see his plan was the best. He had been positive she would understand that faking her arrest and having every person who came to the jail to see her watched was the best way to identify the vampire. Surely the vampire would come, just to be certain. And surely he would give himself away by some look, some sign, when he found that the person in the cell was not Clio Thornton at all.

But she had not understood. All she had understood was that it meant she was confined to his house, to his room. And that he had kept a secret from her. Well damn her, who the hell was she to berate him for having secrets? She had secrets, too. Such as the name of that man she was in love with. Who the hell was he?

Of course, he had learned that soon enough. Miles dragged the sixth decanter of wine toward him and, not bothering with a glass, emptied it directly into his mouth. He was glad he had given Corin the night off so he would not have to tolerate his subtle, calculating glance at the pile of empty wine bottles that told the story of his debauch. He had already endured it once, when he asked Corin to bring in twelve decanters, and he did not think he could stomach it again.

He had given the order immediately after Justin Greeley's charming call on him. Justin had gained access to him by saying that he came at Clio's behest. Silly foolish Clio, he explained as Miles's guards unhanded him, had asked him to visit the viscount, and tell him that she wanted no more to do with him. She had just used the viscount for retaliation when her lover ran off to France, but with Justin back her need for revenge was at an end. Personally, Justin confided, if he had been a woman he would have preferred the viscount, but there was no accounting for taste, and Clio was adamant on the fact that she loved Justin. Justin averred as how women like Clio might be interesting at the beginning but palled in time, and wondered aloud if he would be clever enough to evade her watchful eye. He sighed and said he envied the viscount's near escape from Clio's snares, and was glad to be the instrument of his deliverance. Miles had nodded to everything Greeley had said, and kept nodding until the hateful house-hound excused himself and left. Measured, steady nodding, like the regular rotation of the gears on a timed bomb.

Justin's story had not felt quite right, but Miles realized he no longer knew what right was. Clio had felt right. So right it hurt.

Miles gulped the contents of decanter number seven and turned to assess his untapped supply. Five decanters left. Five days until his wedding. Five days he intended to spend well and truly drunk.

Damn Clio Thornton.

The messenger came just after midnight. He was more a boy than a messenger, scraggly and underfed, but he refused to take any food.

"Give the message to the lady and leave, them's my orders," he told Snug four times, and finally if unwillingly, Snug showed him into the study where Clio was working.

Or rather, fuming. Toast and Inigo were sitting at the far end, away from her, instinctively avoiding the waves of rage that were emanating from her without her realizing it. Even the puppy, who lay curled at Toast's feet staring up at him adoringly, was strangely subdued by her mood. She had been poring over her version of *A Compendium* all night, into which she had copied all the strange underlining from Miles's copy earlier that day, but the words *'E'en rises and die else young fatter is every moon hide can then and comely'* refused to resolve themselves into any reasonable sentiment no matter how hard she glowered at them. She did not know why she had bothered; Miles had disclaimed any knowledge of how the underlinings got into his book, and they could be as old as the text itself, but at least it was something to do. Or not do, since her eyes kept wandering from the page. The truth was that her mind was distracted, which made her glower harder. As Snug and the boy entered, she looked up and transferred her glower to them.

"He insisted on seeing you, Lady Thornton," Snug said apologetically.

"What is it?" Clio snapped, then was sorry. "I beg your pardon. What can I do for you?"

"Here," the boy said, extending a folded packet. Then, he quickly backed out of the study and ran through the door.

Clio opened the packet, scanned its contents, and yelled, "Wait!" But the boy, following orders, was long gone.

'*I must meet you,*' the message read. '*Tomorrow, at ten o'clock in the morning, be at the west crypt of Saint Paul's. It is of the greatest importance that you come alone.*'

Under normal circumstances Clio would have disregarded the message entirely. She had alienated enough people—besides the Special Commissioner—in the course of her investigations to know better than to attend secret rendezvous. Particularly those held in deserted parts of popular meeting places perfectly designed to let people slip in and out without being seen, a category that might have been invented especially for the crypt of Saint Paul's. But she knew without question that she would attend this meeting, knew she would do whatever the message said as soon as she had seen it. There was no mistaking that the hand which had requested the meeting was the same as the one that had told her *You do not know what you are* three days earlier. It would be a relief, if not a pleasure, finally to find out.

The words left a bitter taste in her mouth. Not at all like the taste of Miles. She shuddered as she remembered the morning, his arms, his hands, his smell. Had it all been a lie? All a ploy to get her to acquiesce easily to his plans. Had he seduced her to ensure her compliance?

When, that morning, she had learned the news that "Clio Thornton" had been arrested and was being held at Newgate as the vampire, she was thrilled. This, at last, was proof that she was not the fiend. Only the vampire himself would have orchestrated such a ploy. She was free of the taint, innocent of the crimes she had feared.

And then Miles had explained it to her. Explained it in calm, measured tones. Explained without apology, as if he could not understand why she would be mad that he had lied to her, that he really had been holding her prisoner, that he had given her false hope. That he had made love to her just to keep her in his house. Although, he had said in an icy tone, he did not know why he was bothering to explain anything to a woman even the Special Commissioner had deemed unfit to investigate.

How could he do this? How could he have acted the way he did. Were all his words false? Had he been forced to struggle through their time together, forced to pretend she was someone else? His voice rang in her ears, saying *I can see fireworks anytime but I will only have you for a few days*, saying *You are spectacular Clio Thornton*, saying *happy birthday*, and suddenly Clio had to know. Had to know if it had all been fake. Had to know before her meeting the next day, had to know before she learned what she really was. Had to know if he had been lying to her the entire time.

She ran to Dearbourn Hall, almost invisible in the feeble light of the quarter moon, slinking around the side of the stables and into the servant's corridor next to the kitchen. She forced herself to stop when she was inside, and catch her breath. She would be reasoned. Logical. Coherent. When she was only vaguely panting, she continued down the corridor, finally stopping at the door that led to his bedroom. It slid open soundlessly.

The place was dark and, as best she could make out by the light seeping in from around the entrance to the outer chamber, empty. Hearing a whisper of voices, she tiptoed toward the door through which the light was coming and pressed her eye against it.

Miles was sitting in a chair, his head back, his eyes closed. He looked like he was sleeping, but that seemed unlikely given that the elegant form of Lady Starrat sat astride his lap. As Clio watched, Lady Starrat deliberately dragged Miles's shirt from his breeches and bent over. Miles gave a low sigh.

"Ahh, Miles, aren't we dangerous," Lady Starrat whispered to him in a heady voice, running her hands over his stomach. "My dearest wasp. I will leave you so you can never sting anyone again." Miles murmured something Clio could not make out, and she did not bother to try. Calmly, silently, she backed away, crossed the room, and left.

As she closed the door of the service corridor behind her she heard Lady Starrat begin to hum *The first time I did see you dear*. "A very good friend used to sing that song often," Clio remembered Miles saying at the Jubilee Fair, remembered his wistful tone and expression. A very good friend indeed.

Clio's calmness abandoned her then. She stumbled blindly through the corridors, rushing out into the deserted street, running without direction.

The footsteps behind her were inaudible to her over the clanging confusion of her thoughts.

4 hours after midnight: Moon—three degrees less than half-full. Waning.

"Darling, wake up," a voice, much too close to Miles's ear, implored.

Miles blinked at the sunlight flooding into the outer chamber of his apartment, then at the woman before him. He staggered to his feet.

"What has happened?" he asked, trying to sort out why he felt like a hundred horses had pounded through his head, as well as why he was sleeping in a chair in the outer room of his apartment, and where Clio was. The pile of decanters he spied behind the back of the blonde woman in a nightgown suggested the answers to the first two and reminded him of the answer to the third one, but did nothing to explain why the woman was wailing.

"I know she only did this to hurt me, to hurt us," Mariana began without preamble, sobbing. "She wanted to force us to postpone the wedding."

"What are you talking about?" Miles growled.

"My cousin. My horrible cousin Clio. She has always been jealous. I knew she would try to ruin everything, Viscount, and now she has."

"What has she done?"

Mariana just looked at him. "Haven't you heard?"

"You mean about her being arrested?" Miles asked. "I do not see—"

"No. Oh dear, I thought you would have heard. Everyone has heard."

Miles's mouth suddenly went dry in a way that had nothing to do with having drunk three quarts of wine. "Heard what?"

"That she is dead. My cousin Clio is dead. They found her body this morning."

Chapter 16

YOU FAILED!

The floor lurched and swayed under Miles's legs. "How did she die," he asked, white knuckles on the back of his chair the only thing keeping him standing.

"Poison they say. I do not know. But I really think we should not put off the wedding."

YOU FAILED!

"Who told you about this?"

"Grandmother. She heard this morning that Clio was in jail and she was just dressing so she could go visit her, with Saunders in case anything disturbed her—you know how he positively dotes on her, for my sake—when they received the news. Saunders says I shall need a new set of pearls to wear with my mourning clothes. That will be all right, won't it, Viscount darling?"

YOU FAILED THE WOMAN YOU—

"How?"

"Well, I suppose I will send over to Beaumond. He has such lovely things. Or per—"

"I mean, how did they receive the news."

"Well, naturally they were upset. I mean, it is such a scandal for the family."

Miles was as close to committing murder as he had

ever been. "By what means did they receive the news," he asked, his grip leaving permanent indentations on the wood of the chair. "Who told them? Or who sent a message?"

Mariana looked confused. "Why should that matter?" Then, apparently recognizing in her betrothed's expression something akin to that of a baby lion ready to make its first kill, she said, "I believe the warden told them. When they arrived at Newgate. Her body had just been found in her cell."

The floor, which had been reeling under Miles, suddenly straightened. The sun, which had gone out, bloomed again. Mariana, who had been about to be murdered, was given a reprieve. Clio was not dead. Clio was alive. But one of his men was dead. It was the decoy for Clio that he had sent who had been killed, the fake Clio—

The floor stayed put, but the sunlight dimmed again. He had sent a man to his death and Clio was in grave danger. If someone would kill her imposter, what might they do to her?

"And the scandal was really unnecessary," Mariana was saying, "because poor dear Clio was not the vampire at all. Another body was found this morning, and she could not have been responsible, could she?"

Miles, halfway to the door, stopped and turned. "What? Another body?"

"Yes. The body of that dear woman Lady Starrat Peters. They found her curled up in her bed with those horrible marks on her neck. But even though poor dear Clio was not the vampire, I am not sorry she is dead. She had such a sad and lonely life. It must have been dreadful to be so unlovely. However, it does present some difficulties for my wardrobe."

Mariana had only begun wondering aloud whether she should have her mourning clothes made in silk or velvet—did the darling viscount think it was going to be a mild summer or a cool one, she would be guided by him—when Miles disappeared out the door.

At that moment, nothing, not Justin, not the vampire, nothing mattered except protecting Clio.

Unfortunately, he was already too late.

Clio stopped walking and the footsteps behind her stopped. She resumed walking and they resumed. After performing this experiment three times she was sure she was being followed. She would have been sure after the first time, but with the way she was feeling this morning, she would not trust her senses.

She had absolutely no recollection of what had happened to her after leaving Miles's house. With any luck, and a little work, she would manage to obliterate the memory of what she had seen there just as completely.

And then she would go on with her life as if she had never made love with him. She had been happy before. She would be happy again. Without him. Without the taste or smell or touch or memory of him. Without—

Damn! There were tears in her eyes. This was not the place for tears. She had determined that she could cry about what had happened from nine to half past nine every morning, and no more. It was now ten o'clock, which meant no crying.

And that she had an appointment.

She stopped, but this time the footsteps continued. She swung around to look behind her, and saw only a wizened old woman with a dusting cloth wearing heavy clogs. Clio watched as the old woman paused to run her cloth over the bronze candlesticks in one of the family chapels that lined the wall, then moved on to the next one, and the next. Just like Miles, Clio thought, moving from one woman to—

She was losing her mind. She had known she could never have Miles, so why did she care who he slept with? And even if she did care, this was not the occasion to dwell on it. Pressing those thoughts deeply away, Clio turned from the old woman and continued toward the end of the nave where the crypts were. She moved away from the walls that contained the family chapels and the footsteps behind her ceased. The crowds, which had been large in the farther part of the church, thinned as she approached the altar, and she was almost alone by the time she reached the stairs that descended into the crypt.

The warmth of the summer day seemed to vanish abruptly at the top of the stairs that led downward. As the staircase wound down and around, the light from the nave above disappeared. Candles flickered in wall sconces but did almost nothing to lift the gloom that intensified as Clio descended. With tremendous relief, she felt her mind prepare itself for work, and all thoughts of Miles, all emotions, receded. Her head became blissfully empty, blissfully sharp, a blank sheet ready to record every impression. It was this feeling—the feeling of being entirely independent and self-contained, entirely cerebral—that she loved, and that kept her investigating. Pain and loneliness, along with love, and fear, meant nothing to her when she was like this. The only thing that mattered was what was immediately around her, and she let her eyes roam.

She had reached the bottom of the staircase and was standing in a low chamber. In the hazy circle of light given off by a lantern hanging to her left, she could see that the floor was made of packed dirt, and that the wall nearest her was badly, and not recently, whitewashed. But the rest of the chamber was hidden in shadow, and she could not even be sure how large it was.

"Hello?" she said, her voice disappearing in the cold, damp air. There was no answer, not even an echo, suggesting that the chamber was large. She took a deep breath, removed the lantern from the peg on which it was hanging, and, holding it above her head, moved more deeply into the shadows.

As she made her way carefully toward the center of the space, the hair on her arms stood up. She took two more steps then stopped. She had heard something—a footfall?—behind her. There was someone else with her. For the third time in four days, she knew she was not alone.

She swung around. The lantern swung in her hand, and the chamber was filled with crazy shadows. Noses and chins and foreheads twisted together as the light bounced off the faces of the people along the walls. Grinning faces, deathly pale, watched her, staring out of lifeless, pupil-less eyes. For a moment Clio's calm abandoned her and she began to tremble and she thought her legs might give out, leaving her there, trapped with them.

"No!" she shouted and this time it did echo—*no no no no no*—and as her words returned so did her reason. Statues. They were statues, funeral monuments made by families in memory of their loved ones.

They had looked so real.

Clio swallowed hard and made herself breathe slowly,

deeply. Statues. She held the lantern up and forced herself to look at each one. There were a dozen of them, all from the same family, there a young boy, then an old man, here a lovely young woman. Clio raised the lantern higher to see more of that one. Someone had obviously loved the woman, for great care had been taken with her statue, every detail of her gown had been rendered, each curve of her face. Her fingers were done with such precision that they could have been alive, long fingers, clasped across her chest, entwined around a single rose bud. Clio extended her fingers toward the woman's hands, and, unable to stop herself, reached for them, letting her fingers slip between those of the statue. The marble was warmer than she would have expected, and in the light of the lantern glowed as if it were alive. She bent down to brush her cheek against the fingers and felt a soft exhale of breath against her neck as a voice whispered, "Clio."

She stood up fast, staring at the woman's face. It was the same, immobile, but it had whispered to her, she had heard it, felt it. Clio backed away, quickly, and that was when she ran into him.

She swung around and then stared, incredulous. "Justin," she breathed finally. "You? It was you?"

"I know," Justin replied coolly. "I always knew."

"You knew? Knew what?"

Justin smiled and spread his hands. "Knew you were in love with me. I never doubted it for a moment."

"What? That is why you asked me to meet you here?" Clio was outraged. "Do you know what I've gone through because of you? I've spent months trying to pay back your debts. I don't love you."

"You will admit it. In time."

"I'll do nothing of the kind. Why did you send me that strange note? Why did you want to see me?"

Justin's hand closed around her upper arm. "Because I want what I deserve."

There was something in his tone that made her shiver. "What you deserve? It will be easier for me to disembowel you if you unhand me," she said sweetly.

"Clio, my silly little fool. That love note you found to Plootie, when I wrote it, I was thinking of you. I really was."

"I was not talking about the correspondence you had her landlady forward to me. I meant the other note."

"Clio, Clio, Clio," Justin shook his head. "I can't believe you would let the note of debt I left in your name with Captain Black upset you so much. Would you really have money come between us?"

"Money? You think I am annoyed at you because you cost me five hundred pounds?" Clio was so angry she was almost shaking. "Tell me why you sent for me, Justin, so I can go."

"Why do you keep asking me that? I didn't send for you."

Clio frowned. "How did you know I was here?"

"I followed you. I know you wanted me to. Up there, in the church, you kept turning around to make sure I was still behind you."

"Then you are not the person I am supposed to meet," she said as much to herself as to him.

Justin gave her a strange smile. "If you are waiting for Dearbourn, he is not coming. I had a conversation with him last night and we got things settled between us."

"What are you talking about?"

"I offered to take you off his hands, and he was only too happy to oblige. Said you were amusing at first, but now everything has palled." When Clio did not say anything, he went on. "You did not really think he would devote himself to you? Poor, foolish little Clio."

"I think you should go now," she replied, her voice cold but not as cold as she felt.

Justin moved closer to her and tightened his grip on her arm. "You do not understand, do you?"

"Understand what?"

"That you are mine now and there is no way for you to escape."

"The only way I will ever be yours is if you take me by force," Clio told him. "Just because you managed to assuage Viscount Dearbourn, does not mean you can kidnap me with impunity. There are other people who care about me. Other people who will notice, and report, my absence."

"Your certainty is touching, my dear, but I would not count on that," Justin said with a grisly smile. "With the precautions I have taken, I assure you that it will not occur to anyone to report you missing." He was obviously trying to keep his voice level, even, calm, but Clio did not miss the manic undertone.

She saw that there was only one thing to do. She shuddered slightly and her shoulders slumped. "Perhaps you are right," she said after a pause in a voice that was equal measures disbelief and contrition. "Perhaps I have been a fool."

Justin smiled. "I knew you would understand. Now come with m—" the last syllable was more of a strangled gasp than a word, as Clio drove her knee into Justin's groin. His grip on her arm loosened for a second, and she dodged away, dropping the lantern to the floor and plunging them in darkness.

"Bitch," Justin whimpered behind her.

She had only examined the chamber for a brief time, but her mind told her that there was a corridor in front of her and to the left. Groping with her hands over the marble faces of the statues, she heard Justin behind her fumbling in the dark to relight the lantern. She was close to the opening of the corridor, she knew, but not there. She heard the sound of metal on metal and saw a spark and the protective darkness disappeared.

"Where are you?" Justin demanded, holding the rekindled lantern over his head. Clio, crouched behind the statue of the young boy, thought the pounding of her heart would surely give her away. She heard his footsteps slowly circling the chamber and carefully peered out from alongside the statue. Justin's back was to her and he was on the other side of the crypt, next to the stairs that led out, leaning over the statue of a married couple, checking behind it.

"You cannot escape me," he announced to the room, moving toward the next statue, the one farthest from her, leaving her part of the chamber deeply in shadow.

She seized her chance. Pressing herself against the wall, she slid from the niche behind the statue toward the opening of the corridor. Justin chose that moment to spin around, and his lunge for her was good. He got his hand around her arm again, and dragged her toward him.

"Stupid bitch," he told her, crushing her against his chest. "You are coming with me."

"Why?" Clio demanded, struggling to pull away from

him. "What do you want with me? You don't even care about me. Why—"

Then nothing.

Miles had not expected it to be easy, but, he asked himself, did it really have to be this hard?

"Don't you have any idea where she went?" he demanded again of Mr. Williams. "Did you see which direction she went in?"

Mr. Williams regarded Miles skeptically. "Why are you asking me if those were your men posted out back. They could have seen her come and go just as well as me."

At the mention of his men, Miles's jaw tightened. Three men. There had been three men assigned to watch Clio at all times. Three men who had all inexplicably taken ill at the same time in the night. It was just too damn convenient. "My men were posted in front. I did not—"

Mr. Pearl's soft voice interrupted him. "Clio's in danger, isn't she?" he asked, and his eyes were worried.

"Yes. Do you know where she is?"

Mr. Pearl shook his head and looked at Mr. Hakesly who said, "She went on an appointment. Appointment at ten, that's what she said. And if you know anything, boy, you know it's not good to ask her too many questions, not if you like your head about your shoulders."

"Ten?" Miles interrupted ferociously. "It's nearly eleven. Where was this appointment? With whom?"

"Don't know," Mr. Hakesly replied, pulling away from Miles slightly. "Looked strange, though. Told us all to stay here."

"What do you mean, strange?" Miles demanded.

"Bit like you do right now. Scary. Or maybe just scared. Yes, I'd say scared. Wouldn't you, Mr. Pearl?"

"Yes."

"Of course, she looked strange all yesterday," Mr. Williams put in, with a pointed look at Miles. "Not at all herself since she came back from your house."

But Miles neither heard his words nor saw his rancor. His mind was racing. Clio had gone out and no one knew where. Or even what direction she had gone in. Which meant that she could be anywhere in London. Alone. With the vampire. Without even her monkey for company.

One woman in a city of sixty thousand. One woman and a deadly killer.

Not one woman. Clio.

"I've got an idea," Miles said, abruptly. It was probably the strangest plan he had ever devised. It was also, he knew, his only chance of finding Clio while she was still breathing.

Consciousness came slowly to Clio, as if she were fighting her way through a vat of sticky pudding. There were faces and voices all around, people touching her, fingering her head, her side, whispering to each other. She wished they would stop, because it hurt, but then the hurt disappeared and above all the whispering, she heard another voice, a voice she recognized from the dream she had after the fair, the voice of her father. "I love you Clio," he said and she called out to him, begging him to tell her what she was. She saw him holding something, and heard him whisper, "Look in the mirror, Clio. It is not how you begin, it is how you end up that matters." She did not understand and she pled with him to stay, but he just backed away, repeating, "What you are you are you are you are," over and over again and she could not tell if it was a statement or a question. She pushed as hard as she could to the surface, struggling to catch him, reaching for him. "Wait," she wanted to call to him, "Wait, wait I am coming," but the sticky pudding clogged her mouth and she could not speak.

She awoke coughing and gasping for breath. Her eyes flew open but she could see nothing. It was black in the crypt, and quiet. She could tell that she was propped against a wall, and when she tried to stand, she felt a sharp pain in her side. Wincing, she used the wall to support her and dragged herself to her feet. Over the pain, the only thing she was aware of was the need to escape. She could not remember what had happened, had no recollection of how she had freed herself from her pursuer, but she knew she had to get away. Justin might come back at any moment.

She felt her way around the wall to the opening she had tried to leave through, and then to the staircase. She paused before she stepped onto it, summoning her energy. Every step up felt like a stab wound in her side—which, later, she would learn was exactly what she had—but she forced herself to keep going. She was so weak. She counted the stairs to distract herself, twenty-eight, twenty-nine, thirty, thirty-one. At thirty-two she had to stop and rest. At thirty-six she saw a faint light and knew she was getting close.

That was when she heard the footsteps behind her. They started out faint but got louder as they got closer. Whoever it was had more strength than she did, and was actually running. She wrapped one arm around her aching side and with the other supported herself against the wall of the staircase. Thirty-eight. Thirty-nine. At forty she tripped and fell forward. She was so tired. So exhausted. Maybe if she just rested for a moment. Maybe—

The footsteps were closer now, and she could hear panting. She dragged herself to her feet and kept going. Forty-one. Forty-two. It was getting lighter. Forty-three. Forty-four. Forty—she tripped again. This time there was no strength left. The darkness tugged at her, pulled at her mind, warm, soothing darkness, a place beyond consciousness, beyond pain. She would just slip into it and everything would be fine. Her eyes, so heavy, began to close.

The footsteps kept coming, pounding up toward her. With a great act of will she opened her eyes and saw that one of her hands and her entire dress was covered in sticky brown blood. Then she looked behind her and saw Justin's face emerge from the stairs below.

She shook her head, struggling to keep the darkness at bay. Just a little longer, she told herself. Clutching her side, she stumbled to her feet and up the remaining ten stairs. She threw herself into the nave of the church, reeling into the crowds like a pilgrim who has journeyed without food or water, and then collapsed. She lay on her back, gasping, waiting for the darkness to come and take her, waiting to feel Justin's hand close around her leg, willing her eyes to stay open just until it happened, just to know. And then a miracle occurred.

From out of nowhere, Miles appeared, golden and smiling and so beautiful he looked like an angel. She knew she was mad at him, but at that moment she felt nothing but supreme joy at seeing him, at feeling him bend toward her, feeling his arms around her. "Justin," she panted as he lifted her into his arms. "Must get Justin." Then the darkness took over and she was gone.

"Are you sure she is all right?" Miles demanded for the thirtieth time as the clock in his bedchamber showed five in the evening. They had put Clio to bed six hours earlier and she still had not awoken.

Bianca, Ian's wife and Miles's cousin by marriage, exchanged a look with Corin, then pasted on her most compassionate expression. "Yes, Miles. She will be fine," she replied, using the exact same words she had used all thirty other times. "If you do not trust me, you may call in another physician."

Miles tried to smile but ended up grimacing. "Of course I trust you. You are the world expert on female medicine. She could not be in better hands. I am just worried."

"I know," Bianca assured him, also for the thirtieth time. "But you do not need to be. You found her in time. You saved her life. She will be fine."

Corin decided to change the subject. "How is your other patient, ma'am? Doctor LaForge."

Bianca answered animatedly, grateful for the respite. "He is not really my patient. He seems to have some familiarity with medicines on his own and is looking after himself, but I hear he is much better today. Almost miraculously so. And actually, I was surprised because—"

Miles allowed his mind to drift. He hadn't saved Clio, not really. It had been Miles's idea, but Toast was the one who found her. It was the monkey that had led them through the city to Saint Paul's, following Clio's scent. Recalling that procession—Inigo on his shoulders to follow Toast's every movement through the crowd, the Triumverate panting behind to keep up—almost brought a smile to Miles's lips. But only almost. He would save the smiling for when Clio's eyes opened again.

"She really will be okay?" he demanded again then, interrupting Bianca. Before she could express the annoyance that showed in her eyes, Miles was apologizing. "I'm sorry, I do trust you. It's just—" He paused, then resumed in a different voice. "I was wondering about something, Bianca. It is not really necessary for you to tell Ian and the rest of my cousins about this visit, is it? About Clio—I mean, Lady Thornton—being here?"

Corin made a strange noise. Bianca bit her lip and she looked at Miles with wide open, innocent eyes. "Of course not. And you will be pleased to know they do not suspect a thing. The sight of you whistling in the corridors, smiling spontaneously and for no reason, and occasionally having your steps followed by a small monkey has not come to their attention at all."

Miles stared at her. "They know?"

"Know? No, not exactly. But they are suspicious. You have not exactly been, ah, normal for the past few days."

A low moaning sound came from the bedroom behind them, and as if in confirmation of her words Miles brushed the hair off his forehead, sprinted into the chamber, and nearly leaped to the bedside, followed distantly by an amused Bianca.

"Clio?" he asked tenderly. "Clio are you awake? Are you all right? Can you hear me?"

Clio's eyes fluttered open. For a moment a smile crossed her lips. Then, abruptly, it left and she pushed herself up on one arm. "Pall," she said, her eyes flashing.

"Paul?" Having Justin's name be the first—and last—words on her lips after her harrowing experience had been hard enough for Miles, but hearing this other man's now, the first words when she awoke, was worse. "Who is Paul?" he asked in a strained voice.

"That is what you told Justin I did. Pall. Bore you. Is that why you hauled me back here? To bore you more?"

Behind them, Bianca inched out of the room, not even daring to close the door for fear of drawing attention to her presence.

"Clio there are many things I could say about you, but I could never say you bored me." Miles felt something tense inside of him. "And if you respect Justin so much, why don't you go to Newgate and be with him? I will call my coach for you at once."

"Are you trying to get rid of me so you can visit Lady Starrat?"

"Lady Starrat?"

"Where did you leave her when you came to get me? At home? In bed?"

Miles frowned. "Yes, actually. She is dead."

"I guess I am not surprised after the night she had."

"What do you mean?"

"There is no reason to lie to me anymore," Clio said, trying to look worldly. "I am not as needy of protection as you might think."

"Ah. So you know."

"Yes. I know all about it."

"I was going to tell you in a little while."

"Really? Why?" Clio waved an airy, unconcerned hand. She hoped he did not see it trembling. "What difference could it possibly make to me?"

"I am glad you feel that way. I thought you would be upset."

"Upset? Upset to learn that she had been *stung*?"

Miles cleared his throat. "I think pricked would be the more accurate verb."

"I agree," Clio hissed in an offhanded way. Then she took a deep breath. And began to cry.

Miles reached for her but she pulled away. "You are upset. But you know, you had nothing to do with it."

Clio wiped the tears from her face with the corner of the sheet. "Is that supposed to make me feel better?"

"Yes." Miles was confused.

"Is it your way of saying that I am naturally inadequate and there is nothing I can do about it?"

"Clio, there is nothing inadequate about you." He paused, then added, "I think you are stupendous."

Clio goggled at him. "You have the audacity, after everything with Lady Starrat, to say that to me?"

Miles held her shoulders and looked right at her. "Clio, Lady Starrat is dead."

"My God you are arrogant," Clio said, shaking his hands off. "There is no need to brag about your prowess. You already said that once."

"Yes, but I don't think you understand."

"I understand everything. I saw you with her last night."

Miles suddenly went very still. "What did you see last night?"

"I saw you getting ready to sting Lady Starrat with your pricker. Or prick her with your stinger. Whichever you prefer."

Under other circumstances, Miles could see that this might be funny. Very funny. But the hair at the nape of his neck was standing on end. "You saw me? With Lady Starrat? Where?"

"Here. Or rather, there." Clio pointed through the open doorway into the other room. "In one of the leather chairs." Clio shuddered at the memory. "Shall I describe it to you?"

"I think you had better," Miles said. The grim seriousness in his voice dissipated some of Clio's anger.

"You were lying in the chair, or perhaps it is better to say you were sprawled, and Lady Starrat was astride you."

"Was I clothed?"

"Yes. But while she sat astride you, she pulled up your shirt and started massaging your chest and talking about your stinger. It was clear that you would be unclad soon."

Miles cleared his throat. "My stinger?"

"Yes. And she called you her big wasp and said she would make it so you could not sting again. Very charming. And very apt."

Miles seemed to be lost in thought for a moment, then he pinned Clio with his gaze. "Are you certain? Are you certain that she pulled up my shirt? And called me a wasp?"

"My lord, I have rarely been more certain of anything in my life." Or in more pain than I was at that moment, Clio thought to herself.

"This is bad." Miles looked over his shoulder and saw Corin silhouetted in the doorway. "Did you hear that?"

Corin nodded and his expression was even more grim that Miles's.

Clio looked from one to the other with confusion, and then a scowl. "What are you two talking about? It was clear that you had been having an affair with Lady Starrat for some time. I am sorry I stumbled across it but there is no reason to act so distraught. If you are worried that I will tell Mariana, I promise nothing is less likely."

Miles turned back to her, and his expression was deeply earnest. "Clio, I have never had an affair with Lady Starrat. You are the first woman I have touched in over two years, and the only one I want to touch ever again. Last night I passed out in that chair after drinking ten—"

"Twelve," Corin corrected.

"—carafes of wine. Whatever happened, whatever you saw, took place entirely without my knowledge."

Clio looked down. "It is not good to drink so much," she said in a small voice.

"I only did it because I was afraid I had lost you."

But you will lose me. In four and a half days, Clio thought to herself. Then she said, "Why would Lady Starrat come to your apartment and behave, ah, that way?"

Miles looked from Clio to Corin. Corin hesitated, then nodded his head. "Because she was working for someone who wanted to kill me, Miles said."

Clio's eyes got large. "The vampire?"

"No. Someone else. Someone who, I surmise, had never seen my face but had seen my body and was trying to identify me by the scar on my stomach." Someone who had known about the rendezvous at the bathhouse. Someone who had seen all the Arboretti go in at the appointed time and who had sent a very clever spy to learn which of them possessed a scar on his stomach. "I suspect that was what she was doing the other night, in the library, with Sebastian."

Clio frowned. "But why?"

"The less you know about this right now, the better." Miles saw that she was going to protest, and rushed on. "This has absolutely nothing to do with our investigation, I swear to you. And one day, I will explain it all. For now, I only hope that she died before she was able to make her report."

"What do you mean, she died?"

Miles swallowed hard. "Clio, another body was found this morning. Another of the vampire's victims. It was Lady Starrat."

The color left Clio's face.

"I assumed that you were at home last night but now it seems you had come here. Did you go back to Which House afterwards?"

"I don't know," Clio said, looking at her hands. "I have no idea of what I did."

Or what I am.

Miles turned from her and began issuing orders. "Corin, send a messenger to Which House and find out when Lady Thornton returned there last night. Then, go to Newgate and learn everything you can about the visitors to our agent's cell. I want you to handle this yourself. I'll await your return here with Lady Thornton and then go to the ball when you get back." Corin was already leaving when Miles's voice at his back stopped him. "Wait, Corin." Miles turned to Clio. "Do those arrangements suit you? Do you have any better ideas, or different errands to send Corin on? Can you think of anything I am missing?"

Clio felt color rising in her cheeks. "Are you really asking me for my opinion? The opinion of a woman who

you are holding prisoner and who even the Special Commissioner deems useless? Or is this some sort of trap so
you can laugh at me?"

"I have been a fool, Clio," Miles admitted, "but I
know when to stop. I know that without you the Special
Commissioner would not have solved the majority of his
recent cases, and I suspect that without your help I won't
solve this one. Is there anything we should be doing that
we haven't?"

Corin left the room, shaking his head as he entered the
service corridor. He should have gone right, toward the
kitchen and the stables to order one of the footmen who
waited there to go to Which House and to choose a
mount for his ride to Newgate, but instead, he turned
left. He would see to it that all of Three's orders were carried out. Just as soon as he had taken care of a little errand of his own.

Chapter 17

"Why don't you just lie down an' I'll play with Toast," Corin suggested with a sigh. He shifted uneasily in his chair next to the bed.

"What?" Clio looked up with surprise. "What do you mean?"

"I've been waiting these eighteen hours for you to make your move, my lady," Corin explained. "You'd think you were planning a military campaign not playing a game of backgammon, and that not even for money."

Clio tried a smile. "I'm sorry, I'm a bit distracted." She paused, biting her lip. Then she looked up. "You really should have seen him rescuing me, Corin. He was incredible."

"So you've said," Corin replied wryly. "About a dozen times."

There was a long silence, and then Clio asked in a voice she hoped was neutral, "Do you plan to stay on here after the wedding?"

Corin shrugged. "Course. Reckon the viscount will need me more than ever after that. Going to earn my place in heaven by sticking by him."

Clio nodded to herself and cleared her throat. "Would it be possible, do you think, maybe, from time to time, for you to write to me and tell me how he is? Just so I could know?"

Corin eyed her closely. "Aye. Reckon I could do that. If you really want me to."

Clio pressed her lips together and nodded vehemently. She felt as though her throat was closing up.

"Lady Thornton, may I ask you a question?" Corin said.

"Of course." It came out as more of a whisper than a statement.

"Seeing how it's my job to protect His Lordship, would you mind telling me what exactly your intentions are toward him?"

Clio stared at the manservant. "My intentions?"

"Aye." He crossed his arms over his chest.

"What do you mean?"

"Well, from what I know of your history, you are not one to go casually having an affair, and yet here you are with His Lordship. I'd say it's rather suspicious."

Clio's mind flashed from sadness to outrage. "Just what are you implying?"

"Well, His Lordship is a very wealthy man. And you are a woman with many financial commitments."

Clio's mouth opened and closed. "You think that I am here for the viscount's money?"

"Could be. And no one would blame you. In fact, I've been told to offer you ten thousand pounds."

"For what?" Clio had to clench her hands to keep them from shaking.

"For your departure. You see, it has been suggested that you might be doing this just to interfere with His Lordship's wedding to your cousin. And there are those who have a hefty investment in seeing that go forward. So they were thinking, what if you just left?"

Clio struggled to keep her hiccups at bay. "You wrong me, sir, with your accusations, and your filthy offers. Do you remember how I said I was sorry you hurt your head bending over to get my spoon the other night?"

"Yes," Corin replied, nodding.

"Well, I am not. In fact, I wish I had a platter here right now so I could hit you over the head myself."

The air crackled with tension for a moment, and then Corin smiled widely. "I was just checking. I had to be sure, you know. I don't want to see Miles get hurt again."

"You mean—you mean you said all that just to test me?"

"Aye."

"You could just have asked me. There was no reason to insult me like that."

"There certainly was. If your plan was to interfere, or make some money, you would have been surprised by my offer, and possibly pleased, but not insulted. Your being insulted is a credit to you."

"Do you remember, before, when I said I wished I had a platter to hit you over the head with?" Clio asked sweetly, but her eyes were narrowed. When Corin nodded, she went on. "I was wrong. I wish I had a hundred platters. Actually, make that a thousand."

"A thousand what?" a voice asked from the threshold of the bedroom.

Corin and Clio both jumped. "You might try entering a room like a gentleman, Thr—Your Lordship, when there is a lady present," Corin rebuked him as Miles strode toward the bed. "How long had you been there eavesdropping on us?"

"Not long, why? Did I miss something good? What does Clio want a thousand of?"

"Platters," Clio explained in a strangely tight voice. He was dressed from head to foot in black, which exaggerated every fabulous angle of his body. The sight rendered her entirely breathless.

"That's right, platters to hit me over the head with," Corin stepped in to explain, a little too eagerly. "I was cheating at backgammon again."

Miles looked at Clio. "Is that the problem?"

She just nodded, glad for the obfuscation and still too stunned to speak.

"Very well. Corin, as punishment for your ungallant behavior, I order you to go and get a thousand platters for Lady Thornton. Heavy ones. And don't hurry. We won't be needing you any more tonight." Miles was speaking to his manservant but he was looking at Clio. Her body was tingling all over.

Clio was so entranced by the sight of Miles, by the expression in his eyes, by the heat in his voice, that she forgot all about Corin's insulting test. The sound of the door shutting behind him and Toast was the only thing that broke the spell of Miles's gaze.

"I have interesting news," he told her, crossing to the bed and taking her hand.

"You are feeling subtle?" Clio inquired.

The corners of Miles's lips curled up into a half smile. "I always feel subtle when I am with you. But this is too important. I just received this from Which House." He held out a wrinkled piece of paper.

A line zigzagged through the middle of it, twisting around groups of squares and rectangles, and ultimately ending up where it began. It took Clio a moment to understand it. "A map. This is a map."

"Of your itinerary last night," Miles agreed triumphantly.

"Where did you get it?"

"Inigo drew it. Apparently he was worried you were not working hard enough and followed you to see how the investigation was going. Your clients certainly are demanding." Clio blushed and was about to interrupt when Miles went on. "It goes from Which House here, and from here around the neighborhood. But nowhere on that map do you even approach Lady Starrat's house,"

"Which means—"

"You did not kill her and you are not the vampire," Miles finished the sentence for her. He watched quietly as the news really settled in and felt a strange sense almost of loss. She had needed him when she thought she needed someone to protect the world from her. Now that need had vanished.

"Then the note must have been sent by the vampire himself, to upset and confuse me."

"Note?"

"The afternoon of the day we found Flora in my bed, I received a note that said, 'You do not know what you are.' I assumed that someone was warning me that I was the vampire. But now I think it must just be part of the vampire's plot to scare me. It was because of that note that I went to the meeting today, in the crypt. Because the message was written in the same hand. I was hoping that whomever had summoned me—" Clio's voice trailed off as she caught at an idea. "If the vampire sent me those notes, then it must have been him I was supposed to meet. He must have hurt Justin after I lost consciousness. But Justin's presence scared him away before he finished with me."

Justin. Miles did not like the idea of being beholden to Justin Greeley for anything. "Are you sure Justin was not the person responsible?"

"Positive. He just followed me there and decided to take advantage of finding me alone." She paused. "He really is locked safely away in Newgate?"

"Yes," Miles answered, amazed that he had ever been jealous of the man. "He is safe inside Newgate." He was reminded of something. "Do you have either of the notes you received? Can I see one?"

Clio shook her head. "I no longer have them. I destroyed them."

"How?"

"First I tore them into very small pieces. Then I, well— I ate them."

Miles stared at her for a moment. "You ate them," he repeated. He tipped his head back and laughed. "Of course. So that no one would see them and be concerned. You did it because you are always trying to protect other people from yourself."

Clio spoke without thinking. "At least I am not always trying to protect myself from other people." She regretted the words almost as soon as she had spoken. "I am sorry, Your Lordship, I shouldn't have—"

"If you are going to probe the secrets of my soul," Miles said, interrupting with a wry smile, "you really should call me 'Miles.' "

"Miles," Clio repeated.

"Better. I never trust anyone who addresses me 'Your Lordship.' "

"Corin does," Clio pointed out.

"Exactly," Miles nodded. "I met Corin when he broke into my country estate years ago. Definitely not to be trusted."

"What about people who call you 'viscount'?"

"Worse. Miscreants of the lowest order." He rose, crossed to a table, picked up a silver salver, and returned, holding it toward Clio. "Does this look anything like either of the notes you received?"

Clio reached for the piece of parchment on the silver platter, but Miles pulled it from her. "Don't touch it. Just look."

" '*Do not try to fool me, Dearbourn,*' " Clio read aloud. "No. Why?"

"It was found clutched in the hand of the person I sent to Newgate to impersonate you," Miles explained succinctly.

"Clutched in her hand?"

"His hand. I had a man impersonate you. And yes. He was dead."

"Someone killed my imposter?"

"Yes. Just before someone tried to kill you."

"Not kill. Justin only wanted to kidnap me. But—" She got a faraway look.

"What?"

Clio shook her head. "Nothing." She did not really think Justin was the person behind the death of the imposter. Although it would clarify what he had meant when he had spoken of the "precautions" he had taken to prevent anyone from reporting her missing. If everyone thought she was dead, no one would notice her absence. "How was sh—he killed?"

"By this," Miles nodded at the paper. "He crushed it

in his hand when he died, but you can still make out the lines of the original folds. I've seen it before in Europe. When you unfold the packet, the center leaps up, propelling whatever is there into the air. In this case it was poison, probably white arsenic. The warden reports hearing a sneeze when he opened the message, which would certainly have expedited things, but that would not have been necessary. One good breath and he was dead."

Clio shivered. "Do you have any idea who could have sent it? Any idea who went to see him? Or rather, me?"

"Yes. You are very popular. Sixty people materialized to try to get a look at you, but they were only allowed to peer in through a small slit so that the imposter would go undetected, and they had to leave their names. My men are still going over them."

Clio nodded, lost in thought. Then she looked up. "At least the note shows that whoever did the murder knew it was an imposter and was not deliberately trying to kill me," she said with an attempt at airiness. "That counts for something. And the vampire, or whomever ordered the meeting today, also failed to kill me. I must be very lucky."

"Yes, I expect that explains it. One sharp blow to the ankle, one blunt object to the head, and one knife to the ribs. Luck."

"My ankle does not hurt at all anymore," Clio said. "At least not compared to my side." A frown flickered across her features.

"Are you in a great deal of pain, Clio?"

"No. But I am very frustrated. In a normal investigation, you can try to figure out why someone is doing something bad, and at least use that as a guide and possibly a lever. But with a fiend, there is nothing to hold on to, no rational explanation. The vampire is killing people because he needs their blood to live. Period. Which leaves us no closer to catching him than before. And I feel like time is running out."

In so many ways. She looked toward the window, toward the sliver of moon that hung high in the sky. Learning that she was not the vampire did not bring her the relief she had expected, did not make the waning moon any easier to look at, and she knew why. It was because it still meant the passage of time. It was past midnight. In four days she would still lose Miles.

"Tell me again about finding the vampire three years ago," she said, breaking the silence. "About exactly what it was like when you came upon him."

Miles stiffened, but he answered. "We followed him into a room. He was leaning over a girl. I put my sword behind his back. He turned around. There was blood everywhere. Blood on her pillow. Blood on his clothes. Blood on his hands. Blood on his lips. We fought. He escaped. I chased him."

Clio continued to stare out the window, but she did not see anything. She was lost in thought. She knew she was missing something, something vital, but she could not figure out what it was. Finally, she turned her gaze to Miles. He had begun fiddling with an object he had picked up from the table beside the bed and she realized it was the inner workings of the clock she had kicked over three days earlier.

"I am sorry I broke that," she offered.

"It does not matter. Time marches on indefatigably whether or not the clock counts it," Miles replied with a hint of bitterness. "Besides, it's not broken. Only mis-aligned." He tinkered with something, then turned a little knob and the clock began to click in a steady rhythm.

Clio could see the spring moving, the golden gears spinning, each into the next, with finely tuned precision. "It's like an ideal little world, where everything fits to-gether perfectly," she said with real admiration. "It is beautiful."

"It is an illusion." Miles brought his fist down on the clock, hard, reducing it to a pile of bent metal, and now the bitterness was palpable. "Even the slightest change in pressure or temperature can upset the balance, and as soon as the balance is upset it stops working." With a ca-sual motion, he swept the pieces onto the floor, then looked at her with strangely blank eyes. "Nothing per-fect can endure, Clio. No matter how much money you have, you can't buy time."

He stood and began moving from her, but Clio reached out and grabbed his hand. "No," she agreed in a low voice, crackling with urgency, "but you can steal it."

He turned back toward her, slowly. "Steal it?"

Clio nodded. "By ignoring it. By filling it impossibly full. By losing track of minutes and hours." She pulled him toward her and he came. "I will show you how."

He looked down at her, her magical smile, the hope in her eyes, and his face was impassive. But his mind was reeling. He did not, could not, deserve her. "Why me?" he asked finally. The question was almost inaudible.

"What?"

"Why me? Why did you let me make love to you?"

Clio hesitated. Looking at him, gleaming in the moon-light before her, she felt her breath catch in her throat.

She longed to tell him the truth, but she was terrified of his reaction. What if he laughed at her? What if he frowned? What if he did not say anything at all? What could he say, really, that would not make her ache inside? What could he say besides 'thank you but I am marrying your cousin in four days'? What could telling him possibly accomplish except to make him pull away faster?

"Because I love you, Miles," she said simply.

He frowned. "You do not know me. You can't mean that."

There was so much pain in his voice that Clio knew she had to tell him everything. She swallowed hard. "I do know you. You were my first investigation. I began reading about you and following you the summer I was fifteen, simply out of curiosity, to see what Mariana's betrothed was like, and once I started I could not stop. I followed you every night, when your father thought you were out drinking and your cousins assumed you were with one of a dozen mistresses. I know where you went and what you did. When you stood outside the glass-less windows of those small houses on the outskirts of the city through the night, watching as parents held their children and laughed with them and kissed them fondly even though they barely had enough to eat, I stood next to you. I saw you leave piles of gold for them on their dusty windowsills after they went to bed. I saw you wait to see that the food you sent them anonymously each day arrived, and I saw you leave every time before they began to eat it. I saw the children go out in new clothes, the fathers walk around with the confidence of men who have found better jobs, the mothers smile, really smile, for the first time in years. I saw you bring enormous joy to thirty families that summer. And none to yourself. Every night, before the sun came up, I followed you to the river and watched as you stood at the edge and I knew exactly how you felt. You were alone. Like me." She paused. "You were the best man I had ever seen, Miles. You still are. That is why I wanted you to make love to me. Because I love you. Because I have loved you with my entire heart for ten years."

He stood rigid, looking at her, his eyes, his face, his posture unyielding, unexpressive, and Clio feared the worst.

Then he said, "It was you."

Clio gazed at him. "What?"

"I thought it was some sort of apparition, but I should have known. It was you all along."

"You mean, you saw me? Ten years ago?"

"No. But I knew you were there. When you were close by I felt peaceful. Like everything inside me made sense. And then one day you just disappeared." He moved his glance from hers. "Do you know how long I looked for you? I went back to the river every night that fall but you were never there. I finally gave up and decided that it had been a figment of my imagination."

Clio could not believe what she was hearing. "Why didn't you ever speak to me?"

"I was afraid to do anything in case I scared you away. That was why I went to the river. I hoped you would come out and talk to me." He returned his eyes to hers. "Why did you leave?"

"We moved back to the country and there was no way that I could stay behind. But I read all about you, everything I could put my hands on." Clio put her palm on his chest. "And in the end you did find me. You have me now."

"Yes." Miles looked down at her, no longer a grown man but instead the boy she had followed along the Thames years earlier, the boy who chose to spend his nights not in pleasure but in watching parents treat their children with love, the boy whose loneliness had resonated so powerfully with her own, the boy who had wanted her to talk to him. "Tell me again, Clio," he whispered forcefully, almost pleading. "Please, Clio, say it again."

Clio did not need to ask what he meant. "I love you Miles," she told him, not whispering it. "I love you."

He would have liked to make her promise she would never leave him again, that she would always be his, but it was a promise he could not ask and she could not give. Instead he bent down and pulled her to him and held her against him with a fierce, overwhelming possessiveness.

"Say it again," he begged, over and over again, as he pulled her nightgown over her head, "again," he implored as he admired her in the moonlight, as he kissed her breasts, her neck—his, all his, only his, had always been his. "Again," he entreated, tumbling her onto his lap, her wetness leaving a glistening trail up the black velvet of his breeches as he pulled her toward him. "Again," he demanded as she ran her hands across his chest, pulling his doublet off, kissing him, short nails scratching down his smooth, hot skin. "Again" he ordered as she pushed him onto the bed, "again," he pled as he slipped inside of her. "Again," this time a ragged cry as she sat astride him, touching herself while he moved into and out of her body. She was incredible and gorgeous and everything he had not known how to name, and she was his and she loved him. "Again, again again," he shouted as she collapsed on top of him, panting and moaning, her body pulling him into her, pulsing around him, squeezing him, teasing him, demanding him through one release, and then another. For a long moment Miles floated outside his body, somewhere between consciousness and death, hovered, soared, rose higher and higher on a steadily building surge of pressure and pleasure commingled, and then all of a sudden he heard her say "I love you Miles," one final time, and his climax slammed through him with an intensity that left him gasping and pleading and shouting her name.

They held each other tightly, neither daring to move, to upset whatever fragile balance they had attained.

Then, suddenly, Clio rolled over and said, "E'en rises and die else young fatter is every moon hide can then and comely."

Miles had begun to grow accustomed to her flashes of insight, but this was something else. Something more like insanity. "What?" he asked, suddenly worried that the exertion had not been good for her wound. Wounds, he corrected.

But Clio only beamed at him. "Of course," she said with the air of someone who was not speaking nonsense. "Look in the mirror. It is not how you begin, it is how you end up. I need a piece of paper and some ink."

Miles, still bewildered by her earlier disclosure, managed to decipher that at least the last sentiment was lucid and reached to the table next to his bed to get her some.

"E'en rises and die else young fatter is every moon hide can then and comely," she repeated, then added, "E-R-A-D-E-Y-F-I-E-M-H-C-T-A-C," pronouncing the first letter of each word as she wrote it.

"He are a dee if I'm ache sea tea?" Miles asked, misunderstanding what she had said. "Is that supposed to be a poem? Because, *amore,* I'm a bit rusty bu—"

"No. It's E-R-A-D-E-Y-F-I-E-M-H-C-T-A-C. Which, read backward, as in a mirror, is C-A-T-C-H-M-E-I-F-Y-E-D-A-R-E. 'Catch me if ye dare.' "

At least now she was speaking in sentences that resembled English. "Catch me if ye dare. Is *that* part of a poem?"

Clio held the paper out to him. "No. It is what is underlined in your copy of *A Compendium of Vampires.* I saw it two nights ago when I was waiting for you to yell at me. Remember, when I asked you why you had marked up your book?"

"I would like it to be noted that I didn't yell at you," Miles put in, studying the paper. "I did nothing like yell at you."

"You have a remarkably forbearing nature," Clio said. "Which is one of the things I love most about you, and which we will discuss at another time." At the word "love" Miles smiled enormously and it was all Clio could do to stay focused on her explanation. "Those were the words underlined. At first I could not figure out what they meant, but then in the crypt it became clear."

"How did you find the passages with the underlining in the first place?"

"I don't know. I think—that is right. When I picked up the book there was a page marked with a yellow ribbon. As if someone had been reading it."

"Or wanted to draw our attention to it," Miles said, growing suddenly more serious. "Was that the first time you had noticed the bookmark?"

"Yes," Clio began, then stopped. Braided yellow

ribbon. Braided yellow ribbon. Something clicked in her memory.

A hundred eyes, a hundred mouths, leering at her, calling to her. An ear, an eye, a *braided yellow ribbon* lying on a worktable, waiting to be sewn on to the head of a doll. "A souvenir," she breathed. Her fingers were trembling. "It was a souvenir. The vampire took it from the doll house, where I found the first body. And he left it for us to discover."

Miles watched her. "Are you sure?"

She nodded. Then she looked at him. "He is taunting us. Daring us. 'Catch me if you dare.' "

"He is doing more than that. He is laughing at us. Because the fact that he had access to my library means that he is part of my household. And unless I am mistaken, it is the same person who entered the library the night we, ah, discovered that the vampire was from Devonshire."

Clio's eyes got enormous. "Do you mean that he was the intruder? The person who walked in while we were—"

"—curing your hiccups. Yes. Because the *Compendium* was here in my chamber constantly from that time until you saw the bookmark. No one would have had access to it since that night."

"What about your staff? Are there any members from Devonshire?"

"I am sure there are, but none of them are part of the contingent designated for my apartments. Each of them was handpicked."

Clio wondered at that, but decided to ask why another time. "That seems to settle it. The vampire is here. Which means all we need to do is figure out who it was that entered the reading alcove the night we were in there."

"Unfortunately, it will not be that easy. I already asked the men who were stationed at the top of the stairs to discourage guests from wandering into the private apartments who they had seen go by, just in case whomever entered the alcove spotted you and needed to be subdued with an explanation. Apparently, every member of Mariana's party, and all my cousins, drifted upstairs at one point or another during the evening. The only person they did not recall seeing was your grandmother."

"Too bad," Clio mused. "Of everyone she is the one I should most like to imagine as a vampire." They were both silent for a moment, thinking, and then she went on. "Eliminating your staff and your cousins and my grandmother—and I suppose," she added reluctantly, "Mariana—leaves only those two men who are with her. Her tutor and my grandmother's secretary."

"And Sir Edwin," Miles added gently.

"Sir Edwin? My uncle?" Clio was incredulous. "That makes no sense. He may be fairly vacant, but I am sure he is not evil." She paused. "At least, I think I am." But he had been around twenty-five years earlier when the first vampire attacks began. And he had acted strangely when they discussed the vampire. Still, it was hard to believe. "Besides," she added, "he is not from Devonshire."

"But his nurse may have been," Miles pointed out. "Fifty years ago no noblewoman would have dreamed of nursing her own child. And, unless I am mistaken, he is the only one who actually managed to visit you at Newgate."

"How nice of him," Clio replied. "He has always been the only member of the family to care about me. It would

be fitting if he were the vampire. Very well. We can in-
clude him as a suspect. Which means that we have three
rather than two."

"I'll order my men to search their chambers tomorrow
for evidence that one of those three might be from Devonshire. As well as for more souvenirs."

"And disguises."

"Disguises?"

"Whoever it is, must have a very good disguise or you
would have recognized him from three years ago."

"True. I'll have them search for disguises as well."

Clio scrunched up her nose. "Why wait until tomorrow? Why not do it tonight? Why not confront all
three of them right now?"

"Because I like the thought of the vampire passing an
uncomfortable night. I would be willing to wager there
will not be a body tomorrow, simply because he is sitting
in his room wondering what is taking us so long and
waiting for us to act. As I see it, making him anxious is
about the only leverage we have over him." He paused
while Clio thought about it.

"I think I believe that. But we lose the advantage
as soon as we search. Wouldn't it be better to do it
clandestinely?"

"Perhaps. Or perhaps we can use his expectations to
our advantage as well." Miles warned to his theme. "I
can have my men go through the motions of making a
thorough search tomorrow during the day, and then, tomorrow night, when everyone is at the ball, we will go
back and really search ourselves."

"We? Together?"

"Do I have any choice? I would not trust this to

anyone else, and if I go without you, you will just follow me."

Clio blushed. "Am I that predictable?"

"Rarely," Miles assured her. S'teeth she was beautiful.

She made a face at him. "Although I do not enjoy admitting it, I like your idea. But how will you justify the search?"

"I'll just say I lost something," Miles explained vaguely. There was something he had been planning to lose before his wedding anyway and this would be a perfect cover. "Do you think Toast would be willing to help us?"

"Does your cook make meat pies?"

"Good," he answered definitively. "Then it is settled."

"Yes," Clio agreed. A thick silence settled in the air. "Isn't it rather incredible? From out of hundreds of possible suspects, we have been able to narrow it to three in less than a quarter of an hour."

"It is too easy," Miles said.

Clio nodded slowly. "Maybe he is deliberately trying to deceive us. Maybe, somehow, he managed to sneak in here and leave the book, to deflect guilt from himself and make it seem like someone in the house."

"Maybe," Miles agreed, but it did not feel right to him. "Or maybe he is deliberately leading us to him. Reeling us in."

"Why would he do that?"

"To show us how confident he is. To emphasize that he knows who we are but we do not know him. That he is right here, sharing a house, a roof with us, every day. That he can get to us anytime he wants."

"To terrify us," Clio whispered.

"Yes." The word hung cold and precise and still in the air.

Clio felt a chill pass down her spine. "I think it is beginning to work."

Miles wrapped his arms around her, around the most precious possession he had ever had, and pulled her back onto the bed, next to him, to his warmth. "I won't let anything happen, *amore*. I will protect you. The vampire will never hurt you. I promise."

4 hours after midnight: Moon—quarter-full. Waning.

Miles really did not mean to lie.

Chapter 18

"I still cannot believe it," Clio whispered to Miles as they pressed themselves into the darkness alongside the Curious Cat Tavern and waited for their man to come out. Tendrils of mist swirled in front of her face, and seemed to curl inside of her, leaving her ill at ease and with a bad taste in her mouth. "I cannot believe it is him. Or that we are here. That it has been this simple."

"Neither can I," Miles said in a voice that seemed almost dead. "But I am more convinced then ever that he is the vampire."

"Why?"

"I'll explain later." Miles spoke without turning around. He hoped his tone was dismissive.

He looked up at the sign swaying creakily back and forth above the door he was watching. It was peeling, but the outline of a black cat within a cage was still visible. At least he thought it was. He might just be remembering it from the last time he had seen it.

"I wonder what he is doing in there," Clio whispered, just to make conversation.

"Don't," he told her in the same dismissive tone.

"Don't what?"

"Wonder. Talk. Anything."

Miles clenched his hands and tightened his muscles and wished like hell that he had a drink.

And that he had not brought Clio along. That he had not let her help in the search, that he had found some way to keep her locked away, safe. In his house. In his room. Like she had been that morning.

That morning. Hours ago. Years ago. That morning he had felt like anything but a failure. He and Clio had still been lying in bed—he had just been working up the nerve to ask her if she still loved him, even in sunlight— when Lady Alecia's raised voice in the outer chamber of his apartments made the walls seem to vibrate.

"I thought you said my grandmother was not in the habit of visiting your apartments," Clio had whispered to him urgently.

"She wasn't," he replied, pulling the linen sheets over her head and moving quickly from the bed. He had grabbed a robe from his armoire and had just gotten the belt knotted when Lady Alecia burst into the room, dragging a harried looking footman with her and trailed by Mariana.

"This is an outrage," Lady Alecia began.

"I entirely agree." Miles had given her one of his steeliest looks. "I do not take well to having my sleep invaded." He stood, hands on his hips, legs spread wide, barring the entrance to his bedchamber.

Lady Alecia, unfazed, stepped past his blockade. Mariana followed behind her, craning her neck to take in the furnishings. "I shall have to redo this room," she announced, interrupting Lady Alecia's renewed shouts. "This color gray does not suit me at all. I prefer blue like the color of a baby rob—"

"Be quiet," Lady Alecia told her, and for once Miles thought he could like the woman. "I do not apologize for upsetting your sleep, Viscount, for I do not take well to having my privacy invaded. This man says you ordered him to search my room."

"Not your room," Miles corrected, but before the gleam at the prospect of disciplining the young man violently could settle into Lady Alecia's eye, he went on. "I ordered him to search all the rooms in that wing of the house. He and his men have already been through this wing and the connecting rooms."

"Then you do not deny it?" Lady Alecia spoke with such vehemence that her Lisbeth Willard wig—the red ringlets of a dear little seamstress who sewed her mother's mouth shut so the woman starved to death—slipped sideways on her head.

"Why should I? The men were acting on my orders. Now if you would please leave my chamber—"

"Your orders?" Lady Alecia glared at him. "You had them checking on my guests. Mine?"

"They were not checking on your guests, Lady Alecia. They were looking for something I had lost."

"What?"

"I would rather not say." Miles crossed his arms over his chest. "And I would like to remind you that this is my house."

"I am afraid, Viscount, that you do not have that luxury. This may be your house, but my granddaughter will be mistress here in only five days—"

"—four," Mariana corrected. "Since we are not going to postpone the wedding because poor dear Clio died. It is only four days until my birthday."

"—Four days," Lady Alecia went on, "and neither she nor I will tolerate this behavior."

"Really, viscount," Mariana said, moving toward him, "you are acting like a naughty baby bear. Bad viscount. Bad, bad, bad," she scolded, shaking a finger at him.

Miles thought he heard a choking noise from his bed, but it might have been from his own throat. He had never felt quite so much like running from an adversary as he did at that moment. "Very well," he conceded finally, addressing Mariana. "I did not want you to worry, so I was keeping it from you. I lost a necklace. The famous Loredan amethyst necklace. In the commotion of the parties honoring our betrothal, it was misplaced. My mother received it as a wedding present on her wedding day. I had hoped to find it before—" Miles stopped, swallowed, and resumed, "—before the happy day of our marriage."

"The Loredan amethysts," Mariana proclaimed. She had never heard of them, but they were famous, the viscount said so, which meant they must be large. And they were to be hers. Perhaps she could trade them in for sapphires. Or even emeralds. Purple was not her best color. "I am so sorry we distributed you, Viscount," she said with her loveliest smile, taking her grandmother by the arm and pulling her from the room. "By all means have your men search every inch of the house. We should not keep them any longer."

The door closed behind Mariana with a thud. Clio just had time to flip the covers from her face and then flip them back before it swung open again.

"Oh, Viscount, darling, how thinkful of you," Mariana gushed as she swept back into the room.

There was a long pause and Miles seemed to be having trouble speaking, so Clio made a peep hole in her cocoon and peered out. Only Mariana's complete self-absorption covered Clio's gasp of horror.

Clutched in Mariana's arms, straining vainly to escape, was Toast.

"You knew I had been loitering for a baby monkey like this one and you got it for me to show that you are not mad about the scandal my horrible cousin caused," Mariana cooed. "Oh, look how darling he is," she went on as Toast tried to climb her hair and poke out her eyes. "He absolutely loves me."

Miles found his voice then, largely because he was worried that if he did not Clio would leap naked from his bed. "Why don't you have Corin look after him? So he will not trouble you. Leave him here, and I will have him bring the monkey to you before the ball tonight."

Miles heard a strangled grunt from his bed at the suggestion, but fortunately Mariana did not.

"I couldn't dream of such a thing," Mariana said. "I would not want you to think I did not fancy your present. I shall call him 'Darling Baby.' That is a nice name, don't you think? And I shall have a new suit of clothes made for him at once. This one is so musty." Then she frowned at Toast. "Don't you think he would look dreamy with some darling little earrings? I know just where to get them. You will send your man for them, won't you? Tell him they must have pearls. Baby pearls." She fluttered her long eyelashes at Miles, simpered, "Oh, Viscount, you are a naughty baby bear," and, finally, left.

Miles had locked the bedroom door then, but he and Clio could not escape from what they had started forever.

Reports filtered in from the various footmen assigned
to the search, as well as from Which House where messengers with notes of condolence about Clio's supposed
demise had clogged the streets since morning, and a pile
of flowers left by well wishers had turned the front steps
into an impromptu and impassable shrine. But none of
that—not even the information that Princess Erika had
apparently been dreaming of Clio's death every night for
a year and did not know whether to be sad at the loss of
her friend or delighted that another of her prophesies
had come true—could take Clio's mind off the fact that
Mariana had kidnapped Toast and wanted to make him
wear earrings. Her primary consolation was that Toast—
or rather, Darling Baby—could undoubtedly hold his
own against Mariana and that, according to Miles, he
was already wearing his Jungle Beast expression, which
always proceeded his Shrieking Wild Monkey Tantrum,
by the time she carted him off.

Their afternoon had been spent listening to Miles's
footmen recount the details of their searches. Clio had
been impressed by the questions Miles asked—where did
Saunders Cotton's eyes move first when he heard you
were looking through his room, did Doctor LaForge
fidget with his hands, how did Sir Edwin's voice sound
when he answered your questions—and even more impressed by the degree of observation evident in the answers his footmen gave. During one of these recitals they
had received a frantic visit from Elwood, who had suspected there was something untrue in the reports of
Clio's demise and in the tepid confirmation of them he
received at Which House. Over his protestations of relief, Clio managed to ask him if he had been responsible

for sending her the hazelnut cakes five days earlier. With much embarrassment, he had admitted that he had not, but that he should have, and in the future he would send her dozens. He had finally left, with a curiously probing glance in Miles's direction.

But even this lengthy interruption had not bothered the footman, who had resumed his narrative exactly where it had been interrupted. From him and the others Clio and Miles had learned that Doctor LaForge had to mop his head with a kerchief every three seconds whenever anyone approached his bed, that Sir Edwin clenched and unclenched his fists when people touched his writing desk, and that only Saunders Cotton had reacted to the search with anything like outrage or indignation—that is, reacted in what Clio described as a normal way.

"If you call going pink in the face, stammering about the unholy imposition it is on Lady Alecia, and almost losing your voice you are so mad, normal," Miles had demurred.

"At least it approximates the sort of outrage you would expect. The sort of thing my grandmother was exhibiting this morning," Clio offered.

"I suppose you are right," Miles had conceded. "Which means we have two people who acted in individually strange ways and one who acted normal. Who stands out most?"

Clio did not hesitate. "The normal one."

Miles nodded. "Exactly what I was thinking. We start with Saunders's room."

Clio, dressed in the yellow doublet and breeches of a Dearbourn footman, had waited in Miles's apartments for him, and once the ball was underway they had

crossed to Mariana's wing together using service corridors. When they entered the peacock sitting room, Miles
had stopped dead in his tracks.

"My God," he muttered in a whisper. "This place is
horrible."

"You haven't seen it before?" Clio asked.

Miles shook his head, his mouth a thin, grim line. "It
terrifies me to think that any portion of my house looks
this way."

"If I recall from her outburst this morning, Mariana
did not like the way your part of the house looked
either."

Miles made a sound between a groan and a snort, and
crossed toward a row of three gilded doors on his left,
leading to the three rooms they had come to search.
From the plan of the house she had studied, Clio knew
that Saunders's door was at the far left. It was unlocked,
so Miles only had to push it open. He did, waited a few
moments before entering, and when he was sure there
was no one within, motioned Clio inside.

The furniture consisted of a bed with a writing table
next to it, a large armoire and a small chaise, all done in
peacock blue silk. Besides being outraged, Saunders had
not seemed particularly sensitive about any part of his
chamber, so they had decided to go over the entire thing.
But after opening every piece of furniture that bore
opening, looking under every surface that had an under,
examining inside all the insides there were in the room,
and even sniffing every bottle of ink in Saunders's secretary box, they were forced to conclude that there was
nothing there. Miles remembered a secret compartment
in the mantelpiece that they slid open, but there was
nothing inside it, not even dust.

"I wish Toast were here," Clio sighed. "I can't believe she dressed him in a toga."

"Yes. I was unaware that there was a Baby Monkey God on Mount Olympus. But when I left he seemed to be enjoying himself."

Clio shook her head at the fickleness of males. "Which room next?"

"Why don't you take Sir Edwin and the writing desk, and I will do Doctor LaForge and the bed. I am worried about hanging around too long."

Both of these chambers were identical in furnishings and layout to that of Saunders Cotton, except that Sir Edwin's was deep forest green while Doctor LaForge's was a bright scarlet that made Miles's eyes vibrate.

He was just checking the fourth leg of Doctor La-Forge's bed to ensure it was not hollow when he heard a low whistle from Sir Edwin's room.

"Miles, come here. I've found a secret compartment in the desk," Clio called hoarsely. "I cannot get it open," she explained when he arrived, "but there is definitely something in there. You can hear it when you kick the desk. Will any of your keys work on this?"

The lock was ingeniously hidden inside the eye of what had to be a baby rabbit who, along with other baby animals, was frolicking around the bottom edge of the table. The baby rabbit's eyes were closed, but if you flicked them with your little finger, one of them slid open in a sly wink entirely unbecoming to such an innocent looking animal. Miles glared at the small gilded lock hidden beneath the eyelid, decided he probably did have a key that would fit it, but instead slipped one of the knives from his boots, jammed it in the space between the top of the desk and the location of the secret compartment, and pushed. There was a low squeak, splinters of wood fell to the floor, the baby rabbit's head cracked in two with a satisfying noise, and a drawer sprang open.

Clio and Miles stood and stared at its contents. It contained about ten medium-sized, round pebbles whose surfaces were smooth, as if from being handled frequently. Miles brought one of them to his nose, and then another. He looked bemused

"What do they smell like?"

"Rocks." He faced her. "Do you think they could be souvenirs?"

Clio shuddered. "Yes. In fact, I can't think what else they could—"

Miles clapped a hand over Clio's mouth and blew out the candle in their lantern with one move. The sound of footsteps crossing a thick carpet was faintly audible from the other room. Hidden by the darkness, they moved toward the door of Sir Edwin's room and peered around its edge.

At first Clio saw nothing, but light pressure on her shoulder from Miles's fingers showed her where to look. Her uncle was standing in the middle of the peacock chamber as if transfixed. His eyes looked large and dead. In the moonlight his face was a jumble of planes and shadows, like a misassembled puzzle. A sinister puzzle. The face of a demon.

But what caught and held Clio's eye, what made her body chill completely, made her bite her lip to keep from crying out, were his hands. Because clutched between his long fingers, he held a perfect, white, gardenia.

Miles's fingers massaged her shoulder, instinctively

holding her where she was, instinctively reassuring her. "Wait," his touch seemed to say, "you have nothing to be afraid of. I am here. Wait and watch."

Sir Edwin turned his head slowly about and for a moment Clio felt as though the dead eyes had seen her, had to have seen her, but they kept moving steadily around the room. Then he apparently found what he was looking for. Abruptly, he turned on the heel of his boots and moved toward the door of the service corridor through which Miles and Clio had entered, which now stood slightly ajar. Moving fast, faster than Clio could ever remember seeing him go, he disappeared through the door, leaving it swinging violently behind him.

Clio and Miles exchanged a look but did not speak. They had not needed to. Leaving the pebbles and decapitated baby rabbit in plain view, they had taken the same door, and had been following him ever since.

The Curious Cat was not the first place Sir Edwin had stopped, but it felt as if they had been heading there, circuitously, all along. Up until they reached the tavern, Clio and Miles had been holding hands, sneaking along walls and in shadows in order not to be seen, but always in contact. But as soon as they arrived at the Curious Cat, Miles had moved away from her, crossed his arms over his chest, and become cold and distant.

She studied his back through the misty haze closely now and saw the outline of tensed muscles. She noticed that he was clenching and unclenching his fists. "Miles, has something happened? Is something wrong?" she asked, disregarding his order not to speak.

"No."

"Could you explain then why—"

"There he is," Miles said, cutting her off. "Come on."

Clio was still puzzling over Miles's abrupt coldness as they followed Sir Edwin again into the night. She was not familiar with this part of London, and even if she had been it would have been hard to know where they were with the thickening mist sliding up from the Thames. The regular echoes of Sir Edwin's footsteps were audible even when the fog swallowed him up, and they gauged his direction and progress by those as much as by the occasional glimpses of him they caught when the air cleared.

They followed him around a corner and it seemed to grow colder and darker simultaneously. The sense of foreboding Clio had felt at the Curious Cat redoubled, and she realized that it had been some time since they had heard any sound besides Sir Edwin's footsteps, or seen even the faint outline of candlelight behind a shutter. Clio surmised they must be around the docks at Old Fish Street, where the houses had been slated for destruction and where not even the Watch patrolled any longer. It just kept getting darker and more quiet, darker and more quiet, until, abruptly, the footsteps ceased.

Miles put his hand on Clio's wrist to stop her and Clio was acutely embarrassed that he would now know her pulse was racing. Without releasing her arm, he moved forward, taking her with him. They were about halfway down a narrow street. Up ahead, where it junctioned with a wider one, they had seen Sir Edwin turn to the right.

Soundlessly, their backs pressed against the street walls of the houses, they inched forward, toward the corner. Miles put himself in front of Clio, and was almost close enough to peer around when a sound like a wail pierced the air.

It came again, shattering the silence, and Clio realized it was not a wail at all. It was a laugh. Somewhere a girl was laughing in a high falsetto. And then she began to sing, her voice creaky and strangely thick. She ran the words together, but Clio had no trouble making them out.

"The first time I did see you dear, my heart in me did pound. I knew that day as I know now, that my true love I'd found," the girl sang tunelessly, and the words seemed to come from all around them. There was something terrible about it, about the sound, something desperate and unnerving about the way it echoed and multiplied off the walls around them. *Found-hound-ound*, it rebounded, as if it were surrounding them, following them. Hunting them.

"Where is it?" Clio demanded feverishly. "Where is it?"

Miles did not reply at first and Clio was suddenly filled with the horrible thought that maybe she was the only one who heard the ghastly music, that it was some figment of her imagination like that expression of horror on the face of the first victim, that the vampire was somehow—

"I don't know," Miles replied. "It seems to be coming from all around."

Relief washed over Clio but only for a moment because the singing started again, louder, more piercing.

"The second time our lips did meet"—it was closer now—*"t'was better than the first."* Much closer. *"I felt*

the air float under me, and like me heart would burst."
Burst-cursed-cursed, Clio heard, and felt like the word
was pressing down on them—*cursed cursed cursed*—
chasing them, seeking them out, leading the Vampire to
them.

Suddenly she understood why it was so horrible. "It's a
man," she whispered to Miles. "It is a man singing like a
girl—" but before she could finish the unnerving laughter
came again, the fake, clunky, pretend laughter, like the
laughter of a wicked child in the face of punishment. It
was coming for them, getting louder and louder, more
and more harsh. She could hear it getting closer, could
hear footsteps, it sounded like three sets of them, coming
and the laughter above them and suddenly the hair on
her arms stood up and it was right behind her. If she
turned around she would see it, but if she did not it
would have her. She swung around, her mouth open to
cry out, her arms coming up to ward off whatever it was.

Nothing. There was nothing. Only mist, curling and
twisting in the street behind them, thick and noxious.

She stood staring at it for a moment, watching as it
furled and unfurled itself in endless eddies. She felt as if
she were rooted to the ground by a supernatural force,
utterly unable to move. And as she watched, a form took
shape in the middle of one of the eddies, first a shoulder.
A leg. A torso. Finally a head. It had not been there a moment ago, it appeared as if generated by the mist itself, a
creature of vapor. A creature of horror. One moment
nothing, the next a man, from nowhere. A demon.

A demon with long, thin fingers, pale and white in the
scrap of moon, appearing and disappearing as the mist
swirled, long fingers still clutching a gardenia. They
reached out, straining toward her, toward her neck.

"Clio, Clio, Clio," it said in a voice that was a death rattle. "You should not have come, Clio. I will have to take you home now."

On the word "home" Sir Edwin opened his mouth wide, and the horrible, mirthless laugh rebounded off the walls of the street with crushing volume.

Clio screamed.

Chapter 19

"No," Sir Edwin said, coming toward Clio fast. "You mustn't scream, he won't like that." He had his fingers touching her lips, his palm over her mouth one moment, and then next he was collapsed in a pile on the ground with the gardenia lying next to him.

Clio spent an instant panting and staring down at the body, then felt Miles's arms close around her and she began to tremble.

"It's all right, *amore*, he cannot hurt you," he whispered into her head as he hugged her hard. "You have to believe me. Have to trust me. Because we don't have much time before he wakes up and there is a good deal we need to do."

"He isn't dead?" Clio asked, and she did not know if she felt relief or dread.

"No. Only momentarily knocked out." He would have to thank Sebastian again for teaching him that trick. "We have about a quarter of an hour before he regains consciousness and we can talk to him." He looked down at her. "I want to go in that building over there," he gestured with his chin to a structure a few yards down the street. "Would you like to come or stay here?"

"Come," she answered instantaneously.

The door of the building was closed but opened easily when Miles pushed it with his foot. They paused on the threshold and Miles reached into his doublet and produced a tinderbox and a stump of candle. He got it lit and held it up.

The entire structure consisted of a single room. Clio had been wrong in thinking that no one lived in the neighborhood, because it was clear that someone had been living there. Crumbs from a meal recent enough not yet to have been devoured by mice were still scattered over the top of a table, a plate and tankard were stacked neatly in a corner, a cracked bit of mirror hung on the wall, and a pile of straw had been covered with a thin blanket as a makeshift mattress.

But more interesting was the second door, the one opposite that through which they entered, which was swinging open. Miles poked his head out, then came back in.

"That explains Sir Edwin's miraculous entrance. One of these doors opens onto the next street and he must have come from there. In the mist it looked like he had just appeared, but really, he had come through a door."

It had looked so real.

Clio struggled to bring her rational mind into control. Sir Edwin had come through a door. He had not been generated by the mist. When they went outside he would still be there, he would not have disappeared, he—

"Clio," the death rattle voice called out from the street, through the door. "Clio, where are you?"

Miles went out in front of her. Sir Edwin was sitting up in the middle of the street looking dazed and rubbing his neck.

"What did you do to me, Your Lordship?" he asked Miles. "Never felt anything like that."

"Be careful, Miles," Clio called from the doorway. "Don't get too close to him."

Sir Edwin turned around and looked at her. "Ah, there you are, Clio. They said you were dead, but I knew better."

"How?" Miles demanded.

"Went to Newgate myself, didn't I? I can't think why that fellow used her name to get arrested, though," Sir Edwin mused to himself. "I suppose he had a perfectly fit name of his own."

Miles nodded at this bit of insight. "Why didn't you tell Lady Alecia and Mariana that Clio was alive?"

"Man's got to have secrets," Sir Edwin replied with a ghoulish smile. "But I did tell them later. Mother was so upset."

"Did you tell them you are the vampire?" Clio asked, emerging from the dark building.

Sir Edwin lost all color. "What are you saying, Clio? What are you saying?"

Miles tried a different approach. "What made you decide to come out tonight?"

"Why, I was following him."

"Who?" Miles and Clio said in unison.

"The whistling man. I thought I had him, too."

"Whistling man?" Miles repeated, pronouncing the words carefully.

"Yes. Man who stands outside my window whistling all night. Well, he wasn't there last night, but every other night. And I could not figure it out, because Doctor LaForge said he never heard him. But you will agree with me, Viscount, that is simply not possible, what with his window and my window being almost the same window, and on the same side of the house, won't you?"

Miles took a moment to recollect the placement of the rooms and had to agree that anything Sir Edwin heard, Doctor LaForge would also have to hear. "Yes."

"So, I said to myself, this is very curious. And then it comes to me. Doctor LaForge doesn't hear the whistling man because he *is* the whistling man. So I came out here tonight to follow him and see if he whistles at anyone else's windows. And when I catch him, I'll say 'hey!' and make him stop."

"You were following Doctor LaForge," Clio asked. It was the longest and most coherent speech she had ever heard from her uncle, but it made almost no sense.

"Exactly. Following Doctor LaForge."

"And was it a success? Did you catch him whistling."

Sir Edwin shook his head. "Not once. Singing, yes, singing aplenty. And in that high voice. Don't know what he was thinking of. But whistling? No. Not once."

"So you followed Doctor LaForge from Dearbourn Hall," Miles began.

"And then we went to that place, that Cat place. And he goes and talks to about half the women, chatting them up, but doesn't do anything. Then, wouldn't you know, just as I settled into a bit of ale—not bad, neither. You'd think at a place like that they'd water it down, but not a bit, I tell you. Not that I get to drink that much ale, what with Mother watching me all the time and—where was I?"

"Ale," Miles reminded him. "You were drinking at the Curious Cat."

"Right. I'd taken only one sip before that LaForge fellow goes and leaves." Sir Edwin reached up and scratched his chin. "I wonder if I paid for that tankard. My, it was delicious. Anyhow, off he goes and off I go after him, and we go here and there and in a big bold circle and then I follow him into that house, but it's so dark inside I get myself mixed up and by the time I've put myself right, he's gone and then, out of nowhere, comes you two. I was so startled, I began to laugh like you heard."

"Where did you get the gardenia?" Clio, who had moved to stand next to and just behind Miles, asked.

Sir Edwin looked down at the flower and a childlike smile covered his lips. "I found it on the ground. In that room Mariana decorated with all the feathers. Someone just dropped it, I reckon." He held it out toward Miles and Clio. "Isn't it beautiful? Smells like angels, I swear it does."

There was an awkward pause, and then Miles said, "Would I be wrong in guessing that this was not your first attempt to rid yourself of the whistling man?"

"No, sir, you would not. I tried more direct measures—"

"Such as?" Miles interjected.

"Such as pelting him with rocks. Yes I did, for three nights. But then I lost the key to my desk and couldn't get at 'em. Not that it made much difference—when I did use the pebbles, they didn't work at all. He just kept right on whistling."

"*The pebbles,*" Clio murmured and Miles nodded. "That is what they were for. Not souvenirs." She paused. "Then uncle Edwin is not the vampire."

"No," Miles agreed, "it certainly looks like he is not."

"But you said you were sure it was him," Clio reminded Miles.

"What I meant was that I was sure whomever led us to the Curious Cat was the vampire."

"Which means, if Uncle Edwin was following Doctor LaForge—"

"Exactly."

"Then we should find him. He must still be here. Somewhere."

Miles gestured widely at the thickening mist. "Two people do not stand a chance against him, especially since I am fairly sure he knows we'll be looking for him."

"Why? How could he know we are here?"

"Above and beyond the fact that he could be listening in the shadows right now, I think he knew we were behind him the entire time." Clio opened her mouth to ask him another question but Miles went on without seeming to notice. "I think our best bet would be to find a member of the Watch and have him call out constables to patrol this area. While they are doing that, I will go to the Curious Cat and find out who LaForge was speaking to and if he left with anyone."

"I'll go with you," Sir Edwin, whose head had been rotating from one to the other as they spoke, volunteered happily. "Tell you the truth, I've got a fancy for another tankard of that ale afore I go home." He hesitated for a moment, as if on the brink of speaking, then blurted, "You won't tell Mother will you?"

They accompanied Sir Edwin back to the Curious Cat, alerting a watchman to the presence of a prowler in the neighborhood along the way. Giving Clio stiff instructions to wait for him outside, Miles entered the tavern accompanied by Sir Edwin. As soon as their backs had disappeared through the door, Clio followed him through. She was not in the mood to take orders from anyone.

She stepped across the threshold and found herself in a long, skinny, but otherwise perfectly ordinary tavern. There was nothing about it to explain its strange fascination for the vampire, or its dangerous effect on Miles. She was just about to stop one of the hostesses and ask if perhaps there wasn't another area devoted to something more exciting than drinking, when she felt Miles's eyes on her.

She was stunned by his reaction. She had just raised her hand to wave at him when he crossed the tavern in three great strides, took her wrist in his hand, and dragged her out.

In the street she could see that he was breathing quickly, and that his lips were pressed into a single tight line, but even when she tried she could not get him to stop walking.

"Where are we going?" Clio asked after they had careened down the street for a minute.

"Dearbourn Hall." His mouth barely moved as he formed the words, and he increased his pace, dragging Clio behind him faster.

"Don't you think we should stay here and assist in the search for Doctor LaForge," Clio ventured.

"No," came the reply.

"I do," Clio told him, almost running to catch up. "And you still have not told me why you are so certain that whomever led us to the Curious Cat is the vampire."

"I will tell you when we get to Dearbourn Hall," Miles muttered. They stalked the rest of the way home in silence, Clio acutely aware that something was wrong. Despite their speed, the house was almost entirely dark by the time they reached it. They entered through the stable yard, and instead of taking the servant's stairs up to his wing, Miles stopped in the large, stone kitchen, in front of the smoldering cooking fire. All the servants had gone to bed and they had the cavernous chamber to themselves.

"Sit down and stay there. I will be right back," he said to Clio, pointing her toward a stool at the wide wooden table alongside the fire, and there was something in his tone that made her comply. He disappeared for about five minutes, and when he returned he stood studying the remains of the fire, so that as he spoke she saw only his back. "You asked how I knew it was the vampire who took us to the Curious Cat tonight," he began without prompting. "I knew, because that is where he found Beatrice three years ago."

"Wh—?" Clio began to ask, but Miles cut her off.

"After I found Bea dead, I retraced her steps. She had gone to the Curious Cat. I learned that after she left there a man asked questions about her, and seemed ready to follow her. That man was the vampire."

Miles's tone was horribly devoid of emotion, and Clio tried to keep hers equally colorless. "I see. That is why you think he knew we were following him, because he led us there. Do you think he intended it as another sign, another challenge, like the one he left in the *Compendium*?"

Miles did not reply, merely shrugged and continued to study the fire. A clock nearby clicked monotonously, once, twice, three times, until the silence stretched to five minutes. Unable to stand the palpable distance between them, Clio rose and reached out to touch Miles's arm.

He reacted as if he had been stung. He brushed her

fingers away, and rounded on her. "Don't do that," he said in a low, almost menacing voice.

"Do not push me away, Miles," Clio urged. "I can tell that you are still upset about what happened to Beatrice, but maybe I can help you."

"No one can help. No one can change what happened. Only I could have. But I didn't."

Clio struggled with a pang of pure jealousy. What would it be like to have been loved as much as Miles loved Beatrice, to be missed as much as he obviously missed her, she asked herself. "Beatrice's death was not your fault, Miles."

"Wasn't it?" Miles demanded fiercely, facing towards her.

"How could it have been? She went to the Curious Cat on her own. How were you to know the vampire would see her there and follow her?"

"If it wasn't for me, she would never have gone to the Curious Cat."

"You sent her there?" Clio asked, confused. "You sent your mistress to a tavern?"

Miles pined her with his eyes. "Beatrice was not my mistress, Clio. She was my sister. My illegitimate sister. I learned about her only after my parents' deaths, when I saw provisions for her support in my father's will."

"But everyone said she was your mistress. Everyone thought—"

Miles waved her words away with an impatient hand. "People believe what they see. Everybody just assumed she was my mistress because we spent all our time together, and neither of us thought it was important to dispel that. It meant people left us alone. And we had so much catching up to do. There was so much—" Miles broke off, and his eyes got a faraway look in them. "My father had not treated Beatrice and her mother well. He had not told her mother that he was married when he seduced her. When she became pregnant, he promised to leave my mother, promised to get a divorce, promised to marry, promised a host of things he never did. Never had any intention of doing, apparently. He left Bea a modest income but nothing else—no family, no name. Her mother's family, an old Devonshire clan, threw them out when Bea was born because of the shame they brought. Bea always felt like her mother blamed her for wrecking her life."

When her confusion at the information that Beatrice was not Miles's mistress cleared, Clio saw that her being his sister made everything far worse. "I am so sorry, Miles. You must have loved her very much."

Miles's eyes refocused on Clio and he nodded. "You should have seen her, Clio. You would have liked her. She was lovely. And sweet. And she had the nicest voice. But she also had a terrible temper. Her governess, who raised her after her mother died, warned me about Bea's temper. Said she thought deep down there was anger inside of Beatrice, anger at her father and her mother, anger at everyone for abandoning her, and that sometimes a little of it leaked out. But I saw no sign of it, at least not for the first six months we were together. Then, one night, I came home and found our apartments destroyed. She had pulled down the window hangings and cut open the couches and shredded her dresses. And she sat in the middle of this mess she had made, sobbing. I tried to hold her, comfort her, but she flinched away. When I asked her what was wrong, she said she was miserable. She said that she no longer knew who she was.

She couldn't be a simple country girl anymore, not with all I had shown her and given her, but she also felt she could never really fit into aristocratic society because everyone would know about her, about her being illegitimate. She said that by giving her all these things, showing her another way to live, I had destroyed any chance she had at happiness. She said I ruined her, ruined her life, the same way that my father had ruined her mother. She said I was just like our father."

Miles stopped and looked down at his hands. His fingers were clenched into tight fists, and he willed himself to open them. "She said that I had promised to make her happy but that I had lied, that she was unhappy, desperately unhappy. Just like my father had made her mother. She said she wished I had never found her, that I would just leave, just leave her alone. So I did. I left. Even though I knew I should stay."

"Miles, there was—" Clio broke in, but he silenced her.

"She followed me, Clio. When her rage cooled she went to all the taverns she could find, went into each of them, looking for me. Only, she did not find me. But the vampire found her. And then, the next day, so did I— dead. Do you know what else I found?"

Clio shook her head mutely.

"I found notes. In every one of the taverns she visited. Notes she left. Apologizing to me for what she had said and begging me to come back." Miles stood very still, his face a shadowy mask. "If I had not failed, Clio, if I had not failed to make her happy, to protect her, she would still be alive."

"That is not true, Miles."

"You would not understand," Miles told her coldly.

"I do understand. I understand that you did not fail to

make her happy, that she was happy, or she never would have followed you to apologize. And I understand that you are blaming yourself for something that you had no control over. The vampire killed Beatrice. Not you, Miles."

"He would not have gotten near her if—"

"If what? If she had not gotten angry? Or if your father had not abandoned her and her mother all those years earlier?"

Miles stared at Clio and she felt as if she were watching her words seep into his mind, into his thoughts, watching them wend themselves into his consciousness. Then she saw his eyes go blank. "You are right. I cannot erase my father's mistakes. But I can avoid them." He looked at her with those blank eyes. "I think it is time for us to end our involvement."

"What?" Clio whispered in a voice that faltered. "Are you—" She stopped, as if the words repulsed her. "Are you saying that I am a mistake?"

"No. But it would be a mistake to allow this to go any farther."

Clio lowered herself onto the tabletop, her knees suddenly unreliable. "What do you mean? How much farther could it go?" Her mind cleared and understanding hit her like a bolt of searing pain. "I see. You could start to feel something for me. You might start to care about me. And then if something happened to me, you would feel bad. By all means, we should end it before you have to *feel* anything. End it right now."

"I am glad you agree."

Clio stared at him incredulously, his words seeming to come to her from a great distance. "What is this? Some sort of torture? You make me tell you a hundred times that I love you, make me humiliate myself by saying it, admitting it, over and over again, and then you turn away from me?" Her voice shook.

"Don't be ridiculous. You knew this could not go on forever."

"Not forever. But for three more days. It does not have to end yet. And not like this."

Miles looked confused. "What difference does that make? Why not now? Why not like this?"

"My God, I never dreamed you could be so cruel."

"It is good that you are learning it now."

"No, it is not. I am not learning it. I refuse to learn it. *I will not learn it.* And I will tell you something else, Miles Fraser Loredan. It is too late. You already care about me. I know you do. Because I love you and I would never have fallen in love with the man you are now pretending to be." Her voice took on a cool sheen. "Isn't it ironic that the more afraid you are of acting like your father the more like him you become? The more selfish? The more hurtful?"

"Stop it, Clio. Can't you see that I am only trying to protect you?"

Clio laughed mirthlessly. "Do not lie to yourself, Miles. I do not need a guard dog. It is yourself you are trying to protect. It is yourself you are afraid of hurting."

"No," Miles said, shaking his head. "No. It is you. I don't want to hurt you, Clio. But I will—it is inevitable. I will never be able to give you what you deserve."

"Why not?" she demanded and a sliver of despair cut through her cool mockery.

"Because I am as good as married to your cousin," Miles said with a flash of anger.

"But I am not asking you to marry me, Miles. I just

want to be with you. Now." Despair took over entirely. "Why can't we be together now? For the time that remains? How can you hurt me when I know it will all have to end? I have never asked you for anything you could not give me."

It was true, Miles knew, but still he shook his head. "It would not work."

"Why?" Clio demanded and implored at once.

Miles was quiet for a moment. Then, in a voice barely steady, he said, "I could not love you for three days, Clio. I could only love you forever. And forever is not mine to give."

Clio stared at him, stunned. "What are you saying, Miles?"

"That it would be better if you went. Now. Better for both of us."

Clio nodded to herself quietly and rose from the table on unsteady legs. She started moving toward the door that led to the stables but stopped, her heart leaping up, when Miles spoke behind her. He was going to stop her, he was going to say this had all been a terrible mistake, he was going to tell her, in his warm, husky voice, that he did not want her to go.

But what he said was: "Why don't you stay here until the coach is ready? You will be warmer."

I will never be warmer, Clio thought to herself, her heart thudding back down. She shook her head. "I would rather walk home, anyway." She reached the door and, with her fingers trembling on the latch, turned around to face him one final time. He might lie to himself, but she was not going to, not going to lie to either of them. "I want you to know that my memories of the time we stole together are the most precious thing I have. The days I spent with you, Miles, were the very best days of my life." She swallowed hard and added, "I guess you were right. Nothing perfect can endure. Good-bye."

Miles was surprised at how easily it happened. The control mechanism he had spent so many years refining within himself shifted out of balance and he let it go. He knew it was going to cost him too much, that it was going to cause him unimaginable pain, but knew it was worth it. Only a madman would refuse such a gift. He crossed the room, wrapped Clio in his arms, and said, "They were the best days of my life, too, *amore*. I have been a fool. Please don't leave. I never want you to leave me."

Chapter 20

Clio later wondered if they would have behaved differently had they known that one of them had only fifty-eight hours to live, and she decided that they would not have changed anything.

Miles brought his mouth down over hers and kissed her with a force that seared through her, illuminating every sinew in her body until she felt like she must be glowing. They stood in the middle of the kitchen like that, lost in one another's embrace, in one another's need.

The clock behind them struck three, and Miles pulled away from her lips. Pain flickered across his face for an instant, then disappeared, doused by her smile. They stood quietly apart, holding hands, as they listened to the chimes. Time was too precious now to waste in anything besides pleasure.

Clio reached up, brushed the lock of hair off Miles's forehead, and said, "I read in a book once that, after the strain of battle, the soldiers of the Roman Empire could consume twice their weight in food."

Miles smiled despite himself. "Plutarch only wrote that as propaganda to get more money for the troops from the penny-pinching Roman senators," he said, distractedly rubbing his chin against the crown of her head.

"Perhaps," Clio conceded. "But he gave a very per-suasive example in which the soldiers grew faint from lack of sustenance and were taken as captives by the very people they had just captured."

"Ah," Miles commented with complete unconcern. "I don't quite remember that part. Did he, in this example, give any idea of what these soldiers liked to eat?"

"Their favorite thing was hazelnut cake," Clio ex-plained. "But they would be happy eating anything. After battle."

"And do you feel as though you just fought a battle, *amore*?"

"No. I feel as though I just single-handedly waged an entire war."

"Against whom?"

"Your past. Time. Fate. The universe." She waved a hand at the forces arrayed against her.

Miles pulled away slightly and let his glorious golden eyes rest on hers. No one had ever struggled for him be-fore. He was always the one doing the fighting, doing the protecting. It was an odd feeling. And, he found, he did not mind. "Thank you, Clio."

The power of his gaze was melting her. "For what?"

"For fighting. For winning."

You do not know what you are the voice in Clio's head reminded her, but with Miles's eyes on her, she did. She was a conquering hero. She had never felt as strong or as happy as she did in that moment. "You are welcome."

Miles smiled and his tone lightened. "We had better prepare a feast for the victor before she perishes."

Clio nodded, then stopped. "Do you think we should check to see if Doctor LaForge came back here first?"

"That is what I did when we first got home," Miles

assured her as he moved around the kitchen, peering into cupboards. "I also stationed a guard in his room should he decide to sneak in for anything. I gave the orders as soon as we returned." He studied the items he had laid out on the table. "No hazelnut cake. Ah, but this should do well."

"What is it?" Clio asked, straining to see.

"Surprise," Miles replied, touching the bellows near the flames a few times. Then he took a small copper pot from its hook on the wall, dropped into it a handful of deep red dried cherries, filled it with sweet wine from a ceramic pitcher, and hung the entire thing over the newly awakened fire.

He turned to Clio, who had seated herself on one of the stools while he worked. "Stand up," he ordered with mock ferocity, and she did. He walked around her, as if inspecting her footman's uniform, and shook his head. "This does not fit you at all. You will have to remove it."

Clio looked at him. "Here? You want me to undress here?"

"We have harsh punishments for footmen who do not obey their master," Miles warned her.

"But someone might come in at any moment."

"Not likely. Sirus, my cook, hates to be up before six bells and the rest of the staff only get to work an hour before that. We have at least two hours to ourselves. Now start, or I shall have to do it for you."

Behind him, the mixture in the pot began to give off a fabulously aromatic smell, sweet and warm, and intoxicating. Miles turned around to stir it and remove it from the fire, and when he turned back, Clio was sitting on the edge of the table before him, entirely naked.

She was extraordinary. His body sizzled with desire,

his member straining hard against his breeches. "Lie down," he ordered, moving alongside her and placing the pot on a stool.

She hesitated for a moment, until Miles dipped his finger into the warm liquid, brushed it against her lips, and then covered them with his.

"Delicious," she murmured, "More."

"Only if you do as you are told," Miles taunted her, and she lay down. The table felt cool and hard beneath her bare bottom, and curiously exciting. It was smooth from years of oiling, and smelled faintly of sandalwood.

Miles took a long thin cookie from a platter he had placed on another stool and dipped it into the pot, then held it over Clio's lips. She nipped at it lightly at first, then hungrily as the flavors of the cherry-infused sweet wine and the caraway and nutmeg of the cookie mingled on her tongue. He fed her three more and she felt her body grow warm. She thought at first it was from the wine, but she realized after that Miles was using his other hand to trace long, warm lines over her chest and down her stomach. The heat was concentrated with fabulous intensity on her nipples and between her legs, and she saw as she craned her neck up that he had placed small groups of the warm cherries there, glistening with wine in the firelight.

"Open your mouth," Miles ordered and when Clio complied, he slipped one of the wine-soaked fruits between her lips. Then, he moved his mouth over her left nipple, and carefully corralled a deep red cherry into his mouth, using only the tip of his tongue.

Clio's senses were saturated. Her eyes were riveted on where his mouth touched her body, her skin was overcome with the slow, warm caresses of his tongue, her mouth was suffused with a delicious sweetness, her nose was filled with the exotic perfume made from the mingled scents of sandalwood, warm white wine, and her arousal, and her ears rang with the sound of her moans. She watched as he suckled the last of the cherries off her breasts, letting his tongue trace a wide hot circle across her erect nipple, then gasped as his mouth moved lower. She knew what would happen next and the excitement, the expectation, almost made her climax before he touched her.

But her thoughts were nothing compared with reality. His teeth came down over the vermilion cherries and her sensitive jewel simultaneously, enfolding them together in his lips. The cherries in his mouth moved in a circle around her nub, rolling over it and hugging it and tugging at it as Miles applied more pressure, always letting his tongue rest hot and wet on its very tip. Miles bit into one of the cherries and the warm wine flowed around her. Miles gulped it down, gulped her, and Clio felt her sanity, her reason, her life, take flight. She clawed the table. "Don't stop," she moaned, begging. She was so close, this was it. But instead of complying, Miles pulled away, brushing his cheek against her thigh, leaving her trembling with desire.

That did it. Clio was out for revenge. She sat up and dragged his face to hers.

"You will pay for that," she told him, her lips on his, sampling the flavor of her and wine and cherries all together.

"What are you talking abo—?" he began to ask, then felt her hands on his breeches. She had no trouble undoing the laces—she ripped them—and she pushed the fabric to the floor with her feet. His boots came off next and then her fingers went to work on his jacket, and soon he was out of that as well, standing before her entirely naked.

His rock hard member stood at attention in front of his body, but Clio was more enamoured of the wonderful curves and valleys of his chest and stomach. He simply got more beautiful each time she laid eyes on him, and she found herself almost overwhelmed by his power. And by the fact that, for now, he was hers.

She slid off the table and stood in front of him. "Lie down," she ordered.

Her eyes were more purple than Miles ever remembered seeing them, and his desire for her a hundred times more intense. Nothing he had ever done made him worthy to possess her, he knew, and knew that meant he had to cherish her that much more. He climbed onto the table and lay down.

Clio lay on her side next to him. She dangled her fingers over his chest and warm wine dripped from the tips like a hot summer rain. Miles was surprised it did not boil as it hit his hot skin. She leaned over his body to lap at the drops, her breasts brushing over his chest, and Miles reached around and hauled her on top of him.

"I want to be inside of you," he said. "Now. Please."

But Clio only smiled mischievously and shook her head. "You were in charge before. Now it is my turn. Let me go or you will regret it."

"How," Miles queried. "What will you do?"

"Learn at your own peril."

The idea was tempting, but temptation, as well as everything else, left Miles's mind as Clio plunged her fingers in the warm wine and then ran them in long smooth strokes up the entire length of his member. She sat up and straddled his chest, facing away from him, so that he could not see her front, or what she was doing to him. He felt her hands, both of them, sliding up his shaft, felt her palms form a small tight cup over his tip before spreading to let him through, felt her body growing wetter on his chest as he responded to her touch, finally felt her bend forward and encase his organ between the soft globes of her breasts.

She slid backwards, going up on her knees so she was not straddling him any longer, but kneeling above him. Miles could see now, could see her nipples, hard, dangling over his stomach, could see her mouth go coasting down over his member. Pleasure made him squeeze his eyes shut for a moment, but fascination opened them again. She moved her lips over his body slowly, and he could see the indentations in her cheeks as she sucked him in. Above him, her body glistened with arousal, and as she joined her hand to her mouth to stroke him more entirely, he craned his neck up and kissed the swollen bud of her body.

Clio moaned against his member and he did it again, loving the vibrations that his pleasuring caused in her mouth. Her lips tightened around him, sucking him in harder, her tongue lapped at his tip as it passed by, and at the same time he sucked her in, sliding a finger inside her as his tongue grazed over her with his teeth. Each time she stroked him with her mouth he returned the caress with his. Clio pulled his entire length into her mouth, cradling him from below with both her hands, making a ring of her thumb and index finger to pull him taut, and moved up and down with quickening pressure, until his groans resonated between her legs. He spread her bottom wide and traced the valley between its two halves with one finger, pressing against the sensitive place just below her opening as the fingers of his other hand tickled her and his lips suckled at her tiny tip, and he felt her mouth tighten around him in a gasp.

They soared together, each moment of pleasure echoing through the other's body, more intimately aware of one another than they had ever been, until the coils of their desire were wound so tight that they could no longer bear it. Clio felt Miles grow bigger inside her mouth, felt his body pull up toward her, and she sucked at him harder, running her fingers behind her lips, from the very base to the tip, twirling her tongue around him, moaning as he licked her back, until Miles surrendered, shooting himself into her mouth, pressing and gasping and hollering, "I love you, Clio."

It was the feel of his lips forming those words against her body, of him shouting it into her, around her, while he sucked her, that sent Clio spinning helplessly out of control. Still savoring the sweet taste of him, she pulled her mouth from his spent organ and pressed her body against his lips until he said it again and again, his tongue and teeth converging around her on the word "love," his lips curving and tightening around her bud on the word "you." "I love you, I love you," he repeated, over and over into her, propelling her into such a shattering, roaring, powerful explosion that she was astonished the entirety of Dearbourn Hall did not tumble down around her, kennels and all.

I love you, she heard echoed through her ears and through her body. She let herself hold onto the words, for just one moment, let herself hug them to her mind, as she slid away from Miles's mouth and settled herself alongside him on the table, her head pointing toward his feet. She knew he had not meant the words, could not mean them the way she did (it had felt so real), knew they were something you said at the height of passion, but that only dimmed their luster slightly. *I love you,* she heard him say again in her head one final time as she rested her neck on his thigh and he leaned his cheek against her. Then she pushed the words from her mind, closed her eyes—

And said, "Spaniels!"

Using every ounce that was left of his energy, Miles half opened one eye. "Have you solved the case? Do you know where Doctor LaForge is hiding?"

"No. But I know who killed your guard dogs," Clio replied.

Miles displayed his astonishment by half opening his other eye. "Who?"

"The vampire. It happened the last time as well. If you look over the accounts of his activities, you will see that just before and at the beginning of his killing spree, an inordinate quantity of dogs around London died. There were reports in the news sheets about the large number of dead stray dogs, and the occasional obituary for a pampered pet. Those obituaries always said the dogs died of mysterious causes. Nobody made the connection to the vampire at the time, but now . . ." her voice trailed off. "Does anything about how your dogs died contradict this?"

Miles blinked. "I do not think so. My dogs began to die two weeks before the vampire appeared, just after Mariana and her party arrived. The first to die did so slowly—we found them lying about listlessly and then several hours later they died. The last two were different. There were no scuff marks in the dirt around them to indicate protracted death throes, so we assumed they died on the spot. That is part of what has been confusing us, the different manners of death. The dog keepers assured us it was not in their food, and the victims did not appear to have been strangled."

"It could just be a coincidence, but I doubt it. Did you look for wounds on the dogs' bodies?"

"No. Only marks that they had been tortured. Do you really think the vampire was drinking their blood as well?"

"I don't know. It does not make sense according to the *Compendium*, since I have never heard of anyone being nursed by a dog. But the parallels are very striking. Is there any chance we could look at the body of one of the dogs?"

"Yes. My dog keeper buried them in the corner of the stable yard. I can have them exhumed tomorrow. I can't promise he'll be thrilled about it, though."

"No, I don't imagine it will smell very good, either. But if there are puncture wounds at least it would clear up the mystery of how they died."

"I thought you did not work on cases involving dogs," Miles told her wryly.

Clio elbowed him. "How hard would it have been for someone staying at the house to get at the dogs?"

"Easy. Anyone could have gone to the kennels without arousing suspicion. As a matter of fact, Mariana and her entourage spent a good deal of time out there when she first arrived."

"That is strange," Clio said with a frown. "Mariana hates dogs. The reason I bit her when we were younger was because she was torturing one. I wonder what she was doing out there."

Now Miles really got energetic. He raised his head and looked at Clio. "I believe it was her tutor's idea. Unless I misremember, Corin told me that Doctor LaForge was teaching her the names of the species. One of the prerequisites of being a good aristocratic wife." He reached for Clio's hand as he said the last words and held it tight. Then he released it slightly. "Do you remember, two days ago, when there was no victim and we had expected there to be one?"

Clio nodded.

"Doctor LaForge was ill that day," Miles rushed on. "He did not get out of bed at all."

"Ill like the vampire would be if he had not drunk enough blood," Clio put in.

"Precisely. And the next day, after Lady Starrat's body had been found, he was fine. As a matter of fact, I think Bianca described his recovery as 'miraculous'."

"That seems to confirm it then." Clio paused, then shook her head sadly. "I wish I had figured this out earlier. Then we would have known it was someone in your household right away and we would not have wasted any time. Two girls—possibly more—died because I was not smart enough."

Miles sat up, reached for Clio, and pulled her to his chest. "You did not kill those girls. The vampire did," he told her, repeating her earlier assurances to him. "But you did make it possible to capture him."

"Hopefully. I hope that when we search his chamber tomorrow, we find proof of his guilt. And perhaps a hint about where he is hiding. And then it will be over."

Miles nodded, and they subsided into silence for a moment. Clio was about to fall asleep when she became aware of his eyes on her face.

"What is wrong, Miles?" she asked, propping her chin on his chest.

"Did you mean that? Really? That the days you spent with me were the best of your life? That—" he paused, mustering his courage, all the courage he had. "Did you mean that you love me?"

Clio looked at him wondering how he could not know. Instead of answering, she took his hand and laid it on her chest, where her heart was suddenly pounding furiously.

"I, Clio Thornton, dedicate my heart to you, Miles Loredan," she said solemnly. "It is, and will always be, yours. Only yours. For as long as it continues to beat."

4 hours after midnight. Moon—one degree less than quarter full. Waning.

Which was almost exactly fifty-seven hours.

In his room at the Painted Lady, Doctor LaForge, the man known as the Vampire of London, waited.

At Dearbourn Hall, the search was underway. Forced to remain invisible, Clio stayed in Miles's apartments, avidly collecting each piece of information Corin brought her, concentrating hard in order to keep her mind from wandering back to the previous night.

Every crevice of Doctor LaForge's room was probed, every rug looked under. The floorboards and wall paneling were dismantled. The bed was slashed to ribbons. His armoire was disassembled down to the last hinge. But this proved to be unnecessary, for the clues were lying in plain view.

His clothes were shown to have been padded to conceal his real figure. He had a paste that was known to be used for adhering false mustaches. He had the lost key to Sir Edwin's desk. All of his books were found to be in English, including some translated from the French, showing that he was not a foreigner at all. With the help of Toast—who had fallen from Mariana's good graces when he nearly ruined the strand of pearls she was using as his leash during the ball the previous night by trying to eat it—they found a blue kerchief hidden among the tutor's papers that was identical to the one Clio had found next to the first body.

Perhaps most damning of all was the white linen shirt, crumpled in a ball in the back of his armoire, that was covered with a brown stain that could only be dried blood. It turned out that there was an even more important and obvious piece of evidence, but the searchers did not find that until later.

In his room at the Painted Lady, Doctor LaForge worried.

"I never really liked him, you know," Mariana confided to the footman who Miles assigned to question her. "He was always collecting me."

"Correcting you," Lady Alecia told her. "And you know it was only for your own good. I thought he was rather a nice man when we met him in Paris." She did not add that he had nicely advanced her a rather large sum to cover a gaming debt she had accrued. That came out only later.

"Well, I don't think I needed a tutor," Mariana pouted. "And I am certain I learned more from Saunders than I did from Doctor LaForge."

"Please do not say that, Lady Mariana," Saunders said stiffly, color rising in his face. "You wrong the Doctor, Lady Mariana, and overestimate me. I would not want anyone to get the idea that I overstep my role."

"It's all right, Saunders," Mariana assured him with a coy look. "There is no need for you to be so modest. Doctor LaForge did not know the first thing about clothes or jewels. Everything important I know, I learned from you and you cannot deny it, you baby goose."

In his chair next to the chess table, alone now that his partner was gone, Sir Edwin shook his head. "What's a vampire want with whistling, I ask you?" he murmured to himself. "Don't make any sense at all."

In his room at the Painted Lady, Doctor LaForge fidgeted.

The fourth victim of the Vampire was found at two in the afternoon, in an abandoned building near the docks on Old Fish Street, lying on a mattress that consisted of a pile of straw with a thin blanket over it. Crumbs from a recent meal were still scattered on the table, a plate and tankard were neatly stacked in the corner, and a broken piece of mirror hung from the wall.

She was one of the hostesses from the Curious Cat and had been found in the exact room Clio and Miles had seen, the one that Doctor LaForge led Sir Edwin through. As if he had known they were behind him the entire time. As if he were taunting them.

In his room at the Painted Lady, Doctor LaForge fumed.

At four in the afternoon, the dog keeper completed his examination of the last of Miles's dead guard dogs. He had discovered that each of the dead animals did, indeed, have a set of twin pricks in the sides of their necks, which had been concealed by their coats. He also remembered that when he found them, they had smelled strange.

Clio puzzled over this report for two hours, and over the fact that increasingly, something felt wrong.

In his room at the Painted Lady, Doctor LaForge packed.

A delegation from Which House arrived at Dearbourn Hall to see Clio, and present her with a picture drawn by Inigo.

"The lad was very insistent that you have it right

away," Mr. Hakesly explained to her as he handed it across the table. "Like he thought it would help you with your investigation."

Clio looked hard at the picture. It was a drawing of a young man. A good drawing, Clio saw with some surprise. Inigo was definitely talented. Even still, the face was vaguely familiar, but not in any way she could place. Certainly not in any way that inspired her about the investigation. She thanked Mr. Hakesly and Mr. Pearl for coming.

As they were leaving, Mr. Hakesly paused. "Almost forgot," he said, scratching his head. "Told Princess Erika that you were alive and she was so happy she wept for joy. Then, just as sudden, she started to cry in real earnest. I asked her why and she said it was because she had seen a portent in the water jug that morning and it looked like you, only you were hanging by your neck. Either that or Elton Michaels is going to slaughter one of his cows soon and give us the steaks. Said she couldn't be sure. Anyway, thought I would pass that along."

Clio felt her hand go to her neck inadvertently to rub it, and dragged it back. Princess Erika's predictions never came true, she reminded herself, and went back to the document she had been studying before they arrived. It was a copy of the betrothal contract between Miles and Mariana that had been found in a strange cubby beneath the top of LaForge's desk. She was fairly certain that it had nothing to do with the investigation—it seemed more than likely that he had it because he had to explain its provisions to Mariana, a surmise born out by the fact that the portions relating directly to her birthday had been underlined, probably the only way to get her to pay attention—but Clio found it fascinating on its own merits.

She had been hearing about the betrothal for her entire life, but she had never seen its exact terms before. They chilled her.

"On this, the first day of July in the year fifteen hundred and sixty-five, in gratitude for Sir Edwin's saving my life, I do hereby betroth my son to the first-born daughter of my dear friend Sir Edwin Nonesuch," she read. *"<u>Twenty-five years from today, her hand shall be joined with his in marriage, and her fortunes likewise. From the day of her twenty-fifth birthday forward, Sir Edwin's daughter will be sole heir to my son's estate.</u> Only if the Deity sees fit to take one of them to himself before that day, will this betrothal be voided. Otherwise, it is my firmest wish that it proceed. To that end, I pledge my son's complete obedience. If my son should prove to be craven or unworthy of his blood and my title, if he should behave with dishonor and break this contract, then I disown him, and order that he shall forfeit his entire fortune to Sir Edwin Nonesuch."*

It was the last sentence that really held her attention, not the provision—she knew that Miles forfeited his fortune if he broke the betrothal—but the language. She immediately recognized the incandescent power of the words, of "craven" and "unworthy," knowing without question that it was these which bound Miles. By using such words, Miles's father had staked not only his son's fortune, but his honor, on the marriage to Mariana. Clio decided she would not have liked any man who could speak about Miles that way.

She studied the paper a bit longer, wondering at how

six sentences could wield so much power over so many lives. Then she folded it up and shoved it under the picture by Inigo. She was annoyed to realize she had been rubbing her neck.

In his room at the Painted Lady, Doctor LaForge grew pensive. ⁃

The clock had only finished chiming eight when Miles burst through the door, waving a book in front of him. He and Clio had not seen each other all day, and the first glimpse of him took her breath away. Then she noticed the object in his hand.

"Another souvenir," he announced, slapping the cheaply bound volume onto the table before her.

"Did we miss a body?" Clio asked reaching for it. "Did he kill someone we do not know about?"

Miles shook his head and opened the cover. On the left side someone had pasted a bookplate with a coat of arms on it. And on the right there was an inscription.

"For my brother, Samuel, to help preserve him in London. His ever-loving, Theolinda," Clio read aloud. Then she studied the bookplate. "Theolinda Rightson," she breathed as Miles nodded. "The last woman killed by the vampire three years ago. The woman at whose bedside you caught him. He took this book from her." Involuntarily Clio pushed the object away from her as if she recoiled from touching it.

"Yes. My men missed it in the search the first time because it was piled with the rest of the books. But this one isn't like the rest. Nor is it just a memento of his murder of Theolinda Rightson. It is also probably what saved his life last time."

Miles pointed and Clio realized that one of the corners of the book was missing. "As if it had been shot off by a pistol," she said, understanding. "Your shot must have gone through the book before hitting him in the heart. Now we know for certain he is the same man you caught three years ago."

"Yes. We seem to know everything. Except where he is."

"There have been no sightings of him at all?" Clio asked hopefully.

"None. I have got hundreds of people out on the street and along the wall of the city. He cannot have gotten out, so he must be hiding somewhere." Miles turned to look out the window and Clio did not have to ask what he was looking at. The thin sliver of moon hung midway in the sky, its dim light doing more than helping conceal their quarry.

"Where is Toast?" Clio inquired conversationally of his back.

"Dining with the cook. Corin decided it was easier to take the monkey to the kitchen, than to bring the entire contents of the kitchen to the monkey."

Poor Toast. What would he do when he no longer had an entire kitchen staff to wait on him? When they were back at Which House? What would she do? "Don't you have a ball or a concert or animal viewing to attend?" Clio asked, trying to keep her tone light.

Miles faced her. "Unfortunately, they were all canceled. Mariana informed me that while she is certain the vampire would never interfere with her celebrations, her maid is so upset by the idea of having shared a roof with a fiend that she cannot stop shaking long enough to tie a corset, let alone pin up hair. When I left, I had the curious feeling that Corin was loitering around to comfort her."

"Mariana?" Clio asked with enormous surprise.

"No, her maid, Jocelyn. And now that I think about it, he's been more jovial than usual for the past few days."

"How perfect for him," Clio said, and there was only a hint of deeper emotion in her voice. She paused for a moment. "Does this mean that we have all night together? For going over the evidence," she put in hastily, hoping that he had not noticed the catch in her voice, that he would not pull away from her because she seemed too needy. "All night together to go over the information we have gathered today. Or to go out and join the search for the vampire."

Miles shook his head. "No. I am afraid not. We will be too busy this evening to work on the investigation."

"What do you mean?"

"There are over two hundred men looking for the vampire. I thought we could do something more useful."

"Like what?"

"Dine. On the roof. Just the two of us."

He wanted to be with her. Alone. "When?"

"As soon as you put on your purple gown," he replied.

Clio was changed in less than ten minutes.

In his room at the Painted Lady, Doctor LaForge began to plan.

The sky was velvety blue-black and the stars seemed to twinkle, not above them, but all around them. The terrace had been transformed from the unruly Eden of days earlier to an unearthly, enchanted paradise. Where before they had tread on rose petals, Clio now saw that the entire area was paved. Most of its surface was covered with gleaming white marble, crisscrossed by mosaics of tiny glass mirrors, but where they stood was a path that shimmered opalescently beneath their feet, as if lit from below. A short table covered with a finely embroidered cloth had been set in the middle of the terrace, on a plush gold and deep purple carpet with unicorns and other mythic animals woven into it. Atop the table glasses with filaments of gold swirled into them glittered alongside a dozen lidded silver platters. There were no candelabrum, but small lanterns twinkled from the hedges that lined the patio, suffusing the entire place with a magical golden light.

The old Clio would have looked at this and whispered "impossible," under her breath, but she knew now that nothing was impossible. She held Miles's hand very tightly as she stood, overawed, and admired the terrace. This was a place out of a book, not real, a place of illusion. For illusion. Their entire relationship was an illusion, a moment stolen from time, a moment that should not exist, and would cease to exist in less than three days when Miles married Mariana. Clio could hardly have known that she would cease to exist before that.

She did not move from the threshold of the terrace, as if not going forward herself could stop the night from starting, and then from ending. There were no clocks up there but somewhere in the distance a bell rang out the hour, underscoring the futility of her gesture. And reminding her that she had known all along it would have to end.

"I want to give you something," Miles said abruptly, leading her toward the table. She saw that in addition to the plates and glasses and fine silver spoons and knives, there was a large, tarnished box. "This is for you," Miles said, pushing it toward her.

"I do not want anything from you," Clio told him, almost desperately. It was a lie.

"Open it," Miles half commanded, releasing her hand.

Clio kneeled next to the low table, and flipped up the clasp. The box itself might have been silver under the tarnish, and she had assumed the clasp was brass because it was so dirty. The underside, however, gleamed in a way that made it clear that it, and the rest of the fastenings, were gold. Clio looked up at Miles but he just nodded at her to continue.

The lid of the box opened smoothly under her fingers, and then crashed back down as she released it suddenly.

"What is wrong," Miles asked, kneeling next to her. "Clio, why are you crying?"

"These are the Loredan amethysts," she said. "They are not mine. They cannot be mine. You have to give them to your wife."

"No," Miles shook his head. "My father was able to dispose of me, my fortune, and my name as he wanted, but not of these. These were my mother's."

"I cannot accept them."

"You must." He gave her a smile. "You see, on her death bed, she made me promise to give them to you."

Clio smudged the tears over her face and scowled at him. "That is impossible. I never met your mother, Miles."

"No. But she knew about you. She knew you existed. And she said 'One day, *amore*, you will meet someone who makes you better than you are. When you do, give these to her. But only to her. Only to the woman you love.' "

Clio's eyes were riveted on Miles's face. "You made that up," she whispered.

"No, she really said that. In Italian, of course. It sounds better that way."

"Impossible," Clio breathed.

Miles sat back on his heels. "I have never had a harder time giving jewels to a woman in my life. Very well. Do not take them. I will shove them back into my old trunk to rot and tarnish in the cellar."

"Did you mean that?"

"That I will put them back in my old trunk? Absolutely."

"No. I mean about giving them to the woman you love."

"Yes, she was very insistent on that point. Now if you would just take them we could put to rest a nice old woman's ghost. You would have liked her, Clio. And she definitely would have liked you."

"Do you love me, Miles?" Clio stammered.

Miles raised one eyebrow. "Have you been listening? I—"

"Say it," Clio implored. "Please."

Miles took both her hands in his and his eyes rested on hers. "Clio Thornton, I love you beyond all comprehension. I loved you before I even met you, loved you when I thought you were just the best figment of my imagination. I wasted my life chasing shadows, when all along it was you I was looking for."

In his room at the Painted Lady, Doctor LaForge prepared.

Later, when they had sampled the veal cutlets in sage and the juniper-berry fed capons stuffed with apples and raisins and the asparagus wrapped in puff pastry and the globe artichokes drizzled in butter and the tiny hens glazed with apricot marmalade and the beef stewed in rich red wine over caraway seed noodles, later, after they had eaten steamed pudding studded with gold currants and let lemon ices slip down their throats and of course had large pieces of hazelnut cake with honey-infused cream poured over it, only then did Miles lead Clio from the table into the little clearing behind it.

They laughed and talked and whispered and kissed and held hands and smiled shyly at each other as they ate, but they were both strangely silent as they approached the large square building at the center of the clearing. Clio's first thought was that it was an oversized jewel case, but then she saw it consisted entirely of fabric. It was a tent, made of silver silk embroidered so that when it was lit from within, it looked like the walls were covered with flowering vines, and as if the ceiling were a canopy of leaves. Yellow pennants lined with small disks of gold and bearing the Dearbourn arms flapped at the four corners of the tent, and the gossamer drapes of the entrance billowed toward them welcomingly.

Inside was a bed, covered in purple satin painstakingly embroidered with sliver thread. From the bedposts hung two silver burners that scented the air with an exotic mixture of jasmine and cardamom. The floor was strewn with lavender rose petals, atop which, in front of the bed, lay an enormous silvery gray fur rug. Outside, a light breeze rustled though the gold disks hanging on the flags, filling the tent with their soft, tinkling music.

Beneath the music of gold on gold, unspoken, lay another message. Clio understood what all this luxury meant. This would be their last real night together. Tomorrow the final, ceremonial betrothal ball would take place, the last one before the wedding, and the viscount Dearbourn would have to spend the entire event glued to his betrothed's side. Tomorrow if Clio came here she would come alone, and she would be able to watch as the viscount and his soon to be viscountess greeted their guests in the garden, watch as the handsome couple circulated arm in arm. Tonight was their last chance to be Miles and Clio, together, just them, for hours. This was their wedding night, their wedding bower. Clio knew this was Miles's real present to her, the gift of time, from the master clockmaker himself.

Miles and Clio undressed one another silently, tenderly. Hands moved across shoulders and down arms, across chests, along stomachs and waists and hips and thighs and bottoms, memorizing them forever. These were not erotic touches, not really, but something far more powerful, something that left Clio and Miles feeling more naked than they ever had before.

Wearing nothing but the Loredan amethysts, Clio lay down on the fur rug next to the bed and pulled Miles toward her. They did not speak. They did not make love. They just held each other tightly, exchanging a lifetime worth of hugs and caresses, making a few hours count for the years they could never have together. They breathed only one another, filling their lungs for a life apart, looked at one another, storing away each wrinkle, each dimple, the way lips curved into smiles, the way cheeks shined through tears.

Below them, as London slept, the search for the vampire went on. Below them, soldiers, guardsmen, and constables patrolled the streets, passing his description from mouth to mouth, from informant to tavern owner. Below them, hundreds of men searched for the closest thing to evil incarnate any of them would ever encounter. On the roof of Dearbourn Hall, Miles and Clio conducted their own search, a search for something to hold on to as the hours between this night and the rest of the nights of their lives added up, for a way to preserve the closest thing to pure happiness they would ever know.

Much later, they moved to the bed, sliding under the cool satin cover. Then they did make love, the satin slipping around them, their bodies twining together entirely. Their joining was slow and gentle and perfect. When it was over, Miles felt a tear roll down Clio's cheek. And into his chest he heard her whisper, "Nothing perfect can endure."

4 hours after midnight. Moon—three degrees less than a quarter full. Waning.

In his room at the Painted Lady, Doctor LaForge smiled.

Chapter 22

"Nothing perfect can endure," Clio repeated, sitting up. "Miles, don't you see?"

"Yes," Miles said through clenched teeth. He understood that lesson all too well.

"No, I am not talking about us. I am talking about the vampire. I knew it. I knew there was something wrong. It is too perfect."

"Now I am afraid I do not see."

"Everything about the vampire conforms exactly to his description in the *Compendium*."

"Not the gardenias. Or the guard dogs."

"True, but everything beyond that. Down to the last detail. He kills women from only one region. He always takes souvenirs. And if his rate of killing is any indication, he is getting stronger."

Miles propped himself on one elbow. "So?"

"It is as if the book were patterned after him. Or, to put it another way, as if he were patterned after the book."

"What do you mean?"

"I mean that I think he is not a vampire after all. I mean that it is too neat. I mean that he is a regular if somewhat evil man trying to cover his murders under the guise of being a fiend." Miles was about to object when her eyes grew enormous and she rushed on. "And it makes sense of the gardenia and the guard dogs. My God, why didn't I see this before?"

"What?"

"He kills his victims by poisoning them. He pricks them on the neck. And he uses the gardenias to cover up the smell of the poison."

"Poison does not smell," Miles pointed out.

"This one does. He is using ourali."

"Ourali? That stuff taken from New World savages? If someone were buying large quantities of ourali, I would have known about it." Miles had made a slip, but Clio did not seem to notice.

"He wasn't buying it. He stole it," Clio explained, remembering the apothecary Copperwith's accusations against Toast, and her having to promise him ten pounds in order to spare the monkey's ears. Then a strange smile crossed her face. "Not only that, you paid for it."

"What?" Miles asked, then waved it away. "Never mind. I do not want to know. Assuming what you said is true," he went on in a voice that made it clear he was prepared to assume no such thing, "what does it have to do with my guard dogs?"

"Experimentation. He was experimenting with different quantities of poison, different doses. You said it yourself. The first dogs did not die right away but slowly, over time. Whereas the last two were dead on the spot."

Miles frowned over this for a while. He shook his head. "But I saw him. I saw him with blood on his lips. I saw him with his mouth on that woman's neck."

"That is why it has to be ourali," Clio explained excitedly. "Because ourali can make you ill if you ingest it, but it is only *lethal* when used to prick someone. The savages use it to poison their spears and arrows."

"How do you—never mind," Miles interrupted himself. "I am sure you read it in a book." Clio nodded. "So you surmise that he actually does bite the woman he is killing? That he puts the ourali on his teeth and then sinks them into her neck."

"Not exactly. I suspect he attaches some sort of pointed device to his teeth first and puts the poison on that. Otherwise the marks would be different."

"Why would he bother to bite his victim if he was actually murdering her with poison? No man would do that."

"No sane man," Clio pointed out. "In some ways, his not being a vampire makes his crimes worse."

Miles was pensive. "You said the other night that his being a fiend meant we did not have to look for a reason behind his killings. But if he is a man, we do. What could possibly be motivating him?"

"I don't know," Clio said, shaking her head. "That is the one thing I cannot figure out."

Very shortly, she would have an opportunity to ask him.

When the chambermaid went to Doctor LaForge's room the next morning with his breakfast, she found it empty. "I knew something wasn't wholesome," she reported in her testimony to the Special Commissioner later. "T'was tidier than usual, and everything was all moved around. Looked like he was expecting a visitor. And I'll tell you plain, I'm glad it wasn't me."

*   *   *

Clio's eyes snapped open. Her heart was thudding and it was daylight. It took her a moment to realize where she was, because she had left the bed and was standing in the middle of a clump of shrubbery. A clump which she saw was the only thing between her and plunging off the edge of the Dearbourn Hall. There were footsteps behind her and when she turned around Miles was standing there, his arms crossed over his chest.

"You look marvelous in green," he told her. "And I think you should always sport twigs in your hair. But if you wanted something to wear, you only needed to ask." He reached toward her and wrapped her in his arms, the tightness of his embrace belying the lightness of his tone. "Are you all right, *amore*?"

Clio nodded into his chest, and pressed her palms against his back. "I was dreaming. At home, I often walk in my sleep, but I have not done it since I have been here. I sleep better with you."

"I sleep better with you, too," Miles returned, remembering the years of long nights that ended only in drunken oblivion. "What did you dream about?"

"I don't know exactly." Clio closed her eyes and tried to summon back the images. They floated through her mind like ghosts. "Women. Flying around, calling to me. And they all had stains on their dresses. Like blood stains. But then the stains went away. I must have tried to follow them. It was nothing."

The sun shined down on them, warming their skin, and Clio took several deep breaths of Miles. Her hands were moving down his back, along his bottom, and she was just considering slipping one of them forward to caress the long shaft straining against her stomach when there was a knock, followed by a squeak, and the door that led back into the house opened slowly.

Miles pushed Clio behind him as Corin stepped onto the terrace. "Sorry to bother you, my lord," he said, his eyes looking everywhere but at the naked form of his master, "but you've got an appointment with your cousins and Sir Edwin and the lawyer to go over the settlement papers in half an hour."

From her vantage point, Clio saw every muscle in Miles's body ripple.

"Thank you, Corin," Miles said. "I will be down shortly."

The door closed and Miles turned to Clio and she saw that his face had changed. Before he could speak she was pulling his lips over hers, demanding him.

She would siphon his pain from him. She would show him it would be all right. She would be strong for him, for both of them. He had given her so many gifts, this was the least she could give him back. She pushed him down onto the terrace, warm now with the heat of the sun, and made love to him, milking the anger and hurt and tension from him.

He wrapped his hands around her bottom and pulled her over him harder, as if he were trying to lose himself inside her body. He was wild and wanton with her, pressing into her, holding her with desperation and desire, with insatiable need. He felt he loved her more with each thrust, needed her more, possessed her more. And then, just before he was going to find his release, he took one of his hands and slid it onto her chest, between her breasts. "Mine" he whispered as he arched into her the final time, and Clio thought at first he was referring to the amethysts she still wore.

Then she realized he had been feeling for her heart.

When he was slightly recovered, she heard him whisper, "Thank you," into her hair.

She drew herself up on both elbows and looked down at him. "You are welcome. But I have to go now. I have things to do today and cannot waste all this time dallying."

"What things?" Miles looked puzzled. He did not want her doing anything or going anywhere. He wanted her to stay right where she was. Forever.

"I do have a client, you know," she told him, sliding away from him onto her side. "And a household to run."

"They don't need you," he said with solemnity that was only partially pretend.

"Oh?"

"No. Not like I do."

She brushed the hair off his forehead. "Miles, you are not even going to be here today," she told him, struggling to keep the pain out of her voice. "I will come back tonight, *amore*."

Miles smiled at her. "I like it when you say that."

"I like it when you say it, too." Something about the heat of the sun and his body and the deep blazing gold of his eyes all together broke through Clio's reserves then. "Go on," she urged him, helping him to stand and pointing him toward the door. "Corin is waiting for you."

He kissed her one last time on the lips, then disappeared down the stairs, pausing twice to wave good-bye.

"Do not go alone to any mysterious meetings in dank old churches," he ordered when he turned the last time, and Clio nodded.

Then she sat down in the middle of the terrace, hugged her knees to her chest, and sobbed.

She had hoped all the sadness had drained from her then, but as she sat behind her desk at Which House four hours later with Toast curled comfortingly on top of her head, she felt a tear steal down her cheek. The monkey reached out to dry it with his little hand, letting it rest tenderly on her face for a moment. The gesture restored Clio to herself and she looked at the clock, saw that it was well after noon and therefore much past the nine-to-nine-thirty slot she had allotted days earlier for sobbing over the Viscount Dearbourn. She would have to discipline herself.

But before she could undertake any rigorous punishment, Inigo entered and slid a picture onto her desk. It was almost identical to the drawing Mr. Pearl and Mr. Hakesly had delivered to her the previous day, the same face, rendered from a slightly different perspective. Inigo stood in front of the desk and jabbed a finger at it.

"Yes, I see, but I do not recognize him."

Inigo sighed and rolled his eyes, then began jabbing his finger anew.

"Should I recognize him?"

He nodded vigorously, and jabbed his fingers a third time, now toward his throat.

"He knows the vampire?"

Inigo shook his head and stomped his foot, and had

just embarked on the finger-jabbing pantomime again when Mr. Williams burst into the room.

"Messenger from across the sea," he proclaimed, then stepped aside and let a small woman scurry in.

"Are you Clio Thornton?" the woman asked, marching straight up to the desk, leaning across it, and eyeing Clio at close range.

Clio drew back slightly. "Yes. Can I help you."

The woman then squinted around the room. "Who's he?" she demanded, waving her arm dramatically toward the bust of King Henry the Eighth that stood behind Clio's desk.

"No one," Clio assured her. "I can guarantee that he will not repeat a word you say."

"Not me saying a word," the woman replied, returning her squint to Clio. "It's me tenant, Miss Kimberley. Wants to see you. Think it's a bad idea, I do, but no one ever asks old Annie for her opinion."

"Is Miss Kimberley outside?" Clio coaxed.

"An how would that be, seeing as how she's sick in bed? Wants you to come to her, she do. And right away." The woman leaned closer and Clio could see the pores in her nose. "Twixt you and me and that gen'lman over there," she motioned toward Henry the Eighth again, "she's not fitting to live another three hours."

A client who only had three hours to live was not an ideal client, Clio thought, but at least going to see Miss Kimberley would be a diversion from sobbing, wondering if Doctor LaForge had been found, and watching Inigo jab himself in the throat. Grabbing Toast's leash, she followed Annie to Miss Kimberley's bedside.

Annie's estimate turned out to be slightly pessimistic, although Clio could see the basis for it when she walked into the sick woman's room half an hour later. It was a small room in the middle floor of an old and dilapidated looking boardinghouse. A smartly dressed young man was lounging against the door outside as they approached the house, but slipped away as they neared.

"That's Bad Harvey," Annie told Clio in a loud whisper. "Thinks I can't see him hanging about like that, but I know."

"Bad Harvey?" Clio inquired. At the beginning of a case, it was important to get as many facts as possible.

"That's what I said, isn't it? He's got a fancy for our Kimberley, but she'll have none to do with him. He's a bad'un."

"Hence the name," Clio said, more to herself than to Annie.

"Exactly," the other replied, seriously. "Not that he'll be able to give her much trouble, where she is going, if you know what I mean."

Clio did, especially when she glimpsed Miss Kimberley's room. Heavy blankets had been tacked up over the windows, and the air was thick with the smell of an invalid. Toast, strangely subdued, dashed into a corner and curled up there. At first Clio did not see anyone lying on the narrow bed, but then Annie bent toward the pile of blankets and shouted, "I brought her like you asked, Miss Kimberley."

Delicate fingers pushed the blankets aside, revealing a thin, pale face with heavy lids and dark circles under the eyes. Clio could see that Kimberley was young, younger than herself, perhaps not even twenty. "Thank you so much for coming," the girl whispered with an accent far more refined than her setting.

"Of course," Clio replied, moving toward the bed and seating herself on the edge. "Can I help you?"

The fingers groped for something in the space between the bed and the wall, and brought up a rumpled piece of news sheet. As Kimberley extended it toward Clio, she saw a circle of bruises on the girl's wrist. Instinctively, her eyes went to the girl's neck, and she saw it was wrapped in a bandage.

"The vampire," Clio breathed, her voice almost as throaty as the girl's. "You were attacked by the vampire and lived."

Kimberley nodded, crumpling the news sheet in her hand. "Yes. Barely. I awoke yesterday, but only today was I strong enough to speak. I remembered your advertisement and sent for you." She coughed slightly, and Clio saw her lips were cracked and dry.

"Can I get you some ale? Or some food? You must eat. Has a doctor seen you?"

Kimberley shook her head and reached her hand out for Clio's arm. "I must speak to you first," she rasped. "You must find him." Her eyes, glassy, burned into Clio's, and Clio nodded. Her heart was pounding.

"Can you tell me what happened?"

Kimberley reached toward a cracked glass filled with something that smelled faintly of mint. The girl took a sip, gagged slightly, then swallowed. "I was coming home from work," she began. "I was humming to myself, a song from home." Her expression changed. "I just came from home two months ago, you see, and I still miss it."

"You are from Devonshire," Clio stated rather than asked.

Kimberley nodded. "I work for a dressmaker, a famous one. She sent me to drop off some dresses at a big fancy house, and the manservant there gave me a fine tip for promising not to tell anyone where I dropped off the dresses. So I was feeling happy, and I was singing. But all along I have this idea that there is someone following me. I turned to check but there was no one there. Finally I got home and closed my door and went to see if there was anyone waiting in the street, but there was not."

"And then, that night, the vampire came," Clio said.

"No," Kimberley shook her head. "It was the next night. The night your advertisement appeared in the news sheet. I always like to read the news sheets, when I can, to see what all the fancy folk are doing," Kimberley confided, and Clio saw a touch of color on her cheeks. "So, since that man had given me such a good tip, I decided to buy myself one. This one," she held up the sheet, which she was still gripping in her hand. "I looked at every word on it, and then I blew out my candle and went to bed. The next thing I know, I wake up with the feeling that there is someone in my room. I looked over there," she pointed toward the door, "and saw there was a man coming toward me."

Clio's stomach tightened. "What did he do?"

"He put a hand over my mouth so I couldn't scream and he used the other one to hold my arms over my head like this," she said, crossing her wrists. "And then—" she broke off, gulping hard. "Then he starts whispering to me."

"What did he whisper?" Clio heard herself ask. She felt as though she were listening from a great distance.

"He told me that I was going to help him. That through him I was going to play a role in history. That he was going to make me a great lady. I was terrified, I tell you. I thought he was going to rob me of my virtue."

"Did he?" Clio forced herself to inquire.

Kimberley shook her head miserably. "He told me to sing. To sing the song I had been singing the day before. The one from home. And so I did. I sang it to him, just like my mother used to sing it to me. *'The first time I did see you dear,'*" Kimberly began to sing in a terrible, throaty soprano.

"I know the song," Clio assured her, interrupting. Willing her to stop.

"Then, just when I got to the last verse, he smiled at me. And that was when I saw them."

Clio waited for Kimberley to go on, but the girl said nothing. "Saw what?" Clio asked softly.

"His tears. He was crying. He kissed me on the cheek and said everything would be fine. He put his hand on my neck and told me that my blood was pumping so hard, I must be scared, and I told him I was and he said I was a good girl. And then I felt something sharp on me and I tried to scream but I must have fainted. When I woke up, he was still leaning over me, sucking on my neck, and I opened my mouth to call out, but there was fabric in it and I couldn't. And when he saw that I was awake, he looked almost scared, different than he had before, and he said, 'Be a good girl.' I tried to scream again, then, but I think he struck me because I cannot re-member any more. When I woke up it was days later and he wasn't here. But this was." She pulled the bandage around her neck down slightly, and Clio saw the two familiar pricks.

"What did he look like?" Clio asked.

Kimberley bit her lip. "My mind is so jumbled. I do not really know."

"Did he have light hair or dark hair?"

"Light. Light-ish dark hair. Or darkish light hair. I am not sure. I cannot really recall." Kimberley made an effort to sit up, imploringly. "I was so afraid."

"Of course," Clio said, soothingly, pressing her back into the pillows. "Do you recollect if he was tall or short?"

"He seemed tall when he was coming toward me, but when he was leaning over me he seemed shorter."

"How did he smell?"

Kimberley shuddered. "When he opened his mouth and smiled at me, it smelled horrible, like the smell of death. But after that it went away."

Clio nodded. It all made sense. "Can you tell me anything else about him?"

Kimberley was quiet for a long time, lying still with her eyes closed, and Clio thought she might have gone to sleep, or worse, but then her lips parted. "He was wearing a mask over his eyes," she said, finally. "But I could tell that it made him glad to see me scared." She turned her head toward Clio and said. "I am so tired. But I had to tell you. You will find him? You will fi . . ." her voice trailed off.

Clio rose and crossed silently to the door, startling the eavesdropping Annie when she opened it.

"She dead?" Annie demanded as Toast gleefully dragged Clio from the room.

"No." Clio motioned the woman down the stairs. "But she needs a doctor."

"What that girl needs is a priest," Annie corrected. "She doesn't have a cent to pay a doctor. And I already give her those new linens for free."

"That was kind of you," Clio assured her.

"Kind, nothing. Them flies were all over the other ones. Never seen so much blood in my life."

"Her blankets were covered in blood?" Clio asked, shaking her head. She felt as if she were coming out of a fog.

"Soaked through they were."

"Here," Clio said, handing Annie her entire purse. It was one of the reasons she never had any money. "Repay yourself for the linens and pay the doctor I will send to her. Do you understand?"

Annie poured the contents of the purse into her hand, held them very close to her eyes, then put all but one gold piece back. "I don't need that much," she told Clio, returning the purse. "You keep it, miss. Give it to someone else. This one coin'll do Annie and the doctor right enough."

Despite the story she had just heard, despite everything, Clio smiled. "You'll take good care of her, won't you?"

"Do my best." Then Annie looked around and sniffed the air. "Bad Harvey is 'round here somewhere. I can smell him."

Clio left the old woman on her doorstep, checking the air for Scent of Bad Harvey, and let Toast lead her toward home. It was Saturday, after midday, and the street was crowded with people gossiping and buying and selling. There was one fellow selling meat pies, next to whom Toast danced dangerously close, but Clio hardly noticed. She was going over Kimberley's story, word by word, to be sure she had it completely. Everything about it confirmed what they suspected about Doctor LaForge's methods. Except that Kimberley had lived.

The image of him leaning over the girl, his lips, his teeth on her neck, was so clear in her head, so *real*, that it chilled Clio clear through. And what was worse, she knew it was supposed to. The vampire thrived on the fear of his victims. Even Kimberley had sensed that. He might not have needed their blood, but he needed their terror.

Clio pushed this disturbing thought from her mind. The girl said the vampire had come the night Clio's advertisement appeared in the news sheet. Clio knew exactly when that was. It had appeared on her birthday. The day there were fireworks. The day she and Miles had—

"Lady Thornton," a voice called to her from across the street. Clio looked up and saw that it came from a coach with the Dearbourn arms on it. Waving to her from beside the coach was Jocelyn, Mariana's maid. "Lady Thornton," Jocelyn cried again, and, scooping Toast up so he would not be run over, Clio crossed toward her.

"Thank goodness I found you," Jocelyn breathed. "They want you back at Dearbourn Hall immediately. Corin told me to tell you they found Doctor LaForge and that you should return with me." Jocelyn opened the door and motioned Clio through it.

"They found him?" Clio asked with excitement, pushing Toast into the vehicle and climbing in after him. "Where?"

"Here," an eerie voice said from deep within the dark shadows of the coach as the door clicked shut behind Clio. "I have been waiting for you right here, Lady Thornton, for well over an hour."

Chapter 23

"I was under the impression that the lock you designed for my door could not be opened without the key," Miles said to Tristan tersely as his cousins ambled uninvited into his apartment. "And I have that right here."

"I accidentally made two of them," Tristan replied with an unapologetic smile.

"You know," Sebastian explained. "In case anything should happen to you."

"The only thing that is going to happen to me this afternoon is that I am going to be left alone with my thoughts. Now go away."

"Your thoughts?" Sebastian asked, looking pointedly at the four decanters of wine that stood in the middle of the table.

Miles looked up to glare ferociously, but Ian moved into his line of vision. His expression was grim. "We have something to say to you, Miles."

"I don't want to hear it," Miles said, turning away from them. He had been staring at the decanters of wine he ordered from Corin since returning from his meetings at one o'clock. It was now half past three and he had not touched them. Somewhere inside he recognized that they would only make what he was feeling worse. But now, seeing his cousins, he stood, reached out for one of them, and poured himself a glass.

Ian's hand closed over his before he could take a gulp. "You are going to listen to us, Miles. Sober."

Miles put the glass down and regarded them bitterly. "You have nothing to worry about. I am not going to disgrace the family. I will behave with perfect courtesy tonight and go through with the betrothal tomorrow," he said. "You have my word. Are you satisfied?"

"No," Crispin replied for all of them. "That is not why we came. We—"

"Then what is it? Do you want my promise that I will not see Clio after I am married? You can have that, too. I would never do that to her. I could never treat her that way."

"Damn it, Miles, sit down and let us speak," Tristan said, and it was so unlike him to be serious that Miles did what he said.

"Good." Ian, who had been designated as spokesman, nodded. "We have a proposal for you, Miles. We know that by the terms of your betrothal, if you do not marry Mariana you must sacrifice your assets, your property, everything. We cannot do much about replacing your title, although L. N. is working with the queen on that, but we will each give you a quarter of our fortunes to make up for what you will lose."

"What?" Miles asked, thunderstruck.

"We want you to be happy, Miles," Crispin explained. "We have never seen you as happy as you have been during these past nine days. And we are fairly sure it has nothing to do with the approach of your marriage."

When Miles still looked dumbfounded, Sebastian spelled it out in clear language. "We want you to marry Clio Thornton."

Craven and unworthy, the contract said he would be if he did not abide its provisions. "I can't," Miles answered plainly.

Crispin looked at him, uncomprehending. "But you will have plenty of mone—"

"It's not about the money," Miles interrupted his cousin. "It has never been about the money."

"It's about proving your worth to your father," Tristan said, reciting the line they had heard from Miles so many times. "But damn it, Miles, your father is dead."

"It is not my father. It is about proving something to myself."

"What?" Tristan demanded.

"That I am not the man he thought I was. That I am not craven and unworthy. That I am not dishonorable."

Tristan waved his hand. "Those are just words."

"No," Miles shook his head and his cheeks were flushed. "Not when they are said by your father. Not when they are said about you." Suddenly anger edged his voice. "But I wouldn't expect *you* to understand," he went on, glaring at Tristan. "You don't even know who the hell your father is."

His words seemed to scorch the air, and Miles was immediately sorry. "Oh God, Trist, you know I did not—"

"You are right," Tristan interrupted, not stiffly. "I am a bastard. And a thief."

"That is not what I—" Miles began, but Tristan cut him off again.

"Perhaps you remember that I was fairly troubled by that when you all rescued me from the hanging cells at the Doge's prison, what was that, sixteen years ago? Remember how I growled at you and told you that a thief and a bastard could never be accepted as one of the famous and honorable Arboretti? Remember how I tried to drive you away?"

Miles, chastened, nodded.

"Then maybe you remember what finally convinced me to come with you and assume my birthright. No? It was this very young and idealistic poet, one of my cousins, whose hair kept falling in his eyes and who was already at that time a half head taller than me, who would not accept my arguments. He grabbed me by the collar of my best shirt and said, 'Honor does not mean blindly acceding to somebody else's expectations, Tristan del Moro, it means making your own and living up to them. Stop acting like a fool.' And then stormed off. Of course, he could not get far because the cell door was closed, but he had made his point."

Miles's expression was distant. "I had forgotten about that."

"I hadn't. And now, even though you are still taller than I am, I'm going to do the same thing to you." Tristan dragged Miles up by the collar and looked in his eyes. "If you love Clio Thornton, you should marry her, Miles Fraser Loredan. And if you don't, I'll marry her myself and then you'll really have a reason to call me a bastard. Personally, I do not want to be the only Arboretti not wed to a woman who was once wanted for murder."

All of a sudden, Miles found that he was smiling. And

laughing. He hugged Tristan around the neck. "Thank you," he said.

"It was the least I could do. If it wasn't for you, I would not be here now," Tristan told him. "Now I think it is time you introduce us to your bride-to-be."

He was going to marry Clio. Unable to contain himself, Miles let out an enormous celebratory holler.

Corin burst into the room then as if he had been fired from a cannon.

"Corin, listen to the news," Miles began, but the expression on his manservant's face stopped him cold. It would have been enough to sober Miles even if he had drunk all four decanters of wine. "What has happened?"

"I think there is something you should hear, my lord," he said, stepping aside to let one of Miles's handpicked footmen enter the room. He was panting.

"We found Doctor LaForge, sir," the footman said between breaths.

"Where?" Miles asked in a voice none of his cousins had heard in years. They exchanged perplexed glances.

"He was in one of your coaches," the boy elaborated, still breathing heavily. "Apparently your betrothed's maid, Jocelyn, borrowed it for him. That was how we found him. Coachman passed the word to Arnold when he saw us on the street."

"Did you know about this?" Miles demanded of Corin, who shook his head and looked gray. Miles returned his attention to the footman. "Go on."

"We caught up with him in Whitefriars, waiting outside some old house. When he started to move, I came to inform you. Arnold is still following him, on foot."

"Good work. Stay with him. Keep us notified." Miles began to turn away.

"Yes sir. There is just one thing, sir."

Miles turned back. "What?"

"There's a lady with him. A lady with a monkey."

"Is it Lady Thornton?" Miles asked and his voice was deadly calm.

"I did not get a perfect look, sir, but I am almost certain that it was."

Clio realized four things at once: the figure hunched opposite her had no accent and no beard, but there was no mistaking that he was Doctor LaForge; she was alone with a man who brutally killed women; he had a pistol aimed at her forehead; and he looked like he knew how to use it.

That meant she had two choices. Pray the coach hit a bad spot in the road, upsetting LaForge's aim long enough for her to get away. Or learn what he intended to do with her and start planning an escape.

The coach bumped over something then, and swerved abruptly, but Doctor LaForge's aim did not waver.

One choice.

"Where are you taking me?" Clio asked in what she hoped was an engaging tone.

"Shut up," Doctor LaForge replied.

No choices.

Clio did as he said, pressing herself into the corner of the coach. Toast huddled against her, every now and then peering at the man with the pistol, then turning and hiding his face. Nor could she blame him. Doctor LaForge's expression was one of such complete malevolence that it was chilling just to look at him.

Clio felt his eyes boring into her, seeing but not seeing,

almost feverish in their menace. But she would not be afraid. She would not give him the benefit of her terror.

Not until she could not help it.

Unhelpful thoughts flitted through her mind. How many victims had he taken? Two dozen? More? Would he kill her with the pistol or with poison? Which would be more painful? What was going to happen to Toast? Would she at least get answers to her questions before he killed her? Would Miles still get married the next day?

This last thought rattled around her head, preoccupying her, until the coach drew to a stop. She was astonished to see they were at the Painted Lady. And relieved. Surely, Lovely Jake would be able to help her.

But he was nowhere to be seen as they entered and ascended the back stairs, and before she could even think of calling out she felt the pistol pressed hard against her back. She did as LaForge indicated and pushed open the door of a room, but when she saw what was inside she almost could not make her feet cross the threshold. It was some combination of Toast's running ahead and the pistol at her back that propelled her.

He shoved her into a chair that had been set up opposite the door. As soon as she saw it, she knew that he had been planning whatever was about to happen, because the chair had been modified. Attached to each of the arms were leather straps, with which, despite her attempts to stop him, he managed to bind her wrists. She flexed her hands and pulled against the straps, but they held fast. She was immobile. There was no way for her to escape.

It was one thing to sit across the coach from a madman and remain calm, she realized as she became aware of her growing panic, but quite another to stay tranquil as he tied you into a chair.

"I am not afraid of you," Clio told him, as much as herself, and was surprised by his unconcern.

"Your feelings are of no importance to me. You are merely a pawn."

Had she misunderstood? Was he not interested in her fear? "A pawn? What game are we playing?"

"The game of revenge," he explained smoothly, testing the leather thongs holding her hands to ensure they were tight. "A game that requires you to die. Preferably in a great deal of pain."

You will pay for this Dearbourn, Clio remembered the vampire saying before he plunged into the river last time. "Revenge on Viscount Dearbourn?"

"That is only part of it," he told her, lifting a satchel from under the bed and opening it.

"Tell me the rest," she urged. "Tell me how you survived after Dearbourn shot you."

"I swam," LaForge answered plainly. "Then I went to Europe, where I had the pleasure of meeting up with your idiot cousin and that bitch you call your grandmother."

"How? Did you seek them out? Did you know Mariana was betro—"

"I don't like your questions," he interrupted, removing three rusty knives from the satchel, each one longer and thicker than the other. "The only sound I want to hear from you is the sound of the life draining from you as you cry out, in vain, for help." He spoke entirely without emphasis or inflection, which only made his words more hideous.

Her one chance, Clio saw, was to find a way to delay

him. "But I want to know," she said, and she allowed a hint of desperation to creep into her voice. She had read in a book once that leather became malleable when warm, and she wriggled her wrists slightly to create friction around her bonds. "I want to understand, Doctor LaForge."

"My name is not Doctor LaForge." He turned and stared at her now. "My name is Samuel Rightson."

Samuel Rightson. The name was familiar to Clio, but— "You are Theolinda Rightson's brother," she blurted suddenly. "The one she inscribed the book to."

"Ah, you found that," he said in a disaffected voice. "I figured you would."

His coldness was horrible. She had to slow him. "Tell me about your sister. What was she like?"

For a moment something like emotion whisked across his face. "She was wonderful. She had come to London to visit me. She—" his face grew black again. "She died."

"It sounds like you loved her very much."

"I did."

"Then how could you do it? How could you suck your own sister's blood? How could you kill her like that?"

His face became a hard mask. "I did not kill her. Dearbourn killed her."

"What are you talking about? You bit her neck. You sucked her blood."

He bent down and brought his face close to hers, so that she could feel his spittle on her cheek as he spoke and the pressure of a knife against her throat. "You think you know everything, but you know nothing. Nothing. Mark my words, Lady Thornton, you have been blind. Crime is a virtue and virtue is a crime. You will understand that soon enough. But by then you will be dea—"

The sound of a pistol shot rang out in the air, startling them both.

"What is that?" the man formerly known as Doctor LaForge demanded, spinning toward the door. "It is too early. I am not ready." Silence followed the loud noise. He opened the door an inch to peer out.

And then came crashing backward into the room, falling in a crumpled heap beside Clio. The knife he had been holding flew from his hand and nicked her on the shin, but she barely noticed, her relief was so great.

"Thank God you have come," she panted, twisting against the bonds in her chair. "He was going to kill me, Miles, he was—"

"Good afternoon, Clio," a voice, not Miles's, said from the threshold of the room. "I hardly expected such a warm welcome."

Clio stared at the person standing in the door with cold horror. One by one the thoughts that had been tickling her mind clicked into place. Blood! There was none around Inigo's sister, but Kimberly had been soaked in it. Doctor LaForge, the man known as the Vampire of London, was right. She had been blind.

Doctor LaForge had not been killing his sister when Miles came upon him, he had been trying to save her, Clio comprehended. He had not been sucking her blood but rather the poison in it, trying to stop it before it took over her body, just as he had done with Kimberley. He had been ill the morning they found no body, not because he was the vampire and had failed to drink enough blood, but because he had saved Kimberley's life and the poison, diluted, was in his body. That was why there was so much blood around both women, why Miles had seen blood on his face and on his lips. Because he had been sucking the poison *out*. And that was why there had been so little blood around the other victims. No one had tried to save them.

Crime is a virtue and virtue is a crime, he had said and suddenly she understood. His padded clothes and false mustache, the blood-soaked shirt in his armoire, his presence at the Curious Cat, they were not signs of his guilt but of his innocence. He wanted to revenge himself on Miles for the death of his sister. But he also wanted revenge on the vampire. Like she and Miles, he had been searching for the fiend. Indeed, she had no doubt that he had been following the vampire the night they followed him to the Curious Cat and that it had been him singing the song, to drive the vampire mad. It had all been in front of her eyes the entire time and she had misunderstood everything.

But not any longer. She no longer had that luxury. Because Doctor Lal'orge was lying in his death throes at her feet. And standing in the doorway was the face from Inigo's drawing.

The face of the real vampire.

"No one has come out," Arnold whispered to Miles as he and his cousins joined him outside the Painted Lady. "They must still be inside."

"Ian, you and Crispin go around the back. Tristan, Sebastian and I will enter through the front door. If you hear us whistle three times, come in as fast as you can."

None of the Arboretti thought to hesitate. Miles waited until Ian and Crispin were out of sight, then he,

Tristan, and Sebastian crossed the street and slid through the door.

The first thing they saw was Lovely Jake's body stretched across the staircase. A sticky stain oozed across his doublet from the bullet hole in his chest.

Miles turned to say something to his cousins, but Tristan interrupted him. "Don't even think of ordering us to stay down here," he told Miles firmly. "We are going with you."

Unwilling to waste any time arguing, Miles shrugged, then crept noiselessly up the staircase.

One of the doors was slightly ajar and a low moan came from behind it. Miles kicked it open with his foot, then pressed himself back against the wall of the corridor.

"Help me," he heard someone call from inside. "Please. I am dying. Help me."

Miles spent an eighth of a second weighing the odds that it was a trap, and went through the door.

The man known as Doctor LaForge was lying on the floor in a ball, clutching his arm. His hands were red with blood, and his face was entirely devoid of color. Miles stopped and stared for a moment when he saw him, astonished that he had been living under the same roof as the man for weeks and not realized he was the person he had fired at three years earlier, and even more astonished by his transformation.

Suddenly, Miles understood what Clio had figured out an hour earlier.

"The vampire has got Clio," Doctor LaForge whispered as Miles entered and kneeled next to him. "The vampire took her."

"Where?" Miles demanded, ripping a piece of his shirt and wrapping it around LaForge's arm. "When?"

LaForge watched with fascination as Miles bound his arm. "Why are you doing this?" he asked finally. "I hate you. Why are you saving me?"

"Because you are the only person who can help me find Clio," Miles explained. "Where is she?"

"How do you know you can trust me?" LaForge asked, and madness gleamed in his eyes. "How do you know this is not a trap?"

"I don't, but if it is I will no doubt be able to get out of it. Now, damn it, tell me where Clio is and how long ago she left."

Doctor LaForge shook his head. "Arrogant. Too, too arrogant. I do not know where she is. It happened over an hour ago. I was going to use her as bait. To reel you in. And then the vampire." Doctor LaForge's eyes got a strange, serene look in them.

Miles knew that look. He shook LaForge hard, demanding that the man hold on to consciousness a few seconds longer. "Who is it? Who is the vampire?"

LaForge's eyes focused slightly, but his speech began to slur. "You must find her before midnight or she will be dead. After midnight, she is expendable."

"What are you talking about?" Miles demanded.

"You have not figured it out yet, have you?" LaForge told him, his head lolling to one side. He fixed Miles with an opaque eye and an eerie smile spread over his features. "Well I suppose I will have my revenge after all." Something like a laugh escaped his lips, and then his body slumped forward, unconscious.

"Where is Clio?" Sebastian asked as he and Tristan pressed into the room.

Miles stood up and pushed LaForge away from him, wiping blood from his hands on his breeches. "I don't have the damndest idea. But if our friend is to be believed, we've only got eight hours in which to find her and all of London to search."

Chapter 24

"I know what you are thinking. I always know what you are thinking.

"Don't shake your head, Clio. How else do you suppose I have been able to control you for so long? We are very alike in some ways. You are like a shadow of me, with a shadow of my power. But it lives inside both of us. I can feel it coursing through your blood. Your father's blood.

"They call it evil, but that is only the name envy makes them speak. And who would not envy us? Who would not envy the power we can exercise over people's lives? The way people look at us when they see what we really are?

"You cannot deny that you have felt its potency, Clio dear, felt its pull. That you have never known the urge to cause pain. To bite or hit or hurt. You may struggle against it, but it is within you, longing to come out. Of course, I suppose you cannot be blamed. You are not strong like I am. You do not have my capacity, my power.

"Really, it was quite audacious of you to think you might catch me, Clio. You would have been better off chasing chimeras. At least then you would have stood a chance of success. You did not understand that I was leading you the entire time. Like a stupid dog you devoured whatever bait I threw at you, without even stopping to sniff and see if it was rotten.

"When I began, I had not even thought of you. But then you foisted yourself onto the scene, and I immediately apprehended what you could be. My plan was so clever. Drug you, leave Flora in your bed. I wondered about fixing your ankle, but I never do anything by half measures. I used the water pitcher, lest you were curious. One sharp blow was all it required.

"It was perfect, a beautiful plan. A beautiful trap. It would buy me the precious time I needed and get you out of the way. And everything went just as I had intended. I was sitting outside in the apple tree when you found the body and I saw your face. The sheer, exquisite horror and self-loathing. I wish you could have seen it, too, I really did. You see, I am not ungenerous.

"Why did you dawdle so at the fair? I had expected better of you. You are known for your tenaciousness, yet there you were, wandering around, ignoring all my carefully placed hints. I was tempted to give you a push myself, but my patience worked. Finally you arrived at the cockfighting pit, and what happened was better than anything I could have dreamed.

"Even with the viscount interfering I knew I had you. There was nothing else for you to think, nothing else for you to believe, other than that you were the vampire. You were mine, your mind was mine. I had you.

"It was then that it unraveled. You did not go to the constables. You did not go to prison. You did not tell anyone what you were, what I had made you. You did nothing. You wasted all my efforts, all my work, all my waiting, you selfish, ungrateful bitch. You stopped being scared.

"But only temporarily. Indeed, in a way I am glad it went this way. I am glad I shall have the opportunity of watching the life drain from you slowly, watching the terror rise in your eyes as you watch the clock clicking off the final minutes of your existence. You know, I have never really seen you properly frightened. Even when you found Flora's body, you were not afraid, not as I would have liked. You were scared for others, but not for yourself. You have not tasted real terror yet. But you will. You will see how sweet it can be.

"No, no, don't struggle. You must stay alive awhile longer. But I promise the time will not hang heavy on your hands. I have so much to tell you."

Clio pressed herself with apparent fear against the post to which her hands and feet were bound. "I do not want to hear what you have to say, Saunders. If that is even your real name."

"It is. But I am not Sir Saunders Cotton. Since the death of my father four years ago, I have been Lord Mayhew."

"Mayhew." The name was familiar. "Then you are not from Devonshire."

"No. But my stepmother was."

"Serena Mayhew. The vampire's third victim three years ago." Clio stared at him. "Did you begin all this the first time just to kill your stepmother?"

"You may speak of the act as it deserves. It was brilliant. Everyone assumed she was merely another victim.

When in fact, she was *the* victim. The one around whom the entire scheme was built."

"Why?"

"She deserved it. They all deserved it. They were all bloodsuckers. She preyed on my father, stealing away his life, stealing away the fortune that was supposed to be mine. Mine. My blood rights. She sucked away my title, my property, my money, sucked them from my father. When she first came, she used to sing to me, sing me that song. She used it to lure me. I knew what she wanted to do to me, I could tell. I had seen her do it with my father. She would sing to him afterward, and I knew she wanted to do it to me, too. But I would not let her. I would not be seduced by her wiles. She used her song and her body to steal everything from my father. When he died, she had everything. And I knew I would have revenge. I would make her sing her siren song. And then I would suck the blood back out, suck out what was mine, suck it out until she was dead. I would rid London, rid England of the bloodsuckers. I would make it safe."

"And you did."

"Yes. I was tremendous. No one suspected anything. And it was thrilling. When they understood what was happening, when they understood what I was doing to them, for them, you should have seen the expressions on their faces. They loved me. They pled with me. They begged me to release them. I was a god to them. A god." He closed his fist in tribute to himself. He looked at her and saw terror, his victim's terror, sparkling in her eyes. "You begin to understand, I see."

"I understand that you are mad," Clio replied with an unconcealed shudder.

Saunders shook his head. "They always say that when they do not comprehend. They always say that when they are overawed by your power. Mad? Mad am I? Because my brilliance is beyond your appreciation? Because my thinking leaves you awestruck? How can you be so ungrateful, Clio? After all I have done for you, all the attention I have lavished. No one has ever thought so much about you, about your well-being as I have. Use your petty words if you prefer. Retreat into them. But I am not mad. I shall triumph tonight."

"You mean you did all of this to kill me?"

"No. Clio, Clio, Clio. What are you to me? Was it you I took to the cockfights? Was it you who loved to see the birds bloody one another so much that you fell and hurt your ankle? Was it you who captured my heart and showed me what it was to love? Who could have impersonated you so perfectly at the fair? Do you really think I would do all this for you?"

"You did this for Mariana," Clio breathed, letting the mask of fear she had been struggling to wear drop for a moment as she grasped everything. "You did it to kill Miles."

"Exactly. Mariana, my perfect angel, must be liberated from the prison of her betrothal. She must be uncaged, so her exalted spirit can fly free. And that bastard Dearbourn will have died in pursuit of the vampire. Just like Serena. Just another victim of the clever fiend."

"Does Mariana know of your plan? Is she helping you?"

"My pure saintly Mariana? She knows nothing of all this." He gestured about as if castles and land grants werc scattered at his feet. "She knew only that we had to attend the fair in disguise so her reputation would not be sullied. She loved the idea of dressing up as you. She said she wanted to know what it felt like to look so ill."

"How charming," Clio murmured despite herself.

"Yes, she is. She was my helper. And my muse. Do you understand now?"

Yes, Clio nodded. She understood many things. She understood that the bonds on her wrists and ankles were insoluble. She understood that she was in the hands of a lunatic. She understood that Toast, hunkered in a corner, could never get past him to summon help. She understood that her only power was in convincing her captor of her fear while actually keeping it at bay. And she understood that unless the note she had dispatched from the inn where they changed horses made it into Miles's hands soon, they were both going to die.

"None of you were following her?" Miles demanded, looking ferociously over the assembled inhabitants of Which House as if he suspected them of having broiled and eaten Clio.

"After the threats she gave about what would happen to anyone who dared endanger his life by following her when she heard about Inigo the other night?" Mr. Hakesly shook his head.

"Why weren't any of *you* following her?" Mr. Williams asked, eyeing the Arboretti. "Strong men. Good for following. Look like you'd be willing to risk having your toes licked for ten hours straight by this puppy."

"Is that what Clio threatened as punishment?" Sebastian inquired, barely repressing a smile.

"That, and drawing and quartering," Mr. Pearl elaborated quietly.

"But you know she would never do anything like that," Miles ranted. "You should have—"

"Miles," Ian said, putting his hand on his cousin's shoulder. "You had two guards following her, remember, and she was still abducted. These men are not to blame, and your storming around is not getting us anywhere."

The room fell silent but for the sound of men shifting uneasily in their leather boots. Then Miles said, "You are right." He nodded to Snug, Inigo, and the Triumvirate. "I am sorry."

He would have gone on, saying he knew not what, but a messenger in golden Dearbourn livery puffed into the study then like a bitter wind. "This just came," he said, flapping a paper in front of Miles. "This just arrived at Dearbourn Hall."

Miles snatched the grimy sheet from him.

My lord,

The vampire has me. This shall be my last chance to get a letter to you. I overheard at the coach stop that we are going to the Garden House near Hartwell Heath. Please, my lord, come as quickly as you can. I am terrified.

Your Lordship's own, Clio.

Miles handed the sheet to Mr. Hakesly. "Is this Clio's writing?"

"Looks like it," Mr. Hakesly averred, showing it to Mr. Pearl.

"Yes." Mr. Pearl confirmed.

"Hartwell Heath is close to my sheep pasture. It's three hours hard riding away," Crispin said hesitantly.

Miles looked at the clock. It was after six. Six hours until midnight, and a three hour ride in each direction. What if Clio was wrong about where the vampire was taking her?

"Saddle the horses," he said grimly. "We had better get started."

"You know," Saunders confided, "the hardest part is not the waiting. The hardest part is the pretending."

Clio would have liked to disagree. She was finding the waiting, the steady click of the clock in front of which she was tied, extremely tedious. Pretending to be afraid of Saunders was not a problem at all.

Her mouth was still dry and tasted bad from whatever he had used to make her sleep during the coach ride from the Painted Lady. He had shoved something warm and wet between her lips when she tried to scream, and it must have been coated with a sleeping drug. She remembered telling herself that it was crucial she stay awake, alert, crucial that she know where she was going and what was happening, but no matter how hard she struggled her eyes would not stay open. Her last clear thought was of seeing Lovely Jake napping at the strangest angle on the stairs, and she recollected thinking that if he did not clean it off soon, all the red wine on the front of his doublet would ruin it. It was only when she regained consciousness in the coach that she had realized Lovely Jake was dead, and she had wondered who would look after his pig.

Her first thought on waking in the lurching vehicle, however, had been one of relief, because Toast was nowhere to be found. He had gotten away. And perhaps he could lead help to her. But when, midway through their journey, they pulled up outside the inn where Saunders had forced her to write the note to Miles, she saw that Toast had been tied behind the coach with a sturdy chain, forced to grip its outer edges or run in order to avoid being dragged to his death. Exhausted, he now lay almost motionless in the far corner of the room.

The chamber had no furniture beside the post to which Clio was tied, if that could be considered furniture, and the large clock that stood directly in front of her. Saunders paced back and forth across the floor in bare feet, his quiet footsteps keeping exact time with the steady ticking of the timepiece.

"Yes, that was the worst part. Not being able to show people what I really am," he was saying. "Not being able to reveal what I am really capable of. That was what made me suffer. You see, I learned long ago that they would not understand. That their jealousy would force them to call me names. As you did. But you won't anymore, will you?" Saunders stopped pacing the room and turned to stare at Clio with burning eyes. She noticed that one side of his face had begun to twitch.

"No," she said in what she hoped sounded like a meek voice. "I won't."

"Good. I am tired of being insulted by you, and people like you. How dare you have tried to fool me with that idiot impersonator in Newgate? A child could have seen through that."

"You are right. We were fools."

"No," Saunders hissed, delight flashing in his eyes as Clio recoiled from him. "You are fools."

Clio nodded. "But when we saw how ingeniously you disposed of the man, we knew we had been wrong. Where did you learn so much about poison?"

Saunders smiled. "From my stepmother, Serena. Her first husband had been an apothecary. She taught me everything I know." He looked pensive for a time. "I certainly hope Miles will appreciate all I have done for him. Appreciate the lengths I have gone to orchestrate a hero's death for him, even though he is my enemy. To lose one's life in a final battle with the vampire—what a marvelous way to die. Serena did not understand the gift I was giving her. I kept trying to explain it to her, explain that I was making her part of something special, a part of history, but she fought me. She stood no chance of course. Like you."

Clio shrank away from him, from the twitching lips. "Why do you need me if it is Dearbourn you want?"

"Because I want him to wait. I want him to feel each minute that passes. I want him entirely under my power. He must die in pursuit of the vampire, but first he will taste what it is like to be in someone else's control. He must follow my timetable, be my creature. And you will make him that."

"What do you mean?"

"He will come after you. He must. And then he will be mine. My puppet. My servant. Mine to command. For as soon as he attempts to enter this room, you will be shot."

"Shot?"

"Yes. With that pistol." Saunders gestured behind him and Clio saw that there was indeed a pistol there. It was secured on a stand bolted to the floor so that it was just above the level of her head, but it was pointed downward, at her heart. A thin cord ran from its handle to the top of the door, the only door in the room. "When that door opens, the cord will go taut and the trigger will be pulled. That way, Miles will know it is he and he alone who has killed you."

"You cannot know the shot will hit me, much less be mortal," Clio pointed out to him, her air of terror dissolving in the face of his madness.

"I rather hope it will *not* be fatal," Saunders assured her kindly. "I would rather have you die slowly, in a puddle of your blood. The shot will hit you, some part of you, depending on how still you stand, and it will injure you too gravely to leave here. But that is not the important part. That is just the crossfire. What is important is that Miles will rush to you, run to bathe his hands in your blood, stand right here—" he moved and stood directly in front of her, "—to support you and hear your last, rattling breath. And he will stay that way, with you, until midnight."

"What if he comes soon? It's hours until midnight. Why would he stay here that long?"

"I have seen to that. There is no way he could get here for another four hours and by then . . ." He smiled secretly to himself.

Clio looked at the clock in front of her. Its hands showed a quarter of an hour shy of eight bells. "Why is midnight so important?" she pressed. "What happens at midnight?"

The tick in Saunders face disappeared and it grew smooth, almost beatific. "There will be no moon in the sky at all. And I shall be invincible."

"You are not the vampire," Clio told him, having entirely thrown off the mantle of fear. "You are just a man. The moon has no power over you."

"Just a man," he said with a strange smile and a sideways glance at the clock. "You shall see, Clio Thornton, if I am just a man. You shall see soon. Because it has begun. My plan is moving forward. Your viscount is on his way to Hartwell Heath. I can sense it."

Please, Clio thought to herself, her eyes moving from the pistol to the door. Please let him be wrong.

"Whoever named this the Garden House must have had a wonderful sense of humor," Sebastian murmured to Tristan as they rode around the perimeter of the old building. There was nothing near it for miles, not another house, certainly nothing that looked like a garden. It just sat, low and dark and glowering in the middle of the heath.

The group had split into two detachments, each of which was to take up a station near a different part of the house. They had made good time from London, arriving in under three hours, but they forced themselves to go slowly now. They had agreed on a plan of action, and on the fact that once in place around the house, they would not speak but only communicate by whistling, to minimize the chances of alerting the vampire to their presence.

Tristan, the group expert on breaking and entering, was to go in first, accompanied by Sebastian, and quiet any dogs that might be waiting to announce visitors. He had been hoping for an open window, or even just an open shutter, but he found none. As far as he could see, the house was completely dark, which meant that the vampire had to have Clio in an inside room, possibly on the upper floor.

He and Sebastian had just reached the backdoor when they heard a noise from inside, like the sound of a body hitting a wall.

A low whistle alerted the others, and they were all there by the time the lock yielded to Tristan's expert touch. Once inside, they moved silently through the rooms, finding nothing. Somewhere in the distance they could make out the sound of footsteps, pacing, with the regularity of clockwork. Somewhere above them.

They found the main stairs and scaled them slowly, walking along the edges of the boards to keep from making them squeak. They were about halfway up the second set, growing closer to the pacing feet, when they heard it again, the sound of a person falling. This time it was accompanied by a piercing shriek.

They ran up the rest of the stairs, pursuing the noise, and traced it to a small door. It was louder here, a sound of terror unlike anything they had ever heard before. One of them reached for the handle and jerked the door open.

The ancient hinges gave a hideous wail and suddenly there was an enormous explosion. Black objects came hurtling toward them in a sea of inhuman screeching. The air pulsed with the force of a hundred wings flapping as the bats, disoriented, spun wildly through the hall, careening off the walls and each other. The men ducked beneath the black cloud and ran into the room.

There was no one there. Off to one side stood an enormous, ancient clock. The rhythmic tone of its timekeeping seemed, even this close, like the sound of footsteps. The hands on its face showed a little past nine. And below it, written on a long pieced together strip of parchment, large enough to be seen without a light, were the words, "Fooled you, Dearbourn. She dies at midnight."

Clio's breath caught in her throat.

"What?" Saunders demanded, turning around. "What is it?" His eyes followed hers to the pistol over the door.

"I just cannot stand to see that thing pointing at me," Clio replied in a voice edged with panic.

Saunders studied her, as if he knew she was lying, then returned to his careful, quiet pacing.

Clio let her breath out, slowly this time. It was the only sign of her discovery she allowed herself.

It had taken two hours, but she had found it. She had forced herself to study the clock opposite her, in part because it kept her eyes off the pistol aimed at her, and in part because there was something about the way Saunders had looked at it and about his being barefoot that triggered her imagination. She watched each piece of it in turn, isolating what she could see of the mechanism through the clock face, forcing herself to look for something that might not belong there.

As if she would know that thing when she saw it. But she had. Finally, at last, she had. Because while she was not an expert on clocks, she was fairly sure that they did not usually contain an archer's bow inside of them that was gradually being pulled more taut with each advancing hour, or, being pulled with it, an arrow.

Aimed exactly at her. Or at the spot where Miles

would be standing if he was tending to her pistol wounds.

It did not require a mind like Saunders's—which, as he made a point of telling her at regular ten-minute intervals, she did not possess—for her to guess that the arrow was poisoned, most likely with ourali, or that the probable time of release, the moment when the bow would be pulled as tightly as it would go, was midnight. That way he could kill without having to be present. It would be the ultimate display of his power—the power to take a life without moving a finger.

And it would happen in less than two hours.

There was nothing she could do about the pistol, yet, but perhaps there was something she could do about the clock. *Flawless balance*, she remembered Miles saying of the clockwork mechanism. *As soon as the balance is upset, it stops working.* All she had to do was upset the balance. Easy.

Or it would have been, if she had not been bound to a post. Not only was her range of motion severely limited, but any sort of unusual activity would undoubtedly draw Saunders's attention to what she was doing. He might have been insane, but he was not stupid.

Suddenly, she narrowed her eyes at him. "Do you really think Mariana will marry you when this is over?" she asked.

He spun around and stared at her. "What do you mean?"

"Once she is free of her betrothal, she will have her pick of men. What makes you think she would want anything to do with you?"

"She loves me."

"Of course," Clio said with undisguised sarcasm. "How often has she told you that?"

"She has never said it. That would be dishonorable while she was betrothed to someone else. But I know. I *know*."

"How?" Clio jeered.

Saunder's eyes flashed. "You are just trying to upset me. But it will not work. I am in control here. I am in charge. What do you know of love anyway? No one has ever loved you in your life."

Clio let the words sink in, soaking them up like a sponge. "I know that Mariana is incapable of loving anyone but herself," she said quietly.

"You say that only because she did not love you. And why should she? You are nothing. Nothing at all. Like your wicked father. He was so wretched that your grandmother had to drive him away. She fabricated a spate of vampire killings in the village and framed him for them, so that he would be thrown in jail."

It was working better than Clio had expected. "What are you talking about?" she demanded, truly confused.

"That is how I got the idea. Your grandmother, Lady Alecia, confessed it to me. She told me of how your father beat your mother, her dear daughter, and how in order to avenge her she made it look as though some of the cows and things had been killed by a bloodsucker. Your father had always been interested in such fiends, and it was only too easy to convince the local constabulary that he was responsible. They locked him up and he died by his own hand in prison." Seeing that she was truly shocked, Saunders pressed on. "Once your mother had died, Lady Alecia wanted to do the same thing to you, make it look as though you had been killed by the vampire, but something stopped her."

Clio got a faraway expression on her face. In her mind she was no longer in the tense, hot little room with the pacing madman and two death traps aimed at her heart. She was in a bed, like the beds she had found the girls on.

She is lying there, helpless as someone comes toward her, leaning over her, breathing hot breath on her face, someone is fumbling for her neck, struggling with one hand to pin her down and keep her from crying out, and with the other—

Then her assailant is being dragged away, yelling and screaming, arms flailing. She cannot see who is responsible for her salvation. But she can see the face of the person who had been leaning over her. Who had been trying to hold her down. A younger face, but still the face she knows, the face that has so often looked on her with hatred and contempt. Her grandmother's face.

It had happened to her. That was why she had felt such horror when she saw the dead girls, why she had beheld the terror on their faces. It had almost happened to her. Her grandmother had tried to kill her when she was an infant.

Rage began to boil inside of her and her eyes refocused on Saunders.

"You should know," he went on, grinning malevolently, "that your grandmother confided to me that she has always been sorry she did not go through with it."

Clio was breathing shallowly. "I don't believe you. You are a liar."

Saunders's eyes darkened. "You would dare to call me a liar? You, who are not even worthy of sharing a room with me? Not even worthy, really, of listening to me speak? You are nothing but a stupid idiot, Clio Thornton. You thought you could catch me? You thought you could investigate me? You? You are not even fit to go after a three-legged dog." Saunders watched the color rise in her face, watched the anger take over, and was thrilled. "You see? I told you that it was inside you. I told you—"

"Stop it," Clio hiccuped, interrupting him. *Upset the balance.*

"Have I grieved you, Clio?" Saunders asked with mild amusement. She hiccuped twice more. "Is it the truth you do not like to hear?" She hiccuped again. "Does it make you sad to know that you are a stupid fool?" he demanded, his voice meaner now.

"No," Clio told him, hiccuping so hard her feet stomped. "It makes me," she hiccuped, "angry. It makes me," she hiccuped again, "feel violent."

"Poor, poor angry Clio," Saunders said, closing his eyes to laugh. "Furious because you cannot destroy my perfect plan."

Clio stole a glance at the clock. The hands were quivering in one place, as if caught on the verge of motion.

"You poor unlovable fool."

Nothing perfect can endure.

Clio hiccuped five times in quick succession, powerfully, hiccups that made her body strain against the post, her feet kick, and the clock hands freeze. Inside, she could see that the gears had ceased to turn. The clock was no longer going forward.

She had stopped it. She had stolen time. The hiccups had upset the balance enough to halt the clock. She knew that Saunders would discover the deception soon, but hopefully she would have thought of some way out by then. Now there was only the pistol left to deal with. She had just shifted her attention there, ignoring the taunts Saunders continued to heap upon her, when two things happened, scaring her hiccups away. With one eye she saw Toast sit up. And with the other, she saw the handle of the door begin to turn.

Chapter 25

Saunders saw where she was looking. In a single, swift motion, he crossed to the door and put his arm against it, forcing it to stay closed. "Good evening, Viscount," he said. "I am so glad you have come."

"Good. Why don't you invite me in?" Miles asked through the door.

"I would, but we are not quite ready. We were not expecting you so soon. You are a bit early."

"Open the door or I will break it down."

"Oh, that will not be necessary. It is unlocked. But if you open it, Clio will die."

"Is that true, Clio?"

Saunders looked at her and nodded.

"Yes Miles, it is true." Her voice changed to one of supplication and she became more formal. "If you got my note, my lord, then you must understand. No small amount of time will save me."

"She is right," Saunders assured Miles. "And you must wait until midnight."

There was a long pause. Then Clio heard Miles's voice say, "Very well," and the sound of receding footsteps.

"What are you doing?" Saunders demanded.

"Leaving." Miles spoke through the door. "You said I

could not see her until midnight. That's almost two hours from now. I'll be back then."

Saunders was incredulous. "Where are you going?"

"To get something to eat. I am hungry. It has been a long day and I missed my betrothal feast."

"But you cannot leave."

"Why not?"

"Because I will kill her. I will kill Clio."

Clio could almost hear Miles's head shaking on the other side of the threshold. "You are not going to kill her. If you do, I will march right in there before midnight and kill you before you can get to me, and Mariana will inherit nothing."

Saunders stood up a bit straighter and smiled. "Ah, so you figured it out."

"Yes. Ingenious. You noticed that the betrothal contract only specifies that she shall inherit everything if I die on or after the day of her twenty-fifth birthday, not after the marriage has been celebrated. I should have realized it earlier. You are very literal. And following the letter of the contract you decided to kill me on July first. As soon after midnight as possible."

"Before you could touch her with your filthy hands. So she would be rich and pure when she came to me," Saunders rhapsodized.

"Yes," Miles sounded skeptical. "But you see, that guarantees that you will keep Clio alive, because you need something to lure me back here to my death. I am going to go to a tavern. I'll be back before midnight."

"Wait," Saunders commanded. "Don't you want to hear me tell how I killed the women?"

"I would prefer to be killed quickly than bored to death slowly."

If Clio had not been preoccupied, the way Saunders jerked in front of the door would have caused her to laugh. "Bored to death? You find the prospect of hearing about my crimes boring? I assure you, Dearbourn, they are fascinating in the extreme."

"I have never really been interested in tales of murder. I much prefer romances. Now if—"

Miles's interesting literary commentary was cut short by Clio, who began to sing.

"The first time I did see you, dear, my heart in me did pound. I knew that day as I know now, that my true love I'd found."

Saunders swung around to face her. "Stop it," he said. "Stop singing that. Don't sing that song."

"The second time our lips did meet, t'was better than the first," Clio went on. *"I felt the air float under me, and like me heart would burst."*

"Stop it," Saunders ordered, turning back and forth between her and the door. "Not that song. Do not sing it."

Clio saw that his eyes were getting a strange tint in them. *"The third time we pressed mouth to mouth,"* she continued, singing louder, *"We lay under the starry sky. And when you said 'you are my love,' there was none happier than I."*

Saunders crossed the room, his eyes roving in their sockets. "Stop. Singing. That. Song. I shall have to kill you, Clio, if you continue. That is her song. The song of the bloodsuckers. I shall have to—"

"And now your breath goes from you love, and your lips have grown so thin—"

"Stop it," Saunders whispered, stretching his hands for Clio's neck.

"And one last kiss I'll give you dear, for all those there

have—Now Miles!" Clio shouted, reaching with freed hands and pulling Saunders in front of her.

The door flew open, the pistol sounded, and for a moment, there was complete silence. Then Saunders's body slumped to the floor, Miles picked Clio up in his arms, and Toast began to dance in circles.

"It's over," she said, hugging him as tightly as she could. "It's over."

"I love you Clio," was all he could say in reply.

"Tell me again about how you found us," Clio asked as she and Miles and Toast dined at the round table in Miles's outer apartment. They had arrived home only half an hour earlier, after dropping the Triumvirate, Snug, and Inigo back at Which House. The puppy had been allowed to stay with them, since it was entirely thanks to him that they had been recovered at all.

"I sent my cousins out to Hartwell Heath after I got your note, just in case I had misunderstood what you were saying."

"You told me yourself that you never trusted anyone who called you 'my lord,' " Clio reminded him.

"Yes, but under duress—Anyway, I remembered from my last adventure with your household how fond the puppy was of Toast, so I decided to see if he could follow him. And, after several missteps, including one that almost got us killed near the bear pits, we found you." Miles reached out to touch her cheek. "Not very exciting compared to stopping a clock with hiccups, using the body of a madman as a shield against getting shot, and having your hands freed by a kleptomaniacal monkey who just happened to steal a knife from the other madman who tried to murder you today."

Toast, overcome by this praise, hid his head in his hands.

"You two were marvelous," Clio told them both. "I could not have survived without you."

"Yes you could have," Miles said, and for the first time in their acquaintance, Toast took sides. He leapt onto Miles's shoulder, and nodded furiously. "Your giving me that hint to delay Saunders by calling me 'my lord' again while Toast undid your hands despite having a pistol aimed at you was really remarkable, Clio."

"Anyone could have done that," Clio said, waving the compliment away. "It was the only thing to do."

"Of course. It was easy," Miles said rolling his eyes, and Toast rolled his as well.

The clock at the far end of the room struck two then, and the smile that had taken hold at the corners of Clio's mouth abruptly vanished.

"There is something I need to speak to Clio about, Toast," Miles said addressing the monkey. Toast nodded and crossed his arms. "Alone," Miles added.

With an expression of deep betrayal, Toast leaped from his shoulder, dashed across the floor, and plopped himself into the middle of an enormous suede divan. The puppy followed him doggedly, and sat on the floor, wagging his tail and staring up at his idol as if he had never been happier in his life. Taking Clio's hand, Miles led her into the bedroom and shut the door behind them.

"I shall miss this room," Miles said, somewhat absently.

Clio swallowed hard. "Will you be moving?"

Miles, his back to her, said, "I think it is inevitable."

Clio felt deathly cold inside. She did not want to talk

about this. She did not want to think about it. "I am sure your new quarters will be lovely."

"I doubt that."

She wanted to scream at him, scream at him to stop, not to think about it, not for a few moments. Why could she not stop this clock the way she stopped the one earlier? Why was she so powerless when it mattered most? "In time, my lord, you will grow accustomed to Mariana's taste," she said, hoping her voice did not crack.

Miles swung Clio toward him. "I doubt that, too. Because I am not marrying Mariana. I am going to marry you. If you will have me."

Clio stood stock still. "What are you saying, Miles? You cannot. The betrothal. Your father. You cannot break the contract."

"Why?" Miles asked simply in return.

"I cannot ask you to sacrifice your entire fortune for me, Miles. You have no idea what it is like to be poor."

"Yes I do. Because I know what life would be like without you. And that would be an impoverished existence indeed." He took her hands in his. "You are all I want in the world, Clio. You are all the riches I need."

Now her voice cracked. "Do you really mean that, Miles? Really?" Her heart was beating so fast she thought she might take flight.

"Yes, Clio. I do."

She threw herself into his arms, crying and laughing at once, clinging to him, kissing him, wanting to lift him up and spin him around. "I love you Miles," she repeated over and over again, and for the first time, the words had no biting aftertaste.

Miles had ordered a tub of water to be brought to his bedroom and it stood, still steaming, in the corner. He undressed his future wife lovingly, and led her to it. He climbed into the rose-scented water after her and while she lay in front of him, in his arms, he used a soft sea sponge to bathe her. He washed Saunders's blood from her chest, washed Doctor LaForge's sweat from her wrists, washed the horror of the day from her, washed away the bittersweet anticipation of the night.

He filled the sponge with water and then squeezed it out, letting it trickle over her head. She bent her neck back to drink it in, pressing herself against his chest, and he wrapped his arms beneath her breasts. He marveled at her perfection, at her size. She was so small, her entire length could not cover him, and yet she was the most powerful being he had ever met. He kissed her behind the ear, and on the neck, and she turned around and kissed him back, holding his shoulders with her hands.

"I read in a book once that making love in the water is different than making love out of the water," she whispered to him.

"No you didn't," Miles replied.

Clio smiled. "You are right. But perhaps we should try it anyway."

"There is no rush, you know," Miles said. "We have the rest of our lives together."

But the effect of those words on Clio made delay impossible. They made love in the water, Miles using the sponge to rub against her sensitive place until she moaned and begged him to stop and never to stop. They made love on the floor, Clio finding the foxtail he had worn to some betrothal ball what felt like years ago, and sliding it wrapped up and down his hard member until he thought he was going to go mad. They made love on the bed, passionately and wildly and eagerly, mingling their bodies together in a luxurious shower of I love you's. And when it was over, when the first signs of dawn were beginning to tinge the sky outside, when they lay together in one another's arms, Clio wondered what amazing insight would come to her.

It came slowly, in bits. At first it did not seem amazing at all. It began with the realization that Princess Erika's prediction had been true. That Inigo had brought good fortune to Clio. The best fortune. Inigo had brought her Miles. And he was hers forever.

She would have to tell Princess Erika the next day. That made two perfect predictions for the water jug. That left only "You will never find true love until the fireflies come out at noon." But she had found true love. She had.

She had.

"Impossible," Clio breathed to herself. It was not possible that she was questioning her relationship with Miles over a prediction made years ago by her neighbor, the notoriously unreliable psychic. But she realized, even as she thought about it, that the prediction was not all. She could already hear her grandmother hollering, yelling about how spoiled and selfish she was, about how she had deliberately inserted herself into Miles's life, deliberately ruined Mariana's wedding and dishonored the family. How Lady Alecia had known all along Clio would do something like this, because she was wicked and evil and this only confirmed it. And how she had disgraced not just her family, but Miles's family, the Arboretti as well.

Her own words, her own question, posed days ago, came back to her now. "My lord, do you possess anything so precious you would rather suffer than lose it," she had asked him after the Jubilee Fair. And he had answered, "my cousins."

Worse than knowing she had made true all her grandmother's horrible predictions about her, was the thought, the terror, that one day Miles would regret everything he was forced to give up. Not his house and his title and his money. There had been people who wanted her to go away, Corin had said so, and she suspected they were the Arboretti. If she did not, if instead she heaped infamy on their honorable name, how could they ever accept her? She would act as a wedge between him and his cousins, driving them impassably apart forever. The sacrifice was too big. What could she possibly offer in recompense? How could her love possibly be enough to make up for that? She did not have enough to give him in return for that loss. There was no such thing as enough.

If she stayed, she saw now, it would only be for selfish reasons, because she loved Miles so much. But if she really loved him, she would not force him to give up everything that mattered. She could never separate him from his family. True love, uncluttered with selfish motives, unclouded by her own needs, true love demanded that she go. And God knew she loved Miles truly.

She did not let herself look at Miles as she slid from his arms. She did not let herself glance toward him as she picked up the gown, the purple gown, and quickly pulled it on. She did not let herself touch him as she sat on the bed to tie her boots. Only when she was fully dressed did she turn around and face him. He was sleeping peacefully, soundly. One arm was stretched out, where she had been lying, and the other was thrown across his stomach. His hair, unmonitored in sleep, dangled over his closed eyes. He had the faintest hint of a smile on his lips.

In his sleep, Miles was painfully beautiful to look at. Unable to stop herself, Clio bent over and touched his mouth with hers. He brought his arm up and pulled her toward him. He nuzzled against her neck with his nose, and she fought unsuccessfully to hold back a sob.

The tears came out slowly, drifting down her cheek and onto Miles's. His face burrowed more deeply against her and she felt his lips on her throat.

"I love you, Clio," Miles said in a voice heavy with sleep. "I love you forever." Clio breathed deeply, forcing herself to remember this, this smell, this touch, for always. His arm slipped away, then, releasing her. For a long horrible minute, she wavered.

Then she picked up Toast and left.

She was barely outside the gates of Dearbourn Hall when a black hood was thrown over her head and she was dragged into a waiting coach.

Chapter 26

Corin was going to have to die. First. He was the first one who would die. Then all of his cousins. Everyone would die. Until Miles found out who had done it. Who had paid Clio to go away.

It was easier to blame them than to think about what it really meant. He remembered the conversation clearly, remembered overhearing her say "a thousand," as if sealing a bargain. If she wanted money, why hadn't she just asked for it? She could have had all the money he poss—

The thought caused Miles so much real pain that he had to stop where he stood. He did not have any money if he did not marry Mariana. She left him because he had no money.

The words they had exchanged the night before flooded back to him. "You have no idea what it is like to be poor," she had said, stressing that. At the time he had discounted it.

At the time he had been a fool.

No he hadn't.

Yes he had.

This argument might have gone on quite a bit longer

if Corin had not stumbled on Miles then in the hallway outside his apartment. The fact that his master was wearing exactly one boot and a not very long shirt alarmed him less than the expression on Miles's face. Corin thought he knew them all but he had never seen this.

Pure, unmitigated pain.

"She is gone." Miles squeezed the words out. "What did you do to her?"

"Nothing," Corin assured him, leading Miles back into his apartment.

"You did not offer to pay her?" Miles asked, his eyes burning into Corin's.

Corin looked away.

"I knew it!" Miles declared. "What did you offer her, who gave it to you, and how the hell do you propose to get her back?"

"I did not pay her anything," Corin answered.

"Then it must have been my cousins. Yesterday they tell me to marry her, knowing full well that she was going to leave. That sniveling bunch of scoundrels."

"That must be us," Ian deduced as he, Crispin, Sebastian, Tristan, Sophie, and Bianca entered the room. "What have we done now?"

"Bastards," Miles said, including Sophie and Bianca in his sweeping scowl for good measure. "How much did you pay her?"

"You paid Clio to go away?" Sophie demanded of her husband, outraged.

"No," Crispin pled innocence. "I didn't." He looked at his brother. "Did you?"

"You had best hope not, Ian Foscari," Bianca said

pointedly. "Not if you don't want to be the subject of some very unpleasant medical experiments."

"I did not either," Ian assured her.

"Tristan and I would just have eloped with her," Sebastian pointed out before Miles could transfer his glare to either of them.

"Then why did she leave," Miles asked, and the fury slipped away, leaving only the pain.

"I think that might be my fault," Corin put in after a moment. "The other night I *did* offer her money to go away. She said no," he added quickly, reflexively moving away from Miles. "I just wanted to make sure she was sincere in her feelings about you. But as a sort of test, I told her that people would talk if she interfered with the betrothal, and that they might say she did it on purpose. Might say some mean things about her. And about you."

Miles could see exactly what had happened. Could see how Corin's words would have affected Clio, would have made her afraid that marriage with her would hurt him somehow, cut him off from his family and friends. And Clio, his Clio, would never do anything to cause another person harm.

"You're fired." Miles hurled the words at Corin. "After you find her and explain what you did and bring her back."

"Have you looked at Which House?" Ian hazarded. "Perhaps she just went home for a few things."

"That is right," Miles said, brightening considerably. "Perhaps she just went home. Good idea. Corin, you go to Which House and—why are you shaking your head?"

"That was what I was coming to tell you, sir. Messenger came from Which House wondering where you two and Toast and the pup were. Said you had promised to come this morning so you could all celebrate together, but you had yet to appear."

For a moment, Miles just stood and ground his teeth. Then he started staring around the room like a crazy man. He bent on his knees and began crawling around, peering under the furniture.

"She is rather small, but not that small, my lord," Corin told him gently.

"I am looking for the puppy. He can find her. If she has Toast with her."

"The puppy wasn't here when I came up to clear the table earlier. He must have followed after them," Corin said, grimacing.

Miles got to his feet with the clear intention of wringing Corin's neck, but Ian stepped in front of him. "Before we do anything else, I think you should inform Mariana and Lady Alecia that you are terminating the betrothal," Ian suggested. "Since your wedding was to take place in fifteen minutes."

"You are right," Miles nodded and began to head out the door.

Tristan and Sebastian blocked his way.

"I might also suggest that you put on some clothes," Ian continued. When he saw Miles about to argue, he added quickly, "Not for the chapel. Who cares what they think? For the search. In case our search requires us to ride, for example."

"Or leave the house," Crispin added.

Miles was dressed in two minutes. Trailed by his cousins, he quickly made his way to the family chapel in the bottom corner of his house. There was a sizeable

number of guests all of whom grew very silent as Miles
and the Arboretti marched down the aisle toward the
front where Mariana, Lady Alecia, and Sir Edwin were
standing.

"I just wanted you to know that I am not marrying
Mariana," he told Lady Alecia. Then he turned to Sir
Edwin. "Congratulations, sir. This house is yours. The
roof on the east wing needs repair before winter. Good
day." He turned to go, when Lady Alecia's clawlike hand
closed on his arm.

"What are you talking about? Is it because of Saunders? Because he was a murderer? You can hardly blame
my sweet Mariana for that."

"Saunders was not a murderer," Mariana said. "He
was just pretending to be the vampire. He just stuck that
woman from the fair in the neck for fun and paid her to
lie still so I would be afraid. It was a game, Viscount. He
was not a killer."

Miles was so startled by this information that he momentarily forgot what he was doing there. But then he
thought of what Clio would make of it, and that he had
better tell her immediately, which reminded him that he
did not know where she was. "It is not about Saunders.
It is because I love your other granddaughter Clio and I
want to marry her."

Lady Alecia's face grew mean and pinched. "You would
sacrifice all this," she gestured around with her hand,
but ended up at Mariana, "for that stupid, trouble-
making girl?"

"It is no sacrifice," Miles said. "I am the clear
winner."

"You are my boy, you are," Sir Edwin said jovially.
"Let me—"

"Shut up, Edwin," Lady Alecia ordered, but her eyes did not leave Miles. "You cannot have Clio. You can never have her."

"What are you talking about?" Miles demanded.

"I've taken care of Clio once and for all," Lady Alecia said gleefully. "She is gone. Gone. She will never meddle in my affairs, never disobey me, never look at me with those wicked eyes again. Me or anyone else."

"I demand you explain what you mean."

"I exchanged her for something I wanted," Lady Alecia explained. "And there is nothing you can do about it."

Miles sensed that Lady Alecia would not elaborate unless compelled. He crossed his arms over his chest. "Tell me what you did with Clio or I shall have Mariana arrested for assisting at a murder."

"You bad, bad baby bear," Mariana said, starting up. "It is my birthday."

"Shut up, Edwin," Lady Alecia put in before her son could even open his mouth.

"Lady Alecia, where is Clio?" There was something about Miles's tone that made the entire chapel go very still.

"She is with Captain Black. It seems that she managed to antagonize him and he wanted her dead. He offered to relieve me of a three-thousand-pound gambling debt in exchange for my promise not to undertake an inquiry when her mangled body was found." Noticing Miles's expression, she added, "Oh, he did not use the word mangled. I did. I suggested it. I said I would only take the offer if her body was mangled. She mangled enough of my plans in her lifetime."

"You traded Clio for three thousand pounds?" Miles asked with horror.

"And her hair," Mariana corrected. "Grandmother made them promise not to do anything to harm her hair. I overheard her."

Lady Alecia smiled and patted Mariana on the arm. "She is quite right. I have always had a fancy for Clio's hair. It is a pity I could not have it today. I really had hoped to wear it for the wedding."

Miles was assailed by a wave of queasiness. He forced it aside. "Where did Captain Black take Clio?"

"I don't know. I have never met the man, only his representative. That charming man, Justin. He used to whistle outside my window to give me messages," she explained. Comprehension dawned on Sir Edwin's face, but before he could give voice to it, Lady Alecia went on. "You really cannot blame me, Viscount. It is Clio's fault that she upset a man as powerful as Captain Black. He was going to kill her anyway. I just chose to profit from it."

"I knew Clio would find a way to ruin my birthday," Mariana put in then. "I am sure she upset that man on purpose just to make sure she had all the intention."

"Attention," Lady Alecia corrected.

If he had not had something better to do, it was likely that at that moment Miles would have been guilty of murder. Instead, he turned on his heel and began marching out the way he had marched in. Sir Edwin called after him and Miles turned to see what he wanted, but the man was too busy being chastened by Lady Alecia to say anything. When Miles turned back, the chapel door was blocked by Inigo.

He stood with his hands on his hips, glaring with all the power in his twelve-year-old-boy frame at Miles.

"What is wrong?" Miles demanded.

From behind Miles, a voice said, "He thinks you are the one responsible for sending Clio to Captain Black's and he wants to make you pay for it. He has come to challenge you to a duel and wants to know whether you prefer pistols or swords."

Inigo began to nod, and Miles turned to look at Sebastian. His cousin had often demonstrated an amazing ability to decipher codes and understand languages, but never to make sense of silence. "How did you know that?"

"I am not sure. I can just tell. Apparently he followed Clio from here last night—don't worry, I won't tell her," Sebastian paused to address the boy, "and saw her taken to Captain Black's. Then, this morning he saw someone in Dearbourn livery go there to make sure she had been captured. I think you should explain that you did not do it, and that, if he leads us to Clio, you will rescue her."

Inigo's posture relaxed and he looked inquiringly at Miles.

"It's true," Miles told him. "I did not send that servant. Where is she?"

Inigo looked at Sebastian, who frowned for a moment. "Captain Black has her in his house on London Bridge. The large house in the center. There are guards and dogs. Big guards." His eyebrows shot up. "*Very* big guards. And lots of dogs. Oh, and pirates."

"Excellent," Tristan commented. "I haven't seen a pirate in ages."

*   *   *

"Do you hear that, Clio?" an oily voice inquired from Clio's right. Her blindfold prevented her from seeing the pasty face and the pointed red beard of the speaker, and from being blinded by the bright scarlet sash covered in golden medallions he always wore. It also kept her from having to look at the multitude of animals, stuffed and attached to boards, that hung on every inch of wall space in the tower room—every space apart from the empty one reserved especially for Toast—but she could picture all of it well enough. Captain Black and his collection made an indelible impression on the memory. "You hear those bells?" he asked again. "I left the window open especially so you would be able to hear. Those are your cousin's wedding bells. Perhaps you thought the wedding was not going to take place? The bells would not be ringing if Dearbourn had not gone through with it."

"How interesting," Clio remarked. "I thought you were going to kill me. I do wish you would hurry. I feel as though I have spent the past twenty-four hours waiting for someone to kill me and it is getting tedious."

"Perhaps it would be less tedious if I removed your blindfold. That way you could watch as I run you through with my sword."

After the careful machinations of Saunders, Captain Black seemed positively pedestrian as a villain. "I've never been run through with a sword before, so I would not know. Do whatever you think is best."

Captain Black frowned. He did not like Clio Thornton. He had expended a great deal of time, money, and manpower trying to capture her and her monkey, consoling himself for each new expenditure with the assurance that killing her would be a pleasure. It had been her idea, after all. The words "only if I were dead" with regard to his possession of that delightful little specimen Toast who was now furiously jumping around in his cage and would soon grace the wall behind his desk, had been spoken from her own lips. The least he could do, Captain Black had told himself as he waited for her to be brought in, was oblige her. He had looked forward to this moment with relish. But it was proving to be far less interesting than he had planned.

Frankly, he was hoping for a bit more of a reaction from the girl. Killing people was what he loved to do, it was how he had gotten his start years earlier, and now, what with the constraints of running all his nefarious businesses, he rarely got a chance to take a life with his own hands. When the opportunities are scarce, you must enjoy them to their utmost, he knew, and decided that for this to be enjoyable, he needed Clio to grovel.

"You know it is your monkey I am interested in, not you. And I owe you something for getting the vampire. He killed one of my best operatives."

"Lady Starrat," Clio said.

"Yes. Damn shame. Perhaps if you beg for mercy, I shall grant you your life," he suggested.

"I doubt it," Clio replied. She could not see what it would benefit her anyway. Without Miles, without Toast, what good was her life? Although, perhaps if she lived, one day someone would kill her just for herself, on her own merits, rather than to get revenge on someone else.

Captain Black decided to try a new tactic. "The less cooperative you are, the more painful I shall make this."

"I am not sure how much more cooperative I could be. I am just sitting here, in this chair. I have put up no fight at all," Clio pointed out. "Are you asking me to run myself through with the sword? If that is what you want, you shall have to untie me. I read in a book once that stabbing yourself through the heart requires both hands."

"This is nothing to jest about," Captain Black insisted.

"I was not jesting. The book really said that. It also had some very useful tips on skinning rabbits."

"If you are trying to delay until Dearbourn comes to save you, you delay in vain. Even if he were to come, which he will not, I have an entire kennel of dogs outside to alert me of his presence, and a dozen guards. There is no way he could reach you before you died."

"I do not expect him to come. Weren't those his wedding bells we just heard? It would hardly be suitable for a bridegroom to leave the side of his bride."

"Good. I am glad you understand. Now, prepare yourself to die."

In his cage in the corner of the room, Toast gave a low keening sob, and Clio felt a sharp pang of sadness. Yesterday Toast had helped save her life and today there was nothing she could do to save his. She could not believe that after everything, her life had come down to this, this horrible man, this inconsequential ending. Clio had never felt she needed rescuing before, but she realized that she had indeed been listening for the barking of dogs, for the noise of a scuffle on the stairs. For the sound of someone who cared about her coming to her aid. But there was no noise. No sound. Nobody.

"Good-bye, Clio Thornton," Captain Black said, and

she could sense him hoisting up his sword as clearly as if she could see it, could sense him getting ready to rush toward her. Could sense him hesitating, turning around, gasping in surprise. Could sense him backing up, raising his sword, but at a different adversary now.

"How did you get in?" Captain Black demanded, and Clio could tell from the way he was huffing that he was dodging thrusts from a rapier as he spoke.

"I let myself in the back way," Miles explained. His voice was smiling.

"But the kennels—" Captain Black panted.

Swords clanged against each other. "One of my cousins is a marvel with dogs."

"Dearbourn, listen," Captain Black began. His voice was oily again and Clio had the feeling that he was waiting for something.

The door of the room thudded open then, confirming her suspicion. "Ha!" Captain Black shouted. "Get him boys."

The swish of two knives being thrown with absolute precision was followed by the obscene curses of two guardsmen and the fleeing footfalls of two others.

"Are there any more coming?" Miles asked. "If there are, I shall have to call in my cousins. They would never forgive me if I got to have all the fun."

"I will take you myself," Captain Black growled, and blade clashed with blade again. The two men fought, Clio following their strokes around the room by sound. Captain Black was known as a very capable swordsman, but she thought she sensed he was growing tired. Or was it Miles? It was a strange and unnerving experience to sit in the middle of a battle and be entirely impotent, and Clio decided she did not like it. Nor was she thrilled about having her wrists bound for the third time in two days. In the future, she decided, she would carry a knife up her sleeve for such emergencies.

The future. If Miles was here—

Clio felt something brush against her legs. A sword clanked onto the stone floor, a breeze blew past her cheek, and then she heard someone screaming in fear, a scream that moved farther and farther away.

"Miles," she whispered. "Miles?"

There was no answer. Then, close by, a body shifted.

"Miles?" she asked, hesitantly. "Who is there? Who are you?"

The body shifted again. "Clio," Miles said, his voice weak. "Clio, Clio are you all right?"

Clumsy hands struggled with her blindfold and then Clio could see again. "My God, what happened, Miles?" she demanded, trying to get out of the chair but finding she was still stuck.

Miles's forehead was covered with blood, some of which had run down the front of his doublet. "Nothing serious," he said, his voice stronger now. "He hit me over the head." There was something about his tone that worried Clio.

"What is wrong?"

"He fell out the window and into the river. I had not meant to kill him."

"He was a terrible man," Clio said. "Look what he wanted to do to Toast. And that is not all. I am convinced that he was behind half the crime in London."

"You are right. He was. Among other things. But I had hoped to keep him alive to ask him some questions."

"Then you *are* Three."

Miles looked at her. "How did you know that?"

"Your footmen are too well trained," Clio answered simply. "It was obvious. By the way, Lady Starrat was working for Captain Black."

"It would seem then, that in the space of two days you have managed to uncover not only a vampire, but also the largest traitor in England."

"*We* managed to uncover them," Clio corrected. She twisted against her bonds. "Would you be kind enough to untie me?"

Miles shook his head. "I want to ask you some questions, too."

"In your official capacity?"

"Yes. In one of my official capacities."

"Which one?"

"As your fiancé."

"Miles, you must go through with your betrothal. You have no choice. The sacrifice is too great."

"You mean the money."

Clio looked confused. "No. I mean the honor. One day you will look at me and think of everything you gave up—your name, your family—and suddenly being with me will not be enough to compensate you."

"It would always be enough."

"You cannot know that. And I cannot let you ruin your life."

"Ruining my life means not going through with the betrothal my father contracted for me?"

"Yes. You must do it."

"Yes indeed, my boy, you must." Sir Edwin spoke from the doorway. "I've got a suspicion you've already dishonored my daughter. If I were younger and you were less good with a sword, sir, I would challenge you."

"I can assure you, Sir Edwin, I have not laid a hand on your daughter."

"Ho ho, and I say, sir, that you are a liar." Sir Edwin's eyes sparkled and Clio wondered if he knew he was about to get himself killed.

"Uncle Edwin, I—"

"Not your uncle, Clio. No, no, no. Wanted to tell you that for ages. Not your uncle at all."

"What are you talking about?" Clio and Miles demanded in unison.

"You do not know what you are. That's what I—"

"Shut up, Edwin," Lady Alecia commanded as she entered the room. "Before it is too late."

But Sir Edwin shook his head. "Nope. I'm sorry mother, but I've been shutting up about this for almost as long as I can remember. But no more. Today—"

"*Shut up!*" Lady Alecia screamed, flying at her son with her hands outstretched. "Don't say another word."

Sir Edwin caught his mother's hands in both of his and held them. His gaze on hers was loving, and a bit bemused. "Don't worry, mother. Clio will understand. She is a good girl. She will understand what we did." Then he looked at Miles who was quickly untying Clio's hands lest she have to defend herself against her grandmother. "Maybe you understand already. You see, Clio is really my daughter. Lady Clio Nonesuch. Mariana was my sister's daughter with that man Thornton. They were born only a week apart, and my mother thought it would be best for Mariana to be the one to marry you so we switched them. She never did like my wife, you see. I think she fancied having her daughter's daughter be a viscountess." His eyes moved to Clio. "I tried to let you know about it in my own way, but you did not understand."

"Your own way. Then it was you who sent me the note and asked me to meet you at Saint Paul's," Clio said.

"Yes. Wanted you to know what you really are, you see, but I was afraid to tell you directly. I did not want to upset mother. When you did not figure it out from my note, I tried to talk to you in the crypt, at the place where I first met your mother, but there was someone else there so I could not."

"If Clio is your daughter," Miles put in, in a tone that made clear he had been thinking very hard, "then all along, it is Clio I have really been betrothed to."

"Yes. Mother said it was better the other way. She said Mariana would be a better wife for you. And mother always was right before. But not this time." He smiled down at his mother. "Just one time for not being right isn't too bad, mother."

Lady Alecia wrenched her hands from his and stepped away to level the full force of her glare at him. "You fool. You are a bloody fool. Just like your Clio. You are all fools." From her sleeve she brought out a pistol. "You, Clio," she said advancing with the weapon outstretched. "You have caused trouble for the last time."

"It's all right, grandmother," Mariana said, coming into the room then. "You do not need to kill her. I'll be just as happy with the other birthday. I always felt older and more wisedomful than poor, dear Cl—"

"Shut up," Lady Alecia commanded, elbowing her aside. She pointed the pistol directly at Clio's heart and her fingers closed over the trigger.

Time stood still. In the space of a heartbeat, the puppy entered the room, brushing against Mariana's ankle as he made straight for Toast's cage. Mariana shrieked and leaped away, careening into Lady Alecia just hard enough to cause her to lose her footing. As she flew through the air, the pistol fired, sending the ball of gunpowder into the stomach of a perfectly innocent but long dead rabbit hanging on the wall behind Clio's head. Then time started up again and Lady Alecia was wailing and Toast was chattering and Mariana had fainted, twice, and Sir Edwin was staring about with a smile on his face and the Arboretti had run in and Clio felt Miles scoop her up into his arms and carry her out.

He carried her down the stairs of the tower, all the way down, until they were standing in the small garden on the side of Captain Black's house. There was a bench there, and he set her down on it and turned to face her.

"I would like to introduce myself," he said, formally. "I am Miles Fraser Loredan. The viscount of Dearbourn. What is your name?"

"I—I am not sure," Clio stammered. "I think it must be Lady Clio Nonesuch."

"Are you very attached to it?"

"Not very. I haven't had it long."

"Then you won't mind changing it."

"That would depend on what you have in mind."

Miles nodded. Then he slid down onto the ground beside the bench and said, "Lady Clio Nonesuch, will you marry me?"

"Miles Fraser Loredan, I would like nothing better."

She bent down, brushed the hair from his forehead, closed her eyes, and kissed him deeply.

It happened gradually. Throughout London, first one, then another clock began to chime midday. As the air filled with their peals, the sun dimmed until, when they rang out for the final time, it disappeared completely. The entire city fell dark and quiet simultaneously. Struck by the unnatural silence, Clio opened her eyes.

The garden was filled with fireflies.

Chapter 27

Five minutes later . . .

"Miles, I think I hear someone coming."

"Really, *amore*? I don't hear anythin—" The sharp point of a sword against his back stopped him.

"All right, Dearbourn," a stern voice said. "Your time is up."

Miles turned around. "What are you talking about, Tristan?"

Tristan gestured to the other Arboretti. "We have been extremely forbearing. But if you do not introduce us to Clio this minute, things will happen."

"What kinds of things?" Clio and Sophie asked in unison.

"Oh no," Miles said, shaking his head. "It's begun. She's mine," he told his cousins, gripping Clio firmly by the wrist. "She is on my side. Do not think to bend her to your evil purposes."

"But I thought she was a murderess," Bianca said, with a touch of disappointment. "I thought she knew all about evil purposes."

Clio began to look alarmed, but Miles leaned over and

said, "It's a compliment. Arboretti men seem only to marry women involved in murder."

"Really?" Clio looked from Bianca to Sophie. Neither of them looked much like a hardened criminal.

"Yes," Sophie nodded. "And Tristan used to be a thief."

"Does that mean you know how to pick locks?" Clio asked, turning away from Miles. "I read in a book once that—"

"She is perfect, Miles," Ian said.

Miles gazed at her while she discussed the fine points of dismantling hinges with Tristan, Sophie, and Bianca, and his heart overflowed with happiness. "I know."

As he watched, Tristan lowered his voice and whispered something in Clio's ear. She blushed deeply, then put her arms around Tristan's neck, and gave him a warm kiss.

Later, much later, when he and Clio were home, when the wedding had been quietly performed and an enormous ball scheduled for the next week, when they were standing on the roof, Miles's arms wrapped around from behind her, watching the stars glitter against the velvet backdrop of the sky, only then did Miles dare to ask what Tristan had said to earn him such a response.

Clio turned around to face him. "Are you jealous, Miles?"

"No," Miles answered firmly. When Clio kept looking at him, a little smile on her lips, he said, "Damn it, yes."

The smile got broader. "I don't know if I should tell you. It might make you mad."

"Your not telling me is going to make me madder," Miles assured her.

Clio sighed. "You are sure you want to know?"

"Yes." Miles set his teeth.

"Very well." Clio reached up and brushed the hair from his forehead. "What he said was, 'Thank you for bringing Miles back.' "

Epilogue

"I demand that you have this man arrested at once," Mr. Williams brayed. Behind him, Mr. Pearl and Mr. Hakesly nodded.

"I am not sure that is within my powers," the Special Commissioner told the men.

"It is your job to keep London free of criminals and murderers," Mr. Wiliams replied. "This man is a criminal of the worst order. He has murdered English. He has murdered our names."

The Special Commissioner looked down at the broadside. "It does not seem so bad to me. I like the title."

"You like the title? Never mind about the title. Look at this. Who wants to hear a play by a man named after torturing fruit? It will never work. Never." Mr. Williams threw his arms into the air. "You explain it to her, Toast. Explain that it will never work."

Toast, resplendent now with four medals pinned to his doublet, seemed to contemplate this request for a moment. Then he snapped his fingers, hopped on the back of the large dog who ran over in response to his summons, and disappeared out the door.

"You should know better by now than to ask favors of

Toast within two hours of any meal," Clio told him. "Besides, I really—"

The clock on the mantelpiece chimed gently. Clio turned to glance at it, and her eyebrows went up.

"I beg your pardon, gentlemen. You will have to excuse me."

"Clock's broken," Mr. Williams told her. "It's nowhere near four o'clock. Now Clio—"

"I'll see what I can do," she said, rising from the desk and smiling as she bundled them out the door. Then she used her special key on the clock in her bedroom and disappeared.

Without pausing, she ascended the stairs. She passed through an inconspicuous looking door and entered a recently expanded room that, despite the absence of windows, was filled with light. All twelve desks appeared to be occupied by young men dressed in the yellow and gold livery of the Dearbourns, until closer examination revealed that five of the young men were actually women.

When the hands of the clock on the mantelpiece pointed to four, it meant that the Special Commissioner for the Security of London, the fourth person behind the queen in charge of England's security, was urgently needed. Since she had finished hearing all the testimony in the Vampire of London case the week before—all but Inigo's of course, which had to be sent in written form from Venice where he was staying with Tristan and Sebastian—she could not imagine what the urgent need was. Then she spotted it, lounging in the doorway of his office at the back of the large room. He had a devilish smile on his face and for a moment, Clio had to stop and just stare at him. The fact that he was her husband still took her breath away.

Miles crooked his finger toward her and motioned her into his office.

"Did you do that?" she asked, pointing to the cords on the wall that controlled what the clock in their apartment said.

Miles nodded solemnly as he led her into his office and closed the door. "I have very important business with the commissioner."

"Really? What?"

"Secret. Close your eyes." Miles gathered Clio into his arms, carried her up a new flight of stairs and out onto the terrace, depositing her gently in the middle of the bed. The sides of the silver gray tent had been pulled up, so that the sunlight streamed across it. Off to one side, a plate of hazelnut cakes glistened with sugar icing.

"I am going to tell Two on you," Clio said, playing with the golden brown hairs that curled around the throat of his shirt as he lay down next to her.

Miles cupped her chin in his hand. "You don't know who Two is."

"Neither do you, but I will find out and then I will tell. Luring the Special Commissioner from her duties must be a grave crime."

"Luring? Who said anything about luring? Surely you have an insoluble problem that I can assist you in sorting out."

Clio looked at him. "Actually, I do."

"I knew it," Miles said happily.

"Is this why you wanted me to be the special commissioner?" Clio asked.

"As you are aware, I had no say in the matter. It was Elwood who put your name in. Someone had to take over once the previous commissioner started his interesting job as the London dogcatcher."

"Assistant dogcatcher," Clio corrected.

"Right. Everyone said you were the best candidate. Who was I to disagree?"

He kissed her lushly and settled her on the bed. With the sun setting around them and the fireflies dancing in the bushes, they made love. Afterward, they lay together lazily and watched the stars begin to twinkle in the pinkish-blue night sky.

"Do you know how proud I am of you?" Miles asked in a dozy voice as they held each other.

"Mmmmemslffff," Clio replied.

"Yes," Miles agreed, drifting off to sleep. "That about sums it—"

Clio's eyes snapped open. "Seven," she announced all at once. "Three plus four. That is it."

Miles did not open his eyes. "Ah. You solved your problem."

"Yes," Clio said, and he could feel that she was looking at him expectantly.

He opened his eyes and formed the now familiar words. "What does it mean, *amore*?" He noticed that her eyes were very, very purple.

Clio raised herself on both elbows. "Seven. What she should be called."

He was never able to guess what she would say, and this time her response was even more cryptic than usual, but something about it made his heart skip. "Who?"

Clio took the hand of her husband—her husband, the man she had loved so long, the man she now loved more than ever—and placed it on her stomach. "Her."

It took Miles a moment to understand. When he did, he was filled with a pleasure and joy he had never imagined existed. He smiled at her so radiantly that the stars dimmed in comparison and said, "Impossible."

"Actually, Miles, I read in a book once that when a man and a woman—"

The rest of her words were lost in his kiss.

The solar eclipse of 1590 was not predicted by any astrologer, and still cannot be scientifically accounted for.

Nor can the wild success of the play, written in honor of Clio and Miles's wedding, called *A Midsommer Night's Dreame*, unless you believe—as eventually Masters Williams, Hakesly, and Pearl came to—that it was the work of the divine through the drunk printer's apprentice, who jumbled their names together on the playbill so they read "William Shakes-Pear."

Click. Squeak. Slide.

The sound of a door opening slowly. Tuesday's eyes came unshut in an instant but the rest of her was paralyzed, listening. She had drawn the hangings of her bed closed so she could not see anything, but she thought she felt the fabric flutter.

Shuffle, Shuffle.

Her heart was pounding and she felt the hair on her arms standing up. She felt horribly trapped. . . . There was someone else. There in her room—

Scrape.

—near the foot of her bed. *Don't let him know you are awake* her mind screamed. *Don't shout. Don't move.* This is what she had wanted, to make the killer come after her, to trap him. The fabric swayed again—

shuffle

—closer to where she was laying now. She gripped her hands into fists and tried to make her dry throat swallow. *Breathe, lie still, breathe, lie—*

"No!"

SECRET
ADMIRER

Michele Jaffe

BALLANTINE BOOKS • NEW YORK

A Ballantine Book
Published by The Ballantine Publishing Group
Copyright © 2002 by Michele Jaffe

ISBN 0-7394-2546-3

Manufactured in the United States of America

This book is dedicated to Jennifer Sturman,
for whom my admiration is no secret and
whose friendship means the world to me.

There are but four things that all men must do to have a happy life, but do them they must. And these four be: Sleep, eat, love, die.

—JOHN HARRINGTON, *An Alphabetical Miscellany*, London, 1587 (Entry for "Contentment")

PART I

Sleep

Chapter 1

She lies in the field of tall grass, her arms and legs stretched out as far as they will go, breathing in the smell of summer dirt and heat and Mr. Eliot's trimming in the garden. The dragonflies loop over her, their blue-green wings gleaming like the lids of Chinese boxes.

She thinks of that time when she was younger and she climbed the yew tree and the branch fell off and made a crack like a lightning bolt in the garden wall that cost thirty-one pounds to fix. She had lost her allowance as a result, but she can't remember if it had been repaired. It is so pleasant here, with the sun and the dragonflies and the grass tickling and—

The ground beneath her vibrates with the angry pounding of his boots as he comes toward her, for her. He is nearly on top of her before she realizes it, bearing down, fast. She lies there, completely still, her fingers digging into the dirt, paralyzed with fear. Thinking, not again, please not again. Thinking, don't let him see me, don't let him find me, *oh god*—

"You can't hide from me you stupid bitch! Show yourself *now*."

She gets up and runs for her life.

*   *   *

The Lion examined his reflection in the mirror scrupulously, running a hand through his hair.

Who is the most dangerous man? The brave man? The wise man? The rich man?

None of these, sir. It is the mediocre man.

Why?

Because he is invisible.

No one would remember anything special about him, the Lion decided. Nothing he didn't want them to, anyway. Done up like this, he would look just how he was supposed to look for where he was going.

When he was not on a job, the Lion was a snappy dresser. He spent a lot of money on his clothes, but he felt it was worth it. He didn't talk much so he let clothes show what kind of a man he was. They drew attention to him, made people remember him, hid his other identity. And he liked to look good, liked the way women eyed him, then blushed. He liked it a lot; it gave him satisfaction.

Not like this, though. Not like the satisfaction of being the Lion.

The Lion was, in his own opinion, the best killer in England.

Crunch, crunch, crunch.

Sunlight slants at crazy angles between the boughs of the trees, making a corridor of irregular golden beams. They dance over her arms and hands like fairies as she flees through them, running as hard as she can, biting her lip to keep from screaming.

Crunchcrunchcrunchcrunchcrunch.

"I see you!" he calls from behind her, not sounding

winded. Heavy footsteps follow hers, filling the air with crunching and the smell of decaying leaves.

"When I get my hands on you I'll flay you alive."

She can hear him thrashing through the branches behind her. She has the advantage, being smaller, but not for long. He is gaining on her. She can feel his fingertips inching closer to her, smell his sweat now, oh god he's—

She trips on a rock hidden beneath the leaves and falls, headlong. She scrambles to her feet, gets caught up in the hem of her gown for a moment, then keeps running. She wills herself not to look behind her.

"You idiot," he says, and she can feel his fingers first graze, then grab her shoulders. He drags her, her feet leaving long brown lines in the dirt as he says, "There is no escaping from me. Don't you know that by now?"

The Lion had read everything he could get his hands on about every other killer and he knew that none of them even came close to him. Only one man had ever even approached his numbers, and he'd been caught three years earlier. Besides, he wasn't impressed. That man had only killed girls.

The Lion killed men. Lots of men. And no one ever caught him. He was sure he'd done more kills than anyone else he could think of, maybe even more than anyone in Europe. And nobody knew who he was.

The people who saw him every day—men like Joey Blacktooth and "Can Can Kyle" the barman who kept the tankards full at the Dancing Fawn—didn't think much of him. They'd call him the Loin or sometimes even the Groin after the way he looked at the ladies, but only behind his back. Truth was, they were a little scared of him. The man—more like a boy really—was strange.

He came in at night and sat alone at the table in the back, pulling scraps of paper out of his doublet and studying them. They elbowed each other in the ribs and laughed at him and pointed him out to strangers as a curiosity, but only when he wasn't looking. If they had been more forward or if a single one of them could read, they would have died. As it was, they were no threat to him and the Lion was content to let them stare.

It's not what you are, it's what you seem to be that matters.

Right now, the Lion seemed just like anyone else. But soon. Soon would be different.

When goddamit? I have waited—

What is the true knight's most important ally? Is it his master?

No.

Is it his weapon?

No.

What is it? Answer me!

It is patience.

I am so tired of being patient.

Aaaaaaaaahhhhhhhh! he cries when the heel of her boot lands in his groin.

His fingers lose their grip on her as he reaches between his thighs, moaning, staggering sideways.

She throws herself forward, away from him. The woods thin and she is in a garden, in view of the house. If she could only get there, only get in, she thinks, she could be safe. Late blooming roses flash by her in blurs of red and yellow as she runs across the paths, weaving drunkenly as her feet touch the uneven stones. Gravel sprays up behind her as she runs like loud rain, *pat pat pat pat patpatpatpatpat,* and over this she hears the sound of his moans.

Then she hears his footsteps.

"You'll never get away, you two-faced whore," he calls. Calls, not yells. Calm. Not running, walking. Too calm.

Why?

Ha ha ha he laughs. Then he says, "No way you'll get over the wall, is there? And I've locked the gate. May as well stop and get ready for what's coming. You'll need all your strength to pray for mercy, you heartless bitch."

The Lion came up with that name for himself late one night when he was lying in a noisy room with one of the beauties from Fleet Street. She'd traced the scar on the inside of his forearm with her finger and said, "Where'd you get this, love?"

"Nowhere," he'd replied gruffly, pushing her hand away. There was one thing whores were good for, and it wasn't talking. Plus, he didn't want to think about his past that night. It was his future that was preoccupying him. He'd been working in the same way for a while now, and he saw that it was time to change, move on. He needed something bigger, more taxing. There had to be better challenges for a man of his talents.

"Looks like a sun," the whore had said then, stupid bitch, not getting that he didn't want to discuss it with her. "Or like a lion's head."

The fact that it was a whore who gave him the idea for his name made him a little queasy, so he never told anyone. And because he didn't like to owe anyone anything, he saw to it that she couldn't ever tell either. He could have hurt her, but as a favor, sort of a thank you present, he made it painless.

Still, he didn't like thinking about it, thinking about her. Especially—well, especially now.

It's just a coincidence, he told himself.

There is no such thing as coincidence.

The Lion swatted the memory away and turned to the table behind him. There were a variety of weapons on it, mostly knives. He had found that a knife worked best for almost every job. They were more elegant, more gentlemanly than any other weapon. And he was, of course, a gentleman.

Plus, he liked to see his victims' blood close up, liked to sample their last breaths. Liked to savor the taste of death from their lips. There was nothing else like it.

She is a caged animal she thinks, she is doomed, she is going to die at his hands, and then she sees that he lied. The gate is not locked, the gate is open, the gate is her escape and she runs through it.

She does not stop to think how he could have made such a mistake but turns to the left, toward the kitchen yard, hoping he will think she went into the stables in front of her. She can barely smell the roses anymore—where is everyone?—her legs are burning, her chest aches, her mouth stings with dryness.

"Stop where you are, you stupid bitch!" he orders, not far behind her, not fooled.

She is not running now, she is stumbling, swerving crazily, slipping on the mud of the yard. She plunges toward the door, blinded by the dimness inside.

With unsteady hands she gropes along the wall until she finds—

"*Where the hell are you?*"

—a door. It opens, she falls through it, stumbling over boxes, falls to her knees, to the floor.

She can't run anymore.

What is the loudest sound?

A whisper

What is the most powerful weapon?

Cunning

What is the path to control?

Fear.

Very good. I think you are ready.

"I think so, too, master," the Lion said to his reflection in the mirror. He pronounced the last word with amusement. It was part of the game he played, the mask he wore. But just as he had no peer, he had no master. He was his own man. He patted down his hair one last time and smiled at himself. He liked what he saw.

He was the best.

Not long now, everyone would know it.

"Where are you bitch?"

She knows not to answer, not to say where she is. If she is quiet he won't find her.

"Come here right now, Tuesday!" He is standing just outside the door; she can hear his boots crackle under his weight. The wall shudders when he pounds his fist on it. "I know you are here," he calls, almost coaxing now. "If you come out I won't hurt you."

He is lying, Tuesday knows.

"Get out here you stupid whore bitch and show yourself."

A door opens somewhere, diverting his attention, and she hears his footsteps disappearing down the hall.

Now! She moves on tiptoe to the door and pushes it open. Her arms are trembling. The corridor is empty and not empty. His anger fills the air still. From behind other doors voices whisper. Tuesday thinks someone is watching her, a dozen someones, eyes pressed to the cracks beneath the hinges, but she doesn't care.

Now.

She slides into the corridor. Everything is eerily precise, her vision extraordinary. She sees a crack in the wall, a place where the iron nail was not set flush with the wood, the dark red lines on the petals of the roses that he crushed under his boots, dark red like trails of blood. She notices everything, yet she is running, fast, running hard down the corridor, watched by the unseen eyes. She looks behind her to make sure he is not there. She cannot hear his footsteps anymore, she can only hear her breathing, short gasps that sound almost like laughter, *ha ha ha*.

Ha ha ha she breathes hard, running, turning corners, left, then right. But the corridor never seems to change; it just goes on, more doors, more crushed roses that look like they are bleeding. *Ha ha ha*. Run, she tells herself. Keep running. You can escape. You can—

"I told you I would get you, whore," he says, thundering up behind her.

It had been a trap. Tuesday pushes desperately against the nearest door and then another, but they won't budge, the weight of too many eyes holding them up. *Ha ha ha* laugh the people with the eyes. Now we'll get a good show.

Tuesday keeps running but he is behind her now, bearing down, she can smell him on the air moving toward her. She can't turn around, won't turn around to see him, but she can see his shadow looming up against her. She is stuck. The corridor ends. His shadow crawls up the wall, bent by the corner, leisurely now.

Ha ha ha. Her breathing. His laughter.

The shadow grows an arm, the arm a hand, the hand a knife.

"You are mine now, Tuesday. Mine. I warned you. You just keep your whore mouth shut or I'll do the same to you as I did to him. Do you understand, bitch? *Answer me!*"

Tuesday woke up gasping for air. She was curled in the bottom corner of her mattress, trembling. Her night dress, soaked through with sweat, was clinging to her skin but she had goosebumps on her arms. The room was dark, it was nothing like the dream, and she was alone. Outside, at the level of her two windows, the street was empty. In the distance she could hear the shout of the night watchman saying that it was three in the morning.

She unfolded herself, put on the old silk dressing gown lying on the floor next to her bed, and moved toward her easel. She knew what she had to do, that there was only one way she would ever get back to sleep that night. She used the blank side of the preparatory sketch of the countess of Launton—mouth 22, nose 34, forehead 12, eyes, uneven, 33—and began to paint. She did not bother with undersketches, but divided the thick paper in half, drawing a line down the center to represent the corner across which the shadow had spread. Bold strokes of dirty gold for the oak-paneled walls of the hallway, fast lines barely suggesting the doors, a huge knot in the wood at the end that looked like a death's head.

This painting was different from her by-the-numbers portraits, ironic since they were similarly born of desperation, but she liked it. There was something more interesting in its bold lines than in the staid renderings of highly preserved aristocrats with failing marriages and mercenary young lovers, which paid her. The greatest challenge she faced in those portraits was to avoid painting the weariness that suffused even the set of her subject's shoulders, the weight of the lies they told themselves to keep going.

The watchman, closer now, was calling half five when she began to clean up. She could still get three more hours of sleep before she had to take her father his breakfast. Maybe today she should tell him. It had been weeks and weeks, more than two months. Of course, since it had already been that long, maybe it could wait until tomorrow.

"Blast," she murmured as her wrist cramped and the brush she had been drying skidded out of her hand. It slipped across her palette and stopped at her easel, leaving a rust-colored splatter down one side of the painting. Fixing the mess would take another hour. She felt tears prick the back of her eyes, not because of the ruined painting—no one was ever going to see it, so it hardly mattered—but at this further proof of what she already knew: she always ruined everything. It had been like that from the day she was born—on a Monday, instead of on a Tuesday like every other woman in her mother's family since the time of William the Conqueror—and continued on with no appearance of abatement.

They had given her the maternal family name, Tuesday, despite her lapse of breeding, and she bore the paternal surname, Worthington, but she wore them like ill-affixed labels. She did not fit in with her family, did not look like any of them, could not sing or play the lute or do embroidery like them. Six generations of Worthingtons had been ladies in waiting to the queens of England by merit of their extraordinary skills as needle-women. But everything Tuesday touched just unraveled.

Like her marriage to Curtis. It was her fault, she knew, that Curtis was not happy. She had been lucky to have Curtis, beyond lucky, and she had not tried hard enough to meet his needs. Even as her heart broke, she could not blame him for leaving. She could not give him what he wanted. What he deserved.

With him gone, she could add "wife" to the list of Ws she had failed at being: Worthington, woman, wonderful, wanted—

Taking up his position to watch her as she put away the last of her brushes and slid back into the bed, the Lion would have disagreed completely. He wanted her. He needed her. And he knew everything about her.

He knew that it was her aunt's dressing gown she wore, he knew the old trunk in the corner of the studio was her mother's, he knew that all her garters were light purple, that her father was an invalid living on the second floor, that there were only three servants left in the house, knew where they slept, how deeply, and how long. He knew how to get in and out through the loose door in the cellar without anyone being the wiser, knew when Tuesday was most likely to be alone, what she looked like close up while she was sleeping, and when she was awake. And although Tuesday would speak of it to no one but her maid, CeCe, he knew all about the dream. And about her late night painting. Oh yes, he knew all about that.

Reluctantly, the Lion made ready to leave. But he would be back. Back to watch, and wait, and dream his own dreams. Dream of the day when he would be who he deserved to be. Have what he deserved to have.

He gave the woman and the painting one last glance.

A day very soon.

Chapter 2

Grub Collins kept his fingers hooked over the cracked leather belt slung around his hips in order to keep them from fidgeting. Over the years he'd learned how to control his face and his voice and his walk to keep from showing excitement, but his damn fingers seemed to have a mind of their own.

It was a perfect summer day and the inhabitants of Ram Alley were taking advantage of the fine weather to do all their washing. Laundry hung on lines from almost every window, creating a canopy of lacy petticoats and well-worn trousers. It looked just like any other morning, perhaps a bit quieter than usual. Even if someone had noticed the strange feeling of expectation that fluttered on the breeze with the petticoats, they would not have been able to put their finger on it.

Grub peeled himself off the wall he'd been leaning against for the last hour and lounged slowly down the street, squinting at the laundry. An ancient tavern keeper in high leather boots stopped his sweeping long enough to try to coax him in for a drink, but Grub pressed on. He dropped a coin in the outstretched hand of a one-legged beggar, then continued slowly down the street toward a drunk stretched out next to the street door of the Little Eden.

Roused by the shadow being cast over him, the drunk opened one eye, slowly, then the other.

"Nothing doing," Grub started to say, but stopped as the drunk's gaze moved behind him. He turned and saw the beggar, now in possession of both legs, running hard down the center of the street.

Men and women filed from the doorways of about half the buildings to watch as the beggar spoke urgently to the drunk man, and calm turned to acute expectation. This was not the voyeuristic interest of gossipy neighbors, because these were not the normal inhabitants of Ram Alley. Every chamber maid, shopkeeper, and butcher's boy was a highly trained operative, part of an elaborate surveillance operation designed to catch one of England's biggest enemies. The laundry was not merely hung out to dry, but actually spelled out a report. Grub Collins was not a loafer but a messenger, and the surly drunk was no less than Lawrence Pickering, the earl of Arden—the man Queen Elizabeth herself called "Our greatest hero," now the head of Her Majesty's operation against smuggling.

"It's off," Lawrence announced, getting quickly to his feet, and everyone began talking at once. He silenced them with a look. "I am going with Tom—" he gestured to the agent who had been dressed as a beggar, and whose face had gone sickly pale, "—but I want the rest of you to stay at your posts until I return." Halfway down Ram Alley he stopped and retraced his steps to the old tavern keeper. "Christopher, send word to the Special Commissioner that someone got to the Lark before we did," he barked, then turned and continued down the street.

Lawrence Pickering knew this area intimately. It was here that he had built, with his own hands, the empire that made him one of the wealthiest men in Europe. Two years earlier he had owned almost every one of the newly refurbished buildings he and Tom were now passing, and had funded most of the now thriving businesses. It was also here that he had grown up—sometimes in the buildings he would later own, more often taking whatever shelter he could in the bleak and filthy alleyways between them. From these, he watched the men and women of Alsatia, and watching them he learned the two most important things he knew: that there was a huge difference between living and living well; and that it had nothing to do with money. He knew that for certain.

After volunteering to fight against the Spanish and doing everything he could to get himself killed, from sail a burning ship into the middle of the Spanish fleet to lead a jailbreak of 200 prisoners—

("I just wasn't lucky," he'd said with a beguiling smile and a shrug when he returned to England.

"You don't believe in luck, Lawrence," his best friend, Crispin had reminded him. "But I do, and I am glad you are back."

"So am I," said Lawrence, sounding like he meant it.)

—he had returned to London a hero. His attendance became the most crucial ingredient for a successful dinner or ball, his title the most valued accessory a marriageable young woman could hope to wear, and his presence the most sought-after accouterment for every boudoir.

("Last year it was diamond shoe buckles, this year it is

me," he had joked with one of the women who invited him to her bed.

"My diamond shoe buckles broke," she commented, looking him over with a sweep of long lashes. "There does not appear to be anything broken about you."

Lawrence had chuckled, acting like he meant it.)

But even his most ardent and attentive admirers would have been hard pressed to recognize the earl of Arden in the filthy but determined figure who now accompanied Tom away from the tavern, which was, of course, the point. His men had only been undercover and in position for the past three hours; Lawrence himself had been there all night, checking and double checking. He had enough enemies that he knew better than to go to an anonymously called meeting without real precautions.

He would not normally have responded to an anony-mous summons, but at this point he would do anything to shut down the smuggling operations that had been damaging Her Majesty's coffers and war efforts for the past five years. In the three months that Lawrence had been in charge of the anti-smuggling operation, illegal trafficking had gone from a torrent to a trickle, but that was not good enough for him. They even thought they knew who was responsible for it, but they could not prove it, and even if they could, just grabbing him would only upset, not end, the selling. What they needed was someone who could explain the organization, some-one who could name names. Someone like the man they code named the Lark because in his letter to Lawrence he requested a meeting at the crack of dawn. He offered them all the information they might desire about the smuggling in exchange for immunity and a hideout in the countryside. For that information, Lawrence would gladly have risked his life. Twice. Unfortunately, it was the Lark's life that went instead. And with it whatever he knew.

With his jaw clenched, Lawrence followed Tom around a corner and into a narrow alley. They had to skirt a group of mangy looking dogs fighting over a piece of meat, and then duck under a short arch before reaching the door of the abandoned house where the Lark had been found dead.

It was dark inside but the circle of light given off by the lantern Tom held illuminated a figure slumped half against the wall and half on the floor. Lawrence bent down toward the motionless form and wrinkled his nose. Of the three things Lawrence disliked most in the world, one of them was lilacs, and the dead man must have drenched himself in lilac water before going out. Close inspection revealed no wound on the man's back, so Lawrence reached out and carefully turned the corpse over. And froze.

Behind him, Tom inhaled sharply, then retched and dropped the lantern. The light flickered madly back and forth as it fell and crashed on the ground, spluttering out. With their eyes unused to the dim interior, they were instantly plunged into impenetrable darkness. But even in the darkness the corpse seemed to hover before them.

Lawrence felt as if the image had been seared into his mind, joining so many others and trumping them. There was the agonized expression on the man's face. The long, red gash that crossed his pale throat above his ruff like a bloody smile. And then, below it, the gaping cavity in his chest where his heart should have been.

"Tom," Lawrence turned to call behind him into the

darkness. His voice sounded hoarse and strange to his own ears. "Tom, are you all right?"

"Yes," was the unsteady reply.

"Good. Do you think you could do me a favor?"

"Yes." A little more steady.

"Please go outside and stop those dogs from eating— whatever they are eating."

There was a gag, a pause, a scratching noise, and then the sound of footsteps clumsily receding.

When he was sure the young man was gone, Lawrence steeled himself and relit the lantern. Until that moment he believed he had seen all that man could offer in the way of death and destruction, both on the streets of London and on the field of battle. And until that moment he had not understood the security that such a belief offered.

Those other killings, while pointless, at least were motivated by something: patriotism, greed, love, loss, rage. But even if that had been the case here, the violence of the killing moved it beyond that, beyond the space of motive. There was something chillingly malevolent, hauntingly calculated, about the way this man's life had been taken. Something that went beyond mere murder.

As he looked at the heartless body in front of him, Lawrence perversely remembered one of the axioms he used to drill into his men: *It is not what you take away that matters, it is what you leave behind.* He had always considered it as a way to control his enemies, send them the message he wanted them to see.

What message was the killer sending through this violated body?

Lawrence knew with overwhelming certainty that he did not want to find the answer to that question, did not want to again find himself wading into a dark pool of violence and death and betrayal. He knew that finding it would cause him to suffer in ways he could not even imagine.

Just as he knew, with equal certainty, that he had no choice.

He was right on both counts.

Chapter 3

Tuesday bit the inside of her cheek and glared at the half-finished portrait on her easel ferociously. She would have given anything to be able to concentrate on it. But her eyes kept looking past it, toward the door.

When she had first set up her studio in Worthington Hall's unused laundry rooms, she had angled her easel so that she painted facing the large windows that opened onto the street. But after only three days she had turned around. Her neighbors, who enjoyed peering in and trying to guess the identity of whomever she was painting, thought she changed it for their benefit. She let them think it, because she hated the real reason.

She did it so she could watch the door. So she would know the very instant Curtis came home.

If he came home.

She wanted to kick herself for still waiting, for still looking up anxiously every time there were footsteps in the hallway, wondering if this time, this day, was the day-week-hour when Curtis would come back to her. A dozen times she had consciously turned the easel back toward the windows, and a dozen times, without realizing it, she had found herself staring again at the damn door.

She dragged her eyes from it and forced them back onto the portrait.

Living in this constant state of vigilance was taking its toll on her. It was not just the dreams, although those were part of it. She had begun to feel like someone was watching her all the time. She found herself eyeing shadows in the street and jumping at loud noises. Just that morning she had been convinced that someone had rearranged her linens. She hated feeling afraid all the time, as if she were under siege, as if right this moment—

"Good morning, fair princess."

Tuesday gave a start at the sound of the familiar voice, saying the familiar phrase, behind her. She turned as George Lyle was in the act of climbing through the open window.

"Sorry to scare you," he said, scowling at a fleck of dirt on his meticulous breeches. "No one answered the door."

Annoyed at herself for being so edgy, Tuesday waved away his apology. "It's nothing. I think CeCe has Morse helping her put up some new experiment. He must not have heard you knock." She mustered a smile. "How are you this morning, George?"

"Better now that I have laid eyes on you."

Tuesday looked at him closely. George had been one of her closest friends for a long time. He was just past forty, and grew only more handsome with each passing year, each encroachment of gray around his temples. His square jaw, deep green eyes, and flirtatious smile managed to hold allure for even the most chaste aristocratic wives, and had made having a George Lyle Original

Portrait one of the requirements for stature in the fashionable world. But recently, at least to Tuesday, George had begun to look different. Something—the tightness of his smile, the newly metallic edge of his laugh—had changed. Today she noticed that there were bags under his eyes where there weren't usually, as though he had not been sleeping.

Pretending not to notice her scrutiny, George bent to eye the painting she was working on, then stood up abruptly. His face was a mask of exaggerated horror. "Ugh. Dowager Castenough. She is terrible. I absolutely refuse to do this in front of her."

Tuesday nodded as if she understood. "Perhaps today we ought to let it go. Just skip it."

George looked injured. "You don't mean that." He took a deep breath and looked soulfully into her eyes. "Tuesday, will you run away—"

"No thank you, George."

"You didn't even let me finish."

"I knew what you were going to say. You say the same thing every morning."

"That does not mean you can just interrupt. I never interrupt when you say 'let's just skip it,' which you do almost every morning. Besides, it is quite rude to interrupt when a man is proposing to you."

"Not if you are married and he does not mean it. Can—"

"Lady Tuesday Worthington Arlington, will you run away with me and be my love?"

"No thank you, George. Do you have any—"

"No thank you? That is all?" George frowned. "You usually at least say 'that is very kind of you but I shall have to decline.'"

"I was striving for variety."

"Let us try this again. Tuesday, will you run away with me and be my love?"

"That is very kind of you, George, but I shall have to decline. Now, can you tell me what is wrong with this picture? I've been working on the nose for an hour and I can't quite get it right."

"Everything is wrong with it. The dowager of Castenough should never let herself be painted."

"You were the one who sold her on the idea."

"It was only to punish you for not running away with me. I thought it might make you jealous. Look at me." George interposed himself between Tuesday and the canvas. "Look at this face. How can you say I don't mean it?" He turned heavenward and gripped his chest, but his eyes stayed on Tuesday.

"I do not mean to be callous, but could you have your fit a little farther from the wet paint on the left ear? Thank you."

With a sigh, George seated himself on the arm of the settee next to Tuesday's easel and began to twirl a paintbrush between his fingers. "Really, princess. How can you be so cruel?"

"George, don't be absurd. You knew when you walked in here that I was not going to run away with you."

"But why not?"

"What reason did I give yesterday?"

"I think it was your shoes being too tight for running. No, I'm wrong. Yesterday was the one about not abandoning your father. I've always thought that one rather unconvincing. Bad Sir Dennis would hardly notice."

"Very well. Which reason do you like best?"

"Truthfully, I think they are all rather weak, but if I had to choose, I'd go with 'Curtis will come find us with murder in his heart and pistols at the ready.' At least that one has some drama to it."

Even, Tuesday thought to herself, if it wasn't true. As if Curtis would come for her. As if he would even care.

"George, it is very kind of you to offer, but I must say no. It would utterly destroy our friendship—you know how messy I am, and how you hate chaos."

"I would learn to live with it."

"No. Your esteem means too much to me."

"Now be serious, princess. I've got it all planned out." He took a sip from the glass on Tuesday's work table, choked, and put it back. "What the devil is that?"

"Water," Tuesday replied, vaguely amused. "It comes—"

"I know where it comes from." George wiped his mouth on his hand and stared at her as if she had tried to poison him. "And I know what it is good for. Cattle. No wonder you look so listless today. What you need is some strong wine."

This was another manifestation of the new George. He had always been a man who liked spirits, but now he was almost never without a drink, or the lingering scent of one. And he suddenly looked agitated. Tuesday opened her mouth to ask him what was bothering him, but he spoke instead. His usual playfulness seemed to have drained away, leaving him businesslike, abrupt.

"Never mind. We can get some on the road. It's time we were going. Curtis might return at any moment, you know, princ—"

"Oh George, thank goodness you are here!" a female voice exclaimed from the open door. The voice—genteel, sweet, and very feminine—matched the woman to whom it belonged perfectly. With her reddish-blonde wavy hair, milky skin, luscious figure, and huge, guileless blue eyes, CeCe had managed to capture the imagination of every man in the neighborhood from the moment of her instillation as Tuesday's maid at Worthington Hall, and at the same time befriend most of the women. There were those—the Mean and Uglies, as CeCe called them— who mocked her "hoity-toity" manners and the way she would lecture to younger housemaids about what colors not to wear and how to hold their shoulders just so, but they were in the minority. Tuesday could not remember a day when CeCe hadn't received at least one marriage proposal, which she always politely declined with the explanation that she was waiting for her fiancé—lost during the war against Spain—to make his way back to London. This denial served only to make both her male and female admirers sigh louder as they added "loyalty" to her list of virtues.

Indeed, George Lyle was one of the only men in the metropolis who seemed immune to CeCe's charms, and she regarded him in about the same light as a leper. Which was why, when she came flying through the air at an unseemly pace, said "George, dear, you will save us, won't you," and threw herself into his arms, he and Tuesday simply stared at her, dumbstruck.

Tuesday recovered first. "What is wrong, CeCe?" she asked in a voice of real concern.

"Everything. There is a man. Outside. Prowling. I was not sure so I went outside and there are *footprints*, men's footprints and—" she drew away from George and eyed him with suspicion. "Why aren't you going out to capture him?"

George's former look of surprise had by this time changed into a sneer. He shook his head. "Haven't you tired of that game yet, CeCe?" he asked, brushing at the front of his tunic as if close contact with her had left behind a dirty residue.

"Game? It is not a game," CeCe said, her cheeks pink. "Didn't you hear me? There are footprints out there. There is someone out there. Waiting to rob us!"

George's sneer deepened. "You think all men are potential robbers, especially when I am trying to be alone with your mistress. Those footprints are probably mine, since you and your boyfriend Morse were too occupied, doing God knows what, to do your real jobs and open the front door for me."

"Morse is *not* my boyfriend. And my job is to wait on Tuesday, not man the door."

George waved her objection away. "You know you only pretend to see robbers because you are jealous of the attention Tuesday is paying me."

CeCe's eyes narrowed. "Me? Jealous of *you*? If I did not know better I would have thought you'd already begun drinking rather than waiting until the afternoon."

"I do not get drunk in the afternoons," George said stiffly, glancing fast in Tuesday's direction.

CeCe's tone was light and informative. "That isn't what Albert next door says. He says he's seen you staggering around as early as noon." Taking advantage of George's momentary silence, CeCe turned her attention to Tuesday. "I swear, Tuesday, there was someone out there. Besides George. Last night, when I came back from helping Josie take in her new gown so it would show off her lovely wrists, I saw him just there." She pointed directly across the street, to the mouth of a dark alley. "I tried to remind myself of what you said, of how no one would bother to rob us since we haven't anything, but I just know he was watching us." She hugged her arms around her slight figure, suddenly trembling again. "*You* believe me, don't you Tuesday?"

"Of course."

George snorted and, ignoring the glare Tuesday leveled at him, said to her, "I am telling you, princess, you have to leave here. Another day or two in this madhouse and you'll be as insane as the rest of them."

"I'm not mad," CeCe insisted with new vehemence. "There is someone out there. I can feel his eyes on us. On us right now."

At that moment there was a scratching noise above them. The three of them looked up. CeCe's mouth formed a terrified O and her lips moved but no words came out. There was a pair of eyes staring intently down at them through the open skylight.

But they did not belong to a robber. "Oh good, you're home," ten-year-old James Burns said cheerily and dropped through the opening into the studio without waiting for an invitation, a breach of etiquette that would have made his mother blanch, if he'd had one. He was followed by his younger brother, Baby, and his sister, Lucy, who at fourteen had an inkling that this was no way for a lady to enter a room, and consequently always arrived blushing. It was not clear whether Tuesday had unofficially adopted them or they her. What was obvious was that the three Burns children were almost as at home in Tuesday's studio as she was, and certainly more at home than they were in their own deluxe establishment next door, with their stiff father and his profusion of servants and mistresses.

Their toes had barely reached the ground before they all began speaking at the same time.

"Where is he?"

"Can you undo this knot?"

"What rhymes with 'oozed'?"

Tuesday spent a minute sorting through these questions, then reached out a hand for the knotted gold chain dangling from Baby's fingers, asked "Who are you talking about?" and, addressing the girl, said, "I thought we agreed that you would stop writing poetry about death."

"I have. This is a love poem," Lucy explained, looking at her toes and blushing more.

Before Tuesday could inquire further, two astonishing things happened: there was a thundering crash in the hallway outside the studio; and CeCe, after turning to him and saying "I told you so," fainted into George's arms.

Lawrence had been banging on the front door of the house for a full five minutes before anyone noticed him. Even then it was only a young man who leaned listlessly out a window next to the door, glared at him hard, and asked, "Why d'you want to do that for?"

Lawrence had stared at the man. "Do what?"

"Knock like that. Drive a body batty."

"I was hoping someone would open the door."

"Oh," the young man replied.

Since he did not seem about to move, Lawrence decided to forego subtlety. He smiled. "Could *you* open the door?"

"Me?" the man asked, surprised. "Certainly not. Not my job."

"But you are standing right here," Lawrence pointed out. Not pointing out that the man's throat was close enough for him to wring it.

"Demeans a man, doing tasks not in his job. Cheapens him. Makes him less. Demeans him."

"You already said that."

"I'm studying to build my vocabulary," the young man explained. He had turned from Lawrence for a moment, and when he turned back he extended a broadside out the window. "See, studying up the hard-word list. Comes out every week, a different letter each time. Bet you don't know what those words mean."

Lawrence ignored the paper and focused instead on the young man. He was still smiling—these days he was almost always smiling—but it kept away from his eyes. "Do you know what the word immediately means?"

"Of course. Everyone knows that."

"And the word excruciating? Do you know that one?"

"Yes sir," the young man replied, proud. "Also excursive. They was on the same sheet, one next to each other."

Lawrence's smile was hearty. "Good. Then you will understand what I mean when I say that if you do not open this door immediately, you shall be in excruciating pain."

"Yep, got that clear as—wait a moment. Are you menacing me, sir?"

"No. I am warning you. There is a difference. You have until I count to three. One. Two—"

The door opened abruptly then, and Lawrence found himself face to face with a nattily dressed man with a sour expression on his face. "You did not have to heckle me," the man said, stepping aside to let Lawrence pass.

He stopped short as he crossed the threshold. On first glance, it looked like he had walked into any other entry hall of any other moderately wealthy nobleman, with a staircase running up one wall and a table holding a bowl of fruit, a classical style bust half obscured by a plant, and two gilded chairs upholstered in red velvet pushed against the opposite wall. But something was not right, and in his second glance Lawrence had realized what it was: the staircase was real but everything else—the table, the fruit, the chairs, the bust, the plant—they were all illusions. The hall was, in fact, completely bare except for an enormous painting on one wall that depicted the furnishings with exquisite skill. In his amazement at the painting, Lawrence momentarily forgot all about what he was doing there until he realized that the man was disappearing up the stairs.

"Wait," Lawrence called after him. "I am looking for Lady Arlington. Does she live here?"

The young man, already halfway up the stairs, paused. The hint of a smile crossed his face. "See that door right in front of you? Take that, then go left. At the second door, not the first. You do that, you're guaranteed to find her. Guaranteed." Then he disappeared.

Lawrence had followed these directions, making his

way through a labyrinth of dusty service corridors, until he came to an unpainted door behind which he could hear the sound of voices. There was a moment of silence as he put his hand on the door pull, and then suddenly he found himself flying headlong into a stuffed rooster while a gong went off in his head.

Chapter 4

"It works," pronounced in a tone of muted awe, were the first words Lawrence could make out when the ringing in his ears quieted, and he was not sure he agreed. Whatever 'it' was, it certainly was not his jaw, which felt like it had been slugged, or his vision. He blinked twice and was about to try to push himself to his feet when he realized that there was something on his chest. Something squirmy.

The squirmy thing leaned its face directly over his and said in a voice whose shrillness could have come only from a young boy, "His eyes are open! He is alive!"

Before Lawrence could reply to this, he felt the boy being lifted off of him. Something tugged at his arm and he found himself in a sitting position.

Gradually, the world came into focus, but it still made no sense. All the furniture that had not been in the entry hall seemed to be here, along with a hundred random items ranging from a suit of armor to the five-foot-tall stuffed rooster that had broken his flight, and whose feathers he was now wearing. And among these items were scattered a handful of people of assorted ages and sizes, who could scarcely have had less to do with one another. The only thing they had in common was the direction of their gazes, which were locked on him.

Under their scrutiny Lawrence rose to his feet. He looked behind him, at the door through which he'd, ah, entered, and saw that it had been rigged with what appeared to be a pot lid at chin height. About a handswidth above the ground, a cord crossed the opening, tripping over which, he surmised, had caused him to take flight.

Lawrence turned back around when he heard himself being addressed by a woman. "The top part of the burglar alarm was supposed to hit your head, not your chin," she explained, pointing to where his hand was massaging his jaw. "You are too tall."

No apology, nothing. She just stated these things as if they were facts, as if it were his fault that he'd been attacked by her doorway. And Lawrence let her.

She was taller than average, with hair the color of autumn grass, and she was holding a badly knotted gold cord in her hands. Her eyes—the gray-green of summer thunderheads before a storm and, Lawrence suspected, capable of flashing like them—rested on his face, but she was not meeting his gaze. In fact Lawrence had the strange feeling that she was studying his chin.

Later he was able to identify what he felt at that first moment, what had stopped his tongue and made him incapable of speech, as a warning alarm. But at the time, it just translated into a single thought: he hoped like hell she was not Lady Arlington.

Before he could ask her name, three children rushed on him and, in a flurry of elbows and knees and curtsies and bows, said simultaneously:

"Is it true that you lived on rats when you were in prison?"

"And that you have so many mistresses that you have to buy silk stockings by the boatload?"

"My dog can dance, shall I go get it?"

"Did you come just to see us?"

"Do *you* know a word that rhymes with 'oozed'?"

The woman stared from him to his chorus before demanding, "What is wrong with the three of you?"

"That is Lord Pickering," the oldest looking boy replied, gesturing with his head.

"The earl of Arden," the younger one elaborated in a half whisper.

"The hero," the girl put in for good measure.

Lawrence was growing accustomed to being stared at and interrogated and greeted awkwardly. It had almost stopped bothering him, like it no longer bothered him when women circled near, but not too near, him at balls, as if he were an exotic but dangerous beast.

He was not, however, used to people bursting into uncontrollable laughter when he was introduced, which was exactly what the woman did. "You think that is the earl of Arden?" she repeated, slightly out of breath from chortling. "Oh. Certainly."

Silence fell over the room.

"And you are?" Lawrence asked with annoyance. What the hell was wrong with him? It was his practice to be suave and charming and polite and smiling. It was how he was known. By everyone, even his enemies. But all he could do was frown at this woman and act haughty.

"I? Hmm, let me see." The woman seemed to ponder

it. "I am—oh yes. I am Minerva. The goddess of war. No. Sorry. I am a gypsy named Samantha."

The girl gave her a reproving look, then said apologetically to Lawrence, "That is Lady Tuesday Arlington. You should excuse her, my lord, she really ought to learn better manners. CeCe and I have told her that a dozen times, but she does not listen to me."

"And with good reason," an expensively dressed man of about his same age stepped toward Lawrence to say. "What proof do you have that you are who you say you are?"

"Proof?"

"If you were an earl, Morse certainly would not have told you to come in the servant's entrance, especially since he knew there was an alarm on it. Besides, I've seen many earls and you don't look much like one. More like a vagrant if anything."

He gestured toward a looking glass on one wall and when he glanced in it, Lawrence could see what the man meant. He had come straight here from the murder scene, not bothering to change out of the clothes he had worn to be a vagrant, nor to shave or bathe or even run a hand through his hair.

His eyes moved from his own reflection to the room behind him. He'd been so preoccupied at first with the bizarre array of furnishings that he had not noticed the walls, but he did now, and what he saw took his breath away. If the illusion of the entry hall was a masterpiece, this room was a tour de force. Each of the walls had been painted to look as if they were draped in light poppy-colored silk. Along each of them hung brilliantly executed renditions of some of the greatest masterpieces of the previous two hundred years—Lawrence recognized a

Michelangelo, a Jan van Eyck, a Botticelli, two Leonardo da Vincis and a portrait by the crazy venetian Paolo Veronese—complete with ornate frames.

From the paintings Lawrence's eyes shifted to the face of Lady Tuesday Arlington. She had been looking away but now she looked at him, right at him, and for a moment their eyes met.

In that moment Lawrence forgot all about the events of the morning, of the past weeks, of the last two years. He was aware only of her eyes on his. And a weird tickling sensation inside his head, like someone was peering around inside.

Without permission.

It was not pleasant. He wrenched his gaze away from the reflection and turned to face her, the lines of his frown deeply etched on his forehead. "You are Lady Arlington?"

"Yes," she answered, strangely subdued. He wondered if she had felt it, too. She handed the gold chain, unknotted now, to one of the children. "And you are Lawrence Pickering. Can I do something for you?"

"Are these paintings your work? And the one in the entry hall?"

"No they aren't."

"Yes, they are," the three children corrected in unison, and Lawrence did not miss the look of surprise bordering on alarm that the woman sent them.

She asked, "Are you a connoisseur of paintings?"

"I know a little about them. That one—" he pointed to her copy of a Leonardo da Vinci painting of a mother and child, "—is one of my favorites. Where did you see these?"

"She didn't. She copied them from a catalogue of an auction of the finest collection in England," the girl said.

"But now you must give your word of honor not to tell. Everyone around here knows but if her father knew that she was painting he would be mortified."

"Jenks, our steward, says that if it weren't for Tuesday, her father wouldn't even have shoes," the older boy confided.

The younger boy said, in a whisper, "But we must keep it secret. That is why George gets all the credit—"

"—Even though he never picks up a brush," his brother finished.

The girl shot her siblings an angry glance, then looked back at Lawrence and asked, "Lady Arlington is very talented, don't you think, sir?"

This speech had been delivered over the protests of Lady Arlington who now turned to Lawrence. "Please disregard what they just said. George Lyle—" she gestured toward the well-dressed man, "—is the artist. Did you wish to commission a piece?"

"No, I am not here about painting. I need to discuss something with you."

George Lyle, who through this indictment of his artistic powers had done nothing but watch Lawrence uneasily, spoke up now. "Do you want me to stay, Tuesday? I have an appointment elsewhere but I can—"

"No, of course not." She didn't even look at him.

His malaise increased. "Very well." He turned to address the children. "That means you, too, you terrors. Off with you."

Three groans were followed by three haphazard bows and curtsies and murmured "It was a pleasure to meet you, sir"s. As the girl was shuffling out the door, Lawrence bent down and whispered something to her.

Her face lit up. "Bemused! Of course. Thank you, Your Lordship!" she exclaimed and ran from the room.

"That was a good suggestion," Tuesday said as the door closed behind all of them. "Bemused."

"For some reason it sprang to mind."

Tuesday nodded and bit her lip. There was something about the man that seemed to suck speech from her. For years she had been berated by her father for talking too much. Now she could not think of a single thing to say. Finally she managed to come up with, "Ah."

The room would have been blanketed by an uncomfortable silence then if a woman who Lawrence had not even noticed stretched out on a settee at the end of the room had not chosen that moment to open her eyes, look at him, cry "Oooh!" and faint again.

The interruption brought Tuesday back to her senses. "Pay no attention to CeCe, Mr. Pickering. What was it you wanted to see me about?"

No one had ever called Lawrence "Mr. Pickering." Even before he had been made an earl, everyone who valued their head addressed him as "My lord." But it was not worth it to correct her, he decided, and settled for frowning. "I am afraid I am here on official business. I have some bad news for you, Lady Arlington. Something has happened—"

"To Howard," Tuesday supplied, the words *official business* ringing in her ears. She reached a hand behind her for support and caught the edge of a table. Her older brother Howard, her father's joy, had joined a merchant packet to sail for the new world three months earlier as a way to evade the friendly gentlemen to whom he owed several thousand pounds. Tuesday had arranged the whole thing, had stayed up for weeks painting portraits to earn enough to pay his embarkation fees, and insisted on his going despite his protests that he could put the money to better use gambling. If he had met with some trouble it was her fault, and her father, who had no idea that Howard was anywhere but in London too busy to visit, would never, ever forgive her. She should have known this would happen, since she arranged it. She bit her lip, blinked back tears, and demanded, "Where is he? Is he alive?"

"This is not about Howard. This is about your husband. Sir Curtis Arlington. When was the last time you saw him?"

It took Tuesday a moment to recover. "Not about Howard," she repeated with visible relief, then recalled the man's question. "The last time I saw Curtis? I don't know the exact date but it was, ah, recently." There was a hint of defiance in her eyes. "He said he had business in the countryside so he went away, but it could not be more than a few weeks."

"Are you on good terms with him?"

"Of course. He is my husband."

"Then I am sorry to tell you, Lady Arlington, that he is dead."

"Dead? Curtis, dead?" Instead of sinking more deeply against the table she had been leaning on, she came up off of it like a shot. She had a flash memory of Curtis standing before her, his shirt open at the neck, his lips parted in a cocky smile under the thin line of his perfectly trimmed mustache, hands on his hips, virile, alive. So alive. Could he really be dead?

"How long were you married?" she heard herself being asked as if from a great distance.

She tried to shake away the image of Curtis. "Two years."

"Can you think of anyone who would have wanted to kill him? Anyone who would benefit from his death?"

"No."

"Did he have any enemies?"

"Not that I knew of."

"What about his business associates?"

"I did not know any of his friends."

"Yet you were on good terms?"

Tuesday leveled her storm cloud eyes at him. She was not going to share her failure as a wife with this man. "I cannot see how—"

"Did you know he was in London?"

Her eyes skidded nervously around the walls of the room, then came back to him. "No."

Lawrence did not like being lied to. "I should tell you, Lady Arlington, we know that your husband was involved in illegal activities. I've had a man watching him on and off for a few months." More off than on, Lawrence had to admit. According to Tom's reports, Curtis Arlington had been immensely slippery, but no one needed to know that. "The more forthcoming you are with me now, the better off you will be. It is in your best interests to tell me everything."

"Illegal activities?" Tuesday repeated. Lawrence raised an eyebrow at her tone and Tuesday felt her face flush. She did not know that skill was something he had practiced for months as a boy, and it probably would not have made her feel any better if she had. "I don't know anything about illegal activities," she protested against the eyebrow.

"Lady Arlington. You have clearly lied to me at least

twice in the—" Lawrence consulted a small clock he carried in his cloak, "—four minutes I have been here. That is approximately one lie every two minutes. Why do you think I would believe you now?" There was the eyebrow again.

"I haven't the faintest idea," Tuesday replied, unintimidated. She wanted to be alone, to think about what it meant that Curtis was dead. "Nor do I care. If you have a specific charge to level at me, or a specific question to ask, then ask it. Otherwise, you can go."

"Happily. But first I would like to search your husband's possessions and the rooms he occupied."

"You want to search Curtis's chambers?"

Lawrence had expected indignation. He had not expected her to look like she was going to laugh again. "Yes," he confirmed. "And any papers or clothes you may have."

She sounded absolutely apologetic when she said, "I am afraid that will not be possible, my lord."

"Lady Arlington, I do not think you understand. Your husband was murdered. Left lying at the end of a deserted corridor in a puddle of blood. Whoever did that was determined to—"

Lawrence stopped talking because the color had drained from her face.

She asked, in a voice not more than a whisper, "A corridor?"

"Yes. In one of the old houses along—"

"An unpainted corridor?"

"Yes." A pause. "Do you know something about this, Lady Arlington?"

"Take me there."

What Lawrence said next was, "If you have any information about your husband's death, you would do well to tell me at once."

But in her head Tuesday heard:

You just keep your whore mouth shut or I'll do the same to you as I did to him. Do you understand, bitch? Answer me!

Chapter 5

"Take me there," Tuesday repeated. There were goose-bumps on her arms. "Take me. Now."

"You cannot evade my questions that easily, Lady Arlington."

"Please." She was almost begging. "I need to see it. I need to see the place. If you take me there, afterward, I promise, I'll answer all your questions."

Lawrence weighed the wisdom of taking her deal. He could give orders to his men to make sure nothing left Worthington Hall while they were gone, and he needed her pliant. Plus, the body had already been moved. There was no reason she should not see the place where her husband had died. There was nothing horrible about the *place*.

Her reaction, when they got there, would have suggested otherwise. She stood in the middle of the long, wood-paneled hallway looking down toward the corner where Curtis's body had been found, and began to tremble.

Come here right now, bitch.

Tuesday shrugged off the hands that reached out to support her and walked slowly down the corridor. She collected details as she passed, like she did when she was painting a portrait, details to keep the voices away.

The hallway was dustier than she remembered from her dream. She paused to push open the doors on either side, to make sure there were no eyes there. One of the doors would not open at first and her heart began to pound, but her second attempt succeeded. She walked inside.

Get out here you stupid whore bitch and show yourself.

The room was empty, the dust undisturbed, but she closed the door behind her as she left. With slow steps she made her way toward the place where the floor was sticky from Curtis's blood. There was a dark line on the floor next to the wall, about halfway there. She bent and found that it was a strip of fabric as wide as her hand and knotted. The edges smelled like the lilac hair pomade Curtis always wore and the center, stiff with blood, bore three indentations. Two eyes and a nose, she thought mechanically. The killer must have blindfolded Curtis.

She absently ran her fingers over the knot, her eyes still on the floor.

Something was missing.

"The rose petals," she said aloud, as if musing to herself. "Someone took away the rose petals."

The corridor got very quiet. "What did you say?" the man named Lawrence Pickering asked.

Tuesday, still scowling at the floor, ignored him. "How many men have you let come down here?"

"Two, my assistant and myself," Lawrence replied. "But what do you—"

"Does the other one also have blonde hair?"

"What?"

Tuesday waved the question away. She knew she was

delaying on purpose, stalling. She felt the end of the corridor tugging at her inexorably. Instead of running there as she had in her dream, she was being pulled toward it, dragged there, against her will. She knew what waited for her at the end of the hallway—*I told you I would get you, whore*—but she could not stop herself from moving forward. It was as if she were under someone else's power, as if she were someone else's creature. Somewhere behind her Lawrence Pickering was talking but she could no longer hear his voice. She let the blindfold fall from her hand and walked toward the corner, each step hard and heavy, until she was standing in front of the place where Curtis was killed.

She reached out her fingertips to touch the knot in the wood paneling that could almost be a death's head. Just below it was a smudge of dirt. She bent to examine it and saw that it was a handprint, as if Curtis had fallen and put out his hand to stop himself. No, the angle was wrong for that. She let her right hand hover over the print and felt the hair on the nape of her neck stand up. It wasn't Curtis's. It was the killer's. He had stood exactly where she was now standing, exactly *as* she was now standing. Slightly bent, leaning over her victim. *His* victim. His.

She was about to straighten when she caught something out of the corner of her eye. *Don't look,* her mind screamed. *Whatever it is, you don't want to see it. You don't want to be involved. You don't want to—*

Her head turned to the left. On the side of the wall, a hint of rust-colored paint—or blood, she realized now, that is what it was, blood—had been splattered. Exactly as it was in her painting.

Tuesday's coolness evaporated. She had not done that

on purpose, it had happened by accident, *by accident,* when her wrist cramped and the brush slipped from her fingers and slid across her palette and onto the canvas.

And then she had the terrifying thought that there were no accidents. That she had not been in control of her brush. Or, perhaps, worse, that she had. That somehow she was bound to the killer. She remembered the feeling of the cramp, like someone grabbing her wrist, jerking it. It was as though somehow she and the killer acted together. As though she was just as responsible for the murder as he was. That every gesture she made, he also made. That her wrist had cramped, her brush had fallen, because Curtis's throat was slit.

Or had Curtis's throat been slit because her brush had fallen?

Lawrence saw her shudder and reach out to the wall for support. Her eyes stayed glued on the corner where her husband's body had been found, but her free hand now covered her lips, like a portrait of unspeakable horror.

You are mine now, bitch. Mine.

"No," she said aloud, shaking her head. "You can't do this."

"I beg your pardon," Lawrence Pickering called from behind her.

Turn around, Tuesday told herself. Turn around and tell him everything. Tell him about the dream and *(You just keep)* about the painting *(your whore mouth shut)* and about Curtis *(or I'll do the same to you as I did to him).*

Her eyes rested on the handprint against the wall. What could the killer have been doing to leave it? *Heartless* she heard the killer saying. *Ha ha ha.*

Tuesday whirled to face Lawrence. "Did he—did he cut Curtis's heart out?"

Lawrence hesitated for a moment, then said, "Yes."

Do you understand, bitch?

"Lady Arlington, you seem strangely familiar with this crime scene. Do you know something? Something that would help us catch your husband's killer?"

Answer me!

"No." Tuesday moved her eyes from Lawrence. "I don't know anything. I just saw the handprint on the wall and figured . . ." her voice trailed off. She felt as if her body were made of lead, the weight of her self-loathing pulling at her. She wanted to go home and wash herself, endlessly, wash off the horror of having a killer inside of her, of her husband possibly dying because of her, but she knew it would not work. Nothing was going to purge the killer from her head but catching him. *(Keep your whore mouth shut!)* And she was going to have to do that alone.

She made a decision. She would sneak away and leave London. Perhaps if he did not know where she was, he could not use her to kill. Or perhaps he would follow her. Either way, she would put an end to this. She took a deep breath and, her eyes stuck on Lawrence's nose, said, "I think I need to go home now. I don't feel very well and I must—my father must hear about this. I know I promised to answer your questions, and I will, but not right now. I don't think I have anything useful to tell you anyway." She was a terrible liar, she knew, but she hoped the apparent strain of what she was going through would cover for the tightness in her voice and the way she was blushing.

Lawrence frowned at her. She was being evasive, no

question. And she had not held up her portion of their bargain. But he could use more time to decide how to handle her.

Plus she did, suddenly, look very ill.

"I'll drive you."

"That is very kind of you but I would rather walk. Good—"

"I am driving you," Lawrence repeated, a command now, and steered her forcibly into his coach.

They made the trip in silence, each sunk in their own thoughts as they inched through the crowded streets.

How could a killer be in her head, Tuesday wondered. How could he control her? And, most frightening, what was he going to do, going to make her do, next?

She knew too much about the murder scene, Lawrence thought. She'd tried to cover up mentioning the rose petals; that must have slipped out because of the shock, but he'd heard it. There was too much she wasn't telling him—too many inconsistencies. Too many lies for an innocent woman. She was smart and clever and, he realized, he had to press her now before she had time to arrange a story that could take his men weeks to penetrate.

Lawrence trailed her, uninvited, up the steps of her house.

"Thank you," she said as she opened the door and stepped into the entry hall. "For taking me there. And for the ride." She turned to face him and their eyes accidentally met and Tuesday saw again—

Dark night, a man silhouetted against the sky, it's so cold, so cold.

—emptiness. She had never seen such empty eyes. "I am sorry about before," she stammered, abruptly ill at ease. "About how I behaved. Sometimes I—"

Of the three things Lawrence hated most in the world, the second one was gratitude. "I do not want your thanks, Lady Arlington. Or your pity. I want answers to my questions and I am not leaving until I get them."

That was too much. Her husband was dead, her life was in ruins, there was a killer in her head telling her not to speak to anyone, and now an imperious earl who smelled like he'd been sleeping in alleys and didn't give a thought to anyone beyond himself was frowning at her and threatening to camp at her house. Something in Tuesday's head snapped. "My goodness, Mr. Pickering. You do not need to waste all that charm on me."

Lawrence goggled at her. "The title is Lord Pickering."

"No. It is Lord Arden. At least, that is what everyone said earlier, although I still think—"

"Tuesday!" a voice shouted from above them. "Tuesday, damn you girl, get up here this instant."

"Father," she said in a half whisper, then turned and made for the staircase, sarcasm gone. She dashed up to the first landing and was slightly breathless when she entered the large, sumptuously furnished chamber her father occupied. The old man glared at her from a chair near the window. "Where the devil have you been all day, girl? I've been calling you for hours."

"I am sorry father. I had to go out."

Sir Dennis Worthington looked at his daughter from the corner of his eye, pretending to be looking elsewhere. It was an old habit, and a good one. Caught things people didn't want you to see. But Tuesday's face was impassive, like always, contrary girl. "Out? I suppose you had something more important to do than care for your poor father?"

"Actually, father, there is—"

"Don't interrupt me! Do you know what that scoundrel Morse did? He brought me the same meat pie for lunch today I had yesterday. And you were not here to stop him. Impudent swine. Do you know, Tuesday, what the neighbors will be saying when they hear?"

"Why would the neighbors hear?"

"Can't you ever think of anyone besides yourself, girl? Of course they will hear. And they will say poor Denny Worthington, even his kin don't pay enough attention to him to remember what he ate the day before and see that he gets some variety. Poor old Denny, they'll say, neglected by those who should be most dutiful to him. Poor, poor Sir Dennis—" he was quite wound up now and appeared almost ready to rise in the style of great orators—"whom nobody thinks of, nobody cares for, nobody waits on."

Nobody bit her lip. Sir Dennis, having collapsed back into his chair, was not too busy mopping the corner of his eye with the lawn cuff of his shirt to notice.

"You know I don't usually give in to my condition this way, Tuesday," he resumed with a sad glance in her direction. "But this time of year, the time of year of your beloved mother's death, is always hard for me. And then, the same pie twice. Really, it is too much. Too too much."

"I am sorry, father. I will see that Morse doesn't do it again."

"I've already seen to that. I fired him."

Tuesday closed her eyes for a moment. If Morse left, she would have to give him his back wages, and she would not be able to afford to do that until she finished the portrait of Dowager Castenaugh as Venus. Morse had stayed as long as he did only because he was in love with CeCe. She opened her eyes. "Father, I am afraid you can't fire him. You see—"

"Can't fire him? This is my house, ain't it? Won't have surly numbskulls waiting on—who the devil are you?"

Tuesday turned and saw Lawrence standing in the door. He must have followed her up. Before he could answer, she blurted. "That is no one. Father, something dreadful has happened."

Sir Dennis's eyes were immediately riveted on her. "What did you do this time, Tuesday?"

"Nothing. It is just—Curtis is dead."

"Dead? What did you do to him?"

"He was murdered."

Sir Dennis's mouth worked for a few moments before he managed to find words. "Murdered?" he repeated, his color rising dangerously. "You've done it again, Tuesday. Best thing that ever happened to you, Curtis was, you were damned lucky to have him. Young, handsome. From a good family. What he wanted with you I'll never know. And now you got him murdered!" Sir Dennis, who appeared to be boiling, flopped back into his chair, rage vaporizing into self pity. "Must you destroy everything? Every last shred of my happiness? Murdered! I suppose everyone will be talking about it now. Tuesday, girl, you are my torment." His eyes moved from Tuesday back to Lawrence. "Who the devil did you say you were?"

Lawrence took two steps into the room. "The earl of Arden."

"An earl huh?" Sir Dennis's color was quickly returning to normal. "You must know my son, Howard. Not a thing like his sister. Marvelous boy, Howard. Don't judge us all by Tuesday. Been a disappointment since the day she was born. You don't look much like an earl."

"So I have been told."

"What are you doing here, then? Did you come with the musicians?"

"Musicians?" Tuesday asked.

"Musicians," Sir Dennis repeated in a falsetto, mocking her tone. "Yes musicians. Man in my position is entitled to some entertainment. Told Morse to send up some musicians and do you know what he did? He laughed in my face. Tuesday, go get some musicians."

"Father, I—"

"What do I ever ask you for? Too busy going and getting your husband murdered to find me musicians are you? Too busy sullying the family name? Will you continue to torment me with this disobedience, child? I told you to go. Now get. And take that man with you. Don't like the look of him."

Tuesday hesitated for a moment, then turned and left. Lawrence stepped aside to let her pass, then followed her down the stairs. As they went by the mirror, he saw that the painting he had admired that morning was reflected in it. If he had not known better, he would have thought the hall was filled with furniture, instead of being empty.

In marked contrast to Sir Dennis's handsomely furnished suit. It was then that Lawrence understood.

"He doesn't know, does he?" he asked in a low voice.

"Know what?"

"That you are ruined. That you have been selling the furnishings of the house in order to survive. You leave that mirror there so that if he were to look down the stairs everything would look normal. That is what you meant this morning about not being able to show me your husband's chambers. You and he share the studio."

"Not exactly," she replied.

He saw a flush rise up the back of her neck. The knowledge that the family fortune had been decimated, even if he had been the salient force behind its decimation, would surely kill Sir Dennis, Tuesday's brother had argued, and therefore the news was to be kept from him at all costs. His suit of apartments was the only one that still retained its old appearance, although Tuesday had found herself guiltily wondering the other morning if he would really miss the small ivory casket with the gold hinges that stood, apparently unused, on the corner of a table. The musicians needed for an afternoon concert were as out of her reach as a trip to the Indies in a gold-encrusted boat. But her father could not know that, just as he could not know that she supported the household by painting portraits. "Please, Lord Pickering, lower your voice."

She had called him Lord Pickering. And she was having one hell of a day. He decided he could humor her. "Are all the rooms empty?" Lawrence asked in a whisper as they entered the service corridor that led to what he now understood was not only her studio but her living quarters.

Tuesday was overwhelmed by the need to be by herself. She wanted to think, alone, without some hulk of a man following her and badgering her with questions. Questions she could not answer. "You may look for yourself. None of the doors have locks on them."

"I will. As soon as you have—"

"—answered your questions," Tuesday finished the sentence for him. She opened the door to her studio, not the one he had entered through earlier, and turned to face him. "Where shall we start? With the fact that my husband has not been living here for the past two months?"

She stopped because he was not listening to her. He was not even looking at her. She followed the direction of his gaze.

He was looking behind her, to her work table. Where someone had left a good sized round box, about the size of a man's hand with the fingers outstretched.

The box was decorated with brightly colored enamel. On the sides, unicorns and maidens inconceivably danced together while swains played pipes and leaned on trees. On the lid, a garland of roses surrounded a bright red heart pierced by an arrow. Around the edge of the lid ran a band of lettering in dark green enamel, set off in gold. Tuesday moved to the box and read the message.

Then she set it back down on the table and wrapped her arms around her body and said, "No, please God, no."

Chapter 6

The Lion watched them from outside Worthington Hall. It was warm in the shadows of the alley that faced the woman's windows, but that was not why his heart was racing. It was because it had started.

He had seen them pull up in the carriage, had watched with glee as Lawrence Pickering scanned the street before he let Her out.

Look all you want, Your Lordship. You won't find me!

It was going so perfectly. And this was only the beginning. If it felt like this now, what would it be like later when it got really serious? When they were hunting for him night and day? When he was leading them around by the hair?

The Lion watched Lawrence Pickering with admiration. Even wearing day-old clothes that were supposed to be a drunk's, the man looked good. It was something about the way his garments sat on his body, not just hanging there like other men's. But it was also the way he wore them, something about the way he walked, carried himself. The Lion had practiced in the mirror and could do it pretty well.

It was exhilarating, finally, to have a real adversary. Up until now, no one had much bothered about his

killings. But that was all over. He and Lawrence Pickering, our nation's greatest hero, going head to head. My
God it was good. And what made it so rich was that his
Lordship didn't even know about it. He didn't know
someone else was running the show. Didn't even know
the Lion was watching him right that second. Figuring
ways to kill him without ruining his clothes.

Something rattled in the areaway behind him. He
swung around and saw a dog nosing through a pile of
kitchen scraps. It didn't even notice he was there, stupid
dog. It was ignoring him. Ignoring *him*.

The tingling started in his stomach and moved out
through his body. The Lion bent down to scratch the
dog's head and it looked up. For a moment it studied him
curiously, its tongue hanging out of its mouth, its tail
wagging. Then it plopped down and rolled onto its back,
to have its stomach scratched. When the Lion didn't
move, it waved its paws and looked expectantly at him.
The Lion stared back, and all of a sudden the dog's eyes
changed. They were no longer expectant. Now they registered disgust.

Dragon eyes a voice in the Lion's head said.

Just like the whore. The tingling got stronger. She was
supposed to be scared, supposed to look scared, but instead she looked at him with contempt. No respect,
looked at him to make him weak, to mock his greatness.

The tingling filled his head. She was the last one to do
that. Stupid bitch. The tingling roared in his ears, flickered in front of his eyes. He'd showed her. He'd show the
dog, too. He'd—

It was over before the Lion even realized what he had
done. He looked down at his hands and saw the blood,
but he was good at his job and hadn't gotten any on his

clothes. The dog, not quite dead, whimpered a few times, then went still.

He hated dogs.

He returned his attention to the windows, to his real adversary. Lawrence Pickering was standing over the table, cool, nonchalant. The man sure had style.

He would do Pickering the same as he had done the dog, the Lion decided then. Use his knife, aim for the stomach, make it clean and fast. That way he would have enough time to get the name of the man's tailor before he died.

Chapter 7

My Heart is your Heart is my Heart is your Heart is my Heart.

The words were emblazoned around the lid of the box in an unending band, like the unending nightmare Tuesday had woken into that morning.

She braced herself against the edge of the table to keep from trembling. "Do you think—" She stopped, swallowed. "Do you think that it is—that it could be—Curtis's . . . ?"

Lawrence picked up the box. "I don't know. I'm going to have one of my men take—"

She shook her head. She said, "Open it. Here. Now."

Lawrence was tempted to argue, but her expression, the whiteness of her knuckles, changed his mind. He undid the small clasp and flipped up the lid.

It was empty.

Tuesday stared at the burgundy velvet interior for a moment. Then she collapsed against the table and began to laugh.

She had been a bloody fool! Had she really thought the box had Curtis's heart in it? She was trembling more now than before. How absurd she had been. How completely—

"There is something inside," Lawrence said, and her laughter vanished.

Lawrence lifted a gold chain from the box, from which dangled a burgundy enamel heart the same color as the fabric lining. He dropped it into his palm and turned it over.

"'*For Tuesday, as always,*'" he read the inscription aloud and looked up at her.

"Is today Tuesday?" she asked. When he nodded, Tuesday was tempted to laugh again and again with relief. "This has nothing to do with the murders," she explained to Lawrence. "This happens every Tuesday."

"This?"

"Presents. He leaves one every week."

"'He'?"

"Yes. The Secret Admirer. At least, that is what CeCe calls him," she explained, and seemed to wince a little. "He won't reveal himself, you see, and we don't know anything about him. No one can describe him and as far as we know, no one has ever seen him."

Tuesday had tried repeatedly to find the source of the gifts and put an end to them. They added to her edginess, to the feeling that she was being watched. But none of her efforts yielded any answers. No one saw him come or go. No one saw him leave his packages at the back door as was his invariable custom. No men who excited any kind of abnormal notice bought flowers or sweets from the vendors in her neighborhood. He was as good as invisible.

Compared to everything else that had happened that day, however, Tuesday thought, a man so inconspicuous that no one had ever noticed him was hardly something to worry about.

"How long has this been going on?"

"For about two months. Since Curtis stopped living here."

"Always on Tuesday?" She nodded and he went on. "Your name day. It appears that someone is trying to honor you. Who is it?"

"Honor me," she echoed, shuddering. "I told you, I have no idea who."

Lawrence began straightening the sketches on her work table into neat piles. "Lady Arlington, it is extremely challenging for me to believe that you do not even have a guess about the identity of your invisible lover."

"He is not my lover. He does not *love* me, he is just lonely and confused," she insisted, and the words had the sound of a well-worn argument. Probably, Lawrence suspected, with her maid. He could not think of many women who would deny that men loved them. Most of the women of his acquaintance were just the opposite— so eager to be perceived as attractive that they destroyed their reputations by claiming affairs they had never had. Was she telling the truth?

"For a while I thought it was a joke," she went on, absently upsetting the pile of papers he had made. "Then, when it kept going, I tried to learn his identity but, as I said, no one had seen anything. Ultimately I hoped that by just ignoring the presents, they would stop."

Lawrence was astonished by how little she knew about men. Ignore them and they go away? "You realize, Lady Arlington, that whoever has been sending you these presents could very well be the murderer. If he was in love with you—or just thought he was in love with

you—he would undoubtedly benefit from your husband's death."

"Of course. You are right." It sounded from her tone
like she had not realized it before. But she did now. She
nodded slowly.

Lawrence put all her brushes in a row from smallest to
largest. "Yet you still maintain you don't know who the
Secret Admirer is."

"No. I told you." She had picked up the box and was
turning it around in her hands *(my Heart is your Heart is
my Heart is your Heart)* as he spoke.

Avoiding his eyes, Lawrence thought.

"That is too bad. It would be in your best interest to
suggest a substitute."

"A substitute?" she asked. "For what?"

"For yourself. As the murderer."

Her head snapped up. "You can't—You don't—" She
could tell by his expression that he did and he could. He
was dead serious.

She turned her face away from Lawrence, to buy herself a moment to think.

And then she saw it.

On an easel, at the far side of the room just beyond
Lawrence's left shoulder, stood a painting.

A painting of a corner in a wood-paneled hallway with
a knot in the wood that looked like a death's head and a
splattering of blood. A painting of the murder scene they
had just come from. A painting she knew she had carefully hidden away in the earliest hours of the morning.
Hard, cold fingers of fear closed around her heart.

*There is no escaping from me, don't you know that by
now?* the voice from her dream whispered. *You just keep*

your whore mouth shut or I'll do the same to you as I did to him.

She looked back at Lawrence. She had to get him out of there before he saw it.

She faced him, holding his gaze now. "You do not really think that I am the murderer."

Lawrence was impressed. He would have expected an accusation of murder to illicit a tantrum, or at least a blush, but the only visible effect of his words was to make her grip the box so tight her knuckles went white.

"Feel free to persuade me. I do not know what to think. You knew about the rose petals at the murder scene—rose petals my men had taken away an hour before. Only someone who had been there or been told of the murder could have known about those. How would you explain that?"

"I could have smelled them. I mean, I did smell them," she stammered. It was clear that he was not buying it, but that was the least of her problems right now. "Besides, I often mention rose petals. I adore them. It was just a coincidence that I said 'rose petals' when—"

"I do not believe in coincidences."

She paused. "Really? How boring for you." She was speaking as if they were making light conversation, passing the time at a ball or dinner. "If there are no coincidences, do you believe that everything is planned and ord—"

It was Lawrence's expression that stopped her. He looked up from the glass jars of pigment he was arranging in a line by color. "I do not think you understand how serious this is, Lady Arlington."

"I promise you, you are wrong. And if I did not, the

way you are frowning and grinding your teeth would surely inform me."

She was mad. She was mad and was going to drive him mad. "Lady Arlington, unless you start talking, start giving me true-sounding and compelling answers, I am going to have to conclude, however unwillingly, that you are lying because you murdered your husband."

"True sounding? What would be a true-sounding motive for me to have killed my husband?"

"Perhaps when you kicked him out he took—"

"I did not kick him out."

It took Lawrence a moment to get it. "Curtis left *you?*"

"Yes."

"You are lying." Lawrence said the words before he realized it, without thinking. They hung in the air for a moment.

In a flash her playfulness was gone. She said, "Get out."

"What?"

"I said, get out." She moved backward—toward the door, away from the painting. "If you think I am lying, I do not see that we have anything else to discuss. And I don't like the way you are organizing everything. Get out. Now."

Something about her insistence that he leave pricked Lawrence's suspicions. Instead of following her, he seated himself on an uneven gray velvet chair and moved it so it was at a right angle to the settee. He spent a moment frowning at his hands, then pinned her with his gaze. "What is it, Lady Arlington? Did he refuse to leave so you took other measures to get rid of him?"

Standing with her hand on the door latch she stared

him down. "You know, Mr. Pickering, I do not think there is a question you could put to me that I would answer."

"Aren't you being just a bit too evasive? If you are trying to convince me you killed your husband, you are doing a very good job."

She gave a strange, mirthless laugh. "I should imagine it would be slightly harder than this. With all the evidence to overlook."

"What evidence?"

Keep your whore mouth shut! the voice from her dream screamed in her head. She said, "You know as well as I do that I am not the murderer."

"I beg your pardon?"

"The murderer is a left-handed man with brown hair and a limp." She said it as if it were the most obvious thing in the world.

"What?"

"It was clear just looking around the place where Curtis's body was."

"Explain."

"You told me that only you and your assistant, Tom, had gone down the hallway. But there were three sets of footprints leading away from where Curtis was killed. And one of them was heavier on the left side than on the right, showing the man had a limp."

"Left side. That is how you know he is left-handed?"

Her eyes narrowed, like she suspected he was putting her on, but she continued her explanation. "No. I suspected it from the way the blindfold was knotted, and then I saw the handprint. On the wall. It was of a right hand, and Curtis had one finger shorter than the others on the right hand, so it couldn't have been his. From the angle, it looked like it was made when the killer was steadying himself while he—while he leaned over the body. Since it was of his right hand, he must have been using his left."

"And the hair color?"

"Didn't you see the brown hairs caught in the boards above where you must have found the body? The killer must have leaned against them, hard, and some of his hair came out. Certainly you noticed this, too. It was all there, in plain sight."

It is not what you take away that matters, it is what you leave behind.

Staged. That was what the crime scene had felt like, Lawrence realized. Like it was somehow planned. To lead him to certain conclusions about the murderer. Just like her behavior here. His eyes went back to her white knuckles, the only part of her performance she seemed unable to control. "That is very clever but—"

A loud knocking on the door interrupted him, followed by Tom bursting in, his face red. "You are wanted at your office, sir. Urgent."

Tuesday could have kissed Tom for the effect this news had on Lawrence. He was on his feet and at the door—his back to the painting—in an instant. With his fingers on the handle he said, "Tom, did you come with the guards?"

"Yes sir. They are right behind me." Two large men each armed with a sword entered the room then.

"Excellent. I want you two to insure that Lady Arlington does not leave this room."

The urge for kissing left Tuesday. "Are you imprisoning me in my own home?"

Lawrence turned to face her. "Would you prefer New-gate?"

"Newgate? On what charge?"

"Murder, Lady Arlington. Good day."

"Murder? But I told you! I am not—You are going to be sorry for this, Mr. Pickering. You are going to owe me an enormous apology."

"Feel free to wait for it." And then he was gone. She stood facing the two guards and listened to Lawrence's footsteps recede down the hall.

Ha ha ha, they seemed to say.

She walked over and slammed the door behind him.

It was then, as she faced the closed door, that it hit her. Curtis was gone. Curtis was never ever going to walk through the door again. He was never going to come home. He was never coming back to her. The waiting was over.

Her hand reached behind her for something to lean on, and not finding anything, she stumbled slightly. She felt drunk, light-headed, dizzy. Black spots flickered in front of her eyes. Blindly she moved to her work table and set the box down with an accidental jerk that sent her brushes careening to the floor. Then, guiding herself with her hand, she crossed the room toward the easel with the painting on it. The painting someone had delib-erately left there for her to see. The painting of Curtis's last resting place.

No! This could not be happening. Her mind fought for ways to deny it, deny the morning, the dreams, her failed marriage, but there were none.

She looked at the painting and knew there could be only one conclusion: the killer had been in her room. And he had wanted to be sure she knew it. Leaving the gift, the macabre box, was not enough. He left the painting out so that the evidence of their collaboration—

my Heart is your Heart is my Heart is your Heart is

—their inescapable union, would be in plain view.

With fingers she fought to keep steady she lifted the picture and carried it to her bed. Using the canopy to screen her from the direct observation of the guards, she leaned over and fumbled around alongside the wall for a moment, biting her lip. When she withdrew her hand she held a parcel that had been tied together with a tattered silver satin ribbon.

She untied the bow, opened the makeshift portfolio, and slipped the painting back inside. But even as she did, she heard the unmistakable voice whispering, *You are mine now, Tuesday. Mine.*

Chapter 8

"That is Salome. And Susannah," the man said. "And over here, Eve and Delilah. I have all the temptresses."

Grub Collins wiped the back of his neck with his sleeve and nodded at the four gold cages politely. "Nice birds," he said.

"Oh yes, they are," their owner agreed. "You have no idea. Do you know what Salome did this morning?"

Grub Collins could hardly guess, nor did he much care. What he cared about was finishing up this last visit and getting down to the tavern below where it was cool. And where he could enjoy a tankard of ale and the sight of Kate North's bodice at the same time. "She came and danced on my face!" the little man announced gleefully.

Grub eyed the bird. There were a few birds of a different, ah, breed who he would gladly have dancing on his face, but the scrawny black one in the cage did not interest him in the least. "Must have been nice," he said noncommittally. The man spent too much time with his birds, that was a fact.

"Actually, to tell you the truth—" the man got confidential, cocking his head like a sparrow, "—it hurt a bit. Don't tell her, though, it will make her ever so sad. But I finally had to get up and put her in her cage. That is when I saw him."

That grabbed Grub's attention. "Who would that be?"

"Big Joe. The mean cat who terrorizes the neighborhood. Even the dogs are afraid of him."

"Must be quite a cat," Grub said, not as politely as he might have. He did not take disappointment well and he had been sure this man was about to reveal having seen something useful. Like the killer. Not a damn mouse-eater.

"Oh yes. Usually he stays in that abandoned house and leaves us alone, doesn't he—" this was addressed to the birds, who all began to twitter deafeningly, "—but he must have left when the man went in."

Grub stopped hearing the birds. "What man?"

"The man who was in the alley last night. Skulking, that is what he was doing. Then, when I got up to put Salome back in her cage, I saw him going into the abandoned house."

"Did you happen to catch a glimpse of him?"

The little man had reached into one of the cages and removed a small red bird, whose beak he was kissing. "More than a glimpse, seeing how he was down in the alley, practically outside my window all day. I could have used less of him. The ladies did not like him one bit. Did you Susannah?" This addressed to the bird again.

Grub cleared his throat. "What did he look like?"

The little man gazed at Grub over the head of the red bird as if surprised to see him still there. "Look like? Oh. I don't know. A man. With dark hair. And he walked with a limp. I noticed because Eve has a slight limp, you can see it from how she is standing, and I am always curious—"

For the first time that afternoon, Grub wanted to smile, but he knew better. "You sure about that? Dark hair and a limp?"

"Oh yes. Quite sure."

"Interesting. See anyone else?"

The man thought for a moment. "No. It is very quiet here."

"Ah well. Thank you, Mister—?"

"Marston," the little man supplied helpfully. "Albert Marston."

"Mr. Marston. You have been extremely helpful. Will you be in later today if the boys or I have any other questions?"

"Oh, I am always in. Where would I go? The ladies need me. Don't you my precious ones?" The birds all began to squawk in unison, and Grub headed hastily for the stairs.

He should probably rush right back to Pickering Hall and tell his boss the good news, but didn't a man deserve a reward? Besides, what difference would a few minutes on Kate's bosom make? He felt positively triumphant. It had worked. How his Lordship had hit on the exact description of the killer so quickly was a mystery to him, but he was not really surprised. He'd spent some time studying his boss and knew that overestimating him was pretty much impossible. Like every member of Lawrence Pickering's staff, Grub Collins regarded his boss as a sort of god—omnipotent, omniscient, and invulnerable.

Almost, anyway.

The man who had introduced himself as Albert Marston

watched Grub saunter down the alley toward several of his colleagues, and frowned. There was something—

Ah, never mind. Turning from the window, he reached into Susannah's cage and adjusted the pebbles on the bottom for a moment. When they were exactly even, he slipped her back in and stepped away, murmuring, "The ladies always need me."

Chapter 9

Lawrence stared at the gently lit windows across the street, tossing the gold coin in his hand and reviewing the events of the day.

She was innocent. He tossed the coin.

Heads.

She was guilty.

She was, according to her neighbors, the sweetest, most docile creature on the planet.

She was, according to the reports he had seen that day, the most dangerous woman he had ever encountered. He had sent two men to interview her: one had come back with a story about her being a Portuguese countess; the other with her having a twin sister who was locked in a tower by an evil Spanish count and needed desperately to be rescued. Both had believed her entirely. When he sent a third man she had told him innocently that no one had specified that the answers to the questions needed to be *true*, only true *sounding*, and her life was so dull she did not want to bore them. Didn't he think being a Portuguese countess was much more interesting? Did she know that in France they had special locks that bit the hands off of people found trying to pick them?

All three of them came back talking about what a sweet, docile creature she was. They had all been fired.

Miles Loredan, Viscount Dearbourn and Lord High Commissioner for the Security of England, had looked across his desk at his friend earlier that day. "So what you are saying is that you don't like her much."

"No. What I am saying is that unless we find a way to make her work with us, I am not going to have any staff left."

"Sounds like a puzzle. Just your thing. According to the news sheets, you kept sane in that Spanish prison by doing puzzles. Puzzles and riddles. You love them."

Lawrence grunted. "You know as well as I do that was all made up—probably better than I do, since you wrote it."

One small part of Miles's work during the war with Spain had been to make sure the Spanish knew only what the English wanted them to, which often meant well-placed stories in the daily news sheets. But part of what Miles had caused to be published about Lawrence's time in Spanish prisons was true. Lawrence had stayed sane when locked in solitary confinement not by solving hard mathematical problems and logical conundrums, but by dreaming up an escape plan. An escape plan so perfect that it allowed him to evacuate two hundred British soldiers and half the Spanish underground with the loss of only three men. The Spanish still didn't know how he did it, but thanks to Miles's efforts, they assumed it had something to do with isosceles triangles or Plato, or both.

The two men were meeting in Miles's secret offices, on the attic floor of his London town house. Miles's occupation as the Lord High Commissioner was a national secret, known to almost no one, as was Lawrence's position as one of his top men. Although most of the population of England would never be aware of it, the success of the English war effort against Spain could almost exclusively be laid at the feet of these two men. And if the frown on Lawrence's face was anything to go by, he would rather have been battling the entire kingdom of Spain than Lady Tuesday Arlington.

Miles studied the ruby red wine in his glass for a moment, then said, "Does she have something to do with the smuggling?"

"I am almost positive of it. The way she reacted to my questions—it was strange."

"Yet you do not think she did the murder? Despite the fact that you threatened to have her arrested for it? And despite the fact that she asked you about evidence at the crime scene that she should not have known existed?"

"I just threatened her with arrest to make her nervous, you know that as well as I do. As to her knowing about the rose petals—that was probably just a coincidence," Lawrence said, shrugging it off, to Miles's utter stupefaction.

"Have you started drinking again? You don't believe in coincidences."

In reply, Lawrence gulped down the remainder of his glass of lemonade. "Anyway, we found a witness. The killer appears to be a left-handed man with brown hair and a limp."

"How did you find him?"

"Lucky, I guess." Miles openly gaped at him, but Lawrence just went on. "And they found some brown hair both at the crime scene and clutched in the victim's hand. But even with this, we aren't anything like close to catching him. I am working on the assumption that the murder and the smuggling are related. Lady Tuesday certainly has information about one of them, if not both, and I need to know what it is."

"Fine. Why don't I send some of *my* men to question her? They have all had special training and—"

"I don't think it will work and I would not ask you to risk it. There is something about her, something that exudes from her. Wherever she is, people behave insanely."

"Insanely?"

"Yes." Lawrence made it definite, entirely unaware of the amusement in his friend's voice.

"I see. So we need to learn what information she has *without* interrogating her."

"Precisely."

"Then we have to make her think she is working with us. That our goals are the same. Let her ask the questions rather than us. And then, from what she asks, we will be able to figure out what she is thinking and, hopefully, what she knows."

"That is an excellent plan," Lawrence said with a touch too much admiration.

Miles eyed him closely. "It was your plan. You had it in mind before you came here."

"No," Lawrence said, shaking his head slowly. "It was all your idea."

Miles stared at him for a moment, then put his head back and laughed. It was an extremely rare occurrence those days. "I see. She is as fond of you as you are of her."

"Fonder. If I might suggest, just as an adjunct to *your* plan, that the way it works is you assign me to stay with her, at all times, for her protection. I will make it clear that I find the assignment displeasing, which will cause her to leap at it."

"You just happened to come up with this spur of the moment, sitting right here."

"Yes." Lawrence nodded feverishly.

"Liar." There were only five men in the world who could call Lawrence a liar without risking death. Fortunately Miles was one of them. He sighed. "What if you are right about her not being a killer but wrong about how to motivate her? What if she really is a nice, sweet woma—" Lawrence's snort interrupted Miles. "Fine. She is not sweet. But what if she doesn't leap on the opportunity to antagonize you?"

"Then you threaten her. Subtly—" Lawrence added as Miles began shaking his head, "—threaten her subtly with public exposure. Feel free to phrase it however you wish. She will do anything to keep her name from being bandied about because it will upset her father."

"What are you not telling me, Lawrence?"

"Nothing."

Miles knew better than to call Lawrence a liar twice, which was what Lawrence was banking on. "I'll help you," Miles said finally, "but I don't like it. I'm only doing it because I want to meet the sole woman in London not in love with Lawrence Pickering." Then, with a hint of a frown: "I hope you know what you are doing, Lawrence."

"I do," Lawrence had assured him with a smile, like he meant it.

Now, eight hours later, stationed outside her window to keep an eye on her, he tossed the coin. Do I?

Do I have any idea what the hell I am doing? What I am doing here in London? What I am doing in this charade where I pretend to be a hero? What I am doing every single day I wake up when I should be dead? Do I—

Despite the heat of the summer night, his right shoulder suddenly got very cold. Then his arm. Then his hand, until he could not feel his fingers. *No*, he commanded himself as his fingers went totally numb.

She needs you, Lawrence, my friend.

He pried open the freezing fingers of his hand and flexed them. For a moment he stared at the coin lying on his palm, clammy now; then, despite the pain, he made himself toss it into the air and catch it overhand. He put on his smile.

He was just fine. He knew what he was doing.

He looked at his knuckles, still white from the strain, and remembered Tuesday's earlier that day. *She needs you* he heard again in his head, and frowned. Since his return from Spain, his mind seemed to operate on two distinct and entirely separate levels, one which was sane and the other—the one sending him this message—which was absolutely untrustworthy.

He had never met a woman who needed him less than Lady Tuesday Arlington. Or who interested him less.

When did you start lying to yourself, my friend?

SHUT UP.

He had spent what remained of the evening, after his meeting with Miles, loafing in the back alleys of the houses that surrounded Worthington Hall, cajoling from the neighbors' servants every detail he could about Lady Tuesday and her father, Sir Dennis. As Lawrence knew well, gossip ran between the kitchen yards of the large establishments like old bath water, carrying with it all the day's dirt.

And like bath water, it could use some filtering. Everyone Lawrence had spoken to that day about the Worthington household was extremely forthcoming, but none of them had said the same things. There appeared to be enormous disagreement about whether, in fact, Sir Dennis was an invalid as he claimed or some sort of demon who flew over the rooftops at night (two chambermaids swore they had seen his face peering into their windows as they changed for bed); whether the household's handsome valet, Morse, had been forced to leave his last employer because he had been caught with his hand beneath Lady Beryl's petticoats, or because he had been caught with his hand inside Lord Beryl's cash box; whether that over-dressed fellow, George, who was around so often was in love with Tuesday or with her maid, CeCe; and whether CeCe could in fact be called a maid when Tuesday waited on her more than she waited on Tuesday. On three topics, however, there was perfect agreement—that Lady Tuesday Arlington, who somewhere had picked up the nickname "Lucky," was supporting the household with her painting, that she had some sort of ability to know what was in your head just by drawing you, and that she was by far the sweetest, most even-tempered, most docile, most respectful, most dutiful, and most gentle creature anyone could ever hope to know.

Docile.

Given that assessment, Lawrence was tempted to toss all the other information. But there was one tidbit that he hung onto. It seemed that for years she had been keeping a book in which she sketched every kind of nose, eyes, chin, forehead, lips, and ears she saw. Each entry got a number and from these, so her neighbors claimed, she could draw anyone. One of his men had gotten a look at it, and returned to the office proudly displaying a quick charcoal portrait of himself and explaining in an undertone to his colleagues that no matter what Lawrence said it had been done "by a real Portuguese countess. From France."

After that, he had moved his men to the other side of the studio door, fearing for their reliability if they spent too much time near her, and eager to see if with the illusion of greater privacy she might give something away to the men he stationed outside her windows. But so far, during his watch anyway, she had given away nothing except the fact that she was a perfectionist.

For the last hour she had been pouring over her face book, flipping back and forth among its pages, then rapidly making sketches on a paper lying next to her. After doing that four times she would pull away from the paper she had been drawing on, stare at it, glare at it, and scratch out whatever she had drawn. Lawrence had watched her repeat this process three times.

The last time she worked with intense concentration for seven minutes, during which she flipped furiously back and forth through the book but drew almost nothing. Suddenly she stopped flipping and dropped her arms with frustration. It looked like she was going to put her head down on the table, but the door in the wall behind her opened to admit two people and she shoved the paper under her palette.

CeCe was first, and behind her George Lyle, the supposed artist. It was impossible to say for certain, but it appeared that George's collaboration with Tuesday had begun at least two years earlier, when the new young artist had taken London by storm. From what Lawrence had been able to learn that day, George received a commission; went to visit with the sitter, bringing Tuesday along in the guise of his assistant; chatted with the subject while Tuesday made sketches; and then went away, reappearing in a few weeks with a mouth-watering finished portrait no part of which he had painted. It was not even clear that he *could* paint. Indeed, there had been a period the year before when George refused all commissions, which Lawrence would have been willing to wager corresponded exactly with Tuesday's honeymoon, that is, exactly with the time she would have been too busy enjoying the delights of marriage to pick up a brush.

Lawrence did not know how much of the profit George took for his services as a front man, but given the quietly expensive tailoring of his Florentine silk suit and the size of the emerald that formed the eye of the boar's head handle on his cane, Lawrence decided Tuesday was being much too generous. Also he thought George was taking liberties. Like the way he just sat down on the settee without making a bow to Tuesday or waiting for an invitation, and the possessive, smug expression in his eyes when he looked at her. It was clear to Lawrence that George was deeply in love with Tuesday and equally clear that she had no idea of just how strong his passion was.

Lawrence had been surprised at his own feeling of disappointment earlier when his men came to report that George Lyle had apparently spent the previous night and morning drinking at a tavern, and therefore could not have murdered Curtis. He did not have anything, really, against the man. Except the way he was standing so close to Tuesday now. Or the way he accepted when she offered him a glass of whatever was in the decanter on her worktable. Couldn't he tell she was exhausted? Couldn't he see the way her shoulders were sloping downward and the corners of her smile were trembling slightly? Why was Tuesday taking care of CeCe and George when they should be taking care of her? Her husband had been brutally murdered that morning, and here they both were, coming in and bothering her—

Lawrence cut his own thoughts off by reminding himself that whatever else he did not feel for Tuesday, the top of the list was sympathy. She was a liar and a consummate actress. He watched unsympathetically as she assured her friends that she was fine and then politely but firmly moved them toward the door.

As soon as it was closed, she began again with the book, working more quickly this time. After a quarter of an hour of intense labor she sat up, rolling her neck in a circle and lifting her arms above her head to stretch them. She arched her back elegantly, pressing her chest out, tilting her head slightly toward the left. Lawrence unconsciously moved nearer to the window.

He was close enough now to see her face change when she returned her gaze to the paper on which she had been drawing, and to hear her dispirited sigh. Something was wrong. All at once she struck the table with her fist, stood quickly, took her candle, and moved away from the window toward her bed. As she brushed by the table her skirt skimmed its edge and sent the paper fluttering to the floor, but she did not seem to notice. In another minute she would be shrugging out of her gown, blowing out the candle, and climbing into bed. Lawrence was debating the propriety of seeing her undress when the decision was made for him.

There was a noise from the alley behind him. He had

been plagued all day with the feeling that someone was following him, so when he turned, his hand was already on his sword, his muscles flexed for fight.

"Oh. It's you," he said, relaxing slightly.

"Yes, sir. To relieve you. It is midnight."

Lawrence nodded, suddenly aware of how tired he was. "Good night, Tom."

"Good night, sir."

Lawrence turned back to Tuesday's windows and saw that the light was gone. *Good night, Lady Arlington,* he thought to himself as he walked away, tossing the gold piece in his right hand. *See you in the morning.*

Although he was not consciously aware of it, for the first time in a long time Lawrence was looking forward to the next day.

That feeling lasted approximately seven hours.

Chapter 10

Tuesday lay very still in bed. She could sense it, hovering nearby, on the edges of her mind. Not the dream, she never had the dream two nights in a row. What she was waiting for was more diffuse than that. She was waiting to feel something. Anything.

Principally she knew she should be sad about Curtis. She had tried to cry, tried to make herself cry, earlier, but she could not. Maybe if every sign of his presence had not been removed from the house two months earlier, if she could have spent hours lovingly fondling his precisely folded linens, packing up his carefully polished gold shoe buckles (*don't rub too hard or the gilt will come off*, she remembered him scolding her), or running her fingers over his shaving brush, it might have been easier. She could almost hear Curtis commenting without surprise that she would make as unsatisfactory a widow as she had a wife.

It had been raining, a spring shower, the day they met. Howard had brought Curtis to dine one afternoon, and although he had not shown any interest in her at all during the meal, he had materialized the next day and asked for her hand in marriage. He said he had been too overcome to address her before, but he knew he had to make her his. All five of her previous engagements had been called off and after The Blot—the unfortunate incident when Tuesday managed to fall out of a tree and into the Thames, smack in the center of the dozen naked guardsmen who she had been sketching while they bathed—it had been assumed she would never get another offer. But then came Curtis and his proposal, and her entire family was thrilled.

Tuesday shared their elation. It was as if Curtis's approval of her was contagious, and for the first time in her memory her father and brother were pleased with her. She and Curtis were wed the next week.

"Were you and your husband happy?" the third man sent by Lawrence Pickering to question her had asked that afternoon.

She had not meant to be evasive. She imagined what Lawrence Pickering would think, that she was hiding something from him, that she knew more than she was saying. Which was true, of course. But the real reason she told all those stories was the same reason she always had. Stories kept you from remembering. The wilder the better. In stories, no one ever died or left you. In stories you never had to admit that you were a failure; in stories you never disappointed anyone.

If you're not happy with Curtis, it'll be your fault, her brother, Howard, told Tuesday on the day of her marriage, and Tuesday had agreed. How could she not have been happy with the man who made her family love her? He was handsome and sought after and taking her despite the fact that she was twenty-six. If she made him happy, she would be happy herself.

Happy. The way she felt when a portrait went well.

The way she felt when she could make CeCe or George laugh. The way she had felt before.

She had not known how to make Curtis happy.

"Reasonably," she had replied to her questioner. "We were reasonably happy."

"Reasonably," the man had repeated, painstakingly forming the letters, and in the scratching of his pen Tuesday could have sworn she heard him mocking her. He could tell she knew nothing about making a man happy.

He looked up from his paper. "When was the last time you saw your husband? Can you tell me the date?"

How could she explain that time for her did not consist of dates? It consisted of events: the last time there was a chair in the house, the last time she had gone to the pawnbroker, the last time Curtis had taken her in his arms.

He had rented a coach, a closed one, very fancy with a dusty red velvet interior and taken her for a drive out into the country one afternoon. She recalled the scenery they passed, the smell of freshly cut grass, a lazy cow suckling her rust-colored calves. She had watched all of that as he had pounded himself into her with the jerking of the coach. It had gone on for hours, she thought, past a village, *pound*, past an encampment of gypsies, *pound*, past other people's lives. A young girl in a yellow dress with dust on her feet stood by the side of the road carelessly eating a red apple, and their eyes had almost met, but Tuesday had looked away so the girl would not see her embarrassment.

"What are you thinking about?" Curtis had asked her when the pounding was done, his voice rich, warm, as if he really wanted to know. "What's in your head today,

Lucky?" Lucky. His own personal name for her—*you're lucky to have such a young handsome husband you're lucky anyone would take you at all you're damn lucky I picked you out when I did at twenty-six or you'd never have been married you're so lucky—*

"I was noticing the fine scenery, my lord. It is an exceptionally lovely day."

She knew even before she was finished speaking that she had said the wrong thing. Curtis's face clouded. "I give you the lay of your life, and all you can think about is the scenery? Have you been getting it from someone else, too? Is that it? I don't impress you anymore?"

The pain of these accusations had once been worse than the physical pain. "No," she rushed to appease him. Why? It never worked. "I was just so satisfied that my mind wandered."

His hand snaked out and slapped her cheek before she even realized what had happened. "Lying bitch," he said. "If I had known what you really are, I never would have offered for you. Not for all the gold in Spain. I ought to tell your father about you. Tell him that his daughter is a cheap hussy." His eyes glittered with malice.

Tuesday had slid to her knees, practicing the subservience she knew he wanted, keeping her eyes riveted on a spot of dirt staining the red upholstery next to his shin. "My lord, Curtis, I am sorry if I did anything to displease you. I know I have been a disappointment to you, but I want to change. Please show me how. Please teach me to be the wife you've always wanted." She looked up at him now and saw that he had not softened. "The wife that you deserve," she added.

It worked. The fire left his eyes and he pulled her onto

the cushioned seat next to him. "Lucky, Lucky, Lucky. Why can't you be that reasonable all the time?" He reached out and put a sweaty hand on her breast, holding it so tight it hurt her. "If only you showed your better self all the time, things could be sweet between us. You want that, don't you Lucky?"

Tuesday nodded and worked not to flinch as his lips came over hers, then his teeth. Soon, she knew, if she was lucky, the pounding would start again, and then the whole scene would be replayed. She was fighting not to gag as the coach pulled to a stop and the coachman banged on the roof.

"We're 'ei, sir," his muffled voice called into the interior of the vehicle.

"Damn," Sir Curtis muttered. His hand, which had been urging Tuesday's head into his lap, instead hauled her up. "Get dressed. I don't want everyone thinking my wife is a whore."

He had left her at the inn, saying he had business to conduct elsewhere. He did not think to leave her any money for a room and she did not dare ask for it, so she sat with her back against the wall in the corner through the night. In her entire life she had never felt as humiliated as she did then, abandoned by her husband, abandoned by her courage. She no longer recognized herself.

The next morning Curtis had reappeared at the inn, unshaved, still drunk, and reeking of some other woman's rose water. That was the moment she had remembered when Lawrence told her he was dead, the moment Curtis stood before her at the inn, his shirt open at the collar, smiling cockily beneath his mustache, hands on his hips. Tuesday had sensed what was about to happen. She could almost see the words hanging in the air before they were spoken. Could almost feel the label, "REJECTED" being stitched to her chest.

He had not even bothered to sit. "You are a terrible wife and a terrible screw," he announced loud enough for the tavern keeper and all the stable hands to hear. "I don't know why I've put up with you for so long, but I've got better ways to spend my time. Goodbye, Lucky." Then he had turned and left. Left her there, six hours by horse outside of London, with no money and no husband and no one to blame but herself.

"Do you know what day it was when you last saw your husband?" Lawrence Pickering's man had asked again, puncturing the web of her memory.

"Not exactly," Tuesday answered, grateful for the respite, the way back to the present. For a moment she wished she could explain to this stranger: it had been long enough so that her breast no longer bore the marks of his thumb. Long enough so that the bruises on her cheek and shoulder *(yes, I fell down the stairs again; yes, Father, I must learn not to be so clumsy)* had healed. Long enough so that the blisters on her feet from walking for four days were gone. Long enough so that she had been able to repay the money the gypsies had lent her. She had looked for the girl in the yellow dress, just to touch her, maybe to warn her, but all that was left was an apple core.

Not long enough so that it no longer hurt. "About two months I would say."

She knew Lawrence Pickering would think she was lying, but she did not care. And as she lay alone in the dark she realized that for the first time in her life, she did not care about pleasing a man.

Curled in a tight ball in her bed, knees hugged to her

chin, she did cry then, hard, but not out of sadness or grief. She cried out of shame. Shame that she would have done anything to make Curtis happy. Shame that she had not had the strength to hate him. Shame for what she had become. What she had let herself become.

Shame because she had lost herself.

Where are you, bitch?

Tuesday's eyes flew open but the rest of her was paralyzed. She heard the voice, the voice from her dreams, so clearly that it sounded real. And close. Her heart thudded against her knees.

You are mine now, bitch.

"Who are you?" she demanded. No response. Of course not. There was no one there, she knew. She would have heard them come in. She was alone in her studio. Just her and her memories.

And the voice in her head. The voice of another man trying to bend her to his will. This one was more awful even than Curtis because he was *inside* her. She had often felt like she understood things about people, hidden things, when she looked at them, as though she had a special sense, but she had never experienced anything like this. This was not just knowing about someone else. It was almost like being them. She was trembling, terrified. No, not terrified.

Angry.

She saw red, red everywhere: red upholstery, red apple, red roses, red spot of blood on her canvas. In that instant, shame burned away and became rage. She uncurled from the ball she had been in and sat up in bed.

She would not let this happen again. She would not be another man's pawn. This time she would not give in.

She would leave London and find the killer and make him stop. Somehow she would free herself.

Find herself.

Ha ha ha the challenging laughter echoed in her head, mocking her resolve. You are a prisoner. The queen's own guardsmen are standing outside your door.

Damn the killer and damn Lawrence Pickering. There had to be a way—

You keep your whore mouth shut or I'll do the same to you as I did to him.

—a way to escape them both.

Or use them both.

The thought and the answer came simultaneously.

She wouldn't. She wouldn't keep her mouth shut. She would disobey the killer, make him come after her. Then, using the guards Lawrence Pickering had so kindly provided, she would trap him.

And neither of them, not the killer, not Lawrence Pickering, would know what she had done.

She had one errand to do in the morning, and then she would set her plan in motion. Feeling more optimistic than she had all day, she lay her head back onto the pillow. In less than three minutes she was asleep.

The Lion separated himself from the shadows at the foot of her bed and inched toward her. His hungry eyes roamed her body as he moved, past a naked ankle, a bare wrist. Slowly he bent down until his face hovered right over hers, until he could taste her breath on his lips. Her night shift had come unknotted at the throat and exposed the W-like swell of her décolletage. His fingers ached to touch one of her breasts, to weigh it, to feel its yielding softness.

There was no one outside to stop him. There was no one to interfere.

Her heart could be his forever, with just four cuts.

At seven o'clock the next morning, Tom stumbled into Lawrence's office. The side of his face was bruised and he had a bump at the back of his head. In short mumbled sentences, he recounted how he had been knocked unconscious the previous night shortly after he assumed his post.

Five minutes later, another guardsman arrived to say that Lady Tuesday Arlington was gone.

Chapter 11

"What do you mean, she disappeared?" Lawrence asked, his eyes blazing. "How the devil can a woman just disappear?"

"I'm sorry, sir," Tom mumbled. The side of his face was bruised and his jaw was swollen. "Knocked me out from behind just after you left, and I'm afraid I was unconscious for quite a while. It was light when I opened my eyes. She would have had plenty of time to get away."

Lawrence stalked back and forth across the length of his office as if he were measuring it for new rugs and wanted to be sure to get it just right. His mind was reeling.

Tom was the only man actually watching the room, but there had been guards at all the doors. How had she gotten out?

The answer to that question arrived a few minutes later. "Skylight," Grub reported. "Didn't know it opened. Goes out onto the roof and there's a ladder nearby. From there she could have climbed down into the neighbor's courtyard and sneaked out without us seeing. One of the servants, a Mr. Jenks, says he thinks he heard someone there about two hours ago."

Lawrence didn't say anything, just nodded. "I want to see her maid, CeCe, and that artist, George Lyle. Now."

Two men evaporated from the office in search of them.

Where the hell had she gone? The obvious answer was that she was meeting with someone she did not want them to know about. Maybe Curtis had left her some instructions to act on when he died, the names of people to get in touch with to continue his smuggling activities. Or maybe, despite all of Lawrence's best instincts to the contrary, she really had been responsible for his death. Either way, her sneaking off to a clandestine meeting only confirmed that she knew more than she was telling. But not for long.

"Grub, I want you to go back to her house and search her studio. I am looking for—wait," Lawrence interrupted himself. He was remembering watching her the previous night, watching as she sketched. Or appeared to sketch. Then went to bed, brushing her work—"The settee. In the studio. There should be a paper underneath it. Bring it to me."

Grub was out the door before Lawrence finished his thought.

Why had he moved the men outside her door? Damn damn damn.

His pacing brought him to where Tom was propped in a chair. The boy looked terrible and Lawrence cursed himself for putting him in danger. Tom was one of his youngest men, but also his best. He had served him loyally in Spain and shown himself to be smart and brave. He did not deserve to be beaten up.

"Tom, have Christopher show you to my apartment to clean up and rest. You should take the next few days off."

x96 Michele Jaffe

"If you please, sir, I would rather help. Unless you don't think I am up to it."

Damn damn damn. "Of course I think you're up to it, Tom. I just don't like seeing you get hurt."

"Its not as bad as it looks, sir," Tom assured him. Then, in a different voice added, "I want to get him. I want to make him pay."

Him, Lawrence thought grimly. *Or her.*

The Lion had observed the activity at Pickering Hall with enormous amusement. All those men running around in search of Lady Arlington. He knew exactly where she was. He had followed her there that morning.

The Lion had often thought his life would make a good book. One of those books that his grandmother liked, with knights that went around on adventures slaying other knights and dragons. He was like them. He slayed knights and dragons, too. One day he would slay the knight of all knights. Slay Our Greatest Hero. Would sneak up on him while he slept and run him through. *Sweet dreams!*

It had been so hard to keep himself from killing her the night before. She had looked so perfect, so ripe. But he knew from his reading that something easily won was not worth having. There was so much more to do before he could have her, have her properly, the way he deserved to. Have her pure heart all for himself.

She had been put there like that, at his fingertips, to tempt him, and it had almost worked, but he would not let anything turn him from his quest. He wasn't a fool.

Not like them. God they were idiots. They had found the clues he left for them at the other murder scene pretty fast, but they still had so much to learn. It was almost sad to see them trying so hard.

He gave Pickering Hall one last lingering glance as he sauntered off. He would have liked to stay and watch them go in circles awhile more, but now he had work to do. It was time to start preparing the next adventure, the next chapter.

He thought it could be called *Rest in Peace*. Or maybe *Rest in Pieces*.

"If I were you, I wouldn't move. Not unless you want to feel the point of my sword any deeper in your back."

Tuesday stood stock still.

"Good," the man's voice said behind her. "Now turn around, slow like. And don't think to try nothing funny because funny isn't what I'm in the mood for at this time o' the morning."

Tuesday turned and found herself staring into empty air. The top of the head of the man holding the sword did not begin until somewhere around her waist and it was speckled.

"Yer a lass," he announced, squinting at her.

"Yes," Tuesday agreed. She assumed it always paid to agree with men holding swords, even if they were only one half your height.

"What'r you doing here then? Thieving, I suppose."

Why had she thought this visit to Curtis's apartment was a good idea? That it was so important for her to see where he had spent his last months? She knew the answer. She was looking for a cue, a smell or an object, that would make her feel, would touch her.

But there was something concrete she wanted as well. "I was looking for something. Something that is mine."

"And how would something that was yours come to be in a room I know you ain't got no right being in?" he inquired cagily. "You ain't Master Curtis nor his mistress neither."

"His mistress?" Tuesday heard the word and repeated it before it sank in.

"Aye. Poor dear. They were going to be married soon. Pity ain't it, him being dead and all. Still, she's a fine woman and won't have much trouble scaring up another husband."

That should have done it, should have stirred her, but it didn't. She just felt numb. As if she were taking part in the conversation from a distance. She heard herself asking "When were they marrying?"

"Soon as Curtis could get rid of his hag of a wife, he said. But I don't know why I should be telling you anything, seeing as how you're the one should be telling me things. Like starting with who you are."

"I'm, ah, Sir Curtis's—" hag of a wife, hag of a wife, "—sister."

"Don't look much like 'im."

"Half sister," she corrected, her mouth working on its own. "I was looking for some jewelry that was our mother's."

"Were you now?" The man was clearly not convinced. "What sort of jewelry?"

"A necklace. It wasn't very valuable, but my—our—mother loved it. It had a dragonfly pendant."

The man nodded slowly. "I seen that. He gave it to his fiancée that I told you about. Looks nice on her. Suppose she has as much right to it as you do."

That was when Tuesday realized it was not numbness she was feeling. Her brother had laid claim to every piece of their mother's jewelry except an old dragonfly choker, because the choker had no real gems in it and not much gold. It was the only thing of their mother's that Tuesday had and she treasured it as if it were one of the queen's jewels. She would not even wear it for fear of losing it, the only link she had to her mother, a woman she barely remembered. But one day, after Curtis came home and found her painting when he had expressly forbidden her to, he had taken the necklace to punish her. "You'll get it back when you learn to be good," he'd promised.

Tuesday's fingers wrapped around the wrist of her right hand as she remembered that day. The necklace had not returned. She had not learned to be good enough for Curtis.

Her mind clicked off facts. He had left her. He was going to marry someone else. As soon as he got rid of his hag of a wife.

The bastard.

The thought roared in her ears. No, it was not numbness she felt. It was pure, hot, unfamiliar rage.

She had only once in the two years they had been married permitted herself to feel anything like that toward Curtis. She had always believed him when he told her it was her fault she got hit *(If you'd do as you were told, I wouldn't have to punish you)*, her fault they were broke *(If you pleased me more I wouldn't go out gambling)*, her fault they didn't have children *(If you behaved how you were supposed to, you'd be pregnant right now)*. She had always believed him when he told her she was lucky.

Now she recognized that the anger she had persuaded herself she did not feel had not disappeared simply because she willed it to. Now she saw that she had been harboring it locked inside all along, a dangerous monster.

Now that Curtis had taken away what was suddenly the only possession in the world she cared about, she felt it claw at her. Somewhere deep in her mind she might have realized that the necklace was just a catalyst, that what she was feeling went beyond that, expanded around that, but the wave of rage that surged through her washed all other thoughts away.

The force of her anger terrified Tuesday. She struggled against it, pushing it back into its cage. This was not right, it was not acceptable to feel this way, good girls do what they are told, good girls never speak back, never shout, never wish their husbands dead.

The lessons of a lifetime, learned across her father's lap, came back to her, flooding her with voices, pinpricks of recollection. She was a bad girl.

(Please, no, I am sorry, it won't—)

Bad girls deserve what they get.

(It will be all right, dragonfly, don't worry. I won't let him hurt you; mother will protect you. We will go away from here and nothing will ever be wrong again. Dennis, what are you—Dennis, NO—)

Tuesday jolted herself out of the half memory. She was surprised to find she was trembling and it took her a moment to realize where she was.

The short man, Curtis's landlord, was standing in front of her. The sword had dipped slightly in his hand, but he was still regarding her skeptically. She should say something, but she had no idea what. "Thank you for letting me look around," she blurted finally.

"Had no choice in the matter, had I, since you invited yourself in."

Right. She had forgotten that part. "No, but I am sure you would have anyway." She worked to muster up a smile. "Do you know where my brother's fiancée lives? I would very much like to pay her a visit. To commiserate with her."

"Not sure exactly but expect she'll be coming here to collect his things. If you leave me your address, I'll tell her you was asking about her. She'll come and see you if *she* wants to."

Deciding that it would be unwise to leave her real name, Tuesday gave the man CeCe's and directions to Worthington Hall. Then she followed him down the stairs and left by the front door, which was quite a bit easier than climbing up the gutter pipe as she had to enter.

She had the sensation of being hollow as she left. Someone had scooped out her insides and jumbled them around, so that long-suppressed memories and feelings were suddenly rattling around inside the shell of what had once been her. It was as though all the bolts that usually held her together inside had been loosened, or lost. She felt unfamiliar and out of control. She felt like she had nothing to lose. She felt dangerous.

Just right for a meeting with Lawrence Pickering. Which, if her plan had worked at all, should be taking place—

Clouds of dust. Horses whinnying. Coach door banging open. "Where the hell have you been, Lady Arlington?"

—now.

Chapter 12

"Well?" Lawrence demanded, hauling her into the coach. "I'm waiting."

Something about his presence made Tuesday feel much better. It was not that, having bathed and changed from the previous day, he now looked every inch the heart-breakingly handsome earl of Arden. Nor was it that she had never seen lips or a chin—or eyes or a nose or forehead—quite like his before. Nor that he smelled like the woods in November. She noticed none of these things, and besides, she liked him more when he looked scruffier. What made her feel better was knowing what she was about to do to him.

For her plan to work, she had to be kept well enough guarded to catch the killer when he came for her, preferably by Lord Pickering himself. The only way she could guarantee that she would get that much of his attention, she had surmised, was by keeping his suspicions of her alive, keeping him in a state of constant antagonism. As he sat across from her barking questions, she decided it was going to be a pleasure. "Good morning, Lord—Mr. Pickering. I trust you slept well."

"What the hell have you been doing?"

"I *did* have pleasant dreams. I have not, however,

breakfasted as there was something I wished to do first thing this morning, and I am quite hungry, so I would be delighted to accept your offer of a ride back to my house."

"We are not going back to your house. Now answer my questions."

"I believe I told you yesterday, *Mister* Pickering, that while I am happy to talk to you at length on a vast variety of subjects, questions from you of any type are decidedly unwelcome. Plus, you owe me an apology."

"You are insane, aren't you?"

"I wonder why your coach isn't moving."

"Do you know how close you are coming to getting your neck wrung?"

"Perhaps your coachman has fainted. I'll go take a look."

"My coachman is fine. You do realize you are under arrest, don't you?"

"Isn't the weather lovely?"

"Lady Arlington, if you—" Lawrence's threat was cut off midstream by the arrival of one of his men.

"These are her husband's rooms," the man reported. "Landlord said she must have sneaked in. Caught her looking around. Left this behind." He handed the paper on which Tuesday had written CeCe's name through the window.

"Why did you—" Lawrence began, then stopped. "You gave a false name. I would like to know why." Stated, not asked.

Tuesday almost smiled. "It seems that my husband was engaged to marry someone else, as soon as he could get rid of his 'hag of a wife.' That is me. Naturally, I wanted to meet his bride to be, but I thought that if I left my real name she would be reluctant to come forward. You can understand how awkward that might be."

"That is the most preposterous thing I have ever heard."

"I suspect from what I have heard of your history, Lord Pickering, that is a great compliment."

"It's true, sir," the man who had produced the paper piped. "Landlord says Sir Curtis was engaged and that she was asking about it. Also about some necklace."

Lawrence returned his gaze to her. "I should advise you, Lady Arlington, that your life would be much more pleasant in the next few hours if you took greater pains to satisfy my curiosity as to why you came here in the first place."

"Isn't it obvious? I was hoping to run into you."

"She's only been here the last half hour, sir," Lawrence's helpful man put in then. "We still don't know where she was for the hour before that."

Lawrence looked at her. She looked back at him. Finally he barked, "Where were you?"

"Have you heard the riddle about the lettuce and the eel, Mr. Pickering?"

"It would give me great pleasure to learn from your lips where the hell you've been."

"I doubt that."

"If you do not tell me where you were I shall be forced to assume that you are hiding something or protecting someone."

"I have never in my life met a man more determined to be mistaken."

Instead of saying anything, Lawrence made a low growling noise and scowled at the air in front of him. He was debating whether to go ahead with the scheme he

and Miles had devised. Through a quick interview with
CeCe he had learned that Tuesday had not left her
chamber the night before, so she had not been the one to
knock Tom out in the alleyway. But of course, if she had
an accomplice, she would not even have had to get out
of bed.

Whether she was responsible for Tom's injuries or not,
sticking to her side was still the best way to learn what
she knew, Lawrence decided. He rapped once on the roof
of the coach and the vehicle rocked into motion.

Tuesday did not recognize the house they pulled up in
front of, but it had to be one of the largest in London.
She imagined the façade was lovely, but it was impossible
to tell with the number of workmen swarming all over it,
scrubbing each brick by hand and hanging huge garlands. Inside the scene was even more impressive. She
had never seen such a lavish establishment, or so many
servants tearing around under stacks of linens or huge
trays of glassware. She tried not to stare too openly as
Lawrence guided her up a staircase, past a Michelangelo
painting, and into a large room, made larger by the fact
that it was practically unfurnished.

There was a desk at one end, with a man leaning
against it. He got up as they came in and gestured Tuesday into a chair that appeared never to have been sat in.

"That is the viscount Dearbourn," Lawrence said in
clipped tones. "Miles, this is her."

Miles could barely keep the amusement off his face.
He had never seen Lawrence quite like this before and he
was sorry his cousins weren't there to witness it, too.
They had all been worried about him since his return
from Spain—unlike the rest of London, they were not

fooled by Lawrence's constant smiles, or the vague ru-
mors of his love affairs. They knew that he had not been
happy since he got back, had not, really, been anything.
At least now he seemed genuinely annoyed. Definitely an
improvement.

Tuesday momentarily put aside her own annoyance
in favor of surprise. She had heard of Miles Loredan
but never thought she would be meeting him. According
to the news sheets CeCe was always quoting, he and his
cousins, known as the Arboretti after a company they
owned, were the richest and most important, not to
mention most famous, men in England, if not all of
Christendom. And, she now remembered, their names
almost never appeared—at least not when their more
astonishing and outlandish escapades were mentioned—
without being linked to that of Lawrence Pickering.
Which, of course, figured.

She began a low curtsey but Miles stopped her. "It is a
pleasure to meet you, Lady Arlington. Lawrence had
told me a bit about you."

"Probably the bit about my being a murderess."

"That did come up. In fact, that is why you are here."

"Is this the processing center for Newgate?"

"Not quite. We now have a witness who saw a man—"

"A witness? You have a witness?"

"Yes. Albert Marston. We were hoping you could help
us with him. I have been told that you have a book of
faces, pieces of faces. Could you make a portrait from—"

She was not looking at Miles anymore but had craned
her neck around to stare behind her at Lawrence, who
was tossing a gold piece in his hand. "You found someone who saw the killer and it was not me, but you still
kept me under arrest?"

Lawrence caught the coin and looked at her stonily. Miles, who had decided he liked her a lot, said, "Actually, they found him using the description you provided."

Lawrence glowered at Miles. They had not discussed telling her that. In fact, Lawrence hadn't even told Miles that much. Whoever had leaked the information was going to be in trouble.

But Lawrence's glower was no match for Tuesday's. Any urges she had once felt to smile were eradicated. She turned around to address him. "You *believed* what I told you yesterday about the murderer being a brown-haired man? You called me a liar."

"I was exploring possibilities," Lawrence said coolly. Very big trouble. He tossed the coin in the air.

"I wish I were a murderer," she hissed, and there was no question about who her first victim would be if she decided to take up the vocation. "Now you owe me two apologies." She turned to face Miles again. "Mr. Pickering has abominable manners when he does not get his way."

"Yes, he does," Miles agreed heartily. *Mister* Pickering, and Lawrence hadn't even flinched. "Now about—"

At that moment the sounds of someone bashing into furniture interrupted him, followed by a discreet knock on the door. Miles crossed to open it, and found himself facing one of Lawrence's men. He made an urgent gesture to his boss.

Lawrence and the guard conferred together in whispers for a moment until Lawrence turned to Miles, his eyes blazing, and said, "She tried to bribe one of my operatives this morning."

The guard shook his head and pulled Lawrence back into conversation.

"What do you mean I—?" Tuesday asked, but Lawrence put up a hand to stop her. The blaze in his eyes changed, then changed again.

"Show him in," he said finally, rubbing his hands together.

The guard disappeared, then reappeared with one of his colleagues. Between them they were supporting an enormous man, half a head taller than either of them, who was writhing in their arms and bleeding from a cut above his eye.

"Oh my God, Jack, what have they done to you?" Tuesday cried, coming out of her chair and reaching for the man.

At the sight of her, at the sound of her voice, the man named Jack threw off his guards, wrapped his arms around her, and let loose a torrent of unintelligible words. She held him and rubbed his back and moved him gingerly into the chair she had just vacated. "Keep your eyes closed," she told him in his ear, and he did, using his entire face to smash them shut.

She kneeled next to him, cleaning the wound to his head with the sleeve of her gown, the whole time whispering to him in an undertone. Lawrence moved closer to hear what she was saying and she looked up, giving him, in a split second, a glance that could have singed the bristles off a boar.

He decided to talk to his men instead. "Who is this?"

"Man she was with this morning. Name is Jack, sir. Traced her ladyship's movements backwards, like you said—bit of luck, her trying to pay off Cassandra—and discovered that she'd been at this one's apartment. And it ain't the first time, neither," the man added ominously. "Seems she goes three, four times a week, according to the landlady. Makes no secret, neither, of her feelings. One day Mrs. Peach, that's the landlady, she saw these two embracing and kissing, very familiar. And," he paused for emphasis, getting ready for the good stuff, "Sir Curtis as was her husband? He used to go there regular, too. Then one day he goes and finds this one—" thumb jabs at Jack, "—with her, and there's a regular big fight and then Sir Curtis never comes back again. Want my opinion, these two is a couple and Sir Curtis gets wise and—"

Lawrence cut him off. "I'm not interested in your opinion. What did the man himself tell you about her visit?"

"Nothing. Not said a bloody word. We don't even introduce ourselves and he starts swinging. He's like an ox."

Lawrence turned to Tuesday. "How do you explain this report, Lady Arlington?"

"How do you explain what they did to him, Mr. Pickering?"

"He lunged at us, sir," the man put in defensively.

"He was terrified," Tuesday challenged.

"Terrified?" Lawrence snorted. "He's twice the size of my men."

"Yes but he is—"

"Grub said you were looking for a paper. He got one, all right, but we had to tie his hands just to pry it off him," the man continued and Tuesday went completely white. "He tried to deny having it, tried to deny knowing Lady Arlington, but we cornered him and made him hand it over."

The man held out a folded sheet of paper. Before Lawrence could take it, Tuesday said, "Give that to me." When no one moved, she grabbed for it.

Lawrence got there first.

"Give it to me, please," she said, and now the defiance was gone from her tone, replaced by something desperate that made Lawrence almost sorry for her. Almost. He grabbed the paper and unfolded it brutally. He stared.

It was a drawing of a horse. Just a drawing of a horse.

"Please give it to him if you don't want to give it to me," Tuesday implored now, leaning over Jack. "He won't be able to breathe right until you do."

Lawrence looked up and realized that the large man was gasping for air and rocking back and forth.

"Please, he is terrified. I'll tell you anything you want to know. Please, Lord Pickering—"

Jack had moved his hands to his eyes and was watching Lawrence and Tuesday in the gaps between his fingers, but as soon as Lawrence extended the paper toward him, his hands came down. Jack held the paper right in front of his face, inspecting it, then lovingly refolded it and slipped it inside his doublet. He straightened up in his chair and smiled at Lawrence.

Lawrence frowned but Jack didn't seem to notice. As soon as Jack smiled, the nature of his relationship to Tuesday was clear. They looked almost identical, except where her eyes were stoked with fire, his were uncannily serene. Jack was like an overgrown infant, pleased with everything and completely dependant on Tuesday, who was unquestionably his sister. He was obviously not anyone's accomplice. He was just a sweet, slow boy that Tuesday cared for deeply.

"Why didn't you tell me about him when I asked you?" Lawrence demanded. "Why keep Jack a secret?"

"Because I didn't want your men going there and terrifying him."

"Jack is scared of soldiers," Jack put in then. "When Jack is scared he can't breathe. One time Jack almost died."

Lawrence was absolutely furious. He was furious that he had been so wrong, furious at his men for making such a mistake, furious at her for turning out not to be a cunning criminal, for being willing to do anything—even look guilty—in order to protect her brother. Damn her.

As he watched the two of them together, he felt like there was more he did not understand. He rolled the gold coin between his fingers. "Your father does not know you are seeing Jack," he stated.

Tuesday nodded. "Can he go home now? It isn't good for him to be out so long."

Lawrence could tell something was making her tense. What was he missing? He tossed the coin. What—

"Jack, were you friends with Curtis?"

Jack looked quickly up at Tuesday. Her hand rested affectionately on his shoulder, and Lawrence saw her give it a small squeeze. But there was no affection in her eyes when she turned them to him. "Jack is a very special man," she said, and Jack grinned big. She smiled down at him, then returned her cool eyes to Lawrence. "He has some special skills that Curtis liked to make use of."

"Such as?" Lawrence asked.

"Jack has an incredible memory. He knows everything he has ever heard or read or seen. He can remember the exact location of every item in a room after visiting it for only a second. Curtis used to take him to taverns and make wagers against him getting answers right."

"They called him the Genius Boy," Miles put in then. "I've heard of him."

Tuesday nodded. "Sometimes people did not like the fact that Jack never made a mistake. Once some men, soldiers, followed him home and beat him up. Since then, he has been terrified by men, especially men in uniforms. He is scared to even leave his house except to play with the children in the yard at Bridewell."

Lawrence stole a look at Jack, expecting him to be tense or wary at being discussed, but was surprised to see that he merely looked impassive. In fact, he did not seem to be paying attention to them at all.

"He likes anything shiny," Tuesday explained, gesturing with her chin toward the coin Lawrence was tossing. "Curtis told him that if he got enough shiny things he could have a real pony, so he's been fascinated by them ever since."

Lawrence looked down and realized that Jack's gaze was indeed trained wistfully on the coin he was tossing in his hand. It was a coin he'd had for a long time, had kept on purpose. It held a wealth of memories and reminders. He threw it to Jack, who caught it nimbly and began tossing it in his hand as Lawrence had been.

"You are Jack's friend," a beaming Jack told Lawrence. "Mr. Pickering is Jack's friend."

Tuesday looked like she wanted to bite someone. The truth was, she was torn between making Jack give Lawrence Pickering back his stupid gold coin so that she would not have to hear endless monologues from Jack on the subject of his friend Mr. Pickering, and letting Jack keep it so that Lawrence could not stalk around tossing it. But the decision was made for her when Lawrence told his men to escort Jack home.

She was seething so thoroughly that she barely acknowledged Jack's good-bye wishes. She pretended not
to hear when Lawrence told his men to allow Jack to ride
home on one of his horses. As soon as the door was
closed she turned to him and began, "How dare you
drag him out of his house and—"

Lawrence cut her off clean. "Next time you try to
bribe one of my operatives, you'll need to offer them
more than four pennies. I pay very well."

"I don't know what you are talking—" Tuesday
began, then stopped and gaped. "She—? You—?"

On her way to Jack's room that morning, Tuesday had
noticed a very poor girl following her. She'd had only a
few pennies and the meat pie she was taking to Jack, but
she offered the lot to the girl who had kindly, but surprisingly, refused it. "That girl is an operative? She is not—?"

"A beggar?" Lawrence finished the sentence for her.
"No. She was once but she's been working for me for five
years. She's one of my best operatives—the head of that
whole quarter of London."

Tuesday did not like his smug tone or what he was
saying. She did not like having to replace her black-and-
white image of what he was with a more nuanced portrait of a man who took beggar girls under his wing and
gave them legitimate jobs. She did not like anything at all
about Lawrence Pickering. Only the way his frown was
digging deep furrows across his forehead and his hands,
now without their coin to toss, were clenched tight made
her feel any better. And gave her something to work for.
She wondered if it was true that muscles under strain
could freeze that way.

Although Miles was finding watching Lawrence open
and close his fists and Tuesday bite ferociously on her lip

amusing, he decided the best thing would be to speed the happy couple on their way. He picked up where they had left off before Jack's arrival. "Is it true, about your book, Lady Arlington? Could you produce a sketch of the man observed leaving the scene of the murder from the witness's description?"

Tuesday had to grind her mind back to the conversation as she considered Miles's request. She had used her book to draw someone absent before, and both times had been a disaster. The first time, with the Burns children, their disagreement over the color of their dead mother's hair had left one of them bloody and another with a whole new rhyme for the word "itch." But the second time was worse: CeCe had become positively incensed with Tuesday for "having every other forehead known to man and not my dear, dear fiancé's" in her book and burst into tears, accusing her mistress of being part of a conspiracy to obliterate her and everyone she loved from the earth as if they had never existed. The memory of that scene and of the tearful apology that followed still made her feel wretched. She would try that again only for a very compelling reason. "I might be able to make a sketch, but what good will that do?"

"We could have a team copy it and then our men could blanket the city, showing it around, to try to locate him."

"And if I refuse to help you?"

"Then we shall be forced to conclude that you are hiding something or shielding someone. Your arrest would stand."

"Imagine how hard that would be on your father," Lawrence put in from behind her.

Miles moved past that. "Of course, in return for your assistance, we would provide you with protection."

Tuesday had been staring at her hands in her lap, turning over ideas. Now she looked up at Miles, a strange expression on her face. "Protection?"

"Yes, a bodyguard and men to watch your house. Lawrence—Mr. Pickering—and I have been trying for several months to break a ring of smugglers, the ones we think your husband was working with. They are not nice characters and if they think you are helping us, you may be in some danger. Whoever killed your husband might come after you."

Tuesday shook her head and said, "I appreciate the offer, but I am sure I would be in no danger."

"I have to disagree. If they think you know something or are working against them, they will come after you."

"But I don't know anything. Besides, if there were guards in my house, they would upset my father. His condition, as Lord Pickering so thoughtfully pointed out, is fragile."

"We could disguise them so that they did not seem to be guards," Miles volunteered.

Tuesday shook her head again, then stopped as if something had just occurred to her. "I don't see—could they appear to be servants? Like a valet?"

"Yes. Of course," Miles agreed.

"Or musicians?" she went on.

Out of the corner of his eye, Miles saw Lawrence's frown deepen. Miles said, "I suppose so."

Tuesday nodded. "Very well. As long as my father is protected, I will be fine. I don't need a guard."

"Actually, Lady Arlington, we think you need protection most of all. In fact, Lord Pickering is going to assume the office—"

"No." It was a flat denial.

"I beg your pardon?"

"I will not have him circling around me, haunting me, all the time. No. Under no circumstances. Never."

"I assure you," Lawrence said from behind her, "that I will enjoy it as little as you will."

Tuesday twisted all the way around to face him. "I doubt that, Mr. Pickering. I do not think it is possible for anyone to enjoy anything less than I enjoy your company."

"What a charming compliment," Lawrence drawled with his fake smile.

"You seem to inspire burning emotions in my breast."

"You are not the first woman to say so."

"It is a wonder to me you have lived as long as you have."

"I know you will soon be making me regret it."

They glared at one another, until finally Tuesday sighed. Her shoulders sagged and she turned back toward Miles. "Fine. If there can be protection for the others, I will endure Mr. Pickering's presence."

"And I will endure hers."

Behind her, Lawrence smiled, this time for real, but Miles was not seeing that. What he was seeing was the struggle Tuesday was waging to conceal her own broad grin.

"It has been a real pleasure meeting you, Lady Arlington," Miles said as they were leaving, and meant it sincerely.

"Thank you, my lord."

Miles watched her go from the room, then stopped

Lawrence at the threshold. "Are you sure you know what you are doing, *Mister* Pickering?"

Lawrence narrowed his eyes at him. "It worked didn't it? It was the only way to get her to cooperate."

"Really? I thought it was the only way for you to avoid apologizing to her."

"I don't know what you are talking about," Lawrence replied innocently and strolled out, leaving Miles shaking his head in the doorway.

Miles was wrong, Lawrence assured himself as his coach took them to Worthington Hall. He would never have orchestrated anything this elaborate just to avoid apologizing to someone. Even someone who deserved an apology as little as Tuesday Arlington.

"Is it true that you lived on rats when you were in prison in Spain?" she asked, breaking into his thoughts.

"No," he replied. The meeting with Miles had gone even better than he had planned. His men would be swarming all over her house, at her request.

"Oh. That is too bad," she said.

"Yes, I can imagine you liked the idea of me living on rodents," Lawrence answered without looking at her. (He was not thinking about the fact that she cared for her brother Jack all alone, probably painted extra just to support him.) She had responded exactly as he had known she would to the suggestion that he be her personal guard, and now he would be by her side if she did anything. *Or if anyone tried to do anything to her.* Nonsense. She wasn't in any danger—except from him if she did not cooperate.

"That *is* a delightful thought," Tuesday was going on, "but it's not what I meant. I told the cook to make you rat pudding for lunch. To remind you of old times."

(He was not thinking about the fact that she had offered one of his operatives what he had to assume were her last pennies.) It took him a moment to realize what she had said. "You told your cook? This morning? Are you claiming you knew I would be coming home to dine with you?"

She gave him a look of innocence identical to the one he had given Miles only minutes before. "Of course. But I will confide something to you, Lord Pickering." She leaned toward him and her gray-green eyes were shimmering. "I had no idea just how much fun it would be to see how it came to pass."

(He was not thinking about the fact that she was the only woman he'd ever met who was, truly, breathtaking.)

Lawrence did not know how she ended up in his arms, half-naked, with his lips pressed against the incredibly delicious spot where her neck met her shoulder. All he knew was that he had been wrong.

He had no damn idea what he was doing.

Chapter 13

There was not a place on Tuesday's body that was not on fire. Not a part of her that did not *need* to feel Lawrence Pickering's touch. Her lips pressed against his and she felt his heart racing against her chest, felt his fingers on her shoulders, on the edge of her bodice, smooth and sure on her skin.

He was the most beautiful man she had ever seen, even when he was filthy and disheveled. Now, freed from having to be loyal to her disloyal husband's memory, she could admit that he made her knees weak and her heart pound and her skin tingle and had from the first moment she had laid eyes on him. Yearning built from years of neglect, from the maelstrom of emotions that had engulfed her that morning, coalesced into searing desire.

Lawrence molded his lips to hers, urging them open with his tongue. It had been two long years since he had been intimate with anyone, and he knew, now, that it had not been by choice but by need, the need to find her, this one woman. She fit against his body as if she had been made for him—she was made for him—her arms twined behind his neck, her fingers in his hair, pushing his mouth over hers harder. His fingertips slid inside the bodice of her gown, slid along the sides of her full round breasts, finding unimaginable softness. When they found her nipples she arched against him, pressing into his hard member until he thought he would die.

She moved away from him and he looked into her eyes and saw a thousand questions there and, beneath them, a yawning abyss of insecurity. He was stunned. But that was something he could take care of. He reached up and stroked her cheek.

"I did not know a woman could be as beautiful as you are," he said huskily and was astonished to see tears form at the corners of her eyes. She bit her lip, his lips for biting, and he ran his finger over where her teeth were. Not just sweet but soft and full. He kissed them again, gently this time, and she kissed him back and even though it was the chastest of kisses, they were both trembling.

This was a terrible idea, the worst possible idea, whatever they were doing was everything they shouldn't be. They didn't even like each other. They couldn't even be in the same room without glaring at each other. She might have killed her husband, he might be her jailer. They were both too fragile for this, both too broken. They were both too damaged not to do it.

Tuesday held onto Lawrence, pressed against the hard planes of his chest, hugged the deep muscles of his back. Killers, dead husbands, paintings, fathers, remorse, nightmares all seemed like vague memories against the powerful, delicious reality of his presence. The world turned upside down and the only thing that mattered was being here, like this, with this man.

Then, suddenly, he was pulling away from her.

Tuesday put her hand on his cheek and whispered, "Lord Pickering, what is wrong? Did I hurt you?"

Lawrence turned to face her. Their eyes met and where before Tuesday had seen a world, a future, redemption, she now saw nothing. Empty. They were empty again.

No, not empty. There was something in them.

Contempt.

There was no way for her to know it was contempt for himself. She slid off his lap, hastily tugging her bodice back up with quivering fingers. She could feel the letters, "Rejected" burning into her skin as if they really were written there. She was a terrible wife and a terrible screw. How could she have thought they were both feeling the same thing? She was a hag. She was—

"You did not do anything wrong. That whole thing was wrong. I am sorry, Lady Arlington. It should not have happened. We have both been under a strain."

Tuesday shook her head but kept her face down. A strain, she was a strain, a hag and a strain and a—"It is my fault. I should not have thrown myself at you."

There was a pause, then, "You didn't. I started kissing you."

"No, I started it."

"You are wrong," he corrected, a little more heated. "I distinctly remember pulling you onto my lap."

"No, I was the one who moved over to your side of the coach."

"Because I pulled you."

"You did not."

"I did too."

"You are mistaken, Lord Pickering. I moved over and then I forced you to kiss me."

"Forced me? Exactly how?"

"By—by forcing you."

"That is not an explanation. I am afraid you are going

to have to do better than that to answer me, Lady Arlington."

His tone was so infuriatingly imperious that Tuesday looked up from her lap.

He was smiling at her.

At that moment, emotionally raw, Tuesday felt the world sway under her again. She felt her stomach flutter, felt as though she were tumbling headlong into empty space, felt as though all the normal laws that governed human behavior had been suspended.

At that moment, she looked into Lawrence's smile and knew that she was falling—

Chapter 14

—onto the floor of the coach. It was something about the rapidly changing angle of Lawrence's face above her that made it clear, but not for long, because almost instantly he was also on his knees.

The vehicle swerved sharply, sending Tuesday rolling on top of Lawrence, and jolted to a stop. They lay there, his arms clutching her tighter than necessary against the length of his body, for a single instant. Then they pulled away from each other fast, and were just in the process of disentangling legs and petticoats and fingers, when the door flew open and George filled it.

"Don't tell me you've taken up wrestling, Tuesday," he said.

Tuesday glared at him. "George, what happened?"

"That is an extremely good question," he replied airily. "It seems that your charming maid, CeCe, threw herself in front of the coach—"

"Threw myself? You pushed me," said an outraged CeCe.

"Why would I do that?"

"Who can say? You probably thought it was amusing. I suppose you like hurting animals as well."

"Adore it. Such a feeling of power."

CeCe turned from him to address Tuesday. "What actually happened is that as I was drawing your bath—oh bother, I'm afraid it will be cold now—I thought I heard someone calling me from across the street, from the alley, and since I could not see who it was I went out and was just about to cross when George came out of nowhere and grabbed me up and—"

"Saved her from being trampled to death," George concluded. "I won't do it a second time, though."

"Good, then I shall not have to mend a second gown from where you ripped it," CeCe shot back.

Lawrence's face appeared then and CeCe momentarily looked like she might swoon when he said to her, "I am glad nothing happened to you." After which he peered over her shoulder out the door, added "Please excuse me," and stepped from the coach. Tuesday leaned out to see where he went.

CeCe's eyes also followed him, and under her breath she murmured, "He has the loveliest manners." Then a look of alarm flooded her face and she turned to Tuesday. "You don't think he got hurt, do you?"

"I doubt it," Tuesday said with an audible hint of disappointment, which earned her a smile from George and a reprimand from CeCe. Tuesday was not really listening, however. She was watching Lawrence as he talked to a young man on horseback who had just ridden up. "George," she said abruptly. "Could you take CeCe inside so she can recover from this ordeal? I have to speak to His Lordship."

George opened his mouth to say something in protest, but Tuesday was out of the coach past him before he managed to articulate it. "Thank you," she called to him over her shoulder, then moved toward Lawrence and the mounted man.

They were speaking intently, so neither of them noticed her approach. She arrived just in time to hear Lawrence say, "We already know his identity, Elwood. And why he was killed."

The man called Elwood nodded. "I am afraid it is not as simple as you think, at least, not if you think he was killed because of the smuggling."

Lawrence looked concerned. Elwood had once been his employee and was now the Special Commissioner of London's second in command. There was nothing that went on in the city that Elwood did not know about, particularly nothing nefarious, and his tone was worrying. "What exactly do you mean?"

"There have been three other men killed the same way in the last month."

Tuesday moved forward and joined them. "The same way? With their hearts cut out?"

Lawrence's face instantly broke into a frown as he turned to her. "What are you doing here?"

"This is my house. I live here. What a pleasant surprise, Mr. Pickering, to find you on my front steps as well."

Elwood watched with barely concealed amusement as Lawrence tightened and loosened his jaw, then said, "Elwood Marsh, this is Lady Tuesday Arlington. The corpse's wife."

It was as ungallant an introduction as possible, but that was not what made Elwood looked startled. "It is a pleasure to meet you, Lady Arlington," he stammered. "I am sorry it has to be under these circumstances."

"Thank you. You were saying, about the other corpses—?"

"Right. Yes, they were all killed exactly the same way. All with their hearts, ah, missing. We did not know what to make of the first one. We thought maybe wild dogs had gotten to it or something, but when, a week later, we found the second one, and then a week after that the third, we had to see a pattern."

"Could the others have been part of the smuggling ring?" Lawrence put in.

"That is the problem. Our preliminary research has not turned up anything to suggest a link to your smugglers, but we will want to run their names by your men anyway. There could be some connection to Sir Curtis that we don't know about."

Tuesday, pensive, asked, "Were they all killed in hallways?"

"No. Carter Smyth was found in the woods behind the Rose in Southwark, although he seemed to have been dragged there judging from the tracks. Amory Lockland appeared near the wall in the far corner of the pleasure garden at Richmond. And Richard Ellington's body was discovered in an unused storeroom next to Old Cartson's wine shop over on Cheapside."

Elwood had been studying her. Now he saw her swallow hard before saying, "Could you repeat that? About the woods and the garden and the storeroom?" Elwood did and she murmured, "I see."

Tuesday's hands were clenched into tight fists, but Elwood did not notice because Lawrence claimed his attention then. "So the only similarity between them is the way they were killed?"

"Not quite. When I rode over it was just to say that we

should coordinate our efforts because we were running out of time, but now I think it might be something else." His eyes shifted between the two of them. "You see, all the murders were committed on Tuesdays."

The Lion hummed to himself as he pressed the black powder into place. Some of it floated on the air and he stuck his tongue out to taste it. It tasted gritty and bitter and sour. It tasted marvelous. It tasted like death.

His head was buzzing with excitement and it took all his energy to stay concentrated on what his hands were doing. His mind raced ahead, raced to the deed, then beyond it. This was it, the last quiet moment he would have. After this everything was going to happen fast.

How do we make people believe?

We persuade them.

And if they won't stay persuaded?

We force them.

He liked that. They would be forced to believe. They would be made to see that he was the best.

He had considered hiring someone else to do the job, so there would be no chance of him getting caught for such a little thing, but there was no one he could trust to do it right. He had to be sure the man got the treatment he deserved. He had invested too much in his disguised identity to let it come unraveled by something as simple as a missed shot.

No, he would have to take care of the Witness himself.

"I'm going to check on the guards," Lawrence announced as they entered Worthington Hall, raising his voice to be heard over the sounds of a concert getting underway upstairs. "Wait for me in your studio." Tuesday said nothing, just turned and did what he said.

He should have known then there was something wrong. He should have had an inkling, a suspicion. But somehow his instincts, honed like a fine instrument through years of practice, were dead asleep where Lady Tuesday Arlington was concerned.

Five minutes later, when he walked through her studio door, he should not have been surprised to find that she was not there, but he was. His first flicker of emotion—his first flicker of emotion in two years—should not have been pain, but it was. For a moment, under the combined onslaught, he missed the rest of the scene. But then, gradually he saw a large tub of water standing in the middle of the floor. And around it, each set on its own stand as if arrayed for viewing from the bath, were four paintings.

Four paintings on four easels of—

A wooded glade with two long brown marks as if a body had been dragged.

A garden wall with headless flowers scattered at its base and a crack like a thunderbolt from which small yellow weeds were growing, running up one side.

A dark store room, with boxes and a mildewed barrel in the background.

A corner in a wood-paneled hallway with a knot in the wood that looked like a death's head and a splattering of blood.

—murder scenes.

Lawrence took a step forward and stopped. What stopped him was the feeling of something sharp poking into his shoulder.

"Take your clothes off," Tuesday said, emerging from her hiding place behind him, behind the door.

He started to turn around and the poking got more insistent. "I have a sword pointed at your heart through your back. I suggest you do what I say."

She did not want to see his eyes, not yet. She did not want to see him looking at her the way he would be. With accusation and distrust and anger. That, she realized, was why she had hesitated telling him about the paintings before—paintings she had done in the earliest hours of four different mornings, paintings she had tied up and hidden next to her bed so no one would ever see them, paintings of four dreams, of four murders. But seeing them there, placed on display by a hand that was not hers, waiting for her when she had come in, she had understood she had no choice. She had to at least tell him that.

The killer must have taken advantage of—caused?— CeCe's absence to set the paintings up. And just as Tuesday knew she could have put them away again, could have hidden them once more, she knew more profoundly that it would be just a matter of time before they reappeared. Better to get it over with.

It was as if the killer wanted them to know, wanted them to link the killings to her. He threatened her to keep quiet in the dreams, but now *he* was telling them. The inconsistency nagged at her, because the only explanation was one she did not like: that he wanted control, that he was playing with them, that he was crafting an intricate puzzle whose pieces he could scatter around as he wanted them found. If they continued like this, continued playing by his rules and following only the clues he left for them, they would always be one step behind. The murderer was running things and the only way to change that was by telling Lawrence everything.

Or almost everything.

"Are you going to kill me?" Lawrence asked casually. "Because if you are, it would be easier through the chest."

"I have no desire to kill you."

"You expressed one earlier, at Miles's house."

"Take off your clothes and get into that bathtub."

"Thank you but I prefer to bathe at night."

The only response was a bit more prodding with the sword.

"I presume these paintings are from your brush," Lawrence went on as he loosened the ties on his doublet and slipped out of it. "Or are they more presents from the Secret Admirer?"

He did not see her shudder. "I will tell you everything as soon as you are in the tub."

"Why are you doing this?"

Because it is hard to talk to you when you look so austere and earl-like. Because after what happened in your
coach I feel more vulnerable than I ever have in my life
and I need you to be vulnerable too. "Because I don't
want you stalking around, interrupting me. I want your
undivided attention. Now get in."

Lawrence, naked, stood at the edge of the tub. "You
could just invite me to sit. Like a polite hostess would do."

Tuesday's mind was buzzing with the realization that
her previous experience with the male anatomy was
hugely inadequate. The sooner he was submerged, the
better. "I am notoriously impolite. I pride myself on it.
And I want to guarantee that you will be immobile."

Clenching his teeth, Lawrence slipped into the water
that CeCe had drawn earlier, which was now chilly. It
smelled familiar, spicy, like jasmine and cardamom and
roses. Like her skin. He blocked the memory of her taste
from his mind and asked, "Well?"

"I suspect seeing these paintings is going to make you
jump to a conclusion but please keep an open mind until
I am done."

"I always have an open mind about women pointing
rapiers at me. Now tell me about these—"

"Murder scenes," she supplied helpfully.

"Yes. Why did you paint them?"

"I did not have any choice."

Lawrence was looking at the nearest painting, the one
of the corridor where her husband's body had been
found the day before. He had read his men's reports of
Tuesday's movements the previous day and knew exactly
how she had spent every hour. She had not painted anything while she was under surveillance. So she must already have painted her husband's murder scene when he

had arrived to tell her Curtis was dead. *Where are the rose petals* she had asked. Which meant—

"Before or after? Did you do that—" he gestured at the picture of the corridor, "—before or after you killed him?"

"Neither."

He rose from the tub. "I am telling you, Lady Arli—"

"Sit down." She pointed the rapier at him, trying not to notice that the cold water had no effect on his ability to loom. "This is exactly why I wanted you immobilized. I knew you would overreact."

"I never overreact."

"Really? I am surprised that water is not boiling."

"How else do you expect me to react? What other option is there than that you killed your husband and for some reason memorialized the place? Kindly tell me how you would have me view this."

"During."

"What?"

"I painted it during the murder."

Lawrence frowned at her, uncomprehending, and she went on. "That is what I want to explain. For the past month I have been having these strange dreams. Each time the dream gets a little longer, and they have become more frequent. I thought they came on days when I have been under a strain, days when I get headaches, but now I understand that they have all been on Tuesdays. I always woke up at the end of them and could not get back to sleep, until CeCe suggested I paint them. I did and afterwards I always hid them. I didn't think anyone knew where. Until today, when I came in and saw them arranged like they are now."

"This water is too damn cold for me to sit around listening to nonsense about how you killed your husband in a dre—"

"Stay where you are, Lord Pickering." Tuesday glowered at him. He glowered back. She won and went on. "At first the dreams were all of being chased through a forest. Then they started getting longer, so they would start at the forest and move on to a garden, then a storeroom. There is always someone chasing me, calling my name, calling—" she hesitated, "—calling me mean, horrible things. And saying he is going to get me. Early yesterday morning, I had the final one, which ended with me being chased down a corridor. When I woke up I painted it and went back to sleep. But then you came and you told me about Curtis and I went there and—it was the same. Exactly the same. I don't know how but the killer is in my head. It is like we are collaborating. Like what George and I do but—but much worse."

"Why didn't you tell me about this yesterday?"

"Because the killer threatened me. He said '*You just keep your whore mouth shut or I'll do the same to you as I did to him. Do you understand, bitch?*' " She suddenly looked scared and frail and Lawrence found himself tempted to pull her into his arms and hold her and tell her it would all be fine and no one would hurt her again and he would stay with her forever to make sure she never had another nightmare.

That snapped him out of his sympathy. "You expect me to believe this?" he demanded. "That somehow a killer is making you have a dream and when you paint something he kills someone, but that you have no idea who he is? I would have thought you could come up with something a bit more plausible."

"I could have. I scarcely understand it either. Unfortunately, this is the truth." Not all of it, but enough. The rest, Tuesday assured herself, did not matter. And even if it did, she could not bring herself to tell him. Not after what had happened in the coach. Not after— "I don't care if you believe it."

"You had better care. I can arrest you for murder."

"You wouldn't."

"Why not?"

"It would not be honorable—you know I am not the murderer."

"I must tell you, Lady Arlington, it would be easier to remember that if you were not pointing a rapier at me."

She looked down at the weapon in her hand as if she had never seen it before. "Oh, it's not real. It is just a prop for my painting."

"It is very realistic looking. And feeling."

"Yes," she said animatedly. "George found it somewhe—what are you doing?"

"Getting dressed and then packing up your possessions. You are leaving London."

She dragged her eyes from the scar on his right shoulder. "No! That is the point. I have to be here. I have to find him."

"We will find him better without you."

"You won't find him at all without me. In order to know where those paintings were hidden, he would have had to watch me for days. He is close by, close to me. If it is the Secret Admirer, which now seems likely, I am the closest link you have to him."

It was true. She was a link to the murderer. Which meant she was in grave danger. Lawrence dressed more quickly.

"You would not even have a witness if it weren't for me," she pointed out.

"We don't know he is a real witness. We have no guarantee that it is our killer he saw. For all I know you are in cahoots with him and paid him to describe a man with brown hair to remove suspicion from yourself."

"That is untrue and you know it."

"Feel free to call me a liar."

"Thank you. If you really believed it were that simple, you would not have orchestrated that elaborate ruse today with the viscount Dearbourn to get your men into my house. You would just have arrested me and shipped me off to Newgate. You must let me work with you."

"That is out of the question."

"Why? Wasn't that the whole point of this charade, you pretending to be giving me protection? So that you could learn what I know? Well you will. And you will also get my help. But you have to let me see what you know as well."

She has you Lawrence, my friend.

"No."

It was a last, desperate act. Tuesday crossed to where he was standing and fastening his breeches. She put her hands on his bare arms and he froze. Slowly his eyes came up to meet hers. "Lord Pickering. Please. He is toying with me, with all of us. He has invaded my life; he is inside my mind and I hate it. *Hate it*. You don't have any idea what it is like to have your enemy living in your head."

Because he knew exactly what that was like. Because she was a connection to the killer. Because she had noticed things a dozen of his men together had overlooked at her husband's murder scene. These were the reasons he agreed.

It was not because he wanted to have her close to him.

He shook her hands off of him. "Very well. But you must do what I say. Whatever I say. If I tell you to sit still in a corner and not move or speak for ten hours, you do it. I will not be responsible for your death."

"No." Tuesday shook her head.

His head was halfway through his linen shirt. "What?"

"I would not be able to sit still that long. Five hours is probably as long as I—" Lawrence looking like he might explode was what cut her off. "All right," she rushed on. "I agree. I shall do anything you *say*."

Lawrence did not miss the emphasis but before he could wonder at it, Tom appeared in the doorway. He quavered slightly under the double glares that met him. "I—I am sorry if I am interrupting, sir. They told me to come in."

"You aren't. Lady Arlington and I are finished. What is it?"

Tom swallowed. "We've got a problem, sir. It is the witness, Mr. Marston. He is missing."

Chapter 16

The inanimate body of Albert Marston was found by Grub twenty minutes later in the alley next to his house, the same alley where he had seen the killer. That was where, while on an excursion to get more food for the Ladies, he had fallen when the pistol shots had whizzed by his head.

Inanimate, but not dead. The killer, it appeared, was not as good with a pistol as he was with a knife. It was a shaken yet very much alive Arthur Marston who was shown into Tuesday's studio an hour later. He was slightly dazed but not so much that he hesitated at all in his description of the killer they had begun calling the Secret Admirer.

"Nose like that one, number twelve," he said, singling it out for Tuesday from the drawings in her book. "And lips like these—" he pointed to number thirty-seven, then squinted, then said, "—no, these," with his finger on thirty-one.

Tuesday was feeling some apprehension as she sat down with Albert Marston, but it soon evaporated. Although he did not look like a man borne for decision and observation on the best days—and now, with his clothes at odd angles and a smudge of something on his temple, he seemed to be a prime candidate for disorientation—he turned out to have a keen memory and a good eye. Except for his darting, frequent apprehensive glances at the windows, presumably looking for assassins with pistols, everything went smoothly. There was no name-calling, there were no tears, and they were done with the sketch in forty minutes.

The Secret Admirer was invisible no more. The attack on Mr. Marston erased any lingering doubts that the man he had seen was the killer, which meant that as she stared down at her sketch, Tuesday was staring at him. *Him.* This was the man who had somehow entered her mind, the man who had been watching her for weeks, the man who had killed her husband and threatened her and chased her in her dreams. She expected his face to look familiar or at least menacing. But nothing in its lines, in the combination of nose 12, lips 31, forehead probably 46 (Mr. Marston hesitated between that and number 96), and chin 5, looked sinister or even moderately strange. The Secret Admirer just looked like a man. Any man at all. He could be standing outside her window right that moment, staring at her and she wouldn't know it.

He was.

He was right there as Lawrence's men fanned out with hastily recopied versions of the sketch, right there as the daytime shadows lengthened into night, right there as the musicians left and Sir Dennis tried to bribe his new valet to bring one of the chambermaids from across the way up the back stairs "just for a little visit, is all," right there as she and His Lordship argued briefly, then ate supper without speaking to each other. He had watched with interested amusement as Lawrence's friend Tristan del Moro, a former thief-turned-security-expert, arrived after dark to check out the locks on the Windows in order to keep him from getting in.

Fools. Locks were nothing to him.

He was invisible. Just like the knights in the books with their magic rings and cloaks. Only he didn't need any magic. He was *that* powerful. He could walk right in easy as you please, anywhere he wanted. Have anyone he wanted.

But they didn't understand that, just like they didn't understand anything about him. Like that stupid name they were calling him. The Secret Admirer. "Secret" was alright, but he wasn't his Lady's admirer. He was so much more than that. Secret Lover would be better. Or Secret Knight.

And the killings. They all take place on Tuesdays, that was what they thought. Stupid stupid stupid. Certainly it was all about his Lady, but they were miles from grasping how. Especially if she kept her little secret. He had suspected that his Lady was falling in love with him—sometimes she left her brushes arranged the way he liked, with all their hard ends sticking up, the way that made him think of—

(Wicked boy!)

—lances. Then other times she'd opened her curtains just when he came on the scene, as if she'd been waiting for him, at the Window. And, of course, the dreams. But it wasn't until now that he had proof of how she was feeling. Because she wasn't telling His Lordship everything she knew. She was protecting him, the Lion.

She needn't have bothered, though. They weren't going to figure anything out. They weren't even close. And they wouldn't be, not before he had a chance to kill more men. He knew what they were going to find next and it was so good. So good. He wanted them to find it *now*, right away. Maybe he should just walk right over and—

What are a knight's best weapons?

Cunning and deception.

And? And? Answer me, dammit. Don't look away. You worthless idiot hell cat, if you don't say—

Patience.

Right. Don't make me ask again.

The Lion winced from the imagined blow.

I hate you!

He would allow his Lady and His Lordship to sleep undisturbed this one night, he decided. Lull them into security. That way it would be better when they saw what he could do. More surprising. More exciting for her.

Besides, it looked like there might be a storm coming and he didn't want to get his boots muddy.

Albert Marston stood at his window, a golden bird perched on his finger, nipping at his nose.

"She reminded me of you, Judith," he said to the bird. "Lovely lovely lovely."

Judith responded to the compliment by plucking his eyebrow.

"It was a real pleasure to watch her work," he mused on. "She is quite a good artist. And I don't think she suspected anything."

Judith showed her agreement by climbing on his head.

"No, everyone believed me completely." He reached up and lifted the bird from his head. He cradled her in his hands for a moment, rubbing her chest with his thumbs, then circled the bird's neck with his long fingers. Judith's dark eyes began to dart around the room, fast, and she made a squawking noise in her throat. "Oh, don't worry, my love," Albert Marston said, releasing the pressure slightly. "I won't hurt you. I love you. We do not hurt what we love."

He broke her neck with a clean, painless snap.

"No, no, we never hurt what we love."

Chapter 17

"I won!" Tuesday announced. "Hand them over."

Lawrence took three biscuits from the three neatly stacked rows in front of him and pushed them across the table toward her messy pile. In the course of the evening, Lawrence had learned that she was a dangerous card player. He had also picked up several other pieces of information about Lady Tuesday Arlington—that she had always wanted to ride an elephant, that she had once kept a snake as a pet until her father found out, that since the death of Mrs. Burns she had been the children's surrogate mother and confidant and they arrived and left at all hours to tell her jokes or have her fix a knot or complain that their dog was missing, that she preferred him dirty and scruffy to "puffed up and ready for a royal visit," that she had never read any of the news sheets about him—but nothing as interesting as what he had learned from CeCe earlier.

Those revelations had come just after supper when, despite Tuesday's protestations—

"I am not taking a bath with him in the room."

"Of course you aren't," CeCe replied authoritatively. "I am certain His Lordship will agree to step into the kitchen with me."

"I wouldn't trust him to stay there. I wouldn't trust anything he said." Tuesday leaned toward CeCe and added by way of explanation, "He is prone to lying."

"Tuesday!"

"I may not be of your moral caliber," Lawrence admitted gallantly, "but I do have a nose. A sensitive one. I would do anything to spare it discomfort."

"Are you saying I smell bad?"

"Yes," Lawrence lied. "And I might remind you that you agreed to do whatever I said. Right now, I order you to bathe."

"You cannot just bark orders at me like you do to your unsuspecting men."

"Why not?"

"You are a muddle-headed gargoyle."

—she had been forced, still hissing insults at him, into the tub. This gave Lawrence a chance to corner CeCe on her own. After watching her and Tuesday together that afternoon, he'd realized that the neighbors underestimated CeCe. Whether they liked her or not, they were taken in by her carefully cultivated surface, her studied manners and painstakingly practiced accent, and none of them paid attention to the intelligence below it, an oversight he was increasingly convinced CeCe enjoyed. Only Tuesday seemed to see the sharp wit and mind beneath the polished exterior, and he had quickly realized that the two women were more friends than mistress and maid. Which was why he wanted to ask CeCe a few questions. If only she would sit still for three seconds together.

Any time he started to ask her anything, she'd get up from the kitchen table they were sitting at to respond to some noise she'd thought she'd heard Tuesday make, or to put something away, or to sigh at the cook's messiness as she rubbed at an all but invisible spot of gravy near the fire. Then she would return to her seat opposite his, give him a lovely, sweet smile and say, "I'm sorry. I just cannot stand for anything to be out of place. Now what were you asking me about?"

She did it so smoothly that Lawrence did not realize what she was up to. It was only after the third time she'd gone to the door in response to an inaudible summons that Lawrence saw the quick gleam of merriment in her eyes, and realized he'd been had. She had spent the last half hour evading his questions, and he hadn't even recognized it. He decided to get even.

This time when she sat down, clasped her hands in front of her like a good girl at school, and looked at him with bright, eager eyes, he did not say anything. He just leaned back farther in his chair and watched her. She was extremely pretty, with a heart-shaped face that dimpled slightly when she was amused and reddish-pink lips that looked made for kissing, so staring at her wasn't hard. Keeping a straight face was tougher. When the silence had stretched to almost a minute, she smiled knowingly at him with just a hint of dimple and said, "You are figuring out all my secrets, aren't you, Lord Pickering? I am afraid at the end you will be very disappointed. I am quite dull."

"I believe that is what you want people to think, CeCe. I'm convinced, however, that you are a very clever woman."

Mock horror flooded over her, her ultrablue eyes growing huge. "Oh, please don't say that. Clever people have all sorts of problems I'd rather live without. I'd rather be like the Mean and Uglies than be clever."

It was another diversion, Lawrence knew, but he decided not to call her on it. "The Mean and Uglies?" he asked.

"Some of the women in the neighborhood. You would think they would want to know if red would be a better color on them than black, or if their gowns are twenty years out of style, but instead they just glare at you when you try to tell them." She shrugged. "They make fun of me and call me uppity and say I'm trying to get above my station, but what is the harm in that? If I don't think about bettering myself, who will?"

Lawrence looked at her and his expression was serious. "You are right to try it, CeCe. Don't let them stop you. They are just threatened by what you are doing, so they condemn it. You are holding up an accurate mirror to them, showing them that they could have lived a different way if they'd tried." He smiled crookedly. "That's why the most expensive mirrors are the ones with flaws in them. People never like to see their true reflections." Then, after a pause, he added as if musing to himself, "It probably doesn't help much that you are Tuesday's best friend."

The sweetness in her face was instantly replaced by an expression of real pride, and Lawrence knew that he would have no more trouble getting her to answer his questions. He had guessed that her relationship with Tuesday meant an enormous amount to her, that it was her weak spot, and he saw now that he hadn't been wrong.

CeCe nodded to herself and said, quietly, "You are

right, Lord Pickering, I am Tuesday's friend. I owe everything I am to her. She saved me—saved me from myself,
gave my life a purpose."

"How? How did you come to work here?"

CeCe's eyes looked beyond him, into a space of
memory and she smiled a little. "It was all Lord Cardmore's doing."

"Lord Cardmore? The horse breeder?"

CeCe nodded. "Tuesday had been working on his portrait in the park and lost track of time so she was rushing
home and she ran right into me. I ended up wearing the
better part, if there was one, of Lord Cardmore's face
across the bodice of my gown. She was terribly upset, not
about the painting but about me, about having ruined
my dress, and she insisted I come home with her so she
could clean it up. She had no servants, so I offered to stay
on as her maid. I had been walking in the park trying to
decide what to do with—with my life." CeCe paused and
her eyes came to rest on Lawrence. "Tuesday appeared
like the answer to a prayer, and I have been with her ever
since." It was only part of the story. It left out the fear
that CeCe had seen in Tuesday's face when Curtis burst
into the washroom and saw that she had unauthorized
company, as well as her terror about asking him if she
could take CeCe on.

But CeCe had been determined to stay close to
Tuesday, to attach herself to the only person she had met
whose company did anything to mitigate the bone-deep
loneliness she had been sunk in since her fiancé left. She
had offered to work for free at first, and, unable to object
to that offer, Curtis had agreed.

Lawrence Pickering did not need to know any of that,

she decided, at least not until she could be sure of his exact interest in her mistress. She said instead, "I should warn you, I won't tell you anything that might hurt Tuesday. Her friendship means everything to me and I'll do nothing to jeopardize it."

"Such as tell me her secrets?"

Now CeCe laughed. "Hardly. Tuesday cannot keep secrets. Everything she thinks is either written on her face or bursts out of her mouth. No," CeCe said, regarding him coyly, "such as being seen to be working with the enemy."

"The enemy. You mean me? I'm not the enemy. I am trying to help."

"Then perhaps you should try not to frown at her all the time as if you suspected her of murder."

"Do you suspect her of murder?"

"No. Absolutely not. She was here when Curtis was killed—ask anyone on the street; she never closes her curtains, so they can all see her in her studio, and I heard her moving around. There is no chance she killed Curtis. Not even if—no."

"'Not even if' what?"

CeCe looked at him defiantly. "Not even if he deserved it."

"Why?"

"Because he was a lying, cheating, scoundrel."

"You did not like him?"

"I used to like him. I used to be taken in by his nice manners and lovely accent, just as Tuesday was. But not anymore."

"What happened to change your mind?"

She eyed him carefully. "I would not like Tuesday to

know what I am about to tell you. You will keep it from her, won't you?"

"If I can."

"That is hardly a gentlemanly promise, Lord Pickering."

"I'm hardly a gentleman," Lawrence said, and he wasn't joking. "Look, CeCe, I am interested in catching Curtis's murderer, who it is. If passing along what you tell me to your mistress is going to help, I'll do it. I don't lie, even when it would be more polite."

CeCe thought about this as she studied the tabletop for a moment. Finally, she said, "I had a visitor today. A woman. She claimed to be Sir Curtis's mistress. She said her name was May Dew and she had gotten my name and address from the landlord at Sir Curtis's lodgings and that she was stopping by as I had asked her to. Which is impossible, because I've never been anywhere near that unworthy liar's chambers. But she seemed to think she was telling the truth so—" She finished the sentence with a flutter of her hand and looked up at Lawrence. "Do you know what this woman, this May Dew, told me? She told me that Curtis was going to get rid of his wife and marry her. Marry *her*. That is why I said he deserved it. Because he was getting ready to break Tuesday's heart again."

Lawrence leaned forward, asking, "Did she leave an address? Mention how we could find her?"

"No."

"Do you think you could describe what she looked like? So Lady Arlington could do a sketch?"

Indignation left CeCe speechless. Her lips worked but no sound came out until she said, "I thought you told me we were on the same side. Why would you want to make Tuesday suffer that way? Hasn't she been through enough? Or would you like to see—"

"Tuesday already knows Curtis had a mistress, and that he was planning to marry her." Lawrence broke in, to calm her. "She found out about her this morning from the landlord. She *wants* to meet her. Tuesday is the one who left your name because she was afraid that if she left hers, the mistress would not come."

CeCe was shaking her head. "That is absurd. I don't believe it. Tuesday said she would never go to Curtis's rooms! Never."

"She claimed she went there looking for a necklace. Do you know anything about that?"

"A necklace? No, of course not. Tuesday has no jewelry whatever. Her brother claimed every—*oooh*." CeCe's demeanor softened abruptly. "Now that I think of it, there was that one piece with the dragonfly on it from her mother, but Curtis took it away ages ago. She said he was going to have it cleaned but he never brought it back." She looked at him as she explained. "I only remember because that was the day she fell and broke her wrist. It still sometimes cramps if she's been working too long but at least she can hold a brush again. While it was healing, she could not paint, which made her particularly miserable to be around. She has a rather unfortunate vocabulary when she is in pain."

Lawrence absorbed all of this. "Where did she break her wrist?"

CeCe pointed to her own wrist and said, "Here."

"I mean, where was she when it happened?"

"Oh. Where." She paused, thinking, with one finger

under her chin. "I'm not sure, actually, but it could have been anywhere. Tuesday manages to find things to walk into even if a room is entirely empty. I can't complain; after all, if she hadn't walked into me in the park that day I would never have met her, but she is a bit clumsy. And it doesn't help any that she leaves everything in such disorder. I used to try to put things away, but they were always scattered around by the—"

As if on cue there was a loud bang from behind the door leading to the studio, followed by a thud, a yelp, and a "blast Lawrence Pickering and his blasted furniture moving" in Tuesday's voice.

Lawrence looked toward the closed door, then back at CeCe who was trying hard to conceal a smile behind a look of dismay at the outburst. "I suppose that means she's finished her bath. Does she do that—" Lawrence pointed in the direction of the noise with his thumb, "—often?"

"Trip over the furniture? Yes. Well, actually, yes and no. She used to be more accident prone. Almost never a day that went by without my finding some new bruise when I helped her undress, but she's gotten better since she moved downstairs. I suppose because there are fewer opportunities to fall down them."

"When did she move?"

"Recently." CeCe got up and began floating around the kitchen again. "Would you like something to drink? Some wine? Oh, that's right, I read in the news sheets you only drink milk."

"Actually I prefer lemonade if you have it." Lawrence watched her closely as she poured some into a chipped glass. While she was still cleaning up whatever minute drop might have fallen he asked, "Did she move down-stairs when Curtis left?"

She turned toward him with a look of concentration and took her time answering. "Now that I think of it, yes. It was just at the same time."

Lawrence pretended to believe she'd just realized it. "How long had Curtis and Tuesday been married before that?"

"Two years," CeCe supplied without hesitating.

As if to reward her forthrightness, Lawrence stood up. "You've been very helpful, CeCe. I can't think of any other questions right now."

"Really? That was not nearly as bad as I thought it would be."

"I'm glad." Lawrence smiled and moved toward the door to the studio. He hesitated with his hand on the door pull and mused, "Two years. Two years and no children. That's strange."

CeCe had turned around when he rose and he now saw her shoulder blades come together sharply. She looked over her shoulder at him with a slight smile and said, "I'm sorry? Were you talking to me?"

"Two years is a long time to be married without having any children, don't you think?"

CeCe tried to keep smiling but her voice caught. "No."

"Really? It isn't?"

"No," CeCe said facing him now. "It happens all the time."

"When there is something wrong in the relationship. But it is much more normal that there would be a child."

"I would not know about that, and even if I did it is certainly not my place to speak of it."

"You are right," Lawrence said. "It would be better for me to ask Tuesday all about it. Find out what became of her child."

CeCe grew stony. "I don't think I will ever speak to you again, Lord Pickering. You tricked me."

Lawrence smiled at her. "I'm not nearly clever enough for that. I promise you will feel better once you tell me."

"I doubt it, but I also doubt that you will go away if I don't." CeCe glared straight at him as she spoke, her tone clipped. "Tuesday was pregnant, once. It was a very hard pregnancy; she was ill all the time, but she was happier than I had ever seen her. She loves children and could not wait to have some of her own. To have Curtis's. She thought it would please him." Something bitter flitted across her expression. "Then one day she was standing on a ladder, painting, and her wrist, the one that had been broken, cramped as it often did and she dropped her brush. As she was climbing down to get it, she fell and, well . . ."

"She lost the baby?"

CeCe nodded once. "It was a dangerous fall; she was badly bruised all over. What was worse, she was utterly desolate about the child. She tried to act happy, for my sake and Curtis's, but nothing anyone could do could break her out of her sadness. That was why Curtis took her into the country. He hoped the fresh air would restore her spirits."

"When was this? How long did they stay away?"

"It was a few months ago. They were not gone long." Her eyes did not move from his, as if she were defying him to ask her anything more. "Have you learned enough now?"

"Almost," Lawrence conceded brightly. "Just one more question. Why did they come back from the country so quickly? Did Tuesday recover that fast?"

"Curtis had business to attend to so she came home."

"Alone?"

"Yes."

"How did she explain that to you?"

"She did not need to. I am only her maid. And you said only one question."

"Of course. Sorry." Lawrence apologized sheepishly. "I should be asking Tuesday herself about it."

"You would, wouldn't you?" CeCe challenged, friendship beating out her pretence of being a maid. "You would, just to hurt her."

"Why would it hurt her?"

"Because he left her there," CeCe whispered, her composure gone, her voice shaking. "He left her at the inn in the country, left her because, he said, she was not a good enough wife. She was so bereft that it was two weeks before she even admitted it to *me*. When she first came back all she could talk about were some gypsies she'd seen whose faces she had to get into her book, and she worked feverishly at it. Then one day I came into the studio when she wasn't expecting me and she had her head down on her arms and she was sobbing. I'd never seen her cry before, not even when she lost the baby. That was when she finally told me the truth. Now if she knew I had told *you* she would be furious." She paused to blot the tears that had come into her eyes with the sleeve of her gown. As she finished, a little smile crossed her face. "Actually, she'd probably be more furious at the fact that I told you she had been crying. She sees it as a sign of weakness. She is so worried about always being strong, strong for everyone, that she never lets herself go."

Lawrence nodded, reflected for a moment and said, "I don't think I will have to tell her about any of this."

"Really?" CeCe looked up at him. "You mean that?"

"Yes."

A cunning look came into CeCe's eyes. "On your word of honor? I've read in the news sheets that your word of honor is like gold to you and after your performance tonight, I am not sure I would trust you on a mere promise. Before you give it, though, I must warn you, Lord Pickering. If I find out that you told her, that you have done anything to hurt Tuesday, particularly anything based on what I have told you, I will become your sworn enemy."

Lawrence raised an eyebrow, then agreed, adding, "I would not like to have you for an enemy, CeCe."

"No," CeCe concurred, smiling at him mischievously, "you wouldn't."

His was not a difficult pledge to keep because as he sat across from Tuesday while she trounced him at cards two hours later, he could barely believe that any of what CeCe had said was true. By far the more difficult task was to reconcile the image of the clumsy, sobbing, abandoned wife CeCe had drawn with what he was seeing.

Because she did not seem hurt and upset.

Because her movements were graceful and sure and deft.

Because it was impossible to believe that any man who once possessed Lady Tuesday Arlington would ever let her go.

"You are not very good at this," she informed him, dealing out the cards. "How did you ever make any money in gambling clubs?"

Lawrence, jolted out of his thoughts, replied stiffly, "I owned them, I did not play in them." Tell her about the visit from Curtis's mistress he commanded himself, but he couldn't get the words out.

"Ah, that's the key. Do you still have any?"

"Why?"

She looked up at him and he could see she was genuinely curious. "I was just wondering. It seems as though we should know more about each other if we are to share such close quarters."

"I do not see how my relationship to gaming hells is any of your business." Tell her!

"You sound like my brother Howard. Do you have any siblings Lord Pickering?"

"Yes. One. A brother."

"Is he also an earl?"

"No. He is a hangman."

If he expected that to shut her down as it did with every other woman of his acquaintance, he was wrong. Curiosity turned to blazing interest. "Really? Of course. Bull *Pickering*. Bull is your brother? You don't look anything like him. He is so much more—"

"So much more what?" Lawrence was about to demand, then thought better of it. He did not care. "How do you know Bull?"

"I don't know him. I've only heard of him. CeCe loves to read all about every hanging in the metropolis. It soothes her. Makes her feel like there are fewer thieves, robbers, and general blackguards loitering around to prey on her."

"Why is she so concerned about robbers?"

"I believe they offend her senses of propriety and

cleanliness. Anyone who opposes robbers, on the other hand, is a hero in her eyes. She has told me all about Bull Pickering. Wait—if you are his brother, then you are the one who made sure he went to school every day even though you did not go yourself."

"CeCe told you that?"

"Read it to me. There was an exclusive interview with him in one of the news sheets where he told the story of his life. Apparently if you don't think your brother still resents being packed off to school while you got to dilly dally the day away, you are wrong."

Lawrence found he was not thinking as clearly as he wanted to be. He knew she was jesting; he had heard Bull say things like that a hundred times, and yet he heard himself saying a little too vehemently, "I was trying to support us. We had to eat. We could not both go—"

"I do not think he really meant it, Lord Pickering," Tuesday said soothingly. She had not expected him to react so—well, reactively. "From what CeCe read to me, the rest of the interview was filled with Bull talking about you as if you were something the Deity molded with his own hands. No wonder I didn't realize *you* and *that* Lawrence Pickering were one and the same."

"What a lovely compliment."

"You can hardly blame me. According to Bull you practically turn water to gold, you daily save millions of boys from the streets, the corridors of your house are always swarming with hundreds of women who would rather be hanged for adultery than miss the opportunity to share your bed, and you cared for him when he was only five and you were eight and your mother left you both standing in the stable yard of a—"

"That is not true," Lawrence said tightly.

"Ah, yes. The news sheet went into this at great length. Bull says you claim she got sick and died and that is why you had to raise him. But he remembers your mother saying to sit on this one particular rock and not let go and she would come back for you, and so you did and watched her drive off and the two of you stayed there over night, afraid that if you let go or left she would never forgive you, and then the next morning you realized she wasn't coming back, so you went out and—"

"That is not what happened!"

The force of his reaction stunned them both. The lie shimmered uselessly in the silent air between them. Because Tuesday was looking right at Lawrence and she saw—in the lines of determination around his eyes from years of hard work, in the firm set of his shoulders that showed he could face anything, in the strong hands that had done everything from haul garbage to escort a queen, in the quick easy smile that hid more than a frown—the larger boy huddling protectively over a smaller figure on the flat gray stone in the dark courtyard, scared and cold and wondering where his mother was and determined at all costs not to let his brother ever know the rejection he felt at that moment.

His hands evened out the small pile of biscuits he had left. "If Bull wishes to romanticize our childhood he may, but I will not be a party to it," he said, his voice and his face, at least, back under control.

"I am sure you are right. I'm sure that is what he was doing." She paused. "It must have been hard when your mother died. I was eleven when I lost mine, older than you, and part of me still misses her."

Lawrence made a dismissive gesture. "It is harder when you are older. I barely remember her."

"Of course." Tuesday gathered her biscuits into a disheveled pile. Silence settled around them again, until she said, "I started my book, the book of faces, when my mother died. I forgot what she looked like and I hoped that if I collected enough noses and mouths and chins I would get her back." She had never admitted that to anyone before.

"What an interesting idea," Lawrence commented.

"It only partially worked," she went on. "One day I realized that I could just draw what I wanted and tell myself it was a picture of her. That she could be anyone, any way I wanted to remember her."

"So you did not care about the truth. It was just the illusion you were after," he said absently, now ordering his biscuits in two controlled stacks.

He wasn't even listening to her. She had told him one of her secrets and—"You are right, Lord Pickering. And that would have made it completely indistinguishable from the hundreds of other lies we tell ourselves to mask what we don't want to know. Not you, of course. The rest of us mortals."

Silence. Then the sound of two stacks of biscuits being smashed to pieces under a strong fist. Lawrence did not offer any apology, any explanation. He simply swept the crumbs into his hand, dropped them in the fireplace grate, dusted his palms off and said, "I find myself rather tired. I will have a lot of work to do tomorrow if my men find the Secret Admirer and I will want to be rested. Good night, Lady Arlington. Wake me if you have one of your nightmares."

Tuesday watched him walk to the settee and lie down

on it. It was about three feet too short and, she knew from experience, horribly lumpy. Through the muddle of her confused emotions, she found herself hoping he had to sleep there for a long, uncomfortable time.

His feet poked off the end and as he settled into sleep he wiggled his toes. There was something about the gesture that startled Tuesday, made her chest feel tight. It was the gesture of a little boy. It was, unlike the rest of him, so human.

Suddenly she hoped he would not sleep there long at all.

PART II

Eat

Chapter 18

Lawrence woke up in the middle of the night to the feel of her naked body pressed along his on the settee.

"What are you—"

"Shhh," she told him, placing a finger over his lips.

"But—"

She kissed the words away and climbed on top of him. Outlined by the moonlight, her body was even more incredible than he had imagined it to be. She led his hand to her breast and cupped his palm around it, urging his thumb over her nipple.

She slid her own hands down his chest, to his breeches, slipping them along the edge of the waistband as she purred, "Make love to me, Lawrence."

His name from her lips blazed through him, setting his body alight. He pulled her to his chest and kissed her hungrily. He was starving for her, aching for her with his entire body. His mouth found her nipple and she arched against him, brushing her thigh along his humming member. He was going to make love to her for hours, for days. He groaned and reached down to touch her, and woke up for real.

Lawrence was aware of layers of discomfort in his body

as his eyes shot open, but nowhere more than in his sto-mach. His back hurt, his neck twinged, and his—well, other parts of him ached like they were on fire, especially with the soft purr of her imagined words in his head. But it was his stomach that bothered him because he could not figure out what was wrong with it.

Then it hit him. He was hungry.

He had not been hungry for two years.

He was also thirsty. And he had an itch. And he had been having an erotic dream about—

It was a dream wasn't it? He sat up abruptly, wincing at the pressure on his aroused member. Overcast morning light barely filtered into the room through the windows but it was enough to show him that he was alone and not just on the settee. The bed was empty.

His mind ticked off observations: Good that it was only a dream. Bad that Lady Arlington was not in her room where she should be.

There would be no more erotic dreams he decided. And where the hell *was* Tuesday?

He was about to start—what had she called it? barking orders?—at his men when a solicitous voice behind him asked, "Are you all right?" He turned to see CeCe hov-ering in the doorway. "You looked just now like you were in pain," she said, and he was not sure if, after their conversation the night before, she was glad or sorry. "Is there something I can do to help you?" she asked.

"What time is it?"

"Half past nine. Would you like some breakfast? Tuesday had hers before she went—"

"Went where?" he demanded harshly.

CeCe took a step backward. "Only upstairs. To see her father. I believe she is with him now."

"She had better be." Lawrence combed his hair with his fingers, leaving it standing up in clumps. He needed to shave and his clothes felt and looked slept in but he could not be bothered with that. Not even if they made Tuesday Arlington gape at him the way she did when she came into the studio at that moment.

The sight of him, tousled and unkempt, sent a shock wave through her body that made it hard to stand. Then she reminded herself of what had already happened that morning and bit out, "It is not as though I had a choice."

"About what?"

"Whether I was here or not. I wanted to go see my brother and your men would not let me out of the house. My own house."

Lawrence was delighted to learn that some of his employees were able to follow orders about her. Looking at her as she stood there, radiating anger, he was not sure he would have been able to. He spoke as gruffly as possible. "You are not supposed to go anywhere without me. I go where you go. Besides, you don't know where Jack is."

"Why—what have you done with him?"

"I had him moved. For his protection."

All the color drained from her face. "You put him in an institution."

"Not exactly—"

"Take me to him." She was trembling.

"That is not a good idea and—"

"Take me to him right now!"

"—besides we have an investigation—"

"I swear to you, Lord Pickering, if you have done anything to hurt my brother, if you have arrested him or put him somewhere that scares him, I will make you suffer in ways you could not imagine, let alone dream."

Her choice of words was unfortunate, reminding Lawrence of what he had done and what he was not going to do in the future. "Jack is fine and that is all you need to know," he said crisply.

"Take. Me. To. My. Brother." She stood with her chest practically touching his, her breath hot on his chin, her eyes flashing. "Now."

Lawrence saw that he had two choices. He could pull her onto the settee and make love to her. Or he could take her to her brother.

He ordered his coach made ready and half an hour later they were passing out between the city gates. Tuesday saw that they were driving into the suburbs but she was too furious to see anything else. She looked down and realized that she had begun to unravel the elaborately embroidered "LP" on the seat cushion behind her. She put it aside, then unseeingly picked it up again. By the time, two hours later, their completely silent journey ended, her lap was covered with silver thread and the only monogram remaining on the interior of the coach was the one on the pillow Lawrence had stashed under his head as he pretended to sleep.

He had not wanted to tell her about Jack. He did not want her visiting Doom Manor. He did not want her to see what it was like, what he had done. Not just with her brother. With everything. The thought of Tuesday looking at it made him extremely self-conscious and uncomfortable. Although it would probably be fine provided he could keep her out of the Basking Room.

They had pulled into the stable yard of what appeared to Tuesday at first glance to be a medieval fortress. The walls of Doom Manor were made not of bricks but of impenetrable slabs of sandstone and the roofline was punctuated every four feet or so by a strange—ominous, Tuesday thought—series of turrets and towers. Over the bulk of it grew red ivy, which many people found pastoral but Tuesday thought resembled a huge blood stain.

She took all this in as she leaped from the coach and rushed headlong toward the nearest open door. Before she could enter, a dozen chattering boys came streaming out, bowed quickly to her, and formed a cluster around Lawrence as he alighted from the coach. They were joined by a dozen more and a dozen more, until Tuesday found herself being buffeted on all sides by a sea of boys.

Happy looking boys. None of whom were her brother.

"Where is Jack?" she demanded as Lawrence pushed through the crowd. He was about to answer when Jack himself appeared out of the stables, leading a beautiful gray mare.

"Tuesday!" he whooped, throwing his cap—a new cap, it looked like it was blue velvet—in the air and rushing to her. He picked her up easily and spun her around. "Tuesday came, Tuesday came," he said, happier than she could ever remember seeing him, brilliantly, spectacularly happy.

"Come meet Frank," he insisted, dragging her through the boys toward the stables. "Frank is this horse. Jack's friend Lawrence says Jack can have any horse he wants," he confided to Tuesday. "Or a different one every day as long as Jack does his job."

Tuesday swallowed a lump in her throat and tore her gaze from her absolutely glowing brother. "What job?" she asked Lawrence warily.

Lawrence avoided meeting her eyes. That was all the answer she needed. "Jack," she began, "I am afraid—"

"Our library is in pretty bad disarray and I thought

Jack's skills would be perfect for helping to organize it," Lawrence interrupted to explain.

"Jack has to remember where the books are. And Jack can read however many Jack wants. Or how few," he chortled to himself and winked at Lawrence as if they shared a joke. "And Jack can have a different pony each day. And Tuesday can come visit every week. Do you want to see where Jack works?"

Tuesday nodded, biting her lip. This was Jack as she had always wished he could be, confident and unafraid. And happy. This was Jack as she had always hoped she could make him. Lawrence Pickering had done something she'd been unable to do, and for a moment she felt a prick of something like envy. But then Jack reappeared, a grin literally splitting his face, and all she could feel was gratitude.

The library astonished her. The room itself was three times the size of her studio, and it was heaped with books. Lawrence had not exaggerated when he said the collection was in disarray. It looked to Tuesday as though someone had left a standing order to have every book printed in London delivered and then dumped on the tables of the room without caring where they went, nor was she far off. And although she could not precisely say why—could sense but not really see the figure up all night for weeks and months of nights reading every book he could put his hands on in the hopes that one of them would evoke something, *anything*—she had the sense that Lawrence had read them all.

A short boy with freckles over his nose skidded into the room and said, "Master Jack, do you know where *Plutarch's Lives* is?"

Jack went to a huge pile of books and reached into the middle. "English or Latin, Ryan?"

"Better stick with English," the boy replied, taking the huge volume and scooting on his way.

Jack beamed at Ryan's back, then motioned Tuesday toward him to whisper, "Ryan was living on fish tails behind the old market before Jack's friend Lawrence found him. Now he is the best historian in the world." Three other boys came in and asked for Jack's assistance, and as each of them left he filled Tuesday in on their backgrounds. One of them had been a stowaway on Lawrence's ship to Spain—"but they found him just in time and sent him here and now he is the best lawn tennis player in the world." Another one, with a slight limp, had been found beaten half to death by some under-world thugs for trying to see his mother, who worked at one of the brothels, and he was now the best tumbler in the world. A third couldn't speak that well because his stepfather had yanked out all his teeth and sold them as saint's relics—"but Lawrence is having a new set made, out of diamonds, and they'll be better than the first; they will be the best teeth in the world." Although the ve-racity of some of Jack's superlatives was suspect, the main thrust of the stories rang true. Tuesday managed to piece together that Doom Manor had been Lawrence's country house until, just before leaving for Spain, he had used the money he made in business to turn it into a home for abandoned boys. Or, as Jack put it "the luckiest boys in the world."

"Jack has so many friends now," Jack confided bliss-fully as they walked around the grounds after having what Jack described as "a snack" of capons and trout, and lime and raspberry ices on a table under a rose arbor.

When Jack told her afterward that the cook was the best in the world, Tuesday was tempted to believe it. "Jack is very happy here."

"I am glad," Tuesday told him, and she was. She was.

Jack stopped suddenly and hit himself on the head. "But Jack has forgotten to show Tuesday the best part," he said, and began dragging Tuesday at a breakneck pace toward the house. They had just reentered when Lawrence, who had been mercifully absent for the preceding two hours, materialized in front of them like the specter of old Lord Doom himself.

"I think it is time we were getting back to London," he told her, frowning.

Jack's face fell. "But Jack has not shown Tuesday the Basking Room."

"The what?" she asked.

"The room with all the pretty women in it," Jack explained. She just had time to give Lawrence a glare as Jack dragged her past him.

Of course. There would be a room where women were kept as slaves or something. She had known this was too good to be true, that Lawrence Pickering would have done something sleaz—

Tuesday stopped on the threshold of the room and gaped openly. It was not a large room or a particularly elaborately furnished room. In fact, there were only a few outsized couches all shoved in the middle. But the eyes of a dozen beautiful women gazed at her with various expressions. Gazed at her from the dozen paintings hanging on the walls—the paintings she had copied on the walls of her studio. Only these were the originals. The real pieces that comprised the finest collection of modern painting in England.

"This is where they come to bask in the attention of the pretty ladies," Jack explained into Tuesday's dumbstruck silence. "And Jack comes here, too, whenever he wants."

Tuesday nodded mutely and turned her head from side to side and tried to make sense of what she was seeing. She was standing in a home for abandoned boys with the best cook, the best library, and one of the best art collections in England, if not the world. Her brother was ebullient. It was all Lawrence Pickering's doing. And unless she had threatened him that morning, he never would have told her, she never would have known about any of it.

"There's even Tuesday's favorite," Jack said merrily, pulling her to a painting in the center of one wall. "The one of the man and the statue lady."

"Titian's *Pygmalion*," Tuesday breathed, staring at it with awe. Up close the painting of the sculptor Pygmalion bringing to life with a kiss the stone maiden he carved and fell in love with was almost painfully beautiful.

"You can touch it, you know," a very short boy said from somewhere near her elbow. "I licked that one of the Madonna once and Lawrence did not mind."

And they called him Lawrence. "Did it taste good?"

"Nope. Like rubbish. I wrote a poem about it."

"I see," Tuesday said, not really seeing anything. Turning, she realized that Lawrence had followed them in. He appeared to be making a careful inspection of one of his lintels.

"Why didn't you tell me?" she demanded.

"Tell you what?" he asked without taking his eyes from the door frame.

"That this, what I painted, was your collection."

"Why should I have told you?"

"So I did not make a bloody fool out of myself," she heard herself saying, furious now. "I knew mine weren't good but you didn't need to lie to me."

The force of her anger took Lawrence by surprise. "I did not lie to you. You never asked if it was my collection that was auctioned off."

"If it was your collection, how did you get it back?"

"Some friends of mine bought it and forced me to take it when I returned from Spain."

She hated the blasé way he said that. She hated everything about him. "You also should have told me about Jack. It was not fair of you to take him and just—" Just what, she asked herself? Give him a place? Give him a life? Make him happy? Do what I had never been able to do. "You should have asked me."

"So you could say no?"

She bit her lip and swallowed hard. "I think we should go back to London. Something may have happened."

Lawrence agreed. It was only when they had been bumping along for over an hour that he realized he was feeling hungry. Again. The second time in two years. The second time in one day. Strange.

In the coach on the way back Tuesday made herself stare out the window with tremendous interest in everything. She made herself count the cows—four, or forty-six, she wasn't sure—and notice the way the fences were made extra straight and examine the skirt of that old woman's gown, and smile at the pretty woman and the little boy who were waving, and wonder why that man who looked like George was ducking behind a tree (what would George be doing in the country?) and pay attention to the things she knew should be there but which she could not make her eyes see.

Blast! Why was it so hard to concentrate? Why did she feel like her chest was too big or too small, like her muscles were all fraying. Why did she feel so angry? She realized that she was furious at Lawrence Pickering. Furious at him for having the best art collection in England. Furious at him for generously leaving it hanging so that the boys he gave homes to, boys who had been abandoned, could enjoy it rather than keeping it all for himself. Furious at him for having turned his country house into a school. Furious at him for having given Jack a place and a job, for the way Jack smiled at him, for the worship in Jack's eyes, for the joy there. Furious at him for again not being what he seemed to be—what he should have been. Furious at him for being so much more.

"You are not angry about the paintings," Lawrence told her coolly, as they reentered London and neared her house.

She tried to take a deep breath but felt like there was a weight on her chest. "Yes I am. And you are wrong if you think I am angry because you pulled away for no reason when we kissed yesterday." Tuesday was stunned by her own words, but Lawrence wasn't.

He didn't even pause. He said, like a slap in the face, "I had a reason."

"I don't care. That is not what I am angry about." She looked away. She felt like her teeth were cramping. Her eyes burned. Something was weighing down her arms. And yet they were trembling, trembling with rage. She felt like she could not count on herself, like she might do or say anything, like she had spun entirely out of control.

Good girls didn't get angry, nobody loved girls who were angry, angry girls get punished, angry girls are bad, everyone hates angry—

(It's my fault, dragonfly, I made your father angry—*thwak*)

(I promise I'll be a good girl, Daddy, just please don't make Jack—*thwak*)

(I will be better, Curtis, I will be a perfect wife I will be—*thwak*)

Stop it!

Across the coach she could feel Lawrence's eyes on her but she did not care. She did not care what he thought of her. She cared so little that she could be angry in front of him, could feel out of control in front of him, and not bother to hide it. That proved she was indifferent to his opinion of her, she told herself.

"I don't care what you think of me," she announced and the note of joy, of triumph quivering in her voice nicked Lawrence.

"No, I don't think you'd care for it at all," he agreed.

"That is not what I mea—" she stopped. It did not matter. She did not care. He could hang himself and his opinion of her from the nearest bough of that tree—the sixteenth tree they had passed, she noted, noting also that she was concentrating again, that she was breathing again, that she felt calm again—as far as she was concerned. "In the future I think we should limit our conversation to discussions of the investigation," she informed him suavely.

"You could not have expressed my own wishes any better."

"Good."

"Good."

The silence lasted about three minutes after their return to Worthington Hall. That was when Grub burst into the studio and announced, "We got something, my lord. We got him!"

The Lion carefully filled a jug and set it on the floor next to two others.

He was having trouble keeping his hands steady he was so excited. He could feel it in the air, taste it. He knew what was about to happen. His glory, his genius, was getting ready to be known. Our Greatest Hero was about to begin to see what he could do. Boy would his, would all of their, jaws drop then.

He dusted off his hands and looked around.

How do we protect our fort?

We disguise its strength.

How do we fend off our enemy?

We outlast him.

The hideout was all set. There was enough there to keep him going for months. Probably he wouldn't need it for a few days, but it paid to be on the safe side.

It was almost a pity he wouldn't be right there to watch their faces when it all started. See the looks of amazement and admiration. See the fear. But he would be busy elsewhere.

He lifted a heavy satchel from the floor and hoisted it over his shoulder. It had his tools in it, along with something he'd bought that day. Sort of a present for himself. A celebration. It would make them rock back on their heels when they found out about it.

He was singing to himself as he locked the door behind him and went down the stairs. One of his neighbors poked her scrawny neck out to see what all the noise was about and the Lion started to smile good naturedly at her, then remembered she was blind and wiped it off. No reason to waste one of those. He stuck his tongue out instead and made a lewd gesture at her. Stupid old bat. Her neck wasn't even worth breaking.

At the bottom of the stairs he turned and entered the miserable jewelry shop on the ground floor.

"Going away again, then?" the faded man behind the desk asked politely. In the dim candlelight his face looked like he was already dead, the Lion thought.

"That's right, Mr. Carter."

"You work too hard, boy. Make them give you a few days off."

The Lion chuckled. *Ha ha ha.* Work. "I'll do that. Tell them it was your idea."

Mr. Carter grinned, showing both his teeth. "How long'll you be gone then?"

"Can't say. Probably not more than a night or two. But I wanted you to know so you wouldn't worry."

"Good lad," Mr. Carter replied. " 'Preciate it, I sure do, your being so friendlylike."

What is the difference between a friend and an enemy? One you should kill. The other you must.

"Of course. No other way to be."

"Report come in just now from over near Whitehall," Grub explained excitedly, pacing around the studio. "A Mr. Potts sees a fellow of our description going up the stairs of a respectable looking house over there, above a jeweler's. I sent over five men to watch and make sure he doesn't get out, but I thought you'd want to be there, yer Lordship, when we make the catch."

"Excellent work, Grub," Lawrence commended him. "Are Phillips and Nielson here?"

"Yes sir. Also Coolidge and Jackson."

"Good. Leave those two to guard Lady Arlington. Have the rest follow me—"

"I am going with you," Tuesday informed him.

"No."

"Yes." When it was clear that he was going to object again, she pointed out, "You are my personal guard. You are supposed to go everywhere with me. What if I need to go somewhere while you are gone?"

"Do not be absurd. I am doing this for your protection."

"My protection? I thought you were my protection." She planted herself in front of the door, arms crossed, legs apart, scowling ferociously. "I thought we had to go everywhere together."

"Step aside, Lady Arlington."

"Only if you protect me like you are supposed to. Only if you agree that where you go, I go."

Many men had felt their insides seared by the glance Lawrence now gave her, but it did nothing to wipe away the hint of triumph dancing in her eyes.

Triumph, damn her.

I don't care what you think of me.

A muscle twitched in Lawrence's jaw and for a moment the sound of three of his teeth being ground down to powder was the only noise in the room. Then he said, "Very well. Then neither of us goes. We both stay here."

The triumph died. "You are just doing that to be stubborn. Come on, we will—"

"Be careful," he said to his men over her head. "And report back as soon as you know."

Then he turned and seated himself in the gray-velvet

lopsided chair. "You may as well make yourself comfortable, Lady Arlington. There is nothing for us to do but
wait."

"That is my chair."

"I go where you go."

She flopped onto the settee. The next three quarters of
an hour gave Tuesday a chance to observe Lawrence's superior charcoal-tossing skills. (What had possessed him
to give his coin to Jack?) It gave the musicians upstairs
the opportunity to play the same tune twice. It gave Lawrence time to neaten up her worktable. And it gave them
both a chance to showcase their better natures.

"What the devil is that?" Tuesday demanded as two
men came grunting in under a huge burden.

"I am not spending another night on that inquisitor's
rack you call a settee. Put it there," Lawrence directed the
men. "And take that thing—" he pointed unceremoni-
ously to the piece on which she was reclining, "—away."

Tuesday held onto the sides of the settee with both
hands, planting herself firmly. "No. Take the one you are
carrying away and leave this one where it is." She faced
Lawrence. "It is bad enough you are always straightening everything up, tidying everything. How dare you
buy furniture for my house? If you don't like it, you can
sleep somewhere else. This was your idea, not mine."

"And better proof of my becoming feeble minded I
could not ask for. Right where the other one is will be
fine," Lawrence continued, ignoring her. "And move
that trunk so—"

"Do not touch that trunk," Tuesday said in a voice
that made Lawrence hesitate.

"Never mind about the trunk," he told his men,
bowing to her. "But put that down there."

"I am not leaving this settee," she said as Lawrence moved toward her, wrapped her in his arms, lifted her from the old piece of furniture, and set her down on the new one.

"Thank you, that will be all," he announced, his eyes not leaving hers, his lips only two fingers' width from hers.

She gulped. "This isn't very—"

Grub's heavy footsteps in the corridor outside the studio interrupted them. They just had time to fly to opposite ends of the settee before Grub trudged in and announced dejectedly, "False alarm." His men filed in after him. "Nothing. Not a thing. Seems this Mr. Potts knew that his wife was getting a bit on the side and hoped that having a dozen of Lord Picky's own men bursting in on her and her paramour might fix her for good."

"You mean, he hadn't seen our man at all?" Lawrence asked.

"Yessir. Not hide not hair not face not rear." Then, realizing he was speaking in front of a lady, Grub blushed. "Sorry, ma'am."

"She doesn't care," Lawrence answered for her and was surprised that Tuesday did not object.

She was too distracted, and not with straightening out her skirt from Lawrence's aggressive approach to furniture moving. She had not realized it, but when the news that they had found the Secret Admirer had come in, she had felt not excitement but relief: relief that the doubts that had begun to creep into her mind, doubts about whether she had understood the evidence properly, or been fooled by it, were unfounded. Doubts fueled by how long it had taken them to find his trail. Doubts that were now reawakened and stoked.

Her anger had died down to a steady ache that felt like

a cross between sadness, exhaustion, and hopelessness. As Lawrence and Grub reviewed for the eightieth time the shifts of men detailed to show the Secret Admirer's picture around London, Tuesday rose and moved across the room. For a moment she stood in front of her copy of the *Pygmalion* painting. Hers was very similar to Lawrence's, to the original, but her colors were wrong. They were muddier, and lacked the clarity and definition of the original. She used to imagine the moment Pygmalion sensed the girl become real under his lips, imagine the way he had felt, but she saw now it was just a placating fantasy designed to make people feel powerful. To make them believe that maybe with the right kiss, they could arouse a spark of life in something dead. Stupid. Who would even want to?

She had strayed over toward the mantelpiece where the clock showed her it was past ten. Next to the clock stood a porcelain dog and without thinking, she picked it up and smashed it into the back wall of the fireplace.

Grub and Lawrence turned to stare at her.

She said, "I have a headache." Then she crossed the room, slipped into her bed, and pulled the curtains closed.

Their voices outside were just a low murmur but they were enough to mask the quiet sound of her sobs.

She had a headache, the Lion echoed. *A headache a headache*, he repeated to himself in a strange voice, like a song, a mantra. He was so excited he could barely wait. He did not care that it was going to rain. He did not care about getting his boots wet. She said she had a headache. That was the sign. Tonight, she would open the Window of her mind to him again.

*　　*　　*

Click. Squeak. Slide.

The sounds of a door opening slowly. Tuesday's eyes came unshut in an instant but the rest of her was paralyzed, listening. She had drawn the hangings of her bed closed so she could not see anything, but she thought she felt the fabric flutter.

Shuffle, shuffle.

Was this another dream? She drove her fingernail into her thigh to make sure she was awake. In an instant, her heart was pounding and she felt the hair on her arms standing up. Without being able to see, she felt horribly trapped, like she was being smothered. *Stay calm!* She forced her mind to pay attention, organizing her observations. The rain had stopped, and in the silence, she could hear Lawrence's breathing on the settee. That meant it wasn't him moving around the chamber. That meant it was someone else. There, in her room—

Scrape

—near the foot of her bed. She felt like she was in a black box, like she was interred in her death hangings. The air was closing in around her, suffocating her. Don't let him know you are awake her mind screamed. *Don't shout. Don't move.* This was what she had wanted, to make the killer come after her—

You just keep your whore mouth shut or I'll do the same to you as I did to him.

—to trap him. She felt hot, her palms were sweating. The fabric swayed again—

shuffle

—closer to where she was lying now. *Don't move don't move don't move.* She gripped her hands into fists and tried to make her dry throat swallow. *Breathe, lie still, breathe, lie—*

"No!"

The one loud syllable cut through the air. It took Tuesday a moment to realize the shout had not come from her own throat but from outside the dark cocoon of her bed, from beyond the curtains.

"No! Stop!" it sounded again, muffled but loud, from the settee. There was no mistaking the pain in it.

Reason fled. She was out of bed and through the curtains and into the studio in the space of a heartbeat. Moonlight came weakly through the windows, outlining the familiar shapes of furniture, tables, suit of armor, no one else in the room, Lawrence's figure thrashing on the settee, back and forth—

"Ever!" he shouted again and then a long, wrenching, "Noooo!"

She heard the sound of his teeth grinding together as she rushed toward him. That must have been what she had heard before, not hinges, not footsteps. "Lord Pickering," she whispered, reaching for his shoulder, "Lord Pickering, wake up. Wake up!"

His head turned from side to side, his eyes closed, his jaw tense. "Don't," he commanded to his unseen adversary. "Don't let go!"

A hand snaked out and caught her wrist, then slid down to her fingers. Palm pressed against palm and she could feel his pulse racing.

"I've got you," he shouted. He gripped her hand harder, strong fingers closed around her knuckles. "Keep holding on!"

"I will," she said back to him, holding tight.

"Hold on," he yelled, his tone different. His free hand

cupped his right shoulder and his jaw clenched with some sort of effort and he pulled her to him. "Tighter!" he commanded, and she used all her strength complying. "Just a little more, trust me! I've got you," he repeated, this time triumphant. Suddenly his breathing changed, from frantic to exhausted, then slowed to almost normal. He was holding Tuesday against him but she could see his face relax, could feel his heart stop pounding, hear his jaw unlock. After a few minutes she tried to rise, but he held her fast, her cheek pressed against his shoulder, her chest pressed against his, her body half off the settee. It was the most awkward position in the world. It was the world's most delicious feeling.

Three hours later, as the first streaks of dawn lighted her windows, Tuesday woke up in Lawrence's arms. She had never been held like that by anyone before—no one had ever wanted her to be that close to them—and she felt warm and safe and deeply confused. She felt like she knew Lawrence Pickering well and did not know him at all and she was not sure which she really wanted.

He was still sleeping and she allowed herself to study him for a moment before sliding away. Even in repose, even without the benefit of his sparkling blue eyes, he was magnificent looking. The careful control he kept over his expression by day slipped away like a mask. There was no frown, no smile, just him. He looked younger, a boy, and yet not more vulnerable. She wondered if anything ever made him feel less than strong. She wondered what it would be like to touch him deeply.

He let her go this time without protest and without waking. She would not tell him about his nightmare. She would not tell him that waking up surrounded by his embrace was the best feeling she had ever known. Telling him would only make his rejection, when it came, that much more embarrassing. As she registered these decisions she stretched her neck from side to side to work out the stiffness and turned toward her bed.

That was when she saw what the Secret Admirer had done.

Fear sliced through her body, and for the second time in her life, Tuesday fainted.

Chapter 19

Even as he paced around the room, tossing a stick of charcoal in his hand, Lawrence could not keep his eyes off the knife, buried almost to the hilt in her pillow. The rest of the mattress was in shreds around it, but it was the knife, cold steel and full of menace, that riveted his gaze. Looking at it made his stomach fill with fury, but it was better than looking at the bruise on Tuesday's forehead from where she had hit the floor fainting. Every time he saw it he felt like it was an indictment of him and his inability to keep her safe.

Things that had been fuzzy to him before had assumed razorlike sharpness in his mind. Curtis had beat her, he was positive of it, and now, although he had not inflicted the blow himself, he was no better. The difference between letting her get hurt and hurting her himself was negligible. Lawrence Pickering did not allow such things to happen.

She had given him only a vague answer for why she wasn't asleep in her bed, but he did not press her. He was not sure he wanted to know. Something that felt like a memory of her hair against his chin, her fingers wrapped tightly with his, nagged at him distractingly. The other possible reason for her vagueness, that she had attacked her bed herself, that she had murdered Curtis because he abused her and then slashed her linens to deflect suspicion, just could not make sense to Lawrence, even if it offered the simplest explanation of the facts. And whatever the truth, all that mattered at the moment was that she was not in bed when the knife was driven into it. He did not want to think about what might have happened if she had been. There would be years for self-rebuke later.

The Secret Admirer had been right there with them, right in the room as he slept. Right there—he could even point to the exact spot where the muddy footprints, one slightly larger than the other, indicating that it was made by someone with a limp, circled the bed—and yet somehow managed to slip by all of them.

The footsteps led to a service corridor and from there to the cellar, where a door overgrown with weeds that none of them had noticed opened directly onto the streets. The Secret Admirer seemed to know the layout of Worthington Hall better than its inhabitants and had managed to skirt all fifteen of the men posted inside the house. Fifteen trained guards who should have been aware of *something*.

Those men, the night guards, had already gone home to bed when Tuesday's fainting that morning awakened him, and it had taken some time—several of them seemed to prefer sleeping in beds other than those occupied by their wives—to reassemble them. They filed in now, followed by an older man, one Tuesday had not seen before. The man crossed to Lawrence, said a few words in his ear, and received in reply a scowl and a "Damn."

Tuesday was glad to see that Lawrence did not reserve his scowls expressly for her. "Is it news?" she asked from behind him. She was leaning against the wall next to the window, her arms crossed around her stomach. She had been standing like that for hours.

"Not about this, Christopher," Lawrence addressed the old man. "Tell them I'll come as soon as I can. And not to worry."

"Where are we going?" Tuesday asked.

"Nowhere."

Whatever the message had been, it had done nothing to improve his mood. "If this is about the investigation—"

"It's not." Lawrence turned to the men now arrayed in front of him and set about questioning them minutely. He had been at it for three quarters of an hour when Tuesday, exasperated, interrupted. "This is pointless, my lord. They did not see or hear anything. They would not. I told you, he is invisible."

"No one is invisible," Lawrence pushed out through his clenched jaw. "We know what he looks like."

"Do we?"

"Don't we?"

"Do you see that?" She pointed to the wreck of her bed. "That is a message. He was not trying to kill me. He wanted us to know that he is not afraid of us. And I want to know why." She paused, then voiced the fear that had been dogging her since the previous day. "I am beginning to wonder if he tricked us. If he purposely left all that evidence of his appearance at the crime scene to make us look for someone as unlike himself as possible."

"What do you propose we do then? Look only for right-handed men without brown hair who doesn't limp?" Lawrence demanded curtly. "Besides, if his intention was to mislead us about his appearance, why shoot at our witness, the man who could confirm how he looked? Wouldn't he want us to hear from Albert Marston?"

"I suppose so." Her agreement was half-hearted. "I just have this sense that we are missing something."

"You were the one who found all the damn evidence of the Secret Admirer's existence that we've been going on in the first place."

"Do you think I have forgotten that for a second?"

The pain in her voice, the first real pain he had heard, sliced through Lawrence's anger and suspicion. How had he not considered what she must be feeling? Her husband dead, her bed destroyed, a killer stalking her, an investigation hinging on her observations, and, so far, going nowhere. He crossed to her, took her arm, and pulled her toward the door.

"What are you doing?"

"Come with me."

His tone dismissed any chance of protest. He led her out of the studio, into the main hall and up the stairs. The sound of yet another concert floated past them, but Lawrence did not pause. He wanted to find a quiet place to talk to her. He continued up another flight, went to the nearest door, flung it open, and motioned her inside.

He saw her hesitate but he went in ahead, pulling her behind him. His men had been all over her house, but he himself had seen only Sir Dennis's apartment, her studio, and the entry hall. While those were large, the room they were now in was like a little jewel box. The walls and ceiling were gilded and exotic vines and flowers had been painted over them. Butterflies and dragonflies flitted between the leaves of the plants, and an enormous tree with glossy green leaves covered half the ceiling. A leopard peeked between the fronds of a fern in one corner, and a unicorn's horn showed from behind the painted tree trunk. Through Tuesday's incredible artistry, the room had been transformed into a magical garden. And unlike most of the other rooms in the house, Lawrence saw it still contained a few pieces of furniture.

Pushed into a corner were a wooden chair, a small table, a three-stepped ladder, and a very small bed, just the size of an infant, the kind one would find—

"In a nursery," he said aloud. "This was going to be your nursery."

Tuesday stood with her fingers on the handle of the closed door, her back to him. She nodded. Then she faced him. "Why did you bring me in here?"

Lawrence wanted to apologize. Wanted to tell her that he knew. Wanted to say that he thought her paintings were wonderful. That he thought she was wonderful. Wanted to admit—"Lady Arlington, you have to stop this." He spoke more harshly than he had intended.

"Stop what?"

"Stop doubting yourself and your judgement. You were the only person who saw any of that evidence at the scene of Curtis's murder."

"But what if I was wrong? Your men have been looking for over a day and found nothing. What if he doesn't exist? What if I have misled everyone?"

"Your information is the only lead we have to finding the Secret Admirer. We have to trust it. It's not useful to second-guess yourself like this."

She did not say anything, just moved away from him, trailing the fingers of her left hand along the wall. She stopped in front of a shimmering dragonfly.

Lawrence followed her. "While you are at it, you should stop boxing up your feelings. Your husband has been killed. Your bed was brutally attacked. Most women in your situation would be lying down somewhere with cool cloths on their foreheads being waited on."

"CeCe is lying down."

"It is not good for you to be so stoic."

She reached out and lovingly traced the contour of the dragonfly's wings with her pinkie. The gesture made Lawrence's knees tingle. She asked without looking at him, "Have you ever wondered what it would be like to be a dragonfly? To be able to go in any direction you wanted? To be so beautiful?"

"Don't change the subject."

Her eyes swept the room and she said in a flat voice, "I'm afraid you do not know the first thing about what is good for me, Lord Pickering."

"Very well. Then your acting this way is not good for my men. They are all half in love with you and hearing you so dispirited is destroying their morale."

"That is rot."

"Look, we need everyone to concentrate if we are going to catch the Secret Admir—"

She stiffened. "Please. Please stop calling him that."

Lawrence said, quietly, "I thought that was what you called him."

"No. CeCe came up with the name. I went along with it at first, but now I know it's wrong. He doesn't admire me."

"He certainly seems to."

Lawrence was not prepared for her expression when she turned toward him. There was pain etched in every perfect feature. "He is not my secret admirer," she insisted. "He does not admire me. There is nothing to admire and he knows it better than anyone because he knew about all of them."

"All of whom?"

She squared her shoulders. "All the men who did not want me. All the men who were momentarily blinded but soon saw the truth. The men who—" she made herself say the word, "—rejected me. The men who knew that I'm not worth anything."

"What are you talking about Tuesday?"

"I should have told you before, as soon as we knew but—" she stopped and swallowed hard. "All the men who were killed? All the others? They were all engaged to me once."

Lawrence stared at her.

She nodded. She knew what he was seeing. She could feel the letters "Rejected" as if they were inscribed on her forehead. "They proposed to me but then, right after our engagement, they broke it off and married someone else. Someone more suitable. More lovely. More interesting. More charming. Someone better than me."

She saw anger in Lawrence's eyes and rushed to add, "I know it looks like I was covering it up, and you will probably now think that I was responsible for the murders, but I'm not. The reason I did not tell you before was because—" she took a deep breath and let it out slowly. Then she said, fast, "The reason I didn't tell you was because I was embarrassed. I didn't want you to know. I didn't want you to think about me—that way. At least not yet."

Lawrence could not find the words to tell her how much he believed her, and how much it pained him. He only managed to say, "Thank you. For telling me."

She gave a small, cold laugh at his tone. "You are welcome. But now do you see? Now do you understand? You tell me not to be stoic, but what do you want? What exactly would you have me feel, Lord Pickering? Rejected? Abandoned? Four fiancées broke their engagements with me because I couldn't hold their attention. Curtis only married me because we did it quickly, before he could change his mind. And then he left, too. Do you know why?"

Lawrence did not want to know.

"My husband left me because I was a terrible wife and a terrible screw. I don't want to remember that, but somehow I can't forget it. Forget any of it. What I want, more than anything, is to be numb."

Lawrence surprised them both by saying, "No you don't."

She stopped rubbing her right wrist and gazed at him. "How do you know?"

"Believe me. That is not a way to live."

There was a pause and then she asked, "Isn't it working out for you?"

Lawrence was stunned. "Do you ever not say what you are thinking, Lady Arlington?"

"Do you ever not change the subject when someone asks you a personal question, Mr. Pickering?"

"This is not about me."

Not about how he no longer bothered to drink because it had no effect on him. Not about how until the day before he hadn't felt hungry or thirsty or cold in over two years. Not about how he constantly reminded himself of the words—monster, filthy, low-life, vile—that Constantia Grosgrain, his former mistress, had used to describe him at their last encounter, to remind himself of the glorious freedom, freedom from caring, they'd given him. Not about how he wanted to holler at anyone who called him a hero. Not about how his smile felt like it was a mask, his emotions like they were gaudy theatrical props to be picked up and shown around, then dropped into storage. "This is not about me at all," he repeated forcefully.

"Why not?" she asked, looking not at but into him with those gray-green storm cloud eyes. "Why am I the only one to confess? Why can't we talk about the way you live your life, too?"

Yes, Lawrence my friend. Why not?

Lawrence took a step closer to her. He again experienced what he had in the coach when they kissed, the sense of disorientation, of confusion, but with a strange center of serenity. He took both her wrists in his hand and looked at the right one. It was slightly crooked.

Behind her he saw the chair, the crib, the ladder. Short, only three steps up, but still tall enough to reach the highest point in the room.

She had not fallen.

Curtis had struck her.

That was how she lost the child.

With those bare realizations, something that had been burning steadily inside him flamed up dangerously. "Do you know what I thought the first time I saw you?" he heard himself asking.

Her eyes were locked on his. There was insecurity and wariness. And also hope. She bit her lip and shook her head. Under his fingers on her wrist he could feel her heart racing.

"I thought you were the most un—"

CeCe's blood-thinning shriek sliced through the air.

Chapter 20

Tuesday and Lawrence left the nursery at the speed of a cannonball leaving a cannon. They were out of the room and halfway to CeCe's chamber when she came streaking out of it, still shrieking.

"He's in there, he's in there," she wailed, and threw herself into Tuesday's arms. "He came in through my window, he attacked me. *He is in my room!*" As Tuesday tried to calm her maid, Lawrence sprinted down the corridor toward her room. CeCe had flung the door closed, but from inside issued the sound of someone crashing around. In the moment before he kicked down the door Lawrence realized that he was unarmed except for the piece of charcoal he'd been tossing around, but it was too late to care. The hinges squealed in protest and then broke, the door hit the floor with a loud bang, and Lawrence felt himself being slammed into the wall by the force of another body.

"Relinquish your hold on me!" the other body screeched as Lawrence wrapped his arms around it. "Unhand me! Liberate me! I must resuscitate her! Dammit, let me go!"

Grub Collins had come panting in then, and grabbed

the struggling man from behind. Lawrence stepped away to look at him. He would have recognized the voice, even if the words had not given the identity away. It was the man he had met the first day, the one who had refused to open the door for him and then sent him walking into the burglar alarm.

"You are Sir Dennis's valet, Morse," Lawrence said.

"Was," Morse corrected, fighting valiantly but in vain against Grub's strong arms. "But that is not my occupation any longer. Now let me go or I'll rend both your arms and all your legs."

"Did you hear that, Grub?" Lawrence inquired.

"I'm willing to risk it, sir."

"Excellent." To Morse: "Why should we let you go? What are you doing here if you don't work here?"

"CeCe," Morse called over Lawrence's shoulder. "CeCe, my ardent love, I shall arrive briskly."

"You won't arrive at all unless you answer my questions."

"But she requires me!" Morse protested. "Did you hear her bellowing? Something has attacked her!"

"I believe she thinks that was you."

"Why would I attack her? I love her. I yearn for her. I climbed up the bloody water spout to get into her room, didn't I?" he griped. Then twisting his head over his shoulder he asked the man who was holding him, "What is your name?"

"Grub Collins," Grub answered amiably.

"Grub, Mr. Collins, could you let me go?"

Grub looked at Lawrence who shook his head and said, "Maybe after you explain why you came through a window rather than using more conventional means."

"It's like this," Morse confided, putting aside his astonishing vocabulary. "I've been trying to get CeCe to run away with me. No place for her, this house. She's head and shoulders above all of them, that girl. She's not a maid, she's—" Even his advanced vocabulary failed him. "I just think she is wonderful. She's the reason I've taken to improving myself, see. Going to be someone, for her. But no matter how many times I ask her to run off with me, she won't go. Says she loves her mistress and must wait for her fiancé and won't go away. Fine, I say, but I'm going to watch over her, make sure she is all right."

"Don't you have another job?"

"Not yet, exactly. Got to find just the right station. Won't work for a nobody, if you see what I mean. Demeans a man of my skills."

"Of course. Go on."

"So I'm watching and I'm seeing all these new servants you brought in here, all these *men* servants. And I seen the way they look at her. And I worry that maybe she's not safe with them. Last night I crawled up the water pipe and tapped on her window, but she didn't answer. Probably couldn't hear over the rain. And then today I watch and watch the studio windows, you know you can see them from the street, and I don't see her once. So I decide to come up here and take a look. And then she starts running around screaming."

CeCe had refused to enter the studio once she heard about the attack on the bed, so Morse's statement that he had not seen her and had therefore taken the window approach to visiting made some sense.

"Were you out there last night? While it was raining?"

"And for a bit of time afterwards."

Lawrence looked at him closely. CeCe's window and the drain pipe were on the same side of the house as the door through which the killer had to have entered. "Did you see anyone? Anyone on the ground?"

Morse shook his head. "Not a soul. Course some of the time I was up here. But then I spent an hour or so in those bushes," he tilted his head toward the window where a clump could be seen, "so I suppose I would have seen someone."

"You sat in the bushes?"

Morse straightened himself up as much as he could with Grub still holding him, and his accent became aristocratic. "Dreamed in the bushes. About my celestial CeCe."

Lawrence turned around and saw that Tuesday, having shuffled CeCe to the safety of the kitchen, was standing in the doorway. "Morse, what are you doing here?" she asked.

Morse blushed.

"He came to visit CeCe," Lawrence explained, clearly skeptical.

Tuesday's forehead wrinkled. "Why didn't you just come through the door?"

"Not letting anyone in that way, are they?" Morse demanded rhetorically, then corrected himself. "Passage is impossible through that opening."

Tuesday was immediately sympathetic. "They have turned the place into a bit of a prison, haven't they?"

"Yes, ma'am. Don't know how you stand it."

"Me either." She tried hard not to look at Lawrence. "I am sorry if this upset you, Morse. You might wait a few days to come back. By then things should have settled down. Grub, I think you can release him now."

Grub looked to Lawrence who shook his head. "Hold him."

"But he is not the man we are looking for," Tuesday pointed out.

"How do you know?" Lawrence asked. "You yourself said our man might be using disguises."

"Yes, but Morse simply isn't him. Believe me," Tuesday said, then regretted it. Why should he? Why should anyone? She had been wrong so far. "Besides, he is not cut out to be a killer."

Morse did not like hearing this. "I could be if I wanted to be," he told her acidly. "If you are saying that I do not have the courage to—"

Lawrence eyed him closely as he struggled to prove he could be as good a killer as the next man and concluded that Tuesday was right. This was not their murderer. This was just a man pathetically in love with a housemaid.

Still, he did not like the way she had barreled in while he was questioning Morse. Didn't like the way she had started giving orders to his men. Didn't like the way his self-control fled around her. This was his damn investigation, not hers, and he was going to make sure she knew it.

"Hold him," Lawrence said to Grub. And when she opened her mouth to protest he turned away and started down the corridor.

The Lion thought he knew what had gone wrong the night before. His Lordship was trying to take over her Window, too. The Worthington Widow's Window. Trying to compete. Not likely, the Lion knew.

He understood all about what she was doing with His Lordship, and he'd left her a sign so she'd know. To show her that he had come when she called. That way she would feel his love. Just as he felt hers growing inside him.

Unless it had been a trap?

Never underestimate your enemy, he reminded himself.

It did not feel like a trap, he thought as he listened to the guards around him talk. If it were a trap, someone would have known about it, and someone would have spilled it to him. Eventually he found out everything.

Where do we hide?

Where we are most visible.

Why?

Because no one ever looks there.

Never underestimate your enemy, but make sure he underestimates you.

He thought he'd seen to that pretty well. Something may have gone wrong the previous night, but nothing was going to go wrong tonight.

He moved closer, listening to the guards more intently. Tonight was his. And they had no idea.

Lawrence's behavior in CeCe's room set the tone that persisted through the rest of the afternoon while they waited for news. He quietly had Morse released an hour after ordering him held, but he did not let Tuesday know. It was almost a relief to both of them to have a dispensation from having to be nice to each other. They slipped gracefully and gratefully back into the pattern of mutual—

"Is it really necessary for you to sigh like that, Lord Pickering?"

"I am not sighing. I am breathing. Would you rather I held my breath?"

"Absolutely. Then you would not be able to speak."

"I wasn't speaking. You were the one who started speaking."

"I wish you would just leave me alone. I've had enough of your idle prattle. It's almost as annoying as the way you keep tossing that stick."

"My idle prattle? I am not the one who started picking on the way someone breathes."

"Picking on? Who wouldn't mention it? You sound like a cow mooing in the fog."

"A what?"

"Never mind."

"How many cows mooing in fog have you heard, Lady Arlington?"

"I can't see why that, or anything, is any of your business. I wish you would please stop disturbing me. And rearranging everything."

"I am not rearranging. I am trying to give this place a semblance of livability."

"Then perhaps you should remove yourself. It was far more livable before you got here."

—hostility and antagonism they had established early on.

Tuesday could not stop her mind from returning repeatedly to his words in the nursery before CeCe screamed. *The first time I saw you I thought you were the most un—* seemed to her to be the most provoking sentence in the world, particularly since she could not seem to stop herself from listing words that began with "un," each one more unsavory than the next.

She had been trying to make herself paint in an unsuccessful effort to silence her mind, when the clock in her father's room upstairs chimed five and Lawrence addressed her for the first time in hours.

What he said was, "It is time for you to change."

"Change?" She accidentally dropped her brush and followed it with an unladylike expression. "Into what? A sweet-tempered creature who does your bidding unasked?"

"Into a formal gown. And don't try to lie—I know you have one; I asked CeCe. We will leave in less than an hour."

And she thought she could trust CeCe. "Where are we going?"

"A ball."

"I don't want to go to a ball."

"What a pity. Unfortunately, I must attend. It is Miles—you remember Miles, came up with this terrible idea of me protecting you—it's his betrothal ball. And since, as you pointed out yourself, where I go you go, you are going."

"That was different. That was about finding the killer. This is—" she interrupted herself. "How can you talk of going to a ball when we still haven't gotten a hint about where the Secret Admirer lives?" *Or even if he exists.*

"All the more reason to keep you by my side."

"Absolutely not."

"I am afraid you have no choice. Since she refuses to reenter this room, CeCe is waiting for you with your clothes in her room. We leave in less than an hour. Can you find your way, or do I need to send one of my men with you?" The amusement in his voice was palpable. Amusement and triumph.

Very well, Tuesday decided as she walked, chin up and

unescorted, out of the studio. She would change. She would attend the ball with him. And she would make him very, very sorry.

"Time for you to change," the Lion repeated to himself happily as he moved away from Worthington Hall. Indeed it was. It was time to change. Time to slip back into his other persona, his other Wardrobe.

Time to toy with their minds once more.

Chapter 21

"The total is now seven," Tuesday informed Lawrence as he entered the coach.

"Seven what?"

He smelled marvelous. She breathed through her mouth. "Apologies you owe me."

"Really? Are they collecting interest?"

Don't look at him don't look at him don't look at him. She looked at him.

She forgot everything she was going to say. She forgot English.

He was wearing dark gray but not like any other man had ever worn it. It brought out the silver flecks of his eyes, the gold of his hair, the lean planes of his jaw, the rugged scent of his skin, the sheer power of his body. He looked stupendous in it. And yet she wanted to rip his clothes off.

"Are you going to enlighten me about the seven ways I have offended you, Lady Arlington, or would you prefer a blanket apology?"

Right. Apologies. And she was going to make him regret dragging her to this ball. "There are the two uncollected from before," she began holding up two fingers. "Then one for embarrassing me by dragging me out of the room in front of your men, one for unfairly refusing to let me go with you to investigate what we thought was the killer's apartment, one for unreasonably making me go to this stupid ball, one for not telling me that Curtis's mistress came to the house." *And one for saying I am the most unremarkable woman you've ever seen. Or whatever you were going to say.*

"I only count five."

"Fine, five."

"How did you find out about May Dew?"

"Who?"

"Curtis's mistress."

"CeCe told me as I was getting dressed. She said she had not wanted me to know but you convinced her I would want to. Yesterday. And then you didn't even tell me."

"I forgot."

"Forgot? Unbelievable."

"Why did you want to see her anyway?"

"To see what she was like." *What women who men desire are like.* "Because she had my necklace and I want to—"

"Actually, she doesn't." Lawrence pulled a box out of his doublet and held it toward her. "Thank you for reminding me."

Tuesday opened the box and saw, with a pounding heart, that it was, in fact, her mother's necklace. But something was different. "What did you do to it?"

"Had it cleaned."

She looked up at him with an unreadable expression. He had given Jack a future and now this. "The stones are different."

Lawrence glanced away. "A few of them needed to be replaced," he said as he stared intently at the doorframes on the houses they were passing. He did not explain that he had ordered they all be replaced with real gems, that four jewelers had worked unceasingly since one of his men had awakened the owner of a dingy pawn shop two nights before and found the piece, that it had cost more than the bracelet he had sent to the queen for her birthday, or that he hoped she would use it, when he was gone from her life, to buy her furniture back.

Because as soon as the investigation was over, he was putting as much distance between himself and Lady Tuesday Arlington as modern navigational tools would allow. The effect that seeing her sitting across from him in her dark gold satin gown that set off her eyes and made her hair look as if it had been spun by some demon somewhere to tempt men was enough to warn him against any repeat of what had happened in the gallery that day. Ever.

She did not know it, but Tuesday need not have worried about making Lawrence regret bringing her to the ball. Watching other men look at her looking like she did was going to be one of the most painful experiences of his life.

"Lord Pickering," she whispered. "Lawrence."

He looked up, surprised to hear her say his name. Surprised, dammit, that was all.

"Thank you." She reached a hand up and touched the choker, which settled perfectly around her neck. "Thank you for—"

"We have arrived," Lawrence interrupted with a frown. "Come on."

He might go to Constantinople, he thought as he took her arm and did not look at her or smell her or feel her or long for her. Or maybe it would be better to go a bit farther.

They made such a ripe pair, the Lion thought as he watched his Lady and Lawrence Pickering descend from the coach in front of Dearbourn Hall. He knew why she was with His Lordship and he didn't blame her. The Lion knew she was just trying to lure His Lordship on to increase the challenge for him, make her heart more Worth Winning. The lady of a great lord is a great prize.

The crowd broke into wild cheers as she and His Lordship emerged and the Lion joined in, letting the energy, the love, the adulation course through his body as if it were meant expressly for him. It was a sign, a sign of the honor to come for him. Cheering, part of the group, he became breathless, as if they were already Worshipping him, as if, at last—

"Beg pardon," a large man apologized, brushing up against him hard.

The Lion shrugged casually. "Don't worry about it," he said, nothing wrong, could happen to anyone, not giving a hint that the touch of the other man made him feel filthy. Smiling genially, he reached a finger under the cuff of his shirt, where his scar was, slipped out his knife, and slashed the man through the stomach.

He was so quick, so good, that the man did not even realize what had happened. He was six feet away through the crowd when he looked down and saw blood spurting from the front of his tunic, ten feet away when he lost consciousness, fifteen feet away when he died. The Lion hoped he would slip down and be trampled into nothingness, but the crowd was so thick that he did not even fall, just stood sandwiched between them all, staring at the spectacle with eyes only slightly less perceptive than theirs. Some time soon a Woman—the Lion hoped—in a dreary shawl and a hat she yelled at her husband for sitting on, would look over and realize the man she thought, had delighted in imagining, was groping her, was a corpse. Priceless!

He did not need to wait to see that, though. His fantasy of it was enough. He cleaned his knife on a passerby's breeches, then slipped it back into his wrist holster. It was tempting to stay here all night and kill as many of them as possible, but he had to check on the rest of his operation. Plus he'd soon be wanting an audience.

By the time they had woven their way through the crush of guests, the ball was well under way. Everyone seemed to know Lawrence, and everyone—especially the women—wanted his undivided attention. The way hundreds of smiles died early deaths on the lips of society's beauties when they saw Tuesday made her feel like she was a rare but foul fungus growing on his sleeve.

"Lady Arlington, I was hoping you would come," a male voice said with genuine welcome from behind them, and Lawrence whirled them around. She felt his forearm clench under her hand.

"Tristan," he said with a very polite smile, and Tuesday recognized the extremely handsome and charming Tristan del Moro, the former thief who had come to secure her house the day before.

Tristan ignored Lawrence and spoke only to her. "I know you have already met Miles, the honored bridegroom tonight. Allow me to introduce you to the rest of my cousins. Sebastian, Ian, Crispin, Sophie, and Bianca, this is Lady Tuesday Arlington."

"The murderess!" the woman named Bianca proclaimed, smiling widely.

"Don't worry, it's a compliment," Sebastian leaned in to explain when he saw the expression on Tuesday's face. "We Arboretti men only marry murderesses."

"You can't propose," Tristan objected strenuously. "I met Lady Arlington first."

"That was sheer luck. Not sporting of you to take advantage of it."

Tuesday surprised herself by starting to laugh.

But her laughter died when Sophie, pointing across the room announced, "I don't believe it. He's fled." Tuesday followed her finger to the spot where Lawrence was standing, engulfed by a dozen women.

"I am afraid he does not like my company very much," Tuesday confided in what she hoped was a breezy I-don't-care-a-bit-if-women-swarm-around-him-like-flies tone.

"On the contrary," Tristan put in. "You have a very powerful effect on him. Just watch how he keeps looking over here."

"Glaring over here," Tuesday corrected.

Sebastian raised an eyebrow. "Even better."

"Yes," Tristan agreed, rubbing his chin, "but it does present complications. I for one do not wish to meet Lawrence in a duel."

"Neither do I," Sebastian averred. "Nor would I want to be the one to destroy his happiness again."

"I don't think there is any danger of that," Tuesday assured them.

"Lady Arlington," Tristan said with a half smile, "I am afraid you have quite a lot to learn about men."

* * *

The Lion was lit by his success in front of Dearbourn Hall. He wanted to kill everyone he saw.

Patience.

Screw patience. The world was about to change. This was it, his moment to shine. He was surprised that he could just stroll among people without them seeing it on him. Seeing how great he was. That he was the Winner.

He was the best. Lawrence Pickering thought his men—his stupid men who were walking right by him—were searching for the Lion, but really the Lion was ruling over them. They took no step that the Lion did not somehow suggest to them first, did nothing without the Lion's approval. The Lion was in control.

God it felt amazing.

He was trembling and his fingers were tingling. Just one more, he told himself. Let me have just one more. He grabbed one of the undercover men sent to look for him—not one of Lawrence's personal stable but good enough—by the wrist and tugged him into the alley.

"I think I saw something," he told the man breathlessly.

"Who are you? Hey, what—" the man began to ask, then stopped. His eyes got huge. He looked down at his stomach. He looked back at the Lion.

He died right there.

The Lion stripped off the man's bloody clothes and stood looking at the naked body. It was so ugly, that stupid body. Not like his Lady's. Her body was spectacular. His mouth got Wet just thinking about it.

He was great tonight. Tonight he was alive. Tonight, he was in charge.

Tonight London would be his.

*   *   *

Large insects, Lawrence decided. That was what the men swarming around Tuesday looked like in their black-and-green coats.

"I beg your pardon, my lord? Insects?"

He had not realized he'd spoken aloud. He dragged his eyes from Tuesday's face to that of Olivia Waverly, who was standing at his side.

It was the place she seemed always to occupy at balls this season, other women moving aside as she approached like commoners before their monarch. Despite his best efforts not to hear the gossip about himself, even Lawrence knew of the widely circulated rumor that he and Olivia would soon announce their engagement.

He did nothing to feed the rumor, but nothing to quell it either. As far as he was concerned, at least until four days earlier, the beautiful Olivia Waverly would have made as good a wife as any of the available women that season. Better, in fact, than many because she was a widow and therefore would not require much coddling, and because she was smart. She was also ruthless, he knew, having an idea of just exactly what kinds of maneuvering had been required of her to overawe the entire field of young women vying for his title and install herself as the prime candidate, which did not entirely bother him. But she would no longer fit the bill. Not at all. Because it would hardly be fair to marry a woman and then drag her to the ends of the earth, which was exactly where Lawrence was determined to go.

He was calculating how long it would take him to get to—

(the other side of the ballroom where Sir Bottlebuck had his hand twined around Tuesday's elbow like a grasping vine)

—Morocco, when he realized that Olivia was speaking to him.

"I knew her, as a girl," she said, following Lawrence's gaze across the crowded floor of the ballroom. When he turned a puzzled frown on her, she added, "Lady Tuesday Arlington. We were neighbors for one summer."

"Oh," Lawrence said. "That must have been unpleasant."

Olivia looked at him quizzically for a moment, then laughed. "Not at all. She was—" Olivia broke off as if groping for the right word. Really, she was torn. She'd worked so hard to get this close to Lawrence, and she could tell by the intensity of his interest in Tuesday that she was a viable threat. Olivia had learned the hard way to take what she wanted, whatever the cost, whatever the means, because everyone else was doing the same. She had learned to be as unscrupulous as her first husband, and as cold. But seeing Tuesday again cut through her cynicism, shuttling her back to an earlier time. She said, "Tuesday was a marvelous girl."

Still, marvelous hardly did her justice. Olivia had never again felt as thrillingly glamorous as she had at the age of twelve when Tuesday, two years younger than she but somehow ages more mature, had asked if she could draw her portrait. Or as bold and alive and joyful as she had when they had lay on their backs in the rickety hayloft over Tuesday's brother Jack's room in the stables and stared at the stars through the cracks and imagined what their futures would be like. Olivia shook her head ironically at her young self as she recalled her dreams of being married to a powerful, rich man with a fantastic title, a duke or an earl. Sometimes, when Tuesday's influence was strongest, Olivia had even dared to dream of an exotic European count. But Tuesday's plan, like everything about her, was different. She wanted to travel around the world with her brother Jack and ride on camels and climb mountains and taste every flavor and draw every face and have dozens and dozens of children. Neither of them knew for certain where children came from, but Tuesday felt fairly certain she would be able to find that place during her travels and get some.

Their friendship lasted only two months—Olivia had a vague recollection of Tuesday's brother Jack being sent away, and the family moving shortly after—but images from it had stayed with her, haunting her better dreams, since then.

"She was a really marvelous girl," Olivia repeated. "I always knew she would be an extraordinary woman."

"Oh," Lawrence replied, wondering—

(why Tristan and Sebastian weren't breaking Lord Alcott's fingers for touching Tuesday's shoulder)

—what she had said.

Not long after, Olivia drifted away from Lawrence and toward a circle of her admirers, all clamoring to know every word he'd spoken.

"Something about insects," she answered, shaking her head in confusion. "And then something about catching the next boat to India."

"Move it or prove it," the freckle-faced boy behind the news-sheet stall said to him saucily. "Ye gots to pay if ye wants to read them."

The Lion thought the boy's belt, of strong leather and wrapped three times around his waist so he could grow into it, would make a perfect noose. The Lion thought the cash box would work ideally to batter the boy's brains out. The Lion considered whether he could strangle the boy just by shoving his goddamned news sheets down his throat until he could not breathe, let him choke on those Words, on the black ink that said nothing, nothing important, nothing worth reading, *nothing at all about him!*

"Ye gonna pay, mister, or ye going to get along?"

I'm not going to pay, the Lion thought, feeling the guard's bloody shirt drying under his own, next to his skin. But you are. Everyone will.

Tomorrow everyone would be talking about him. Tomorrow his name would be on the top of every news sheet. Tomorrow he would be as famous as Lawrence Pickering, Our Greatest Hero. Or more famous.

Because tomorrow Lawrence Pickering would be dead.

Crispin crossed the ballroom floor, moving purposefully toward Lawrence. He and Lawrence had been best friends since they were boys, long before Crispin became an earl or Lawrence became Lord Pickering. They had met by accident one day when, on a bet, Lawrence had dived into the Thames without giving a thought to the fact that he could not swim. Crispin had saved his life and from that moment on they had been nearly inseparable whenever Crispin was in England. Lawrence always claimed that he would still be an ill-mannered pauper if it wasn't for Crispin and his cousins, but they knew better than anyone that he had been a gentleman even when he was wearing tattered breeches and finding his meals behind the kitchens of houses like the one he now lived in.

Lady Olivia and her entourage were just floating away as Crispin reached his friend. Lawrence, oblivious to their departure, stood alone, frowning. He was heedless of the fact that he was clenching and unclenching his fists. He had no idea that he had just unwittingly and mercilessly cut the most important widow in London. Indeed, he was so unaware of everything going on around him that when Crispin came up and put his arm on his friend's shoulder, Lawrence almost socked him.

"I thought you had forgiven me for that scene with Constantia Grosgrain two years ago," Crispin said, stepping hastily away.

"I'm sorry." Lawrence dusted off the smile. "You startled me. It is good to see you. What are you doing here?"

"This is Miles's betrothal ball," Crispin explained as if speaking to a child. "He is my cousin. I—"

A normal Lawrence would have gotten annoyed by being addressed this way. Normal Lawrence might have made an acerbic comment. Normal Lawrence would absolutely not have said, "Oh."

Crispin stood and blinked at him for a moment.

The stranger who had taken over Lawrence's body was gazing at the dance floor. He said, "Miles and his betrothed certainly look good together."

"That is not his betrothed," Crispin informed him, not bothering to fill him in on the mad arrival of the woman with the monkey through a service corridor just before Lawrence's own.

"Oh. Oh no."

"Exactly." A pause. "I am surprised you even noticed them, Lawrence."

Lawrence kept his eyes on some point just beyond the dancers. "What do you mean?"

"You've been so busy glaring at Lady Arlington I

didn't think you'd seen anything else. Why don't you just go ask her to dance?"

"Why would I want to do that?"

"Because you can't keep your eyes off of her—"

"I'm protecting her."

"—And because you have already fallen half in love with her."

"I have not," Lawrence said, glaring balefully at Crispin.

Crispin was undaunted. "All right, all the way in love with her."

"I am not falling in love with anyone. I am not going to fall in love with anyone."

"Don't let the memory of Constantia ruin this Lawrence."

"Oh is that what is ruining it? I thought it was the fact that she might be a murderess. And I've already had the experience of falling in love with a murderess. Remember? Constantia? How she murdered her husband among others and tried to pin it on me? Once was enough for that kind of fun."

Crispin waved the reminder away. "I am serious, Lawrence. You know Lady Arlington is no murderess. And I have not seen you this happy in a long time."

"I am not happy."

"Yes you are. You are having a wonderful time. You are just too pig headed to admit it."

"Are you calling me a liar."

"Will it help?"

"Don't you have someone else to torment?"

"Not right now. Besides, it's the least I can do. You saved my life when we were boys and I was drowning."

"I was the one who was drowning. You saved *my* life."

"All the more reason for me to ensure you make the most of it."

Lawrence glared into Crispin's wide grin one final time, stalked across the dance floor and pulled Tuesday onto it.

The pungent smell of ale and bodies hit Tom as he pushed through the entrance of the Dancing Fawn. Several patrons were still scattered around but only one of them looked up from their tankards as he walked in. Behind the long plank bar, the young girl dozing against a cask of ale grunted and turned over.

Many of Lawrence's men, discouraged by turning up continually empty-handed, had already slid off to bed, but Tom stuck with the search. As he reminded himself by periodically running his fingertips over the scab on his cheek from the attack on him in the alleyway two nights earlier, he had a better motivation. He was determined to be the one to bring Lord Pickering the killer's address.

"Whatreyewantingson," the one patron who had looked up when he entered, a slight man, called to him from across the room.

"I beg your pardon?"

"Placesclosed but ye can help yerself. If ye leave the money with Becky that is," the man expanded, waving a limp wrist in the direction of the sleeping girl.

"I am not looking for a drink, thank you," Tom said. He saw the man's attention waver, so he moved to him quickly. "I am trying to find someone. This fellow." He unrolled the now smudged copy of Tuesday's drawing on the table, smoothing it with his hands. "Have you seen him?"

The man picked the picture up, held it close to his face and squinted at it.

He eyed Tom closely. "Whowouldyoubethen?"

"I beg your pardon."

"Im asking who you be. Who is it is wanting to know about this cove?" He tapped the paper with a dirty fingernail.

"I am working on a special operation against smuggling with—"

"So yer from the queen's stable, eh? Official are ye?"

Tom nodded. "Do you know who that man is?"

The man picked his black teeth with his fingernail for a moment. "Can't say for certain. Need to consult with my colleague. There's a reward for knowing who he is, didyesay?"

"Not an official one," Tom began, saw the man's attention drift again, then revised, "But Lord Pickering, the earl of Arden, is heading the investigation and he knows how to show his appreciation to those who help him."

"Lawrence Pickering ye say? Know his brother well. Not a bad cove. Ye just wait here a moment."

The small man rose and Tom expected him to go somewhere and do something. Instead he cupped his hand around his mouth and bellowed "Kyle! Kyle get yer lazy self down here if ye want to be rich afore ye die!"

This was it! Finally this was it!

"If you don't want to dance with me, you don't have to," Tuesday told Lawrence as he spun her around the floor.

"If I didn't want to dance with you I would not have asked."

"You look miserable."

"I am trying to figure out why CeCe told me you were clumsy. You are a very good dancer."

"That is kind of you, Lord Pickering but—"

"I would not say it if it weren't true," Lawrence told her abruptly.

"Oh." There was silence until Tuesday said, "Are you having a good time?"

"You seem to be," was Lawrence's reply. "With all your admirers."

Tuesday rolled her eyes. "They're only interested in me because I came with you. But actually, I am enjoying myself." She barely avoided adding "now," and said instead, "This isn't how I pictured a ball would be."

"Really? What did you imagine? People being nice to one another? Delighting in each other's company?"

She chuckled despite herself. "No. I think I always pictured it from above. All the colors, all the movement. I imagined it being more like watching dragonflies in the summer, the way they move from one place to another, however and whenever they want. More like that and less, well, stiff."

"More chaotic you mean," Lawrence said dryly. "What a surprise."

"I'm sorry, I must sound like an idiot to you, my lord." She was staring at his shoulder as she added, "Actually, being here tonight has made me think I owe you a more serious apology."

Lawrence made a show of peering around them. "Have we entered one of those enchanted circles where everything goes backwards? I thought *I* was supposed to do all the apologizing."

"Very witty, my lord," Tuesday complimented him. "I wanted to tell you that I am sorry if I have been difficult in the course of this investigation. I have, um, a hard time submitting to other people's rules." Lawrence grunted, but it was a laughing sort of grunt. She looked at him with mock hardness and said, "You have not exactly been a lamb to deal with yourself."

"You astonish me, Lady Arlington. It was my impression that I have been charming."

"Be careful or I shall stop apologizing."

Lawrence pressed his lips together in enduring silence.

"Good," she went on. "What I wanted to say was that, until tonight, I had not really realized everything you've given up to help me. All this—" she looked around the splendid room, "—all these lovely people, all this luxury, all this order. This is what you are used to. And instead you've been forced to sleep on a lumpy settee in my disorderly studio. I promise that I will be more cooperative from now on and that I will do anything I can to make the investigation go faster, so you can move out of my house as soon as possible and get back to your real life. So we both can. I want you to know that I am very grateful for the sacrifices you've made and—"

"You have nothing to thank me for," Lawrence said brusquely, interrupting her. Halfway through her speech his smile had drained away and his eyes had moved beyond hers. "And there is nothing to be grateful for. I have just been doing my duty. Nothing more."

Tuesday looked over her shoulder, then back at him. "Why do you always stare at doorframes when I am trying to speak to you seriously? Are you making sure there's nothing to block your escape route?"

"I do not stare at doorframes."

"You were doing it just now. And you did it tonight in the coach on the way here when I tried to thank you for my necklace."

"That is ridiculous. I don't—"

Tuesday took her hand from Lawrence's shoulder and placed her fingers lightly on his lips to silence him. When she spoke, her voice was choked, little more than a whisper. "Please, Lord Pickering. I don't know what it was, but obviously I said something wrong. I did not mean to upset you." She moved her fingers away and looked up at him. "Could we not talk anymore? Could we just dance? I—I have been waiting all night for you to ask me."

She was never able to learn what the strange expression that came over Lawrence's face then meant, because at that moment Tom pushed through the crowd on the dance floor and announced feverishly, "This time we've really got him."

Chapter 22

"'E calls hisself the Lion," Joey began, and it flowed from there. The Lion dressed expensively, showed up often at the Dancing Fawn, limped, and liked to eat walnuts. He gave himself his nickname because of a mark on his forearm shaped like a Lion's head. Apart from this, all their information was a long list of nevers: the Lion never ordered but one ale a night, never touched the women who came in—not to say he didn't look hard enough at the merchandise—never chitchatted, never met anyone there, never ate the mutton stew—pretty good, tis, if ye haven't eaten in a month—never told anyone where he lived, or what he lived on. From time to time he had received written messages at the bar, which made them think he lived nearby, but neither he nor Can Can Kyle, who came along with him to make the report, could read so they didn't know what they said. Once they had speculated that he was an apprentice in one of the printer's places around the corner in Saint Paul's churchyard because he was always going around with them little books, unbound, but Kyle had observed that he never had ink on his hands.

Lawrence sent home the men who had been out all

night and ordered a fresh set to blanket the neighborhood around the Dancing Fawn, despite the duo's admission that they had not seen the Lion in over a week.

Reports came flowing in fast then. A fruit vendor up the street thought a man who looked like the Lion had been loitering around recently, but hadn't seen where he went. Two of the girls from Helen's Harem swore he had stood on the street opposite the place for three nights running but had never entered.

As witnesses and reports filtered in, the large table was cleared off to make way for a map of London. By half past two in the morning, the map was speckled with red marks indicating places the Lion had been seen. Although they were scattered around the city, they definitely clustered in a circle around the Dancing Fawn. Unfortunately, that zone was also densely populated, and finding anything in it would take either days or luck or both.

Lawrence and Tuesday were individually mulling over this fact when the skylight squeaked open. Three guards instantly had their pistols out and aimed at it, so that when Lucy Burns, the eldest of the Burns children, poked her head through, her eyes got huge. "I saw the light on," she explained awkwardly.

"It is all right. Come in," Tuesday assured her. Lawrence motioned for the guards to stand down and Lucy dropped to the ground. She stood shifting from one foot to the other. "Do you want to sit down, Lu?" Tuesday asked finally. "Is there something I can do for you?"

Lucy thoughtfully gnawed on the end of a braid. "Not really."

"Oh."

"How did your poem go?" Lawrence asked.

Lucy blushed and the braid fell out of her mouth. "Very well, Lord Pickering, sir, thank you."

"Is everything all right at home?" Tuesday asked.

Lucy nodded. Then in one motion crossed the studio, threw herself on Tuesday, and began to sob.

"H-h-have you ever been in love, Tuesday?"

If Tuesday had been making a list of questions she most wanted to answer at that moment in front of three armed guards and Lawrence Pickering, that one would not have made the top hundred. "Of course," she said vaguely.

"Then you understand. I am desperately worried."

"About what?"

"Not what. Him."

"Him?"

Lucy dried her eyes and looked soulfully up at the ceiling. "George."

"You love George Lyle?" Lawrence asked with unconcealed astonishment. Tuesday glared at him, but Lucy just nodded.

"Yes. He is a dear dear man. I know he is years older than I am, but I think we have twin souls and—"

"Why are you worried about him?" Tuesday asked.

"He's missing. Since yesterday."

It was true that George had not appeared for his daily proposal that morning, Tuesday reflected. "I am sure he is just out—" on a binge, she almost said, but stopped herself.

"No. I have asked everywhere and been to his rooms. No one has seen him."

"Perhaps a trip to the country," Tuesday offered, then

seemed to remember something. "I distinctly recall him saying he wanted to see his aunt in Essex. I am certain that is where he went."

Lucy brightened. "Do you really? So you think he is safe."

"Of course."

"Oh good. It is just that, with Sir Curtis being murdered and everything, I just worried. But I am sure you are right. Good night, Tuesday—" she gave her a warm hug, "—good night Lord Pickering, sir—" gave him a deep curtsey, and then exited via the window.

As soon as she was gone, Tuesday's frown returned.

"George did not really mention going to visit his aunt, did he?"

"He has no family that I know of."

"Are you worried?"

"No. Not really. I suspect George is somewhere with a new mistress."

"Not likely given how he was carrying on about you the other night, ma'am," one of the guards put in.

"What do you—"

"We've found him!" Grub announced, bursting into the room and pushing all thoughts of George Lyle from everyone's mind. "No mistake this time. We've found his lodgings."

Before anything else could be said, Lawrence shot out of Tuesday's favorite chair and stood blocking her path to the door. He gave her a serious look. "There isn't anything I could say to persuade you to stay here, is there?"

"No. Not if you are going."

"And if I weren't?"

"I would go anyway."

"Be reasonable, Lady Arlington. It is not safe."

"Why is it safe for you? Because you are a man? I might point out that he seems interested in killing only men. By that logic it would be safer for me to go alone."

Lawrence muttered something and clenched something and frowned at something and led her to his coach.

"He came back tonight." The windows were all closed so there was no reason for Mr. Carter, the jeweler, to be whispering but he felt bad, as though somehow he was conspiring against his nicest tenant, and he didn't want the lad to know about it. "I can't believe what you're saying about him. He's a lamb, I say. Never had no trouble from him at all."

"You are very fortunate," Lawrence told him. He seemed to fill the small kitchen where they were gathered, awaiting word that the men were in position outside the building. It was a four-story house, one story more than the law proscribed, and at first Mr. Carter had been unwilling to talk to them for fear they were the building inspectors. But when Grub had first pointed out that most building inspectors did not do their work at three in the morning, and then made it clear that he didn't give a damn about who built the place, just who lived there, Mr. Carter had knotted his dressing gown, unlatched his door, and let them in.

The man called the Lion, who he knew simply as Edward, had taken the rooms on the top floor a year earlier, he explained. He was a tinker, traveling around the countryside fixing people's pots and things, and wasn't home that often. But when he was there he was quiet like a mouse, kept good hours, didn't bother no one. He never had guests in, but he didn't seem really to miss them. Mr. Carter's only complaint was that he used extra candles, staying up reading, but that was hardly a problem compared with blind Mrs. Slipson always falling down the stairs or what the bloke on the second floor got up to. One time there had been four different women in there at once, each of them—

A glance at Tuesday had ended that story, although she had been the most interested auditor. "How's this going to work, then?" Mr. Carter asked nervously.

"As soon as my men have surrounded this area and escorted the other tenants out of the building we'll take Edward away with us."

There had been disagreement between Tuesday and Lawrence in the coach about whether it would be necessary to empty the building of its inhabitants. Tuesday, claiming to know the killer's mind better than anyone, said yes, that he was liable to take hostages or hurt anyone he could. Lawrence disagreed, pointing out that clearing the area would give him more time to run away.

"Very well. It can be on your conscience if he does something horrible," Tuesday acquiesced politely.

Deciding that his conscience had enough to bear at that moment already, even without knowing what lay in store, he decided to evacuate the building.

"In fact," Lawrence went on now, "If you, Mr. Carter, would not mind waiting outside, I think we can begin."

"I'm not leaving the store," Mr. Carter said with finality. "I built this with my own hands and no one is going to drive me away."

But Lawrence Pickering was not no one and his powers of persuasion—which included the offer of a ride in his coach around the city—were too much for the jeweler. Mr. Carter and all but one of his tenants were duly escorted out, Lawrence's men were silently escorted in, and the operation was underway.

Lawrence was the first up the stairs. Tuesday had agreed to let him lead, and to stay behind the first group of guards, in case shots were fired. Waiting in the unlit stairwell now she studied the shadowy silhouettes of the men in front of her. The small space vibrated with their tension, with the silent racing of nine hearts and the sweating of eighteen palms. Time seemed to have stopped as they hovered there in the dark.

Thwack-groan-bang rent the silent air, and light trickled into the corridor as the door of the Lion's apartment fell to the floor under Lawrence's kick. Heavy footsteps rang out over shouts of "don't move" and the muffled sound of shoulders hitting as the men crammed through the door, weapons ready.

The apartment was small. There was only a single room, single door, single window. On one side was a bed, the other a chair. Jugs of what looked like water were tidily lined up along a wall next to a small fireplace hung with few cooking implements, a mirror, and a basin. There was a square table next to the chair with a lit candle and a book, a manuscript it looked like, lying open on it as if someone had just been there reading it. *Had* been there. Was now gone.

Lawrence shouted something along the lines of "Damn hell damn!" but it was hard to make out the exact words because his head was out the window. The open window, through which, he surmised, the Lion, alias the Secret Admirer, alias Edward, had made his escape.

Lawrence was too angry to even spare a glance at Tuesday as he stalked out of the room, issuing commands for his men to blanket the area. He stopped the last four from leaving and instructed them to keep Tuesday there, right there, in that room, until he got back, his suspicion that she was at the very least a co-conspirator in the murder rekindled—after all, evacuating the building had been her damn idea.

The near pleasure Tuesday had felt only a half hour that the man as described and then drawn by her existed, was now completely extinguished. For a brief moment, when Mr. Carter confirmed the man was his tenant, she felt exalted, as though the voices of doubt were not her instincts but her insecurity. As though she should, she could, trust her judgement.

She had been wrong. She moved around the room, not really seeing, berating herself. Why had she even interfered? Why not let Lawrence Pickering do the sorts of dashing things he was famous for? Why—

Why didn't she see more books, another part of her mind asked. Everyone commented on how this man was always reading, but there was only the one book there. She moved over to examine it. It was in manuscript, a small neat hand. Across the top of each page was written *"The Prince by Nicholas Machiavelli,"* and the text appeared to be about how to be a good leader. It seemed an odd choice for a homicidal maniac. Even stranger was the line that had been underscored in dark red ink: "In addition to all this, at the appropriate time of year the ruler ought to keep the people occupied with spectacles and festivals."

Once again she had the sensation of being duped, of

being given not real evidence but instead pieces of a carefully constructed puzzle. Even the room she was standing in felt staged, like it was drawing in around her, trapping her. Nor did it smell very good. She was moving toward the window for some air when a door, recessed in the wall and almost completely hidden, caught her eye. Probably where all the books were. She pushed at it gently and to her surprise, it swung inward.

The guards were standing by the window, longingly observing their colleagues engaged in the exciting search for a deadly criminal, so they were surprised when they heard her muttering, "Blast blast blast blast!"

"What is it, Lady Arlington?" one of them asked as they lined up behind her around the opening of the narrow cupboard.

"Oh!" another exclaimed when he saw.

Tuesday had not found books. She had found something more like a shrine. Made of pieces of ribbon clipped from the hems of her gowns, the lace that she had thought snagged and ripped off the collar of her night shift, four locks of her hair, a garter, a key to her house, and a half-dozen sketches of people's faces she recognized as her discards. All of which only confirmed that the previous night had not been the Lion's first visit to her room.

You are mine, Tuesday. Mine.

Tuesday did not think that there could be anything worse than seeing such bald evidence of the fact that someone had been observing her, following her, *touching* her for months, evidence that her suspicions had been right, that she had been stalked by a murderous lunatic who was killing men to—to what? To get her attention? To get *her*?

Then she saw the neat pile of items stacked off to one side of the cupboard and knew she was mistaken. There was something worse. The stack contained:

One brown wig

One metal tub hand-labeled "Noodle's Theatrical Wax: for noses, chins, ears, and scars"

One pair of shoes, specially made so one was wider and higher than the other, causing its wearer to limp

One left-handed glove with blood on it

Which, added together, made one disguise. Meaning that the man who had been watching her, touching her, observing her could be anyone. And that Lawrence and his crew did not stand a chance of finding the killer they were looking for.

He had tricked them all. She was so furious that she could barely breathe and she felt like her blood really was boiling. Now she understood the meaning of the underlined passage, "keep the people occupied with spectacles and festivals." He had kept them occupied. He had been fooling with them—God she was hot—and she had fallen for it—she could use a glass of water—and now they were looking all over London for a man—maybe from one of the pitchers—a man who did not—what was that smell?—even exist, a man who, who—oh my God, the—

Half a mile away, Lawrence heard the explosion. For a second he was struck by the eerie beauty of the orange flash against the predawn blue of the sky. Then he realized where it was and what it was, and he ran like hell.

—a man who had booby-trapped the entire building

so it exploded into an infernal spectacle that lit up the night sky around London and kept Lawrence's men occupied digging through the wreckage for survivors for hours afterward.

They did not find any.

Chapter 23

Lawrence stood over the line of bodies but did not really see them. He wanted to clench his hands, but they seemed to be locked in place. Later he would learn that it was because they had been seared by the heat and were badly burned. Even then he didn't care.

He had charged into the mass of rubble before the flames were out. It was he who recovered blind Mrs. Slipson's precious silver-plated goblet from King Edward's coronation celebration. He who brought out the strange globs of gold and gems that had once been the prized merchandise in Mr. Carter's shop. He who dug through the scalding bricks, heedless of the blisters on his hands and arms or the fact that his pants were smoldering. It was he who uncovered the bodies of all four of his men. He worked harder than all the others put together, and they all knew why.

It was he, Lawrence Pickering himself, wiping the soot out of his eyes and leaving clean streaks on his otherwise blackened face, that finally had to admit they weren't going to find Lady Tuesday Arlington's body.

There were only two conclusions he could draw and he forced himself to draw them. Either she had been closer to the source of the explosion than his guards and been entirely burned. Or she had not been in the building. Which meant that she was somehow working with whomever had done this and had managed to escape.

He fairly well hated both options. Because as he had combed through the debris like a madman, clawing away bricks and tables and charred pieces of other people's lives, he had realized that he wanted to see Lady Tuesday Arlington again. Wanted it so bad that it made him ache inside.

If she really were responsible for exploding the building, my friend, would she have told you to evacuate everyone?

Maybe she only wanted to get away with her husband's murder and could not bring herself to kill innocent people.

Then why hadn't she gotten rid of the guards. Surely they were innocent, too. And—

Shut up, Lawrence said to the speaker in his head. He was tired of having him there, tired of hearing Rafael's subtly accented voice like some Spanish conscience whenever he had a single negative thought about Tuesday. About Lady Arlington.

Besides, if he agreed with what the voice in his head was telling him, that she was not responsible, then she was dead.

He was not ready to believe that yet. Not until he saw some trace, until some small piece of her surfaced. Lawrence found himself hoping that she was a murderer and hardened criminal and had escaped, rather than that she was gone. Only because he did not want responsibility for her death. Only because he wanted to yell at her for staying in the building, for making him bring her with him. Not because she had been more full of life, stronger and more courageous and more exciting than anyone else he'd ever met. Not because he needed to see her smile at him again the way she had when he'd kissed her in his coach.

Let her be alive.

Shouts, arms waving, jolted Lawrence from his thoughts. Tom was barely visible through the smoke, but his voice carried. It would have reached Lawrence across two continents, because what he said was: "I've found her!"

Lawrence took the shortest route to his man, crashing straight through the still hot ashes of the building, sending a stream of red sparks up in his wake.

Grub stepped in front of him when he was only six feet from Tom. He put a hand on Lawrence's chest. "I don't think you should, sir."

"Get out—"

But Grub did not budge. "I mean it. There's no reason you need to see. She's gone, sir."

Lawrence did not say anything, just stepped around the other man.

She was lying in a field across the street from the former building. It looked like she had been thrown from it with the force of the explosion, then buried under the chimney. She lay in a ditch, the chimney lay across her body and her body on top of her arm, which, judging from its strange angle was probably broken. But that hardly mattered since there was blood caked around a huge gash to her head and since, as far as Lawrence could make out, she was not breathing.

She had been blameless. Not a murderer, or a murderer's accomplice. Somehow he had known that all along. And still he had gotten her killed.

She was not going to smile again.

He bent over and lifted the chimney off of her, an act three of his men could not have performed together, but which he managed and made look easy. Then he stooped and gathered her to his chest and walked by the cordon of his men, all silent now, to his coach.

No one knew what happened in that ride back to Worthington Hall, but reports said that Lawrence's face was pretty streaky when he got there.

PART III

Love

Chapter 24

Lawrence's first act upon getting back to Worthington Hall was to summon Ian's wife, Bianca, the famous doctor, and make her do things to Tuesday. From her he learned that he had been right about Tuesday's arm being broken but wrong about something else. She was still breathing. Barely. And, Bianca explained, she had lost quite a lot of vital fluids from the gash on her head.

"Is she going to live?" Lawrence demanded. "I mean, past today?"

Bianca guided him away from the bandaged, still figure lying on the bed. "Let me look at your burns, Lawrence."

"Bianca, tell me."

Bianca faced him. "She may regain consciousness for a brief time, but I would say that the chances of her coming back permanently are remote."

Remote was a word Lawrence understood well. It was what he became as soon as she had spoken. He did not notice as she rolled up his sleeves and applied a special ointment and bandages, did not flinch even when she advised him that the preparation she was putting on his calf was going to sting, did not respond when she noted that from what she had seen of Lady Tuesday Arlington the night before she was a strong woman and had as good a chance as anyone of surviving, did not say anything as she left. He just sat in Tuesday's gray chair, her favorite chair, pulled up to her bed and was remote.

After many hours, when daylight had returned, he started talking to her.

"You know, I really enjoyed fighting with you," he said, then felt stupid. Why would she care about that?

He lapsed into silence again for an hour, then startled himself by saying, "You can't die, Tuesday. It is all wrong. Because—"

And suddenly he was telling her a story. He hadn't thought about the incident since it happened, but for some reason he had to share it now. He knew he was practically babbling nonsense but it didn't matter.

"There was a man, one of the sailors, on the first ship I commanded in Spain. His name was Orlando, a name from out of one of those old romances, and it suited him. He was a quiet, nice, charming man. And he was an artist in the galley. I have heard people say that men signed on to the *HMS Phoenix* because they wanted to sail with me, but I actually think it was word of Orlando's cooking that spread." Why was he telling her this? And why was it so hard? It was not as though she was listening.

"We were only three days out from our last reprovisioning when we encountered a Spanish galleon. We engaged and eventually blasted them out of the water. But they managed to get one shot off at us, at our kitchen, and Orlando was hurt." Actually, it had blown the entire bottom half of his body away, but Lawrence was not going to tell her that, even if she couldn't hear. "It was pretty clear that he was not going to make it. I was passing through my cabin, which was being used as the surgery, when he reached out and took my hand. He said he wanted to say something to me, wanted it to be a warning to others. And he told me a story. About how he had been in love with a woman back in England, deeply and completely in love, but too shy to ever tell her so. He always thought that if he did something, made himself worthy, then he could propose to her, which was why he had signed on to serve with me. But instead, he was dying, dying loving her, dying without ever telling her his feelings. He wanted me to make sure all the men on the ship knew his story so they would not be too shy with the women they loved." Lawrence snorted. "With that group, shyness around women was not the problem."

Then he grew serious again. He raked a hand through his hair. "Everyone laughed when they heard. But as I listened to him all I could think of was how lucky Orlando was. Because he had never looked into the eyes of the woman he loved and seen disappointment or hate or contempt." Never had to hear her call him a monster and a lowlife. Never had to watch her disappear from the coach yard and leave you sitting there, trying to believe her promises that she would return for you and your brother in just a few hours even when you knew they were lies. Never had to face that same woman years later when you were rich and she was poor and tell her you forgave her and put her up in a house in the country on the condition that she never bother your brother because he believed she was dead, it was just easier that way, dammit, and none of her goddamned business.

He put his elbows on his knees and his chin in his hands and gazed at Tuesday's unmoving figure. "I was a fool, Tuesday. I should have listened to Orlando. I should have told you I was falling in love with you."

Lawrence did not know what he had expected, but the fact that she did not stir made his insides clench tight. He moved closer to the bed and took her unbandaged hand in his. God it was cold. She was so cold.

I just want to be numb, he could hear her saying.

No you don't.

Why, isn't it working out for you?

"No," he answered aloud. "It isn't. It wasn't. But if you die, I am going to be numb. Forever. And it will be your fault."

He must have lost his mind. He never spoke like this with anyone, and he certainly did not hurl idle threats at all-but-dead women. "If you die, Tuesday, I am going to hole up in a cave and never come out. Except to get dressed up in the way you don't like. Puffed up for a royal visit, I think you said. Every day. In my cave."

Nothing.

"And I'm going to breathe loudly. And toss coins in the air constantly." He stopped.

He hung his head over their joined hands and whispered, "Tuesday, I can't believe I let this happen to you."

He was about to pull his hand away when he felt it. A squeeze, a slight pressure. Maybe.

"Tuesday can you hear me?"

Nothing.

"Tuesday?"

Nothing again.

But he had felt it. He *had*. He needed something that would illicit a strong reaction from her. Something that would pull her back to the surface. His ran his mind backward over everything that had happened in the time they had spent together. The ball, giving her the neck-lace, their conversation in the nursery (God there was so much he wanted to share with her), playing cards, her forcing him to strip at the end of a fake rapier and get into the bath (he smiled despite himself), that kiss in the coach, the scene at Miles's (she had been in control the whole time, he now understood), meeting Jack, standing outside her window as she painted, listening as she de-scribed the murderer from four pieces of evidence he had barely noticed, coming into her studio for the first time and being utterly and completely overwhel—that was it.

He leaned close to her ear and whispered, "Uncivilized."

Nothing still.

"The first time I saw you, Lady Tuesday Arlington, I thought you were the most uncivilized-looking woman in the world."

If that did not agitate her, nothing would.

It didn't. She did not move. She did not respond. Her pulse did not even change.

Lawrence dropped her hand, no pressure restraining him this time, and moved away from the bed. He leaned his forehead against the wall and made his face very hard and rubbed his aching right shoulder with his hand. He had let her die, he had as good as killed her, he was a killer, like that other time, just like in Spain with—

He was a fool and an idiot and he did not deserve her anyway, he told himself. Which was good, because she was not coming back.

"What does it mean?" a hoarse whisper asked from the bed.

Lawrence turned around and stared. His heart stopped.

"You can't just revive me from death with riddles and not tell me the answer." Her eyes were open and she was looking at him. She had bandages around her head and across one arm and bags under her eyes and her lips were chapped and she was the most exquisite being he had ever seen.

She tried to reach out to him with her bandaged arm and winced. "Tell me. What it means. To look uncivilized."

The chances of her coming back permanently are remote, Lawrence heard Bianca warning. He stood beside her and took her hand and let the words fall out. "It means that you are the kind of woman men duel to do a favor for. The kind of woman over whom wars are fought. The kind of woman who makes words like 'reputation' and 'duty' sound pretentious and empty, but who gives 'honor' new luster. The kind of woman who is completely incompatible with the dictates of polite society."

Her forehead creased. "Is that good?"

"It depends on how you feel about polite society."

A pause. "How do you feel, Lord Pickering?"

"I've spent my life working to get it to accept me."

"Oh." Her eyes moved away from his.

"Only to discover that I am allergic to it."

"Allergic?"

"Yes. I knew a man once whose tongue lost feeling any time he ate anise seeds because he was allergic to them. Polite society seems to have the same effect on me. I just did not realize it until I met you."

Lawrence never knew how he ended up, boots off, carefully stretched out on the bed next to her. They faced each other on her pillow, their clasped hands between them. Gently, he placed a kiss on her forehead and wrapped an arm around her. Her eyes closed and her

cheek rested against his shoulder, and he felt extraordi-
narily marvelous.

"Tuesday?" he whispered a moment later, but she did
not answer.

For a long time they lay there like that, Lawrence
afraid that if he moved, if he shifted at all, she would go
away forever. The burns on his arms and legs ached but
he did not notice. He was aware only of her too shallow
breathing and the too cold length of her body next to his.

What if this were all? What if she were gone now?
What if she had slipped not into sleep but unconsciousness again? There were so many things he needed to say
to her. To show her. He still hadn't given her a proper
kiss. Or found out what her favorite food was. Or seen
her in a silver gown. Or a lavender one. Or in nothing.
He still hadn't shared with her his plans for Jack. He still
hadn't spent an entire night with his face nuzzled in her
hair and her legs tangled with his and his arms wrapped
around her. He wanted to tell her everything, about
growing up, about how proud he was of some of the
things he had done, about what had happened in Spain,
about Rafael and—at least about some of it.

It had been a long time since Lawrence had prayed,
but he prayed that night to anyone who would listen.

He must have dozed off because when he opened his
eyes evening light was filtering through the windows. It
took him a moment to remember why he had a knot in
his stomach, but then he felt Tuesday's limp body on his
arm, in the exact position she had been in before, and it
flooded back.

He was half-afraid to look at her. He finally forced
himself. Slowly, he tilted his chin down and out of the
corner of his eye saw her smiling up at him.

"I didn't want to move because I was afraid I would wake you," she purred. She did not say that having him in her bed was like having a dream come true and she did not want it to end.

"You are alive."

The way he said it made it sound like he was accusing her of a crime. "I'm sorry. Would you rather that I—"

His lips came down on hers, and her heart stood still and he kissed her the way he should have kissed her a dozen times before. His mouth tasted sooty and delicious to her, his tongue skimming the edges of her lips was a firebrand stirring sparks throughout her body. The aches in her legs, the sharp pains in her arm and head and shoulder and back all vanished in the heat he ignited inside her.

Lawrence did not want to hurt her, knew he should move slowly or not at all, knew she had been badly bruised, but when she brought her good arm up and twisted her fingers in his hair and urged his lips against hers harder, he could not stop himself. His bandaged hand slid down her body and cupped her bottom, pulling her on top of him. She arched her hips into him and her neck went back and he lost himself in the magic of its silky smoothness.

Through her nightshift the hard points of her nipples rubbed against his chest, making them both moan. Everything they had almost lost became kindling in the heat of their desire. With one arm she ripped his linen shirt from him, and with his bandaged fingers he took a ridiculous amount of time unknotting the stays of her night shift. They laughed at their ineptitude and held each other and helped each other and each delay only made their hunger that much more intense. When they later made a hasty attempt to gather up their clothes, Tuesday's nightgown appeared to have been sliced down the middle, Lawrence's boots were lodged in the next-door neighbor's yard, and his breeches were at the other end of the studio with tooth marks on them.

The planes of his naked, warm, hard body pressed against her was the most extraordinary feeling. She smoothed her good hand down his rippling back, along the curves of his chest, across his stomach, her eyes following her fingers, marveling at his beauty.

Lawrence made a small noise in his throat as her fingers stroked the side of his bottom, and she turned back to look at him. Her eyes were alight with pleasure and expectation and invitation.

He ran a finger down her cheek and said, "The other night I dreamed about making love to you."

Something flickered behind her gaze. Recognition? "Was it like this?"

"The first part," he said huskily, and pulled her toward him. "Would you like to know what happened after this?"

"Yes," she said, because it was the right answer.

She knew what making love was like. And if she had endured it for Curtis she could certainly do it for Lawrence. She braced herself for what came next, closing her eyes and concentrated on relaxing.

Nothing happened.

Had she failed already? She opened her eyes. Lawrence was staring down at her. She expected him to look angry or upset. He was smiling a little. He looked amused.

"We don't have to do this," he said.

"No, let's." She reached up to touch his chest.

He caught her hand. "Why?"

"Because I want to."

"No you don't."

"But you do."

For some reason this caused him to laugh. "You have never done anything in the past just because I want to." He studied her. "I think we should put this off for another day."

"No, let's get it over with now." The words were out before she knew it. This would have been a good time for Lawrence to laugh, she felt, but he just looked at her seriously.

"Tuesday, making love is not supposed to be something you want to get over with."

She tried a smile. "I was jesting."

The way her smile wavered, the way her voice got tight, the way she had stiffened and shut her eyes tight as if expecting to be punished made Lawrence furious at Curtis, and more in love with her. "Come here." He gathered her to his chest and held her and kissed her gently. "You feel wonderful in my arms."

He held her like that for an hour, rubbing her back, reveling in her smell, ignoring the pounding insistence of his arousal.

"Lawrence," she whispered when he thought she was asleep. "Please make love to me."

He looked down at her. She was incomparable. She did not look scared anymore, but he did not want to do anything wrong.

"Please."

His hand moved down her back. "Maybe. I want to show you something first," he whispered.

"What?"

He arranged three pillows against the wall, lowered

her gingerly onto them so that she was half sitting up, and propped himself on his elbow next to her. For a moment he just looked at her, speechless. "You are magnificent," he murmured, running a fingertip between her breasts. She wriggled, astonished by the sensations fluttering through her body and Lawrence seized the moment to tip his head down and kiss the freckle he had just spotted underneath her right breast. His hair tickled over her nipple and her wriggling turned to a long sigh.

"What are you showing me?" she asked, the words coming slowly like individual breaths.

"You'll see."

Lawrence's hand rubbed the sides of her breasts, then slid along the curve of her waist, resting on her hip, the fingers splayed so that his thumb touched the rectangle of dark brown curls between her legs. His touch, which seemed to have a medicinal effect on every other part of her body, worked precisely the opposite magic there. Instead of being soothed, the place between her legs was aching and throbbing in a way that was exquisite and painful at once. And utterly unfamiliar.

"What are you doing to me?" she slurred now, the words and breath no longer slow.

"A medicinal procedure."

"How?"

Lawrence appeared to think about the best way to explain for a moment as he watched her stomach rise and fall. "First, I am going to rest the palm of my hand here." He moved so it was nestled in the soft curls and she made a tiny noise. "Then I am going to let my index finger slip down and stroke you gently like this." His finger found a place on her body that Tuesday had never visited before. When she made no noise, he added, "Unless you object?"

She was not going to object. She was going to beg him to keep touching her there, like that, forever. As soon as she could speak again. She had been married for two years but no one had ever made her feel the way she was feeling now; she did not know it was possible to feel that way. She was beyond objecting, beyond noises, beyond moaning or sighing or breathing.

Lawrence used his other hand to part the curls and between them she could see his finger skating in devilish circles over her newly awakened body. With each caress he added another finger, and with each caress the sensation built, until Tuesday was dizzy with pleasure and alarm and wonder. He suckled on her caramel colored nipples, he planted feathery kisses along the S of her waist, and let his tongue dip into the pool of her navel, his fingers never relieving her ache, but increasing it, making it build and spread steadily, until her entire body felt like it was filled with molten gold.

Lawrence rested his chin against her hip and breathed in the potent scent of her arousal. Her hand strayed softly through his hair and he glanced up and saw her looking at him. He had planned to do this in stages, to teach her about lovemaking slowly, bring her to her first climax over hours, but suddenly he could not wait to see the expression in her eyes. Holding her gaze, he shifted so he was lying between her legs, reached out his tongue, and wrapped it around the sensitive bundle of nerves there.

"Oh*hhhhhhhhhhhhhhhhhhhhhhhhhhh*," Tuesday half moaned, half shouted, as if she had just made a marvelous discovery. She wanted to observe everything, remember everything, but she could not think. Her brain, her body, had been replaced by tingling fibers, all of them wrapping themselves tighter and tighter into knots, each time past the point of bearability, each time stretching that point a little more, until suddenly, as she watched, Lawrence's beautiful lips closed over her glistening pink bud. She felt him suck it deeply into his mouth, felt his tongue and teeth flickering around it, felt him swallow and tug at it harder, and felt the world fly out beneath her.

She pressed herself into his mouth as wantonly and insistently and brazenly and unwittingly as she could and called his name and the name of every deity she knew and prayed that she was dying because nothing would ever feel that good again. A pounding wave of pleasure rushed through her body and seemed trapped there, reverberating through every limb and sinew, sending fresh eddies down her legs and across her breasts, until she trembled and begged Lawrence never to stop and dragged his face up her body to hers.

"I thought you said not to stop," he started to ask but couldn't finish because she was kissing him, licking her flavor from his chin and lips, teasing his tongue with her own, repeating "thank you thank you" over and over again into his hungry mouth.

When she had almost stopped trembling, she moved her lips from his and just looked at him.

"I would describe that as extremely medicinal," she said, her voice the lowest purr he had heard yet. It sent ripples through his body.

"Yes. Well you have a lot of injuries."

"So do you. I want you to teach me how to be medicinal back."

"You seemed to master that pretty well."

"Make love to me, Lawrence."

"I just did, sweetheart."

Hearing him say sweetheart made her heart stop then start again. "No, I mean—I mean the other way."

"The 'Let's get it over with' way?"

She nodded.

"Why? There are so many other things we can do."

She looked right at him and said, "I want to know what it feels like to have you inside of me. I want to be that close to you."

It took him a moment to find his tongue. "I don't want to hurt you."

"I don't care. I'm not a virgin. And I just learned that I am not frigid. I feel like I have missed out on so much and I want to experience it all right now."

"There is plenty of time."

"Bianca said I might die."

"You heard that?"

"Please. Let me hold you inside of me." As she spoke, her hand slipped down and rested on Lawrence's shaft. It was rock hard and feverish and it jumped when her hand closed around it.

"You can't do that," Lawrence eked out. "Not if you are serious."

"About what?" Tuesday asked, moving her palm from the tip to the base.

Lawrence's hand wrapped around hers, stopping her. "Tuesday, you don't seem to have any notion of the effect you have on me, but if you—stop squeezing!—don't move your hand at once, there will be no lovemaking."

"Is it going to break?"

"Tue*aaaahhhhh*!" She did not move her hand. She

moved her entire body. So that she was lying on top of him with her wet curls trailing over his aching member. She glided up, down, and up again along his length, then arched her back and in a single graceful motion slid him inside of her.

This was nothing like the raw, painful scraping of having Curtis inside of her. This was smooth and silky and completely magical. She sat atop Lawrence, savoring the feeling of his body in hers, reveling in the expression on his face, the one he wore when something she said made him summon up all his self-control. It was her favorite expression.

"Don't move," he ordered through clenched teeth, and for once she would have been happy to obey him.

Except she couldn't. Because she accidentally discovered that the feeling of having him inside of her became so much more intense when she moved just slightly up or down, that she could not stop herself.

"Tuesday," Lawrence moaned as she slid her body up his organ. He clutched at her bottom, pulling her toward his chest and held her very still. "You are cruel," he panted, the strain of the discipline he was exerting visible in every feature of his face. "You make me feel weak."

Knowing that Lawrence Pickering, the war hero, the demigod, felt weak with her, could feel weak for her, overwhelmed her. She realized that the reason she could be angry in front of him was not because she did not care what he thought, but because she trusted him, trusted him entirely and implicitly. With him she felt powerful and sensual and whole. She wanted him to trust her completely, to give himself to her with nothing held back. She needed him to lose himself inside her. She evaded his grasp, shifted her legs, and took him into her as deeply as he could go.

All the strength that Lawrence had been pouring into restraining himself, all the longing that he had denied and pushed away over two years, over thirty-two years, now flooded out as he buried himself within this most extraordinary woman. He saw lights dance in front of his eyes and felt his toes wriggle and heard someone that sounded like him laughing uproariously, and he smiled in a way he had forgotten and he knew he had never been more alive in his entire life. Then he felt himself explode into her, felt her climax around him, heard her saying his name over and over and saw what was written in her eyes and knew he had been wrong.

He had lost control and shown her what he'd never shown anyone before, the real man beneath the careful surface, and she had not run away or flinched or called him a monster. She had looked into him and said, "I love you Lawrence."

It was the best moment of his life.

It was the worst mistake of hers.

Chapter 25

"When I get my hands on you, Tuesday, you are going to be sorry!"

Tuesday woke up sharply, confused. It was evening (Still? Again?) and she did not think she had been dreaming, but she had heard someone hollering at her an—

"Dammit, girl, where the devil are you!"

"Father," she breathed, trying to slow down her racing heart. It must have been days since she'd seen him. No wonder he was yelling for her.

She rolled toward the side of the bed, and practically fainted from the pain. She had forgotten her broken arm. Carefully, she curled onto her back and started shimmying to the edge of the mattress. Halfway there she realized she was naked and remembered everything that had happened and blushed a deep red.

That was when Lawrence strolled into the room. He saw her, naked except for her sling, caught in a tangle of sheets, and smiled hugely.

"Good afternoon, sweetheart," he said, moving to her and kissing her on the lips.

"Good afternoon, Lawrence." This was not really

happening. He was not really sitting with her, calling her sweetheart and looking like he loved her and knew she loved him back. Her life was not like this. Her heart was not slowing down.

"What are you doing up?"

"I thought I heard my father calling me."

Lawrence shrugged. "He was but I explained to him you weren't available."

"Explained? How?"

"I said that I wanted you all to myself and you would no longer have time to see to his needs."

"Ah. How did he take that?"

"Very well. Understood perfectly." He had, too, after a bit of negotiation. "You have had about a hundred visitors," he went on, changing the subject. He pulled a list from his doublet and read from it. "Tristan and Sebastian have been most insistent. They each sent a dozen proposals in the event that you recover and I think Tristan might have said he would marry you even if you didn't. Then there were Sophie and Bianca. And what appears to have been everyone in the neighborhood, the lords and ladies as well as the cooks and coal maids. And all three of the Burns children. Oh, they wanted to send something called Captain Gumpkins—they felt it would really help your recovery—but it appears to be missing."

"Not it. He. Their dancing dog."

"Right. I can see where that would help. Also, of course, CeCe, who now regards me as no better than a robber for almost getting you killed. I think she'd be happy to see me hang on the gallows."

Tuesday chuckled. "Anything else?"

"George Lyle came over. He said he had to speak to you urgently."

"I'm glad he is back. Did you tell him about Lucy Burns?"

"I did not think it was my place." Also, Lawrence had not wanted to be bitten, which was what it looked like George Lyle would have enjoyed doing to him if they had stood close enough together for another moment.

"How do you feel?" he asked after studying her.

"Like a house fell on me."

"You've really got to stop exaggerating. It was just the chimney."

There was a long pause. "Lawrence, I am so sorry."

"Why are you sorry?"

"It was my fault we were there in the first place. My fault we followed all that fake evidence."

"What do you mean?"

"It was a disguise. The brown hair and the limp. A costume. I saw it in his chamber."

"You told me that earlier. And I told you that does not make it your fault."

"Yes it does. And that your men died. And you got hurt. Not to mention that he got away."

"No, if I had evacuated the building like you suggested, no one would have gotten hurt. It is my fault."

"Mine."

"That is completely absur—"

"I like fighting with you, too, Lawrence," she interrupted, smiling. She reached her free hand up and touched his face. "Are there any new traces of the Lion?"

Lawrence shook his head. "And it seems that we've got competition, at least for the Special Commissioner's forces."

"What do you mean?"

"Did you ever hear about the Vampire of London?"

"Of course. He killed all those girls several years ago. But didn't your friend Miles catch him?"

"Everyone thought so, but a new victim was discovered on Friday. It was in all the news sheets this morning but we slept through them."

"Two killers loose in London! I wish we were still sleeping."

"We could be. As a matter of fact," Lawrence leaned over and kissed her lightly, "you are already dressed for it."

The fingers of her good hand had only just slid past the fabric of his shirt to where his heart had already quickened when someone pounded on the door three times, then shouted, "Tuesday, open this door. I know you are awake. I heard you."

"George," she sighed.

"Ignore him. I locked the door."

"It won't matter. I gave him a key."

"I don't mean to be critical, but that was a very silly thing to do."

The sound of a lock coming unlocked echoed through the room and was followed by the quick, agitated tapping of George's walking stick. Tuesday managed to pull the covers up to her chin and Lawrence to assume a respectable distance in the chair beside the bed before George spotted them.

He rushed to her side. "Tuesday, princess of my heart, are you all right?"

"Yes, George. A little bruised but fine."

"I've been trying to get in here since early this afternoon but someone—" the eyes that slid to Lawrence were George's only recognition of the other man's presence, "—told the guards I was a suspect and not to be let in."

"We have to be careful."

George ignored him. "I have to talk to you, Tuesday. It's extremely important. *Alone.*"

Lawrence's "Out of the question," and Tuesday's "Of course," collided in midair.

George smirked at Lawrence. "Good night Lord Pickering. She'll call you when she wants to see you again. But I would not recommend that you wait around."

Lawrence was caught between wanting to laugh and wanting to sock the putative artist. He opted for just leaving the room.

Christopher was waiting for him outside. "All done, sir."

"Good," Lawrence confirmed moodily. "Christopher, I need you to look into something for me." The old man cocked his head and waited. "I want everything you can find on George Lyle. Everything. As soon as possible."

Inside the studio, the object of Lawrence's curiosity was shaking his head. George had not at all liked the way Tuesday's gaze followed Lawrence's departure. He cleared his throat. "Tuesday, I have something serious to say to you."

Her eyes came back to him. Such lovely eyes. She was so beautiful.

"What?" she repeated when he did not answer her immediately.

"Are you really all right?" he asked solicitously.

"Yes. I'm fine. What serious thing do you need to say?"

George took a deep breath. "You know that I have long loved you—"

"Please George, not today," Tuesday interrupted. "No proposals today."

George was willing to wager that she would not have acted the same way if His Lordship had been proposing, but he knew that was about to change. "Run away with me, Tuesday."

"George—"

"It's him, isn't it?" George demanded, leveling a deadly look at the door through which Lawrence had passed.

"George, you've asked me a hundred times to run away with you and I never agree—even before I met Lawrence Pickering. Even when I hadn't just been buried under a house."

"If you run away with me you won't get hurt."

"I don't think I have any places left to hurt."

"He's not what he seems," George said intensely.

"What do you mean?"

"He's untrustworthy. He is a lying, philandering, cheating, low-life thief. And a murderer."

"You are starting to sound like CeCe, George."

"Lawrence Pickering is more dangerous than most."

"Really?"

"Yes. And—" he paused. "I didn't want to tell you this but I think I must. He has a mistress."

"A mistress? Are you sure you don't mean a harem?"

It was clear to George that she was not taking him seriously. He wanted to grab her by her perfect shoulders and shake her. Make her see that he was the man for her. The only one. "He definitely has at least one mistress. One serious one. And there may be others."

"Have you seen her? Any of them?"

"Not yet," George hissed. "But I will. I'm looking."

"Keep me informed."

"If you don't believe me, you can ask him."

"I will."

"Promise? Promise you will ask him?"

"I promise, George."

"If he denies any of it, he's a liar."

"Thank you very much for your concern."

"You will thank me, Tuesday. Wait and see. You'll get down on your knees and thank me." *Soon you'll understand everything I've been doing for you. Soon you'll understand that you were meant for me.*

The Lion dragged that morning's news sheet out of his doublet and looked it over again. He was not reading it anymore, he had already memorized its contents. Now he was counting. Counting how many precious Words the damn Vampire of London had stolen from him.

He had killed six men—men!—four at one time in one genius explosion, and all he got was the bottom piece of the second column. Whereas the vampire had done one stupid girl and gotten a full column and two-thirds. And two woodcut portraits, one of the dead girl and one of the living one who had found the body.

If only he had not decided at the last minute to spare Lord Pickering, then he would have owned the damn news sheet, the Lion told himself. But he had realized that blowing him up was too easy a victory. They had to meet face to face on the field of battle. Only then would the Lion's greatness really be seen.

Why don't we kill our enemy when we have him in our power?

Because defeating him twice brings twice the glory.

Across the street, the hangings on his Lady's Windows were drawn and he knew she was punishing him for not taking her right away. At first it made him mad. How could she not understand how much better it was this way? How much more glory he would earn saving her from deep inside the other knight's Walled fortress? How much more Worthy he would be of her heart?

But she was just a Woman, he reminded himself. The women in the stories always made mistakes like that. They didn't understand how it was with knights. Soon she would gaze out at him again, the way she always did, as if she were just looking at the street but really looking for him. And he would give her a sign and show her that he forgave her for doubting him.

His eyes moved back to the news sheet. Girls, he thought with disgust. Dammit, if they wanted girls, he could kill girls. Hundreds of them. Even though the thought did nothing for him, it would be worth it for the fame.

What the Vampire really had in his favor, the Lion realized, was a sort of signature. That killing he had done in the crowd outside Dearbourn Hall and the one in the alleyway, there was no way for anyone to tie those to him—any more than they could know he did the dog, which was lying under the heap of rubbish behind him. Whereas the Vampire's two tooth marks neatly and instantaneously proclaimed a killing as his.

The Lion wished he'd come up with that. He almost always blindfolded his victims—he hated to see the dragon eyes—but lots of times the blindfolds got lost and it was only recently he'd taken to cutting out their hearts. That was a good marker, he decided. It made people

think a bit. And it showed off his skills, his profession-
alism, not like sucking blood out of someone's neck. Any
fool could do that.

He had been so immersed in thought that he hadn't
heard the noise in the alleyway behind him, but even
caught unawares, only the lightening fast reflexes of a
fourteen-year-old girl saved Lucy Burns from having her
wrist severed by his knife. Before she could shriek, his
hand was over her mouth, pulling her head back, watching her girl eyes fill with terror.

Girl eyes. Like the answer to a prayer.

From the way this girl and the other children had been
carrying on about their missing dog, he assumed the one
molting behind him was hers, and it came to him, how
perfect it would be to slice her up right there and leave
her with her pet. That would be something for the news
sheets. And then he would send the girl's heart to his
Lady, so she would know he had forgiven him.

"What are you doing here?" he demanded of the girl,
staring at her eyes. He saw fear and—something he
didn't understand.

She mumbled in response but his hand was in the way.

What was that expression in her eyes? "If I let you
talk, you won't scream will you?"

She shook her head and he unclapped her lips.
"Well?"

"You are one of Lawrence Pickering's men, aren't
you?" she asked almost awestruck, between heaving
breathes. "Working in secret? Undercover?"

The Lion nodded and motioned for her to continue.

She tried a timid smile. "I knew because I've seen you
out here before. And because of how you reacted just

now. That was amazing." The Lion realized what he was
seeing. It was Worship. She *liked* him. "Did you learn
that from Lord Pickering?"

The Lion wanted to snort. *The true Knight wins
through craft not candor,* he reminded himself sternly.
He said, "Yes."

"Could—" she began, then stopped, blushing.

"Yes?" When she blushed her neck turned pink. It was
a good neck. He began to imagine what his knife would
feel like sinking into her young flesh.

I told you not to touch the girls.

I didn't. She came over to—

Shut up. You know what your punishment is. Now go.

But I didn't—

Get out of my sight wicked boy!

The Lion flinched, then straightened. He would kill
this girl. Just to show he could.

Wondering what he was going to use as a blindfold, he
took a step closer to her. He was watching the girl's neck,
watching its blush deepen as her blood rose to the surface, so he didn't notice that the girl's eyes had moved beyond him.

He had his knife halfway out of his wrist sheath when
she spoke.

"I have to go," she said, gazing behind him and
blushing more. "Excuse me." And in a flash, she was
leaving. She sidled by him, not trying to escape, not even
seeing his knife, just moving on with the lithe agility of a
young girl. When she got to the mouth of the alley, she
turned around and faced him. "It was a pleasure to meet
you, sir." She paused. "My name is Lucy Burns. What is
yours?"

"Grub," the Lion said, not knowing why. "Grub Collins."

"Good-bye, Mr. Collins. I hope to see you again."

The Lion told himself he was glad that she'd gone. Told himself that girls were beneath him. He did not touch girls.

But there was no denying he was in the mood to kill. And it was only Saturday. Which meant there were probably three days left until the next killing. He didn't know if he was going to be able to stand it.

He was so hungry for it. So ready. He knew exactly who it was going to be. He had the tools sharp and perfect.

Patience is the Knight's best friend.

I don't want to be goddamned patient. I want Lawrence Pickering to die.

Lawrence looked up at the man in front of him as if seeing him for the first time that night. "Grub, you look like you are falling asleep on your feet. Go home."

"I don't want to. I want to be here in case anything happens. Anything needs doing."

Almost all of Lawrence's men were smitten with Tuesday and upset by her accident, but none more than Grub. He had been hovering around Worthington Hall and her bedchamber since that morning, begging to be put to use in finding "that weasel who did that to Her Ladyship."

Lawrence appreciated the offer of help but since he felt largely responsible for Tuesday's injuries, not to mention for Tuesday, he kept refusing.

"His Lordship is right," Tuesday said, moving stiffly into the room. "You ought to sleep a little."

What Lawrence had not been able to effect for twenty hours, Tuesday did with six words. Grub was bowing out the door and promising to take a nap on one of the mattresses that had been laid out in the gallery "just for an instant and just so long as you promise to wake me soon as there's cause," before the hand on the clock moved at all.

"How is CeCe doing?" Lawrence asked, pulling Tuesday onto his lap.

"Quite well, actually. I think I've almost managed to convince her that if it weren't for you, I would never have been found. She might even consent to speak to you again in about a week or so."

"What a relief."

"Mmmm." Tuesday was working hard not to think about what George had told her. Even CeCe, who was not exactly favorably disposed toward Lawrence, had agreed with Tuesday that George was just jealous and had made up the whole story about the mistress to upset her. Asking Lawrence about it would only mean succumbing to George's paranoia, which Tuesday decided she was *not* going to do. Instead, she reached across and pulled the volume he'd been looking at toward her. It was a version of the book she had seen at the Lion's apartment, the one by Nicholas Machiavelli. "Where did you get this?"

"After you told me you'd seen it at the Lion's house, I had Jack look for a copy in my library."

The mention of her brother reminded her of the extent of Lawrence's generosity. "There is a lot I don't know about you, Lord Pickering," she said. Like whether you have a mistress. Or rather, *not* like that. "Like where you live."

Lawrence looked around the studio. "Here."

"I mean besides here. And like what you—"

"There is nothing important about me that you don't know," Lawrence replied.

It was true. Everything that mattered about him, she and she alone seemed to understand.

She rewarded him with a wide smile, but it faded as she glanced again at the volume. "Have you learned anything interesting from this book? Anything that might help us find the Lion instead of having to wait until next Tuesday for him to kill again?"

Lawrence understood the bitterness in her tone, even though he hated it. They had spent the evening trying to figure out ways to identity this most faceless of killers, and had come up with nothing. Nothing heartening anyway. Given the shrine Tuesday had found in his room, they surmised that he was likely to stay close to them, to want to be able to see her. Lawrence had the sense that the man craved attention—cutting his victims' hearts out seemed evidence of that—and Tuesday thought that he'd want to stay abreast of what they were doing. Neither thought was enormously uplifting, and neither of them could think of any way to put this information to use. They considered employing the news sheets to disseminate false reports about their investigation, but it seemed that someone had already paid to have them packed with reports about the Vampire of London, and they were not sure it would work anyway: both Lawrence and Tuesday had the uncomfortable feeling that the Lion was too close to their operation to be fooled.

"Have you ever read Machiavelli's *Prince*?" he asked.

She shook her head and he went on. "The basic premise is that it is better to be cunning than honest, better to seem good than to be good, at least if you are trying to rule over men. When I was younger I found it very instructive. There is one passage that seems relevant, though, although I can't figure out how."

"What does it say?"

" *'It is better to be impetuous than to be cautious,'* " he read, " *'for fortune is a woman and in order to be mastered she must be controlled and kept in submission.'* Oh wait," he laughed, flinching from her glare, "that's not it."

"I don't like this book very much. I hope that's not one of the instructions you learned when you were younger."

"By heart. Actually this is what I really meant to read. I think it describes our man's attributes perfectly. *'A prince should adopt the natures of both the fox and the lion: for a lion is defenseless against snares, and a fox is defenseless against wolves. Hence to be impervious a prince must be a fox in recognizing snares and a lion in driving off wolves.'* "

"While I agree that for all we know of his appearance he could be a fox or a lion, the fundamental premise is absurd. Both the lion and the fox are hunted by men. Neither of them are impervious."

Lawrence looked up at her. "You might just have found the answer."

"What do you mean? It is just a metaphor."

"Maybe. But maybe we should hunt him with the things that separate men from beasts."

"Our sense of humor and our opposable thumbs?" she offered, ticking off the attributes that philosophers generally referred to.

"Don't forget about our ability to speak. And our belief in God."

Tuesday started to laugh, then interrupted herself with a gasp. "Of course! That is exactly it. Lawrence, you are a genius."

"We pray a lot?"

"No," she said, moving from his lap to the stack of reports that had been amassed when they were initially looking for the Lion's lodgings. Near the bottom she paused and slipped one out. "Not pray. Listen."

For the next five minutes, while she outlined her plan, Lawrence did. It took a bit longer for him to get the orders out to his men, orders to have everyone involved in the case brought in the next day for questioning, but by midnight the operation was underway.

"If this works, we could know who the killer is tomorrow," Tuesday said. She stifled a yawn.

"Yes," Lawrence agreed, picking her up and carrying her to bed. "If this works."

The Lion trembled a bit as he strolled away from Worthington Hall with the effort to keep from laughing. All the waiting had made him tired and jumpy, but his enthusiasm had been reawakened by their idiocy.

He was definitely glad he had let His Lordship live a little longer. Watching him piece together an investigation was like watching a stupid Worm writhe on the end of a fishing hook.

Nothing his Lordship was doing would take away the Lion's powers of invisibility. But the Lion would sure have a good time watching him Wriggle.

And then at the end, he would remove the hook from His Lordship himself. Stand there, close by his side, seeming like a dear friend until the last possible moment. He could imagine the look on Lawrence Pickering's face when he finally understood the truth. Understood that he was not the best. Understood who was the real Winner.

The Lion hugged himself with glee all the way home.

Chapter 26

Lawrence was up early taking care of the last few details of their operation. Waking with Tuesday in his arms, even if they were still wrapped in bandages, was the most incredible feeling in the world, and he swore he was going to do it every morning for the rest of his life. He never would have believed that she would be gone long before the bandages were.

He got back to Worthington Hall just minutes before they were set to begin, and found Tuesday pacing the studio.

She looked relieved when she saw what he had brought with him. "Thank goodness. I thought—I was getting nervous."

Lawrence knew what she had thought; it was the reason they had agreed that he would go on that particular errand himself instead of sending one of his men. It was the reason it had taken him so long to figure out the exact wording of the orders to his men, the reason he had left and reentered through the kitchen, the reason only CeCe had any inkling of what they were doing. It was no longer safe to trust anyone.

He was leading a spry old woman by the arm. "Mrs.

Slipson," he said, standing the woman in front of Tuesday, "this is Lady Arlington."

"Pleasure to meet Your Ladyship, I'm sure," Mrs. Slipson said, bowing her head slightly. If it had not been for the strange, milky color of her eyes, Tuesday would not have known she was blind. She moved confidently even in the unfamiliar room, and settled comfortably into the chair that had been placed for her.

"Has Lord Pickering explained what we need you to do?" Tuesday asked.

"Explained himself blue, I imagine," Mrs. Slipson replied, smiling. "Some young men don't believe a woman like me can understand anything."

"Madam I never intended—" Lawrence began stiffly, but Mrs. Slipson's gleeful laughter interrupted him.

She leaned toward Tuesday. "Them serious ones never can tell when a body is jesting, can they?" Then she sat back, wiping the merry tears from her eyes and said, "He 'splained it clear as day. I'm to sit here, hidden like, and give a cough when I hear him."

"Exactly," Tuesday confirmed.

"Then hide me up. I'm ready."

"He changes his appearances as easily as we change clothes," Tuesday had said the night before to Lawrence, keeping her voice low so no one would hear. "Which means, we will never be able to find him if we are looking for him."

Lawrence had regarded her as if she had sprung a leak. "Are you proposing that we just stop the investigation and—"

"What we need," she interrupted, "is someone who won't be fooled. Someone who has never *seen* him before."

"Shall I just go drag someone off the street or do you have an individual in mind?"

She held out the paper she had extracted from the stack of witness interviews. "Mrs. Slipson."

Lawrence had frowned at her. "The blind woman?" he had begun to ask. And then, as understanding came, repeated in an entirely different tone, "the *blind* woman."

"Exactly. If we are right and the Lion wants to stay close to the investigation, then the chances are good that he has let himself be questioned by your operatives— maybe even begged to be questioned. He can do that safely because he is a master of disguise, changing his appearance whenever he has to. But I bet, despite how meticulous he is, he has not bothered with his voice or his scent or any of the hundred things someone without sight would recognize. And she lived in the same house with him for over a year."

"The blind woman," Lawrence was still murmuring with awe.

Once Mrs. Slipson was hidden, each of the people interviewed by Lawrence's men were escorted into the room, introduced by a guard, and offered a seat. That way they were able to parade everyone close to the case—including the men working on it—by Mrs. Slipson's waiting ear without any of them realizing it.

Lawrence asked most of the questions, but occasionally Tuesday would suggest one. The idea was ostensibly to see if, probed and prodded anew, anyone could remember anything about the Lion, they had not remembered earlier. Mrs. Slipson was silent through the questioning of the women from Helen's Harem, snored during the fruit-seller's detailed description of how to choose a melon, and let loose audible giggles when her former landlord, Mr. Carter, went into a long rant about his property.

"Ought to put me up in the queen's own palace, losing my house in service to my nation like I did," he told Lawrence.

"Queen's palace indeed," Mrs. Slipson commented after he'd left. "Place was lousy with mites. Did everyone a service knocking it down, I'd say. Queen's palace, ha."

She had barely mastered her indignation when Albert Marston was brought in after that, his posture as he perched at the edge of the seat suggesting that of a bird ready to take flight at the first opportunity.

"He didn't want to come," Tom explained, adding that he had found Mr. Marston barricaded in his apartment and had been able to get him out only by threatening to break the door down. "He's refusing to speak, sir. He seems to think his life is in danger."

"There are three men guarding you, Mr. Marston," Lawrence explained patiently.

"I don't like them and I don't want them," Albert Marston complained. His chest puffed and he sat up straighter. "I can guard myself. And I'm not saying anything to you."

That was the only information they could extract from him, except, finally, that he wished them a good day and hoped never to see them again.

The next witness was Can Can Kyle, the owner of the Dancing Fawn. They had found Joey Blacktooth as well, but he had growled that he refused to leave the dice tables "while on a winning streak"—which looked to Grub to mean he'd only lost half his reward money—and would kill any man who made him.

Kyle seemed to have invested his money in new

clothes, and was only too happy to have an opportunity to show them off. "Man o' our builds," he said, leaning forward to take Lawrence into his confidence, "G-g-got to be fitted by an expert."

Lawrence deftly steered the conversation onto the topic of the Lion without losing Kyle's interest by asking, "Do you know where he got his clothes made?"

"Never confided in me, he didn't," Kyle said sadly. "Fine work thou—"

Mrs. Slipson erupted into a coughing fit then, which only stopped when she began hollering, "It's him, it's him, it's him!"

"W-w-w-w-w-w—" was all Kyle managed to get out before Lawrence's sword was at his throat. At a sign, six men advanced into the room, lifted Kyle from the chair, and dragged him away to manacle him.

When the door was closed, Lawrence crossed to where Mrs. Slipson was still seated behind a screen in Tuesday's favorite chair, and kneeled next to her. "Are you certain, ma'am?" he asked. "Positive that he is the man?"

The woman turned toward Lawrence and looked confused. "Not that stuttering one. The one before. The one who talked about not wanting to come and talk. That one."

"Albert Marston," Lawrence and Tuesday pronounced in unison.

"I don't remember his name, but it was that one. Soon as I heard him my heart gave out and I fainted dead away. I'm sorry if I let you down, dear," she apologized, addressing the place where Lawrence had been standing.

She was speaking now to empty air. Lawrence was already across the room issuing commands and sending out messengers to the men trailing Marston with orders to drag him back as quickly and discreetly as possible. "Tell them not to hurt him," Lawrence added, almost as an afterthought. He did not add that he wanted that pleasure all for himself.

It was only a half hour later, when he shouted for someone to help him, that anyone remembered to unshackle Kyle.

"Albert Marston is dead," Grub reported three hours later. "Has been for fifteen years."

Albert Marston, it seemed, was just one of many other names—including Bob Fish, Lad Carlton, Derrick Egret, Noddy White, Ebenezer Ripple, and Ugly Sluice—all to be found on the grave markers behind the debtor's wing at Bridewell, and all adopted in the course of his career by the man they now pursued.

He had, it seemed, led a very colorful life. Once a bit player in the duke of Norfolk's company, he'd thrown off the yoke of the theater to freelance. He had not given up acting, though, and despite being barely past thirty had managed to act the part of husband to six elderly women who passed away shortly after marrying him, leaving him the bulk of their properties and a handful of mortal enemies in the form of their heirs.

His method seemed to be to earn the affection of these women by taking on their favorite hobby. He had been, at various times, a great admirer of ferns, an aficionado of wooden toys hand painted by orphans, a student of German literature, and a fan of a certain one-armed juggler. His most recent conquest, Dorthea Burthen, was dearly attached to sparrows and other "sweet singing birds."

"Which is why he had all them in his house," Grub explained. "And they was making a racket to raise all hell when we got there."

This was just one of the many interesting facts they collected about Albert Marston in the course of the day. But what they did not manage to collect, from any part of London, was the man himself.

None of the guards Lawrence had following Albert Marston could give a very good explanation of how he had eluded their grasp. Lawrence knew from personal experience that it was not hard to lose a man following you in London, or even two. But it should have been hard to lose three men, and he had assigned four. Which, along with the objects discovered in his house, seemed to confirm that the man they knew as Albert Marston was a professional criminal of some skill.

Arrayed on the table in front of them now were a half dozen pieces of blood caked clothing, a dirty knife, and two pieces of paper. One of them had the names of each of the victims so far written on it. The other showed several attempts to sketch a man. The face of the best one was crossed out in what looked like blood.

"Looks a bit like Your Lordship," Grub observed, pointing to it.

"Looks a bit like your work," Lawrence said to Tuesday.

"It is," she admitted grudgingly. "Part of it. I—I tried to sketch you the first night we met. To figure you out. Don't get the idea that I—"

"I won't." Lawrence could barely conceal his smile. He remembered standing outside her window that night, watching her work, not knowing she was drawing him. "Was the blood part of your original design?"

"Of course," she agreed. "I could sense even then how taxing you could be."

Lawrence's face became serious suddenly. "I had my men search for that paper the next day and they could not find it. And that was the night Tom was knocked out in the alley. The Lion must have paid you a visit while you slept." He saw Tuesday shiver and changed the subject. "It certainly looks like we have found the right man."

"I suppose," Tuesday admitted, but not enthusiastically.

"Are you still annoyed that I wouldn't let you go and look at the rooms yourself, or is something else bothering you about this?"

"I'm definitely still annoyed," she assured him heartily. "But that's not it. All of this—it just doesn't feel right. He staged his other lodgings, the one he had booby-trapped, so carefully. But his place this time was a mess."

"Maybe he wasn't expecting us this time," Grub put in.

"But there are things missing. Things that should be there."

"Like what?"

"Books. Everyone always talked about him reading all the time. And fancy clothes. And—"

"Got something else," Tom announced, rushing into the room. "Found it under the rocks in one of the bird's cages."

"Better man than me," Grub said, shaking his head. "I'd not have touched those scrawny things for gold."

"I had one of the Special Commissioner's men do it," Tom said with a wink. "Anyway, look. I think this clinches it." He held out a scrap of paper.

" *'Nose: 12; Lips: 31; Forehead: 46; Chin: 5'*," Lawrence read aloud. He looked up at Tuesday and saw that her eyes were blazing.

"He used me. He used my book. That must have been what he was doing in my studio that night. Looking up the numbers." She swallowed hard. "Then he faked that shooting to make sure we would believe him. And I fell for it. He tricked me."

"He tricked all of us," Lawrence said, to make her feel better, but it didn't work.

It was horrible enough that he was in her head, that he had invaded her house, stolen things from her room. But somehow even worse was knowing he had used her own work, her own book of faces, to fool her.

"There is nothing we can do right now." Lawrence tried to make his voice soothing. He could imagine what she was feeling—self rebuke, failure—and he racked his mind for some way to ease it. "Every available man in London is searching for him."

"I want to search, too."

"No."

"Why not?"

"Because Bianca says you cannot do anything strenuous."

"Come on," Tuesday said, making for the door.

"Because if anything happened to you, the investigation would go nowhere—none of my men are as good as you are at figuring out the killer's mind."

She snorted. "Are you coming?"

"And finally," Lawrence said, getting the idea on the spur of the moment, "because you have an appointment."

"I do not."

"Yes, you do."

"What are you talking about."

"Yesterday you said you wanted to know where I lived."   ~

"I do, but not right no—" She broke off. "Where are you going?"

"To bark a few orders at unsuspecting men. Be ready in half an hour."

She opened her mouth to protest, but he was gone.

Chapter 27

As they wandered in just after nightfall, what amazed Tuesday most about Pickering Hall was not the fact that it was the largest house in London. Or that it had the most spacious grounds. Or was widely judged to be a modern architectural masterpiece.

What amazed her was that it was empty.

"Not entirely," Lawrence corrected, leading her past suite after suite of empty chambers. "The cook and a few footmen have furniture."

There were lines where chairs had once scuffed paneling, and rectangles and ovals and squares of dark fabric marking the walls where paintings had hung. Eerie shadows seemed to flit across the walls like ghosts of a past life, of past parties, dancing over the rugless floors and through the chairless rooms as they stood together in silence. Tuesday could imagine the house lit with thousands of candles, imagine the balls and the fine furniture and the stupid jokes and unsubtle, unsuitable, flirtations. The duke and the chambermaid sequestered behind one set of curtains, the duchess and another chambermaid tucked more comfortably—why did men always choose such uncomfortable venues for their affairs?—into one of the dozens of spare bedrooms. And she could also hear the whispered comments behind people's hands about how exactly Lawrence Pickering got his wealth, about his low breeding, about his prowess in bed. She could almost feel the jealous looks and the condescending looks and the admiring looks, and knew that Lawrence had to see them all to see any of them.

She was already well aware of his generosity, but standing in the deserted, dead corridor of his house, she understood his courage better than at any other moment. Not every man could lead sailors against an enemy or mastermind an escape from a foreign prison or do any of the dozens of glorious acts the news sheets rang on about. But compared to the effort of being honorable around men and women ready to condemn you because you had the audacity to have once been poorer than them and now were richer, compared with the effort of not succumbing to their vision of you but remembering, every day, to be proud and not embarrassed by what you achieved, compared to that the Spanish were a mediocre enemy.

"I used to like to throw parties," he said as if reading her thoughts. "I loved to see everyone wondering how much a chair or a plate of oysters cost. Men leaning across their wives to inform one another that the wine came from the king of France's own cellar. 'Yes but did the king know about it,' one of them would inevitably ask, laughing at the scandalous implication that I had stolen it. Which just showed that they had never been there, because Henri has his cellar locked up tighter than any of their jewel casks. I used to like it when their laughter or whispering stopped abruptly when I sauntered over because they had been speculating about what sorts of illegal acts I had been involved in to purchase that chandelier or that inlaid table. Their imagination of my business was so much more interesting than what I actually did to make money."

"What happened to everything?" Tuesday asked, skirting around the outline of a long-forgotten rug.

"I sold it all when I went to Spain."

"Everything?"

"I was not planning to come back."

"You wanted to settle in Spain?"

"I wanted to die in Spain."

Tuesday pulled Lawrence to a stop in the middle of a dark corridor. "You were ready to die?"

Her question took him completely by surprise. No one had ever asked him that before. "What do you mean?"

"Weren't there things you still wanted to do? Experiences you still wanted to have?"

He really did not know how to answer. "I guess I was not thinking about that. I was thinking about what I had done. What I never wanted to do again."

She was silent for a moment, then asked, "Is that what the nightmare was about?"

She felt him tense. "What nightmare?"

"The one you woke me up with the other night. You were shouting and I went to see what was wrong and—that is why I was not in my bed when the Lion attacked it."

"What did I shout?"

"Mostly 'Don't let go' and 'Ever.' Or 'Never.' I couldn't tell."

"Everly."

"Is that a name?"

Lawrence nodded and got a very faraway look. "He was one of my men." Tuesday stood next to him, silent, in the dark, empty corridor. She listened to the leaves on the large tree in the back scrape against the window panes, heard an owl's call echoing through the vacant rooms. She knew why her house was empty, but Lawrence did not need money. The emptiness here was both a sort of purity, and a sort of punishment, she felt. Penetence for something? Or an unwillingness to be too attached to life?

Lawrence's voice cut through the darkness, making her jump.

"He died," he said simply. "Everly. He died in Spain." It was the first time he had spoken the words. He'd lived with the memory long enough.

"Did he fall?"

He looked at her closely. "How did you know that?"

"From your dream. The way you acted."

He nodded. His eyes moved beyond her again. "Down a cliff. He let go. I was there and I could have pulled him up but he let go."

Lawrence could still remember the darkness, thick and heavy and freezing. Each gust of wind was a biting slap in the face, making his eyes tear, making it impossible to see what was happening. The raw howling lashed at his ears, obliterating the sound of the waves pounding the edge of the cliff below.

"I don't have any choice, Lawrence."

"No, Everly! Don't."

"Heads or tails?"

"Don't do this."

"You always choose heads, don't you. Look. It's your lucky day!"

"Everly, I am telling you. This is not the right way."

The shot blinded him, hurtling him to the frozen

ground. Frozen but warm, in patches, warm from the blood.

"No!"

He caught the fingers just as they went over the edge, barely. "I've got you," he yelled, straining with all his strength. "I'm not going to let you die."

"It's too late now. There's nothing you can do, Lawrence. Nothing."

Nothing nothing nothing nothing echoed down the cliff, in his mind, indictment and sentence all at once, nothing you can do.

"He just let go," Lawrence said, and silence fell over them like a blanket. Finally, he shrugged, and added in a cold voice, "Maybe he was lucky. There are worse things than dying for your country."

"Like what?"

"Killing for it."

He reached up to rub his right shoulder and found that Tuesday was already massaging it for him. Covering her hand with his own, he brought it to his lips. He should tell her the whole story. About Rafael. About Maria.

"I love you Lawrence."

But not tonight. He did not want to risk ruining it. Besides, he was ravenous.

"Come on," he urged, keeping her hand clasped with his. "Our dinner is getting cold."

The corridor they were in ended in a staircase that took them up to an enormous ballroom, made larger by its emptiness. It was a huge cavernous shadow except in the middle where a hundred candelabra of different shapes and sizes had been arranged in row after row around a square, like a forest of flaming silver trees. It was one of the most dazzling sights Tuesday had ever seen, but Lawrence did not let her stop to admire it. Instead he led her into the center, where, atop a luxuriant Turkish carpet woven to look like a swath of light green grass, a table laid with silver and crystal and a hundred orchids stood surrounded by three-dozen silk-covered pillows, inlaid with mirrors.

"I don't really entertain very much anymore," Lawrence explained, almost sheepishly, "so I am afraid we had to make do with whatever we had lying around."

"You did this in half an hour?" she gasped.

Lawrence had felt self-conscious bringing her here. Two years earlier, before he had sold everything, he could have impressed her with the gorgeousness of his furniture and his art and his wine. He could have set the most sumptuous table for her, put out the salt cellar in the shape of a castle that had been a gift from the duke of Saxony, the golden dolphin soup turreen from the Pope. The house would have glittered and every corner would have held a masterpiece.

But all that was gone, the Lawrence Pickering that had all that was gone, and now there was just him, this empty house, and this most extraordinary woman. He could have had all that again, but he no longer wanted it. And now he knew why. Seeing the expression of wonder and joy on her face made him realize this was better. He wanted to spend the rest of his life doing things that made Tuesday happy, that made her feel cherished, that surprised her. That made her look at him the way she was right at that moment. He felt like a god.

"Tuesday, I—"

She moved to stand right in front of him, to force him to look down at her, to force him to see all her gratitude, all her love, all her admiration in her eyes. "Yes, Lawrence?"

"I think—" He was lost. He was losing himself in her, to her.

She tried to raise one eyebrow and slid her hand down to the waist of his breeches. What she wanted most, at that moment, was to seduce him. To make him feel vulnerable so he would be alive to how much she loved him. She savored knowing she made him feel weak. He made her feel so strong.

"I think we should dine," he stammered.

She stood on her toes and kissed his neck and murmured, "Why?"

"Because I have not been hungry like this in years. And because food is—"

Tuesday kneeled in front of him and smoothed her hand up the front of the bulge in his breeches. Using her lips and her teeth she managed to untie the laces and slide them open. Then she turned her mouth sideways and licked from the tip of Lawrence's newly freed shaft to its base.

"Unnecessary," he finished his sentence in a moan.

Her lips closed around the head of his member and this time she sucked him all the way into her mouth. Her hand slid around to join her mouth and she felt his knees tremble beneath him as her thumb stroked the base.

His moans, deeper now, spurred her on. Her cheeks molded themselves to his contours and the pressure inside him grew until every part of him felt like it was shimmering. Then he looked down and saw her looking up at him. The heat of her gaze loosed whatever restraints were left and the force that had been building surged through his body, pounding along every limb and sending him bursting into her mouth.

Lawrence had never been seduced by anyone before, would never have allowed himself to be, but he let himself go entirely with her. She drank his pleasure from him hungrily, until he protested and begged and ordered her to stop and began to get hard all over again. Only then did he remember where he was and his name and what he had been planning to do and he lifted her from her knees. Kicking his pants off his ankles he carried her toward the cushions around the table and set her down in the middle of a pile of them.

"That was not what was supposed to happen tonight," he informed her, deftly untying the laces of her bodice.

Bringing him to a climax had been one of the most sensational and arousing experiences of Tuesday's life. Every time his fingers grazed her skin, she felt an echo deep inside her body.

"How come you get to say what happens?" she sighed.

"I am in charge."

"Why?"

"This is my house."

"Does that mean I am in charge at my house?"

"No."

"Where can I be—"

His lips teased over hers and when he pulled them away she found that she was no longer wearing any clothes. Lawrence, also naked, lay on his elbow alongside her, unable to take his eyes off of her. Her skin turned gold in the candlelight and the mirrors in the cushions covered her stomach and thighs with circles of silver light. She had pinned her hair up, but it began to fall loose in tendrils that dipped like invitations over her shoulders. One looped just under her nipple, and Lawrence had to run his finger along it.

He wanted to make her feel things she had never felt. To savor her body. To have her lose control, give herself up to him entirely the way he did to her.

"Close your eyes," he whispered to her, but she shook her head.

"I want to see you. To watch you."

"Close your eyes," he repeated, this time in a voice that promised her she would not be sorry. "Trust me."

She closed them and he tied his shirt like a blindfold around them. "Lawrence, I—"

"Trust me," he said again and she relaxed.

It was the most extraordinary dinner of her life. Lawrence had learned all her favorite foods and had his masterful chef prepare them for her. But it was not only the menu or skill that made it so special. It was not being able to see. The candied lemons on the broccoli were more tart-sweet, the rosemary in the wild mushroom ragout that topped the veal was sharper, the hint of sage in the chestnut soup was more woodsy, and the ginger cake with caramel on top was more gingery-caramely-sublime than any before.

Without her eyes, her other senses became stronger. She had never before considered the erotic potential of nubbly broccoli, or the arousing feeling of having caramel dribbled over your lips, then over your body and having someone slowly lick it off while you suck cream off their finger. She could feel each individual strand of silk on the tassel that he dragged with drugging slowness over her skin, leaving her body trembling. The silkiness of the pillows alternated with the coolness of the mirrors against her back as she arched her hips forward, begging Lawrence never to leave off stroking her with the petal softness of the orchids, and the smooth rug caressed her bottom as Lawrence's tongue gave her swollen nub a relentless minty kiss. While she was recovering he iced the silver bowls of two spoons and set them over her nipples, then dripped warm, almond-scented oil around her breasts. The contrast of cold and hot rekindled her arousal instantly, and it became almost excruciating as he began to massage the oil into her body. His hands stroked her shoulders and arms, then gently moved to her breasts. He lifted the cool spoon with his warm tongue, smothered her nipple twice, and let the spoon fall back into place.

As he dabbled the oil onto her stomach and worked it, with his fingertips, down her thighs, down her calves, down to her ankles, it was as if her other climaxes that night only built pressure, not relieved it. Her body was aching for him to touch it, but he ignored her pleas and stretched out next to her, his mouth at her feet, and sucked her toes into his mouth one by one. He started with the smallest toe, licking it first, then engulfing it, then moved to the next, and the next. As he worked he massaged her arch and the ball of her foot with his thumb. The sensations he caused fizzled through her from her heels to her ears but were concentrated, almost painfully, between her legs.

When he had her largest toe in his mouth, her moans were so agonized that he took pity on her. Only then, as she cried out to him, did he slide one hand up the inside of her thigh and begin, barely, to stroke her. Sensation pounded through her body, overwhelming her completely. She arched against him and he pulled away, teasing her, until she relaxed. Not being able to see his hands, only being able to feel his mouth on her feet and his fingers slipping now into her, now over her, drove her mad. Her body was humming with desire.

His teeth skimmed some sort of magic place on her toe and his fingers, one on top of her and one just inside, found her most tender spot and all at once the hum turned into a pounding crescendo. It crested explosively again and again as Lawrence continued to ply her, relentless now, and intensified as he cruelly sucked her into his mouth. She was dying, she was dead, she was soaring, she was unaware that he was now lying next to her, unaware that he was holding her tight, unaware that he was kissing her ear and whispering to her. And then suddenly she heard what he said and everything she was feeling fell away and all she knew were the words echoing in her mind, louder than any other words she had ever heard, the words "I love you Tuesday."

He loved her. He said he loved her. Tuesday pressed her lips to his and kissed the words from them.

"Make love to me," she whispered.

Lawrence hesitated. It was supposed to be a night only for her, for memorizing every inch and scar and secret of her body. But her responsiveness had set Lawrence on fire, destroying all the rest of his carefully conceived plans for how he was going to seduce her. And when she now pressed her fingers against his chest, when she pushed him down and blindly climbed atop him, when she said "be inside me, Lawrence," he was powerless to keep his hands off her, his body from hers.

He slid into her while her body was still vibrating with pleasure. He pulled her to his chest and wrapped her legs around him so she was sitting on him, on his lap, then pulled the blindfold off of her.

Her eyes came open slowly. Their gazes were exactly level and she found she was looking into the blue blue depths of him.

"I love you Tuesday," he told her again, letting her see him, all of him, as her body held him deep inside. "I did not dream I could feel this way with anyone. You are the most—"

"Shhh," she said, kissing the words from his lips. She did not want him to say them, to use them up and forget them. She whispered, "Show me."

He cupped his hands beneath her bottom and moved her up and down his shaft, first tenderly, then, as she took over, more urgently. Her good arm wrapped around his neck and she arched backwards as he slipped a hand between their bodies and touched her again, asserting control. The faster she moved, the softer he touched. When she slid over him in long, shuddering motions, his caress deepened; in short fast ones, they withdrew. The contrasts sparked tiny explosions of feeling all over her body, until, with both his thumbs on her and his member filling her, stretching her, the explosions began to coalesce into one powerful current. His lips found her neck and her shoulder as his fingers rolled over her. He forced himself to concentrate on her, to ignore the overpowering tension in his body, and brought his lips down over her nipple, grazing it with his teeth, and deep in her throat Tuesday purred.

Lawrence felt the reverberations through his entire body, shattering his resolve. This time when she pressed against him insistently, urgently he responded by stroking her against his shaft as it pushed into her. Somewhere nearby fireworks began to explode, filling the room with loud bangs and bursts of light, but Tuesday and Lawrence did not notice. She clung to him and he sank into her and with each thrust he smoothed and teased her a little longer until pleasure crashed through them both like a bolt of lightening, and their gasps and moans and pleas set the candles around them flickering like a summer storm.

Dawn was just getting ready to turn London pink when Lawrence picked Tuesday up in his arms and carried her around to blow out the remaining candles. Then he conveyed her through a discreet door into a small, cool chamber. The only thing in it was a bed covered in silver silk, but the walls and floor had been painted to look like slabs of glowing pinky-orange marble. No, Tuesday realized, putting her hand out, they *were* slabs of pinky orange marble, made to glow with tiny lanterns that hung from behind. The effect was ethereal and became more so when Lawrence adjusted the lanterns so that the room was lit only from below. He moved across the glimmering floor and crawled into bed next to her.

Tuesday had not seen Lawrence give his discreet signal, and did not hear the guards slide into position around the house. She had been too distracted, first with the magic of this room, and then with her own thoughts.

Lawrence was on the tip of dozing off when he had the uneasy feeling of being watched. He opened his eyes, moved them from one side to the other, and saw Tuesday staring at him with a strange expression.

"Is something wrong sweetheart?"

Tuesday shook her head. He studied her and was just closing his eyes again when she blurted, "Do you have a mistress?"

His body went rigid. He rolled onto his side to look at her and he seemed nervous. "I am not sure how to answer that question."

George had been right. Tuesday was biting her lip and telling herself she did not care and berating herself for asking and wanting to rip his heart out and—

"I mean, I've already gotten your father's permission," he went on, interrupting her thoughts, "but I was waiting to ask you to marry me until all of this was over."

She had to sort the words to make sense of them. "You want to marry me?"

"Did you think I was lying about all those things I said? That you are marvelous and I love you?"

"No. I just didn't think—"

Lawrence did not like the way she was taking it. Like it upset her. "I don't want you to decide now," he put in hastily.

"I want to decide now."

"You do?"

"Yes."

"Yes?"

"Yes."

" 'Yes I will marry you' or 'yes I want to decide'? I just need to be clear."

Tuesday sat up and faced him and said in her low, rumbling, unmistakable voice, "Yes I want to marry you, Lawrence Pickering. I love you. I want to be your wife."

When Lawrence was thirteen he had taken all the money he had saved by running errands and taking stupid wagers and bought his first property—his first home with a roof. It was over a tanner's studio, so it stank and was hot all the time, but he didn't care. He pulled Bull out of school and the two of them ate mutton pie for dinner off their own table and drank real ale out of their shared mug and went to bed, Bull on his new mattress, Lawrence with his cheek pressed against the bare planks of the floor—there was a mattress for him, too, but he wanted to be as close as possible to this amazing thing he owned—and felt like they had reached the apex of human happiness. That night Lawrence remembered not being able to stop smiling as he tried to go to sleep, not being able to turn the corners of his mouth down no matter what he did because he was so infinitely happy.

He had never felt that way again, not once. Not until the moment when Tuesday said, *I want to marry you, Lawrence Pickering. I love you. I want to be your wife.*

Listening outside the door, the Lion could not wait to kill him.

Chapter 28

Lawrence had not been completely candid with Tuesday. Pickering Hall itself was empty, but he still kept an office in the small octagonal building—it had only six rooms—called the banqueting house that stood in the garden. That was where he was standing, trying to review the results of the search for Albert Marston, but mostly dreaming up presents he wanted to give Tuesday—he had already sent Tom out twice, once to a jeweler and once to a brush seller to get her a new set of paintbrushes—when Elwood arrived.

"I have some news for you, sir," Elwood began, as if it were just news, as if he were not about to destroy Lawrence's life. As if he were not about to show him, without space for doubt, that Lady Tuesday Arlington was a duplicitous, manipulative, bitch.

"Yes?"

"You are not going to like it."

"Is it about George Lyle?"

"No." Elwood swallowed. "It is about this." Elwood held a piece of paper out to him.

It was badly scrawled, but still legible. Too legible.

"*Lady Tuesday Arlington is a thief and a liar. If you*

don't believe me, believe your own eyes: check the bottom of her mother's trunk and see what you find. Yours, A concerned friend,' " Lawrence read. He looked at Elwood. "Where did it come from?"

"It was delivered by a messenger this morning to my office. He disappeared before I could ask him where he got it."

"So?"

"I sent some men to Worthington Hall to check."

"And you found?"

"The trunk was locked. According to the cook, Lady Arlington is the only one with the key and she keeps it hidden. The cook was under the impression that the trunk contained clothes and mementos of Lady Tuesday's mother and that she valued them very highly."

"And did it?"

"No." Elwood paused. "We had to smash the lock to open it. And inside we found this." Elwood pushed an account book bound in black leather across the desk.

It took Lawrence only a few moments to decipher the entries. He flipped back and forth through it, dropped it with a thud back onto the desk, and stared at Elwood. "My God. This is the ledger of the entire smuggling operation. Every transaction."

Elwood worked not to flinch under Lawrence's gaze. "Yes. And there's more. A thousand pounds in solid gold coins more," Elwood said. "In addition to maps of the three armories from which we know weapons were stolen to be resold in Spain, and detailed directions to two storage facilities where they stored goods before moving them out of the country."

"Have you visited them?"

"Yes. You can't believe what we found. There were—"

Lawrence put up a hand. "I don't want to know." He took a deep breath and stared out the windows. He was remembering the day he'd had the new settee brought in. He had asked his men to move the trunk and Tuesday had reacted strangely. At the time he'd thought she was just being willful, or protective of something that was her mother's.

At the time he'd been a fool. "I suppose there is no question about any of this?"

The fact that Lawrence asked that taught Elwood what this revelation was costing him. The amount of evidence left nothing in doubt. "No. There can't be."

The room filled with a heavy silence.

"There were two gentlemen guarding one of the storage facilities when we arrived. They both managed to get away, but we think we have a lead on them."

Lawrence said, "Oh."

Elwood shifted from one foot to the other, wishing there were something he could do. "If we can catch them, they should be able to give you the names of all the people in the smuggling ring. You should finally be able to smash it," he offered.

It should have been great news.

Again, Lawrence said, "Oh." There was a pause while he pressed his burned palms hard against the corners of his desk to see if he could feel anything. He couldn't. "When you catch them bring them to me. I will want to have them identify Tuesday. Just to be certain."

"Yes sir. I am afraid, sir, there is something more."

"More?" Lawrence looked at him, aghast.

"Yes. You know that each of the victims was at one

time engaged to Lady Arlington. What we have just learned is that they were all summoned to London by notes right before their death. Notes from her."

"Oh. Are there any still alive?"

"One. Lord Ivry."

"Where is he?"

"He is supposed to be at his country house."

"He isn't." Lawrence reached up and rubbed his right shoulder.

"No."

"Oh."

"But we have no evidence that he came to London. Or was summoned by Lady Arlington."

"You will."

"Yes," Elwood agreed unwillingly. "I think we will."

"What day is it?"

"Monday."

"So there should be another killing tomorrow?"

"Yes."

"Find Lord Ivry."

"Yes sir. Sir, my lord, are you—"

"Find him."

"Yes sir."

Lawrence stepped out of his office and surveyed the guards posted there. "Tom, come with me. I want you to stay with Lady Arlington all day today. Do not let her breathe without your noticing. Do you understand?"

"Yes sir."

Despite having one arm in a sling and bruises that were now turning green, Tuesday awoke feeling glorious. Feeling, for the first time in her life, Lucky. She had labored under that nickname for years, but only now, this morning, did it feel right. The light filling the marble room was an incredible peachy color, and a breeze came in through some openings hidden high in the walls. It was a perfect chamber, with a perfect bed, built by a perfect man whom she was going to marry.

"Good morning, Tuesday," CeCe chirped as she entered.

"What are you doing here?"

"His Lordship and I are in cahoots. He thought I would not like to sleep at Worthington Hall without you there, and also that you might want assistance this morning. How are you feeling?"

"Stupendous."

CeCe smiled hugely and sat down on the bed. "You look it. Did you ask him? About the mistress? Tell me everything."

Tuesday nodded. "It was—" she started to say, then broke off because she heard Lawrence's voice in the corridor giving orders to guards. She could not hear what he was saying, but his tone sounded businesslike, as if there had been some news.

"What has happened?" The question died on her lips. It was not just his expression, it was the way he was gripping his right shoulder. "What is wrong, Lawrence?"

Having her say his name was terrible. "When were you going to tell me, Lady Arlington?"

She blinked at him and looked shocked. "What are you talking about?"

"Don't pretend to be confused. About the smuggling? About this?" He held up the black ledger.

Tuesday frowned. "What is that? I've never seen it before."

Lawrence gazed at her for a long time. He shook his head. "Exceedingly well done, Lady Arlington. I think you may be the best liar I've ever met. And God knows, I've met a few."

Tuesday looked as if she'd been slapped. "I am not lying."

"Of course not. Just like you didn't lie to me when you told me you knew nothing of your husband's involvement in smuggling." *Just like you didn't lie to me when you said you loved me.*

"But that was true. It is true. You know that. You know I hadn't seen Curtis in two months when he was found killed."

How could he have been such a bloody fool? How could he have believed her and trusted her, even when evidence pointed the other way? "I know that's what you say."

"Ask anyone. Ask CeCe." Tuesday turned to her maid who was standing against the wall, trembling. "CeCe, tell him."

"Don't bother, CeCe. I know you well enough to know you would lie for your mistress."

Tuesday was outraged. "How dare you?"

Lawrence looked interested. "How dare I? I'll tell you, Lady Arlington. We found a ledger in the bottom of your mother's trunk recording every transaction of the largest smuggling ring operating in England. Don't bother gasping, you don't want to overdo the drama until you've heard it all. In addition to the ledger we found a thousand pounds in gold and enough information to hang you for treason. If you don't hang for murder first."

"Murder? What are you talking about?"

"The neat coincidence of your husband dying and you being in charge of the smuggling ring. The tidy fact that all the victims were at one time engaged to you, and that you summoned them all to London."

"What?"

"Did you or did you not send Silus Ivry a note?"

"How did you—"

"Very good. You can see how this looks, Lady Arlington. Four men die. You are the only connection between them; indeed, they have all inflicted a wrong on you. You tell me you had nothing to do with their deaths and, because I am a fool, I believed you. You tell me you had nothing to do with the smuggling your husband was involved in, and because I am a fool I believed you then, too. But I can't believe it anymore. I am not that much of a fool."

Tuesday was shaking her head. "I have no idea how any of the things you talked about got into the trunk, but I assure you that I did not put it there. I know nothing about smuggling. Or notes to the victims. If I—"

"I'm afraid, Lady Arlington, your assurances are not very valuable to me. Is it true that you have the only key to the lock on the trunk?"

"Yes."

"And that you keep it hidden?"

Tuesday pressed her lips together, then answered, "Yes."

"Then how could anything have gotten in without your knowledge?"

"I'm not—" Tuesday's eyes got huge. "Maybe it was him. The Lion, Albert Marston. We know he's been watching my house. Maybe he saw where the key was."

"The Lion," Lawrence repeated, nodding. "Yes, perhaps it was him. Why don't we proceed a bit farther down that path. Perhaps you and he are in this together. Perhaps you had him kill Curtis to take over the smuggling operation."

"That is absurd."

Lawrence sighed. "I don't know why I expected you to stop lying to me now when you have been so successful for so long."

"I have not lied to you. I have never lied to you."

"Please, Lady Arlington, spare me at least having to listen to that. I can see that we aren't going to get anywhere this morning. I suspect you'll have more to say when you are confronted with your accomplices. For right now, just answer this one question. Satisfy my curiosity on this single point, so I will know the depth of your duplicity. Did you plan to make me fall in love with you all along, to confound me more deeply, or was that just a happy accident?"

She bit her lip and gave him a look that at any other time would have crushed his heart and said, "Oh, Lawrence."

Now it just made him angry. "Can't even answer a simple question straightforwardly. Oh well. At least you did not lie. Tom, escort Lady Arlington back to her house."

Tuesday's face had lost all its color. "It won't be necessary. CeCe and I will go back to Worthington—"

"And Tom," Lawrence interrupted, ignoring her. "Do not let her out of your sight."

*   *   *

Time passed in great black blocks, unfelt and unnoticed by Lawrence, but bearing down on him. There was no sign of Albert Marston but, of course, he no longer expected one. No doubt Tuesday had tipped him off. Or knocked him off. It was growing dark outside and fireflies had begun to hover in the bushes when Elwood, breathless, appeared at the door of the office.

It took him five minutes of steady pounding to rouse Lawrence's attention.

"We found Lord Ivry, sir," he said when he finally managed to get Lawrence to open the door.

Lawrence nodded dully. "He was summoned to London by a letter from Lady Arlington."

"Yes," Elwood confirmed.

"I don't think I need to hear any more. Put him up in my room and send someone to arrest her."

"Are you certain that is—"

"I say, Lord Pickering, is that you?" a bobbing lantern with a man behind it asked, emerging from the encroaching darkness of the garden. "Good evening, my lord. I'm Lord Ivry, Silus Ivry. Be honored if you would call me Silus. Sorry to burst in on you like this, but I was wondering, can you tell me what is going on? What is wrong? Tuesday, I mean, ah, Lady Arlington—is she in some sort of trouble?"

"Nothing she cannot handle herself," Lawrence said icily.

"What if you are wrong? I know I look a sight and I'm not as agile as I should be since I took that ball in the knee during the war, but for Tuesday, for Lady Arlington, I would willingly do anything."

Lawrence's feelings on meeting the man were complicated in ways he had not expected. Lord Silus Ivry was not some ancient ugly man, but a man younger than himself with a jutting chin and handsome face and all his hair. Above all, he did not sound like a man who had rejected Tuesday. "If you feel that way about her, why did you break off your engagement?"

Silus Ivry grew stiff. "I don't see that is any of your business—" he began, then cut himself off. "Oh bother. It's the greatest mistake of my life. Can I sit down? The heat makes my knee ache."

Lawrence gestured for the man to come into his office, then waited in silence.

"I would not want my wife to know, you see," Silus Ivry began, blushing slightly. "Catherine is a lovely girl but, well—she isn't Tuesday. No one is Tuesday." He sighed. "I would have done anything to hold on to her, only, I was afraid."

"Of her?"

"Good God, no. Of her brother. Howard. He charged too high."

"Too high?"

"Yes. He offered her hand in marriage as payment for his gambling debts. But then, once you got engaged, he hit on you again and again. The settlement he demanded was huge. And it was clear it would never stop. The thought of not being able to maintain that glorious creature as she deserved because her brother was gambling away my fortune just sickened me. And I was not the only one. There were—"

"We know." Lawrence could not believe what he was hearing. Her brother had practically sold her. Like—

"I still regret the decision," Silus Ivry said heavily. "And I am sure the others do, too."

"I doubt it. They are all dead."

"Oh dear, then I really must go to her—to help her."

"Right now I think the most helpful thing you could do would be to remain at my house until Wednesday."

"But she needs me now." Lord Ivry rose and leaned over the desk. "If there is anything I can do, I must. Her note made it sound most urgent. Where is she?"

"Ah right. Her note. Is that why you came? Because she summoned you?"

"Well—"

Lawrence reached out a hand. "May I see the note please?" After a moment's hesitation Lord Ivry gave in.

" *'Dear Silus,'* " Lawrence read. " *'I beg you not to come to London this week for any reason. Your life could be in grave danger. Be on your guard at all times. I shall explain all soon. Fondly, Tuesday.'* "

Lawrence looked up at him. "She told you *not* to come."

"Yes, but—"

"Why the devil are you here?"

"Wouldn't you be? If you'd gotten a letter like that from the woman you loved?"

Silus Ivry was still talking but Lawrence was not listening. Had he made a mistake? Had she—

Christopher came into the office, then, rushing with uncommon haste. "I must speak to you, my lord."

Lawrence rose and stood with him at the doorway. "What is it?"

"I have a message for you. From Grub, at Worthington Hall."

Lawrence did not think he could feel any worse than he had all afternoon. But when he heard what Grub had said, he discovered he was wrong.

Ha ha ha, the Lion laughed as he watched Tuesday, his Lady, sitting on the settee in her studio. *You are mine,* he wanted to say. His Lordship isn't very happy, is he?

The Lion spared no sympathy for His Lordship. She wasn't supposed to be Lawrence Pickering's anyway. She was his, the Lion's. They were already collaborators. Working together. And they would soon be so much more.

He had fallen in love by accident. It was all the Watching that did it. Hours spent on the street outside his Lady's Window or hovering over the skylight, watching her in her studio, watching her paint, and smile. Watching her talk patiently to those children who came in all the time. To that little boy whose dog he had killed.

The Lion fingered the chain he wore around his neck as he remembered. She was so kind and good. She made everyone beautiful. When she looked at you, you felt like she understood everything about you. As the days went by and he Watched her more, the Lion had wanted to tell her everything. Share his secrets with her. He already knew all of hers.

They were so much alike, he thought. They needed each other. The way she talked, the sympathy in her voice—like the way she talked to those children—made the Lion quiver to touch her—

lips, neck, breast

—made him quiver to have her heart.

And this one he would not feed to dogs. He would treasure it. He'd already had a special pouch made for it that hung from the chain around his neck. That way they could be together forever.

"Grub swears to it, sir," Christopher repeated. "He searched the trunk two days ago, and yesterday right after you two left to come here. Lady Arlington gave him the key herself and begged him to be careful. Told him that they were the only things of her mother's she had left. And there was nothing in there but faded linens and some old shoe buckles."

Lawrence looked up at Christopher. "What do you think?"

"I think Lady Arlington is innocent, and that someone is trying to make her look guilty."

"Why would they do that?"

"To get you two apart, I would say. To get her—"

On her own, were the words that would have finished off Christopher's sentence, but Lawrence was already halfway to the stables and not letting up on his sprint. He was not going to allow anyone to see Tuesday before him. He had been so convinced that she was manipulating him that he had not even considered she could be telling the truth. He had acted like a boor and an idiot. But he would make it up to her. He would explain why he was like that. Explain about Constantia and Everly and Maria and Rafael, about how it wasn't her, that he did not trust himself. And he would hope like hell she understood.

He felt physical pain to think about how he had treated her that morning. To think about what he had said.

It was nothing compared to the pain he was about to feel.

*   *   *

The Lion twisted the chain around his finger as his eyes followed his Lady.

She had to pretend to be upset about what happened with Lawrence Pickering. Otherwise everyone would Wonder. But the Lion knew what she was really feeling. Worship. For him.

"Was he a good commander?" she asked His Lordship's men as she paced around her studio.

Everyone wanted to talk to her. Everyone loved her. But he knew it was only his answers that interested her really.

"Oh yes," the Lion told her. It was true. He'd learned everything important he knew from him. Learned about planning. About hiding. About what to look for at a crime scene. About how to govern men's minds. Learned to question everything and not to trust coincidences. Learned the most important truth of all, got it right from His Lordship's own lips: *The only difference between a hero and a murderer is which side you are on.*

The Lion had a feeling that when His Lordship said that, just after their escape from the Spanish prison, he was thinking of himself as a murderer. But for the Lion, it meant something else. It meant that he was a hero.

He saw her glance in his direction and then turn away and her shoulders began to tremble. She was overwhelmed by his courage, he knew, and she did not want the others to see it. Not until it was time. Not until he had proven himself Worthy.

At the start, he had killed the men just to honor her, honor what they shared. But then he'd seen the signs and come to understand. Window, Worthington, Widow. Winner Worship, Work. Wisdom, Well done—

Wicked, Worthless, Wretched, Worm.

NO!

—Wanted. The Words were all signs, for him. And once he'd seen that, he had known. The other killings were just the beginning.

Once he'd known how to look, he started to see signs everywhere, urging him on. His quest was to be the greatest, they told him. He, the Lion, was the one chosen to slay the Knight of Knights. To have Our Greatest Hero fall under his sword. He would overcome him and rescue his Lady. But first, the Knight of Knights had to be ensnared.

Who is the most worthy opponent. Is it the strongest knight?

No.

Is it the bravest knight?

No.

Is it the wildest knight?

No. It is the knight in love because in him dwells the strength, courage, and wildness of a dozen.

When she was again in possession of the Knight of Knight's heart, that was when he would be hardest to beat. That was when the Lion would slay him.

The chain bit into his neck.

He saw how he could do it with exquisite clarity. He could distract the other guards, kill her, then use her body to trap Lawrence Pickering and kill him, too.

It would be so simple. He would pull her head back and let her look at him. He would kiss her once. And then he would cut out her heart.

Winner!

The chain snapped.

*   *   *

Lawrence lathered his horse getting to Worthington hall, nearly felling the handful of late-night pedestrians he passed. But he need not have bothered. As he discovered when he stormed into the studio, she was gone.

The only sign of her was a line of blood trailing out the door.

PART IV

Die

Chapter 29

Lawrence followed the track by instinct, almost without seeing it. He did not think to notice the absence of guards. The unnatural quiet of the house. The strange squeaking of floorboards above him.

The blood went up the stairs, past Sir Dennis's room, and up again, and so did Lawrence, taking them four at a time. As he approached the door under which it disappeared, it registered in his mind that he had been here before, that this was the nursery. As he approached the door he braced himself for what he might see. As he approached the door he thought he was ready.

He wasn't.

Nothing could have prepared him for the sight of Tuesday propped against the wall, soaked in blood.

"I felt lucky to be with him," Tom was in the middle of repeating that afternoon when CeCe had rushed into the studio.

"They found Albert Marston's clothes in an alleyway and they want to search the area," she explained urgently.

The other guards piled quickly out of the room when

they heard, but Tuesday could feel Tom hesitating between following Lawrence's orders to stay glued to her
and wanting to see what they had discovered.

"I won't leave the house, Tom," she had told him. "I
promise."

"I'm to stay with you, at all times, ma'am," he said in
his intense way. But Grub—thank God for Grub—had
come back in then and, perhaps sensing that Tuesday
needed to be alone, had literally dragged his colleague
out to join the search. Tuesday's relief had been almost
overwhelming.

As soon as Grub and Tom were gone, Tuesday had
taken the first jar of paint she could find, jammed a
handful of brushes into her sling and run upstairs. The
paint dribbled out of the container, staining the floor and
the stairs deep red, but she did not care. For the first time
in her life she wanted not to make something, to create
something, but to destroy it.

"Lucky to be with him," Tom had said. He hadn't
known that the words were like a knife going into her
stomach. The simple phrase worked like a mocking incantation in Tuesday's mind, speeding her back to that
morning, back to how she had felt when she woke up,
how she'd felt when Lawrence had still loved her.
"Lucky," that one word, reverberated, sending her back
farther, back to the dark place she kept locked up.

"Lucky, get down from there." She could still hear the
timbre of Curtis's voice so vividly, as if he were again
standing behind her in the nursery.

"Just a moment. I want to—"

"I said get down from there."

She turned to look at him. "What is wrong?"

"You're a mess, Lucky."

"I've been painting all day. But I'm almost done." She stood back to study her work. "Do you think—"

"What's this supposed to be?" he asked, pointing to one of the animals half-visible through the painted ferns.

"It's a kind of cat. From Africa. It's called a leopard."

"Is it? You must have painted it wrong. It looks ridiculous." He sneered at it, trailing a finger through the paint and then wiping it on the gilt wall. "Come on, we've got to go."

"Where?"

"To Jack's. You are going to tell him you were jesting when you said he should not come out with me anymore."

She stiffened. "I wasn't."

"Yes, Lucky, you were."

Curtis took a step closer to her and she saw the malice glittering in his eyes.

"Curtis, you can't treat Jack that way. You can't take him to taverns and make him perform tricks as if he were a trained dog."

"Why not? What else is the freak good for?" He tried to pull her from the ladder.

She resisted, gripping the wall in front of her hard. "No. You are not going to make a fool of Jack."

"The freak doesn't need anyone to make a fool of him."

"Stop calling him a freak!"

"Get down here right now, Lucky, or I will make you sorry."

Although his threats were unoriginal, he always made good on them, which was why they worked. But today she had a headache and had been up half the night being sick and could not stand to hear him talk about Jack that way. Today, this one time, she would not be stopped by his threats.

She looked him in the eye and said, "No. I'm not done with what I was—"

He jerked her off the ladder so hard that she stumbled and hit the wall. He twisted her arm behind her. "When are you going to learn to do what I say?"

"When you stop acting like a beast and start acting like a man," she spit back, trying to ignore the pain in her arm.

He flipped her around so she was facing him. "I'm not enough of a man for you?" His eyes looked wild now. "Do you have someone else you prefer? Someone like George Lyle?"

"That is not what I meant, Curtis. I just—"

"It's his, isn't it? This," he poked a finger into her abdomen. "You're just a damn whore."

"You bastard."

"Never call me that again."

"Why? What are you going to do that you haven't already done?"

His palm rested on her stomach. "Whose is it, Lucky? George's? Or someone else?"

That was when her reason snapped. She remembered trying to work her fists up so she could claw his eyes out. "You bastard. How dare you? How dare you accuse me? After everything—"

He dug the fingers of one hand into her stomach, pushing the air out of her. She looked up at him and the expression in his eyes, a viciousness she had never seen before, terrified her. Quelled her. Told her she had made an enormous mistake.

His fingers pressed harder and anger evaporated into

fear. Fear of how he could hurt their child. Fear of how he could hurt Jack. Oh god, what had she done? "I'm so sorry, Curtis. I'll do whatever you say. I will be better, Curtis, I'll be a perfect—"

Thwack!

She heard it, the sound of her head hitting the wall and then felt herself sliding down its surface. She tried to sit up but she couldn't, couldn't move. She got her eyes open just in time. In time to see him pull his leg back. In time to watch as his boot with the shiny buckle—*don't rub too hard or the gilt will come off*—came tearing toward her. In time to feel the full force of his first kick in her stomach. In time to see him smile and hear him say, "This is your fault, Lucky. I warned you." And then, for the first time in her life, she fainted.

When she regained consciousness it was light outside. She was lying by the wall on her side, in a pool of blood. Her body ached everywhere. She sensed somehow that her baby was gone. And all she could hear in her head, over and over again, was Curtis's voice saying, *This is your fault, Lucky.*

It had taken her hours to clean the blood stains off the floor of the nursery that day, she now remembered as she worked to paint over the walls with huge strokes. She paid no attention to technique, just brought her brush down wherever she wanted to, ruining the exquisite painting, the magical garden, covering the walls and herself in dripping blocks of blood-colored paint. It did not matter; nothing mattered now. She had lost Lawrence and while part of it was her fault (she should have told him) another part thought that he should have listened to her, should have believed her, should have trusted her (yes, but she should have told him about writing to

Silus). Not that it could have gone any differently, she knew. It was inevitable that he would reject her, too. But his words, his willingness to believe in her betrayal made her feel inexorably sad for both of them.

How could he not have believed her? How could he not have trusted her? a voice sobbed in her head, but the questions were rhetorical. She knew the answers. It was because he wanted to be rid of her. It made perfect sense. Why would their relationship go any other way? Her paintbrush smacked the wall, leaving splatters shaped like hideous spiders. She painted over the dragonfly, she painted over the butterfly, she painted a huge serpent's tongue on the leopard.

She moved from one wall to the next until she came to the place in the gilding where Curtis had cleaned his finger, the place she had never been able to fix—*don't rub too hard or the gilt will come off*—the place that had always mocked her, a constant reminder of her failure, her easy rejectability. Just under it the wall was slightly dented from where her head had hit it. As she stared at it, the futility of what she was doing almost choked her. No layers of pigment were going to erase what had happened to her or what she knew to be true. No layers of pigment would cover the fact that she was alone, again, rejected again. She dropped the jar of paint and it shattered, soaking the floor and her dress, and beyond caring she sat down in the puddle to wonder what the hell she was going to do with her life.

She heard quick footsteps in the corridor. Tom's she figured, coming to check on me. But when she looked up it was not Tom who filled the doorway. It was Lawrence. Lawrence staring at her as if she were the most hideous creature living.

She could not meet his eyes. She took a deep breath and said, "I will not—"

"I see," Lawrence said as if having just found the solution to a puzzle. "You are redecorating." His gaze took in the ruin of the nursery and it made him want to die inside to see what he had done to her. "It is a nice change, but I am not sure I agree with what you have done on this wall," he said, gesturing toward one covered in broad cross-hatched strokes. "A bit severe. Over here, however," he moved toward the one with the spider-like blotches and the forked-tongue leopard, "this really catches the eye. Some of your best work, sweetheart."

Tuesday gaped at him.

"Ah, now this is a place I can help with." He nodded as he stood in front of the only wall that was untouched. The wall that Curtis had stained. He bent down and dipped his hands into the pool of paint edging along the floor, then planted them firmly over the mark in the gilding. He repeated this a half dozen times until the wall was fairly covered with his hand prints. "I hope you won't think me immodest, but I feel that this really gives the place a good tone, don't you?" He slid down the wall and sat, in the puddle of paint, next to her.

"What are you doing, Lawrence?"

He looked from her to her paint-colored lap. "Stalling while I work up the courage to apologize to you and ask your forgiveness."

Tuesday felt an unfamiliar pricking in her eyes. "You want to apologize?"

"Yes. I was horrible to you. I should have trusted you and asked you about the ledger and the other evidence, rather than accusing you. Can you forgive me?"

"Why did you do that? Why did you say those things? Even think them?"

He stared at her hand, lying next to him. He wanted to take it in his, but he did not dare. "It's hard for me to explain. It just made so much sense to me that you would betray me, lie to me, that I latched on to it."

"Why?"

He brought his eyes to hers. She had a red spot on her cheekbone and another on her chin and the bottom half of her hair on her left side was clumped with paint. God how he loved her. "Because you are too good to be real, Tuesday. Because I don't deserve you. Nobody does."

A tear streaked through the paint on her cheek. Her fingers reached for his.

"I mean it, Tuesday."

"You deserve so much more," she said, and was astonished at how tight her throat felt.

"There is nothing more than you."

Tuesday bit her lip and whispered, "Do you mean that?"

Lawrence wanted to stab himself for the pain and insecurity he had rekindled in her eyes. "Tuesday, I am so sorry. I can't believe I almost lost you. I can't believe what a fool I was. Can you ever forgive me."

"You had no choice. You had to believe what you saw," Tuesday told him, and that made Lawrence feel even more wretched. "Besides, I should have told you that I wrote to Silus Ivry."

"Silus," Lawrence repeated. He saw a way to begin to make up to her what he had done. "I had a talk with Silus tonight."

"You saw Silus?"

"Yes. And I know why he broke off your engagement. Why they all did."

She flinched and tried to pull her hand from his. "So do I."

He held on tight. "I don't think so." He leaned down and whispered in her ear. "He is still in love with you."

She flicked her head as if trying to get rid of a fly. "He was never in love with me."

"He was. They all were. But your brother made it too expensive for them to marry you."

"What are you talking about? That Jack was too much of a burden—"

"Not Jack. Howard. He skimmed money off of them in exchange for your hand."

"That's ridiculous."

"It's true. And I hope you won't mind living in a hovel. Because there is no amount of money I wouldn't give to be with you."

Tuesday was frowning over what he said. She needed to think about that, but later. She shook her head. "Is that what convinced you? That I wasn't—wasn't all the things you said?"

"Yes. And then Grub sent word by Christopher that he had searched your trunk twice, while you were there, and found nothing." Lawrence hated to admit it. He wished he could tell her that he had just believed in her, but he was not made that way.

Tuesday understood. Understood that his doubts were even more about himself than they were about her. "I am glad. I want you to know for certain. And I had forgotten about Grub. Although, you know, I could have put those things in after he searched."

"The last time Grub searched was last night, while you were at my house."

"How do you know I did not sneak over here when you were asleep and do it then."

"Because I did not go to sleep. Neither, if I recall correctly, did you."

"You did doze off," Tuesday pointed out. "I could have done it then, then sneaked back into bed, so you wouldn't know."

"You didn't. You wouldn't."

"Why? How can you be so sure? It would be a nearly perfect cover."

"Because I believe you. I believe in you. You would not do that."

"Ah. Then do you believe that I love you?"

There was a pause.

"Do you?"

"Yes."

"Do you know what that means, Lawrence?"

"That you are daft."

"Stop it." She made him look at her. "I love you Lawrence. That means I would never betray you. I would never do anything willfully to hurt you. Do you understand?"

Lawrence swallowed hard. "Yes."

"Good," she said. She kept meeting his eyes for a long moment, willing him to believe her the way she believed in him. Then her eyes moved and she frowned slightly. "Why did Silus come to London? I specifically told him to stay away."

She felt Lawrence stiffen beside her. "He came because he thought you were in trouble. Because, as I said, he still loves you." He paused. "Did you—ah, were you in love with him, too?"

"Deeply," Tuesday said. Out of the corner of her eye she saw a muscle in Lawrence's jaw pulse. "Are you jealous?"

"No."

She covered her mouth with her hand. "Lawrence, I—"

"I don't want to hear about it."

The hand was not enough to block the muffled sounds of her laughter. "I was jesting, my lord. I was not in love with him."

"Don't say that just to appease me."

"Have I ever done anything just to appease you before?" She was smiling at him and Lawrence felt his insides melt.

"No," he had to admit.

"Lawrence, you are the only man I have ever loved."

"Oh," he said, because once again she had robbed him of words. And then he yawned.

"Very flattering, my lord."

"It's your fault," he told her. "You kept me up all night."

"I did not. It was *you* who kept *me* up," she protested. "I distinctly remember—"

"Don't argue with me, Tuesday." His voice was tight. "Please."

"Why not? If I am right?"

"First of all because you are wrong. And secondly because arguing with you arouses me to such an extent that it is impossible for me to think straight."

Her eyes were huge. "It does? Always?"

"Since the first moment I met you. And I don't have

time for that. I have a murder investigation to consider, which I badly neglected all day."

"Why did you do that?"

"Because my heart was broken."

"Mine, too. I mean, I neglected it, too." Tuesday tried to stifle it but could not keep back a yawn. Suddenly she was exhausted. "I am certain that if anything important had happened we would have known about it."

She made to rise but before she could get to her feet, Lawrence had gathered her into his arms. "Wait, where are we going?"

Lawrence pushed open the door with his back. "I am taking you to bed and then I am going to see how little we progressed today."

"I am not going to bed. I want to know what happened in the investigation, too." It all seemed strangely far away and unreal to her now. She was so weary. And she knew she had better sleep tonight because she was not going to sleep the next night, Monday night, when the killer might use her dreams as a launching point for his Tuesday murder again. But first she wanted to know what had happened. If she could keep her eyes open.

"I will tell you all about that in the morning," he said as he carried her down the stairs.

"I am absolutely not going to bed. I'm not even tired."

"Then why have you been yawning? Right through my declaration of love."

"I did not. You yawned through my declaration of love."

"You did it first."

"No I didn't. You are the one who should be going to slee—"

Lawrence kissed her. "Later sweetheart. When this is over. Then argue with me for hours."

They finally compromised that she would lie in bed, with her eyes closed, while he met with his men to catch up on the investigation in the other half of the studio where she could hear.

"And I am agreeing to close my eyes only because I have a slight headache," she announced as he carried her into the room. "Otherwise they would be open, as I will be wide awake."

"Of course."

Lawrence settled her in bed and went to join his men, who were arrayed around the large table. In the center of the table was a pile of clothes.

"Marston's," Grub told him. "That's all we found."

"I'm not surprised," Lawrence admitted. "He would have changed disguises as soon as he lost the men following him. You searched the area?"

"Twice. No sign of anyone unusual."

After Lawrence had reviewed their lack of progress from every angle and sent his men home, he stood and stared out the long windows of the studio into the darkness of the night. It was a perfect night for hiding. There was only a sliver of a moon and the streets were oddly empty, as if all London were holding its breath alongside him.

He had done everything he could, and he could not have felt more dissatisfied. Albert Marston had gone to ground somewhere. Their only hope now was that he would come back out to keep his schedule of killing every Tuesday. Which was an extremely unpleasant hope.

Everything about the investigation rankled him. Tuesday had been right the previous day—it all felt too staged, too put together. Even their meeting and their collaboration. It was as if the murders were just a vehicle to bring them together, to showcase their precise talents—hers for drawing and observation, his for—whatever he was good at. Puzzle solving. Frowning. It all seemed somehow inevitable, preordained.

That is called destiny, my friend.

It's called coincidence, Lawrence corrected, and he didn't like it. He didn't like it because it made him feel as if someone else were in control. As if, at any moment, whomever had given him Tuesday could take her away again.

He was absolutely right.

Chapter 30

At midnight, the moment when Monday turned to Tuesday, the transformation of London began. It was almost unnoticeable to the naked eye, but a few very astute watchers—largely prostitutes—caught on that something strange was happening. As the night watchmen finished calling the hour, the streets gradually filled with able-looking men. They were all dressed differently and none of them acknowledged one another, but there was no mistaking that even when they lounged, they lounged with an attentiveness and purpose that suggested they were not at leisure.

At one Silus Ivry awoke from a disturbing dream about Tuesday and himself and a tortoise. He put on his dressing gown and wrote a long letter to his wife.

At two Lucy Burns, perched on her rooftop, finally thought of the perfect rhyme for "vaporous" and, with a fond look at George Lyle who had for hours been lurking in the alleyway opposite Worthington Hall below (he lurked better than any man alive, she thought), went inside to sleep.

At three, the Lion traded posts with one of the other men on duty and settled himself on the chair outside of Tuesday's studio.

At four, Tuesday began to dream.

*   *   *

Ha ha ha footsteps pounding behind her, near her. Scenes already painted, the forest, the garden, the storeroom, whiz by her. Now they are in the corridor, now the familiar shadow is crawling up the wall, crawling closer, over her.

"Hello, Tuesday." It is his voice, the voice of the killer. It is uncannily familiar, and terrifying in its intensity. *Wake up,* her mind screams. *Wake up.* But she can't.

"It did not have to be like this, you know," he says, his voice like glittering metal.

If you can see him, you can find him. You must see his face. She tries to turn around but a strong hand holds her head forward.

"Don't." His fingers dig into her scalp. "I don't want to see your harlot eyes."

"Why are you doing this?" she gasps, trying to wrench away.

"You know why. I warned you."

He grips her head tighter so she is staring straight ahead, straight at the shadow on the corridor wall. The knot in the wood, like a death's head, hovers above it, and now, as he comes to rest behind her, it sits on his shoulders, a small, leering face on his grotesquely huge body. She can hear his breathing, regular, steady, hear hers panting, gasping.

Ha ha ha the death's head laughs at her. "It's time for you to get what you deserve, whore."

If you can remember everything you can catch him.

He can read her mind. "There is nothing you can do to stop me. You had your chance. You could have behaved. But now it is too late. Now I am going to be your worst nightmare. Now you are mine, Tuesday. Mine."

It happens in front of her, in slow motion. The shadows moving together. His, large, standing, *familiar*. Hers kneeling, pleading. The knife above her, plunging down.

"*NO!*" she screams, so loud it surprises them both. The shadow of the knife hovers in the air right above her, hovers there, startled, and then comes slashing down for her neck.

But she is gone. Ducking under the arm, she runs, blood pounding in her ears like heavy footsteps behind her. She turns a corner and keeps running, staggering forward to the staircase ahead of her.

Don't let him have control. Leave something behind. Leave yourself a clue. Thoughts rattle around her mind without registering, *leave a clue, leave a clue,* over and over. Barreling forward, she grabs the first thing she passes and carries it with her to the stairs.

Her hand closes on the balustrade and she is running. She turns around to look at him and sees the fabric of his cape is caught in a crack between the steps. This is her chance, if she can just go fast—

Sweet whistles the fabric as it rips, a low susurration over the clunking of his boots, and he is behind her again, reaching for her. She gains the top of the stairs, her burning feet find the landing, and she is nearly to the next flight—the next flight, freedom, the next flight, safety—when he throws himself on top of her, pinning her down.

He smashes her body beneath his and the breath goes out of her in a single gasp. He wraps his arms around her, clamping her hands where they lay, one next to her side, one above her head. Everything stops as they lay like that, his chest rising and falling on her back, his sweat tickling her neck.

"I loved you so much Tuesday," he says to her, and now he sounds sad, small. A boy with a broken toy. "I loved you so much. How could you do this to me?"

Her mouth is too dry to speak. She tries to wriggle free but she cannot fight against him. She feels like she is being smothered. Like she will die under his horrible weight.

She sees where the joiner imperfectly matched the corners of a step. She sees the place where a newly polished boot scuffed the riser leaving a startled looking line. She sees, below her, a strip of his cape wafting like a desolate flag. She sees, above her, her own hand holding the bruised petals of a deep red rose.

He raises one arm and touches her hair, blocking her view.

"I loved you so much and you betrayed me," he whimpers into the golden strands. "You betrayed me, with him."

"With him," he repeats and his caresses change, become gruff, as if under the influence of a powerful memory. He is not stroking, now he is pulling back on her hair, hard.

"You told him all about me. I heard you. I heard you laughing." He says the last word like it is acid on his tongue. He twists her hair, jerking her head around toward him. "Look at me, you bitch," he orders, seeing her eyes, smashed closed. "Look at me and tell me what is so damn funny."

She feels his ragged breath against her cheek, his hand tugging her hair. This is it, this is her chance to look at him, but suddenly she is terrified of what she is going to see. She swallows hard and makes herself open her eyes.

She sees, right in front of her, the knife, pointed down at her throat. She sees his hand, the white cuff of his shirt, holding it. And behind it, she sees *him*.

"No. Oh, God, no—"

Tuesday awoke suddenly, clinging to the edge of the bed, her mouth wide to scream. She lay there, perfectly still, until the panting subsided, until she could swallow again. Then, careful not to wake Lawrence, she rose, went to her easel, and painted. Dawn was just trickling into the studio when she began to shift through the papers on the large table, looking for the calendar. She was suddenly afraid that she had been wrong, that—

"Lady Arlington," a voice whispered close behind her, making her jump. She whirled around and saw Tom standing right there.

"I am sorry to startle you ma'am," he said softly, taking a step closer to her so his voice would not bother Lawrence. "I saw the candlelight from under the doorway and since Grub is asleep outside I wanted to make sure everything was all right."

Tuesday cursed herself for being so jumpy. "Thank you. I—I was just painting." She pointed at the picture on the easel but did not turn back to it, not wanting to see it again. "I was looking for the calendar but I couldn't find it. Do you know what day it is, Tom?"

"What day?" Tom repeated, thinking for a moment. "Why it's June 26, ma'am. Tuesday."

Tuesday reached behind her to steady herself, and found her hand clutching Lawrence's arm instead.

"What's wrong, sweetheart?" he asked sleepily. "I woke

up and you weren't in bed. What have you—" his eyes fell on the painting. "Oh."

"It's Tuesday, Lawrence," she said, and her eyes were filled with terror.

"Don't worry." He turned her toward him and wrapped her in his arms. "Nothing is going to happen today."

He smelled of sleep and bed and comfort and safety. Tuesday inhaled deeply. She desperately wanted to believe him.

Over her head Lawrence spoke to Tom. "What are you doing here? I didn't even know you were on duty. You look exhausted."

"My shift just ended. I was about to leave when I saw that Grub had dozed off at his post outside. There was a light under the door so I came in to make sure there was nothing wrong," Tom repeated.

"Good man," Lawrence praised him. "But enough. You're working too hard, Tom. Go home and get some sleep. I don't want to see you again until tonight. That is an order."

"Yes sir."

At eleven o'clock the body of George Lyle, the well-known artist, was discovered on the staircase of an abandoned rooming house in Whitechapel. From the temperature of the body and the amount of blood, it looked like he had been dead only a few hours. He was lying on his back when he was found, his throat slit, his heart missing. Beneath him, caught in one of the steps, was a strip of fabric. Just above him was the head of a crushed red rose. When his body was moved, they discovered that a word had been written in blood beneath it. The word was "Tuesday."

A quarter-of-an-hour later the man assigned to the day

shift guarding the studio stood looking at Tuesday's painting and shaking his head and repeating, "No one's touched it, sir, I swear." For the first time in his life, Lawrence wished one of his men was lying to him. Because he was having trouble coming up with an explanation, that did not make the hair on his arms prickle, for how the word "Tuesday" had suddenly appeared on the left side of the painting. He had the guard remove the painting so that Tuesday wouldn't see it.

By noon the dogs had been sent out and were trying to catch a scent from the piece of fabric left behind in the staircase.

Chapter 31

She had tricked him. The Lion was so furious he could barely see straight. His Lady, his own lady, had tricked him. It had not seemed dangerous to leave the rose or the piece of fabric. But that was because he had not thought of the dogs.

They had probably been all her idea. Punishing him still.

He had been enjoying himself so much. Enjoying watching the guardsmen as they carefully scanned the buildings for clues. His Lordship wouldn't let his Lady come, but the men had been so meticulous, searching for footprints or telltale hairs. He hadn't left them any of that this time. Nothing that could be clearly linked to him. He knew every one of them and knew they didn't stand a chance at catching him. He was practically right in front of them right now, and they did not recognize him.

But the dogs could.

The barking was getting closer, like a horrible chorus shouting for his death. They could smell him; he could almost smell himself, the disgusting smell of his own body, of his own fear.

Shouting, footsteps now, closing in on him. There

were dozens of people between him and them but he could almost feel the panting of the dogs on his heels. He had to find a way to change his clothes. He knew all about dogs and knew that he had only minutes until they picked up his scent. Calm. Patience. Think.

He scanned the busy street he was on, two blocks from the scene of the crime. Stay calm. The thing to do would be to find a man of about his stature and kill him—patience!—tail him to a deserted alley, *then* kill him and trade garments. The dogs would have the corpse half eaten by the time their handlers got there. Calm calm calm—

Barking at his ankles, barking all around him, barking coming for him, kill that man, kill all the men, kill—

Patience!

God, he hated dogs.

Think.

He spotted a likely candidate on the other side of the street. The man's clothes were nowhere near as nice as his green suit, but he would not be embarrassed to be seen in them. Good—stay calm—move slowly—barking!—don't startle him, be careful, look around—

Then he saw her. Saw her walking down the street, toward him, not recognizing him, like one of the damsels that always give succor to knights. Wench, his mind pointed out. Carrying Wine! He knew exactly where she was going. And he decided he was going there, too.

Wine splattered all over the front of his cape and breeches as she collided with him.

"Oh no, I beg your pardon, sir, oh, I am so sorry," she immediately began apologizing, mopping at the mess she had made of his lovely suit with her handkerchief.

He looked down at her as if he was startled, surprised.

As if he had not purposely Walked into her. He saw her scan his face and was certain she had no idea who he was.

He flashed her a slight smile, the one he'd practiced, and said, "With beauty like yours in the neighborhood, no wonder there are robbers here." He talked, smooth, slow. No rush. No fear.

"Robbers?" the Woman repeated, her hand stopping in midair.

He took the kerchief from her fingers and began daubing at the wine himself. "That's what the dogs are for." They were close now, very close. Hurry up, the Lion's mind told him. Please let it work, he thought. Please let—

"Robbers here? Right here?" She clutched his arm, realized what she was doing, and pulled her hand away.

He looked at her as if just understanding what he was seeing. She was really pretty, the Wench. "You look frightened. May I escort you home? To make sure they don't get to you?"

Gratitude flooded her face. "Would you? Even after I ruined your suit?"

"It would be my pleasure." He slipped his arm through hers and she clung to him tightly. "Which way do we go, Miss—"

"CeCe."

The dogs and guards were now visible at the end of the street but he did not care. It was going to be fine. He was the Winner. "I'm William," he heard himself saying.

"My house is just around the corner, William," she told him, moving more quickly. They stopped in front of a two-story building with a White door. She fished around in her purse and withdrew a set of keys, but her fingers were trembling so much that she could not get them into the lock.

The dogs rushed up the street, sweat flying off them, their teeth barred. The Lion could see them, could see the teeth, could smell their disgusting breath. They were only half a block away, people leaping aside to make room for them, children gripping the hems of their nannies' gowns, a boy dropping his sugar stick with fear, the dogs were coming, they were looking right at him, they were salivating for him, starving for him.

Come on come on come on!

She dropped the keys.

"Allow me," he said, charming smile, no hint of his agitation. He picked up the keys, slid one into the lock, opened it and held the door open for her. He had not quite figured out how to maneuver himself in yet, but she took care of that for him. She was trembling so badly that she could not walk up the stairs to her apartment. He offered her his arm to lean on and she accepted it gratefully.

At the apartment door she turned to look at him, her hand still on his forearm. "I don't know what I would have done if you weren't here, William," she said. "I can't believe how, how silly I've been but the dogs, the robbers—they just terrified me so much. It is hard for a woman on her own. Thank you for walking me home. And for staying with me."

"It's nothing."

"William, you are kind to say that, but what must you think of me?"

She had little dimples and lovely lips. He said, telling the truth, "I think you are charming and beautiful."

She blushed deeply. "I know this is irregular, but it seems the least I can do after—after all that. If you were to step inside with me, I believe I have something that will take the wine stain right out."

Not too eager. "That is not necessary—"

"Oh please. Please allow me to."

"You would do that? For me? A stranger?" Charming smile.

"You are hardly a stranger now. And it is I who made the mess."

"Bosh. A ruined jacket is a small price to pay for making the acquaintance of a ministering angel."

She blushed again and opened the door.

"This is a lovely place," he said, because he knew he should, when they were inside. There were drawings tacked all over the Walls, a bit like at his house, but the rest of the place was much tidier.

"It is not really mine," she confided as she directed him to a chair at a small round table. She hesitated for a moment. "It's—it's my fiancé's. I am engaged. But he won't mind me having you up."

The dogs were downstairs, barking. He could see the cloud of dust stirred up by their feet as they ran in circles in the street, wondering where the scent had gone. And he was upstairs, safe. With a lovely Woman.

"Engaged? Brave man, letting a creature like you alone with other men when he hasn't even made it legal yet," he joked, just like Lawrence Pickering would, as he removed his stained jacket.

He saw her give his fine shoulders an appreciative glance before saying, "He has no choice."

"Why is that?"

She was moving around the room, putting things away, looking for the powder that would remove the Wine, but he could tell that she was eager to share her story. "He is missing. Disappeared during the war. I try to keep the place just as he left it, so that if—when he comes home it will be exactly how it was." She now sat down next to him at the table and looked at him from under her long eyelashes. "You did not fight in the war, did you William?"

He had an urge to seem brave to her. He had vanquished the dogs. Overcome His Lordship's men. And that was just the beginning. "Actually, I did."

"Why? You look like a man of means."

"Well, the truth is—" the Lion paused, trying to figure out what to say, what lie to tell. He felt wonderful. It was very nice being in this little apartment with CeCe. With her not knowing him, not recognizing him. With her Worshiping him. He'd heard the other guards talk about her but he himself had been too busy to notice how pretty she was. And now she was sitting there, right next to him, Watching him. Wanting him. He knew he was a great Knight and that his Lady loved him, but sometimes the Waiting got a little lonely. It was really nice to have someone to talk to. Someone to look at. To look at him that way.

"What happened is that my grandmother died. After that I did not know what to do with myself so I signed up to fight for Her Majesty," he answered, astonishing himself. It was the truth, just like he'd given her his true name. Or part of it.

"You must have loved your grandmother very much," she said.

"Yes." Suddenly he wanted to tell her everything. Share his favorite memory with her. "Her death—

("I told you what I would do if I caught you with your hands on one of the girls again," the old woman said, opening and closing her bony hands like claws. "Go to the kennels, you hideous boy, and meditate on what you are. You will sleep there for a week."

"I don't think so, grandmother."

"Do it, William! Do what I say or you will be sorry." The old woman's eyes were blazing and she was leaning forward in her chair. The ratty blanket that covered her legs slipped away and he could see how thin she was. How feeble.

"There is nothing you can do to me, ma'am," young William, not yet the Lion but on his way, told his grandmother quietly. "I learned your lessons too well." *Men are ruled by fear not love.* He was not going to be afraid anymore.

He held up the glittering knife he had found in his father's ancient trunk so the old woman could see it in the candlelight. Could get scared. But she just looked at him with disgust.

"You haven't got the nerve to skin a cat," she said. "Even the chambermaids you approach think you are pathetic. 'Whimpering Willy' they call you. I tried to make you a real knight but you were too backward. And you go around with your pants down, touching yourself. You are wicked. You disgust me." She leaned forward to glare at him with her dark glittering eyes. And then she puckered her shriveled lips together. And spit in his face.

The feeling of the knife severing her thin neck had been incredible. He was in charge now. He was the master! He was the knight! He had killed the dragon!)

"My grandmother's death changed everything in my life," he explained to CeCe, his hands flexing and unflexing with the remembered feeling of the knife. The same knife he still used for his killings. "It made me think about what was important. Made me realize I needed to aspire to higher things."

They had never caught him, because he had gone to Lawrence Pickering and pleaded to be allowed to serve on his boat. Begged to be allowed to serve him. And the fool had taken him in, without asking about his pedigree, or being bothered by the fact that he ducked his head every time a constable from Worcester came close by. Had taken him in and trusted him and trained him.

The Lion had deceived him entirely—entirely! He had killed Curtis right under His Lordship's nose. He'd been the one to shoot at Albert Marston to ensure that they believed him as a witness and went with his description. He'd led them to the explosive-filled hideout by letting himself be seen regularly in a memorable disguise. He had been directing them, ruling them all along. And every single thing he had done had worked. He was the Winner again!

Every helpful thing he did just made him look better, *more Worthy of trust*. The time he spent around Worthington Hall just made him seem more concerned, more interested in catching the Lion. He had fooled them all, fooled them brilliantly.

Killing his grandmother had been the best moment of his life so far. But killing Lawrence Pickering—seeing His Lordship's face as he realized that he was not the best, that the Lion was the real Knight of Knights—killing Lawrence Pickering was going to be better.

He looked at the Woman next to him and wanted to share it all with her. Wanted to tell her how he had fooled them all, how he was smarter and braver and more clever than even Lawrence Pickering. Maybe he would, he decided. He was not lonely, but it was really very nice to have someone with him.

He had never been alone with a Woman like this, just sitting at a table, talking. Sharing memories. It was a strange feeling, and he was not sure what to do. He said what he thought Lawrence Pickering would say. He said, "Doesn't it get lonely waiting for your fiancé to come back?"

She had her head bent over his jacket, cleaning it, but she glanced up at him with a slight smile and said, "Oh yes. Terribly."

"You must be very loyal to have waited so long. The war has been over for more than a year."

She said, "It—it is not so bad. But it is nice to have a handsome man like you to sit opposite."

He reached out and put his finger under her chin, raising her face from the jacket to his. "You are a very beautiful girl, CeCe."

Her eyes grew huge and the jacket accidentally slid to the floor. They both bent down to retrieve it, their heads knocking, their hands coming together. They laughed, and as they sat up he kept hold of her fingers.

"I don't do this very often," she said, blushing all the way into the bodice of her gown. "Invite men up here, I mean. In fact, I've never done anything like it before."

"I am glad you did it for me." He looked at her the way he'd seen His Lordship looking at his Lady. Then he took her hand and brought it to his lips. He felt her tremble again. "Is CeCe your real name?"

"No," she said, breathlessly. "It is just a nickname. My real name is too absurd to use."

He pressed her hand between his. "What is it?"

"You really want to know?"

Her palm was smooth and delicate. It felt nice. "Yes."

"Promise you won't make fun of me?"

He nodded.

"Patience. Patience is my real name."

His heart stopped beating. *Patience is our most powerful ally.*

It was a message for him. A sign. A sign of his success, of his luck. He had been right to go with her. To trust her. "That is a beautiful name." He smiled His Lordship's smile at her. "May I kiss you, Patience?"

"Oh, I'm not sure. My fiancé—"

He leaned over and kissed her. She did not taste like he thought Lady Arlington would, but she was nice. Her lips were soft and warm. She did not pull away.

"Do you believe two people can fall in love when they first meet?" he asked her.

Her eyes opened slowly from the kiss. "I—I don't know."

"I think I am falling in love with you, Patience."

"Oh." She looked down at their clasped hands and he felt her knee close against his leg. He began to pull her closer, for another kiss, when she started slightly.

He saw where she was looking. His shirt had been pushed up when he moved and her eyes were on his scar.

"Did you get that in the war?" she asked, touching it gently.

Her fingers on his wrist made him tingle. "No," he answered again truthfully. "It is a dog bite."

"How terrible. I hate dogs."

"So do I."

They looked at each other deeply. Her hand was on his thigh, moving up.

Men are ruled by love not fear, he thought, and then realized that was backwards. She was confusing him. Being with her was strange. Upsetting.

Nice.

"Are you hungry William?" she asked.

"Only for more of your kisses." His Lordship could not have said it better.

She blushed. "What if I were to make you supper? And we could dine together. I—I would really like to spend the evening with you. To get to know you better."

No one had ever made supper just for him. No one had ever wanted to sit, just with him, for a whole evening. Especially no Woman. She leaned toward him and her bodice gaped slightly. Inside, her breasts spelled W. It was a sign. He could feel it all the way in his pants. Near where her fingers were.

He made himself shrug, trying to look nonchalant. "All right. If you don't mind."

"It would be a pleasure," she said, looking at him with so much Worship he thought he could fly. "A real pleasure. But I must go out to purchase a few things."

"Like more Wine?"

She laughed. "Exactly."

"I will miss you, Patience. Hurry."

"I will, William." She rose to go and reluctantly took her free hand from his.

The Lion sat quietly at the table and waited for her for two hours, but she did not come back.

He had known she wouldn't. He had seen that she was

sent by his Lady as a temptation. And as a warning, to be patient. Just as he knew that she would betray him. In fact, he was counting on it. But it was still a little sad.

Patience.

He would have liked to have had supper with her.

CeCe ran all the way back to Worthington Hall, rubbing her lips with the back of her hand and trying desperately not to sob.

Chapter 32

The dogs found nothing. "But this flower seller, he got woked up by a bloke wanting to buy a rose," Grub said that afternoon. His feet ached from all his running around but he was glad he'd been able to discover at least someone who had seen something.

"Could he describe him?" Lawrence asked.

"Medium," Grub replied with annoyance. "Medium height, medium-brown hair, medium build. Only noticeable thing about him was his clothes."

"Which were?"

"Bright green, sir. Same as that cloth at the murder scene."

"I guess that is something," Tuesday said wearily. She felt numb. It was as if she had too much to see to, too much to take in, to even absorb George's death. Absorb her part in it. She had never wanted George to die. Never. How could she have helped kill him?

Telling Lucy Burns had been terrible. Every time she looked at the girl she felt reproached. Both for her part—what part? She wanted no part. She had no power, no control—in George's death. And for her own lack of feeling.

But she could not let herself believe it. George had

been her friend, her collaborator, for so long. He could not be dead. He was just away.

Away forever.

Think about that later, she cautioned herself. Today what she needed to do was find the Lion. Find the man responsible for tormenting her.

Ha ha ha, she could almost hear him laughing.

"I'll have to go talk to him and do a drawing of the man the flower seller saw, so we can know what disguise Albert Marston is sporting now," she announced. "What time did he say the man was there?"

"Half past seven o'clock, ma'am."

Tuesday inhaled sharply. "That's impossible. That's after I finished my painting. Long after."

She and Lawrence had the same thought at the same time. "Unless—"

"What?" Grub asked, looking from one to the other of them.

"Maybe the Lion has not been in my dreams at all. Maybe the killings take place after my dreams. Maybe he has just been copying the paintings, not creating them with me." The rush of relief brought with it a rush of grief for George. No emotions, she told herself. Keep them all back.

"That would explain the word," Lawrence said without thinking.

"What word?"

He sorted her painting out from where the guard had hidden it, under a pile of papers. "That word."

Tuesday saw her name inscribed on the side of the paper. "But I didn't write that," she said.

"No. I can't believe I did not see this before. You painted over the calendar and that word bled through because you used a lighter color paint there. It happened while the painting was drying. Which was when the Lion was looking at it."

"You mean my name was written at the crime scene?"

Lawrence pretended to find something very interesting across the room that kept him from meeting her eyes. "Yes."

"And you didn't tell me?"

"I forgot."

"You forgot. And now you think that my name, that word 'Tuesday,' being the only one to appear when I painted over the calendar is—what would you call it, Grub?—a coincidence?"

"Aye, ma'am. A coincidence."

Tuesday was glad to see Lawrence flinch.

Grub shook his head. "But why would he do that? Copy one of your paintings?"

"I don't know." Tuesday moved toward the mantelpiece and picked up a small glass elephant.

"If it's true," Lawrence began, "it means you don't have a killer in your head."

"Yes," Tuesday agreed, turning the elephant around and around in her hands without seeing it. "But it also means that the Lion is deliberately using my pictures as plans for murders."

"It could be another way for him to honor you," Lawrence pointed out. "By bringing your paintings, your artwork to life."

"Or to death," Grub corrected, and Tuesday blanched.

"There is something else," she continued after a moment of silence. "If the Lion isn't causing the dream, why do I keep having it? And if he isn't the one in my head, *then who is?*"

Tuesday had not intended to break the glass elephant, but when CeCe came rushing in calling for Morse and sobbing that she was supposed to be making dinner for the killer, it fell from her hands and smashed against the back of the fireplace.

Lawrence and Tuesday spent the rest of the day arguing and only came to an agreement as it grew dark.

Instead of going to CeCe's fiancé's apartment, which he may well have set to explode again, they would force the Lion to come to them. Unless they were deeply mistaken, he would be unable to keep himself from Worthington Hall, from coming to see what steps they were taking and to preen over how much of a flurry he had put them into. They also wagered that he would chase after CeCe once he realized that she had betrayed him. The best way to catch him, they decided, would be to trap him then.

None of this was up for debate. What Lawrence and Tuesday fought over was whether or not she and CeCe were going to leave London immediately and not return until the Lion was caught. Lawrence's position was that they were. Tuesday's was that every horse, mule, and dog in England yoked together could not carry her away.

"Tuesday, I don't want to argue with you about this."

"Good, then it's decided. We stay. In terms of—"

"No. You are going."

"Look, Mr. Pickering. Unless I am mistaken we are talking about luring the killer here, to my house, and trying to ensnare him."

"Yes."

"And the reason you want me to leave is because it is dangerous."

"Yes."

"Which means that someone, you or I, might die."

"Maybe."

"And you think I would leave when there was the possibility of anything happening to you? I have already lost nearly all the men I have ever known, let alone cared about, to this monster."

"I'm not worth—"

She put her fingers over his lips. "Lawrence, I love you very much and sometimes I even respect your judgement. But about this you are wrong and I am going to keep arguing with you until you either carry me to bed where I will make you forget about it or agree to let me stay."

In the interests of remembering what he was supposed to be doing, not to mention remembering what others were supposed to be doing, Lawrence admitted defeat.

After giving orders to the men who would be stationed on the perimeter around Worthington Hall to keep the Lion from getting in, Lawrence summoned Grub and Tom. They, his most trusted men, were going to guard CeCe.

"There are more men out there than they had watching us in Spain," he told them.

"We managed to escape them, didn't we, sir?" Grub asked cheerfully.

"Yes. That is why there are *more* of them. But there is still a chance he might get in. That is why I want you, Grub, on duty outside CeCe's door. Tom, you'll be at the head of the stairs."

"What about in her room?" Tom asked.

"She doesn't want anyone. She says she just wants to be alone. But I think she has Morse in there with her. I think this meeting with the Lion sort of broadened their relationship."

Grub nodded. "I thought I saw him going up the water pipe. And you, sir. Where will you be?"

"Around." He paused and looked serious. "This man is very dangerous. I don't want you to deal with him yourself. If you have any sign of him, summon me." Then he added, as an afterthought, "And don't kill him if you can help it."

There were a lot of questions Lawrence wanted to ask.

The man in green lowered himself cautiously into the cellar of Worthington Hall through the small window. It was dark and quiet. There was no one there, as he had expected.

He paused to dust his suit off, then silently felt his way to the door that led to the staircase. Here there was a dim light and he was careful not to cast a shadow. It would not do to be noticed on his way to meet his Lady.

He had begun to be concerned that she loved Lawrence Pickering, but he had received her message that day and knew it was him she really wanted.

As he scaled the first set of stairs, he marveled at his good fortune. He was going to bed the woman of his dreams. Going to have her all for himself. For whatever wickedness he wanted.

He had to smother a chuckle.

He crept by the first guard station unnoticed in the darkness, and headed up the final flight of stairs. He was getting so close now, he thought he smelled her.

The second guard was asleep in his chair. Fool. He walked by the man, completely undetected.

Then, just as he had passed, there was a loud cry.

"Who are you?" A voice shouted. A lantern appeared, illuminating the corridor, lighting the man in the green suit.

"It's him!" the voice hollered.

"The Lion!" another added.

"He's armed!"

"Look out!"

"But—" was the man in the green suit's last word. Footsteps pounded down the corridor toward him, guards arriving from all sides. Driven by instinct, he pressed forward, pulling himself out of the grasp of strong arms that held him. Punching like a maniac, he broke free and ran hard in the direction of his Lady, the lady he loved, ran to her for help, ran blindly, ran—

Right onto Tom's sword.

The candles of a dozen lanterns saturated the hallway with shadowless light that gave everything precise, unnatural edges. For an instant the man in the suit and Tom stood face to face, Tom's sword between them, staring at one another. Then Tom let out a low, horrified sob and dropped his weapon and the man in the green suit crumpled to the ground, the sword's hilt sticking out of his stomach.

"I got him," Tom mouthed, watching the body twitch, his face colorless, his eyes unable to move. "I got him. I got him, sir. I got the Lion."

"It's all right, Tom," Lawrence told him.

Tom twitched slightly and turned blank eyes on Lawrence. "I killed him. He ran to me and I killed him. I got him, sir. I'm sorry, sir, I know you wanted him taken alive, but I'm sorry, sir, I've killed him."

"Grub, can you take Tom downstairs?"

"I'm fine, sir," Tom insisted, his voice hollow. "I killed him. I killed the Lion."

Lawrence looked at the floor. Albert Marston lay in a pool of his own blood on the bare planks of the hallway.

His face was a mask of surprise. He was wearing a green suit identical to the one CeCe described.

Lawrence said, "Yes, Tom, you did." He had to hold back his anger. He had wanted the man alive, wanted him to stand trial for what he had done. Wanted him to explain why he did it, why he used Tuesday, why—

Later, my friend.

Tuesday had joined them by then. She stared at the man, the man who had been tormenting her so long and felt nothing. Curiosity, perhaps. Not horror. He looked so harmless. So little like a fiend. What had made him into a monster?

She bent and rolled up his sleeve, just to be sure. There was the scar, the mark of the Lion. She ran her finger over it and the edge peeled off, then the whole thing. She stood up, frowning, and said, "It's fake. The scar. It's just wax."

Lawrence looked at it in the palm of her hand. "We should have guessed that even that would be part of his disguise."

Tuesday could not take her eyes off of it. "I suppose."

"You don't sound convinced."

"It's just odd. Why would he wear it here? Why not conceal himself?"

"He probably needed the entire disguise to feel powerful, to feel like himself."

"Probably." Her eyes moved to the dead figure and she stared at him searchingly. "I guess we will never really understand why he did that. Why he did anything."

Well done, the Lion wanted to tell her. Excellent performance. He was extremely pleased that she had noticed the scar. He had put it there, on purpose, for her. So that even while the others believed he was gone, believed they were safe, she would know that he wasn't really dead. That he was still coming for her.

It had been so easy to lure Albert Marston there. All he'd had to do was say that his Lady loved him and the fool came running. As if she would have anything to do with a Worm like him. As if she would Want him.

The Lion looked around at all of them and wanted to laugh at how solemn they were. None of them knew the good part was still to come. They thought they had killed him, gotten rid of their nemesis. They thought they had vanquished the Lion forever.

They had no idea that was just part of a plan, a Wondrous plan only now about to come to fruition. Just like the knights in the stories, he would reappear at the Great Tournament and slay the knight of knights. Then, as everyone in the land Watched and Worshiped him, he would be crowned the Winner.

No, the Lion knew exactly what his Lady Wanted. He Wanted the same thing.

She wanted him to kill Lawrence Pickering.

Chapter 33

The silence that had fallen over the corridor was broken by the banging of a walking stick on the staircase.

"Father, what are you doing up here?" Tuesday asked, swinging around to face the man as he batted his way through the clutch of guards.

"My house, ain't it? Man's allowed to go about his house."

"Yes, but—" Tuesday was so amazed to see a man who had claimed not to have the use of his legs for three years walking, that she for a moment forgot about the corpse lying on the floor.

"Out of my way," Sir Dennis boomed and the crowds slid apart in front of him. "This is my house and I—"

Tuesday had moved in front of him, to block his view of Albert Marston, but it was too late. His eyes took on a strange, glassy sheen and he staggered forward toward the body.

"What is he doing here?" he asked, looking around, suddenly wild-eyed. "How did he get—" He gripped his chest and his eyes rolled into his head and he fell backwards onto CeCe. She staggered under his weight and began to shriek, but it was nothing compared to the horrible gurgling noises that came from Sir Dennis's throat.

"Father!" Tuesday flew to him, as the gurgling noises went silent. "Father!" she shouted, shaking him by the shoulders.

Lawrence came behind her and pulled her away as Grub leaned over the man. "He's unconscious, sir, but I think he's breathing."

"Someone go for Bianca Foscari," Lawrence called to the group of men standing, dumbfounded now, along the wall. For a moment the room was entirely silent, the sound of the guard's footsteps sprinting down the stairs the only noise in the house. And then CeCe began to rock back and forth with a low keening wail. Everyone stared at her, silent, but in that mournful sound she seemed to be speaking for all of them.

Lawrence did not hear Bianca as she came in. Hours had passed, hours during which CeCe, Tom, and Sir Dennis had all been sedated and put to bed, during which Albert Marston's body had been removed.

He should be relieved, he knew. The Lion was dead. Even if they could not interrogate him, he would no longer pose a threat to anyone. But there were so many questions left without answers. Questions that he knew would plague Tuesday even more than they bothered him.

"Lawrence, Tuesday asked me to check on you," Bianca said, putting her hand on his shoulder.

"I'm fine." He tried a smile but couldn't make it work.

"That was what Tuesday said you would say."

"How is she?"

"She also suggested you might change the subject."

"Bianca—"

"She is fine. She is with her father."

"How is he?"

Bianca looked out the window that Lawrence had been standing in front of all day. "He has suffered some sort of attack. He seems a bit confused, delusional. Sometimes it is hard to make out what he is saying, and at others he seems to be mistaking Tuesday for her mother."

Lawrence nodded. "Can I go to her?"

"I am not sure that is a good idea. I want to keep the number of people in the room to a minimum to diminish his confusion."

"What am I supposed to do then?" Lawrence demanded harshly, and was immediately sorry. "I shouldn't have spoken that way, Bianca. My apologies. I just feel so damn powerless."

"I understand," Bianca said with a laugh. Her own husband reacted identically when confronted with circumstances outside his control. "The best thing would just be to—"

Bianca stopped speaking because she had lost her audience. Her back had been to the door so she had not seen Tuesday come in, but Lawrence had, and had crossed the room in three strides to pull her into his arms.

"Tuesday, sweetheart, how are you feeling?" he asked, nuzzling into her hair.

"Better now." Nothing had ever seemed as precious to her as he did in that moment. She felt as though everything in her life was being systematically taken from her, as if slowly, some malevolent force were gathering the rug from under her feet and drawing her toward itself. She could think of only one way to stop it. "I love you Lawrence," she said, invoking the power of those words like some sort of spell against anyone trying to harm her.

"I love you, too."

"I should go back to Father. In case—" she bit her lip and Lawrence held her tighter. "But I had to see you. Just for a moment."

They held each other close, sharing strength and compassion and understanding from the embrace. They were still clinging together when Bianca showed herself out. They held each other as if somehow they knew that the sun pouring into the windows of the studio marked the dawn of a day that would change everything.

"It was like they sensed what was about to happen and were saying good-bye," Bianca told her husband, Ian, later.

And then Tuesday went back to her father's side, and the guards wrote up their last reports, and Christopher arrived with an urgent message for His Lordship, and Lawrence decided to follow it up in person.

It was the beginning of their last twenty-four hours together.

Chapter 34

"Tuesday!" the scream is hollow, beseeching. "Tuesday come out here."

The dream is different this time. This time she is watching the woman run, watching the killer get closer to her. This time the voice is not in her head.

This time, she knows, he is going to catch her. This time she knows who the killer is.

And who the victim is.

She follows them, the man dragging the woman. She is outside it, an observer, panting behind them, watching from the bushes.

"Stop it," her mother pleads. "Let me go."

"I told you what would happen if I caught you, Tuesday," the killer tells her mother. "I warned you." His tone is eerily bantering but he is dragging her behind him fast. "I killed him. I had to. It was the only way to get rid of him. The only way to get you to behave."

He pulls her into the corridor that runs from the yard into the kitchen and Tuesday follows, hiding now behind a barrel of molasses, now next to a sack of flour. Her mother fights against the killer, trying to regain her feet.

"I'll shout," she threatens the man. "I'll bring the entire household down on you."

The killer stops dragging. He turns around and pulls her mother to him, lifts her off the floor, and gets his face so close, their noses are touching in profile. "Don't even think of screaming for help. I killed your filthy lover and now I am going to do the same to you. And then I'll do the same to your filthy bastard children. Do you understand bitch? Answer me?"

"I understand."

Her mother's voice has changed now. It is calm, not pleading. It is terrifying. Tuesday follows them as they go into the kitchen, through the entry hall, up the stairs. She stands at the bottom of the staircase and sees them fighting on the first landing. Her mother is struggling but the knife is pinned against her throat.

"No!" Tuesday yells from the bottom of the stairs.

The killer turns to look at her and Tuesday sees his face. The face she had blocked from all her dreams. Her father's face.

She understands this is not just a dream, it's a memory.

The killer, her father, turns to look at her and in that instant, from the surprise of seeing her there, his arms go slightly slack.

Her mother smiles. Pulls away from him. Runs forward two steps—

NO!!

—and leaps.

In her memory, her mother comes flying toward her, flying down the stairs, flying like one of her beloved dragonflies, her body now rolling and tumbling, feet then face then feet, *ha ha ha* the noise her head makes as it bangs down the stairs, *ha ha ha,* the sound of Tuesday's sobs.

"Mother!" Tuesday shouted, jolting herself awake. It

was all so horribly clear. Now she remembered everything she had kept locked away, everything about the day she had watched her father kill her mother.

She jumped when her father's fingers closed on her wrist. "Tuesday, my dearest," he said, his glassy eyes fixed horribly on her. "You are as beautiful as I remember."

Tuesday could not find words, could barely stand to have him touching her.

"You are so kind to visit me today. I knew you would come one day. I've waited for you. I've missed you so much over the years."

Tuesday swallowed.

"Our last meeting has weighed so heavily on my mind, Tuesday," her father said and his voice changed, became clouded with tears. "I did not mean for everything to happen that way, you know. I loved you so much. And then when I saw you with him. John Eliot, the gardener. Why did you love him?" A tear slid down his cheek. "You were going to run away with him. I knew it. And I could not let you. What would people say if you left me? For a gardener? No, I could not let you."

"So you killed him?" Tuesday asked.

"Yes. It was the only thing to do. But you didn't understand. I just wanted you to see how much I loved you. I had to make you see." He reached out and touched her cheek. "Have you seen our daughter? She takes after you in every way. I can't tell you how painful it has been for me to look at her all these years. I have loved you, have missed you, so much."

Tuesday bit her lip and felt a tear roll down her cheek.

"I am sorry for what happened, Tuesday. I am so sorry. But you are an angel now. I can see that. I can see from how beautiful you are." Sir Dennis sat up slightly, clawing his way up Tuesday's arm, and something in his eyes changed. "Take me with you, Tuesday. Please. I am frightened. No, don't leave." His grip got more insistent. "Forgive me, Tuesday. I have missed you so much. Please, please take me with—" The last word was just a whisper, no more than a soft breath.

Sir Dennis's body gently went loose and slid backward, pulling Tuesday with it. For a few moments she just stayed there, his dead fingers on her arm, his lifeless body next to her. And then she unclasped the fingers and stood and hugged herself with her good arm.

Her mother had been unfaithful. Her father had killed her lover. He had chased her with a knife, threatening her. And in the end she had chosen to end her life rather than let him end it for her.

She held the image of her mother sailing down the stairs in her mind, her gown billowing around her, her expression so peaceful and beautiful. Her mother had been happy at the end, Tuesday told herself. She had escaped. She had flown away.

And now, so had her father.

Tuesday felt dizzily numb. She did not want to cry. She did not feel loss. She just felt—

"Tuesday, are you all right?"

Tuesday turned around and saw CeCe standing in the doorway, looking concerned. "He is dead," she said.

"I thought I heard something so Morse and I rushed up here," CeCe explained, moving toward Tuesday and putting an arm around her shoulders. "Was that you yelling? Is there anything I can do to help you?"

The thought of explaining it to her, to anyone, made Tuesday feel weary all the way to her toes. She shook her head. "No thank you, CeCe. I think I just need to be by myse—"

"Tuesday? Where are you?" Lawrence's voice sounded from the entry hall below and she knew she was wrong. She needed to be with him. For hours.

She was moving to the door when CeCe stopped her. "I have to talk to you, Tuesday."

She stared at her. "Not right now."

"It is important."

"Please, love. Tomorrow."

CeCe dropped her hand from Tuesday's shoulder and watched as she flew down the stairs and into Lawrence's arms.

"What happened?" Lawrence asked, engulfing her in his embrace. "Did he?"

She nodded and pressed her face into his chest.

"I am sorry."

She was quiet for a few moments. Then she said, "There is something wrong with me, Lawrence."

"What are you talking about?"

"I am horrible." She swallowed. "I am not overwhelmed, or grief stricken, or even sad. And—" she tried to keep the words back but couldn't. "And I am not sorry. There. I've admitted it. I am a terrible daughter."

"You are a daughter who has been through quite a lot in the past week."

"I should be in mourning. If not for my father than for Curtis. And George. I should be tearing out my hair and weeping all the time."

"Why?"

"Because that is what widows do and that is what dutiful daughters do. They do not go leaping into the arms of the man investigating the murder of their husband."

He stroked her hair for a few moments, then leaned down to whisper, "I think this is a special case."

"Why?"

"Well for one thing, sweetheart, I am widely known to be irresistible."

Through their conversation she had kept her face buried in his chest. Now she looked up at him and, to his great relief, rolled her eyes.

"For another thing," he went on, "I think it is their fault."

"How?"

"Maybe not George. But certainly Curtis and your father. The way they treated you forced you to be so incredibly strong that now it is hard for you to let go and feel anything like grief. And there is no denying that you did your suffering for both those men while they were alive. You were living in a nightmare. I do not think there is anything wrong with you feeling relief that the shadow you have been existing under is gone."

She stared at him. "That is exactly how I feel. How did you know?"

"I know a bit about nightmares." He kissed the crown of her head. "At least I did before you. And, of course, there is the fact that I would say anything to make you feel better. What should I say now?"

"Say, 'I don't want to talk. I don't want to think. I just want to take you somewhere and hold you all night.' "

He sought her eyes. "I don't want to talk if you don't want to. When I am with you I don't seem able to think. So I was hoping that you would let me take you to a place I know and hold you in my arms all night."

"Where?"

"Surprise."

"I hate surprises."

"No you don't."

"Yes I do. Surprises and secrets. And beetles. At least the flying—"

Two hours later they lay twined around each other in a specially configured skiff just off the dock of Pickering Hall. On the dock were a gold candelabrum and a number of dishes the chef had labored over intensely. Whenever they wanted anything Lawrence pulled them back along the rope that was tethering them to land. But the chef's labors were largely wasted. They did not want anything.

They lay together on the silk-cushioned expanse of the boat under a linen coverlet beneath the stars, being gently rocked by the motion of the Thames. They were facing each other, bodies pressed close, Lawrence inside of Tuesday. As the boat rocked their bodies moved lazily together and apart, their lovemaking unfolding one inch at a time. It went on for hours, right through the golden cherries Tuesday fed Lawrence from between her teeth, through the setting of the moon. He stayed inside her all night, until his excitement encompassed every pore, until the slightest change in his breathing was nearly enough to topple her over the edge. This was not simple arousal, they had passed that hours before. This was something that took them outside themselves and their bodies. They both felt like they were hovering on a precipice of ex-quisite sensation, shifting closer to the edge with each hour but not quite reaching it, painstakingly balanc-ing the forces urging them forward with the tension of keeping away. They stayed poised there, outside of thought or time, poised on the edge of this well of sensa-tion, until the sky turned from black to inky blue and the earliest birds began to sing. Then, by silent agreement, they both unreigned everything they were holding back and let the pleasure engulf them.

It started small, like a rumble and grew and grew until it blared through both of them from head to foot, rebounding and clanging and pealing through their bodies. They clung to one another, half in awe, half in terror of the battering waves of pleasure that refused to end, that just kept getting more intense until they were both shouting and both unaware of it. Finally the sensation subsided and they collapsed into and onto and around one another, utterly transported, completely exhausted, and sopping wet from the waves they had sent crashing into the bottom of the boat. By the time the fog of exhilaration began to evaporate, they were lying in two feet of water and perilously close to sinking.

Lawrence reeled them in and they walked naked, hand and hand, back to the house.

When Tuesday was tucked between the linen sheets in the marble chamber, Lawrence bent to put a kiss on her forehead.

"That was spectacular, Lawrence."

"No, sweetheart. It was better than that."

"Are you arguing with me?"

"I don't think I have the strength."

She smiled wolfishly for a moment, then frowned. "Where are you going?"

"I have a few things to check on."

"What things?"

"Details from the investigation. I need to get them taken care of before the afternoon."

She gave a big yawn as she considered this. "Very well.

I will let you go. But only if you promise that tonight we get to do whatever *I* say."

"Sweetheart—"

She crossed her good arm over her chest. "No arguing."

She looked imperious and ridiculous and marvelous, and at that moment Lawrence loved her more than ever before. He gazed at her, completely entranced that she could be his, and burned the image of her on his mind.

That memory greeted him every night before he went to bed, and every morning when he woke up. It floated into his mind whenever he had a moment of free time, whenever he saw something beautiful, or heard someone laughing, or saw a boat bobbing on the river, pulling him right back to that instant, right back to the marvelous, transporting smell and taste and sight of her.

Which was why, in the months that followed, he stopped sleeping and started drinking and became so busy with his work that he barely had time to keep his social engagements.

Because by the time he finished with his work that morning, she was gone.

Gone for good.

Chapter 35

"Where are we going?" Tuesday asked, laughing, as Jack hurried her through the thick grove of trees that partially surrounded Doom Manor.

"Secret place. Tuesday will like it."

"What kind of secret place?"

"*Secret!*" Jack had insisted emphatically, then burst into hysterical laughter. Tuesday joined him, overwhelmed by the changes she saw in him.

The security and safety of Doom Manor had worked magic on him. After years of cowering in his chambers he had blossomed into a gregarious, adventurous boy. It seemed as though he spent all his time dashing from one end of the Doom Manor grounds to the other, exploring every niche and cranny. He had already taken Tuesday to the boating lake that filled a corner of the property, and to the top of one turret to show her a rusted set of manacles, but from his excitement and calls for speed she sensed he had saved his best surprise for last.

"We're almost there," he sang out merrily as they rounded a bend in the path. He stopped and pointed. "There."

They had emerged into a clearing surrounded on all

sides by trees. In front of them stood a charming little cottage circled by a low stone wall.

"Whose house is it?" Tuesday asked.

"Jack's new friends. Tuesday's, too. Come on, I will show you."

Never one to stand on ceremony, Jack not only pulled Tuesday into the garden and up the steps but, knocking on the door and getting no answer, stepped inside.

"We can't just go into someone's house," Tuesday balked.

"They won't mind," Jack assured her, nearly dragging her into a large, pleasant chamber. "Wait here," he ordered and walked out.

Trying not to focus on the fact that she had committed a dozen social gaffes and probably an illegal act by entering someone's abode uninvited, Tuesday looked around her. One wall of the room was almost entirely taken up with windows that overlooked the path they had just come up as well as the drive, and filled the space with light. But despite being bright and cheerful, there was something about the room that struck Tuesday as odd. It was not just that the furniture was finer and more luxurious than she would have expected given the remote location of the cottage, or that it was almost incredibly clean and neat. It was—it was that all the chairs, but one, were facing the window.

That lone one, a sort of throne, looked instead at a painting. As Tuesday approached the painting she saw that it was a copy of the Leonardo da Vinci painting of a mother and child, the one Lawrence had said was his favorite the day they first met. This was an exceptional copy, much better than hers. It was so good that—

She turned then to see Jack reentering, leading a beautiful woman slightly younger than Tuesday. She had alabaster skin and Tuesday's favorite nose and very dark hair and eyes. She was small but carried herself regally.

"This is Jack's friend Maria," Jack announced proudly. "And this is Jack's sister, Tuesday."

As Tuesday was beginning to wonder if Jack was trying to tell her that he had fallen in love, he leaned toward her to whisper, "Maria's real name is Lady Pickering, but Jack is allowed to call her Maria. Maybe Tuesday can, too."

Tuesday felt as though the blood stopped running through her body. "Lady Pickering?" she repeated stupidly. When Maria nodded, Tuesday forced herself to ask, "You are Lawrence Pickering's—wife?"

"Yes," Maria said, and two spots of pink appeared on her cheeks. Then she added quickly, and almost in a monotone, "But I am afraid my husband is not here right now. He is away on business. I am not sure when he will be back. He is never gone long."

Tuesday heard the words, the exact words, she had spoken so many times herself, heard them spoken with the same undercurrent of bravery designed to blanket out the knowledge that they were lies, and felt like someone had hit her. Listening to her own speech, knowing everything that lay behind it, made the oddness of the room, its cleanliness and luxuriousness and arrangement, make sense.

She saw the chairs facing the window that overlooked every possible approach to the house and knew all about the waiting, the vigilance, the sleepless nights of pacing and hoping. The lonely mornings of despair. She looked at the one chair, the throne, facing Lawrence's favorite painting, kept just for him, pristine for him how he liked it, and instantly sensed the long days of trying to guess his every whim, trying to be the perfect wife, so he wouldn't go away again. She could almost hear all the questions about where he had been or when he would be coming home, swallowed back for fear of driving him away. And she could feel the uncertainty that came in the darkest parts of the morning and ate into even the happiest moments, uncertainty about which was worse, the weeks of loneliness or the terror of doing that one unknowable thing once he finally came home that would make him leave again.

Beneath all the careful tidiness, the attention to detail, the wondering and hoping and working, lurked the need to keep busy enough never to think of the question of whether this was really what love was.

Only with Lawrence had she allowed herself to ask that question. He had shown her that being in love could be so much more, could be liberating and exciting and exalting, not terrifying and exhausting. But unless there was some other explanation, some other way to comprehend what was so clear in front of her eyes, she now saw that she had learned it at the expense of another woman.

She could not face it. Tuesday's eyes searched frantically for Jack. "I think it is time for us to go, love. I am sure Lady Pickering is—"

"Jaaaaack!" squealed a little boy who had just toddled around the corner. Jack scooped him up and swung him around, then planted him next to Maria.

She looked at the child with such an expression of mingled love and pride that there could be no question he was hers. He had inherited his mother's dark hair, but his eyes were a brilliant, piercing blue.

"He is beautiful," Tuesday said, and it was the truth. "What is his name?"

Maria smiled. "Lawrence. Just like his father."

Tuesday closed her eyes for a moment. This was so much worse than anything she had ever imagined. She was filled with rage, and at the same time with an overwhelming desire to deny it all. It wasn't true, it could not be true. There was a mistake, some enormous, breathtaking mistake. Lawrence would explain it all to her, he would make her understand. It would all be fine.

But another voice, a quieter and more reasonable voice, told her not to kid herself. What explanation could there be? Better to accept it and move on. Get Jack out of Doom Manor. Find a house, somewhere, anywhere. Never see Lawrence Pickering again. Never . . .

No. She had to find Lawrence.

She opened her eyes as Maria was tousling her son's hair—Lawrence Pickering's son's hair—and asking him, "Do you think Jack and his sister Tuesday would like some cake?"

Jack and the little boy let out twin yelps of joy, but Tuesday squelched them.

She tried to smile as she said, "That is very kind but I am afraid Jack and I need to be going," but she could hear the tremor in her voice.

"Jack is hungry," Jack complained.

"I'm sorry love. We'll find some cake somewhere else. There is something important I need to do right away."

Jack did not conceal his disappointment, but he went along with her. They said their good-byes and set out from the house. As they trudged slowly down the path back to Doom Manor, he asked, "What do Jack and Tuesday need to do?"

Tuesday tried to sound cheerful as she explained, "Jack needs to collect up all his things. That way he can come home with me."

"But Jack lives at Doom Manor."

"Yes, he did, but now he is going to have a new home."

"In London?"

"No," Tuesday answered, and suddenly she was having trouble breathing. "I don't know where. Somewhere good."

Jack stopped walking and stood in the middle of the path. "But Jack likes it at Doom Manor. Jack has a lot of friends. Jack does not want to leave." Over Jack's shoulder Tuesday could still see the little cottage.

"I know, love, and I am very sorry but you can't stay here anymore."

Jack reached out to touch her face. "Why is Tuesday crying?"

"It doesn't matter." She slapped at the tears, and then grasped his hand with her good arm and pulled him on.

"Jack can't leave without saying good-bye to his friend Lawrence," Jack pointed out.

A voice from the side of the path asked, "Good-bye? Where's Jack going?"

Tuesday looked up and saw Lawrence there. *There.* He had been smiling but the smile died when he saw the expression on her face. "Tuesday, what is wrong?" he asked. Her only reply was to back away from him. Frowning, he asked, "What are you two doing here?"

She took a deep breath. "Learning your secret."

He looked confused for a moment, then nodded slowly and said, "Maria and Lawrence. You've seen Maria and Lawrence."

No! she wanted to scream. You were not supposed to know about them. It was supposed to be a mistake! Tuesday had to press her knees together to keep from shuddering. "Yes. We just came from their house. Your house." When he didn't correct her, didn't protest, didn't say anything, she went on, "Damn you, Lawrence, why didn't you tell me about them?"

"I was going to."

I was going to? That was not the right answer, not the answer she wanted at all. "Really? You were going to tell me? How were you going to put it?" she asked sarcastically. "Just casually mention on our wedding day that you had a son and a wife already? How pleased you must have been when I only asked if you had a mistress. You didn't have to lie to me, not really. And you were safe. It would never have occurred to me, while you were asking for my hand in marriage, that you already had a wife."

He felt the anger rolling off of her in waves. "You don't understand, Tuesday."

Hearing her name from his lips now was terrible, terrible. "You are right. I don't. But I want to. I desperately want to." Her outrage slipped and she appealed to him. "Oh, God, Lawrence, please, deny it. Deny that she is your wife, that the boy is your son. Deny that I am sane, or that I am awake. Argue with me. Tell me I am wrong. Explain it to me so it makes sense some other way. I am begging you. Please, I don't want to believe what I saw. When George came that time and told me about her I laughed an—"

Lawrence interrupted. "George? George knew about Maria and Lawrence?"

"Yes. He told me you were keeping a woman, he thought it was your mistress, somewhere in the countryside bu—"

"Damn him."

His reaction stunned her. Tuesday's chest grew tight with anger. "Damn *him*? As if this were his fault? As if George did something wrong?" She moved closer to him. "It was you, Lawrence. You are the one who as good as lied to me. I thought you were a gentleman. Better than a gentleman—I thought you were a man of honor, of your word. Was I wrong? Tell me, Lawrence," she challenged. "Answer me. Is that your wife? Is that your son?"

No one else in the world could have questioned his honor and his integrity and gotten away with it. But he knew Tuesday loved him. He trusted her not to mean what she seemed to mean. And there was something he absolutely needed to do that instant. He said, "I'll explain it all later. I don't have time right now and this isn't the place to discuss it."

"I don't want you to *discuss* it," she said icily. "Not discuss it, no. I just want you to answer those simple questions. Can't you spare just a few seconds to convince me? Oh God, Lawrence, you don't know how much I want to believe in you, but you are making it so hard. Just tell me, is that boy your son?"

Tuesday had not heard the fast, irregular footsteps on the path, but before Lawrence could open his mouth to answer, the little boy had come running up to them. He threw himself around Lawrence's legs, his face wreathed in smiles. "Papa, Papa, Papa is home!" he shrieked, laughing.

His laughter was like a fist squeezing Tuesday's heart. She looked from the child to Lawrence.

This time Lawrence did not hesitate. He said, "Yes. He is." He reached out for her. "Tuesday, let me—"

She shrank away from him. "Don't touch me." She moved backward, shaking her head. She had asked for the truth and she had gotten it, and she realized that she had not wanted to know. She had fought against believing, but now she had no choice.

The tears stayed caught in her eyes but the words poured out, poured over him and into him, like shards of glass slicing his skin. "Lawrence, Lawrence, how could you? How could you have been holding me and telling me you loved me and saying you wanted to marry me, when all the time you knew that your wife and your son were waiting for you? Waiting for you to come home to them?" The image of his chair, lovingly arranged, facing his favorite painting, an always ready reminder of his absence, almost strangled her. "How could you? How— how *dare* you? You who pride yourself on being such a paragon of honorability and goodness. Ha! What kind of gentleman are you to treat a woman who loves you that way, *Lord* Pickering? What kind of a monster?"

Her words were like a cold slap in the face, waking Lawrence up to the truth, to the fact that he had been wrong. He had shared himself with Tuesday, shown her everything, entrusted her with his darkest secrets, and this was what she thought of him. If she had really loved him, had really understood him, she would never have believed him capable of such things.

Lawrence made no attempt to answer her questions this time because there was no point. No matter what he said, she would doubt him. And he no longer cared about her opinion. She had betrayed the trust she put in him. He had no more time for her.

He did not feel pain as he made this decision. He did not, from that moment on, feel anything at all.

"Come on, *querido*," he said, hoisting little Lawrence onto his back, not noticing the throbbing ache in his right shoulder. "We're done here, and Mama will be worried if we don't get home soon."

He passed by Tuesday and Jack without a word and made his way quickly toward the little house. Jack gazed after his friends wistfully, but let Tuesday drag him back to Doom Manor. He did not understand what had happened, why he needed to pack his things, why he had to leave all his friends, but when Tuesday, brushing away tears said, "please, Jack, love, no more questions," he grew quiet. As he said good-bye to the boys he assured them that he was only going on an adventure and would be back soon, and Tuesday did not have the heart to correct him. They walked down the road, hand in hand, Tuesday looking only at the ground, Jack turning around every few minutes to catch a glimpse of the place he had so briefly and happily called home.

Lawrence left a few hours after they did. He did not return to Doom Manor for a long time. From that day forward, he was always much too busy.

There was Pickering Hall to furnish and his business (too long neglected) to see to, and so many parties, and his future (he wanted a family of course), and what about that addition to the banqueting house he had meant to do. Not to mention Pickering Hall to furnish and his business and his future and the addition to the banqueting hall and the furnishings he needed to get before his marriage (why did he see Tuesday's profile in every frosty window?), which had to be arranged, and the Cottonwood's ball to attend and furniture and the future and family and festivities and—

He kept on breathing and eating and going to parties. But Lawrence Pickering died that day.

Chapter 36

Tuesday's arm healed very well and the gash on her head left almost no scar. She looked to be in perfect health. In fact, those who saw her every day, CeCe and Jack and the neighbors on either side of the little cottage in the country they had taken, thought that she grew only more beautiful as summer became fall.

She had never felt worse. The depression Tuesday fell into when she saw Maria deepened every day until she became physically ill as well, with nausea and cramps that none of the local apothecary's remedies did anything to soothe. In desperation, CeCe had gone around to the neighbors to round up portrait commissions and had Morse bring paints and an easel from London, but Tuesday would not touch a brush or even flip through her book of faces. She spent her days wrapped in a blanket sitting in the garden of their cottage, staring at the flowers as they lost their summer bloom, then at the grass as it turned from green to brown, and finally at the piles of leaves that littered the ground and were iced, each morning, with frost.

Jack's presence was the only thing that could bring a smile to her lips, but he had begun to take long walks by himself, visiting the local ponies, and when he was not there to care for, to distract her, it took all her energy to keep from thinking about Lawrence Pickering. And about Maria.

She wanted to crawl out of her body when she realized that she had been an instrument of pain to another woman, that because of her someone else had suffered the way Curtis made her suffer. She wished there were some way to restore to Maria what she had taken away, some recompense. She had done the only thing she could—remembering the terror of being on her own, without support, she had sent Morse to pawn her dragon-fly necklace and make sure Maria got the money—but she was too mortified to go and see the woman.

The Lion had been astonished by her desertion. He did not know what he had done to anger his Lady so much, but he knew he had to get her back. Until she returned, there would be no Great Tournament. Until she came back he could not be the Winner. He scoured the country-side for her every day he had off from work.

And then one day his Watching paid off. He saw her brother, Jack. And the next day he had a letter from pretty, devious CeCe. And from then on, he was in control all over again.

"Good afternoon, Lawrence," Crispin said as he breezed, unannounced into Lawrence's study and sat down opposite his friend. "Are you trying to embalm yourself? It is freezing in here. Why are some of your windows broken?"

Lawrence looked up from the pile of papers on his desk. "I like the fresh air. It doesn't seem cold to me."

"You must be very busy then." Crispin leaned forward in his chair and tried to see Lawrence's pile of papers. "What are those?"

"Documents. I am working."

"Working? I would very much like to know on what."

"Why?"

"It's Tuesday. You always do something bizarre on Tuesdays."

"I do not know what you are talking about," he replied, intently studying something interesting on the arm of Crispin's chair.

"You don't? What about four weeks ago when you had your entire art collection taken from Doom Manor and sold? For a fraction of what it was worth? Wasn't that odd?"

Lawrence shook his head. "I was tired of it."

"Or three weeks ago when you had all the doors in your house taken off and burned?"

"They made me feel hemmed in."

Crispin looked down at the sleeve of his jacket to see what could possibly be holding Lawrence's attention riveted to it that way. Finding nothing, he went on. "Very well. What about the custom-made boat you sank with sacks of rocks two weeks ago?"

Lawrence's eyes moved to the other chair arm. "That was an experiment."

"Experiment in what?" Crispin asked.

"Boat sinking. Surely you can see—"

Crispin put up a hand. "And what kind of experiment were you doing last week when you cornered the market on dry biscuits, making them the most valuable commodity in London, and then proceeded to line them up in your garden and shoot them all with your pistol? Sixty of them?"

"Target practice," Lawrence said, looking at his friend as if it were the most natural thing in the world. "It is important to keep the eye in form."

"I should have known. Well, you are right. There is nothing strange about your behavior at all."

"No." Lawrence looked down at the papers on his desk. In his lap his knuckles were white except where they were crisscrossed with scars from the time he rammed them through a window pane. He cleared his throat but did not look up from whatever was busying him on his desk. "I thought maybe you had come to congratulate me."

Crispin looked interested now. "On what? What have you done today? Did you blow up your coach? Or maybe you were going to take up all the planks in Miles's ballroom floor, so they would not remind you of where you danced with her."

Lawrence ignored him. "Congratulate me on my engagement. I am betrothed to be married. To Olivia Waverly. Tell your aunts they can put it in their newsletter. I think Sophie will be glad. Hers is the largest wager on it."

"Is that why you chose Olivia? So Sophie would win a bet?"

"Of course not. She is a lovely woman."

"She knew Tuesday as a girl."

"This has nothing to do with Tuesday."

"Doesn't it?"

"I think you are obsessed with her. You should watch that," Lawrence advised, glancing up from his work. "Thank you for visiting. Give Sophie my regards. Good day, Crispin."

Chapter 37

"Have you seen Jack?" Tuesday asked CeCe as she burst into the cozy atmosphere of the cottage. "I've been looking for him for the past two hours and I can't find him. He's been gone all day."

"I am certain he is fine," CeCe said.

"How can you be certain?" Tuesday demanded.

"Who would hurt him?"

"It's not so much who as what. It is nearly dark out and it looks like there is going to be a storm." Tuesday pressed herself next to the window and looked out. "He has not been really happy since he left Doom Hall. I am worried he might have done something to himself."

"Not Jack," CeCe assured her. "I think he is mostly sad for you. He hates it when you don't smile."

"You are right. I should try to be jollier when he is around." She looked out the window for another two minutes and announced, "I am going out looking for him."

"No," CeCe said firmly. "Tuesday, you are not well. You are staying here. It is sleeting out."

"All the more reason for me to try to find him. What if he is lost and outside? What if—"

CeCe tried to comfort her again. "He has some money. He knows to go to a tavern."

"You don't understand."

"Jack would not want you to worry about him this way," she said, hoping the impatience did not show through her voice. Where were they? She was getting tired of having to keep Tuesday locked up. "He is fine. I am sure he is snug in a tavern smiling at the barmaid right now. Come back inside."

Tuesday spent all night standing in the doorway letting the sleet and cold air in, and CeCe spent it at her own window, but there was no sign of anyone. At the first hint of dawn CeCe came downstairs and found Tuesday putting on her boots.

"What are you doing?"

"Going in search of him."

CeCe put herself in front of the door. "He is fine. I know where he is. No one is going to hurt him. You are staying here."

CeCe's tone was brusque. Tuesday stared at her. "What are you talking about? What do you mean you know where he is."

"I am not going to tell you, and if you don't—"

The sound of carriage wheels crunching over the icy ground stopped CeCe in the middle of her speech.

Tuesday's hands froze with her scarf halfway to her neck. Something had happened to Jack. Jack was dead. Jack had been hurt and the barber was bringing him home. These were the only possible explanations for the arrival of a coach. She had pushed past CeCe and was out of the cottage and skidding down the front of the walk in her slippers as the door of the carriage opened.

Four people looked out at her and she saw that she had not actually covered all the possible explanations.

"How do you do it?" Lawrence demanded as Crispin sauntered into his office.

"What?"

"Get by an entire staff of servants both armed and trained to keep me undisturbed without them even thinking to announce you?"

"Bribes," Crispin answered. The truth was that Lawrence's servants would have allowed in anyone or anything who offered even the slightest chance of bringing their master to his senses.

"Is this going to be another one of your talks? I am very busy today."

"Of course. You are always busy. In fact, you seem busier these days than ever before."

"I am," Lawrence confirmed, glad that people had noticed. His activities had increased and changed slightly in the months since his engagement, keeping him almost constantly occupied.

He had entered into the fast-moving commodity market at the Royal Exchange with a vehemence that left his friends breathless. By Crispin's best guess, Lawrence had managed to lose the better part of an average man's fortune through his speculations in the last two weeks alone. The label "A Pickering Pick" on any stock was quickly coming to be viewed as a sure sign that its value would decrease.

However stimulating this might be for the economy, and Crispin was certain he had seen at least one merchant in negotiations for a new coach, it was not good for Lawrence. He would always have plenty of money, but this carelessness was unlike him. It was as if instead of doing things to obliterate the memory of Tuesday, he had begun to do things to punish it. And himself as well.

"Was there something in particular you wanted, Crispin, or did you just drop in to say hello? Because—"

"There is something in particular. Actually, several people asked me to come today. Triscut Walpole was wondering if he could ask you not to invest in the new stock his bank is offering. They are hoping to raise quite a lot of money and, while I'm sure you aren't aware of it, your interest in anything these days is a bit of a liability."

"You are mistaken. I am aware of it."

"Then why are you speculating like this?"

Lawrence scowled at him. "To make money."

"You are doing a lousy job." Crispin sat forward and said, "Lawrence, you can't take your anger at Tuesday out on every market in London."

"I've warned you about this obsession of yours. Have I done anything illegal?"

"No."

"So why is my investing wrong?"

"Because you are not investing. You are bleeding money."

"I can afford to."

"It's not about that Lawrence. It's about what is good for you."

"Ah. It all makes sense to me. You certainly never objected to my speculations when I just buying gaming clubs, Crispin. But now that I am trying to be a legitimate merchant, just like you, you object? Is it because I was poor? Because I was abandoned by my mother and—"

The only thing that kept Crispin from punching

Lawrence at that moment was Christopher stepping through the doorway and announcing, "Lady Waverly, my lord."

Olivia floated into the room, immediately attune to the thick atmosphere. "Lord Sandal, how are you?" she asked, curtseying to Crispin. Looking from him to Lawrence she said, "I hope I am not interrupting anything important."

"No." Crispin rose from his chair. He stared hard at Lawrence for a moment and then, filled with anger, stalked to the door. When he reached it he forced himself to turn around. He tried to paste on a smile but spotting himself in the mirror across the room he saw it looked like he was choking. He said, "Congratulations on your engagement."

"Thank you, my lord," Lady Olivia said. "We shall see you and Lady Sandal at our ball tonight, won't we?"

"No," Crispin answered at the spur of the moment. "I am afraid neither we nor any of my cousins will be able to attend. We're going out of town."

For an instant something old and familiar flickered in Lawrence's face, but it was gone almost before it appeared. Crispin could not identify it but he hoped like hell it was pain.

Jack—unhurt, unharried, even unrumpled—emerged from the coach first and smiled at Tuesday in a way he had not smiled since leaving Doom Hall.

"Jack has a surprise for Tuesday," he said gleefully.

"Tuesday is just so relieved Jack is back," she said, rushing toward him. "She does not need any surprises."

"Yes yes yes," Jack insisted, putting up a hand to check her approach. "Jack had to stay at his friends' house because of the weather. And now Jack brought his friends to stay at his house just like CeCe told him to."

As he spoke Tom stepped out of the carriage, carrying a dark-haired boy with piercing blue eyes in his arms. He set little Lawrence down, then reached in and gave his hand to Maria.

"Friends for Tuesday," Jack chirped.

The two women stood and looked at each other. Then Maria rushed forward, embraced CeCe as if they were old friends, and said, "Lady Arlington, you must help me."

Tuesday looked from CeCe to Maria. "What is going on? How do you two know each other," she demanded. She looked at Tom. "What are you doing here?"

Tom was beaming. "Just wanted to help. Now that I've seen you three together I'll take myself off."

"Please, Tom, you are welcome to come inside and warm yourself. It is freezing," Tuesday insisted.

But Tom shook his head and mounted the horse that had been running behind the carriage. "I think you three have plenty to talk about without me. Besides, His Lordship might notice I was gone and, given his mood these days, that would land me in grave danger."

He saluted them and galloped off, leaving Tuesday standing, baffled, between CeCe and Maria.

"Come inside," CeCe urged, putting an arm through hers. "There are a few things you need to hear Tuesday."

Once inside, CeCe nudged Tuesday into a chair next to the fire and placed Maria in one opposite. Then, to Tuesday's complete astonishment, CeCe bent on her knees at her feet and said, "Before I start, I want you to know that I will understand if you can't forgive me."

Tuesday's head was buzzing. "Forgive you for what?

You still haven't explained how you two know each other."

"Later," CeCe said. "Right now I have to explain how *you* and *I* know each other."

"We ran into each other at the park," Tuesday told her.

"No. I made you run into me. I had been looking for ways to meet you for a month when that happened. For ways to get into your household. Because I hated you and I wanted to do you harm."

Tuesday gaped at her. "CeCe, have you taken leave of your senses? I think you should lie down."

"It's true," CeCe went on. "Although it's like you not to believe it. But I hated you so powerfully that I was determined to do everything I could to ruin your life. That was why I offered to work for you for free, so I could be close to you and study how best to destroy your happiness. Because I blamed you for destroying mine."

"I did? I never meant to."

"Of course you didn't. But that's not how I saw it. I had been in love with a boy in our village, an artist. To tell you the truth, I threw myself on him. After we had laid together I told him he had to marry me and he agreed, saying only that he wanted to come to London first to try to sell his paintings. He approached you and asked for you to critique his work, but you told him your brother wouldn't let you, that he did not want you to scare off any suitors for your hand by painting. When I first heard that I thought it was a ridiculously romantic excuse, but knowing you now I can see it was probaby the truth. In any event, Orlando wrote to me and said he could not marry me because he had fallen in love with you. That I would, too, if I had seen you and met you. That he could not stop himself, that it was fate. He spent

Michele Jaffe

all his days watching you but he was afraid to talk to you or press his suit because he did not want you to be forced into loving him the way you were with the men your brother brought home. Every time you got engaged it gnawed at him, and when you married Curtis, he wanted to die. So he enlisted in the navy."

"And sailed with Lawrence," Tuesday put in. She remembered Lawrence telling her the story about Orlando, about how he loved a woman and never told anyone, but she could hardly imagine it had been her. "He died."

"Right," CeCe continued. "And I blamed you. I blamed you for stealing him from me and then for killing him. I blamed you for taking away everything I held dear. So I resolved to do the same to you. First I had an affair with Curtis, but I soon discovered that wasn't really going to cause you pain, not the kind I wanted. So I bided my time. And finally got the opportunity. You fell in love with Lawrence Pickering. And I resolved to destroy it."

Tuesday's eyes moved to Maria, who was listening as she watched little Lawrence and Jack make a fort out of the cooking pots on the rug in front of them, but CeCe shook her head. "No, you'll understand that later. Because of my affair with Curtis, I knew all about the smuggling, and I decided to frame you for it. I sent the note, I changed the contents of your trunk, I did everything." CeCe paused. "But it did not work. What you and Lawrence had was stronger than that. And as the days went on, I found I was glad. I used to think you were so self-centered that you did not even know I hated you, but then I realized I was the one who was self-centered. You only cared how others felt, not how they felt about *you*. You would dedicate your life to making someone else happy even if they hated you, like you did with me. When I realized that, I discovered I couldn't hate you anymore. And Morse convinced me that I should confess everything to you. He told me you would forgive me. But I wanted to do more. I spent more than a year trying to destroy your happiness. I've spent the last three months looking for a way to restore it. And now, thanks to Tom, I think I have finally found it." Her eyes went to Maria and her expression changed as she added, "I'm only afraid that I might have wasted too much time."

Tuesday was completely dazed by CeCe's revelations. She took both the woman's hands in hers and pulled her up and hugged her. "I am so sorry if I ever did you harm, CeCe," she said, and CeCe pulled away, a little smile on her lips.

"Haven't you been listening, Tuesday? I'm the one who did you harm. But now, if I can, I'm going to fix it." She gestured toward Maria and said, "I believe you two have met. You have a lot to talk about. Why don't I take the boys outside so you can speak freely."

CeCe was bundling them up when Jack turned to Tuesday and sang out, "Guess what! Maria says Tuesday's friend Lawrence is getting married."

Tuesday's hands made fists and she whispered, "The bastard. How could he do this to you?"

"That is what I want to talk to you about." Maria paused until the door had closed behind CeCe, Jack, and her son, then said urgently, "It is not me he is hurting. It is you. And himself. I need you to help me save him."

"What are you talking about? You are his wife. He is—"

"Lawrence and I aren't married."

"That is worse. He did not even give you his name after getting you with child?"

"Lawrence is my son's father, yes. But only by adoption. My son's real father—" she stopped. "What I am going to tell you, you must promise not to repeat to anyone."

"I promise."

Maria leaned forward in the chair. "Have you ever heard the name 'Everly'?"

"Yes. Lawrence said he was one of his men. That he died."

Maria smiled to herself slightly. "That is all he told you?"

"He said he tried to save him but he couldn't."

"Ah, Lawrence. Too gallant for your own good," Maria mused. Then she looked at Tuesday. "Everly is my son's father. But he was a traitor. And still Lawrence did everything he could to save him."

"I don't understand."

Maria took a moment to marshal her thoughts, then plunged in. "Everyone knows that Lawrence and his men were captured during the war, but no one knows they let themselves be captured on purpose, in order to learn all they could about the Spanish operation and free the hundreds of English who were languishing in Spanish prisons. My brother Rafael and I had been working with the English against our king for several years, ever since the king's nephew—" she paused, waved that away. "But that does not matter. I had been working as a *camarera*, what you call a chambermaid, collecting information in the prison for over a year before Lawrence arrived. That was how I met Everly. He had been captured early in the war and was there during that time, too. I remember the first time I noticed him exercising in the yard—but that is not important either. I was a fool. I fell in love with him. And I believed that he loved me, especially when he bribed the prison priest to marry us secretly. He taught me English and told me about England and I told him about my brother's and my work—I wanted to seem brave and important to him, to show him we could have a life together, that we were on the same side. When Lawrence came Everly put him in touch with Rafe and me. Together, we learned all we could of the prison, and prepared for the escape. Lawrence made the plan and handled the instructions inside the prison, and we were supposed to organize transportation outside.

"But the night before, the *comandante* of the prison learned of the plan. He had all the prisoners, all two hundred of them, dragged from bed and lined up against the wall to be shot. Rafe and I were waiting on a ridge overlooking the camp and we saw it all. It was horrible, the prison yard lit up like sunshine, and all these men standing, not moving. On one side the prisoners. On the other side, the guards with their pistols aimed at their chests.

"Then, like a miracle, the barracks exploded. The building collapsed entirely, trapping the shooters under it. In the confusion, Lawrence rushed the men out. All but two—two out of two hundred—got away. They scattered as they had been told to when the escape was first planned, except that instead of going where he was supposed to, Lawrence followed Everly.

"Everly came to meet Rafe and me on the ridge. He rushed to me and took me in his arms, I thought to celebrate his escape, but in a moment I realized that he was pointing a pistol at my brother.

" 'You tricked me,' he said to Rafe. 'You knew I was selling information to the Spanish and you used me to set them up.'

" 'I'm afraid I did that,' Lawrence said, coming up then. Everly turned toward him, training the pistol on him instead. It was the moment for Rafe to run, but he stayed planted where he was. 'Why did you do it, Everly?'

" 'Money of course.'

" 'Where were you going to spend it? Here in Spain?'

" 'Why not? Spanish women like me.' He rubbed my stomach because I was, by that time, more than eight months pregnant with his child. 'But you've ruined the whole thing. My bosses aren't going to be happy with me. Thank heaven I got at least one part of it right.'

" 'What are you talking about?'

" 'Come see for yourself.' He dragged me farther up the ridge, so we were on the edge of the cliff, and Lawrence and Rafe followed. From there if you looked straight down you could see the ocean. And if you looked to the right you saw the town where Rafe and I had grown up. Where we were living. Everyone in the town was a relative of ours and everyone bore the same grudge we did against the king, so they were all working with us. Or had been. Because the town had been burned to the ground.

" 'I suppose to make further amends I'll have to bring them the heads of the two prison-break ring leaders.'

" 'Only one head,' Lawrence said. 'Mine.'

" 'Do you think I'm a fool, Pickering? You expect me to leave your friend here alive to carry out your orders? I know damn well you and Rafael are a team.'

"He was right. Lawrence and my brother had become

very close friends. Rafe was posing as a roof builder—it was quite windy there and the roofs' tiles were always flying off—which meant that he was very often near the attic cell where Lawrence was kept by himself as punishment when he made too much of a fuss about the bad food or his men's need for shoes. It was a horrible place, not even large enough for him to stand or lie down all the way, but he was able to communicate with Rafe through a hole in the roof. My brother had been a professor of theology in Madrid at the king's university before our sister was—before all of this, so for him to have a man like Lawrence to talk to was a blessing. Sometimes I suspected Lawrence got punished just so he and Rafe could continue whatever argument they were having." Maria paused and shook her head at the memory.

"Of course, their friendship was why Everly behaved as he did. Holding his pistol on my head, here," she tapped her temple, "he made me tie them together, back to back; then he pushed them to the edge of the cliff and had them stand there. One of Lawrence and my brother's favorite arguments was about whether fate and luck existed, and the way Lawrence always argued against it was by pulling out a coin and tossing it to show that no amount of prayer could control which side it landed on all the time. That was what Everly did then. He pulled out a coin and tossed it. It was heads, which was what Lawrence always picked. It was Lawrence's turn to die. Lawrence did not say anything. Everly put his pistol on him and, with Lawrence looking right in his eyes, fired."

Tuesday had not realized that she had taken Maria's hand, but Maria now clenched hers, tight. "Oh God. I hate this. I hate remembering." Maria took three deep breaths. "Rafael—Rafe moved. He moved so the bullet

just grazed Lawrence's shoulder but hit him in the neck.
Blood flew everywhere. Then he fell down and dragged
Lawrence down with him. He did it so that Lawrence
could save me. Could take me to England. He sacrificed
himself for me.

"I could not stop myself. I pulled away from Everly
and threw myself on my brother. Everly was surprised
and he lost his balance and tripped forward, toward the
edge of the cliff. I remember so clearly a moment when
he seemed to be hovering, almost flying, at the edge of
the cliff. And then, at the last second, he was gone."
Maria closed her eyes hard. "I got my brother killed.
And then I killed the father of my child."

Tuesday shook her head. "No. Lawrence caught his
hand, but Everly let go."

"That is what Lawrence says to make me feel better."

"It is the truth."

"Maybe. What is important is what happened after."
Maria's eyes opened. "I was very pregnant and Lawrence
refused to let me cross to England until after the baby
came. He stayed with me, even though he could have
been killed, hiding me in boarding houses, until my son
was born. And then he smuggled us across to England in
a shipment of silk stockings. He had to buy them all because little Lawrence and I made such a mess of them,
but he did not care." She wiped a tear from her cheek.

"When he was made an earl he adopted Lawrence as
his son so he would always be able to give him protection, and so he could inherit his lands. Of course if you
have a son he should be the one—"

"I don't think Lawrence and I are going to be having
any children."

"Yes," Maria said, becoming animated again as she

remembered why she was there. "You must. Don't you see, Lady Arlington. You must go to him. He needs you."

"No, he doesn't."

"You don't know. He has been miserable these three months without you."

"It does not sound like it. You said he is engaged."

"Only to punish himself. To fill the empty place you left him in his heart."

Tuesday looked away. "He would have come after me. If he cared about me he would have come and explained all of this himself." She spoke the words she had not allowed herself to think every minute of every day of the past months. The words that proved again how easily she was forgotten. "If he loved me he would have found me."

"He couldn't. You see, there are people from Spain who consider me a traitor and who would like to punish Lawrence for the damage he did. They cannot kill him, he is too powerful here in England, but they can kill me. That was why we told people I was Lady Pickering, because they would hesitate to hurt me until they confirmed it, and in that time I could get away. He was afraid to tell you, to tell anyone the truth, because it would endanger my son and me. He would not put our lives at risk for anything. He was protecting us. Not from you. From everyone. When he found out you had seen me, that your friend George knew about me, he was terrified of what might happen. He moved us that night and told us to speak to no one. That is why he did not deny what you said that day at Doom Manor," Maria added, as if reading Tuesday's thoughts. "And afterwards he convinced himself that you had never loved him because you had not trusted him enough to believe he would never betray you. Or me."

Tuesday was shaking her head. It made no sense and perfect sense.

"You know him well enough to see how he would react, Lady Arlington. And then, when he discovered you had pawned the necklace he had cleaned for you—"

"—he did not have it cleaned. He had all the stones replaced so that it went from worthless to priceless."

Maria half smiled. "He has a problem with excess, no?" Tuesday nodded. "When he learned that, he thought you were trying to get rid of all signs of him because he disgusted you. After that nothing in the world could have brought him to you."

Something occurred to Tuesday. "You are risking your life by telling me this."

"I would have nothing, no life, without Lawrence. He has given me everything. This is the only way I know to repay him. To win you back for him."

A hundred memories flashed across Tuesday's mind. "He probably won't take me back."

"I think he will."

"What if he doesn't?"

"Do you still love him?" Maria had only to look at Tuesday to see her answer. "Please," she said. "Please just try."

Tuesday felt both better and worse than she had at any time since she first saw Maria months earlier. She took both the woman's hands in hers and asked, "What would you have me do?"

"The horses on the coach outside should be rested now. I'd suggest you take it and get to London as quickly as you can. You see, tonight is his betrothal ball."

Tom spurred his horse back to London as quickly as he could. His Lady was even more beautiful than he had remembered her. That was what made him understand. She had purposely kept herself from him, for three months, just so that he would be more forcefully spurred to action. And it had Worked. Boy had it Worked. He could feel the W poking through his leggings even as he rode.

He had been great before, but never so great as he was now. As he was about to be. The Grand Tournament was finally about to begin.

Chapter 38

Tuesday was astonished at the change in Pickering Hall. Not just the decorations for the ball, which were lavish and omnipresent, but by the fact that it was jammed with furniture. All of it was beautiful and well chosen and elegant. But somehow it felt wrong. As if the place were wearing a dress that was not quite flattering.

"Christopher," Lawrence began without looking up from his work when he heard someone step into the room. "In the future I want you to announce *all* my guests. Not just those, like Lady Waverly, that you disapprove of."

"I'm afraid it is too late for that, Mr. Pickering."

Lawrence froze. The sound of her purr thrilled him. His head came up slowly.

Lawrence and Tuesday stared at each other for a long moment. It was the most painful moment in both of their lives.

"What are you doing here?" Lawrence's voice was a rasp.

Tuesday was asking herself the same question. Why had she believed Maria? Why had she come? This man did not love her. This man, in his perfect house with his perfect clothes and his perfect ball about to get underway, this man who looked at her with eyes she only wished were empty so she would not have to see his hatred; this man wanted nothing to do with her.

Tuesday picked up what looked like an ornate wooden box standing on the small table next to her and it fell into a dozen pieces in her hands. She hastily dumped it back onto the table in a little mound, upsetting the stack of papers next to it so that they slid from a perfect pile into a crooked heap. She clasped her hands in front of her and stared hard at the floor.

"At least you have not lost your ability to create chaos out of order."

Tuesday looked at him again. She would have given anything for him to be smiling, but he was not. "It looks so different. Everything. I mean, with the furniture."

Lawrence did not say anything, did not move.

"Are you happy?" Tuesday blurted.

"Amazingly."

"Oh." Tuesday looked at the expensive rug again. "Because I am not. I haven't been, I—" She looked up. "I have missed you so much, Lawrence."

"My name is Lord Pickering."

He meant it to sting, but it didn't. "Yes, sitting here like this, in your splendor, you certainly do look like Lord Pickering."

Why did it sound like an insult? Why did he care? What the hell was she doing there? He wanted her out. Now.

"Was there something in particular you needed to say to me? I have been barraged with interruptions today and I have a few things to finish before my betrothal ball begins tonight."

"Am I inconveniencing you, Lord Pickering?"

"Does this visit have a purpose?"

"Yes. I came to tell you that I was wrong, that I made a huge mistake, and that I am very sorry. I came—"

"Thank you. Good evening, Lady Arlington."

"I am not done."

"Yes, you are."

"Damn you, Lawrence. You are not mad at me for barging in here and ruining your schedule. You are mad because you think I betrayed and abandoned you. But I did not. I left because I thought you had betrayed me. I thought you were married to Maria."

"I am aware of that. You were, as you no doubt now know, wrong."

"Why didn't you tell me?"

"Why didn't you trust me?"

Tuesday paced in front of his desk, looking for words. "I was too upset. The idea that I had destroyed a marriage, destroyed a family, destroyed the life of another woman just like me, made me furious."

"And yet you could not believe in me? Could not have waited a few hours for me to explain? Could not trust me not to have been a man who would behave that way?"

"Why couldn't you trust *me*? What was I supposed to think when you did not even deny it? How was I supposed to know?"

"I really cannot say, Lady Arlington, nor do I care to give the matter any thought."

"You said you loved me, Lawrence. I was ready to give you my whole life. I shared things with you I had never shared with anyone. I thought we had something extraordinary. Special." She took two steps and put her hands on his desk, sending papers skidding in all directions. "You said you wanted to be with me forever and then you did not even come looking for me."

"I changed my mind."

"Changed your mind?"

"Why is that so hard to believe?" He looked up at her as if puzzled by her confusion. "Certainly you do not think that what we had together was unique?"

Tuesday shook her head. She managed only to mouth the word, "No."

"I can't imagine what you expected to achieve by coming here today and disorganizing my office, Lady Arlington. I will, however, take advantage of your presence to tell you that any feelings I might have thought I had for you turned out to be utterly illusory."

Tuesday nodded, letting the words sink in. She took her hands from the desk and stepped backwards. "I am sorry to hear that, my lord, because mine for you were not. When I thought you had a wife and child that you had been cheating on with me, I wanted to die. To be the instrument of another woman's shame, to have made another woman feel how I felt with Curtis, was the worst punishment I could imagine. And yet I could not stop loving you. Not then. And not now."

Lawrence regarded her blankly.

"Your face, your smile, were in front of my eyes every day. I have relived every moment of our time together, relived it to keep from going mad. I loved you with a love so strong it could not be killed by what I thought of you." There were tears in Tuesday's eyes but she did not care. "You were the best thing to ever happen to my life, Lawrence Pickering. And I think I could have been the best thing to ever happen to you, too."

Now Lawrence did smile. And what he said was, "Don't overestimate your attractions, Lady Arlington."

The words hung in the air until Christopher stepped

into the doorway and announced, "It's Lady Waverly, my lord. Again. I told her you were busy but she insisted."

"I am not busy," Lawrence said, his eyes boring into Tuesday. "Lady Arlington was just leaving."

"Yes." Tuesday turned and almost walked into Olivia Waverly. She said, "Congratulations, Ollie on your engagement. I hope you will be very happy."

Olivia smiled. "Ollie. No one has called me that in a long time. It reminds me of our girlhood." She gave Tuesday a searching look. "Thank you for your wishes. I have—I have always valued your good opinion." Then she moved quickly past her toward Lawrence and began asking about packing for their wedding trip.

Tuesday walked from the room with her shoulders back and her chin up and tears streaming down her face. She walked like that down the corridor. She walked like that into the entry hall. She walked like that almost all the way to the front door.

Then she gripped the wall and let out an anguished breath and collapsed onto the floor, upending a table and shattering the glass vase (a wedding present) into a thousand splinters that glittered like diamonds on the hem of her dress.

Christopher found her there five minutes later. He knew exactly what do with her.

It was just past dusk when Crispin entered Lawrence's office. None of the candles were lit and the place was filled with violet shadows. Standing among them, staring at the window, was Lawrence. He did not hear Crispin enter, and for a few minutes Crispin studied his friend's reflection in the glass.

Lawrence turned around suddenly. "I thought you were going to be in Italy or something."

Crispin shrugged. "Only during your ball. That is still two hours away."

The two men faced each other across the carpet. In the half light of the chamber, expressions were unreadable, but there was something strangely intimate about the encounter.

"It looks like your office was hit by a huge gust of wind," Crispin said, noting the upturned piles of paper and ornaments.

"Tuesday was here."

"Ah."

"She came to apologize."

"Did she?"

"Did she what?"

"Apologize. If you looked at her the way you've looked at me the past few times I came here, I imagine it would have been a challenge."

"She apologized."

"Did you accept it?"

"Of course not."

"Ah."

"Don't say that."

"What?"

" 'Ah.' "

"What should I say instead?"

"Nothing."

They stood in silence until Lawrence said, "I know what you are thinking. You are thinking that I should have accepted her apology. Aren't you?"

Crispin did not say anything.

"Answer me."

"You just told me—"

"Crispin."

"I don't think it would have been compromising your principles too much to accept it, no. Especially as you are still in love with her, have been mourning for her for three months, spend every waking hour thinking about her, and have made fifty families go without their income just because you had to go without her. Yes, I would say that I think you should have accepted her damn apology."

"That is what you think?"

"Yes."

"Ah." A long pause. "I think you are wrong."

"That comes as a surprise."

"I should not have accepted her apology because she does not owe me one. I should have gotten down on my knees and begged for her forgiveness. She came here and apologized and for what? Do you know why she left me?"

"Actually, I—"

"She left because she thought I was married to Maria and she was upset for her. For Maria. Not for herself. She came and apologized for being too generous, too selfless, for caring about other people too much." Lawrence shook his head and looked down at his hands, which were clenching and unclenching as if trying to grasp something intangible. "Nothing is an obstacle to her, nothing is too hard. She has experienced so much, overcome so much, and she is not bitter. She does it gracefully and effortlessly. She makes everything she touches better."

"I don't suppose you told her any of that."

"Do you know what she said to me this afternoon? She said that she still loved me. Can you believe that?

What a fool. She loves me. Me. And do you know how I replied?"

"No, but I imagine it was charming."

"I said, 'Don't overestimate your attractions, Lady Arlington.' I threw it away. Because I was too stubborn and too proud to admit that I had been wrong, that I should have trusted her. Because of that I threw away the most amazing gift any man has ever received."

"It seems that you are both fools."

Lawrence came out of his thoughts enough to glare at Crispin. "I don't know what I am going to do. I have got to get her back."

Crispin shook his head. "It sounds to me like that will be impossible. I think you ruined whatever you might have had together for good."

"Thank you."

"You have never liked to be lied to, Lawrence. I am telling you the truth. You had better go upstairs and change. Your guests will be arriving in less than two hours."

"Do you really think I am going through with this betrothal?"

"What else are you going to do, Lawrence? She is gone. You sent her away. You took her offer of love and pulverized it and stomped on it and—"

"That is enough, Crispin."

Crispin shrugged. "I don't think you have any choice but to go through with this betrothal, to get on with your life. Olivia Waverly is, as you said, a lovely woman. Marry her. Be as happy as you can knowing what you have sacrificed on the altar of your stubborn ego. It is all you can do."

Lawrence stared at him with an expression so bereft

that Crispin almost felt sorry for him. But then he remembered how Lawrence had been behaving the last few months and the urge passed.

Lawrence Pickering deserved exactly what was coming to him.

Crispin waited at the bottom of the stairs to make sure that Lawrence had gone into his bedchamber before he ran to the kitchen to get his bet down.

"Fifteen minutes," he announced as he walked in.

"Bianca already has that. You can have four minutes or ninety-four minutes."

"That is all that is left?"

"The betting has been pretty fierce. Tristan took everything from twenty to forty. Sebastian, Grub Collins, and Christopher picked up most of the rest of the first hour. CeCe staked everything she has on eighteen."

Crispin looked back on the conversation he had just had, did a bit of calculation and made his decision. "Four minutes." He wished Lawrence knew how much faith he had in him.

Lawrence's bedchamber was as gloomy as his office and it suited his mood perfectly. He knew he should start dressing, but he could not face it. He went to the bed and stretched out on it.

And sat up.

She was there. She was there in his bed, right there, right where he could touch her, Tuesday, his Tuesday. She was sleeping it looked like. She did not know he was there.

How had she gotten there? Should he wake her? What did it mean?

He stared at her, willing her to open her eyes, but she didn't.

Tuesday there in his bed. He felt like Jack, he felt like a boy, he felt like the luckiest man in the world.

He began to eye the windows of his bed chamber. Why had he thought it would be nice to be on the third floor? If they were lower, he could have carried her out through the window while she slept and they could have made their escape easily. As it was, he would have to wake her up.

Why was she sleeping?

He looked at her profile, studied it, checking it to make sure it was—what? All there? The same? It wasn't. Something was different. Or his memory was wrong. Because she was even more beautiful to him than she had been before. That had been the very first thing he thought when he looked up and saw her in his office that day, that she had somehow gotten more beautiful, more striking, more lovely, in the time since she had thrown him aside.

Her beauty had been like a goad to him, and then she had stood there and said, "I am sorry" and "I love you" and all those things he did not deserve to hear.

Why wasn't she waking up?

He reached out a finger for her cheek. It was painfully soft. "Tuesday," he whispered in her ear. Her eyelashes did not flutter. "Tuesday."

Nothing. She did not sleep this soundly normally, he knew. What if there were something wrong with her? What if she wasn't asleep.

What if she were pretending?

He leaned close to her ear and slid his arm under her head and whispered, "You were."

She did not move. She was not pretending. Something was wrong with her. He had to get Bianca. He—

"Were what?" she asked sleepily.

"What?"

"Exactly."

"I don't—"

"Lawrence, you can't do this again. Whisper riddles to me and then not give me the answers. What were I?"

Her eyes opened and he put his head down on the pillow so their noses were almost touching. "You already were the best thing that ever happened to my life. Were and are."

"Do you mean that?"

"You can't know how much."

"Where am I?"

"My bed chamber."

Tuesday suddenly had a vague recollection of falling down, of Bianca's face hovering over hers. "How did I—"

Lawrence's laughter interrupted her. "Crispin, you scoundrel," he said aloud.

"What are you talking about?"

"I'll tell you later. It's not important." He curled a piece of her hair around his finger. That was important.

"Lawrence, I am so sorry I did not wait for you to explain about Maria. I should have trusted you. I should have—"

Here she was, this woman he had wronged, who he had insulted to her face, and she was apologizing to him. He put his finger to her lips. "Stop. I never want to hear another apology from you. It is I who should be doing all the apologizing. I know I can never make up for how I treated you today but I want to try, try as hard—"

She looked wary. "What did Bianca tell you?"

"Bianca? Nothing. I have not seen her. Why?"

"Then you just apologized, because you wanted to?"

"No. Because I needed to. Because I want to ask you to marry me and if you say no I'll go out of my mind. Tuesday, I do not deserve you, but I will do everything I can for the rest of my life to try. Because you are the most courageous, the—"

"Yes."

"—most generous, the—what?"

"Do you want to marry me as much as I want to marry you, Lawrence?"

"No." He shook his head emphatically. "I want to marry you more, sweetheart. I want to marry you tomorrow. And later I want to have babies."

"Later?"

"Yes when—" He stopped. "Bianca. That is why you asked. Oh. Oh my. Are you—? Did we—? Sweetheart, is it true?"

Tuesday could not keep the tears out of her eyes at how excited he was. "Yes. But I did not want you to know. I did not want you to think I was manipulating you. I did not want to win you back for the wrong reasons."

"You did not have to win me back, Tuesday. You never lost me."

The ball at Pickering Hall was the most lavish of any season in anyone's memory. There were so many people and musicians and servants there that almost no one noticed the absence of the betrothal pair. By the time the dinner was served, Olivia Waverly was on her way to Paris with her sizeable marriage settlement and the handsome, sweet, charming, and loyal groomsman with whom she'd been in love for four years.

By the time the fireworks were going off, Lawrence and Tuesday were too distracted to notice.

In the unfinished expansion of the Pickering Hall banqueting house the Arboretti—joined by Grub Collins and Tom and Christopher and CeCe—drank a toast to Lawrence's lighted window.

"May they live long and happily together," Grub proclaimed and they all raised their glasses in agreement.

Later they all grudgingly emptied their purses to Crispin.

The Lion lay in bed that night and touched his W and listened to the clocks around London chime midnight. It sounded beautiful, like a death toll. Every passing minute brought him closer to the day. The day of the Grand Tournament. The day when there would be no more Waiting.

The day when there would be a Wedding.

Chapter 39

Tuesday reached up and traced Lawrence's smile with her fingertip.

"Good morning sweetheart," he said, kissing it.

"Good morning, Lawrence." She gazed up at him. "This is real, isn't it? This is not a dream."

"No."

"What happened last night. That was real, too?"

"Yes."

"So you love me? And we are going to get married?"

"And have a baby. Yes."

She gulped. "Oh."

"You don't sound entirely pleased."

She did not say anything.

"Tuesday, is something wrong?"

She reached up and pulled him down to her, so he could not see her face. She whispered, "I am so scared."

"Of what, sweetheart?"

"Of being too happy. Of losing you again."

He pulled away so he could look right in her eyes as he said, "I will always be here. I will always be by your side."

It wasn't strictly true. During the next two weeks, Lawrence and Tuesday were forced to spend at least ten hours apart, between the fittings for her gown and Lawrence's having to seek a special license from the archbishop. But they always spent their nights together. And together they counted down the days. Until their wedding.

The Lion could not hold still. This was it! This was the day!

Already the knights and ladies were starting to fill the stands. They came early to get good positions. They all wanted to be close to him.

And they had dressed up. He loved that they put on their finery for him. Not that he had much use for anyone but his Lady, but it showed they knew how to honor him. Understood how great he was.

He wondered if any knight had ever felt as powerful as he felt then. He had never been defeated! No knight that had gone against him in battle had ever come out alive!

"Tom, you'll be stationed in front of the side door," a voice broke into his thoughts and he almost lost it.

"Don't call me that!" he wanted to shout. "Call me the Lion! Call me by my Right Name." But he knew he had to wait. Only a few more minutes.

"Yes sir," the Lion told the Knight of Knights. "I'll make sure no one comes in that way."

Lawrence put an arm on his shoulder and gave him a smile. "I know I can count on you."

Count on me to kill you! The Lion thought. He could have taken off that arm right there. It would have been so easy. But he knew he should wait for the Watchers.

Despite the impropriety of their wedding—as every London gossip pointed out, the woman ought to have been in mourning, and the man, well, he was engaged to someone else as recently as *two weeks ago*—the nave of the church was packed. Tuesday had hoped that the fact they had not posted any banns or told anyone but close friends would have made the ceremony unattended, and to a certain extent she was right. If they'd done it properly, CeCe assured her, there would have been at least a thousand people instead of only five hundred.

Lawrence's men were stationed around the perimeter, more to keep the courtly guests from having their pockets picked too badly by some of his less upstanding friends, than from any threat he felt to himself. The sheer number of witnesses would keep the weapons of his enemies in check more than any guards he knew.

The Lion stood at his post as the spectators filed in and listened to the mingled sound of the voices. He could not make out many words but they were almost all Whispering, and the soft hissing made his toes tingle. He could pick out the ones who would be cheering against him—that woman in the pink dress, she was of the Knight of Knight's party—and he decided to kill them first. Thin the crowd. That way his people would have a better view of the real fight.

Something jostled the Lion's arm and he looked over to see—

A dog! The dogs had found him they were coming for him

—a young boy. "Sir," the boy said, "could I sit on your shoulders? I can't see anything."

The Lion scowled at him and was fingering his knife when a girl came and pulled him away. "I am sorry, sir," she said, and he realized it was the same girl he had almost killed that time outside Tuesday's house. The girl named Lucy Burns. She looked down at her brother. "James, you must not bother the soldiers."

"But I want to see!" the boy cried.

The Lion decided he would spare the girl but kill the boy. She would thank him, he could tell. She Worshiped him.

He was feeling love, adulation, from everyone. The signs were everywhere, urging him on. Above the altar there were a row of Ws and the heads of the crowd spelled W and he had begun seeing it on people's foreheads. Anyone without a W would die. No, he thought to himself, they would Want one.

He wanted to kill someone right then, just one person, just to tide him over until it was time. The woman in pink glanced at him and he could see her thoughts. "What are you Waiting for?" she was thinking, and he decided he would start with her. He was about to take his knife out of his sleeve when the crowd suddenly grew hushed. They were all looking at him, he knew. Out of their secret eyes. They were all Waiting for him.

He felt himself growing larger as they looked at him. He was too good to kill the lady in pink. She was nothing. He was huge now, huge with the power inside of him. As his Lady appeared from a side door, he thought he might explode.

She was wearing a jade green dress with two dragonflies on the bosom. Everyone else noticed that they were made of rubies, that they trailed a twining path of diamonds in their wake, which circled around the waist of the dress and spiraled down its skirt. Everyone else admired the hem of the gown where an emerald lawn grew, each blade of grass jeweled individually and dotted with snapdragons, sweet peas, carnations, and roses, all made of precious stones. Everyone else was astonished by the bride's exquisite, radiant beauty. But the Lion saw only the way the dragonflies spelled W, spelled I love you, spelled slay the knight, spelled I am your Lady, spelled KILL LAWRENCE PICKERING.

He flew over the heads of the crowd toward her, to welcome her, to embrace her, to lay claim to her as his own. He saw her turn to look at him, really see him for the first time as he was, her Knight, and he could tell from her expression that he impressed her admirably.

His Lordship saw him, too, and tried to move toward him—everyone wanted to touch him, he was the Winner—but he was faster and got to his Lady first. He clutched her to him, hard, and he could feel how glad she was to be in his arms.

"You are doing very Well," he told her as she struggled against him. He knew she had to make it look like he was holding her against her will, so that the Knight of Knights would challenge him. Once that happened, she could admit everything. Admit they had been fooling the Knight. Admit she belonged to the Lion.

"What are you doing, Tom?" she asked, and he loved the fear she put in her voice.

"You know my real name," he chastised her.

He saw her gulp. He put his knife near the place where her throat moved when she swallowed, so he could be touching her. He could see how much she liked it.

"Tell me," she begged. Oh, she was Wonderful. Wonderful.

"My real name is the Lion."

He could see that she was swooning with ecstasy. She was so conscious of the honor he was doing her. He would have liked to kiss her. He put his knife on her lips and traced them slowly instead.

A sword point touched his back. "Let Lady Arlington go," he heard the Knight of Knights say.

A sword point. As if that could hurt him. As if anything they had could. He was immune to their weapons. He did not even turn around. He said, "If you do not back away from me and my Lady I will drive this knife into her chest."

He wasn't kidding either. He was going to do it later, of course, but in private. He thought she would like to meet his W in private.

He felt the sword point retreat. "What are you doing, Tom?" the Knight of Knights asked.

"That is not my name!" Tom shouted. He squeezed his Lady's throat. "Tell them my name."

"The Lion," Tuesday choked out. "He is the Lion."

"The Knight called the Lion," he corrected. He turned so that he was facing the entire church. Everyone was awestruck by him. They all stared and did not say a word.

"You are the Lion?" the Knight of Knights asked.

"Yes," Tom said proudly.

Then the Knight of Knights laughed.

Tom swung toward him, swinging his Lady with him. A trickle of blood appeared on her neck. "You dare to laugh at me?"

Lawrence stared at him. "You're no knight. You're just a boy."

"I am not a boy," Tom said. "I am a knight. The greatest Knight. And I am going to prove it."

"I'd like to see that," Lawrence said, sarcastic. It was taking every ounce of restraint he had to keep his tone light, but he guessed the only way to catch Tom off guard was by antagonizing him.

"I already have," Tom sneered. "I killed all those men and you never knew."

"Anyone could have done that," Lawrence said coolly.

"You think so? What about when I killed Sir Curtis right under your nose? I had to drop the lantern that day when I took you to see the bodies so you wouldn't see me laughing. But you never guessed! You never guessed! And Albert Marston? First I hired him to be my witness, and then I lured him to Worthington Hall and killed him. And you all thought the Lion was dead. I fooled you completely! With a stupid wax scar!"

"That's true," Lawrence admitted. "But it still doesn't make you great."

"My Lady knows I am great," Tom said, then jabbed Tuesday in the throat. "Don't you?"

"Yes," Tuesday whispered.

Tom looked at Lawrence triumphantly but the Knight of Knights only shook his head. "A person with a knife at their throat will say anything."

"I have proof!" Tom declared. "She painted those paintings for me. She painted them by the Window so I could Watch. That was how it started. You had me observing Worthington Hall when the smuggling operation began, remember? I was to keep on Sir Curtis like a fly. But right after I started, Sir Curtis left. She made him leave. So she could have me. And she painted her paintings so that I would keep Watching her."

"Why would she want that? Why didn't she just invite you in?" Lawrence asked.

The Lion stared at him. "I had to Win her. I saw the paintings and I knew they were a sign. For my quest. I learned all about her past. All about the other knights who had tried for her but failed. It was their punishment.

They were not Worthy of her, but they entered the lists in her name and like all unworthy knights they paid with their hearts. Simple."

"And then you decided you wanted me involved," Lawrence suggested.

"Exactly. It was too easy. I needed a more worthy opponent if I was going to win my Lady. So I chose you. The Knight of Knights."

"This all sounds a little far-fetched."

The Lion was getting fed up with him. "That is because you can't see the signs. You aren't the one chosen for the quest. You are not the Winner. No one cares how it sounds to you. No one cares about you. After today, no one will even remember your name."

"Really? What is going to happen today?"

The Lion looked around the room and then at his adversary. "The Grand Tournament. Where do you think we are?"

"This is the end of your quest?"

"Yes. I have completed my adventures. I have slain many knights and some dragons. And now I will slay the Knight of Knights—that is you—at the Grand Tournament."

"Why?" Lawrence asked.

"To prove that I am the best." Tom spoke with impatience, as if explaining something to a child. "You are the best now. When I kill you, it will show I am better. Therefore I will be the best knight."

"What is the prize?"

"My lady's heart."

"But that is hers to give."

Tom scoffed. "She wants me to have it." He looked down at his Lady. He could see the encouragement in her eyes. The way the W in her bodice rose and fell to get closer to him. She did not know what was going to happen next, so he Winked at her to let her know not to worry. Then he said, "Look, I've even had a special pouch made for it."

He pulled the pouch from his shirt and held it toward Lawrence.

The Knight of Knights took a step forward. One more, the Lion screamed in his head. Take one more and you are mine.

The Knight of Knights took another step.

The Lion lunged toward him, knife high, ready to slash down. Victory pounded in his ears as he felt the Knight of Knight's skin under his blade, felt his blood exploding over his chest. He looked down and saw that they were both splattered with it, and he licked his lips to taste it. He was so strong, he was on fire. The Knight of Knights was gazing at him with admiration and he could feel his Lady's eyes Watching him, Worshiping him, could feel them blazing into his chest. Burning into it. Stop, Lady, he wanted to say. You can stop. He looked down and saw the full force of his Lady's love for him spreading across his tunic, spreading red across his lovely blue suit, like a red rose, growing and growing on his chest. Pricking him with love.

He looked at the Knight of Knights. His chest did not have a rose on it. His Lady truly loved the Lion best, he thought.

Then, as the full force of Grub's pistol shot burned into him, the Lion collapsed.

It was not hard to clear the church. Everyone was eager to get home and tell what had to be the most sensational news of the year, and they filed out quickly, leaving Lawrence and Tuesday and their closest companions alone in the hulking nave. And the Lion.

Christopher and Grub were guarding him, off to one side of the dais. He had not moved since he fell down, but they had taken the precaution of manacling his hands anyway. Now they stood with their backs to him, screening him from view. On the other side, Bianca was cleaning the cuts in Tuesday's throat. There were several of them, and one of them was deep so she wanted to make sure it would not get infected. Tuesday, semiconscious, saw Lawrence hovering and whispered something to Bianca, who promptly suggested he go outside and arrange to have his coach brought round.

He refused to move until Tuesday, glassy-eyed from pain, said, "Please Lawrence." It was, he understood, her way of keeping him from thinking. From reflecting on the mistake, the monster, he had made.

That first moment when Tom stood with his knife at Tuesday's throat, realizing that Tom was the Lion, had stunned him like a blow to the stomach. He knew that one day he would have to face the responsibility of having trained Tom, having made him what he was. And having let nine men die because he trusted him. But not now. Now he could only think about Tuesday.

When he came back into the church his face was under control. He inched toward the part of the dais where Bianca was still leaning over Tuesday, and stood, straining to see. Suddenly someone was tugging at his arm.

"Tuesday will be all right," Jack told Lawrence, nodding and rocking back and forth. He smiled, and then his face crumpled. Lawrence put his arm around Jack's shoulders and the boy buried his eyes in Lawrence's jacket. "She'll be all right, she'll be all right," he repeated over and over, clutching Lawrence.

"Yes," Lawrence said, clutching him back, "she will."

The two men Tuesday loved most in the world stood that way, hugging one another, until Bianca made a discreet sign to Lawrence. He gently released Jack and sat him on the edge of the dais promising to be right back.

"I think it would be a good idea to take Tuesday now," Bianca started to say to Lawrence when he reached her, but she could see he was not paying attention. He kept going past her, and bent over Tuesday, caressing her forehead with his hand.

"I am so sorry, sweetheart," he said. "I can't believe that I—"

Her eyes fluttered open. "Shhh, Lawrence," she whispered. "It's no fair starting an argument now. Bianca says I'm not supposed to speak."

She was going to be all right, Lawrence told himself. "Very well, but it's only postponed."

She propped herself up on her elbows and her smile became a wince. "Where is he?"

Lawrence gestured to the left with his chin. "Over there. With Grub and Christopher."

"Is he dead?"

"Not quite."

Tuesday could not read the tone in his voice. She took his hand and held it tight and for a moment they stayed that way, in complete silence, each of them lost in the reflection of how close they had come to losing one another again.

No one noticed the flicker of movement behind Grub and Christopher. No one saw what the Lion slid from his waistband. They almost did not notice the soft swish, no more than a whisper, like the sound of fabric rustling. But then Lawrence made a strange gasping noise. Tuesday looked at him, and for a moment he stayed kneeling next to her with a perplexed expression on his face. He opened his mouth to speak, and a line of blood began to trickle out of it. He reached up to touch it, stared at it unseeing for a moment. And collapsed.

As he went down, Tuesday saw the hilt of the knife with a W engraved on it, buried deep in his side.

"*NO!*" Her cry of anguish rocked the church.

It had worked! the Lion commended himself. He had tricked them to the very end! "I Won," the Lion whispered blissfully. "I won, my Lady. I am the Winner."

Tuesday did not hear him. She did not hear anything. She was hanging over Lawrence, wiping the blood that poured out of his side away with her skirt as fast as she could. Her tears rained down his cheeks.

"No, Lawrence, no!" she urged him, as if she could keep him, hold him with the power of her voice. He was getting pale and his breathing was short, shallow. "You can't die," she told him. "You *can't* die. No. No. *No!*"

Lawrence's eyes had been unfocused, almost stony, but now they locked on her face. He gazed up at her with a strange, almost peaceful expression and his lips moved but no sound came out. She bent closer, bringing her ear right to his lips and she heard him.

What he said was: "Your father was right. You do look like an angel."

Then he closed his eyes. And was gone.

Chapter 40

She sees him in her dreams all the time. Sees him standing at the side of the Thames, his linen shirt stretched across his shoulders, his hair slightly ruffled by the wind. In her dream he turns to smile as she comes over. He reaches for her hand and pulls her close to him.

Everything reminds her of him. Smells, sounds, even the feel of linen against her body. The sun dancing in gold circles on the surface of the water becomes the gold coin he used to toss; the sound of the wind rustling leaves is his sigh of contentment when they made love.

In her dream they stand at the edge of the river, his arms wrapped tightly around her, watching Jack row a golden-haired boy who already has his father's smile around in a skiff. Jack and the boy wave at them and in her dream she can feel his heart quicken at the sight of his son.

In her dream they always stand there until the sun sets around them. He kisses her hair, her cheek, her neck, and she turns around to face him. When she wraps her arms around his waist she can feel the edge of a scar on his side and she kisses him harder to keep back the memory of that night. In her dream every kiss is like their first kiss, and every touch of his hand is like a stolen gift.

In her dream he lifts his son, Rafe, out of the boat, and the two golden heads rub together. He hoists the boy onto his shoulders and wraps an arm around her waist and she takes Jack's hand and together they watch the sky fade from blue to pinkish-orange. In that moment, the final moment of her dream, they are completely happy.

In that moment there is no memory of the funerals. Of the inquest. Of the endless reports and explanations, endless days spent next to endless sick beds. In that moment no one has died and everything is as it might have been. In that moment, that single moment, there is only joy. Joy and the feel of his lips pressed against her forehead, whispering, "I love you."

She always comes out of the dream crying. And when she does she always stretches out her hand. And when she does she always finds him where he said he would be. Right by her side.

Tuesday reached with her fingertips to stroke Lawrence's cheek, as she did every time she awoke, just to be sure he was real. His lips hovered near hers.

"You see, sweetheart, you are not the only one in the family who can wake someone from the dead with a kiss," he told her, catching one of her still-wet tears with his fingertip. "You were having the dream again, weren't you?"

"Yes." She looked at him as the March breeze rustled through his hair and the leaves of the tree shading them cast dancing shadows across his chest. It was nearly impossible to recognize in this vibrant, almost entirely recovered man the lifeless figure at whose bedside she had stood guard for three horrible months. Three horrible months of talking to him and arguing with him and cajoling him and yelling at him and begging him to please, please come back, please show some sign of life other than breathing. Three months of sleeping in fits, and only when Bianca made her, three months of painting horrible paintings, painting out her memories of the days that followed those final moments at their wedding. At the beginning she had shuttled between Lawrence and Tom, who lingered on the edge of death solely because he was waiting to be sure that Lawrence would die. Twice they caught Tom trying to crawl out of his bed in order to finish off the Knight of Knights for good. Finally even his quest was not enough to sustain him, and he had been buried behind the prison in which he died.

They had searched his chambers, trying to understand what had made him that way, and found dozens of cheap editions of courtly romances, with every use of the letter "W" circled. The same letter had been carved into the walls, except in one place in the corner behind the bed where someone had written "William Thomas Watson is a Wicked boy," incising the Ws deep into the wood. Eventually they found the same words written, in a different hand and much larger, over a ratty bed in the corner of the kennels in a house in Worcester. Tom's grandmother's bones, badly mangled, were found scattered outside the house, which was now overrun with wild dogs.

After Tom died, there was only Lawrence, Lawrence who did not move or speak or do anything other than stay slightly, barely alive. He got thinner and thinner as Tuesday, carrying their child, got rounder and rounder. For three months she did everything for him, fed him and bathed him and turned him and cleaned his wound. She slept in his bed with him, at first careful about not letting him feel her tears against his chest, but later uncaring. Her grief was huge inside of her and one night she had let it burst free in a torrent of words and sobs and threats so vehement that it exhausted her.

That was a turning point. After that night, after her hollering had done nothing to break through his unconsciousness, Tuesday had to accept that he was gone. She climbed atop him, to look at him one last time, and was awed by his beauty. Working to keep back her tears, she brought her mouth near his, whispered, "I'm sorry, Lawrence," then kissed him once, passionately, on the lips.

That was when he woke up.

Tuesday's laughter then had brought the entire household into Lawrence's sick chamber. They assumed it was caused by the sheer joy of having Lawrence back. None of them ever knew that his first words to her were, "No, sweetheart, I am the one who should apologize."

After that he healed quickly, regaining his strength and stamina as much by eating everything that Tuesday put in front of him, which was nearly everything that walked into the house, as by his need to rush around finding good hiding places for what he could not manage to consume. He was large and sturdy again, no longer frail, but something inside him was different. He was calmer, as though he now possessed a contentment that went all the way into his bones.

Tuesday was lying on her back on the blanket under the tree gazing up at him with a small, illegible smile.

"What are you thinking about when you look at me that way, sweetheart?" he asked her, twisting a few strands of her hair around his finger.

"How lucky I am to have you."

"No," Lawrence corrected. "I am the lucky one." He

was trying to be better about accepting gratitude, but he still tended to respond by changing the subject. "Tell me, in the dream this time, was it a boy or a girl?"

"Boy."

"And was he called Rafe or George?"

"Rafe. It's been Rafe the past three times. Would that be all right?"

Lawrence put his mouth on her round belly, whispered something, and felt the baby inside, his baby, kick. "He says that will suit him just fine," he reported. He kissed her stomach gently, eliciting two kicks, then moved up to kiss her on the mouth.

"Ugh. Are you two doing that again?" Crispin demanded, strolling up to the blanket they were lying on. "Can hardly walk around here for three minutes together without finding you two kissing."

"You're just jealous because you are no longer the only person who has saved my life," Lawrence told him, rolling back on his elbows.

"Thank goodness," Crispin agreed. "I am glad someone else now has responsibility for making sure you make the most of it. Speaking of which, I just wanted to tell you that I'm finished with that project you asked me to see to." He gave Lawrence a cryptic look, which was returned with a nod, and left.

"What have you done, Lawrence?" Tuesday asked, suddenly suspicious.

"Nothing. I don't know what you are talking about." He could barely get the words out he was working so hard to conceal his grin. "Come on, we'd better go."

"Go where?"

"You'll see."

As they walked toward the Doom Manor boating lake, Tuesday noticed how quiet and empty it was.

"Where did Crispin go?"

"Home probably. He just came to help me with some things."

"What thin—" she started to ask, and then saw. Tethered just off the shore of the lake was a raised platform that was covered with a yellow silk canopy, which had a rainbow of pennants waving jauntily from the corners. The pathway leading to it and the entire surface of the platform itself had been covered in sweet peas and gardenias and jasmine and roses whose fragrance floated on the air. Without saying a word or answering a single one of her questions, Lawrence led Tuesday across the bridge and stood her in the middle of the platform.

He took both her hands in his and looked into her eyes. He smiled gently. "Lady Tuesday Arlington, you have been a challenge to me since I met you. All I have wanted to do was dedicate my life to you, but each time I get close to doing that one or both of us end up nearly dead. I refuse to let this pattern continue. You deserve to have a huge wedding with hundreds of people and a bishop, but we tried that already and it did not work. Besides, I do not want to wait. I am taking matters into my own hands and marrying you right now, this instant."

His voice changed tone, becoming more somber. "Tuesday, you resuscitated me even before I was dying. You reminded me of what it means to be alive and taught me what it means to love. You showed me how to give my heart, and what you gave in return was infinitely more precious. Everything good and strong and virtuous that I am, I am because of you. I want to spend the rest of my life, my life that you gave me, making you as happy as you make me. Will you be my wife?"

There were only the two of them there, on the platform on the lake. It was completely silent but for the sound of the pennants snapping in the breeze and the music of Lawrence's words. If Tuesday could have dreamed of a perfect wedding, this would have been it, just the two of them, pledging their love, dedicating their lives to one another, hand in hand. It was the best gift he could have given her. She reached out and stroked Lawrence's cheek, just to be sure he was real. Then she said, "Yes."

The applause that burst from the bushes and trees and overturned boats that lined the lake then was almost deafening. All the boys from Doom Manor and all the Arboretti and Maria and little Lawrence and Grub and Christopher and CeCe and Morse and all of Lawrence's men and the Burns children and the half of London that either Tuesday or Lawrence had at one time in their lives aided were all there, cheering for them.

But the sound of their cheers was nothing, at least not to Lawrence's ears, compared with the sound of Tuesday's joyful, ringing laughter when she saw it—or rather, them. All of them.

Because every person standing on the shore was wearing dragonfly wings.

The wings were exquisite, completely covered with enamel except where they were studded with what Tuesday—knowing Lawrence as she did—was afraid were real rubies, sapphires, diamonds, emeralds, and topazes. Each set of wings was unique and each caught the sunlight and sparkled just like real dragonfly wings, making the entire party look enchanted.

"It was Jack's idea," Lawrence confided to her as she kissed him for the hundredth time in gratitude and Jack ran up then, wearing the biggest wings of all, and sporting a set of gold antennae. He hugged Tuesday and Lawrence and jumped up and down in transports of joy and danced around in three circles, and then abruptly ran off. When he came back, he was holding out a pair of wings that was unlike all the others. This pair was uneven and scraggily and crazily decorated. There was no enamel and instead of gems it was encrusted with mirrors and buttons and little pieces of rocks, stuck on haphazardly.

"These are for Tuesday," Jack said, grinning hugely. "Jack made them himself. Does Tuesday like them?"

"Oh, Jack, they are the most beautiful wings I have ever seen," Tuesday stammered, and it was the truth.

"Jack's friend Lawrence helped with them," Jack explained, and Tuesday's only reply was to kiss each of them. They both blushed and looked at one another and burst into laughter like old friends and conspirators and neither of them understood why Tuesday had tears in her eyes. Wiping them away she put her wings on and wore them for the rest of the day, to Jack's unending glee.

It was a day of immense chaos and disorder, a day during which every punch bowl was overturned at least once, a local dog ran off with half the roast pig, and at least three boys, wings and all, ended up in the lake.

"I think I could get used to wearing wings," Tristan said as they all lounged together on blankets along the lake shore. "I feel just like an angel."

Lawrence almost choked on the lemonade he was drinking. "I'm sure this is the closest you or any of the Arboretti will ever get to being one," he said.

Tullia, Ian and Bianca's daughter, listened to this with the studious attention she gave to everything, then grew very serous. "Daddy," she asked, "can I be an Arboretti, too?"

"Of course, *carissima*," Ian told her as Bianca groaned. "You already are one."

"And will my children be, too?" she went on.

"Yes."

"And their children?"

"Yes."

"And their children? All the way to forever?"

"Of course," Ian assured her, tousling her hair.

She was silent for a moment. "What do you think the Arboretti will be doing then? In forever?"

"I really cannot imagine," Ian said.

"Funny, I can," Bianca put in then. "Getting involved in things that are none of their business, making trouble everywhere they go—"

"—And wreaking havoc on the lives of innocent women," Sophie finished for her.

"That is not fair," Miles protested, holding his wife Clio tighter. "We never get involved with innocent women."

Sebastian sat up. "I for one hope that is exactly what they are doing. I'd like to know someone followed in my footsteps."

"What a terrifying thought," Lawrence said with a shudder.

Crispin exploded with laughter. "Oh certainly, Lord Pickering. As if your progeny won't be right there alongside them, giving them all their best ideas."

Tuesday clutched her stomach in mock horror then,

but what she really felt was alight, as if she really were in paradise among the angels.

The feeling was still with her hours later as she and Lawrence stood at the open window of their bedchamber, watching the stars come out and being serenaded by the sounds of their remaining guests' laughter. People were still celebrating on the lawn below them, their wings catching the light of the lanterns and making them truly look like dragonflies.

"That was the most beautiful party in the world, Lawrence," Tuesday said, gazing at the remaining guests.

"I wanted to do something special for you. To give you a present. But it is so hard. You never want anything."

"That is not true. It's just that I already have what I want." She looked at him. "Thank you Lawrence."

"For what?"

"For making my life feel like a dream."

Something about the way she was gazing at him gave him a lump in his throat. "It is so much less than you deserve, Tuesday." When she started to protest, he said, "Very well. Tell me what happens next in *this* dream."

She frowned for a moment, then her look became mischievous. "Take this and this off. But leave these—" she pointed to his wings, "—on."

And because for all their years together he continued to make all her dreams come true, she was never sure if she was awake or asleep. And to test it, every morning, she woke up and kissed him.

And he always smiled his special morning smile at her and always said the same thing.

"Good morning, sweetheart."

Then she knew.

"Good morning, Lawrence."

She was so very very lucky.

The inhabitants of London still talk about the strange and miraculous spring of 1591 when the Lion was unmasked, when a spell cast on Doom Manor caused its inhabitants to grow wings, and when England's greatest hero was brought back to life by a woman's kiss.

Tuesday always said that it was not her kiss, but the threat that she would now win every argument, that did it.